PENGUIN BOOKS

HOUSE OF SHADE

M. M. Kaye was born in India and spent most of her childhood and much of her early married life in that country. Her ties with India are strong: her grandfather, father, brother and husband all served the Raj, and her grandfather's first cousin, Sir John Kaye, wrote the standard accounts of the Indian Mutiny and the first Afghan War. When India achieved independence her husband joined the British Army, and for the next nineteen years she followed the drum to all sorts of exciting places she would not otherwise have seen, including Kenya, Zanzibar, Egypt, Cyprus and Berlin. M. M. Kaye is best known for her highly successful historical novels, including the bestselling *The Far Pavilions*, *Shadow of the Moon* and *Trade Wind*, all published by Penguin, and for her detective novels, which include *Death in Berlin*, *Death in Kenya* and *Death in Cyprus* (also published by Penguin in one volume entitled *Murder Abroad*), and *Death in Zanzibar*, *Death in Kashmir* and *Death in the Andamans*, collected together in this volume. Penguin also publish the first volume of her autobiography, *The Sun in the Morning*. M. M. Kaye has written a children's story, *The Ordinary Princess* (1991).

M. M. KAYE

HOUSE OF SHADE

Death in Zanzibar

Death in the Andamans

Death in Kashmir

PENGUIN BOOKS

PENGUIN BOOKS

Published by the Penguin Group
Penguin Books Ltd, 27 Wrights Lane, London W8 5TZ, England
Viking Penguin Inc., 375 Hudson Street, New York, New York 10014, USA
Penguin Books Australia Ltd, Ringwood, Victoria, Australia
Penguin Books Canada Ltd, 10 Alcorn Avenue, Toronto, Ontario, Canada M4V 3B2
Penguin Books (NZ) Ltd, 182–190 Wairau Road, Auckland 10, New Zealand

Penguin Books Ltd, Registered Offices: Harmondsworth, Middlesex, England

Death in Zanzibar
First published as *The House of Shade* by Longmans 1959
This revised edition published by Allen Lane 1983
Published in Penguin Books 1984

Death in the Andamans
First published as *Night on the Island* by Longman 1960
This edition published by Viking 1985
Published in Penguin Books 1986

Death in Kashmir
First published by Viking 1984
Published in Penguin Books 1985

This omnibus edition first published in Penguin Books 1993
1 3 5 7 9 10 8 6 4 2

Printed in England by Clays Ltd, St Ives plc

CONTENTS

Death in Zanzibar

To
the Zanzibar I knew.
With Love

FOREWORD

In the early years of the 1950s there used to be a B.B.C. Radio programme called 'Housewives' Choice', which consisted of popular records — in those days, presumably 78s? — that provided a pleasant accompaniment to tedious and repetitive chores. Any tune in the Top Twenty got played fairly frequently, and one in particular caught my fancy: the first line of the refrain being 'Then I'll go sailing far — off to Zanzibar!'

Since I myself was in the all-too-familiar position of a British Army wife — abandoned, with my two small daughters, in depressing Army quarters in a small garrison town while my husband and his regiment were on active service somewhere on the other side of the world (on this occasion, Korea!) — I would have given a great deal to go 'sailing far', to almost anywhere. But Zanzibar is one of those names that possess a peculiar, singing magic in every syllable; like Samarkand or Rajasthan, or Kilimanjaro; and when the radio was not playing that song I used to sing it to myself, and like Dany in this story, I read anything I could get hold of on the subject of Zanzibar: never dreaming that I would ever see it myself.

Then, when my husband was almost due back in England, his regiment, while *en route* for home, was suddenly diverted to Kenya. And since families were allowed to go out there to join their husbands and fathers, it was not long before the children and I were setting off to Nairobi on a flight that nowadays would only take a few hours, but which in those days, as in this story, took well over twenty-four.

It was during our time in Kenya that I got the chance to visit Zanzibar. And I fell in love with it at first sight, for it turned out to be one of those rare places that live up to everything one has hoped and dreamed that they would be. I also had the honour of meeting its greatly respected and much-loved old Sultan, His Highness Seyyid Khalifa bin Harub: grandson of Thuwani of Muscat and Oman — who was a half-brother of the two successive Sultans of Zanzibar, Majid and Bargash, about whom I wrote in a historical novel, *Trade Wind*, which tells the story of Tyson Frost's grandfather, Rory — Emory Tyson Frost of *Kivulimi*.

Since my husband kept being posted to all sorts of novel and entertaining places, I wrote a 'whodunit' set in each of them. Because of this, I made detailed notes of things I was afraid I might forget. So that when, several years later, I got around to writing this story, all I had to do was to hunt up my Zanzibar notebook, and there it all was. An exact description of everything I could possibly need, down to the advertisement painted on looking-glass in the Mombasa Airport, and the millipede crawling across the floor of the tiny, makeshift one on Pemba.

The Zanzibar I knew has gone for ever, and this book is already a 'period piece' — almost a historical novel, so much has changed. But at least I saw it, and lived in it for a brief while, and it is stored away in my mind for ever.

1

The heavy brocade curtains stirred as though they had been blown by a breath of wind, and a billowing fold touched the corner of the dressing-table and overset a small bottle of nail varnish.

It was a very slight sound, but it woke Dany; jerking her out of an uneasy dream in which she had been hurrying down a long lonely country road in the sad fog and drizzle of an early autumn, clutching a small sealed envelope and listening to the drip of rain off the unseen hedges and the footsteps of someone who followed close behind her.

She had caught brief glimpses of this person when she stopped and turned, and once it had been Mr Honeywood with his narrow, dry, solicitor's face and his small dry disapproving cough, and sometimes it had been a large hearty woman in tweeds, striding through the wet mist, or an Oriental; a dark-faced man wearing flowing white robes and a fez — or was it a turban? But none of them had any right to be following her, and she dare not let them overtake her. It was vitally important that they should not overtake her...

The bottle fell over and Dany awoke.

She sat up in bed shivering in the aftermath of nightmare, and was momentarily surprised to find herself in an unfamiliar room. Then the dream receded, and she remembered that she was no longer in her great-aunt's house, but at the Airlane Hotel in London.

Yesterday, in Market-Lydon, it had been misty and damp; as

though autumn were already far advanced. But here in London on this September morning it still seemed to be high summer, and although it was very early and the city was as yet barely astir, the sky beyond the open window was clear and bright.

The curtains that had been closely drawn last night were now partially open, and the pale light of early morning, filtering into the room, showed a clutter of cardboard boxes, air-weight suit-cases, tissue paper, and the new lizard-skin bag that was Great-aunt Harriet's parting present and which contained, among other things, a brand new passport.

Dany had checked over all the impedimenta of foreign travel late last night, and now all she had left to do was to buy a beach hat, a sun-suit and something for air sickness, and to introduce herself to her step-father's sister, Mrs Bingham, whom she had so far never met but who had been staying since yesterday in the same hotel and was also travelling out to Zanzibar on a Zero Zephyr of the Green Zero Line.

London, Naples, Khartoum, Nairobi. Mombasa, Tanga, Pemba, Zanzibar——

Dany shivered again. A shiver of pure delight that ended unexpectedly in a quiver of unease: a sense of disquiet so sharply urgent that she turned quickly, half expecting to find someone standing behind her. But nothing moved except the curtains billowing idly in the dawn wind, and of course there was no one there. And no one watching her! It was only the effect of that silly dream about people following her ...

Dany Ashton had left school almost a year ago, but this was her first taste of freedom, for despite the fact that, as her mother's daughter, she might have been expected to have led an erratic and entertaining existence, her life had hitherto been a remarkably sheltered one. Her mother, currently Lorraine Frost, was a notable beauty who collected and discarded husbands in a manner that would have done credit to a film star, and Dany, her only child, was the daughter of her first husband, Daniel Ashton.

Lorraine had never been maternally minded, and Daniel Ashton, explorer and big-game hunter, had been more interested in such things as the Lesser Kudu and the upper reaches of the Amazon than in fatherhood. He had met his death at the hands of an unenlightened and excitable tribe of South-American Indians when Dany was three years old, and Lorraine had promptly married Dwight Cleethorpe, an affable millionaire from Chicago, and handed her small daughter over to the care of a maiden aunt, Harriet Henderson.

Mr Cleethorpe, whose hobbies were golf and deep-sea fishing, had not lasted, and there had been three more step-fathers in rapid succession, the latest of whom was Tyson Frost, the novelist. But none of them had taken more than a passing interest in their step-daughter, and Lorraine's visits, though exhilarating, were always brief and did little to disturb the even tenor of life at *Glyndarrow*, the large red-brick house in Hampshire where Dany's Great-aunt Harriet lived in cosy Edwardian seclusion while the world passed her by.

Great-aunt Harriet disapproved of Progress and the Post-War World. She had also disapproved strongly of this visit to Zanzibar, but had been unable to prevent it since she was not the child's legal guardian, and moreover her great-niece had suddenly displayed an unsuspected streak of independence.

Dany had been wildly delighted at the prospect of going to this outlandish spot where Tyson Frost owned a house, and she had not only paid no attention at all to her great-aunt's warnings, but had flatly refused to spend the three nights in London under the roof of an elderly relative, or to be accompanied there by Twisdon, Great-aunt Harriet's austere and aged maid.

Chaperones, declared Dany, were as dead as the Dodo, and she was perfectly capable of looking after herself: or if she were not, the sooner she started learning, the better. In any case, Lorraine had advised her to stay at the Airlane, as there would be half a dozen other people there who were also bound for Zanzibar and the house-party at *Kivulimi*, and who would be travelling on the same plane. Her fellow-guests were Tyson's sister, Augusta Bingham and her friend and companion, Miss Bates; the Marchese di Chiago, who raced (but whether horses, dogs, cars or yachts was not disclosed); Amalfi Gordon, a close friend of Lorraine's, and her fiancé Mr Holden — American and something to do with publishing — who intended to get married on the eve of departure and thereby combine business (discussing terms for a new Tyson Frost novel) with pleasure in the form of a honeymoon in Zanzibar. And finally, Mr Holden's secretary, Miss Kitchell. One or any of these people, wrote Lorraine airily, would be sure to keep an eye on Dany.

'If she means Mrs Bingham or Miss Bates, then possibly they will do so,' said Aunt Harriet, frigid with disapproval. 'But what if it should be this Marchese? I cannot think what has come over your mother. It all comes from living abroad: foreigners are notoriously lax. And *no* one could approve of Mrs Gordon! There was an exceedingly unpleasant rumour going round that she had—— Well, never mind. But she is not in my opinion a suitable companion for any young girl. Besides, she has been married and divorced several times already.'

'I don't see that you can hold that against her,' said Dany with a somewhat rueful smile. 'What about Lorraine?'

'That is *quite* different,' said Aunt Harriet firmly. 'She is your mother — and a Henderson. And I do wish you would not refer to her as "Lorraine". You know how much I dislike it.'

'Yes, Aunt. But you know how much she dislikes me calling her anything else.'

Aunt Harriet shifted her ground: 'It's a very complicated journey. I understand that the Green Zero Line only fly as far as Nairobi, and that you would have to spend a night in an hotel there, and take another aeroplane on the following day. Anything might happen. There have been race-riots in Nairobi.'

'Yes, Aunt. But Lorraine — I'm sorry; Mother — says that Tyson's secretary, Nigel Ponting, will be meeting the plane there, so I shall be quite safe.'

'Ponting ... Yes. I have met him. He came here with your step-father two years ago. You were at school. A most affected man. More like a dancing master than a secretary. He minced and giggled. Not at all a reliable type, and I did not take to him.'

'I'm sorry, Aunt.'

Old Miss Henderson had been compelled to give up the unequal struggle, and Dany — naïve, romantic, eager — had left for London unchaperoned, taken a room with a private bath and balcony at the Airlane, and indulged in an orgy of theatres, shopping and freedom.

She had also had a commission to execute for Lorraine, who had asked her to call on Tyson's solicitor, Mr Honeywood, in Market-Lydon in Kent, to collect a document that Tyson would like her to bring out for him. *'This is the address,'* wrote Lorraine. *'It's his house, not his office, as he's more or less retired now. I do hope this won't be an awful bore for you, darling, and of course the person who should really be doing this is Gussie Bingham, or that hearty girl-friend of hers, as they live practically on his doorstep. But Tyson says Gussie is an unreliable gossip with a memory like a sieve, and so he would far rather you did it. I do hope you won't mind, baby? Tyson has written to Mr Honeywood and told him that you'll call for it on the afternoon of the twelfth, between three and four, and that he's to have it ready for you. You won't forget, darling, will you?'*

Dany had duly gone down to Kent, though as she had wanted to fit in a cinema in the afternoon as well as a theatre that night, she had rung up Mr Honeywood and changed the time to eleven-fifteen in the morning instead. That had been yesterday. And now it was the last day: really the last day. Tomorrow she would be flying eastward — to Zanzibar!

Ever since Lorraine had married Tyson Frost, Dany had dreamed of going to Zanzibar. She had ransacked the local library and spent her pocket-money on books about the island: *Princes of Zinj, Isle of Cloves*, and a dozen others. Books that told the saga of the great Seyyid Saïd, Imam of Muscat and first Sultan of Zanzibar. And of such things as the underground wells whose waters were said to come from far inland in Africa, the haunted palace of Dunga and the sacred drums of Zanzibar, the vast legendary treasure buried by Seyyid Saïd in Bet-el-Ras; the horrors of the slave trade and the pirate raids, and the witch-haunted island of Pemba, home of devils, djinns and warlocks.

Europeans were not permitted to hold land in Zanzibar, but long ago Tyson's grandfather — that rowdy, roving, colourful adventurer, Emory Frost — had done a service to the great Saïd, and his reward had been the lease of a house, *Kivulimi*, for a period of a hundred and fifty years. Tyson's visits there were irregular and brief, but as this year happened to be the seventieth anniversary of Emory's death, and he intended to write a book based upon the life and times of that fabulous character, he had descended upon *Kivulimi*, complete with wife, private secretary and an assortment of guests. And Dany's dream had at last come true.

'Then I'll go sailing far, off to Zanzibar — though my dream places seem — better than they really are . . .' Dany slid out of bed, crooning a snatch from a song that had been popular when she was in the fourth form; and as she did so something moved at the far side of the room and she started violently and bit her tongue. But it was only her own reflection in the looking-glass, and she made a face at it, and going to the dressing-table, picked up the new lizard-skin bag and rummaged through it for a slip of paper on which she had written down the time that the bus for the Airport left the Terminal. It did not seem to be there, and she was about to try one of the drawers when she remembered that it was in the pocket of the camel-hair coat that she had left in the ladies' room on the previous evening, and forgotten to retrieve. She would have to remember to fetch it after breakfast.

Once again something made her jump nervously; a soft slapping sound in the corridor outside that she identified a moment later as the morning papers, dropped by a page-boy whose feet had made no sound on the thick pile of the carpet. She could not understand why she should be so ridiculously on edge this morning; she had never previously been given to nerves. Perhaps this curious feeling of tension was something that everyone experienced when they first realized that they were entirely on their own? If so, she could only hope it did not last long! Giving the page-boy a minute or two to leave the corridor, she crossed to the door. Tea would not be arriving for at least another hour and a half, and she might as well fill in the time by reading the papers.

The corridor was silent and empty, its lushly carpeted length punctuated by white and gold doors, numerous pairs of freshly polished shoes and a varied assortment of daily newspapers. Dany stepped out cautiously and picked up her own selection, the *Daily Dawn*. And as she did so her eye was caught by the heading of a column: *'Man Murdered in Market-Lydon'*.

She opened the paper and stared at it, frowning. Market-Lydon...? Why, that was where she had been yesterday! The little town where——

There was a sharp click immediately behind her and she whirled round. But it was too late. The draught had blown the door shut behind her and she was locked out in the corridor.

Dany dropped the paper and pushed futilely at the door. But it possessed a spring lock and remained blandly impervious to her efforts, and she turned from it to stare helplessly up and down the silent corridor. There was, fortunately, no one in sight, but she could see no sign of a bell either; and even if there had been one she could hardly use it when the chances were that it would be answered by a man.

For the first time Dany regretted the purchase of that diaphanous and far too expensive nightgown. Nylon and lace might be enchantingly frivolous, but its purpose appeared to be to reveal rather than conceal, and she was only too well aware that to all intents and purposes she might just as well be naked. Why, oh why had she flung away those sensible, high-necked and sacklike garments of white winceyette that Aunt Harriet had considered to be the only suitable and modest night wear? If only——

It was at this inopportune moment that footsteps sounded on the staircase that led into the corridor some twenty feet from her door.

Despite the heavy pile of the carpet the footsteps were clearly audible and noticeably uneven, and they were accompanied by a male voice singing in a blurred undertone the same song that had recently been running through Dany's head.

'*"I want to go away — be a stowaway,"*' announced the gentleman on the staircase, '*"Take a trip, on a ship, let my troubles——"* blast!' The singer stumbled noisily on the stairs, and something — possibly a hat? — bounced down them.

Inspiration born of despair descended upon Dany, and snatching up the fallen newspaper she retired hastily behind the front page of the *Daily Dawn* just as the owner of the voice reached the top of the stairs and turned into the corridor.

He proved to be a tall, dishevelled young man in formal evening dress, wearing his white tie several inches off centre, and carrying a gaily coloured balloon and a large and fluffy toy cat with a pink ribbon round its neck. His dark hair was in a state of considerable disorder, and quite apart from his undeniably festive appearance he possessed an indefinable air of what an earlier generation would have termed 'rakishness'.

He stood for a moment or two swaying slightly and looking vaguely about him, and then his gaze alighted upon Dany.

'Well, say!' said the young man, saying it in an unmistakably transatlantic voice: 'what do you know about that!'

He advanced until he was level with her, and then as the full beauty of her situation dawned upon him he gave way to immoderate mirth, and stood before her laughing his head off, while

Dany glared back at him like an angry kitten, scarlet cheeked, helpless and infuriated.

'Be quiet!' hissed Dany, 'you'll wake everyone up! Do you know what time it is?'

' *"Three o'clock in the mor . . . ning, I've danced the whole night through!"*' carolled the young man, throwing his head back and giving it everything he had got in a blurred but pleasing baritone.

'And you look like it!' said Dany in a furious whisper. 'But it's nearly six now, and I want to get back into my room. Don't just stand there laughing! *Do* something! Get me a pass key — anything! Can't you see I'm locked out?'

'I can,' said the young man. 'And let me tell you that I haven't seen anything better in days. No, sir! It's a pity that your taste in newspapers didn't run to a smaller sized sheet, but who am I to carp and c-cavil? Let's face it, it might have been *The Times*. Not, le' me tell you, that you look like a dame who reads *The Times*. No, I sh'd say——'

'*Will* you be quiet?' demanded Dany frantically. 'And if you aren't going to help, go away! No — no, don't do that! For goodness sake get me a pass key.'

'Sure,' said the young man cordially. 'Any li'l thing you say. Here, hold the children.'

He handed over the balloon and the white cat, and Dany, making a rash attempt to accept them, came dangerously near to losing the front page of the *Daily Dawn* in the process. The balloon bounced out of reach and the white cat fell to the floor.

'Now look what you've done!' said the young man reproachfully. 'You've dropped Asbestos. Have you no compassion on dumb animals? He may be heat-resistant, but he doesn't like being kicked around.'

He retrieved the cat and hunted through his waistcoat pockets with his left hand. 'Don't rush me. I know I had it some place. Ah, here we are! Madam — no. No wedding ring. That's good. Miss — your key.'

He held out a door key with a courtly bow.

'But that *isn't* my key,' said Dany on the verge of shedding tears of sheer exasperation. 'It's yours!'

'Why, so it is! You know something? you're a very intelligent girl. You may even read *The Times*. A pity. Well, I'll tell you what. You can't stand there for everyone to take a look at; 'tisn't decent — besides being darned chilly. I'm parked in that room over there, and I guess you'd better go right in and wait while I fetch some gilded flunkey to batter down your door. O.K.? Don't mention it: my fam'ly motto has always been "Never Give a Sucker an Even Break". Let's go.'

He tacked across the corridor, humming gently, and after a couple of unsuccessful tries succeeded in opening the door of the room opposite Dany's.

'There you are,' he said in the self-congratulatory tone of one who has performed an intricate conjuring trick: 'Move right in. We Holdens are nothing if not hospitable. Make yourself at home. And if there's any little thing you fancy, such as a blanket or a bath towel or a bathrobe, jus' go right ahead and wrap it up. The joint's yours. I'll be right back.'

He bowed again, sweeping the floor in an old-world gesture with the white cat, and removed himself.

Dany did not move until he was out of sight (the *Daily Dawn* did not meet round the back) but as soon as it was safe to do so she crossed the corridor at a run and took refuge in his room.

It was in darkness, for the curtains were still drawn, and she switched on the lights and saw that the bed had been neatly turned down and a pair of maroon-coloured pyjamas laid out upon it. There was also a bottle-green dressing-gown hanging over the back of a chair, and she reached for it thankfully. It was far too large, but all the more welcome for that; for Dany, though slim, was by no means short, and it covered her adequately from throat to ankle, allowing no more than a glimpse of bare feet.

A small travelling-clock on the bedside table informed her that it was already ten minutes to six, and from behind the heavily curtained windows she could hear the muted rumble of the early morning traffic. But there were as yet no sounds of movement from inside the hotel, and Dany sat down on the edge of the bed and prepared to wait.

The room was an almost exact counterpart of her own, though a good deal tidier, and it contained one slightly surprising object: a large photograph of an extraordinarily beautiful woman that stood on the dressing-table, expensively framed in silver and inscribed largely across one corner 'To Lash — with all my love for always — Elf'. It was not, however, the film-star features or the extravagant inscription that was surprising, but the fact that someone had draped the frame in a length of black crêpe, drawn a heavy line through the word 'always' and substituted tersely above it, and in red ink, 'September'.

Dany was engaged in studying these interesting additions when her eye was caught by something else: a familiar coloured label on a suitcase that stood on a chair by the dressing-table. Lashmer J. Holden, Jnr, it would appear, was also intending to fly to Zanzibar via Nairobi.

Holden ... Why, of course! Lorraine had mentioned him. American and something to do with publishing. He was going to see Tyson about some book or other, and to spend his honeymoon in Zanzibar. Although if that photograph was anything to go by ... A cold draught of air blew through the room and billowed the curtains, and a quantity of letters that had been carelessly propped against a china ornament on the writing-table fluttered to the ground and lay strewn across the carpet.

Dany rose and replaced them, noting as she did so that Mr Holden's correspondents appeared to be numerous, but unexciting; the large majority of the envelopes being of the strictly utilitarian variety with the address typewritten on them, and having apparently come from various secretarial agencies.

She stacked them in a neat pile and put them back, and then

stopped to retrieve the discarded sheet of newspaper. And as she did so her gaze fell on a word in black type: *'Murder'*.

'Man Murdered in Market-Lydon. Retired Solicitor Found Shot. Mr H. T. Honeywood ...'

But it couldn't be! There must be some mistake. It couldn't possibly be Tyson's Mr Honeywood. That small, dried-up, disapproving solicitor. It must be someone with the same name. People one had met — people one knew — were never murdered. But there was no mistake. Here was his name. And his address: the prim grey-stone house standing back from the road behind a high wall and an ugly screen of wet laurels. Dany sat down slowly on the bed and read the incredible column of close print.

Mr Honeywood had been shot through the heart at close range, presumably by someone whom he had no reason to fear, for there were no signs of a struggle. The safe in his study had been open, and certain sums of money — the funds, apparently, of local societies of which he was treasurer — had vanished, though no one was in a position to say if anything else had been removed. Mr Honeywood had virtually retired from active work and seldom visited the office in the High Street, which was in the charge of a junior partner, Mr John Honeywood, a nephew; but he occasionally saw an old client at his house. It was this scarcity of visitors, allied to the absence of his housekeeper, that accounted for the fact that the crime was not discovered until so late ...

The police were of the opinion that he had been killed some time during the morning, possibly between eleven-thirty and twelve, but his housekeeper, who was elderly and deaf, had asked for the day off to visit a cousin in Tunbridge Wells, and had left the house shortly before 10 a.m. She had not returned until late in the evening, and it was she who had eventually found the body. There was also a charlady who came every morning for two hours and who had left about the same time, but neither lady could say for certain if Mr Honeywood had been expecting a visitor, and the sole entry in his engagement pad for the day read 'D.A.

between 3 and 4.' The police were anxious to interview a young woman who had been seen leaving the house shortly after half-past eleven that morning, and whom they thought could give them some information ...

Why — they mean *me*! thought Dany, horrified. But I can't tell them anything! It can't be true——

She let the paper slide to the floor and sat staring down at it. She would have to go round to the nearest police station as soon as she was dressed. Or did one merely reach for a telephone and dial 999? They could not detain her for long, for there was very little that she could tell them. But all the same it would cut badly into her last day, and she had meant to——

Another and far more disturbing thought suddenly struck her. Wouldn't there be an inquest? And if there were, would she have to attend it and lose her seat on the plane? But if she did that she might not be able to get another one for days! Possibly for weeks——! Or even months, if the Nairobi run was a popular one. Tyson and Lorraine might have left Zanzibar and moved on to Spain or Cape Town or New York before she could get another passage, and she could not *bear* it if that were to happen!

Perhaps after all it would be better to say nothing, and do nothing. She had only to wait one more day and then she would be safely aboard the plane. And the police were not in the least likely to fetch her back from Zanzibar for any inquest. It wasn't as if she could give them any help, and anyway she could always write them a letter.

She straightened up with a sigh of relief as though a weight had fallen off her shoulders, and her gaze fell again on the travelling-clock. Twenty-five minutes past six! She had not realized that so much time had slipped by. What on earth was Mr Holden doing? Had he forgotten all about her? It could not possibly have taken him over half an hour to find a valet or a page-boy and collect a pass key.

She jumped up and had started for the door when it opened,

and Mr Holden was back, still clutching the cat.

'Relax!' said Mr Holden buoyantly. 'Here come the United States Marines! One of those retired ambassadors in striped pants and ten dollars' worth of whiskers rustled up a spare key. The guy seemed to think he should stand by and personally usher you in, but I urged him to spare your blushes, and he reluctantly handed it over. I guess he fears the worst.'

He held out the key and Dany clutched it gratefully.

'Sorry to have kept you waiting,' pursued Mr Holden cheerfully, 'but I got side-tracked by an Alka-Seltzer. They certainly offer service in this gilded flop-house. Hey! — you're not going, are you? Stick around and be sociable.'

'I don't feel sociable,' said Dany. 'Not at this hour of the morning. Thank you for your help. And for the dressing-gown. I'll return it.'

'So I should hope,' said Mr Holden. 'It has sentimental associations. Say, if I can manage that one I must be in better shape than I thought. "Sentimental Associations". Not bad. Not bad at all. That bathrobe was a present from Elf. Embroidered that flashy great monogram on it with her own fair hands — so she says. But you don't have to believe a word of it. The truth is not in that girl. Jus' between you an' me, honey——'

The door shut with a decisive bang, and he was alone.

'No gratitude,' said Mr Holden sadly, addressing himself to Asbestos. 'That's what's wrong with women. No — bloody — gratitude!'

2

The corridor was still silent and empty, and the entire hotel appeared to be still asleep: a fact for which Dany was profoundly grateful. She fitted the key into the lock, opened the door — and stood wide-eyed and aghast.

The room looked as though a tornado had struck it. Drawers had been pulled out and their contents emptied on to the floor, suitcases had been dragged out and opened, and tissue paper, cardboard boxes and bedclothes strewed the carpet.

'So *that's* what he was doing!' said Dany, breathing stormily. 'I suppose this is his idea of a screamingly funny joke! How dare he — how *dare* he!'

She whirled round and ran back across the corridor, and had reached out her hand to bang on his door when she changed her mind. Mr Holden was undoubtedly under the influence of alcohol — a condition that Dany had not previously encountered — and the chances were that he was at that very moment gleefully waiting for her to burst into his room in a fury so that he could enjoy his silly practical joke to the full. It would therefore be more dignified — and snubbing — to ignore the whole thing.

She went back to her own room and, shutting the door with a commendable lack of noise, spent the next half-hour restoring order, so that by the time the room-maid put in an appearance with a tray of morning tea, the place was tolerably tidy again.

Dany had gone down to breakfast at eight-thirty to find the vast dining-room sparsely populated, and had lost her appetite after one glance at the representative selection of the morning papers that had been thoughtfully placed on her table.

Yes, there it was again. 'Murder at Market-Lydon.' Every paper carried the story, and the accounts did not vary much, except as to detail. One paper mentioned that the 'fatal shot' had been fired from an automatic small enough to be carried easily in a coat pocket or a lady's handbag, and another said that the initials 'D. A.' on Mr Honeywood's engagement pad had been duplicated on a lace and cambric handkerchief that had been found under Mr Honeywood's desk. So that's where I lost it! thought Dany guiltily. It must have been when I was hunting through my bag for Lorraine's letter.

There was one point, however, on which every account agreed. The police wished to interview a young woman who had been seen leaving Mr Honeywood's house 'shortly after half-past eleven', and whom they hoped might be able to assist them in their inquiries.

Well, I won't! decided Dany stubbornly. I'm going to fly to Zanzibar tomorrow, and nothing and no one is going to stop me! I'm not going to help them. I'm not — I'm not!

She pushed the papers aside, and snatching up her bag, almost ran from the room, colliding *en route* with a slim man in a pepper-and-salt suit who had just entered the dining-room. Dany apologized breathlessly, the man said it didn't matter at all, and a stately waiter who, if he were not actually a retired ambassador, might well have been a retired ambassador's gentleman's gentleman, looked so gravely disapproving that Dany flushed hotly and returned to her room at a more decorous pace.

She found that in her absence the room had been swept and tidied and the bed made. And on the bed, laid out with some ostentation on the satin counterpane, was a large and unmistakably masculine dressing-gown.

It managed, somehow, to convey the same austere disapproval that the stately waiter had conveyed with a single cold glance, and Dany's flush deepened as she looked at it. She had meant to return it before going down to breakfast, but she had not trusted herself to be civil to Mr Holden, and it had not occurred to her to put it out of sight in a drawer or cupboard.

He'll have to wait for it, she thought. If he's been up all night he'll be sound asleep by now. I'll wrap it up and hand it in to the hall porter.

She sat down in front of the dressing-table and tried on a small cyclamen velvet hat that had been one of her first purchases in London. Her great-aunt would undoubtedly have disapproved of the colour and swooned at the price, but there was no doubt at all that it did things for her that Aunt Harriet's choice of hats did not.

Lorraine was dark haired and tiny, and Daniel Ashton had been tall and blond; but their daughter had struck out on a line of her own. Dany's hair was light brown: soft, shining and shoulder-length, and curling under in the traditional manner of a medieval page-boy's, while her eyes, a happy medium between Lorraine's blue and Daniel's hazel, were large and grey and lovely.

There was no doubt about it, thought Dany, studying herself in the looking-glass, hats and clothes did make a difference — an astonishing difference. She was never going to wear navy-blue serge again!

She pulled open a drawer that contained gloves, scarves and handkerchiefs — one of the few that had escaped Mr Holden's prankish attentions — and was rummaging through it in search of a pair of gloves that could be worn with a cyclamen velvet hat, when her fingers encountered something that had certainly not been there before. She felt it, frowning, and then took it out; wondering if this was another practical joke and if that was why he had not emptied the contents of this drawer on to the floor as he had the others. It was something hard and cold and heavy that had been rolled in one of her chiffon scarves and hidden at the back of the drawer. Dany unrolled it, and instantly dropped it.

It hit the edge of the open drawer and fell with a clatter to the floor, and she sat very still, staring at it, and after a minute or two stooped slowly and stiffly and picked it up. It was a small gun. 'Small enough to be carried in a coat pocket or a lady's handbag...'

Quite suddenly Dany was frightened. Her knees felt weak and her hands cold, and she seemed to be having some difficulty with her breathing. The looking-glass reflected a movement behind her and she gave a startled gasp and turned swiftly.

She had apparently left the door ajar, and now it swung open and Mr Holden was with her once more: changed, and presumably in his right mind, though still accompanied by the cat.

He did not present the appearance of one who has spent the entire night on the tiles, and except for a slight heaviness about the eyes, no one would have suspected him of having had no sleep in the last twenty-four hours. But the sight of the weapon that Dany held clutched in her hand wiped the amiable smile from his handsome features.

'Hey!' said Mr Holden, considerably startled. 'Put that down! My intentions are strictly Grade A. All I want right now is my bathrobe — it's got a couple of letters I need in the pocket.'

Dany gasped and whipped the gun behind her.

'Tell me,' said Mr Holden, 'do you always hold up visitors in that dramatic fashion? Life in London must have gotten a lot brisker since I was last over.'

Something in Dany's white face and wide eyes suddenly struck him, and his own face changed. He came in quickly and shut the door behind him.

'What's up, kid? In trouble?'

Dany licked her dry lips and swallowed convulsively. She found it astonishingly difficult to speak. 'Yes ... No ... I don't know. Would you...? There's your dressing-gown. On the bed. Please — take it and go away.'

Mr Holden favoured her with a long, penetrating look and

ignored the suggestion. He deposited the cat on the nearest chair and said: 'I thought maybe I'd better bring Asbestos along to play propriety. *"When in Rome ..."* you know. He may not be much of a chaperone, but he's better than none. Makes a third.'

He came across the room and stood in front of Dany, looking down at her, and then turning abruptly away he vanished into the bathroom; to reappear a moment later carrying a tooth-glass which he filled almost a third full from a silver flask that he produced from his pocket.

'Here, drink this,' ordered Mr Holden sharply, handing it to her. 'No, don't sip at it! Knock it back!'

Dany complied, and having done so, choked and coughed, and Mr Holden thumped her on the back and inquired with a trace of impatience if she had never come across rye before, and who the heck had been responsible for her upbringing?

'G-great-aunt Harriet,' gasped Dany, made literal by shock.

'She the one who taught you to tote a gun?' inquired Mr Holden, interested.

'No, of course not! I — it isn't mine.'

'Just borrowed it, I guess. Now, look, I know it's none of my business, but are you in some sort of a jam?'

'N-no,' said Dany uncertainly. 'There isn't anything — I mean ...' She looked down at the gun that she still held clutched in her hand, and said: 'Is this an automatic?'

'Yes,' said Mr Holden.

Dany shuddered suddenly and uncontrollably, and he reached out, and taking it from her, jerked back the cocking-piece. She saw his eyebrows go up in surprise and he said in a startled voice: 'Loaded, by golly!'

He removed the magazine and counted the rounds, and finding these one short, sniffed the barrel. 'And fired! Say, look sister — you haven't by any chance been taking a shot at someone, have you?'

Dany said: '*Has* it been fired? Are you sure?'

'Yep. And fairly recently, I'd say.'

He clicked the magazine back into place and, laying the little gun on the dressing-table, thrust his hands into his pockets and stood looking down at her with a crease between his brows. She looked, he thought, very young and scared and helpless, and he wished that his head felt a bit clearer. He had an uncomfortable suspicion that he was about to become involved in something that he would regret, and that were he in full possession of his faculties he would collect his bathrobe and leave the room without loss of time. But he did not go. He picked up the empty tooth-glass instead, and having poured out a second and larger tot from the flask, swallowed it and felt better.

'Now,' said Mr Holden bracingly, drawing up a chair and disposing himself in comfort, 'let's get down to cases. Go ahead — tell me what's the trouble.'

Dany had not previously come into contact with anything stronger than cider cup, and four fingers of rye whisky were beginning to have their effect. The fact that Mr Holden was a stranger to her, and should therefore be treated with proper reserve, did not seem to be of the slightest importance. And anyway he knew her current step-father and was going to marry one of her mother's oldest friends, and perhaps he would be able to tell her what to do.

She said haltingly: 'I — I don't know where to start.'

'Try starting at the beginning,' suggested Mr Holden sensibly.

Dany looked at the gun, and shivered again. She said: 'I found this — the gun — in that drawer just now. Someone must have put it in there while I was at breakfast, or — some time. And I — know it's silly, but I suddenly wondered if it were *the* gun. The papers say it was a small automatic, and though I know it can't possibly be, I thought——'

'Hey, wait a minute,' intervened Mr Holden, pardonably confused. 'What gun, and what papers? You'll have to do better than that, sister. My wits are not all that sharp this morning. And by the way, what's your name? I can't keep calling you "hey" or "you" or "whatsername".'

'Ashton. Dany Ashton.'

'Delighted to meet you, Miss Ashton. I'm Lash Holden, from——'

'I know,' said Dany, cutting him short. 'You're going to *Kivulimi* too, aren't you?'

'What's that?' Lash sat bolt upright, and the movement appeared to be painful, for he screwed up his eyes and winced. 'Say, do you know Tyson?'

'He's my step-father.'

'Well, whatdoyouknow?' demanded Lash in pleased surprise. 'That makes us practically relations. My Pop is a life-long pal of the old reprobate. They used to infest the speakeasies back in the old days when the States were technically dry and Tyson was over on some lend-lease college course. Well, well! It is, if I may coin a phrase, a small world. Yep, I'm off to Zanzibar.'

'On your honeymoon,' said Dany.

Mr Holden winced. 'Who told you that?'

'Lorraine. My mother. She said——'

'The wedding,' said Mr Holden, 'is off. Let's not discuss it, if you don't mind.'

'Oh,' said Dany confused. 'I'm sorry.'

'I'm not. Merciful escape. T'hell with women! Say——' He paused and frowned. 'Haven't we wandered off the point some place? You were telling me something. Yeah; I remember now. That gun. Someone stowed it away among your nylons. Now why would anyone do that?'

'Because of Mr Honeywood,' said Dany.

'Mr Who?'

'Honeywood. I don't suppose you've seen the papers this morning, but he was murdered yesterday, and it says that the police want to — to interview a young woman who was seen leaving his house not very long before it happened. And that was me.'

'*You*? Now listen, kid — let's get this straight. Are you trying to tell me that you shot this guy?'

'*No!*' said Dany furiously. 'Oh, what's the good of telling you anything? Of course I didn't shoot him!'

'O.K., O.K.,' said Lash pacifically. 'I just wanted to clear that point up before we went any further. What were you doing in this Honeywood's comb, I mean house?'

'He's Mr Frost's solicitor — the Frosts live near there. Tyson wanted me to bring a letter out with me, and Lorraine, my mother, asked me to call in and fetch it; and I did. I fetched it yesterday morning at eleven o'clock — no, it must have been nearly twenty past, because the train was late; there was some fog about.'

'Well, go on. What happened?'

'Nothing happened. We talked for a bit, and I left.'

'Meet anyone coming away?'

'No. I passed a few people, of course, but I didn't pay much attention. There was a woman with a walking-stick and one with a puppy on a lead, and an African — or an Indian — anyway an Oriental of sorts, in a white — no, that was the dream. In a raincoat: one of those students. I can't remember any more. But it was rather misty, and I wasn't bothering.'

'And why are you bothering now?'

'Because the papers say that the police think Mr Honeywood was — was murdered some time between eleven-thirty and twelve. And I was there until just after half-past eleven, and it seems that someone saw me leave.'

'The murderer, you mean?'

'No, of course not! He wouldn't have told the police. But someone told them; and — now someone else is trying to make it look as though I did it.'

'Baloney!' said Lash impatiently.

'It isn't baloney! It isn't! It was that kind of gun. It said so in the papers. A — a little gun. An automatic. And that horrid thing there isn't mine. I've never even *seen* one before! But it was wrapped up in my scarf, and it wasn't there yesterday because I wore that scarf yesterday——'

'O.K., sister!' said Lash. 'I get you. Yes, it's quite a point. You think someone planted this on you, so that when the police came around asking questions it would be found right here in your room? Well you don't have to worry. It won't have your fingerprints on it, and—— Yes, by God, it will! Mine, too. *Hmm*. That's a fast one.'

He brooded for a few minutes, and then said abruptly: 'Know what I'd do if I were you? I'd drop that damned thing down the elevator shaft and think no more about it. The cops aren't likely to locate you before you get aboard the plane tomorrow, and once you're out of the country they can go ahead with tracing the guy who did the job. Simple.'

'But suppose they do find me?' said Dany, twisting her hands together distressfully. 'Mr Honeywood may have told someone I was coming down. And I telephoned him. I was going down in the afternoon, but I wanted to go to a film, so I telephoned and asked him if I could come in the morning instead. They might trace the call because I telephoned from here. And — and I left a handkerchief in Mr Honeywood's office. It had my initials on it.'

'You *what*?' said Mr Holden, unable to credit it. 'You're telling me that you actually pulled that corny old gag? Good grief! *Women!*'

'You don't suppose I did it on purpose, do you?' retorted Dany hotly. 'And anyway, how was I to know that this sort of — of awful thing was going to happen? How could *anyone* know? People oughtn't to keep valuable things in safes in their houses and then leave their safes open and — and——' Her lips began to tremble.

'Hey!' said Mr Holden, appalled. 'Don't cry. I can handle anything else — well, almost anything else. But not tears. Not at this hour of the day, there's a good girl. Here, let me lend you a handkerchief — unmonogrammed!'

He handed one over, and Dany accepted it with a dismal sniff. 'I'm sorry,' she apologized, blowing her nose. 'It was only because I'm so worried, and it's all so — so fantastic and impossible and horrid. Mr Honeywood being murdered, and then finding that gun wrapped up in one of my scarves, and — and not knowing what to do. What *am* I going to do?'

'Nothing!' said Mr Holden firmly. 'Masterly inactivity is my advice. It may be regrettably short on Public Spirit, but right now it looks like saving you a helluva headache. We'll make a nice tidy parcel of that gun, address it to Scotland Yard and drop it in the nearest post box. And you can spend your air trip in writing them a full account of your visit to this guy Honeycomb, and post it in Nairobi: allowing it to be supposed that you missed reading the newspapers today on account of one little thing and another. Not strictly truthful, but a labour-saving device if ever there was one. That should satisfy both your conscience and cops. O.K.?'

'O.K.,' agreed Dany with a breath of relief and a somewhat watery smile.

'Good,' said Mr Holden briskly. 'Then that's fixed.'

He stood up, reached for the gun, and having carefully cleaned off all possible fingerprints with his handkerchief, wrapped it in the crumpled square of linen and stuffed it into his pocket.

'And now I'm afraid I must leave you. I have to go out gunning for a secretary-typist. Mine, believe it or not, has contracted mumps. *Mumps* — I ask you! There ought to be a law against it. See you at the airport, babe.'

He collected his dressing-gown and Asbestos, and departed.

3

Dany sighed and stood up. She still felt badly shaken, but at least she was no longer frightened, for Lash Holden's casual attitude towards the whole horrifying affair had reduced it to manageable proportions.

She was not, she assured herself, obstructing the course of justice by keeping silent. Any information that the gun might convey to the police would be theirs by tomorrow morning. And as far as the details of her visit to Mr Honeywood were concerned, she would tell them that too; but, as Lash Holden had sensibly suggested, by letter. Probably by the time they received it the murderer would have been caught; and if not, at least she would be with Lorraine and Tyson, who could support her story and deal adequately with the police.

Dany closed the drawer in which she had found the gun, and having repaired the ravages caused by tears and Mr Holden's handkerchief, reached for the lizard-skin bag. The unpleasant happenings of the morning had driven the day's programme out of her head, but she had made a list of the few things that she still had to buy, and she took it out of her bag and studied it.

Beach hat, sunsuit, something for air sickness? Ticket for matinee of 'Sun in Your Eye'. *Book for journey?* That should not take long.

It was only when she was replacing the list that she noticed that something was missing from the bag. Surely there ought to be more in it? Money, cheque book, powder compact, lipstick, a crumpled face tissue, a pocket comb, a bunch of keys, a leather pocket-book containing tickets, reservations, permits and certificates, and——

With a sudden sickening sense of shock she realized that her passport was no longer there! The brand new passport that Aunt Harriet had impressed upon her that she must on no account let out of her keeping, and which she had carried about in the new lizard-skin bag for the last three days.

She hunted through the bag with desperate, shaking fingers, and finally emptied the entire contents on to the dressing-table. But there was no passport.

It must be there. It *must* be! thought Dany frantically. I couldn't have lost it. It's never been out of my sight, and it was there last thing last night — I saw it when I was checking the plane tickets. *The tickets!* Had those gone too?

She tore open the pocket-book with hands that were so unsteady that she could barely control them. But the tickets were still there. Everything else was there. And none of it was any use without a passport!

Dany dropped the pocket-book and began a frenzied search through the dressing-table drawers. But the action was purely a panic-stricken one, for she knew quite well that it had been in her bag when she had checked over all her various forms and tickets before turning out the light last night. She had taken the bag down with her to the dining-room at breakfast time, and it had never once been out of her sight except——

Dany straightened up suddenly and stood gripping the edge of the dressing-table. She had been locked out of her room for nearly three-quarters of an hour this morning, and during that time Lash Holden had entered it and turned all her things upside down for a practical joke. Had he taken her passport too, as part of it?

She gathered up the scattered contents of her bag in feverish haste, crammed them back into it, and ran out of the room and across the passage.

Mr Holden's door was shut and she hammered on it, terrified

that he might already have left and that she might have to wait the best part of the day before catching him again. But Mr Holden was still at home.

The door opened and he regarded her with a trace of annoyance. 'What, again? Not another lethal weapon, I trust? I've only just finished packing up the first one. Here it is.'

Dany said breathlessly: 'Did you take my passport this morning? When you were ragging my room?'

'Rag——? Sorry; I no speaka-da English.'

'Turning it upside down. Did you? Because if you did I don't think it's in the least funny, and I want it back at once. How *could* you?'

Mr Holden stared, scowled, and then reaching out a hand and grasping her by one arm he jerked her into his room and shut the door behind her.

'Say, what goes on here? I don't get it. No, I have not taken your passport. And just when am I supposed to have roughed up your room?'

'This morning. While I was waiting in here. It *must* have been you. It couldn't have been anyone else! You had the key and——'

Dany stopped: suddenly realizing that someone had got into her room without a key, and hidden a gun there. The balcony——? the fire-escape——?

Lash said: 'Now relax. Just sit right down and have another slug of rye. Looks like you could use one. No? Well I certainly could. You've got me all confused. Chicago was never like this!'

Dany said: 'Then — then it wasn't you. All that mess. I thought it was meant to be a joke, but it was someone looking for my passport. I — I don't understand. Why should anyone want to steal my passport?'

'Probably to use,' said Lash. 'Very useful things, passports. You can't go any place without 'em these days. Some dame may have needed one badly, and thought yours would fill the bill. Or else someone wants to stop you catching this plane.'

He paused for a drink, and then said meditatively. 'You know, that's quite an idea — taking that gun into account. Know what I think? I think someone saw you leave this Honeyball's house, and decided that you'd make a very useful red-herring. Probably saw you coming away as he went in, and—— Say, how did you get back to town yesterday?'

'By train. The 12.5.'

'Well, there you are. Simple! He bumps off this guy, takes what he wants from the safe, and beats it for the station. And who does he see on the platform but a dame who he knows was visiting this solicitor only a few minutes before he was there himself. If he can only play his trump card, it may keep the police dogs baying on the wrong trail for long enough to let him get clear. So he follows you up to town, works out a way of planting that gun among your undies to make the thing foolproof, and—— Has that room of yours got a balcony?'

'Yes. But I don't think——'

'Too easy. The dam' things connect. And there's a fire-escape somewhere. He plants his little time bomb, and then suddenly notices that your bags are lying all over the place covered with air labels — seems you're lighting out for foreign parts. That washes you out as a red-herring, so where does he go from here? Easy: fixes it so you can't leave! No passport, no foreign parts; and there must be a passport around somewhere. He turns the joint upside down until he finds it, pockets the thing and lights out. You are now not only tied by the leg but, what with the newspaper accounts and the fact that you were in this Honeydew's house within the time limit — and that gun and no passport! — it's a cinch you'll panic and start behaving in a manner likely to arouse suspicion in a babe of three: which will be just dandy. How's that for a piece of masterly deduction? Brilliant, if you ask me. The F.B.I. don't know what they missed when father's boy followed him into the business!'

He put down his glass and sat down rather suddenly on the end of his bed, and Dany gazed back at him dazedly. She had taken in very little of what he had said, because her mind was filled with only one distracting thought: she could not catch the plane! She would have to stay here and face the police and questions and inquests and newspaper men, and the scandalized disapproval of Aunt Harriet who would, understandably, feel that all her dire predictions as to the fatal consequences of independence had been fully justified. She was caught!

'No!' said Dany on a sob. 'Oh *no*! I can't stay here. I won't. I *will* go to Zanzibar. They shan't stop me. But — but they can if I haven't got a passport! What am I going to do? Oh *why* did I ever telephone Mr Honeywood? Why did I ever change the times? If I'd only gone in the afternoon instead!'

'And found the body? You wouldn't have liked that.'

'It would have been better than this! Far, *far* better. Can't you do something?'

'Such as what?' demanded Lash reasonably. 'Call up the cops? That would be one helluva help! Now just shut up and let me think for a minute. I don't know how you expect anyone to think while you're carrying on in this uninhibited manner. Hush, now!'

He helped himself to another drink and relapsed into frowning silence while Dany struggled with an overwhelming desire to burst into tears, and was only restrained from this course by a strong suspicion that Mr Lashmer J. Holden, Jnr, was quite capable of boxing her ears should she try it.

She sat down weakly on the nearest chair, her brain feeling as numb and useless as wet cotton wool. The whole thing was impossible and horrible and fantastic: she must be dreaming and she would wake up suddenly and find herself back in her snug, safe bedroom at *Glyndarrow*. This could not be happening ...

But it was Lashmer J. Holden, Jnr, who woke up.

'I've got it!' he announced. 'By God, what it is to have a brain! Can you type?'

'Yes,' said Dany, bewildered.

'What about shorthand?'

'A — a little.'

'Secretarial college?'

'No. Class at school. Why——'

'Never mind. It'll have to do. O.K. Consider yourself engaged.'

'W-*what!*' gasped Dany.

'Oh — in a purely secretarial capacity. Nothing personal. I'm through with women. Now listen, kid; here's the layout — and is it a lily! If someone thinks they're going to use you as a red-herring to cover up their own get-away, let's wreck the scheme. I've been travelling with a secretary — Miss Kitchell. But Ada has developed mumps, and I haven't so far been able to get hold of a suitable substitute who possesses a valid passport and the necessary visas and forms and whathaveyou to enable her to leave pronto. So what do we do? We take you!'

'Don't be ridiculous,' said Dany crossly. 'You know quite well that I haven't got a passport either! That's the whole point.'

Mr Holden made an impatient noise that is normally rendered in print as *'Tcha!'*

'Use your brain, girl! I'm not taking you as you. I shall take you as Miss Kitchell. You aren't too unlike her. Height about right. Eyes roughly the right colour. Shape a whole lot better, but they don't include that in the photograph. She's older of course, and her hair's red, but she wears glasses and a fringe and about a million curls. The thing's a gift! We dye your hair red — it's a pity, but one must suffer for one's art — get it fringed and frizzed *à la* Ada and buy you a pair of glasses. It's a cinch!'

'But — but ... No! it isn't possible! She won't agree.'

'She won't be asked,' said Mr Holden firmly. 'I have all her documents right here in a brief-case with my own, and all the files and things we need. She sent 'em to me along with the bad news, and forgot to take her own stuff out. So there we are. Masterly, I think. And what's more it will enable me to put a long-cherished theory to the test.'

'What theory?' asked Dany faintly.

'That no one ever yet looked like the photograph on their passport, and that anyway no official ever really glances at the thing. Well, we shall know tomorrow.'

'We can't do it,' protested Dany, though with less conviction. 'We can't possibly do it!'

'Why not?'

'Well — there's this secretary of Tyson's — Nigel Ponting. He's meeting the plane at Nairobi, and he's bound to have seen photographs of me, and——'

'By the time I've finished with you,' said Mr Holden blithely, 'you will have ceased to resemble any photograph ever taken. Except possibly the libel that is pasted to Ada's passport, and that only remotely. And he will not be expecting you, because we will cover that contingency by sending your parents an express cable to say 'Sorry. Delayed — writing.' That'll hold 'em! As for this Ponting, he is an elegant tulip of the precious and scented variety that your great and glorious country has suddenly taken to breeding like rabbits. A pain — no kidding. I met him last time your step-father was in the States, and I can assure you he wouldn't know one girl from the next. One of those. So *phooey* to Ponting. You don't have to worry about him.'

'Well ...' began Dany hesitantly; and was caught in another spasm of panic and doubt. 'No! No, I can't. We couldn't!'

'What's to stop us? They can't give us more than a two-year stretch at Sing Sing — or Borstal, or wherever they send you in this country. And what are two years among so many? Haven't you British any guts?'

There was a sudden angry sparkle in Dany's grey eyes, and her chin lifted. 'All right. I'll do it.'

'That's the girl,' approved Mr Holden, and helped himself to another drink.

'I can't think,' he said, 'why I don't write for a living instead of publishing the puerile efforts of lesser minds. It's all here —

brains, dash, fertility of invention and a frank approach to the problems of daily life. What are you just sitting there for? Get going, girl! Jump to it!'

'What am I supposed to do?' inquired Dany, startled.

'Well, pack I guess. You've got to get out of here before the cops catch up on you, so the sooner you check out the better. Get the girl at the desk to call up and cancel your seat on the plane and to send off that cable. That'll help. And tell the room girl and the hall porter and anyone else you meet that you've just heard that your bedridden old grandmother is dangerously ill in Manchester or Aberdeen or some place, and you're having to cancel your trip and rush to her side. Ask the hall porter to get you a taxi to go to whatever station it is where trains leave for the wilds of Caledonia.'

'King's Cross, I think,' said Dany.

'O.K. King's Cross. And when you get there, grab a porter and get him to put your bags in the checkroom, and I'll meet you in the booking hall in an hour and a half's time. Think you can make it?'

'I'll try.'

'Try, nothing! You'll make it or else. If there's one thing that makes me madder than a hornet it's women who keep one waiting around. I've put up with plenty of that in the past, but no more of it for L. J. Holden, Jnr. No sir! Not from now on. Besides, there won't be much time to waste. We have a stiff itinerary before us. Check you in at another hotel, change all your baggage labels, find an intelligent hairdresser and buy a pair of spectacles, for a start. So the sooner you get going the better. See you at King's Cross at 11 a.m. sharp. And mind, I'm not waiting there for ever! Ten minutes is my limit.'

It was, in actual fact, twenty. But he was still there, and in excellent spirits — in every meaning of the words.

'I'm sorry I'm late,' apologized Dany breathlessly, 'but as I was checking out I saw him again — at least it may not have been, but I thought——'

'Saw who?' demanded Lash, confused.

'The African — or whatever he is. I told you I passed one when I was leaving Mr Honeywood's. No, it couldn't possibly have been the same one I suppose. I'm being silly. But he was talking to the man at the desk about some letters, and it gave me such a jolt that I forgot I'd left a coat in the ladies' room, and so of course I had to go back and fetch it, and that made me late. I was afraid you would have left.'

'Another two minutes, and your fears would have proved well founded. But a mish ish as good as a — A miss ish — Oh, well; the hell with it! Let's go.'

He hailed a porter, retrieved Dany's suitcases from the left-luggage office where they had been deposited only a few minutes previously, and half an hour later she was sitting in front of a large looking-glass, swathed in a peach-coloured overall, while Mr Holden explained breezily to a giggling blonde hairdresser's assistant the details of Miss Ada Kitchell's coiffure.

'He's a one, isn't he? Your gentleman friend,' said the blonde, dunking Dany's head into a basin. 'In films, are you dear? Must be ever so interesting. Ever been a red-head before? No? Well I expect it'll make a nice change. You won't know yourself.'

'Not bad,' said Lash, viewing the result some time later: 'Not bad at all. Though I can't say that it's an improvement. Definitely a retrograde step. Or is that because I'm seeing two of you? Never mind — you can't have too much of a good thing. Let's eat.'

They had eaten at a small restaurant in a side-street near the hairdresser's shop. Or rather Dany had eaten while Mr Holden had confined himself to drinking. And later that day he had deposited her at a sedate family hotel in Gloucester Road, with instructions to keep to her room and not to panic. He would, he said, call for her on the following morning on his way to the Air Terminal, and he regretted his inability to entertain her further, but he had a date that evening. In fact, several.

'You won't oversleep, or anything dreadful?' said Dany

anxiously, suddenly terrified by a vision of being abandoned — alone, red-headed and masquerading as Miss Ada Kitchell — in darkest Gloucester Road.

'Certainly not,' said Mr Holden, shocked. 'You don't suppose that I intend to waste valuable time in going to sleep, do you? In the words of some poet or other, I am going to "cram the unforgiving minute with sixty seconds' worth of drinking done". Or know the reason why!'

'But you didn't have any sleep *last* night,' protested Dany, worried.

'What's that got to do with it? Tomorrow is another day. Be seeing you, sister.'

Dany passed the remainder of the day in solitude and acute anxiety, and crept out at dusk to buy the evening papers. But a fire in a large London store, a train crash in Italy, another revolution in South America and the fifth marriage of a well-known film star, had combined to push the murder of Mr Henry Honeywood off the front pages and into small type.

There were no further details, and with repetition the accounts lost much of their horror for Dany, and became more remote and impersonal. Which soothed her conscience somewhat, though not her fears, for there had been nothing either remote or impersonal about the gun that had been hidden in her room at the Airlane. Or in the fact that someone had stolen her passport! The whole thing might sound like an impossible nightmare, but it had happened. And to her — Dany Ashton. Oh, if only — if *only* she had gone to see Mr Honeywood at the proper time!

She had passed a sleepless night, and was looking white and worn when Lash collected her in a taxi at a comparatively early hour on the following morning. But a glimpse of herself in the large Victorian looking-glass that adorned the hall of the family hotel had at least served to convince her that no one would be likely to recognize her. She had not even recognized herself, and for a fleeting moment had imagined that the wan-faced young woman with the over-dressed red hair and wide-rimmed spectacles was some stranger who was standing in the narrow, chilly hall.

Lash, however, apart from a noticeable pallor and the fact that his eyes were over-bright, showed no signs of fatigue. He exuded high-spirits and was accompanied by a strong smell of whisky and the cat Asbestos, and no one would have suspected for a moment that he had not been to bed or had any sleep at all for two consecutive nights.

He had dismissed with a single short word Dany's trembling assertion that she had changed her mind and couldn't possibly go through with it, and once in the taxi and *en route* to the Air Terminal had made her take several sea-sick pills and swallow them down with rye whisky.

She had been unable to eat any breakfast that morning, panic having deprived her of appetite, and the raw spirit, coming on top of a sleepless night and an empty stomach, had quietened her post-operative nerves and filled her with a pleasant glow of confidence which had lasted until the passengers bound for Nairobi were marshalled in the departure lounge, and she had found herself standing next to a slim, youngish-looking man with a thin, triangular, attractive face, observant brown eyes and a square, obstinate chin.

Catching Dany's eye he had smiled at her; a swift and singularly pleasant smile that she found it impossible to resent, and said: 'I see that we're both bound for Zanzibar. Have you ever been there before?'

His voice was as irresistibly friendly and good-humoured as his smile, and Dany smiled back at him and shook her head.

'No? That's a pity: I'd hoped to pick up a few pointers. This'll be my first visit too. As a matter of fact, I never expected to make it. I've had my name down on half a dozen waiting lists for weeks on end, but all the Nairobi planes seemed to be booked solid. I'd almost given up hope when my luck turned — someone cancelled a seat only yesterday, and I got it.'

'Oh,' said Dany, jumping slightly. 'H-how lucky for you.'

'It was that all right! I'm a feature writer. Freelance. My name's Dowling — Larry Dowling.'

'Oh,' said Dany faintly. 'A — reporter.'

Mr Dowling looked pained. 'No. Feature writer. Have you ever heard of a novelist called Frost? Tyson Frost? But of course you have! Well, he's got a house in Zanzibar, and I've been commissioned by a newspaper and a couple of magazines to try and get a feature on him. That is, if he'll see me. He's not an easy man to get at, from all accounts. Still, I ought to be able to get something out of the trip, even if Frost won't play. Might be able to do something on the elections down there. There's a rumour that the local Moscow-Nasser stooges are making an all-out bid for control of the island.'

'Of *Zanzibar*? But it's quite an unimportant little place!' protested Dany, momentarily forgetting her own predicament in a sudden sense of outrage. Was there then no longer any lovely, romantic spot left in all the world that was free from squabbling political parties?

Mr Larry Dowling laughed. 'You know, there was a time when a good many people might have said the same of Sarajevo. But they learnt differently. I'm afraid you'll find that in a world that plays Power Politics there is no such thing any longer as "an unimportant little place".'

'Oh, no!' said Dany involuntarily. 'Why does everything have to be spoiled!'

Mr Dowling lifted a quizzical eyebrow, but his pleasant voice was sympathetic; 'That's Life, that is. I didn't mean to depress you. I'm sure you'll find Zanzibar every bit as attractive as you expect it to be. I believe it's a lovely place. Are you staying with friends there, or are you going to put up at the hotel like me? I hear there is——'

He broke off, his attention sharply arrested by the Vision at that moment entering the crowded lounge. A vision dressed by

Dior and draped in mink, preceded, surrounded and followed by a heady waft of glamour and exceedingly expensive scent, and accompanied by a slim, dark Italianate young man and a tall, distinguished-looking gentleman with grey hair and cold pale eyes.

Her entrance created something of a stir, and Mr Holden, also turning to look, lost a considerable portion of his *bonhomie*.

'Here come some of your step-father's guests,' he observed sourly to Dany. 'The Latin type is Eduardo di Chiago. A Roman louse who races his own cars and is a friend of Tyson's — he would be! The one with white whiskers and Foreign Office written all over him (erroneously, he's oil) is Yardley. Sir Ambrose. He's been getting a lot too thick with Elf of late, and she'd better watch her step — there was a rumour around that his Company might be heading for the rocks; and not the kind of rocks she collects, either! It's a pity it isn't true. But at least we don't have to put up with him for long. He's only going as far as Khartoum.'

He did not identify the Vision, but he did not need to. It was, unmistakably, the original of the affectionately inscribed photograph that had adorned his dressing-table at the Airlane. His ex-fiancée and Lorraine's great friend, Amalfi Gordon.

'She's lovely, isn't she?' sighed Dany wistfully, speaking aloud without realizing it.

'Is she?' said Mr Holden coldly.

He directed a brief scowling glance at the Vision, and turned his back on it. But Mrs Gordon had seen him.

'Why — Lash!' Her warm, throaty voice was clearly audible even above the babble of the crowded lounge, but Mr Holden affected to be deaf.

It did him no good. Mrs Gordon descended upon him in a wave of scented sweetness. 'Lash, darling — it's lovely to see you! I was so afraid you'd decide not to come after all.'

'Why?' demanded Lash haughtily. 'This started out as a business trip, and it can stay that way. You surely didn't think that I'd cancel it just because you decided to transfer your affections to some gilded Italian gigolo, did you?'

Mrs Gordon tucked a slender, gloved hand under his arm and gazed up at him from a pair of enormous sea-green eyes; her long soft lashes fluttering appealingly.

No one had ever been able to stay seriously angry with Amalfi Gordon for any length of time. Exasperated, yes. But it was an accepted fact that dear, soft-hearted, feather-headed Elf simply couldn't help it. If she fell into love, or out of it, and hurt people thereby, it wasn't her fault. She never meant to hurt.

Mrs Gordon made a *moue* and said: 'Sweetie, you're not sulking, are you?'

'Of course I'm not!' snapped Lash, descending rapidly from the haughty to the frankly furious. 'What would I have to sulk about? I am, on the contrary, deeply thankful. And now run along back to your Mediterranean bar-fly, there's a good girl.'

Amalfi gave his arm a little coaxing tug. 'Darling, aren't you being just a *tiny* bit kindergarten? Eddie's marvellous!'

'You mean Eddie's a Marchese!' retorted Lash bitterly. 'That's the operative word, isn't it? And you're just another sucker for a title! Apart from that, what's he got that I haven't?'

'Manners,' said Amalfi sweetly. And withdrawing her hand she turned away and rejoined her two cavaliers without having even glanced at Dany.

'How d'you like that?' demanded Lash indignantly. '*Manners!* I suppose if I bowed and scraped and went about kissing women's hands——'

He broke off and subsided into deep gloom, from which he was presently aroused by another clutch at his arm. But this time it was Dany, and he saw that she was staring in wide-eyed alarm at a thin, boney, dark-skinned Oriental in a blue lounge suit, who carried a brief-case, a neatly rolled umbrella and very new burberry.

'It's him!' said Dany in a feverish, ungrammatical whisper.

'Who? The one you think you saw in Market-something, or the one you saw in the hotel?'

'In the hotel. But — but perhaps it's both!'

'Nuts! The world is full of Oriental gentlemen — they come in all sizes. And anyway, what of it? He was probably staying at the Airlane. You were. I was. And so, as it happens, were Elf and that slick owner-driver. And we're all flying to Nairobi. Why not him?'

'But suppose he recognizes me? I was standing right next to him!'

Lash turned and surveyed her with a distinctly jaundiced eye, and remarked caustically that it was extremely doubtful if her own mother would recognize her at the moment. To which he added a rider to the effect that if she was going to lose her nerve every twenty minutes she had better give up the whole idea after all and run off back to her Aunt Harriet, as he did not fancy the prospect of being saddled with a spineless and probably inefficient secretary who suffered from frequent attacks of the vapours. A trenchant observation that acted upon Dany's agitated nervous sytem with the bracing effect of a bucketful of cold water, and stiffened her wavering resolution. She cast Mr Lashmer Holden a look of active dislike, and preceded him into the aircraft in chilly silence.

No one had questioned her identity, and if there were any plain-clothes police among the crowds at the airport she did not identify them. The stewardess said: 'Will you please fasten your seat belts,' and then they were taxi-ing down the long runway. The propellors roared and the airport slipped away from them: tilted, levelled out and dwindled to the proportions of a child's toy. They were safely away.

'Well, it seems we made it,' remarked Lash affably, unfastening his seat-belt and lighting a cigarette.

He accepted a cup of coffee from the stewardess and added the remains of his flask to it. He seemed surprised that there was no more.

'Why, hell — I only filled it half an hour ago! No — I guess it must have been earlier than that. Oh well, plenty more where it came from. Happy landings! How are you feeling, by the way?'

'Sleepy,' said Dany.

'That's odd. So'm I. A very good night to you.'

He settled himself comfortably and was instantly asleep, and Dany, looking at him resentfully, was annoyed to find that her own head was nodding. She had no intention of wasting her time in sleep. This was her very first flight, and although the circumstances under which she was making it were, to say the least of it, unusual, she was not going to miss a moment of it. Soon they would be passing over the Channel. France . . . Switzerland. Looking down on the snowy peaks of the Alps. On the Matterhorn and Mont Blanc. Over the mountains to Italy. No, of course she could not sleep . . .

4

Dany awoke with a start to find the stewardess once again urging her to fasten her seat belt. 'We shall be coming in to land in a few minutes.'

'Land? Where?' inquired Dany dazedly.

'Naples. Do you think you could fasten your friend's belt? I don't seem to be able to wake him.'

Dany performed this task with some difficulty, Mr Holden remaining immobile throughout. He did not even wake when the plane touched down, and the stewardess gave up the unequal struggle, and in defiance of regulations, left him there.

Dany climbed over him to join the other passengers who were being ushered out into the dazzling sunlight of the Naples aerodrome, and feeling quite incapable of any conversation, affected not to see Larry Dowling, who had given her a friendly smile as she passed him.

A curious mixture of lunch and tea was served in the dining-room of the airport, but Dany was in no mood to be critical, and she ate everything that was placed before her, surprised to find herself so hungry. Prompted by caution she had selected a table as far as possible from her fellow passengers, and from this vantage point she studied them with interest; realizing that among them, still unidentified, were two more guests bound for *Kivulimi*. Tyson's sister, Augusta Bingham, and her friend Miss — Boots? No. Bates.

It was, she reflected, the greatest piece of luck that she should have been suffering from measles on the only occasion on which this new step-aunt had suggested coming to see her, and that she had selfishly put off calling on Mrs Bingham at the Airlane on Wednesday evening. She had so nearly done so. But there had been the film of *Blue Roses*, and then there had been the choice between doing her duty by introducing herself to her step-aunt, or going to the theatre that evening — and the theatre had won.

Glancing round the dining-room, Dany decided that the two women she was looking for were obviously the two who had seated themselves at Mrs Gordon's table, for the older one bore a distinct resemblance to Tyson. The same blunt nose and determined chin. Yes, that must be Augusta Bingham: a middle-aged woman whose greying hair had been given a deep-blue rinse and cut by an expert, and whose spare figure showed to advantage in an equally well-cut suit of lavender shantung.

Mrs Bingham wore a discreet diamond brooch and two rows of excellent pearls, and looked as though she played a good game of bridge, belonged to several clubs and took an interest in gossip and clothes. Her neighbour, in marked contrast, conveyed an instant impression of Girl Guides, No Nonsense and an efficiently-run parish. Undoubtedly, Miss Bates.

Miss Bates, who despite the heat wore a sensible coat and skirt and an uncompromisingly British felt hat of the pudding-basin variety, provided a most effective foil for Amalfi Gordon, who was sitting opposite her. Mrs Gordon had discarded her mink cape and was looking cool and incredibly lovely in lime-green linen. How does she do it? wondered Dany, studying her with a faintly resentful interest. She's old! She was at school with Mother, and she's been married almost as many times. Yet she can still look like that!

The Italian marquis — or was it marchese? — and Sir Ambrose someone (oil) were giving Mrs Gordon their full attention, and Amalfi was being charming to both of them, as well as to Mrs Bingham and Miss Bates and a couple of openly admiring waiters. Even Larry Dowling was finding it difficult to keep his eyes from straying and his attention on what his table companion was saying.

Mr Dowling was sitting two tables away with the dark-skinned man whom Dany had seen at the hotel, and who was talking earnestly and with much gesticulation. His voice came clearly to Dany's ears: 'You do not understand! You are not Arab. It is the iniquity of it! The flagrant injustice! Why should a suffering minority be exploited for the benefit of cru-el and blood-sucking imperialists of a dying pow-ah, who mercilessly snatch their profits from the very mouths of the starving poo-er? Now I, as an Arab——'

So people really *did* talk like that! And, presumably, others listened. Mr Dowling was certainly listening, though perhaps not quite as earnestly as he should. But then he hoped to write a feature, whatever that was, on the elections in Zanzibar, and——. With a sudden sense of acute alarm Dany remembered something far more important. He wanted to interview Tyson! She would have to warn her step-father, and she would have to keep out of sight. It would be disastrous if this Larry Dowling, who wrote for the newspapers, were to find out that she was Tyson Frost's step-daughter, masquerading as the secretary of a visiting American publisher in order to escape giving evidence at an inquest on murder. It would make an excellent front page story for the newspapers, and Dany shuddered at the thought. Supposing — just supposing — someone were to recognize her? The man whom he was talking to——

Once again panic snatched at Dany. Even if the Arab was not the man she had passed in the mist near Mr Honeywood's house, he was certainly the man who had stood almost at her elbow in the hall of the Airlane, and if he should recognize her, and ask questions, she might be stopped at Nairobi and sent back.

What were the penalties for travelling on a false passport? Why hadn't she thought of that before? Lash Holden had made some flippant reference to it, but she had not stopped to think. She should have thought . . .

Mr Dowling's companion was talking again, even more audibly, but on a more topical subject. 'I feel always sick — most sick — in these aeroplanes. It is my stomach. Everything, I take it. It is no good. The height — I do not know. Yes, we do not move, but still I am feeling bad always. But worse over the sea. I am most bad over the sea. For if the engines fail over the sea, what will happen then? We will all drown! It is terrible!'

He's not airsick, thought Dany. He's only frightened! Well, so am I . . .

Larry Dowling caught her eye and grinned, and unaccountably some of the panic left her. He might be a reporter, and dangerous to know, but he was a dependable sort of person, and she had a sudden, strong conviction that Aunt Harriet would have approved of him. Which was odd . . .

She became aware that passengers for Nairobi were being requested to return to their aircraft, and rising hurriedly she snatched up her coat and bag and hastened out in the wake of her fellow passengers.

Lashmer J. Holden Jnr had not moved, and he did not stir as she squeezed past him to regain her seat. He was, in technical parlance, out for the count; and Dany, vaguely recognizing the fact, was conscious of feeling lost and friendless and very much alone. Until this moment she had felt herself to be a mere member of the crew with Lash in charge and steering the ship, and provided she did what she was told he would bring her safely into port. Now she was not so sure. Viewed dispassionately in the bright Mediterranean sunlight, Lashmer Holden looked a good deal younger. His hair was dishevelled and he looked pallid and unshaven and she studied him with a critical and disapproving eye, and then — her maternal instincts getting the better of her — leant over and loosened his tie, which had worked round somewhere in the neighbourhood of his right ear, and drew down the blind so that his face was shielded from the sun.

The two red-faced gentlemen of unmistakably Colonial appearance who occupied the seats immediately behind her began to snore in gentle and rhythmic chorus, and she wished she were able to follow their example and fall asleep again herself, in order to avoid having to think. But she was by now far too anxious and far too wide awake; and in any case there was that letter to be written. The letter that she must post in Nairobi, explaining herself to the police.

Dany stood up cautiously and removed her attaché case from the rack above her head, noting, with a renewed sense of surprise, the label that proclaimed it to be the property of Miss Ada Kitchell. But with the writing paper in front of her and a Biro in her hand, she found that it was not going to be as easy as she had thought.

Looking back over the last twenty-four hours she wondered if she had temporarily taken leave of her senses. Or had Lash Holden's alcoholic exuberance exerted a hypnotic influence over her? She had been frightened and confused, and stubbornly determined that nothing should cheat her out of this long-looked-forward-to visit to Zanzibar. And in that state of mind she had been only too ready to grasp at the preposterous line of escape that he had offered. But now that she had plenty of time for thought, the folly of her behaviour was becoming increasingly clear.

She had done precisely what someone had hoped that she would do. Panicked and behaved in a foolish and suspicious manner, and allowed herself to be used as a red-herring to confuse the trail of a murderer. She was an 'Accessory After the Fact'; and that, too, was a punishable offence. If she had kept her head and rung up the police at once, even though it meant postponing this visit or perhaps sacrificing it altogether, then it would have been the police who would have found that gun — and without her fingerprints on it. And if she had given them what little information she could, it might have helped them to get on the track of the real criminal at once, instead of wasting time trying to trace her.

She had, thought Dany with bleak honesty, been selfish and cowardly and deplorably gullible. She had obstructed justice and played a murderer's game for him, and she wondered how long it would take the police to find out that Mr Honeywood's visitor had been a Miss Dany Ashton if she did not write and tell them so herself? Perhaps they would never find out. Perhaps, after all, it would be better to say nothing at all — having let things get this far. Could she get a jail sentence for having used someone else's passport, in addition to one for having obstructed justice? Yet she had only wanted to see Zanzibar. Zanzibar and *Kivulimi*...

Lorraine had sent her some photographs of *Kivulimi* two years ago. They had arrived on a cold, wet, depressing afternoon in November, and brought a breath of magic into Aunt Harriet's stolidly unromantic house. *'There are jacarandas in the garden,'* Lorraine had written, *'and mangoes and frangi-pani and flamboyants, and any amount of orange trees, and they smell heavenly and keep the place nice and cool. I suppose that's where it gets its name from. "Kivulimi" means "The House of Shade".'*

Dany put away the writing paper and pen and returned the attaché case to the rack. It was all too difficult, and she would wait until she could make a clean breast of it to Lorraine and Tyson. Lorraine would think it was all thrilling, and Tyson would probably be furious. But they would take charge of the whole problem, and know what to do.

She sat down again, feeling cold and forlorn and more than a little ashamed of herself. If only Lash would wake up! But Mr Holden did not look as though he intended to wake up for anything short of the Last Trump, and Dany found herself regarding him with increasing hostility.

It was, she decided suddenly, all Lash's fault. If it had not been for him — him and that ridiculous stuffed cat! 'Asbestos' indeed!

A fragrant breath of *Diorissimo* competed triumphantly with the smell of cigarette smoke, antiseptics and upholstery, and Dany became aware that Mr Holden's pleasant profile was silhouetted against a background of lime-green linen.

Amalfi Gordon was standing beside him in the aisle, looking down at his unconscious form with a faint frown and an expression that was a curious mixture of speculation, doubt and annoyance. In the shadow of the drawn blind, and with the light behind her, she looked blonder and lovelier than ever, and it was impossible to believe that she must be a good deal nearer forty than thirty, and had been at school with one's own mother.

She lifted a pair of long, gilt-tipped lashes that were undoubtedly genuine, and glanced at Dany with the unseeing and entirely uninterested look that some women bestow on servants, and the majority of beautiful women accord to their plain or unattractive sisters.

It was a look that aroused a sudden sharp antagonism in Dany, and perhaps it showed in her face, for Mrs Gordon's sea-green eyes lost their abstraction and became startlingly observant. She looked Dany up and down, noting her youth and missing no detail of her dress or appearance, and the frown on her white brow deepened. She said without troubling to lower her voice:

'You must be Lash's — Mr Holden's — secretary. I thought he was bringing Ada.'

'She couldn't come,' said Dany shortly, disturbed to find that she was blushing hotly.

'Oh?' It was obvious, and in the circumstances fortunate, that Mrs Gordon was not in the least interested in Lash's secretaries, for she made no further inquiries. But something in Dany's gaze had evidently annoyed her, for she looked down again at the sleeping Lash, and then lightly, but very deliberately, stretched out one slender white hand and smoothed back an errant lock of hair that had fallen across his forehead.

It was a sweetly possessive gesture that spoke volumes — and was intended to. And having made her point, Mrs Gordon smiled charmingly and went on down the aisle to the ladies' room.

Dany subsided, feeling shaken and unreasonably angry, and unnerved by the narrowness of her escape. What if Mrs Gordon had asked her name, and she had said 'Kitchell'? What would have happened then? *But you aren't Ada Kitchell. I know her.* How would she have answered that? Two redheaded secretaries, both with the same name, would have been difficult to explain away. Unless they were sisters——? If Mrs Gordon questioned her again she would have to be Ada's sister. Lash should have remembered that Mrs Gordon had met his ex-secretary, and warned her of it.

She turned to look at him again, and apprehension gave place to that entirely illogical anger. She reached out and pushed the lock of hair over his forehead again. That, thought Dany, will show her!

The stewardess dispensed tea, and the two Colonial gentlemen in the seat behind woke up and embarked upon a long and dogmatic discussion of the race problems in Kenya. The thin Arab whom Dany had first seen in the hall of the Airlane — or possibly in Market-Lydon? — passed down the aisle, and one of the men behind her lowered his voice and said: 'See who that was? Salim Abeid — the chap they call "Jembe".'

'Believe you're right. Wonder what he's been doing over in London?'

'Being made much of by our messy little Pro-Reds and Pink Intellectuals, I suppose. Can't think why we allow that type of chap to go there. They're never up to any good, and they never get any good — the Reds see to that! Swoop down on 'em like vultures the minute they land, and cherish 'em and fill 'em up with spleen, and educate 'em in subversion.'

'I've always heard,' said the other voice, 'that he's an able feller. They say he's getting quite a following in Zanzibar.'

'So I believe. Which is Zanzibar's bad luck! That place has always seemed to me a sort of peaceful oasis in a brawling desert of politicians and power-grabbers. But Jembe and his ilk are out to change all that if they can. Ever noticed how for all their bellowings about "Peace and Brotherly Love" the average Red is eaten up from nose to tail with envy, hatred, malice and all uncharitableness? Their gods and their gospel are hate and destruction, and Jembe is typical of the breed. At the moment his target is the British, because that is a sitting duck these days. But he's a Coast Arab, and if ever he should manage to get us out he'll turn his followers on the Indian community next; or the Parsees — and then the Omani Arabs — and so on. There must always be an enemy to kick, so that he can keep hate alive and profit by it. If Zanzibar is a little Eden, then Jembe is the serpent in it! Did I ever tell you ...?'

The speaker lowered his voice again as the subject of his remarks passed again on his way back to his seat, and thereafter made no further mention of Zanzibar or of the man he had referred to as 'Jembe'.

The daylight faded, and Dany drew up the blind and found that they were still flying over the sea. She wished that she had something to read. Or someone to talk to. Anything to soothe her jangled nerves and keep her from thinking of Mr Honeywood — and of murder. The couple behind her, having exhausted politics and settled the fate of Kenya, had advanced — loudly — to the unnerving subject of air disasters. A painfully audible anecdote about a settler who, while flying his family in to Nairobi for a week-end, made a forced landing in waterless country where they all died of thirst before help could reach them, was succeeded by another concerning a convivial gentleman called 'Blotto' Coots who 'pancaked' in the sea off Mombasa and was devoured by sharks, and a third relating to one 'Toots' Parbury-Basset who crashed into the crater of an extinct volcano, killing herself, two friends and her African houseboy in the process ...

'Must have got caught in a down-draught: or else her engine cut out,' trumpeted the narrator light-heartedly. 'We didn't find 'em till the next day. Nasty mess. Bits all over the shop — no idea who was who. Did you hear about that airliner that broke up over the Mediterranean last Tuesday? Come to think of it, must have been just about where we are now. Forty-eight people on board and——'

The Arab, Jembe, rose abruptly and hurried down the aisle once more, casting the speaker a look of virulent dislike as he passed. It was obvious that he too had caught part of the conversation, and Dany remembered his recent assertion that he felt 'always most bad over the sea, for if the engines should fail then, we will all drown: it is terrible!' He had something there, she thought, peering down at the enormous empty leagues of sea so far below them, and wondering if there were sharks in the Mediterranean. She had it on good authority that there were plenty off the Mombasa coast, and it occurred to her that if the timorous Jembe had been tuned in on the fate of the late 'Blotto' Coots, he was likely to feel a lot worse once they left Mombasa on the last lap of their journey.

If he has any sense, thought Dany, he'll take a strong sedative! She was not sure that she couldn't do with one herself.

A star swam palely into the blue immensity above, to be followed by another and another, until at last it was dark. The chairs were tipped back to facilitate sleep, and the lights were dimmed to no more than a faint blue glow; but it was not a restful night — although judging from the stentorian snores, a few people found it so.

In the yellow dawn they came down for breakfast at Khartoum, where the stewardess, assisted by the First Officer, made another unsuccessful attempt to arouse the slumbering Mr Holden. 'We're supposed to turn everyone out at these stops,' explained the First Officer, 'but short of carrying him out, and back in again, there doesn't seem to be much that we can do about this one. He must have been on one hell of a bender. Lucky chap! Oh well — let him lie. Are you with him, Miss — er——?'

'Kitchell,' supplied Dany hastily. 'Yes. I'm his secretary.'

'Tough luck! What are you going to do about him when we reach Nairobi?'

'I've no idea,' said Dany truthfully. 'But he's bound to wake up before then.'

'I wouldn't bet on it,' said the First Officer cheerfully, and went away followed by the stewardess.

Dany and the remainder of the passengers, looking heavy-eyed and somewhat creased, had eaten breakfast and exchanged wan, polite smiles as the sun rose over Ethiopia. Sir Ambrose Yardley had left, looking regretful, and his place had been taken by a stout Indian. But otherwise the passenger list was unchanged, and the weary, yawning faces were beginning to look as familiar to Dany as though she had known them all for several years.

Lash had woken shortly after they had taken off again. He had looked at Dany as though he had no idea at all who she was, and having informed his Maker that he felt terrible, had staggered off to the men's washroom where he had apparently drunk several quarts of richly chlorinated water, and returning to his seat had instantly fallen asleep again.

Dany peered anxiously down at Africa and did not think much of it. A vast, flat expanse of orange-brown, broken by splashes of livid green and dotted with clusters of pigmy beehives which she took to be native *kraals*. But at last there arose on the horizon a blue shadow topped by twin snow peaks.

'Mount Kenya,' announced an enthusiastic passenger who had been studying the flight card. 'We should be coming down to land soon. We're due at Nairobi at eleven, and I make it a quarter to.'

'Will passengers please fasten their seat belts,' intoned the stewardess, and Dany turned her attention to the arduous task of rousing her employer.

5

'L'me alone,' mumbled Mr Holden thickly, and without opening his eyes.

'I can't,' said Dany, continuing to shake him. 'Wake up! You can't go on sleeping any longer. At least, not here. We'll be in Nairobi in a few minutes.'

'What of it?'

'We get out there,' explained Dany patiently. 'This particular plane goes no further. Remember? You've got to wake up. Lash, *please* wake up!'

'Go t'hell,' murmured Lash indistinctly.

Dany shook him viciously, and Lash moaned and attempted to sit upright. He forced open his eyes with a palpable effort and shut them again quickly.

'God! I feel terrible!'

'That's what you said before,' snapped Dany unsympathetically. 'And you look it!'

Lash opened his eyes again, but with caution, and scowled at her. 'Do I know you?' he inquired.

Oh dear God, he means it! thought Dany with desperation. He really means it! he doesn't remember—— Panic threatened to rise and engulf her, but she fought it down.

'You should,' she observed briskly. 'I'm your new secretary.'

'Rubbish! What's happened to Ada?'

'Mumps,' said Dany succinctly.

'Then how in hell——? Oh, let it go! Let it go! I'll sort it out later. God——! Have I got a hangover!'

The aircraft touched down on the runway with a light bump and Lash clutched his head and groaned aloud.

Dany could never remember afterwards how she had got through the next half hour, but at least she had had no time in which to be frightened. There had been no sign of Tyson's secretary, Nigel Ponting, and somehow or other she had collected her luggage, and Lash Holden's, piloted him through a maze of official procedure, steered him through the customs and shepherded him into a taxi. Her passport — or more correctly, Ada Kitchell's — had received only the most cursory glance, and once in the taxi Lash had roused himself sufficiently to recall the name of the hotel where those passengers who were booked through to Zanzibar were to spend the night.

'Holden?' said the receptionist, peering shortsightedly through rimless glasses. 'Mr L. J. Holden? Oh yes. Yes, of course. We were expecting you.' She beamed on them as though their safe arrival was a matter for congratulation. 'Your rooms are reserved. I hope you had a pleasant flight? There is a message from a Mr Ponting. He had to see the dentist — an emergency stopping, and he could get no other appointment. But he will be calling round later and hopes you will forgive him for not having been at the airport.'

'His loss, our gain,' said Lash sourly. 'Let's hope he gets a gumboil as well, and is hung up at the dentist's indefinitely. Suits me.'

'Er ... um ... quite,' said the receptionist with an uncertain smile. 'The boys will take your luggage along, madam. Sign here please, sir. Now is there anything you would like sent up——?'

'Black coffee,' said Lash. 'A bath of it. And some Alka-Seltzer.'

'Er — certainly. Of course. Will the other lady be arriving later?'

'No,' said Lash shortly. 'There isn't another lady. Where's this room? I can't stand here half the day.'

The receptionist left her desk in charge of an African clerk, and graciously accompanied the procession herself, ushering them at last into a sitting-room lavishly supplied with flowers. There was also, somewhat unexpectedly, a bottle of champagne in a bucket of ice, and two glasses.

'With the management's compliments,' beamed the receptionist, and withdrew.

'Wait a minute!' said Dany. 'What about me? Where do I——?' But the door had closed.

Lashmer Holden Jnr sat down heavily on the sofa, put his head in his hands and gave every indication of taking no further interest in the proceedings, and Dany looked at the flowers and the champagne, and struck by an unpleasant thought, crossed the room quickly and opened the only other door. It led into a bedroom where there were more flowers — orange blossom among them — and an impressive double bed.

'It's the honeymoon suite!' said Dany blankly. 'For heaven's sake——!'

She returned in haste to the sitting-room. 'You'll have to do something. There's been a mistake. They think we're married!'

Lash winced and said very distinctly: 'Would you mind not yelling at me?'

'But this is the Bridal Suite!'

'Yeah. I booked it.'

'You *what*?'

'Don't *shout*!' implored Lash testily.

'You mean to sit there and tell me that——? Is this your idea of a joke?'

'Joke!' said Lash bitterly. 'If you think that being jilted on the eve of your wedding, and all for the sake of a grinning, greasy-haired, hand-kissing son of a snake-in-the-grass who—— Oh, go away! Be a good girl and get the hell out of here.'

'Elf!' said Dany, enlightened. 'I forgot. Oh, Lash, I *am* sorry. I didn't mean to ... I mean, I ...' She stopped, confused and remorseful.

'I'll take it as read,' said Lash. 'And now, if you don't mind fading away, I think I could do with some sleep. Thanks very much for your help. Good-bye.'

He dropped his head back into his hands again and Dany stood looking down at him with an exasperation that was replaced, suddenly and entirely unexpectedly, by a strong desire to pillow his ruffled, aching head on her breast and whisper consolation and endearments. And this to a man whom she had met only forty-eight hours before, and who, having been instrumental in landing her in this intolerable and probably dangerous situation, could not now even bring himself to remember her!

I must be going out of my mind! thought Dany, astounded at herself. And anyway, he's in love with that Gordon woman, and he's been drinking himself silly because she threw him over. He doesn't care one bit what happens to me. All he wants to do is to get rid of me as soon as possible. He's selfish and stupid and spoiled and egotistical, and he drinks. *And* drinks!

But it was no use. She could not even feel indignant about it, and she still wanted to stroke his hair and comfort him. Oh dear, oh dear, oh *dear*, thought Dany. I suppose this is it!

In common with all young women she had dreamed of the time when she would fall in love. It would be a romantic and rapturous and altogether wonderful moment, and the hero of it would certainly not be a pallid and dishevelled stranger who was suffering from an imperial hangover, and who was himself hopelessly in love with a glamorous widow who had jilted him for an Italian marquis!

Nothing, it seemed, turned out as one had pictured it or planned it. Life was very disappointing. *'Damn!'* said Dany aloud and deliberately.

Lashmer Holden flinched. There was a rap on the door and a white-robed African entered with a tray that bore coffee, a jug of water, a glass, and some Alka-Seltzer. Dany was relieved to find that he both spoke and understood English, and having given him several precise orders she dismissed him and turned her attention to the tray.

The coffee, though not supplied in the quantity originally suggested, was hot and very strong, and she poured out a cup of it and took it over to the sufferer. 'Try some of this,' she suggested. 'It'll probably make you feel a lot better.'

Lash lifted his head and scowled at her, but he took the coffee and drank it. Dany removed his empty cup, refilled it and handed it back, and went into the bedroom. She had already possessed herself of his keys in the Customs shed at the airport, and now she unlocked his dressing-case and dealt efficiently with the contents.

'I've run you a bath,' she announced, returning to the sitting-room. 'You look as though you could do with one. And you need a shave. You'll find your brushes and things in the dressing-room, and the room waiter will be along with something to eat in about twenty minutes. I'm not sure whether it's an early luncheon or a late breakfast, but I don't suppose it matters. Don't be too long, or it will be cold.'

She left him to it, and went away to sort out the room situation with the desk clerk and the receptionist, and returned sometime later looking thoughtful. A room-boy was waiting with a laden tray, and she told him to leave it on the table, and that he need not wait, and after he had gone she stood for several minutes staring thoughtfully at a forlorn white object that was lying upside down on the floor, displaying a neat satin label that guaranteed it to be washable and heat-proof.

'Poor Asbestos!' said Dany, stooping and picking him up. She dusted him off and replaced him, right-side-up, on the sofa: 'I suppose he's lost interest in you too. Never mind. I'll look after you. And him — if it kills me!'

There was a faint sound behind her and she turned to find Lash standing in the doorway.

He was looking exceedingly pale and there were dark circles under his eyes, but he had shaved, and his hair was wet and smooth. He had apparently found the effort to look out a change of clothes too much for him, for he was wearing pyjamas and the bottle-green dressing-gown, and he looked exhausted and ill and bad tempered.

'Do you make a habit of talking to yourself?' he inquired morosely.

Dany flushed, but ignored the question. She said, 'Your food's come. The soup looks rather good, and it's hot. I didn't think you'd like curry, so I ordered steak.'

Lash shuddered, but he drank the soup, and feeling slightly revived by it, managed to eat a reasonable quantity of steak, and topped it off with two more cups of black coffee. After which he lit a cigarette, and said grudgingly: 'Thanks. I feel slightly better. I guess I must have been pretty well plastered. The whole thing is a blur.'

'Including me,' said Dany.

'Yes — no. I seem to remember thinking it was a good idea to bring you along instead of Ada, though God alone knows why.'

Dany told him. At length and in detail.

'I don't believe it,' said Mr Holden hoarsely, breaking the long silence that had followed that recital. 'I — simply — do — not — believe — it!'

'Well it's true!' said Dany hotly. 'And if you think I'd take the trouble to invent such a — a nauseatingly improbable story, I can only say——'

'I *couldn't* be such a brainless, godammed, half-witted moron,' continued Lash as though she had not spoken. 'I couldn't. No one could! Are you giving me a line? No — no, I suppose not. For the love of Mike, why did you pay any attention to me? Couldn't you see I was higher than a kite and not responsible for my actions? Hell! you *must* have known I was drunk!

'I'm sorry,' said Dany, 'but you see I'd never met anyone who was drunk before. Aunt Harriet, you know,' she explained kindly.

'No, I don't know your Aunt Harriet! But—— Now listen — you can't have thought that I was talking sense. You can't!'

'I thought you were just — cheerful and optimistic.'

'Cheerful and optimistic! God Almighty!' He pushed his chair back violently, and rising from the table began to pace up and down the room like some caged tiger. 'Look — you must have been able to work it out for yourself. That the whole thing was crazy, I mean. Stark, raving crazy. And that I must have been crazy to suggest it! And anyway, how were you to know that I wasn't? You didn't even know me! For all you knew I might have escaped from the local asylum!'

'But you were a friend of Tyson's,' explained Dany patiently. 'You told me you were. And you were going to stay at *Kivulimi* — like me.'

'What's that got to do with it?' demanded Lash unfairly. 'You can't go two-timing the police and skipping out of the country on a stolen passport — well, a borrowed one, then! — just because I happen to know your step-father. Don't you understand? It's illegal! It's criminal! It's — it's — Good grief, it's sheer, shrieking lunacy! You can probably go to jail for it. And so can I!'

'Well, after all,' said Dany, 'it was your idea.'

Lash stood stock still and glared at her for a full minute in a silence that was loud with unprintable comment, and then he sat down very suddenly on the sofa and shut his eyes.

'I give up,' he said, 'I am just not strong enough to compete with you — or this situation. And to think,' he added bitterly, 'that this was to have been my honeymoon! My romantic, orchids-and-champagne-and-tropical-moonlight honeymoon! Dear God, what have I done to deserve this?'

'Drunk too much,' said Dany unkindly.

Lash opened one inflamed eye and regarded her with strong revulsion. 'One more crack like that out of you,' he said dangerously, '— just one! and I shall ring up the nearest police station and spill the whole dam' story, and let *them* deal with you!'

'And if you do,' said Dany sweetly, 'I shall tell them that you persuaded me into it; and then if anyone goes to jail it will be you. For kidnapping a minor!'

There was a brief silence.

'Why you little——!' said Lash very softly.

Dany rose briskly. 'I don't think I know what that means,' she said, 'but I can guess. And I'm afraid that calling me names isn't going to be any help. You got me into this, and you're going to get me out.'

'Am I, by God!'

'Yes, you are! So it's no use saying "Am I, by God!" Once we're in Zanzibar, and at *Kivulimi*, you can wash your hands of me, or tell the police, or do anything else you like. But until then I'm your secretary, Miss Kitchell. And I'm going to go on being Miss Kitchell — or else! Do you see?'

'O.K. I get it,' said Lash grimly. 'All right, Miss Kitchell, you win. And now, as I am not in the habit of sharing a bedroom suite with my secretary, will you kindly get the hell out of here?'

Dany studied him with a faint smile. He was looking completely exhausted and exceedingly cross, and once again it occurred to her how pleasant it would be if she were able to put her arms about him and kiss away his tiredness and ill-temper. She felt, suddenly, a good deal older than him, and that it was unkind of her to confront him with any more problems. But it couldn't be helped.

'I'm afraid,' she said carefully, 'that I can't do that either. You see, there are no other rooms.'

'Oh yes there are. There was one booked for Ada.'

'Yes, I know. But they thought I was your wife, and when that receptionist asked you about the "other lady" — meaning your secretary — you said there wasn't one.'

'So what?'

'So I'm afraid they've given the other room to someone else.'

'Then they can dam' well give you another,' snapped Lash.

Dany shook her head regretfully. 'I'm afraid not. There aren't any more rooms. Not even mine! A Mr Dowling's got that. He told them I'd cancelled my passage, and he'd taken it, and could he have my room as well. There isn't a hole or corner to spare anywhere, though the manager was very kind when I explained that I was only the secretary and not the bride, and he rang up at least eight other hotels. But it seems we've chosen a bad time to arrive. There's some special week on at the moment, and the town is packed out. I said I was sure you wouldn't mind.'

Lash looked at her for a long moment, and then he rose and crossed the room, and planted his thumb firmly on the bell.

'What are you ringing for?' inquired Dany, a trifle anxiously.

'Rye,' said Lash grimly. 'I intend to get plastered again. And as quickly as possible!'

6

Dany ate a solitary luncheon in a corner of the cool dining-room, and drank coffee on the hotel verandah with Mr Larry Dowling, whose conversation she found both restful and entertaining. He appeared to be aware that she was feeling worried and distrait, and cheerfully took it upon himself to do all the talking: for which she was profoundly grateful, as it enabled her to relax and enjoy the view, while the necessity for paying some attention to what he was saying prevented her from brooding over her own problems.

'I must get me a suit of white drill and a panama hat,' said Larry Dowling. 'It's obviously that sort of climate. I suppose you wouldn't be really kind and come and help me do a bit of shopping would you, Miss — Miss——?'

'A — Kitchell,' supplied Dany, almost caught off guard. 'Yes. I'd like to very much, thank you. I want to see something of Nairobi, and I have to send off a cable.'

'That's grand,' said Larry gratefully. 'Let's go.'

They set out on foot in the bright African sunlight, and found the Telegraph Office without much difficulty. Dany had dispatched a brief affectionate message by deferred cable to Aunt Harriet, reporting her safe arrival (after first making quite sure that it could not be delivered in England before she herself reached Zanzibar) and Larry Dowling had cabled an even briefer one, express, to an address in Soho. After which they had visited several shops, and Mr Dowling had duly acquired a tropical suit, a panama hat and a pair of beach shoes. He had also bought Dany an outsize box of chocolates, as a small return, he explained, for her invaluable assistance. But Dany was becoming uncomfortably aware of pitfalls.

It was proving no easy matter to talk for any length of time, even to an attractive stranger, without finding oneself mentioning things that belonged to Miss Ashton rather than to Miss Kitchell. And although Larry Dowling had no more than a friendly interest in Miss Kitchell, he was intensely interested in Tyson Frost and anything and everything to do with him, and the indignant Dany found herself being compelled to listen to a candid thumb-nail sketch of her step-father's career and her mother's marriages, with a brief reference to herself.

'I've heard that there's a child somewhere,' said Larry, strolling beside her. 'Kept well in the background, it seems. Not Frost's — hers. But the Lorraine type don't like being bothered by brats: spoils their glamour. Besides, it makes people start doing sums. Difficult to go around looking barely thirty when you've a lumping great deb of eighteen or nineteen summers tagging along in tow. Ever seen her? Mrs Frost, I mean?'

Dany blinked and opened her mouth, and then shut it again, but his question appeared to be purely rhetorical.

'She's a honey!' he said enthusiastically. 'I saw her in London last year at a Press reception for Frost. Tiny, with dark curly hair like a baby's and blue eyes the size of saucers. Looks as though you could pick her up with one hand. Married at least half a dozen times, and when you see her you aren't surprised. Like that friend of hers on the plane — Mrs Gordon. Now there's another charmer! Though for all her looks she's had a pretty tragic life, poor girl. Her last husband fell down their cellar steps in the dark and broke his neck. Tight of course. And as if that wasn't enough, the man she was going to marry last year, Douglas Rhett-Corrington, took a header out of a top-storey window on the eve of the wedding. Seems someone had been writing him anonymous letters, or else she threw him over at the last minute, or something like that. But whichever it was it must have been sheer hell for her, and she deserves a break with the next one. I wish I were in the running!'

'Are you rich?' inquired Dany, startled to find herself feeling so angry and uncharitable.

'Ah! but she's not one of those. They say she only marries for love — even if she doesn't love 'em for long! It just happened that the ones she married had money, because those are the only kind she meets. And if it was only money she was after, she'd have married your boss. A week ago there were rumours that they were going to stage a surprise wedding at Caxton Hall. But now it looks as though it was off. What went wrong.?'

'I've no idea,' said Dany coldly. 'Mr Holden does not discuss his private life with me.'

Mr Dowling's attractive triangular face lit with amusement. 'The perfect, loyal little secretary!' he said, and smiled his swift, disarming smile. 'I'm sorry. I didn't mean to pry. But there's no need for you to clam up on me. I'm not a gossip writer, you know. Young Holden isn't news as far as I'm concerned. It's men like Tyson Frost who are my bread and butter. Him and the Zanzibar elections! That was why I was so dam' pleased about getting on that plane: there were two people on it who might have been very useful to me. An Arab agitator who hopes to become a little Hitler one day, and Tyson Frost's step-daughter — a Miss Ashton. The one I was telling you about.'

'Oh ... really?' said Dany, swallowing a lump in her throat.

'Yep. And I'd rather hoped I might be able to scrape an acquaintance with the girl,' confided Larry Dowling with rueful candour. 'It shouldn't have been all that difficult, and I might have got a lot of inside information, and even wangled an invitation to stay if I'd played my cards right. I did everything I could to get on that plane, but not a hope. And then at the last minute someone cancels a seat, and I get it. And then you know what?'

'No. I mean — what?' said Dany nervously.

'It's the Ashton girl who's cancelled it! Probably contracted whooping cough or measles or something. A pity. I'd like to have met her. Her step-daddy is news in any language just now.'

'Why just now?' inquired Dany, curiosity getting the better of a strong conviction that she ought to change the subject at once.

'Surely you know? Why, I thought that must be what your boss was after. It's his father who publishes Frost's books in the States, isn't it?'

'Yes. But——'

'Then you can take it from me that's what he's here for. The Emory Frost diaries. They were released this year. Emory was the old rolling stone who was deeded the house in Zanzibar by one of the Sultans. He seems to have been quite a lad by all accounts. There were a lot of curious stories about him — that he was mixed up in the Slave Trade or the smuggling racket, and went in for a bit of piracy on the side, with a spot of wrecking thrown in. He left a whole heap of papers and diaries that he said were not to be read until seventy years after his death, which was June this year. Tyson Frost has had 'em for a couple of months now, so he should have had time to go through them. The betting is that they make pretty racy reading, and that Frost'll publish them in book form. If I can only get him to talk about them I shall be sitting pretty. Is Holden out to get the exclusive rights?'

'Perhaps,' said Dany, trying the effect of a cautious answer.

'Ah!' said Larry Dowling. 'I thought so! It'll go down well in the States. The Yanks had a lot of influence in Zanzibar in the eighteen hundreds, and the first treaty the Sultanate ever made with a foreign country was with America. And then there's some story that Emory ran away with an American girl — rescued her from pirates who attacked Zanzibar, and blockaded the American Consulate in eighteen-sixty something, and ended up by marrying her. What a film that'd make! She must have been Frost's grandmother. They say she was a stunner, and that after she married him Emory become a reformed character and . . .'

He broke off. 'Wait a minute ... Isn't that one of the women who were on the plane over there? Mrs Bingham? The manager of our hotel told me that she's Tyson Frost's sister. I wonder if——'

He caught Dany's arm, and hurrying her along the crowded pavement, dived into a shop that appeared to sell everything from shoes to saucepans, and went up to a counter piled high with sponges which Mrs Bingham and Miss Bates were prodding speculatively under the bored gaze of an Indian saleslady. Two minutes later Dany realized that she had been quite right when she had decided that Aunt Harriet would have taken to Mr Dowling. Mrs Bingham had instantly done so, and in an astonishingly short space of time he was involved in an animated discussion on the rival merits of natural versus foam-rubber sponges.

Dany had attempted to beat an unobtrusive retreat, having no desire to make her step-aunt's acquaintance before it was absolutely necessary. But she had not been quick enough, and before she could prevent it, Larry was introducing her.

'This is Miss Kitchell, Mrs Bingham. Mr Holden's secretary and a fellow-traveller to Zanzibar. She will be staying with the Frosts. Tyson Frost, the novelist, you know. What's that? ... Your *brother*? Now that really is a coincidence!'

He met Dany's accusing eye with a wicked twinkle in his own, and grinned at her, entirely unabashed. But the remainder of the afternoon proved to be trying in the extreme, for he had not permitted her to separate herself from the company, and her step-father's sister had turned out to be one of those exceedingly talkative women who delight in asking endless personal questions, and handing out endless personal information in exchange.

Mrs Bingham wished to know *all* about America; a country she had not yet visited but hoped to one day. Dany, who had not visited it either, did not come well out of this catechism, and could only pray that Larry Dowling and the brisk Miss Bates were equally ignorant.

To Mrs Bingham's loudly expressed surprise at her lack of a transatlantic accent she replied glibly that her parents had only emigrated to America within recent years, and that she herself had been partly educated in England.

'Ah!' said Gussie Bingham with the satisfaction of one who has solved a problem. 'Then that of course is why Mr Holden selected you to come to Europe with him. You would *understand* us. I don't think I ever met this Mr Holden, but his father stayed with me once — let me see, was it in '38 or '39? He is a *great* friend of Tyson's, my brother's. A very pleasant man — for an American. Oh, I beg your pardon, my dear! How very rude that sounds. Do forgive me.'

'It's all right,' said Dany bleakly, wondering how long it was going to be before she was asked something that was so impossible to answer that discovery was inevitable. What a fool she had been to talk to people: any people! She should have kept well out of sight and out of danger. Lash was quite right: she had no sense. All she had thought of was that a stroll round Nairobi with Larry Dowling would be a pleasant way to spend the long afternoon, and that it would be quite easy to keep off dangerous topics. And now look where it had landed her!

Gussie Bingham said: 'Do you suppose this is all there is of Nairobi? Perhaps I should have accepted Mr Ponting's offer to show us round. My brother's secretary, you know. He was here to meet me, and he took us out to luncheon at some club. It was really very pleasant. But as the poor man had spent half the morning in a dentist's chair I insisted that he take a couple of aspirins and lie down this afternoon, and that Millicent and I would look after ourselves. I feel sure he was grateful. You must have met him, of course, when he was in the States with my brother. What did you think of him?'

Dany's heart appeared to jump six inches and then sink at least twice that distance. *Had* Ada Kitchell met this Mr Ponting when Tyson had been over in the States? Certainly Lash had met him, and therefore probably Ada. Why hadn't Lash warned her? Why hadn't she thought of asking him? Why had they both forgotten that angle, and what on earth was she going to do when she did see this man, and he refused to recognize her as Ada Kitchell?

Fortunately Gussie Bingham did not wait for an answer: 'He has been with my brother for several years, but I had not met him before — though he has been to the house, of course. But that was when Tyson was in England a year or two ago and Millicent and I were having a little holiday in Jersey. Still, it was thoughtful of Tyson to arrange for him to meet me. Though I suspect he is really here on Dany Ashton's account — my brother's step-daughter, you know. She was to have been on the plane, but she was not at the airport, and when we made inquiries they told us that she had cancelled her seat. Very odd. Chicken-pox or mumps or something, I suppose.'

It was clear that in this matter Augusta Bingham's mind moved in much the same grooves as Larry Dowling's: school-girl diseases. But fortunately for Dany's nervous system, Mrs Bingham abandoned the subject of the missing Miss Ashton and turned to a less dangerous topic:

'We shall be quite a party at *Kivulimi*, shall we not? You know, I haven't stayed there since Father died. That seems a very long time ago. We spent almost a year there, as children. But Father never really took to the place. Not like his eldest brother, old Uncle Barclay, who was completely besotted with the house. He had a *thing* about it — and about Zanzibar. He loved the place, and hardly ever left it. I suppose that was why he never married.'

'Was he the eldest son of Emory — the first Frost?' inquired Larry Dowling.

'The first Frost to visit *Zanzibar*,' corrected Mrs Bingham gently. 'Yes. The family place is in Kent, of course. I live there now, because Tyson is so seldom in England. Millicent and I keep it warm for him, we say. I don't know what I should do without

Millicent. She came to stay with me when my husband died, and she simply runs everything.'

'Does your brother live much in Zanzibar?' asked Larry, steering the conversation firmly back to Tyson Frost.

'Not really. He's such a restless person. Always on the move. He only lives in it by fits and starts. Asks some of his friends there, and then off he goes again. I've always thought it was such a *romantic* thing to have a house in Zanzibar, but Tyson never really stays in it very long.'

'Probably finds it jolly uncivilized,' said Miss Bates. 'Romance is all very well, but give me H. and C. every time! I always say there's absolutely nothing to beat "All Mod. Cons".'

'I'm afraid Millicent doesn't care for foreign travel,' confided Gussie Bingham in an undertone to Dany. 'She detests the East. And she misses the Institute and the Girl Guides and things like that. She has so many interests: a tower of strength. Our vicar often says that he doesn't know how Market-Lydon would get on without her, and I'm sure she agrees with him. Oh! I didn't mean — that sounds unkind of me. What I meant——'

But Dany had ceased to pay attention, for the words 'Market-Lydon' had brought a chill to the hot day. *Man Murdered at Market-Lydon* ... But it wasn't just 'a man'. It was elderly, pedantic, disapproving Mr Honeywood. And since Mr Honeywood had been the Frost family's solicitor for at least two generations, he was almost certainly Mrs Bingham's too. She would have known him well. Did she know he was now dead? Even if she did, the news of his death could not possibly have shocked her half as badly as it had shocked Dany, who had only met him once and very briefly.

Larry Dowling was saying: 'Does your brother often entertain like this when he is in Zanzibar, Mrs Bingham? Or is this a special occasion?'

'Oh, I don't think it was my brother's idea at all. He's not really very sociable when he's writing, and I believe he is supposed to be working on a book just now. But his wife likes to have the house full of guests. I suppose she gets bored when he's writing all day. And then of course ...'

Mrs Bingham's voice went on and on, and Larry Dowling listened with flattering attention, interjecting interested, incredulous or congratulatory noises whenever the flow showed signs of drying up. He was evidently as good a listener as he was a talker thought Dany uneasily. A very likeable man — but a dangerous one ...

She said with forced lightness, breaking into the bubbling stream of confidences: 'Mr Dowling is a newspaper man, you know.'

But if she had intended this as a warning, it missed its mark.

Larry Dowling threw her a brief, quizzical grin that was strangely disconcerting, and although Miss Bates turned sharply and regarded him as though he were something she had unexpectedly turned up with a garden spade, Gussie Bingham, far from being taken aback, was enchanted.

'A *reporter*? But how interesting!'

'Feature writer,' corrected Mr Dowling patiently.

'The same sort of thing, surely?' said Gussie Bingham blithely. 'You must live such an exciting life. Fires and murders and film stars. Paris today and Bangkok tomorrow. How I envy you! Of course Tyson — my brother — knows a great many newspapermen. He says they are the lowest form of human—— Oh, I *am* sorry. That was *very* rude of me. I really didn't mean ... I am quite sure he would like *you*, Mr Dowling.'

Miss Bates sniffed audibly and muttered something about carrion crows and snooping nosey-parkers, and Mrs Bingham frowned repressively at her, and taking Mr Dowling's arm, walked on ahead, chatting energetically and leaving Miss Bates to fall in beside Dany.

'I'm sure I've seen that chap before somewhere,' said Miss Bates, directing a scowl at Mr Dowling's unconscious back. 'I never forget a face. Probably in the papers, being sentenced for libel and defamation, if you ask me. It'll come back to me. I know the type. All charm and good humour, and thoroughly untrustworthy. Only out for what they can get. No better than confidence tricksters. In fact that's probably what he is! We've only his own word for it that he's a feature writer — whatever that is!'

Miss Bates sniffed again, expressively. 'You know,' she confided, 'Gussie's a good sort, and she's got plenty of brains in her head. But there are times when you'd never suspect it. Look at the way she's letting that reporter pump her about Tyson. Anyone could see that he's up to no good. If he's not a crook, then he's after an article — preferably one with a lot of dirty linen involved. Newspapers are a menace. Garbage — that's all they're interested in. Garbage and Murder.'

Murder! ... Yes, murder was only something that you read about in a newspaper. It wasn't real. People one knew died; but they were never murdered ...

Dany had tea on the hotel verandah, still in the company of Augusta Bingham and Millicent Bates, and the Press, as represented by Larry Dowling. Larry had issued an unexpectedly diffident invitation, which she had been about to refuse when the sight of Lash Holden had made her change her mind. For Lash was also taking afternoon tea on the verandah — with Amalfi Gordon. He was wearing a grey suit and showed no signs of a hangover, and Amalfi was looking soft and sweet and appealingly lovely in something that had undoubtedly run someone into three figures in a cheque book, and whose simplicity of line made every other woman within range look (and feel) like a back number of *Home Chat*.

There was no sign of the Marchese Eduardo di Chiago, and Amalfi was talking earnestly and inaudibly, with an expression on her lovely face that admirably combined a sweetly sorrowing archangel and a child begging forgiveness for some minor peccadillo.

Lash was looking a little sulky, but at the same time bedazzled, and Dany wondered if the Marchese had been sent off on some errand that would keep him out of the way for an hour or two and allow Mrs Gordon to eat her cake and have it. The anxieties of the afternoon, together with the murder of Mr Honeywood and half a dozen pressing and unpleasant problems, retired abruptly from the forefront of her mind, to be replaced by indignation on the score of the predatory Mrs Gordon and the spinelessness of that gullible, besotted and hypnotized rabbit, Mr Lashmer J. Holden, Jnr.

What can he *see* in her! thought Dany indignantly. And instantly realized just exactly what he saw in her. Amalfi Gordon appeared to have everything.

Well she isn't going to have Lash! decided Dany fiercely, and sat down in a chair from which she could keep an eye upon that feckless and intransigent young man without appearing to do so.

Lash did not become aware of her for at least twenty minutes, but when he did, he reacted promptly; though in a manner that could hardly be termed gratifying. Suddenly catching sight of her, he remained for a moment transfixed, as though he could hardly believe his eyes, and then rising abruptly and excusing himself to Amalfi, he came quickly towards her, threading his way between the intervening tea-drinkers on the crowded verandah.

'I've been looking for you, Miss Kitchell,' said Lash ominously. 'There are several things that need your attention, and I'd be glad if you'd deal with them immediately. And another time, just let me know when you intend to take the afternoon off.'

Dany bit her lip and blushed painfully, but fortified by a sense of humour, and even more by the spectacle of the golden Mrs Gordon left abandoned at the far end of the verandah, she rose meekly.

'I'm so sorry, Mr Holden. I had no idea that you would be needing me this afternoon. Will you excuse me Mrs Bingham? It seems that I have some work to do. Thank you for the tea, Larry.'

She introduced Lash to the assembled company, and left. But she had been back in the bridal suite for less than five minutes when the door opened violently to disclose her employer.

He banged it shut behind him and said furiously: 'Say, have you taken leave of your senses? What the heck do you mean by flaunting yourself all over Nairobi and letting yourself get picked up by any Tom, Dick or Harry? Hell! d'you know who you've been getting off with? A newspaperman! Of all people to pick — of *all* people! And that blue-haired dame is Tyson Frost's sister. Your step-aunt, by God! Do you suppose she hasn't recognized you? You'll probably wake up tomorrow to find the whole thing splashed right across the front pages. You ought to have your head examined!'

'Don't worry,' said Dany soothingly. 'I've never met her before, so of course she can't recognize me. And I'm very sorry about Larry Dowling. I didn't think——'

'You never do!' interrupted Lash bitterly. '"*Larry*" indeed!' Her use of Mr Dowling's Christian name appeared to infuriate him further. 'Has it ever occurred to you to take a look at the passport you are travelling on? No? Well let me tell you that Ada comes from Milwaukee — and they don't talk with a British Broadcasting accent there!'

'Oh dear,' said Dany guiltily, 'that reminds me. Did I ever meet this Mr Ponting? Tyson's secretary? — I mean, did Ada Kitchell ever meet him? Because Mrs Bingham asked me about him, and I didn't know if I should know anything or not.'

Lash raised a couple of clenched fists to heaven while his lips moved soundlessly, and then, lowering them, said in a strictly controlled voice: 'No, by the mercy of Providence you did not meet him. Otherwise we'd have been in a worse jam than we're in right now. What did you tell her?'

'Nothing. Luckily she didn't wait for an answer.'

'Lucky is right! And I hope that's taught you a lesson. Can't you see that your only chance is to lie low and keep out of sight, and not talk to anybody — *anybody!* — until you get to Zanzibar? Once you get there it's your step-father's headache. And if he has any sense, he'll give you six with a slipper where it hurts most!'

Lash went across to the table by the window and helped himself to a drink from a tray that had not been there when she left. But she was relieved to see that the bottle appeared to be far more than three parts full, and that the amount he took was unquestionably modest.

'This,' said Lash, intercepting her look and interpreting it correctly, 'is merely to take the taste of that godammed tea out of my mouth. Much as I should like to duck the whole situation by getting roaring drunk, I shall lay off it until I've got rid of you. Going on a bender is a luxury I can't afford while there are people like you around loose.'

Dany remarked pleasantly that it was kind of him to worry so much about her welfare.

'I'm not,' said Lash shortly. 'You can disabuse yourself of that idea right away. It's myself I'm worrying about. Which is why, Miss Kitchell, you will stay right here in this room and keep your mouth shut until we leave for the airport tomorrow morning. And you will continue to keep your charming trap shut until we are safely inside your unfortunate step-father's front door. After that, I shall, myself, take the first plane out again, with Ada's passport in my pants' pocket, and leave you to it.'

He finished his drink and moved to the door: 'You'll find the draft copies of several letters on that writing table. I guess you may as well fill in the time by typing them. Three carbons. And spell them correctly — in American.'

'Yes, sir,' said Dany meekly.

Lash laughed for the first time in twenty-four hours. 'You know, you're not a bad kid,' he conceded. 'Your I.Q. is probably the lowest on record, and I can't figure out how the Welfare State ever allowed you to go around without a keeper. But you have your moments. Don't let this lick you, honey. I'll see you through.'

Dany was aware of a sudden prickle of tears behind her eyes, and she turned away quickly so that he should not see them. 'Thank you,' she said in a small voice.

Lash said: 'The typewriter is in that square maroon-coloured case. I'm not sure where the paper and carbons are. Look around. Oh, and by the way, just for the look of the thing, you are occupying this suite on your own. I fixed it with the management. Officially, I am down as sleeping in Room 72, during the absence of the owner. Actually, as he's put a padlock on it, I shall be spending the night on this sofa. But as long as no one else knows it, the decencies will be preserved. And there's a lock on that door over there, in case you feel anxious.'

He opened the door into the passage, and added over his shoulder: 'I'll see that they send along some dinner for you. Safer than turning you loose in the dining-room, with wolves like that guy Dowling prowling around.'

'You, I suppose,' said Dany crossly, 'will be dining out. I should have thought you'd have more pride!'

'Take a letter, Miss Kitchell,' said Lash austerely, and shut the door with a bang.

7

It was just on two o'clock in the morning when Dany awoke suddenly and lay still; listening.

She did not know what had awakened her, except that it was a sound. Perhaps it was Lash coming back. No, it could not be that. She had heard Lash come back before she fell asleep; and that was over an hour ago, for she could make out the position of the hands on the luminous dial of the travelling-clock that stood facing her on the dressing-table. Besides, the sound had not come from the next room. It had been nearer than that, she felt sure …

Dany had slept little and uneasily in the hotel in Gloucester Road, and worse on the plane last night, so she had confidently expected to make up for it here. But sleep had eluded her, and for hour after hour she had tossed and turned in the wide bed, worrying over her parlous predicament and listening for Lash's return.

He had come back at last, shortly before one o'clock. And presumably sober, for he had made so little noise that but for the fact that she was awake and listening for him, she would not have known that he had returned. She had heard a switch click, and a narrow thread of light had appeared under the door between the two rooms, and Dany had sat up in bed hugging her knees and wishing fervently that the conventions did not forbid her going in to the next room to talk to him.

She was feeling lonely and forlorn and frightened, and much in need of comfort, and Lash had not improved matters by starting to whistle very softly between his teeth as he undressed. It was only the ghost of a melody, but the song was familiar. Too familiar. *'Then I'll go sailing far, off to Zanzibar ...'* He sounded light-hearted enough.

He's made it up with her, thought Dany desolately. What fools men are. She's old enough to be his mother! Well, not his mother perhaps — but his aunt. And she doesn't care a button for him. Not really. She'd rather be a *Marchesa* — or a millionairess — or ... Perhaps he *is* a millionaire? No, he can't be! He mustn't be. That Sir Somebody ... Ambrose Something who got off at Khartoum. Oil. *He's* probably a millionaire, and old enough for her. Perhaps she will marry him instead. Or the Italian. But please, not Lash ...

The light under the door vanished, and Dany had fallen asleep at last. To be awakened very suddenly an hour later by a sound that she could not identify.

She listened for it to be repeated, but it did not come again, and presently she relaxed once more and lay staring sleepily into the darkness. An hour earlier there had been a moon: a bright, white, African moon that had shone in at her window and made the room so light that she had got out of bed and pulled the heavy inner curtains over the muslin ones that were intended to keep out such things as flies and dust during the daytime. But now the moon had set and the lights in the hotel had winked out, and the streets of Nairobi were dark and silent. As dark and as silent as her room.

Dany's eyelids had begun to droop when suddenly and horribly she was aware that there was someone in the room with her.

She had been lying looking idly at the faint green dial of the travelling-clock, and she had heard no sound. But she did not need to. Something — someone — had moved between her bed and the dressing-table, and blotted out that small luminous circle. She could still hear the clock ticking quite clearly. But she could no longer see it.

Dany sat up very slowly, inch by terrified inch; moving as noiselessly as that other presence in the room, until at last she was sitting upright, pressed hard back against the pillows and the padded bedhead. Her hands were clenched on the sheets and every muscle in her body seemed atrophied by fear. She could move no further. She could only sit rigidly and stare into the darkness with dilated eyes, while her breath seemed to fail her and her heartbeats sounded as swift and as audible in the silence as hoof-beats on a hard road.

Nothing moved in the blackness, but there was an odd smell in the room. A queer sickly smell that was somehow familiar and yet very frightening. As frightening as the unseen thing that was in the room with her.

Then all at once the clock face was visible again. The blackness that had obscured it had moved from left to right, and that meant that it — whatever it was — was moving towards her.

Dany opened her mouth to scream and found that her throat was dry and stiff and so constricted by terror that the only sound that emerged from it was a foolish croaking little gasp. But it had been a mistake to make that sound.

There was a sudden sharp sense of movement in the darkness and something touched the side of the bed. And suddenly, born of a desperate instinct of self-preservation, courage and the power of connected thought returned to her. That foolish croak had only served to guide someone to her; and if she screamed, though she might wake Lash, he could not get to her for she had locked the door. And she might not have time for more than one scream...

Dany gathered her strength, and flinging herself suddenly to one side, rolled over to the far side of the bed and was on the floor and on her feet.

The suddenness of the movement evidently took the intruder by surprise, for she heard a sharp intake of breath and a quick movement that was followed by an involuntary gasp of pain. At least it was human, for it had stubbed a bare or a stockinged foot on the leg of the bed. The sound betrayed its position as her own effort to scream had betrayed hers, and that much at least helped her. But only for a moment.

Dany backed away into the darkness, and it was only then that she realized that whoever was in the room with her was not an ordinary thief. A thief, with the window behind him and realizing that she was awake, would have escaped into the night without loss of time. But this was someone who meant to get *her* — Dany Ashton! To kill her ... For a swift sickening moment the pinched, prim face of Mr Honeywood seemed to float in the air before her.

Murder ... That was no longer merely an arresting word in a newspaper headline. It was real. It was here in the room with her. Murder. When she moved, it moved. When she stood still, straining to listen, it stood still — listening too. Waiting to pounce ...

She was shivering so badly that she could hardly stand and she felt as though she would go mad with fear. She had lost her bearings, and though her cold hands were against the wall and she felt along it, she no longer knew in which direction she was moving. Was she going towards the door into the sitting-room or moving away from it? Where was the bed? Where was the window?

And then, for a brief moment, she saw the clock dial again and knew where she was. But in the next instant there was a clatter and the ghost of a chuckle — a horrifying sound in the darkness — and it had vanished. The clock had been deliberately overturned so that it could no longer guide her, or betray a movement.

But she was within a yard of the door now. She must be. Another three steps and she would reach it.

Something struck the wall beside her with a sharp *plop* and almost succeeded in forcing a scream from her. The effort to restrain it and make no sudden movement beaded her forehead with a cold sweat and wet the palms of her hands, but with the next step she knew that she had saved herself: and what had made that sound.

The intruder had thrown one of her heelless velvet slippers at random across the room to trap her into a scream or an audible movement that would betray her position. Her foot touched the slipper and she stooped cautiously and silently, and picking it up threw it in the direction of the bathroom door.

It hit the wall and fell with a soft thump, and once again she heard a harsh, quick-drawn breath, and then a rush of stockinged feet towards the sound. But she had reached the door of the sitting-room and the key was cold between her fingers. She turned it, and twisted the door-handle with hands that were so wet with terror that for a moment the knob slipped sickeningly and would not turn. And then the door was open and she was through; stumbling into unseen furniture and screaming for Lash.

She heard her pursuer cannon into the half open door behind her, but she had reached the sofa and Lash had woken up. 'What the hell——!' he demanded. And at the sound of his voice there came a quick incredulous gasp and a flurry of sound that ended with the slam of a door. And they were alone.

Lash groped his way blasphemously to the nearest switch, his progress grossly impeded by Dany who was clinging to him with the desperate tenacity of a limpet and then the lights snapped on and he blinked dazedly, mechanically patting her shuddering shoulders.

'Lash ... Lash ... Oh, Lash!' wept Dany, dissolved in tears and terror.

'It's all right,' said Lash awkwardly. 'I'm here. Everything's all right. Was it a real bad nightmare, honey?'

'It wasn't a nightmare,' sobbed Dany. 'It was a m-murderer! A *murderer!*'

'Don't think about it, bambina,' advised Lash kindly. 'It's no use letting all this get you down. Stop crying, honey.'

But Dany merely tightened her terrified clutch on him. 'You don't understand — I wasn't dreaming. It was real. It was *real*——'

'O.K., it was real,' said Lash soothingly. 'But you don't have to strangle me. Look, what about a little drink and a couple of aspirins?'

Getting no response to this suggestion, and finding that Dany had no intention of letting go of him, he picked her up bodily, and returning to the sofa sat down on it, holding her, and reached over her head for the tray of drinks that he had thoughtfully placed within range of his temporary bed.

'Now see here, for Pete's sake sit up and get a grip on yourself. Here, drink this — it's only water ... That's a good child. You know, right now what you need most is a handkerchief. Or let's say six handkerchiefs. Come on, honey. Snap out of it! You're soaking me, and I shall catch one hell of a cold.'

Dany lifted her head from his damp shoulder and sat up, displaying a tear-streaked and terrified face, and gazed helplessly about her.

'What are you looking for?' inquired Lash.

'H-handkerchief, of course.'

'If you'll let go of me, I'll get you one.'

He freed himself from Dany's clutching fingers, and setting her down on one end of the sofa, collected a clean handkerchief from the pocket of his discarded dinner jacket, and handed it over.

'I seem to remember that nightgown,' he remarked, lighting himself a cigarette and smiling at her through the smoke. 'You were wearing that and a sheet of newspaper when we first met. This is quite like old times. I'll admit that right now your face isn't looking up to much, but if it's any consolation to you, the rest is a treat to the eye.'

This observation produced no reaction whatever, and the smile died out of Lash's grey eyes, to be replaced by concern. 'You have had a bad time of it, haven't you, brat? But everything will be all right now. You'll see. Come on, you're awake now.'

Dany dropped the handkerchief and stared up at him with shocked tear-blurred eyes. 'You still think it was a dream, don't you? But it wasn't. There was someone in my room. I heard a noise and woke up, and — and then I ... then I saw the clock. It's — I could see it in the dark. It's luminous. And then ... then suddenly I couldn't see it any more, because someone was standing in front of it——'

The sentence ran out into a violent shudder that made her teeth chatter, and Lash's face changed suddenly and startlingly. He flung his cigarette away and was at the bedroom door in two swift strides, feeling for the light switch. It clicked on, revealing the tumbled bed and the curtains stirring idly in the soft dawn wind. But there was no one there.

The room was empty and the light twinkled on the little pearl and diamond brooch and the narrow gold wristwatch that Dany had worn. She had left them on the dressing-table, and near them, face downwards, lay the gilt travelling-clock.

'Nuts!' said Lash brusquely, relief giving place to irritation. 'You dreamt it. If there'd been a thief in here he'd have taken care of that stuff, and——' He stopped. There was something lying on the floor by the dressing-room door, and the door itself was ajar.

He crossed the room quickly and stooping, picked it up. It was a torch, of a type that is cased in heavy black rubber and capable of being focused.

Lash turned to find Dany at his elbow, white-faced and shivering. 'This yours?'

'No. Of course not.'

'Umm,' said Lash thoughtfully, and vanished into the dressing-room. He did not return for several minutes, and Dany sat down on the edge of the bed, still trembling violently and wondering if she were going to disgrace herself by being sick. It seemed only too likely.

Presently Lash returned, looking puzzled. He said: 'Nothing seems to have gone. It looks screwy to me. Why didn't he grab what he could, and scram?'

'Because he didn't w-want anything like that,' quavered Dany, shivering. 'He didn't come for t-that. He was looking for m-me. He was going to m-murder me.'

'Oh, baloney!' snapped Lash exasperated. 'Will you just lay off carrying on like a character out of a soap-opera? It was obviously only some little African sneak-thief. A town like this is probably full of them! It may even have been one of the hotel staff trying a bit of light burglary.'

'It wasn't,' insisted Dany obstinately. 'It *wasn't*. B-burglars don't want to murder people, and he meant to murder me. I know he did!'

'Now see here,' began Lash patiently. 'You haven't a shred of evidence that he intended to do you any harm at all — beyond relieving you of any cash or jewellery you'd left lying about. He probably hadn't gotten around to that when you woke up, and the chances are that you scared him worse than he scared you: which is plenty! Now why don't you just——'

He broke off and looked about him, wrinkling his nose. 'What's that smell?'

'I d-don't know. It was in here before. *He* brought it——'

'Chloroform, by God!' said Lash in a whisper. 'That's what it is! Chloroform——!'

He swept the bedclothes to one side with a single savage jerk, and the smell was suddenly stronger and more clearly identifiable as something fell to the carpet with an almost inaudible plop.

It was an ordinary polythene bag of a size and type frequently used to pack sandwiches in for a picnic, and it appeared to contain nothing more than a pad of cotton wool and gauze.

Lash stooped rather slowly and picked it up, and opening it, jerked his head back sharply with a grimace of distaste as a strong waft of anaesthetic flowed out from it.

He rolled it up again swiftly and pushed it into an empty drawer of the dressing-table, and Dany said, also speaking in a whisper: 'I told you. I *told* you! That was m-meant for me, wasn't it?'

'Maybe,' said Lash curtly.

'Well then why don't you do something? Why are you just s-s-standing there?'

'What do you suggest I do?' inquired Lash coldly.

'Call someone! Wake up the manager. Telephone the police. Something — anything!'

Lash turned away and walked towards the open door into the sitting-room. He said: 'Don't be a fool, Dany. You know damned well that we are in no position to go bawling for the cops.'

He held the door open for her, and having shut it again behind her, went across to the armchair that contained his discarded clothes and picked up his dressing-gown.

'You'd better borrow this again. In fact, if this sort of thing is going to become a part of the daily round, I guess you'd better keep it. Your need would appear to be greater than mine.'

Dany said tonelessly: 'No. You have it. I can use this.'

She wrapped herself in a blanket off his makeshift bed, and sat down in a shivering huddle on the nearest chair, feeling limp and boneless from shock and fatigue and the aftermath of abject panic.

Lash put on his dressing-gown and helped himself to a drink, and sat silent for a time, staring ahead of him in frowning concentration while Dany watched him and did not speak. Presently he stood up abruptly, finished his drink at a gulp, and putting down the empty glass went back into the bedroom.

He was away for perhaps ten minutes, and though Dany would have liked to follow him, merely from terror of being left alone, she found that she was too exhausted to move. She kept her frightened gaze on the open door instead, and presently saw his shadow move once more across the wall.

He came back into the sitting-room, frowning blackly, and mixed another drink which he handed to Dany. 'You'd better take that. You look as though you could do with something stronger than water, and you can't fold up now. I want to talk to you.'

He poured out a second and considerably stronger one for himself, and then sat down on the sofa, facing her.

'I'm coming round to the idea,' said Lash, 'that there is more in this than meets the eye. It looks as though that guy in there had gone to quite a bit of trouble. And he wasn't after cash.'

'I *told* you——' began Dany again.

'*Ssh!* Now I'm telling you. He didn't come in by the bedroom window. He broke the one in the bathroom, and came in that way. There was quite a bit of my stuff, and most of yours in the dressing-room, and he's had a darned good look at it. Forced every lock on the ones that weren't open, and gone through every little thing. But as far as I can see he hasn't taken anything. Unless, of course, you were carrying a clutch of diamonds or something? Did you have much money in your bags? Or jewellery?'

'No,' said Dany in a hoarse whisper. 'I haven't much jewellery. Only that brooch and the watch, and a pearl necklace, a diamond bar pin and some costume stuff that were in my dressing-case.'

'And still are,' said Lash. 'They haven't been touched. And neither have my pearl studs and a rather flashy assortment of cuff-links, or a gold and platinum cigarette case and lighter, and one or two more far-from-inexpensive trifles. Not to mention a good few traveller's cheques. All, or any, of those things are just the size to go comfortably into any guy's pants' pocket. Yet he didn't take 'em. Now why?'

'I told you,' said Dany for the fourth time.

'Look, just quit talking will you? This is a soliloquy, not a dialogue. I'm sorting out the facts. That dressing-room and everything in it has had a real going over. The sort of frisking that it would only get if someone were looking for just one thing: one special thing. And it's my guess that if it had been found, your visitor would have got out the way he came in and there'd have been no more trouble. But because he didn't get what he was after, he came into your bedroom; and as you can't search a bedroom thoroughly while the owner is occupying the bed, that's where the chloroform was going to come in. If you hadn't woken up just then you wouldn't have known a thing about it: you'd have passed out cold, and when you woke up you might have felt a little sickish — but that'd have been all. Except that while you were out for the count your bedroom would have gotten the same treatment as the dressing-room. Now am I right, or aren't I?'

Dany merely shivered and drew the blanket more closely about her, and Lash answered his own question: 'I'll bet I am! But where do we go from here? that's the six-hundred-thousand-dollar question. Well, I'll tell you. Backwards!'

He drank deeply, and Dany said morosely, her gaze on the glass in his hands: 'Yes. I can see that!'

Lash grinned at her. 'The point is taken, honey. But you don't have to worry. I intend to stay strictly sober. This is merely medicinal: an aid to thought. And right now we're going to have to do some fast and fancy thinking, because I see I was way off the line in my first assessment of the situation.'

'I don't know what you mean,' said Dany. The whisky Lash had given her was beginning to make her head swim a little, and she felt better. But not much.

'You're not concentrating,' said Lash. 'Remember how I met you? You'd gotten yourself locked out of your room, and while you were out of it someone took it to bits. But they didn't take your money or your jewellery, which shows that they were after something else.'

'My passport,' said Dany impatiently.

'I don't believe it. Not now; though I admit I did once. It seemed the obvious answer at the time, and that, I guess, is where we tripped up. Why should anyone take a room to pieces looking for something that is exactly where they'd expect to find it? in your handbag and right under their nose. We ought to have seen that one: it stands out a mile. Those balcony rooms at the Airlane were a darned sight too easy to get into — always provided one was a resident. Someone probably meant to try that chloroform trick around six in the morning. Easier than poking about in the dark, and most people are dead asleep at that hour. They were probably already on the balcony or behind a curtain when you saved them a lot of trouble by going to fetch that newspaper, and getting locked out. Taking your passport and planting that gun was probably merely an afterthought, when they couldn't find what they were after. To stop you leaving the country with something that you've got and they want.'

'But I haven't got anything!' protested Dany, beginning to shiver again.

'You must have. And I'm willing to bet you five grand to a stick of bubble-gum that I know what it is! What have you done with the letter that Tyson's solicitor gave you? — that guy who got shot?'

Dany's eyes widened until they were enormous in her white face, and she stood shakily, clutching the blanket about her. 'No! No, it couldn't possibly be that. It was just a letter. It couldn't possibly——'

'Of course it is. It couldn't possibly be anything else! The question is, have you still got it?'

'Yes. I — I think so.' Dany's voice was hoarse and breathless.

'Where?'

'I think it's still in the pocket of my coat. The camel-hair one that's hanging in the cupboard.'

Lash got up and went into the bedroom, and returned carrying a light-coloured loose overcoat. 'This it?'

Dany nodded, and he thrust a hand into one of the deep silk-lined slit pockets and unearthed a crumpled slip of paper, two pink bus tickets, a receipted bill and three ha'-pennies. The other pocket was more productive. It contained, along with a face tissue and a card of bobby pins, a plain envelope addressed to *'Tyson Frost, Esq. By hand'*. Lash dropped the coat onto the floor, and slitting open the flap, drew out the contents.

It was another envelope, but of a different variety. This one was a piece of hand-made paper, yellowed with age and folded and sealed in the manner of a day when there were still a few people who did not use manufactured envelopes. There was no address on it. Only the heavy seal bearing the crest of the Frosts over the arrogant motto *'I Tayke Wat I Wyll'*, a number, 74389, and the initials E.T.F. written in faded ink.

'Women!' said Lash. 'And you had it in your pocket the whole time!'

He sat down on the sofa and gazed at her, shaking his head, and then looked down at the sealed envelope again. 'What beats me is why he didn't find it when he went through your things at the Airlane. I guess he can't know anything about women, or you'd have thought—— Say, wait a minute! Didn't you say something about leaving some coat in a powder room? Was this it?'

'Yes,' said Dany, still having some difficulty with her voice. 'I — I forgot it. It was there all night.'

'So that's why. Then it all ties up.'

He stared at the small sealed packet that he held, and was silent for what seemed a very long time.

The room was so quiet that Dany could hear the tiny tick of his wrist-watch and the slow bubbles breaking at the rim of the glass that she still held clutched in one hand. Lash was looking tired and grim and oddly unfamiliar, and as though he had suddenly become a stranger; someone about whom she knew nothing at all.

The silence began to get on her nerves and she found herself watching the bedroom door again, and listening with strained attention for any faint sounds from the night outside. Was the broken window in the bathroom still open? Had Lash thought to lock the door between it and the dressing-room. Suppose the man were to come back — and with a gun or a knife instead of a pad soaked in chloroform?

Lash spoke at last: slowly and in an undertone, as though he were talking to himself rather than to Dany.

'Yes ... that would be it, of course. It's the only way it fits. I remember now. You said something about telephoning. You phoned this solicitor of Tyson's and asked if you could see him in the morning instead of that afternoon. Which means that you should have gone there in the afternoon, and someone who knew that, but not that you had changed the time, meant to get there first — to get their hands on this!' He tossed the small envelope in the air and caught it again. 'That's why the safe was opened, of course.'

'But Mr Honeywood ... Why should anyone murder Mr Honeywood?'

'Because you can't open a safe without keys. Unless you're a professional cracksman. And whoever was after this, and didn't realize that you'd got in ahead of him, expected to find it in the safe.'

'But — but he had a gun. He could have *made* Mr Honeywood open it. He didn't have to kill him!'

'Suppose your Mr Honeywood knew the guy? I'd sure like to know what's in this bit of paper.' Lash balanced it in his hand thoughtfully and said: 'I'm not sure we oughtn't to take a look at it.'

'But you can't. It's Tyson's! And it's sealed. You can't go breaking the seal.'

'Can't I? What makes you think that? There's something inside this that was worth a man's life. Someone was prepared to murder Honeywood in cold blood in order to get it, and you don't get many people risking the death penalty for peanuts.'

'It's Tyson's letter,' said Dany stubbornly, and held out her hand for it.

Lash shrugged his shoulders and passed it over. 'I won't say "Take better care of it this time", because it seems to me that in your own cock-eyed fashion you haven't done too badly. But for Pete's sake don't leave it lying around, because whoever was after it has got a shrewd idea who's got it.'

Dany gazed at him appalled. 'I — I didn't think of that. That means——' Her voice trailed away and she shuddered uncontrollably.

'Exactly!' said Lash dryly. 'It's someone who followed you from London and must have been on the plane with us. And what is more, it's someone who knows quite well that you are not Miss Ada Kitchell from Milwaukee!'

8

The alarm clock rang shrilly, notifying the fact that it was now 5 a.m., and Dany awoke for the second time that morning; to find herself in possession of a bad headache and sharing not only the bridal suite but the bridal bed.

The proprieties had been observed by the slenderest of margins, and one which would hardly have been recognized as such by even the most broad-minded: Miss Ashton being inside the bedclothes while Mr Lashmer J. Holden Jnr, still wearing his dressing-gown, was disposed gracefully outside them.

Blinking at him in the pale light of early morning Dany recalled with painful clarity that it had been her own hysterical and unmaidenly insistence that was responsible for this scandalous state of affairs. She had, she recalled, refused frantically and flatly to be left alone. A combination of panic and whisky had drastically altered her sense of values, and the ethics involved had ceased to have any meaning for her when compared with the terrifying prospect of being left alone once more in that darkened bedroom.

Lash yawned and stretched, and having propped himself on one elbow, regarded her flushed cheeks and appalled eyes with comprehension and some amusement.

'All in all, a very cosy and domestic scene,' he remarked pleasantly: 'I can't think what the younger generation is coming to. Or what your dear Aunt Harriet would say if she could see you now!'

'Or your dear "Elf"!' snapped Dany. And instantly regretted the retort.

'Puss, Puss, Puss!' said Lash, unruffled; and rolled off the bed.

He stood up yawning largely and rubbing his unshaven chin, and announced that she had better stay where she was while he had the first bath and shaved: 'And don't go ringing for the room-waiter until I'm out of the way. The less publicity we get, the better.'

Dany occupied the time in wrapping the sealed envelope in a chiffon head scarf and then putting it back into her coat pocket as far down as it would go, and pinning the chiffon wrapping firmly to the lining with a large safety pin. That at least would ensure that no one could possibly pick her pocket without her knowledge.

Time being short, she took over the bathroom while Lash dressed, and as soon as she was in a fit state to answer any knock on the door he went away, leaving her to pack.

He had finished breakfast by the time Dany appeared in the dining-room, and had gone out into the verandah, where she could see him through an open door talking to Mrs Bingham, Millicent Bates and a pallid willowy man whose face was vaguely familiar to her. Amalfi, the Marchese, Larry Dowling and the Arab, Salim Abeid, were also on the verandah, standing together in a bored group just beyond them, yawning at intervals and making desultory conversation, while presumably waiting for a taxi, or taxis.

The sight of Salim Abeid was a shock to Dany. She had not realized that he too had been staying at the hotel, and she was digesting this fact, and its possible implications, when Lash came quickly back into the dining-room and over to her table.

'That out there,' said Lash without preamble, 'is your dear step-father's secretary, Ponting. So just watch your step, will you, and keep your mouth shut. He may look like the popular idea of an underdone Interior Decorator — and choose to talk like one — but there's nothing much the matter with his little grey cells, and don't you forget it!'

'So *that's* who it is!' said Dany, relieved. 'I knew I'd seen him somewhere.'

'Holy Mackerel——! Say, I thought you said——'

'Oh, I haven't ever met him before,' said Dany hastily. 'I've only seen his photograph. He was in some snapshots that Lorraine sent me.'

Lash exhaled noisily. 'Thank God for that! For a moment I thought we were going to run into more trouble. Well, if you've seen photographs of him, it's an even bet he's seen plenty of you, so for Pete's sake be careful. His hobby is ferreting out information and gossiping about it, and in that line he can give points to any women ever born! He was being infernally inquisitive last night. It seems that there should have been a Miss Ashton on that plane, and he can't figure out why she hasn't come.'

'Oh dear!' said Dany guiltily. 'He hasn't done anything about it, has he?'

'Nothing much he *can* do, is there? Apart from ringing the Green Zero office, and he did that yesterday. They came right through with it and said that Miss Ashton had cancelled her passage only twenty-four hours before the flight, so he had to be satisfied with that. But he's still making quite a song and dance about it, and but for that providential goddam tooth of his he'd have fetched up at the airport yesterday when I was in no condition to deal with the situation. It's a pity his dentist didn't give him an overdose of gas while he was at it, and save us his company this morning as well. But I suppose one can't have everything. Don't be too long over that coffee. We leave in ten minutes.'

They drove through Nairobi in the cool of the early morning, and once again there was the ordeal of passports and officials to be faced. But at last they were in the departure lounge, and the worst was over. The last lap——

Larry Dowling appeared at Dany's elbow, and relieving her of her typewriter, asked with some concern if she were feeling all right. Larry's eyes, thought Dany, were like a Kentish trout stream with the sun on it. Clear and cool — and friendly. Looking at them, she felt again that he was a dependable person — in a way that Lash was not. And yet...

Gussie Bingham, smart in a suit of lilac-blue linen that toned admirably with her blue-rinsed hair, said briskly: 'You look tired, my dear. I hope you don't allow Mr Holden to keep you working too late. Personally, I had an excellent night. But then I am thankful to say that I always sleep well wherever I am. It's all a matter of *control*. I don't think you have met Mr Ponting yet, my brother's secretary? Mr Ponting——!'

'Dear lady?' said Mr Ponting, hastening to obey that imperious beckoning finger.

Dany turned quickly so that her back was to the light, and shook hands with Mr Ponting. His hand felt limp and boneless and as soft as a woman's, and his voice was high and light and affected.

'Ah!' said Nigel Ponting gaily. 'A fellow wage-slave! A toiler at the oar! You and I, Miss Kitchell — mere downtrodden secretaries: hard-working honey-gatherers among this decorative swarm of holidaying drones. They toil not, neither do they spin, while we are compelled to do both. Gross injustice, is it not? We must form ourselves into a Trades Union. Ah——! Eduardo. *Buon giorno!* I didn't see you at the hotel. How are you? You look *deliriously* fit. I suppose you all know each other madly well by now—— No? Oh dear! I'm so sorry. Miss Kitchell, this is the Signor Marchese di Chiago, a fellow guest bound for *Kivulimi*. Miss Kitchell is Holden's confidential secretary, Eduardo, so we are Birds of a Feather.'

The Marchese bowed over Dany's hand and gave her a long observant look that tabulated her admirable physical assets, added the spectacles, fringe and curls, and subtracted the number he had first thought of.

He was a slim, dark man, handsome in a typically Italianate

manner, and although he was not much taller than Nigel Ponting, he gave the impression of being twice the size. The willowy Mr Ponting, thought Dany, would have made quite a pretty girl. And possibly he thought so himself, for he wore his butter-coloured hair far too long, and allowed a single artistic lock to fall carelessly across his white forehead — apparently as an excuse for a frequent graceful tossing of the head that would temporarily return it to place. His eyes were a limpid and unblinking blue like the china eyes of a Victorian doll, but nevertheless they conveyed a disturbing impression that very little escaped them, and Dany was more than relieved when he took the Marchese affectionately by the arm and walked away, talking animatedly of mutual friends in Rome.

Gussie Bingham, hailed by Miss Bates, hurried off to see to some question of luggage, taking Larry Dowling with her, and Dany retired to a seat near the window and struggled with another attack of panic. Officials came and went, appearing suddenly in doorways and glancing keenly about the room, and each time she was sure that she was the one they were looking for. Every stranger was, or might be, a plain-clothes detective, and every idle glance that came her way turned her cold with apprehension. They *could* not stop her now! Not now, when she was almost within reach of safety. Her head ached and she felt chilled and sick and taut with the strain of trying not to think of the happenings of the last few days, or the dreadful thing that Lash had said last night: 'It's someone who must have been on the plane with us.'

But that was absurd and impossible. It was out of the question that it could be anyone who had travelled out from London with them. Dany turned restlessly to look out across the vast, dun, dusty expanse of the aerodrome, and as she did so a man passed by on the other side of the window. It was the Arab, 'Jembe' — Salim Abeid — who had been on the plane from London. She saw him stop not far away in the shadow of an adjoining building to speak to a man who seemed to have been waiting there. An olive-skinned Arab in a well-cut white suit.

Salim Abeid seemed to be speaking with the same fervour that he had displayed at Naples, and Dany wondered if his conversation was still confined to politics. His hands waved, his shoulders shrugged and his eyes flashed, but his companion showed little interest, and apart from an occasional surreptitious glance at his wrist-watch, remained gravely impassive.

Salim Abeid turned and gestured in the direction of the glass-fronted departure lounge, and for a moment it seemed to Dany as though the Arab in the white suit looked straight at her, and once again panic attacked her. Perhaps he was a policeman. An Arab policeman. Perhaps this man 'Jembe' was telling him about her: that he had seen her in the hall of the Airlane in London. Or worse — far worse! — was *he* the one who had murdered Mr Honeywood, and searched her room at the Airlane — and meant to chloroform her last night?

Dany felt her heart begin to pound and race again, and she looked wildly round for Lash — or for Larry. But Lash was at the far side of the room being monopolized by Amalfi Gordon, and Larry, looking faintly resigned, was collecting a cup of coffee for Mrs Bingham. He smiled at her across the crowded room, and her panic unexpectedly diminished. She was imagining things and behaving, as Lash had said, like some hysterical heroine in a soap opera. Surely her situation was parlous enough without her manufacturing turnip-lanterns with which to scare herself further. And yet . . .

'Will passengers on flight zero three four, proceeding to Mombasa, Tanga, Pemba, Zanzibar and Dar-es-Salaam, please take their seats in the plane,' announced a sepulchral and disembodied voice.

The orange earth of Africa slid away beneath them. A waste of sun-baked earth and flat-topped thorn trees, dotted with slow-moving specks that were giraffe and zebra, wilde-beeste, lion, and drifting, grazing herds of antelope — for this was the Nairobi Game Park.

A lone white cloud, faintly tinged with pink, lay in the cool blue of the early morning sky, and as they neared it Dany saw that it was not a cloud, but a mountain. A solitary snow-capped mountain faintly reminiscent of a Japanese print of Fuji-Yama. Kilimanjaro, the 'Mountain of Cold Devils', looming lonely above the enormous, dust brown plains: a gaunt, burnt-out volcano whose snows defied the burning African sun.

A voice from the seat behind Dany's, a man's voice, fluting, high-pitched and seemingly a deliberate parody of an announcer on the B.B.C.'s Third Programme, said: 'Yes — *rather* spectacular, isn't it? And they say that there is the corpse of a leopard in the crater, frozen into the ice. No one knows how it got there, or why. Deliciously intriguing, don't you think? I *adore* mysteries!'

Dany made a movement as though she would have turned to look at the speaker, but Lash's hand shot out and closed warningly on her wrist. *'Ponting,'* he said soundlessly and Dany turned hurriedly back to her contemplation of the view.

Nigel Ponting's neighbour was apparently Mrs Bingham, and with the object of instructing the ignorant — or possibly because he was addicted to the sound of his own voice — he embarked on a lengthy verbal tour of Kenya.

'And you have simply no idea how primitive those up-country roads are,' fluted Mr Ponting. 'Mere tracks, I assure you. *Torture* to the tyres! Not, of course, to mention one's *spine*! Though actually, when one gets there, it is quite deliciously stark. The natives — the animals — the scenery! Intoxicatingly primitive. Such an improvement on down-country Kenya and the Settler Belt, which is so *painfully* Pre-World-War-One, I always think. *Too* Poona, don't you agree? But the Northern Frontier now . . .'

His voice tinkled on and on like water trickling from a faulty tap, interspersed at intervals by vague noises from Gussie Bingham (herself no mean monologist but at present patently outclassed) and it would have been a soothing enough sound had he not changed to the subject of Dany.

'I can't understand it,' said Nigel Ponting fretfully. 'I simply *cannot* understand it. No word at the hotel, and her room reservation not even cancelled. One hopes that the Frosts have had a cable, but really — one didn't know whether to go or stay! I suppose the wretched girl has been smitten with some form of spots. Measles, or some similar schoolgirl affliction.'

Lash turned his head and grinned maliciously at Dany, but she did not share his amusement. She was getting tired of hearing herself referred to as though she were a school-age adolescent, and in any case she could see nothing comic, in the present circumstances, in having to listen to this particular form of conversation.

'Actually,' said Nigel, 'it was on Miss Ashton's account that I was over here at all. Your brother thought that it would be a graceful gesture to have her met at Nairobi, and probably save you trouble if I could see to her and show her the town. So he kindly arranged for me to take a little holiday at about this time to fit in with the date, and now the wretched girl has not arrived! *Too* tiresome of her, as I fully expect to be sent back to meet her when she finally does so. And I *detest* air travel. I may not show it, but I'm always simply terrified in a plane. Aren't you?'

'No,' said Gussie Bingham, firmly seizing her chance. 'I can't say I am. But then I am a fatalist. I feel that if fate intends me to die in an air-crash, I shall die in an air-crash: and that is all there is to it. And if it does not then there is nothing to worry about. Everything, dear Mr Ponting, is pre-destined. Everything! There is no such thing as chance. Once one has grasped that simple but essential truth, life becomes far less complicated. One ceases to worry.'

Mr Ponting uttered a sharp cry of disagreement. 'Oh no, no, no, no *No*, Mrs Bingham! I cannot agree with you. The doctrine of pre-destination, even if it were proved right, *must* be wrong.

So spineless. Surely one should grasp opportunity and *mould* it to one's will?'

'That's what Millicent says. We have *such* arguments. But it is my contention that when we think we are grasping an opportunity we are merely doing something that we were ordained to do, and cannot avoid doing. For instance, when we left Lydon Gables for London we were half-way to the station when I remembered that I had taken my passport out of Millicent's bag to show to a friend (a really laughable photograph!) and left it on the piano. So of course we had to hurry back, and what do you think! We found that a live coal had fallen out of the drawing-room fire, and the carpet was already smouldering! Mrs Hagby might not have had occasion to come in for several hours, and had we not returned the house might well have burned down!'

'Very lucky,' conceded Nigel Ponting.

'Lucky? No such thing. We were *meant* to return. I was meant to leave that passport behind, and so could not have avoided doing so.'

Nigel gave a little tittering laugh. 'And supposing you had missed your train and had not been able to reach London, and the airport, in time? Would that also have been *meant*?'

'Oh, but we were not meant to miss it! It was fortunately running late. Though even if it had not been we should not have missed the plane, because we came up to London two days early, on the afternoon of the twelfth, and stayed at the Airlane, as Millicent had some shopping to do and——'

Dany was aware of a slight movement beside her, and she saw that Lash's hands had tightened suddenly on the newspaper he held so that it's outer columns were crumpled and unreadable. But surely he had known that Mrs Bingham and Miss Bates had been at the Airlane? And surely he could not think — *Someone on the plane* ... Gussie Bingham ... No, that at least was not possible!

Nigel was saying pettishly: 'But really, Mrs Bingham, one cannot bring oneself to believe that Providence is interested in such matters as a coal falling out of your drawing-room fire or a fog to delay your train, or the fact that passport photographs always make one look so painfully improbable that you were impelled to share the joke with some friend. Now I myself am more interested in psychology, and it is my contention that when you left that passport on the piano——'

Dany rose abruptly. She did not want to listen to any more talk of passports, or the Airlane, or anything else that forced her to think of frightening and horrible things, and she handed her folded coat to Lash and said briefly: 'I'll be back in a minute.'

'Feeling all right?' inquired Lash, half standing to let her pass. 'You're looking a bit green.'

'No. I'm quite all right, thank you.'

She went quickly down the aisle and took refuge in the ladies' room, where she stood staring out of the window at the wide blue sky and the little idling clouds. But her thoughts had only come with her, and she could not hold them at bay.

Gussie Bingham ... Millicent Bates ... Jembe ... Mr Honeywood. *Murder in Market-Lydon* ...

Dany gave it up and returned to her seat.

The tiny, dragon-fly shadow of the aeroplane flitted across muddy green water, mangrove swamps and forests of palm trees ... Mombasa. 'May I have your attention please? The indicator will tell you when to fasten your seat belts. In a few minutes we shall be coming in to land——'

The passengers trooped out dutifully into hard sunlight and a salty smell of the sea, and among them Dany noticed the slim Arab in the white suit whom she had seen Salim Abeid talking to so excitedly at Nairobi that morning.

Apparently there were others on the plane who also knew him, for Nigel Ponting, catching sight of him, left Mrs Bingham's side and hurried after him. They shook hands and stood talking together for a few minutes on the hot, sandy tarmac, and Dany, passing them, heard Tyson's secretary say: 'I do hope you had a lovely time? Frankly, Nairobi is *not* my cup of tea. But of course it's different for you — you've friends there. Now *I* went up to the Northern Frontier with Bunny, and——' The words 'deliciously stark' pursued her as she reached the shade of the airport entrance.

Salim Abeid — 'Jembe', pushed past her, looking far from well, and making for the opposite side of the room he sat down at a small table, ordered himself a cup of black coffee, and began to read an Arabic newspaper which he held in noticeably trembling hands.

The waiting-room of the airport was hot and crowded, and Lash having left her to her own devices, Dany bought a magazine at random off the bookstall and retired with it to a comparatively secluded seat near a pillar. But she did not read it. She sat staring unseeingly at the printed page and listening absently to the medley of accents about her, until her attention was attracted by a large framed advertisement for a local air-line that hung on one side of the pillar a little to her left.

The advertisement, she discovered, was painted on looking-glass, and in it she could see the reflection of Gussie Bingham's blue curls, Millicent Bates' pudding-basin hat, and Amalfi Gordon's flower-like face.

Amalfi, thought Dany, was not looking her best this morning. She looked as though she were hot and rather cross, and the conversation of Eduardo di Chiago, whose handsome hawk-like profile was just visible at the extreme edge of the looking-glass, appeared to be boring her, for she was replying to it in monosyllables and allowing her gaze to wander. Mrs Bingham, on the other hand, seemed to be enjoying herself. She was laughing at something that someone had said, and all at once the wild idea that she might have had anything to do with the murder of Mr Honeywood was exposed as utterly ridiculous.

Perhaps it had been the Arab, Jembe, after all. Or else it was some stranger on the London plane whom she had taken no note of. Or even Sir Ambrose Yardley! The complete absurdity of that last thought drew a wan smile from Dany: she was letting her imagination run away with her with a vengeance! And anyway, Sir Ambrose had not been in Nairobi last night. It *must* be some stranger . . .

The group in the looking-glass broke up and moved away, and she could no longer see the reflection of anyone she knew. Passengers on other flights arrived and left again, and the waiting-room became noisier and more crowded. Dany's head began to ache intolerably, and every separate sound in the medley of sounds became an added irritation: a fretful Indian child wailing with dismal persistence, the crash of an overturned cup and the trickle of spilt liquid, the shrill giggling chatter of a covey of Arab matrons, and the loud laughter of a group of young planters round the bar.

'You never told me you could read Arabic,' remarked Lash's voice behind her.

Dany started violently and bit her tongue, and focusing for the first time on the magazine that she held, discovered that it was indeed printed in a totally unfamiliar script.

Lash reached across her shoulder, and twitching the magazine out of her hands, reversed it and handed it back. He said: 'You'll forgive me for mentioning it, Miss Kitchell, but there's nothing quite so conspicuous as someone pretending to read a paper that they're holding upside down. And that fresh boy-friend of yours, the newspaper guy, has been watching your reflection in that slice of glass with considerable interest. It's a game that two can play. Maybe he just likes red-heads — but then again he might have other ideas.'

Dany said breathlessly: 'Larry Dowling? What ideas? He — he couldn't know anything. And anyway he's only interested in people like Tyson. And politics.'

'That's a buyer's estimate,' said Lash dryly. 'Murder is news any place. So just try and stop acting like you had a ton-load of guilt on your conscience. It shows.'

'I'm sorry,' said Dany in a small voice.

'That's O.K. It's not much longer. We're almost there.'

'But not quite,' said Dany unsteadily.

'Where's your fighting spirit?'

'I haven't any — Not at present.'

Lash said: 'Poor baby.' But without sarcasm. And then once again a quacking, disembodied voice from the amplifier cut through the fog of babel in the crowded room:

'Passengers on flight zero three four, proceeding to Tanga, Pemba, Zanzibar and Dar-es-Salaam . . .'

9

They walked out into the glaring sunlight and a sea wind that sang through the casuarinas and whipped hot grains of sand against their legs, and took their places in the waiting plane; dutifully fastening their seat belts and stubbing out cigarettes. Larry Dowling, from a seat just behind Dany and across the aisle, called out: 'Hi—— Stewardess! we're one short. Don't shut that door. My neighbour isn't here yet. Mr Salim Abeid.'

The stewardess smiled in the tolerant manner of a school teacher coping with a backward new boy, and said sweetly: 'Thank you, I have the list. There is no need to worry. He will be along in a minute.'

But five minutes ticked by, and then ten, and though the plane vibrated to the roar of the engines it did not move, and the passengers began to fidget restlessly, turning to peer over their shoulders at the open door or to look anxiously at their watches.

'What's holding us up?' demanded a stout man from a seat near the front. He rose and looked down the aisle, his red face purpling with indignation. 'We shall be late at this rate, and I've got a conference on at Tanga at 10.15. Hey! Stewardess — Miss!'

The stewardess turned and smiled a bright official smile. 'Just a moment, sir.' She leaned out and spoke to someone through the open door, and then came quickly down the aisle and vanished into the pilot's cabin. Two more minutes passed, and then she re-appeared accompanied by the captain and the First Officer, and all three left the plane.

'*Now* what?' demanded the gentleman who had a conference in Tanga. 'This is the ruddy limit! How much longer do they intend to keep us hanging about?' He lumbered wrathfully down the aisle and peered out into the sunlight, and they could hear him shouting down to someone on the tarmac.

'*Really*,' said Nigel Ponting in a fading voice, 'these business types and their *hustle*! As if half an hour one way or another *mattered*!'

'There I don't agree at all,' said Gussie Bingham tartly. 'Delay is always maddening. And it will probably be most inconvenient for Tyson, who is sure to be meeting us. What do you suppose is holding us up?'

'Whatever it is, dear lady, it is surely a comfort to know that it is *Meant*,' said Nigel with malice. 'But let us trust that it is not some vital fault in the engines, or we shall be pre-destined to wait here for *hours*!'

Mrs Bingham was saved the necessity of finding an adequate retort to this shrewd shot by the return of the Tanga-bound passenger. 'Seems that one of the Zanzibar passengers has been taken ill,' he announced, and went angrily back to his seat. 'Can't think why we should all be held up for a thing like that. Do they expect us to wait until he feels better?'

At this point the stewardess returned, looking flushed and put out, and made a brief announcement: 'May I have your attention, please? I am afraid that we shall be delayed for a further — er — few minutes. We are so sorry that you should be put to this inconvenience, but we hope it will not be too long before we — er — take off. You may smoke if you wish, but will you all please keep your seats.'

Once again a buzz of conversation broke out; to die away as two airport officials and a young European police officer in a starched khaki uniform entered the plane. One of the officials spoke politely and briefly into the microphone: 'Sorry to trouble you, but we have to make another passport check. Will you have your passports ready, please?'

Dany threw a wild, terrified glance at Lash, but he did not return it. He drew out his own passport and held out a hand for hers, still without looking at her, and his complete lack of emotion brought her some measure of reassurance. She could hear the voices and footsteps and the rustle of paper as the officials passed up the aisle, examining every passport, checking it against a list and jotting down brief notes on a loose-leaf pad.

'Holden,' said Lash laconically, handing over his passport as they stopped beside him. 'My secretary, Miss Kitchell.'

Dany forced herself to meet the man's gaze and hold it calmly, and although it seemed to her that he stood there for an appalling length of time, it was, in fact, all over in under three minutes. They had only asked one question: the same question that they had put to everyone on the plane. 'Where can you be reached during the next ten days?'

Even the young police officer had heard of Tyson Frost, and had read his books. 'Another of you,' he said jotting down the address. 'Mr Frost seems to be throwing quite a party. He's a wonderful chap, isn't he? I saw him when he came through here a few months ago. Got his autograph, too!'

The boy grinned and passed on to the next passenger, and Dany relaxed again. It was all just some routine check after all. She turned to smile her relief at Lash, but Lash was not smiling. He was looking, on the contrary, remarkably grim and there was a curious suggestion of alertness about him: as though his nerves and muscles were tensed. It was the same look that he had worn during the previous night, and it frightened Dany.

The three men came back down the aisle, their check completed, and Larry Dowling said: 'How is he, officer? — Mr Abeid? Nothing infectious, I hope? He seemed all right when he got off just now. Is he really bad?'

'He's dead,' said the police officer shortly, and departed.

There was a brief shocked silence. The silence that must always greet such an announcement, whether it refers to a friend or a stranger. The ending of a life.

It was broken by Millicent Bates, who said loudly and incredulously: '*Dead?* D'you mean that Arab chap who was on the London plane with us? What rubbish! They must have made a mistake. Why, he was chatting away to Mr Dowling, on and off, all the way from Nairobi. I heard him. He can't possibly be dead!'

'Heart, I expect,' said Larry Dowling uncomfortably. 'He said he always felt bad in a plane. He looked a bit green. But he can't have been air-sick. We haven't bumped about at all. I think it was just nerves.'

'As long as it's not plague or cholera or one of those beastly Eastern diseases!' said Millicent with an audible shudder. 'I told you we should regret coming out East, Gussie!'

Dany heard Mrs Bingham turn sharply in her seat. 'Don't talk nonsense, Millicent! Of course it can't be anything infectious. If it were they'd quarantine the lot of us!'

'How do we know they haven't?' inquired Miss Bates. 'We're still here!'

The entire plane was silent again, digesting this. Presently the silence was broken by the return of the captain and the First Officer, and five minutes later Mombasa Airport was behind them — a dwindling speck among toy trees.

Dany turned to look at Lash again, and said in an anxious undertone: 'Would they really quarantine us if it was something infectious?'

'If it had been anything infectious they'd never have let us leave.'

'Oh. Yes. I didn't think of that. I suppose it must have been a heart attack. Or a heat stroke.'

'I doubt it,' said Lash curtly.

'Why?'

'They wouldn't have taken all that trouble to check up on the lot of us, and make certain of being able to get in touch with us again, if it were anything as simple as that. They think it's something else.'

Once again Dany was conscious of feeling oddly breathless. She said: 'I don't know what you mean.'

'Then you're lucky,' said Lash briefly, and put a stop to any further conversation by lying back and closing his eyes with deliberation.

Small puff-ball clouds lazed in the hot blue air and trailed their shadows far below across acres of pineapple plantations spiked with sisal, and thick, pale, leafless baobab trees ...

Tanga, and another wait: shorter this time. An agonizing wait: but there were no police officers to meet the plane. The voice of the stewardess again: 'May I have your attention, please. The indicator will tell you when to fasten your seat belts ...'

Now they were over the sea. A glassy sea that merged into a glassy sky with no line anywhere to show where one ended and the other began: blue and green, violet and amethyst, streaked with the pale ribbons of wandering currents; the colours shifting and changing as the shadow of the plane swept across deep water, coral beds, rock bottom or sandy shallows.

Pemba: the Green Island. Rich in cloves and dark with the legends of witches, demons and warlocks. A long, sandy runway and the sea wind rustling the palm-leaf thatch and matting sides of the little hut that did duty for airport office and waiting-room. Amalfi Gordon, looking as out of place as a diamond tiara in the one-and-ninepennies, and gazing in horrified disbelief at an enormous slow-moving millepede that was crawling placidly across the dusty floor. Millicent Bates, her worst fears realized and 'What Did I Tell You?' written all over her. Gussie Bingham, seated on the extreme edge of a wooden bench upon which she had first thoughtfully spread a clean handkerchief, and also watching the millepede with an expression of acute apprehension. Eduardo di Chiago, Nigel Ponting and the Arab in the white suit standing together in the open doorway, silhouetted against the hot empty expanse of sand and sky, talking together in Italian. And Larry Dowling fanning himself with his new panama hat and gazing absently at a framed poster that urged prospective travellers to 'Fly BOAC.'

There were eight other passengers of assorted nationalities in the hot little hut. A stout German business man, a Swedish tourist hung about with expensive cameras, two British army officers on leave, a Parsee, an elderly Indian couple and a citizen of the United States of America — Mr Lashmer J. Holden Jnr, who once again appeared to have fallen asleep.

How *can* he just doze off like that, thought Dany indignantly, when we shall be arriving in Zanzibar in no time at all, and if they've heard anything there we may find police waiting for us at the airport? And if Mother is there to meet us she'll know me at once, even in spectacles and with this hideous hair-fixing, and suppose she says something in front of the passport and customs people before we can stop her, and—— Oh, I wish it were all over! How *can* he go to sleep!

Lash opened one eye, winked at her solemnly, and shut it again, and Dany blushed as hotly as though she had been caught speaking her thoughts aloud. She turned her back on him with deliberation as Nigel Ponting drifted in and introduced the Arab:

'Here's someone you simply *must* meet. Seyyid Omar-bin-Sultan. He has a simply heavenly, *heavenly* house in Zanzibar. In fact two — or is it three? Anyway, if you want to see the island you must lure him into taking you on a conducted tour. No one can tell you as much about it as he can. He practically *is* Zanzibar!'

Seyyid Omar smiled and bowed. His English was as fluent as his Italian had been and he spoke it with barely a trace of an accent. He in no way resembled his compatriot, the late Mr Salim Abeid, for his complexion was no darker than the Marchese di Chiago's, and he was a charming and entertaining conversationalist.

Lash did not open his eyes again until the passengers were summoned once more to take their seats in the plane, but as they left the little palm-thatched hut he took Dany's arm and delayed her, walking slowly until the others had drawn ahead.

'Now get this,' said Lash, speaking quickly and in an undertone. 'When we get there, waste as much time as you can before you leave the plane. Fuss over the baggage — anything. But get right at the end of the line. I've got to see your mother first — if she's at the airport. Or your step-father. Or both. Otherwise we're going to find ourselves in the can before we can blink twice. Got that?'

Dany nodded. And then they were back once more in their seats, facing an illuminated sign that was saying 'No Smoking. Fasten Seat Belts.'

Pemba dwindled in its turn to a little dark dot in a waste of blue, and ahead of them lay something that at first seemed no more substantial than the shadow of a cloud on the glittering sea. Zanzibar . . .

The blue of deep water gave place to the gorgeous greens of sandbars and shallows, and they were losing height and swooping in over acres of clove trees and groves of palms. Above orange orchards and the clustered roofs of houses.

Lash reached out a hand and closed it over one of Dany's, gripping it hard and encouragingly, and then there was a bump and a jolt and they were taxi-ing up the runway to stop at last before a long white building backed by innumerable trees.

Lash unfastened his seat belt for the last time and said 'Here we go!' And went.

Dany never knew what he had said to her mother and Tyson,

both of whom were at the airport to meet the plane. He had had less than five clear minutes; certainly not more; but he had apparently made good use of them.

'*Darlings!*' called Lorraine, greeting her guests as they emerged from behind a barrier where they had queued to have their passports and permits inspected and stamped. 'How lovely to see you all. Elf——! What heaven to see you, darling. And Gussie! Gussie, you look *marvellous.* And madly smart. Hullo, Millicent. Eddie! — *years* since we saw you last! Oh well, months then, but it seems like years; and isn't that a lovely compliment?'

Lorraine never seemed to change, thought Dany, regarding her mother with indulgent affection. She was not beautiful in the way that Amalfi Gordon was beautiful, but she managed none the less to convey an impression of beauty, and that did equally well. Part of her appeal, thought her daughter dispassionately, undoubtedly lay in her lack of inches and that entirely deceptive appearance of fragility. It made even undersized men feel large and strong and protective.

Lorraine was wearing white linen and pearls, and she did not look like anyone's mother. Or, for that matter, like the wife of the burly, loud-voiced, bearded man in the salt-stained fisherman's slacks and faded blue T-shirt, who seemed slightly larger than life and was clearly recognizable to any reader of the Press of any country in the world as Tyson Frost, author of *Last Service for Lloyd*, *Clothe Them All in Green O*, *The Sacred Swine* and at least half a dozen other novels that had been filmed, televised, analysed, attacked, imitated, selected by Book Societies and Literary Guilds and sold by the million.

Lash said briefly: 'My secretary, Ada Kitchell; Mrs Frost,' and Dany, demurely shaking hands with her own mother, was seized with a sudden hysterical desire to burst into helpless giggles.

Lorraine had not blinked, but her small face had paled a little and her blue eyes had widened in dismay. She said faintly: 'So pleased——' And then in an anguished whisper: 'Darling — why *red?* and that *appalling* fringe!'

Tyson's large, sinewy hand descended on Dany's shoulder blades with a smack that made her stagger: 'Well, Miss Kitchell — delighted to meet you. Perhaps you and Bates won't mind going in the station wagon with the luggage. No, Lorrie! you'd better take Elf and Eddie and Nigel. Hiyah, Eddie? Back again like a bad lira? Didn't think we'd see you down this way again after giving you sandfly fever or whatever it was you caught last time you were here. No, by cripes — it was dysentery, wasn't it? Gussie, I'll take you and young Lash. Go on, pile in.'

He opened the door of the car, and suddenly caught sight of Seyyid Omar-bin-Sultan. 'Hullo, you old wolf. Didn't know you'd be back so soon. How was the night-life of Nairobi?'

He took Seyyid Omar by the arm and said: 'Gussie, this is a friend of mine. I'd like you to meet Seyyid — Oh, you've met? Good. Well get on into the car then. We don't want to hang around here all day.'

Gussie got in, followed by Lash. 'Come round and look us up as soon as you can,' bellowed Tyson as Seyyid Omar moved off towards a large white car bearing a Zanzibar number plate. 'Who the hell are you?' He turned to glare at Larry Dowling, who removed his hat and smiled amiably.

'Merely a fellow-traveller — in a strictly non-political sense,' said Mr Dowling. 'As a matter of fact, I came here hoping to meet you, Mr Frost. If I may call sometime——'

'In what capacity? As a member of my public or the Press?'

'Both,' said Mr Dowling promptly.

'Then let me break it to you right away,' boomed Tyson, 'that I despise my public wholeheartedly, and I never talk to the Press. Good day.'

He dived into his car, slammed the door and drove off in a cloud of dust, followed by his wife in a second car, and Dany, Millicent and the luggage in a station wagon. Larry Dowling, who was not unused to this sort of thing, bestowed a brief, good-humoured grin on Dany, shrugged philosophically and hailed a taxi.

At any other time or in any other circumstances, Dany would have found her first sight of Zanzibar fascinating and exciting. But now that she was here at last, all that she could feel was not so much relief as overwhelming exhaustion. She had, as Lash would have said, made it. But it did not seem to matter.

The station wagon, piled high with assorted suitcases and driven by a smiling African in a smart white uniform and a red tarboosh, whirled them along white, shadow-splashed roads, tree-lined or palm fringed. Past pastel-coloured houses and sudden glimpses of a sea that glittered blue as a broken sapphire.

Hibiscus, oleander, bignonia and wild coffee starred the roadside, and brilliant masses of bougainvillaea spilled over garden walls in an extravagant riot of colour. And then they had reached the town and were threading their way at a foot pace through streets so narrow that neighbours living on opposite sides of them could surely shake hands with each other from their upper windows. Tall, whitewashed houses, so high that the streets were deep canyons and crevasses. Hot white walls, hot black shadows, and white-robed black-faced men. Huge, elaborately ornamental doors decorated with fantastic carving and great metal spikes. The smell of strange Eastern spices and hot dust; the scent of sandalwood and frangi-pani and cloves. A sound of laughter and music and drums . . .

On the far side of the town they passed through a fringe of squalid slums: an ugly shanty-town of rusty tin, corrugated iron, crumbling mud walls and decaying thatch, which gave Miss Bates an excuse for a dissertation on the subject of Oriental inefficiency and the inexcusable stupidity of Eastern races who were critical of the benign blessings of British rule.

The road crossed a bridge over a malodorous creek and skirted a shallow bay full of mud flats where the rotting hulks of ancient dhows lay stranded beyond the reach of the tide. And then they were among trees again: forests of coconut palms, thick groves of mango and orderly plantations of clove.

'How much farther do you suppose this place is?' inquired Millicent Bates restlessly. 'I should have thought Tyson would have had the sense to live nearer the airport.'

'There wasn't any airport a hundred years ago,' said Dany.

'What's that? Oh — Oh, I see. Well it's a bally nuisance all the same. I don't mind telling you that I could do with a strong cup of tea. Gussie and I always have one about eleven o'clock, and it's one of the things I miss. But at this rate it will be jolly nearly lunch-time by the time we get to this shady house of Tyson's. Shady house . . .'

Millicent threw back her head and laughed uproariously at her own joke. 'Not bad, that, you know. I must remember to tell Gussie. And I bet it's not far out, either! From all one hears about old Rory Frost, I'd say there'd been a good few shady goings-on in that house. And I wouldn't put much beyond Tyson, either! He's the kind who'd watch his grandmother carved up if he happened to need some first-hand information on dissection for a chapter in one of his books. All the Frosts have been hard nuts; or else crazy, like old Barclay. I can't think how Gussie—— Ah, this looks like it at last.'

The car turned left off the main road and into a narrow side lane that was barely more than a track, and presently they were skirting a long, high wall of whitewashed stone. Bougainvillaea, flowering jasmine and orange trumpet flowers draped it with scent and colour, and from behind it rose the tops of many trees.

'Yes, this must be it,' said Millicent with relief. 'The road seems to end here. There's the sea.'

The station wagon had been the last to leave the airport, and the two other cars, having easily outpaced it, were already back in the garage. The road was empty as they drew up before an ancient, iron-studded door set deeply into the long wall, where a stately Somali servant in white robes and a wide, welcoming grin awaited their arrival.

A scent of orange blossom, frangi-pani and warm damp earth drifted out to meet them, and through the open doorway Dany could see a garden full of flowers and winding paths and freckled shadows, and a tall, square, three-storied Arab-style house whose windows looked out across the massed green of trees and a blaze of flowers towards the sparkling sea and the long blue horizon. *Kivulimi*, at last!

10

'And now,' said Tyson, closing the door of the guest-house behind him and depositing a bottle and a handful of glasses on the nearest table, 'for the love of Allah, let's get this sorted out. Have a drink, Junior. In fact, have several. You look as though you needed 'em — and by God, I do! What in the name of hell's delight is all this about?'

Lash had been allotted the small, three-roomed guest-house that was built on the seaward wall of the garden overlooking a curving bay which was part of the domain: a wall that had once been part of the outer defences of a small fort, and dated from the days of Portuguese domination. Half a dozen armed men could have walked abreast along its crenelated top, and Tyson's father, Aubrey Frost, had reinforced the crumbling stone, and converted a look-out and two guard rooms into a small but pleasant guest-house, shaded by a gigantic rain tree and overhung by a profusion of purple and crimson bougainvillaea.

Tyson had led the way there, followed by his wife, his step-daughter and Lashmer Holden, after first seeing to it that his other guests were safely in their several rooms, unpacking suit-cases and preparing for luncheon.

Lash accepted a drink and disposed of half of it before replying.

'You may well ask,' he said. 'And you aren't going to like the answer. We are, not to put too fine a point on it, in one helluva jam.'

'It was like this——' began Dany.

Lash said: 'Now look——! you keep out of it. Right now I'm doing the talking. You can take over when I'm through.'

He turned back to Tyson: 'There's just one question I'd like to ask before we get down to cases. Why did you send this kid here tracking all the way down to the country to fetch you a letter from a guy called Honeywood, when your sister's living right plunk on his doorstep? Don't think I'm inquisitive, but I'm interested. How is it you didn't ask Mrs Bingham to collect it for you?'

Tyson stared. 'What the hell's that got to do with this? Or you?'

'Plenty,' said Lash. 'How come?'

'I don't see that it's any affair of yours. But if you've travelled out in the company of my sister without learning that she is talkative, untrustworthy and bloody inquisitive, you must have brought lack of observation to a fine art!'

'Tyson, *darling*!' protested Lorraine faintly. 'Gussie isn't——'

'Yes, she is. And well you know it! And don't interrupt. Well, boy, having answered your question, let's have an answer to mine. What the hell is all this fantastic fandango about?'

'Have you,' said Lash, asking another one, 'by any chance heard that Honeywood was murdered a few days back?'

'*Honeywood!* Good God! When — how——' He turned sharply to face his step-daughter. 'Then you didn't see him after all? Does this mean that you didn't get that letter?'

'Yes, she did,' said Lash brusquely. 'That's the trouble. And it makes a long and screwy story.'

He finished his drink, and having replenished his glass sat down on the window seat and supplied the salient points of that story with terseness and economy.

'Is that all?' said Tyson Frost with dangerous restraint, breathing heavily.

'It'll do to go on with,' said Lash laconically.

'Then all I can say,' said Tyson, saying it, 'is that there must be insanity in your family! And, by heck, I always knew it! Were you out of your mind?'

Lash winced. 'To be frank with you, yes. I happened to be plastered at the time.'

'My God! So I should think! Why — it's sheer lunacy. It's criminal. It's——'

'I know, I know,' said Lash wryly. 'You aren't telling me anything. I seem to remember saying all that myself when I surfaced yesterday. And more! There isn't any angle you can put to me that I have not already come up against — hard. The point is, what do we do now?'

'Cut her hair,' said Lorraine in a fading voice. 'And wash it. Darling, *really*——! It's quite *hideous*. Not the colour so much; I could bear that. But that awful fringe! The sort of thing film stars used to wear in the ghastly twenties. Too frightful. And darling, those spectacles! For goodness sake take them off at once. They make you look too dreadfully intelligent.'

'It's an illusion,' said Lash sourly.

Lorraine ignored him: 'That's right, darling. And don't put them on again. You look so much nicer without them.'

Tyson said: 'Your mother, thank the Lord, is utterly incapable of intelligent thought or of grasping the essential guts of any situation.'

'It would appear to run in the family,' commented Lash caustically. And added as a gloomy afterthought: 'And maybe they've got something there, at that. An inability to grasp the essential guts of this set-up is something I wouldn't mind having myself right now. And you're dead right about that hair-style. It's a pain. I never did go for red-heads, anyway.'

'No. You prefer blondes, don't you?' said Dany with a sudden flash of waspishness.

'Hell, who doesn't? Is there any more of that Scotch around?'

Tyson pushed across the bottle and said angrily: 'You're all mad! The whole lot of you! What the blue-asterisk-blank does it matter what Dany's hair looks like? It seems to me, young Lash, that you're taking a ruddy casual view of all this. What do *you* propose to do about it?'

'I?' Lash looked mildly surprised. 'Oh, that's dead easy. I propose to eat a hearty meal at your expense, and then I'm catching the next available plane out of here. And I don't give a damn which way it's headed! From now on this is your headache, brother!'

'*Lash!*' Dany's voice had a sudden break in it.

Lash got up quickly and going to her, took her face between his hands. 'Listen, babe, I know I got you into this, but you'll be all right now. All you've got to do is to make a clean breast of it. Lay all your cards on the table. I can't help you. You know that. All I've done is to give you a wrong steer, and make bad worse. I——'

Dany said in an imploring whisper: 'Lash, please don't go — please!'

'Look, honey; it isn't going to help one bit if I — Oh, hell!'

He released her abruptly and turned suddenly on Tyson Frost: 'What I want to know,' said Lash furiously, 'is why you ever let her get mixed up in this sort of thing in the first place! Couldn't you have got someone else to do your dirty work for you? You must have known darned well that there was dynamite in that letter. What was it?'

'Yes, dear,' said Lorraine, sitting suddenly upright. 'What was in it? Why should anyone else want it?'

Tyson said: 'Why does anyone want three million?'

'*W-what!*' Lorraine sprang to her feet. 'Tyson, darling! What are you talking about? You can't mean——'

'Sit down,' said Tyson. 'All of you. That's better.'

He crossed the room with a step that was curiously light for so big a man, and reaching the door, jerked it open and peered out; looking along the broad open top of the wall and down into the green shade of the garden below, as though to assure himself that there was no one within earshot. After a minute he closed it again carefully, and went over to the window to lean out and look down on the sun-baked slope of rock thirty feet below. At last, satisfied with the result of his survey, he came back to the low cushion-strewn divan that stood against one wall of the sitting-room and sat down on it; the wood creaking protestingly under his weight.

'I shall have to go back a bit,' said Tyson Frost, lighting himself a cigarette and inhaling deeply: 'As you probably know — it seems to be common property! — my revered grandfather, Rory — Emory Frost, who died way back in the eighteen-eighties — left a stack of papers and diaries with the family solicitors, Honeywood & Honeywood, with instructions that they were not to be opened or their contents made public for seventy years, which is reckoned to be man's permitted span. That time limit expired a few months ago, and the stuff duly arrived out here. And good ripe stuff it is! Roaring Rory must have been a hell-raiser and a half in his day, and ... But that's neither here nor there. The point is that it took me some time to go through it, and it wasn't until about three weeks ago that I came across a folded piece of paper that had been pushed in between the leather and the backing of one of the covers. And I wouldn't have found it at all if the backing hadn't split. It was interesting. It was very interesting ...'

Tyson reached for the glass he had left on the floor and took a long pull at it.

'You know,' he said thoughtfully, 'it's astonishing how often life can give points to the movies. Have any of you ever heard the legend of the lost treasure buried by Seyyid Saïd?'

'Yes!' said Dany.

'No, *really*, darling,' protested Lorraine. 'You can't believe that story! I mean, it's *too* ridiculous. I know it's in one of the guide books, but——'

'"But me no buts",' said Tyson flapping an impatient hand,

'I too thought I was too old to fall for that one. But there was something mightily convincing about that bit of paper. If no one else believed in the treasure, Grandfather Emory certainly did. And for a very good reason.'

'I suppose he helped to bury it?' commented Lash with sarcasm.

'In a way,' said Tyson. 'And you can take that damned impertinent superior sneer off your face, young Holden!'

He glowered for a moment, refreshed himself from his glass, and then said: 'No. According to old Rory, when Seyyid Saïd died he left the secret with a witch doctor of Pemba, who promptly and rather meanly put a curse on it to the effect that anyone finding it could only use it to bring evil — something of that description. It was intended, one supposes, to discourage people from hunting around for it, but Saïd's successor, Majid, wasn't going to be put off by a thing like that. According to Grandfather Emory, he tortured the witch, collared the information, dug the stuff up with the enthusiastic assistance of my unregenerate ancestor, and generously went halves with him. Emory's share, if I have worked out its present-day value correctly, must have been close on three million sterling.'

There was a brief silence, and then Lash rose to replenish his glass. 'All this,' he said, 'if you will forgive my saying so, is the ripest slice of pure Gorgonzola that I have come across in an ill-spent life. Me, I don't believe a word of it! But it's obvious that someone else does. And I don't mean you or your grandfather, either!'

Lorraine's eyes were enormous and she spoke in little gasps: 'But Tyson! ... but darling ... three *million*! He can't have ... What did he *do* with it?'

'Buried it,' said Tyson blandly. 'Or so he says.'

'But *where*?'

'Ah! that's the catch. He doesn't say. All he says is that he has deposited the key in a sealed envelope with old Honeywood (that would probably be our Honeywood's grandfather, or else his great-uncle) and that it is only to be handed over if and when someone asks for it, quoting, correctly, a number and some initials that were on the envelope. The number being seven four three eight nine, and the initials being his own, E.T.F.'

'I'll be damned!' ejaculated Lash, startled.

'I don't doubt it: not if this is your usual form,' commented Tyson unkindly. 'Well — there you are. It seemed a damned sight too good to be true, and I didn't believe a word of it. Life isn't *that* much like the movies! But it was worth investigating, and as a first step I wrote old Honeywood, asking if he had such a letter in his possession. He had — which shook me. Deposited with Honeywood & Honeywood in eighteen sixty one. I thought it was well worth looking at, and I didn't want to trust it to the post. *Or* to Gussie! Between you and me, I don't... Oh, well, let it go. The point is that as Dany was coming out, it seemed a good idea to ask her to call and collect it and bring it out with her. And that's all there is to it.'

'Except that you gave him a date and a time for that call,' said Lash.

'And why not? The thing was almost certainly in a safe deposit box in some bank, and he'd have to get it out and have it ready to hand over. It wouldn't have been at his house, and as I still correspond with him and not his junior partner, I said I'd send Dany to get it from him; which meant to his house. And if I know anything of old Honeywood, he wouldn't have had it there very much before he needed it. He's a careful guy. Or rather, he was, poor brute.'

'So that was it!' said Lash. 'Then I was right.' He got up and stood looking out of the window, his hands in his pockets. 'Someone knew, and meant to get there first. But Dany spoilt the game by going down in the morning instead of the afternoon.'

He turned abruptly: 'Who else knew?'

'No one,' said Tyson shortly.

'Oh, nuts! Of course someone else knew.'

'I apologize,' snarled Tyson. 'I should have said: "I myself did not tell anyone." Not even my wife.'

'What about Ponting?'

'Or my secretary!'

'But he could have found out.'

'Oh no, he couldn't. I took dam' good care of that! Curiosity is Nigel's besetting sin, and I had no intention of letting him get a look at the Frost papers — or my letters to Honeywood! I keep those papers in a locked box, and the key to it is round my neck. Some of that stuff could touch off quite a few explosions even now, and I'm taking no chances. Besides there's money in 'em.'

'And murder!' amended Lash grimly.

'So it would seem. All the same, I don't believe——'

'Belief is no good,' said Lash impatiently. 'Could you swear on oath that neither your secretary nor any servant or guest in this house, nor your wife, could possibly, under any circumstances, have seen that paper of Emory's?'

Lorraine gave a faint indignant cry: 'Well, *really* Lash! Why *me*? I mean, even if I had (and I didn't, I hadn't an idea) *would* I have been likely to tell anyone?'

'I don't know,' said Lash. 'Would you?'

Lorraine made a helpless fluttering gesture with her little hands and gazed appealingly at her husband.

'Of course she would,' said Tyson brutally. 'That's why I didn't tell her. I never tell any woman a secret unless I want it given the widest possible publicity in the shortest possible time.'

Lorraine gave a small sigh. 'You know, Tyson darling, I can't understand how it is that you write so well when you so often talk in clichés. Schizophrenia, I suppose. Not that you aren't quite right about me, as it happens. Whenever anyone tells me a secret I always think "Now who shall I tell first?" '

Tyson gave a short bark of laughter. 'I know. But to revert to your question, young Lash, the answer is "No". The key of that box has never been out of my possession, and just in case you are going to suggest that Lorrie might have removed it one night while I was asleep, I will add that I am a remarkably light sleeper. And anyway, I don't believe for one moment that anyone in this house was even aware of the existence of that paper.'

'And what about the letters you wrote this guy Honeywood? They must have contained quite a few relevant details. Enough, anyway, to arouse a considerable slice of curiosity as to the contents of that sealed envelope! The number and the initials, and roughly the date when it was deposited with the firm. Who mails your letters?'

'Abdurahman, when he goes into town. And he can't read English.'

'But he could have shown 'em to some of the local boys who could.'

'Why? My purely personal correspondence is pretty voluminous — quite apart from the stuff that Nigel deals with for me, which is vast. Any house-servant or local snooper who was interested in it would have had his work cut out for months, steaming open envelopes in the hope of stumbling across something of interest. So you can wash that one right out.'

But Tyson had forgotten, thought Dany, that there was at least one other person who had not only read his letters, but who possibly knew something — perhaps not much, but enough — of the contents of that time-yellowed envelope.

She said: 'Mr Honeywood knew something, I think. He didn't seem to approve of my taking the letter. He said something about letting sleeping dogs lie, and that no good would come of it. Perhaps he knew what was in it. His grandfather may have told him.'

'Of course! And *he* may have talked!' said Lorraine.

Tyson let out another crack of laughter. 'What, old Henry Honeywood? That desiccated clam? You didn't know him like Gussie and I did!'

'Perhaps not; but I do know that it isn't only women who

talk,' retorted Lorraine. 'Any dried-up old-maid bachelor can usually leave them at the post when it comes to gossip. And he had a housekeeper: that stout old lady with the hearing-aid. She was probably eaten up with curiosity. It's an occupational disease with housekeepers. I expect she read all his letters and gossiped over the contents with all her friends at the Women's Institute!'

'Not Mrs Broughty,' said Tyson, looking thoughtful. 'She's another clam. But that char of his, Mrs Porson, is quite a different proposition. She often does odd jobs for Gussie, and she talks her head off. Why, once when Elf was staying down there she told her the most staggering details of a case that——. Oh well, that's neither here nor there. But as she could only have got hold of them by taking an unauthorized interest in old Henry's correspondence, I suppose we shall have to take it that there may have been a leak. In fact there must have been! So I think that our next move is to notify Scotland Yard — and see that the letter goes by hand. I'll write it first thing after luncheon, and take it round myself to the Residency and ask the Resident as a personal favour to send it in the next diplomatic bag — they must have one. Thank God I happen to know the Commissioner of Metropolitan Police. That may help. I'll write direct to him, and if he wants to set the local cops on to us, he can. But as it will be at least three days, and possibly four, before he can get a letter, it'll give us time to see if there's anything in this fantastic Buried Treasure yarn. Where's the key, Dany? Let's have it.'

'But it isn't a key,' said Dany. 'At least, not an ordinary key — a metal one. I would have felt it if it was. I think it's only a folded piece of paper.'

'Probably a map,' said Tyson.

'Or clues, like a crossword!' Lorraine's face flushed as charmingly as an excited child's.

Lash said dampingly: 'Far more likely to be one of those rambling bits of abracadabra that say *Walk fifty paces due south from the back porch of Ali Baba's house, and when you reach the blasted fig tree, wait until the sun be overhead, and dig where the shadow of the fig tree joins the ditch.* A fascinating document that fails to take into account that by this time Ali Baba's house has been pulled down and replaced by a fish-glue factory, the blasted fig passed out of the picture seventy years back and someone's drained the ditch in the course of an irrigation scheme! That's all we need yet!'

But Lorraine refused to be damped. 'But the treasure would still be there — *somewhere*! Oh, Tyson, just think if it should turn out to be true! It's the most thrilling thing. Will there be jewels? There ought to be. Carved emeralds and pigeon's blood rubies and diamond hilted daggers and ropes and ropes of pearls. *Marvellous!*'

'It depends on how Emory and his Sultan pal split the loot,' said Tyson, finishing his drink. 'But being a citizen on whom remarkably few flies appear to have rested, I bet he played safe and took the gold. Anyway, that's what it sounds like — if, of course, he took anything, and this isn't the old reprobate's idea of a belly-laugh at the expense of his posterity. I wouldn't put it past him!'

'Oh *no*, darling!' protested Lorraine. 'I won't believe it. It's got to be true. I *want* it to be true. We shall solve the crossword, and creep out at night with spades and dig up buckets and buckets full of gold.'

'And find ourselves in the local lock-up for attempting to steal what is undoubtedly the property of the Sultan of Zanzibar,' said Lash morosely.

'Ah, that's just where you're wrong, boy,' said Tyson, heaving himself up and fetching another drink. 'There was no green in Grandfather Emory's eye. His half was a gift, for services rendered. Duly attested, too. There is a document to prove it. It was inside the opposite cover; and there's a nice clear thumb print attached, as well as the donor's seal and signature. It would probably stand in a court of law even today. However, we haven't got the stuff yet. Where's old Honeywood's letter, Dany?'

'In my coat pocket,' said Dany, and smiled a little wanly. 'It seemed the safest place, and I did fix it so that it couldn't be pick-pocketed!'

She reached for the camel-hair coat that she had carried over to the guest-house with her and hung over the back of her chair, and after struggling with the safety-pin, drew out a soft square of chiffon that was folded about a small yellow envelope with five numerals and three initials written on it in faded ink.

She stood staring at it wide-eyed, feeling it: horror and incredulity dawning in her face. Then she turned it over quickly.

The heavy seal that had closed the flap was broken, and the envelope was empty.

11

'It's preposterous!' bellowed Tyson for the fourth if not the fifth time. 'It's just plain bloody impossible!'

'Oh, darling,' moaned Lorraine, 'don't go on and on and *on* saying that. Besides, it's so *silly*! How can it be impossible when it's *happened*?'

'It can't have happened; that's why! Not the way she said, anyway. You can see for yourself the way that bit of stuff was folded and pinned. I tell you it was humanly impossible for anyone — anyone outside of an astral body! — to do the job unless that coat was out of Dany's possession for at least five minutes. Great suffering snakes — I've tried it! You saw me. No one could unpin it from the lining, take it out, get at the envelope and remove the letter, and then put the whole shooting-match back again just exactly as it was, at the bottom of a deep slit pocket. Not even Houdini! She must have left the coat lying about.'

'But I didn't,' protested Dany, on the verge of tears. 'I had it under my pillow for the rest of the night, and it was perfectly all right when I wrapped it in the scarf this morning. The seal wasn't touched. I tell you, I *know*! I would have felt at once if it was empty. Like I did just now.'

Tyson said: 'You must have washed, I suppose? Or had a bath!'

'Of course I did, but——'

'And you took it with you?'

'No, but——'

'Well, there you are! Someone must have got into the room.'

Lorraine said plaintively: 'Tyson darling, don't keep on interrupting the child. Do let her finish a sentence.'

'Lash was there,' said Dany. 'He was dressing while I had a bath.'

'It all sounds very intimate and domestic,' growled Tyson.

Lash said pleasantly: 'It was. Though quite unavoidable, as I have already explained. But if you make any further cracks like that you are going to find that life is even more like the movies than you had supposed.'

'Meaning that you'll knock me down?' inquired Tyson. 'You couldn't do it, boy.'

'It would give me the greatest pleasure to try,' snapped Lash.

'I daresay it would. But I do not intend to let the sons of my college friends use me as a punching-bag to work off their spleen.'

'Then stop bullying the kid!' said Lash. 'Can't you see that she's had just about all she can take? Lay off her, will you?'

Tyson cocked an eye at him, and said meditatively: 'I well remember your Aunt Maimie describing you once — accurately I have no doubt — as a rakish heel who could hook the average woman with the ease of a confidence trickster getting to work on a frustrated small-town spinster. That was when you were getting into trouble over the Van Hoyden girl — or was it girls? So let us have less of the Galahad attitude from you, boy, and fewer back-answers! Were you really in that suite the entire time that Dany was in the bathroom?'

'I was.'

'Did you know where the letter was?'

'I did. Are you by any chance suggesting that I took it?'

'*Bah!* Don't be tedious,' said Tyson crossly. 'Can you be quite certain that no one else came into the room during that time? No hotel servant, for instance?'

'No one. Repeat — no one.'

Tyson turned back to Dany. 'I presume he didn't stick around while you were dressing?'

Dany flushed pinkly. 'No, he didn't. He went off to have breakfast.'

'And no one else came in?'

'No. I locked both doors. And I took the coat with me when I went in to breakfast, and I've never let go of it since, until I came in here and put it on that chair. No one could have taken that letter. No one but myself or Lash. It isn't possible!'

'Did you take it?'

Lash took a swift step forward and Tyson said: 'Let her answer for herself, boy! Well, Dany?'

Dany looked at him; her cheeks flushed and her eyes wide and sparkling. 'I think,' she said stormily, 'that you are the most odious, selfish, egotistical, *impossible* man I have ever met, and I'm sorry I ever came here!'

'Yes, isn't he?' said Lorraine, giving her husband a fond glance. 'I remember saying just the same thing to him the first day I ever met him. And he gets worse. But baby, you didn't really take it, did you?'

Dany rounded on her, anger giving away to exasperation. 'Mother, you cannot really think——'

'Darling,' protested Lorraine plaintively, '*how* many times have I asked you not to call me that? It makes me feel a *hundred.* No, of course I don't think you stole it or anything like that — nor does Tyson. Just that you may have thought that — what with the murder, and everything being so foul for you — that it would be better if you simply tore the horrid thing up and got rid of it.'

'Well I didn't!' said Dany tersely. 'And perhaps it's a pity I didn't think of it — now that someone else has got it.'

'Meaning me?' inquired Lash gently.

'Why do you have to say that?' demanded Dany resentfully. 'You know quite well I don't mean anything of the sort!'

'But you've just said that only you or I could possibly have taken it. And if *you* didn't, that leaves me, doesn't it? Or is there something wrong with my arithmetic?'

'Don't bully the girl!' boomed Tyson. 'Can't you see she's had all she can take? Lay off her, will you?'

Lash laughed and threw up a hand in the gesture of a fencer acknowledging a hit. '*Touché!* I'm sorry, Dany. Well, what do you suggest we do now?'

'Eat,' said Lorraine firmly, and rose to her feet. 'It must be nearly one o'clock, and everyone else will be wondering what on earth has happened to us, and getting hungrier and hungrier. Come on, darling, let's go and see what they're doing. And Dany will want to wash.'

'Just a minute,' said Tyson. 'Let's get this straight. If we are to subscribe to this theory that whoever was after that letter was also on the London to Nairobi plane, it follows that whoever has got it now was on the Nairobi to Zanzibar one this morning. Am I right?'

Lash said: 'It certainly looks that way, doesn't it? If it weren't for one outstanding snag, on which the whole thing snarls up.'

'And what would that be?'

'What the hell is the use of three million — or three hundred million if it comes to that — if you can't get it out of the island? O.K. for you perhaps, or for anyone who lives right here. But how would anyone else start in shifting it? Me, for the sake of argument?'

'I, boy. *I!* Don't be so sloppy with your grammar!'

'Okay; I. Me, Lashmer J. Holden, Jnr. What do I do with a coupla hundredweight of bullion? Load it into my bags and smuggle it through the Customs just like that, I suppose?'

'Then you suppose wrong,' snapped Tyson. 'Use your head! Do you *really* imagine that anyone who is after that much money, and prepared to kill in order to get it, hasn't worked that one out? Good God, boy, there are literally dozens of ways of getting in and out of countries illegally in these days, if you've money behind you — or the prospect of money. And don't start yapping that "It isn't possible!" Of course it is! A bloody sight too possible! What do you suppose there is to prevent you going for a sail or out fishing one fine evening, and being picked up a mile or so offshore by a dhow or a motor-boat? Or a private yacht? — damn it all, your own father's got one of those! There are hundreds of miles of empty coast-line and little creeks or beaches where you could be landed on a dark night, and be picked up by a plane. Good grief, this is the Air Age! There are any amount of privately owned planes around — and any amount of empty Africa for 'em to land on! You wouldn't be your father's son if you couldn't work out that one, and we can take it someone else has. The problem is, who?'

Lash shrugged his shoulders: 'Someone who was on both plane rides, I guess. I checked up on that, and apart from your personal guests there were only two. That newspaper guy you were so charming to outside the airport——'

'What newspaper guy?' interrupted Tyson, sitting up sharply. 'I don't remember any—— Yes, by God, I do! Some blasted squirt in a panama hat who asked if he could call. Was he on the London plane?'

'I just told you so. And staying at the same hotel in Nairobi.'

'He was, was he?' said Tyson meditating. 'Perhaps I shouldn't have been so hasty. Well we can fix that. As there's only one hotel in this salubrious spot, we know where he is. Lorrie darling, ring up the hotel will you, and ask for—— What's his blasted name?'

'Dowling,' supplied Dany. 'Larry Dowling.'

'Mr Dowling; and when you get him on the line, tell him I'll be delighted to give him an interview, and would he like to come and stay here. Run along and do it now.'

'But Tyson——!' Lorraine's gentian-blue eyes were wide with dismay. 'We can't. Darling — a reporter!'

'He isn't a reporter,' said Dany, but was ignored.

'Everything will be all over the front page of every newspaper before we know where we are,' wailed Lorraine. 'Think of Dany — and all of us. Just *think*!'

'I am,' said Tyson impatiently. 'And I appear to be the only one who is capable of doing so. It's a dam' sight safer to have all the suspects under one roof.'

'With an eye, of course,' said Lash, 'to the cash deposit.'

'If that was meant for sarcasm, boy, you'll have to do better. Naturally with an eye to the cash deposit. What do you take me for?'

Lorraine's hands made their familiar fluttering gesture, and she said: 'I don't understand. I don't understand anything.'

'He means,' translated Lash, 'that one of a reasonably narrow field of suspects has just got hold of the key to grandpop's bank vault. It is therefore quite an idea to keep 'em all right here, where he can watch 'em, and the first guy who is caught borrowing a spade and sneaking out to do a bit of digging is it. See?'

'But of *course*!' exclaimed Lorraine happily. 'Tyson darling, how clever of you. I'll ring up this Mr — Mr Dowling at once.'

'You do that,' said Tyson. 'Get going. No — wait a minute. There were two of them. Didn't you say there were two?'

'Were,' said Lash, 'is right. There's only one now.'

'I don't get you.'

'The other one,' said Lash, 'was an Arab. A shining light in the local Zanzibar-for-Mother-Russia movement, I gather. One Salim Abeid.'

'Oh, Jembe — *"the thin man"*.'

'That's the guy. Or to be accurate, that was the guy.'

'What do you mean by that?' demanded Tyson sharply.

'I mean he's dead. He died rather suddenly this morning at Mombasa Airport, which is why our plane was held up. I thought maybe they'd have told you that one: you must have had to wait quite a while for us.'

'Dead?' said Tyson, his bull voice almost a whisper. 'You don't mean ... What did he die of?'

'They didn't say. He walked off the plane and into the airport with the rest of us, apparently a sound insurance risk, and when we were herded back on, he failed to turn up. There was a certain amount of delay and flurry, and first the stewardess told us he'd been taken ill, and then a squad of cops and officials turned up and took another look at our passports and re-checked our visas — and for all I know got our fingerprints as well. They seemed anxious to know where they could get in touch with us during the next few days.'

'What do you suppose they'd want to do that for?'

'Your guess,' said Lash dryly, 'is as good as mine.'

Lorraine looked anxiously from Lash's face to her husband's, and came back from the door to clutch at Tyson's arm. There was a sudden trace of panic in her light, lilting voice: 'What guess, Tyson? What does he mean? What are you both hinting at?'

'Nothing,' said Tyson brusquely. 'Only that Jembe had a lot of political enemies. There's no need for us to start visualizing burglars under every blasted bed in the island. And anyway he probably died of heart failure.'

'Almost certainly,' said Lash pleasantly. 'Few of us die from anything else.'

'Be quiet, boy!' blared Tyson. 'The young should be seen and not heard! It's all right, Lorrie. You run along now and phone that infernal reporter. And be nice to him.'

Lorraine sighed and relaxed. 'I'm always nice to people, darling.'

She turned from him and directed an appealing smile at Lash. 'I do hope you don't mind being in the guest-house by yourself, Lash?'

'Why should I mind? It's charming.'

'Now that *is* sweet of you! I was afraid you might feel sore about it. Being put up in a sort of honeymoon cottage when——'

'Oh, not again!' groaned Lash. 'Once was enough. I get you — you mean this was the cosy little hideaway that you'd gotten all fixed up for the newly-weds, was it? Well, it was a swell idea and I shall not feel any qualms about occupying it — provided I'm allowed to do so strictly solo. You don't have to worry about it. It wasn't your fault.'

'But it *was*. That's what's so *awful*,' Lorraine's voice was tragic. 'I feel that it's so much my fault: Elf wrote to me, you know. You see it was I who asked Eddie — Eduardo — to look her up when he was in London, because he'd suggested that he might come down here again, so I thought it would be nice for them to know each other, and of course I never dreamed—— But I don't expect it will come to anything: so much that Elf starts doesn't, you know. She's so vague and soft-hearted and irresponsible, and she never means any harm. She's like a sweet, spoilt child who just picks things up and then drops them.'

Lorraine illustrated with a graceful, expressive gesture, and Lash winced. 'I get you.'

'Oh, but I didn't mean *you*, Lash!' Lorraine's eyes were wide with dismay. 'I meant Eddie. He's only a new toy. And rather a novel one. But when that's over, everything will be all right again, won't it?'

'Sure. Just dandy,' said Lash bitterly. 'And now if you don't mind, could we just cut the whole question of my love-life off the agenda? I prefer murder.'

'Yes of course, dear,' said Lorraine hastily. 'I *do* feel for you. And I'm sure it will all come out right in the end. Come on, Dany darling, let's go and get tidy. And you *will* get rid of that awful fringe, won't you sweetie?'

'No she won't!' declared Tyson unexpectedly. 'Here, Dany——' he picked up the discarded spectacles and replaced them firmly on her nose. 'I'm sorry if it worries your mother and fails to please the United States Marines, but it seems to me that you'd better stick to that fancy dress and go on being Miss Kitchell for the next few days. It'll save a lot of explaining. And the less explaining we have to do once that scribbling journalist is on the premises, the better.'

'Are you really going to ask him over?' inquired Lash.

'Certainly,' said Tyson, bristling. 'Any objections?'

'None at all. It's your funeral. But it seems to me that your sense of proportion has slipped a disc. If you import this Dowling guy you can watch to see that he doesn't start in digging up grand-pop's dollars, but if he starts digging any of this dirt instead, how are you going to stop him splashing it all over the tabloids?'

'Murder him!' said Tyson succinctly. 'Now let's get on up to the house and have some food.'

12

The House of Shade stood three storeys high on a wide stone terrace that was approached from the garden by short flights of steps set at regular intervals about it. Each of its storeys was of a different height, for the ground floor had once been a colonnade surrounding an open central courtyard about which the house was built, and the rooms on the first floor had been large and long, and were abnormally high. It had been Tyson's father — who had a mania for improvements — who had divided them into bedrooms, bathrooms and dressing-rooms.

The top storey, by comparison, appeared unduly low, and the rooms were hotter than those on the floor below, for the sun beat down strongly on the flat Eastern roof and the shade of the trees did not reach them. But the breeze did, and by night they were cool.

There was a lily pool in the courtyard, where lethargic goldfish idled in the shade of the flat green leaves, and on each floor the rooms led out on to pillared verandahs that faced each other across it, in a manner vaguely reminiscent of a courtyard in Seville.

Curious, curving stone staircases with shallow, disproportionally wide treads, their heavy banisters of hammered iron wrought in an odd geometrical design and barely a foot and a half in height, rose from each corner of the courtyard, inside the verandahs and leading up on to the next. Dangerous looking things, depending for their support only on the stout metal and the proportion of stone that had been built into the thickness of the wall, and proof that some long-dead Arab builder had known his trade as well as Adams or John Nash.

At the edge of each verandah, stone jars filled with sweet-scented creepers and flowering shrubs stood between the tall supporting pillars, and gave an entrancing impression of hanging gardens. But from the outside the house looked far less decorative and unusual: a square, white, very high building with a flat crenelated roof and rows of green-painted shutters.

It was sometime during the afternoon, and shortly before Tyson left to take a letter in to the Residency, that Mr Cardew, the Police Superintendent of the Zanzibar Division, called briefly at the House of Shade.

His car came and went again, making so little sound on the white coral dust of the palm-shaded road that no member of the house-party heard it, and apart from Tyson, only a Somali servant, a somnolent gardener's boy, and a drowsing cat on the wall above the main gate, had seen him.

He had stayed less than a quarter of an hour, and it was not until much later in the day, when night had fallen and the house-party were seated at the dining-room table in a glow of candle-light, that Tyson had chosen to bring up the subject of his visit.

The dining-room at *Kivulimi* was a long narrow room, with a row of arches along one side that had once been open, but which Tyson's father, Aubrey, had converted into french windows. They stood wide tonight, letting in a heady scent of flowers and luring moths and other nocturnal insects to a fiery death in the candle flames, and from her seat between Nigel and Larry Dowling, Dany could see out into the garden where the tree shadows and the moonlight formed a complicated mosaic patched with gold from the lighted windows.

She had plenty of leisure to enjoy the sight, for Lorraine, in the interests of playing safe, was keeping Larry Dowling engaged in conversation, while Nigel was hotly defending a modern masterpiece, recently purchased for the nation, in the face of

Gussie Bingham's assertion that it was a shocking waste of the taxpayers' money (by which she meant her own) and indistinguishable from a pool of spilt ink and a squashed tomato — which would have come cheaper.

Larry Dowling had arrived in a taxi shortly after luncheon, and much to her surprise Dany had found herself not only pleased, but more than a little relieved to see him. Which was foolish of her, she knew, since Larry's profession made him a danger to all of them. But for some indefinable reason she felt a greater sense of safety and a lessening of tension while he was within reach. Larry, she thought, would not let one down.

Lash Holden had greeted Mr Dowling with a marked lack of enthusiasm, and having commandeered his taxi had returned in it to the airport to inquire into the possibility of reserving a seat for himself in a Nairobi-bound plane on the following day. He had not been back by four-thirty, when Lorraine's guests had assembled for tea on the shaded terrace outside the drawing-room windows, but he had joined them later when they had gone down to explore the sea shore and exclaim over the weird, wind-worn shapes of the coral rocks, and watch the sun go down in a blaze of rose-tinted splendour.

He had not spoken to Dany, and had in fact appeared to avoid her, and she looked at him now across the width of the wide table in the glow of the candles, and wondered if she would ever see him again. I suppose I could always get a job in America, she thought. Tyson or Lorraine could fix that; they've got loads of friends there, and Lash's father is Tyson's best friend. I'd be able to see him. But if Mrs Gordon decides that she likes him better than Eduardo after all...

Dany turned to look at Amalfi, who was being charming to Tyson and prettily petulant to Eduardo, and her heart sank. She knew that she herself had little to complain of in the way of looks, for she had inherited them from her father who had been an outstandingly handsome man. But Ada Kitchell's unfortunate hair-style did not suit her, and neither did Ada Kitchell's spectacles. They combined to reduce her from a pretty girl to a nondescript one, and even the dress she had chosen to wear did not help, though once she had thought it entrancing — a short, smoke-grey dress whose wide skirt, ornamented with two enormous patch pockets appliquéd with white magnolias, reduced her slim waist to hand-span proportions. She had been charmed with it when she bought it; but now it only appeared rather ordinary, and what Aunt Harriet would have termed 'suitable for a young girl'.

Amalfi, looking anything but ordinary, was wearing pale gold chiffon that exactly matched her pale gold hair, and her jewels were an antique set of topazes set in gold filigree. It was a colour that did charming and complimentary things to her sea-green, mermaid's eyes, and she was using them now with dazzling effect on Tyson.

I don't know how Mother stands it! thought Dany resentfully: and turning to look at Lorraine was instantly answered.

Lorraine, wearing a fragile confection of black spider-lace, with diamonds that were a magnificent reminder of the brief reign of Dwight P. Cleethorpe, was, in her own and entirely different way, as entrancing as Amalfi, and she was engaged in employing all her charms on Larry Dowling; who was looking equally dazzled.

They can't help it, thought Dany, feeling depressed and deplorably gauche. They were born with charm. They just turn it on like a tap, and half the time it doesn't mean a thing. They can't help having it, or using it, any more than Millicent Bates can help being — Millicent Bates!

Millicent was sitting opposite her between Lash and Eduardo di Chiago, and 'Dressing for Dinner' meant only one thing to Miss Bates. A long dress, and she was wearing one. An undatable garment in solid blue marocain that made no concessions to frivolity and did nothing for her flat-chested, square-shouldered figure. She was engaged in giving Lash, as an unenlightened Colonial, a lecture on the advantages of a National Health system, when she was interrupted by Tyson who at last elected to broach the subject of the Superintendent of .the Zanzibar Division's afternoon call. His voice boomed down the lengh of the table and successfully terminated an anecdote concerning scheming foreigners in search of free false teeth.

'By the way, Lash, about that plane reservation you wanted for tomorrow, I'm afraid you'll——'

Amalfi turned sharply: 'What plane reservation? Lash, you aren't leaving? Not when you've only just arrived! Darling, don't be silly!'

Nigel gave his little giggling laugh. 'It's all this American passion for hustle. Here today and gone tomorrow! So enervating.'

'On the contrary,' snapped Lash, 'it's a strong instinct for self-preservation.'

'Darling, I'm not all *that* dangerous,' cooed Amalfi dulcetly. 'Are you frightened?'

'Terrified!' said Lash promptly. 'But apart from that, as I find that the business side of this trip can be dealt with in half an hour — provided our host will sit still that long — I don't feel justified in wasting too much time idling; however pleasantly. I have a lot of commitments.'

Mrs Bingham said: 'Poor Miss Kitchell! And I feel sure that you were so looking forward to seeing something of Zanzibar. What a slave-driver your Mr Holden is!'

She beamed sympathetically at Dany, and Lash looked startled. It was a point that had somehow escaped him. If Dany had to continue masquerading as his secretary he could hardly leave without her. Or with her.

Blast! thought Mr Holden with quiet and concentrated bitterness. And was visited by inspiration. He half rose and bowed at Mrs Bingham. 'Ma'am, you put me to shame. You're dead right. I'm a slave-driver, and Miss Kitchell certainly needs a rest. But she's going to get one. I don't happen to need her for the next week or so, and she's going to stay right here, grab herself a nice long vacation, and join me later when I'm due back in the States.'

And now, thought Lash with some satisfaction, just try and gum up that one!

Tyson did so.

'It looks,' he said blandly, 'as though you will be spending it right here with her, my boy.'

'Oh no, I shan't,' began Lash firmly. 'I intend——'

Tyson said crossly: 'If you will all have the goodness to lay off interrupting me every time I open my mouth, perhaps I can get on with what I was saying? ... Thanks! About that plane reservation. I'm afraid you'll have to cancel it, boy. In fact, I have already done so on your behalf. The police have requested that you all remain *in situ* for a day or two.'

'The *police*?' Amalfi dropped the glass she was holding, and it fell with a little splintering crash, sending a red stream of claret across the table. 'What police? Why?'

'Josh Cardew. He was over this afternoon. He says it's just a routine matter, but that they've been asked to check up on everyone who was on the Nairobi–Zanzibar plane this morning, and more particularly, on the London–Nairobi one. So it would help if you'd all stay around for a bit. It's that chap Jembe.'

'Salim Abeid?' inquired Larry Dowling. 'You mean the man who died in the airport at Mombasa this morning?'

'I mean the man who was murdered in the airport at Mombasa this morning,' corrected Tyson. 'It would appear that someone added a good-sized slug of cyanide to his coffee, and they somehow don't think he did it himself.'

Gussie gave her glass of wine a horrified look and put it down hurriedly. 'But how dreadful, Tyson! I remember him quite well. He was on the London plane too. But why on earth should the police want to question any of us? Too ridiculous, when it must have been someone in the airport. The barman who gave him the coffee, I expect.'

'They're checking up on all that. Needle-in-a-haystack job, I'd say. I gather the airport was pretty crowded.'

'Packed,' said Gussie Bingham, and shuddered. 'Besides being abominably hot, in spite of all those fans and things.'

Larry Dowling said reflectively: 'It can't have been all that easy to drop something in a man's drink without being spotted; even in a crowded room. Bit of a risk. It must have been someone he knew.'

'I don't see why,' said Nigel, mopping up claret with a clean handkerchief. 'Anyone — simply *anyone* — could have jogged his elbow or distracted his attention as they went past. *Too* simple. You knock the man's newspaper on to the floor, or stumble over his briefcase, and while he's picking them up and you're apologizing — *plop!*'

He dropped an imaginary pellet into an imaginary glass, and Eduardo di Chiago said: '*Brr — !* this is a most unpleasant conversation. For myself, I do not like to talk of death. It is unlucky.'

'Oh, I do so agree with you,' said Lorraine earnestly. '*Dreadfully* unlucky. And now I suppose there's *bound* to be a third.'

'A third what?' demanded Gussie Bingham, startled.

'Murder of course, darling. Things always go in threes. Haven't you noticed that?'

'But there's only been one murder so far,' objected Millicent Bates.

'My dear — but haven't you *heard*? Why, I thought we only hadn't because we don't get the English papers for days, but I thought you two must have seen all about it.'

Tyson cast his eyes up to heaven, and thereafter, realizing it was too late to intervene, shrugged his shoulders and circulated the port.

'Seen all about what?' demanded Millicent sharply.

'Why, about Mr Honeywood. Tyson's solicitor. He's been murdered.'

'*Honeywood* — old Henry Honeywood?' The thin stem of Gussie Bingham's wine-glass snapped between her fingers, and once more there was a dark pool of wine winking in the candle-light. But she did not appear to have noticed it. She leant forward to stare down the table at Lorraine, and her voice was suddenly strident: 'Where did you get that story?'

But Lorraine was not paying attention. She reached out, and picking up an empty tumbler, lifted it and dropped it deliberately on to the floor, where it shivered into fragments.

'That's the third one,' she said reassuringly. 'And it was an odd one anyway, so it means we needn't bother about losing any more of the set. I do apologize, Gussie darling — what were you saying?'

Gussie turned towards her brother with a rustle of lilac satin and a clash of bracelets.

'Tyson, what is this preposterous nonsense that Lorraine has got hold of?'

'It isn't nonsense,' said Tyson, helping himself liberally to port. 'Only heard it myself today. The poor old boy's been murdered. Shot in his study on the morning of the day you left for London. I daresay you missed seeing it in the papers because of the move — last minute shopping and all that sort of flap. And it wouldn't have been front page stuff.'

'No, I didn't see it. And I still can't believe—— What would anyone want to murder old Henry for?'

Tyson shrugged. 'Ask me another. Theft, I suppose. The safe was opened. I don't really know any details.'

'And where,' demanded Millicent, 'did you get all this from? If you've got the home papers, I'd like to see them.'

Tyson looked disconcerted, and Lash thought with a trace of malice: That'll teach him to watch his step!

'They'll be around somewhere,' said Tyson, rallying. 'But as a matter of fact, I had a letter by the afternoon post. Have some port, Gussie.'

'Who from?' inquired Millicent Bates.

'Oh — a man you wouldn't know,' said Tyson hastily.

'What did he say? When did it happen? How ...'

Tyson rolled a wild eye in the direction of Lash, who refused to meet it, and found himself enduring a lengthy catechism which he replied to as well as he could.

'Why are you so interested anyway?' he inquired irritably. 'He wasn't *your* family solicitor.'

'He happened to be both honorary treasurer of our Wednesday Women's Guild and treasurer to the Market-Lydon Lads of Britain League, and as such was a personal friend of mine,' snapped Millicent. 'What time did you say it happened?'

'For Pete's sake, how am I expected to know? It'll be in the papers.'

'Eleven forty-eight, precisely,' put in Larry Dowling gently. 'They know the time because the murderer evidently pressed the muzzle of the gun against the victim's body — it would have helped to muffle the shot — and the shock of the explosion damaged a repeater watch the old gentleman carried in his breast pocket, and stopped it.'

'Good God,' said Tyson heavily. 'The Press! I'd forgotten we had a newshound in our midst.' He glared at Larry Dowling as though he had found a slug in his salad. 'Did you by any chance cover this case, Mr Dowling? You appear to know a hell of a lot about it.'

'No. Not in my line. But I read the papers. It was in most of them on the 13th. I must have seen five accounts of it at least.'

'Umm,' grunted Tyson, and returned to the port.

'Eleven forty-eight,' said Millicent Bates, and repeated it slowly. 'Eleven ... forty ... eight.'

'And what exactly does that mean?' inquired Nigel of the table at large. 'It sounds *just* like the Girl with the Golden Voice *"On the third stroke it will be eleven forty-eight and twelve seconds precisely"*.'

Millicent Bates scowled at him across the table. 'If you really want to know,' she said tartly, 'I happened to pay a rush visit to a friend of mine on the morning of the 12th. I'd forgotten to give her the key of the Wolf Cubs' hut, and we were leaving that afternoon. She lives at the end of Mr Honeywood's road — it's a *cul de sac* — and I was wondering if I might not actually have passed the murderer. He must have come down that road.'

Nigel smiled with maddening tolerance. 'Do you know, I *hardly* think so, dear Miss Bates.'

'And why not?' demanded Millicent Bates, bristling.

'But surely it stands to reason that a murderer would not go *prancing* along a public highway and in at the front door by daylight? He'd be far more likely to *creep* in by a shrubbery or something.'

'Which just goes to show,' said Miss Bates, 'how little you know what you're talking about. You could possibly creep *out* of Mr Honeywood's house through a shrubbery, because you could use the kitchen-garden door. But it has a slip lock and you can't open it from the outside. And as there is a high wall around the house, the only way in, for anyone who didn't want to do some jolly conspicuous climbing, is through the front gate. And I *do* know what I'm talking about, because I happen to know the house well.'

'So well,' said Nigel gaily, 'that you will soon have us shivering in our little shoes, wondering if you couldn't have done it yourself!'

Millicent Bates' weather-beaten countenance flushed an unbecoming shade of puce, and Gussie rushed angrily to her defence.

'You appear to look upon murder as a joke, Mr Ponting. But the death of an old acquaintance is hardly a joking matter to us.'

'Oh dear! Oh-dear-oh-dear-oh-dear!' wailed Nigel. 'What can I say? I *do* apologize. *Dear* Miss Bates, you must know that I didn't mean it! My wretched, *distorted* sense of humour. *Do* say that you forgive me?'

Millicent made a flapping gesture with one large and capable hand, in the manner of one waving away an irritating insect, and said gruffly: 'Don't talk rot! My fault for harpin' on it. But I couldn't help being interested — realizing that I might well have passed the man.'

'Or woman,' put in Larry Dowling softly.

Millicent Bates turned swiftly to face him. 'Why do you say that?' she demanded sharply.

'No reason. Just that it may have been a woman. Nothing to show it wasn't — if the papers were anything to go by. You didn't read them, or you'd have seen that he had a female visitor that day. She even took the precaution of leaving a handkerchief behind her — complete with monogram.'

'Oh,' said Miss Bates doubtfully. 'I didn't think of that. Yes, I suppose . . . it could be.'

'Some winsome ornament of the Wednesday Women's Guild, stealing through the mist on the track of the funds!' tittered Nigel. 'Oh dear — there I go again! My *wretched* sense of humour. I won't say another *word*!'

Millicent made no retort, beyond staring at him long and malevolently. But there was suddenly something in her face — in her frown and her narrowed eyes, that suggested that his words had reminded her of something. Or suggested something. Something quite impossible, and yet . . .

No one spoke, and for the space of a full minute there was a curious, strained silence in the room; and then Millicent nodded at Mr Ponting. The brief, brisk nod of someone who has been presented with a fresh viewpoint and accepted it.

On the opposite side of the table Larry Dowling leant forward with a small, swift movement that somehow had the effect of a pounce, and said sharply: 'So you *do* think it might have been a woman — a woman he knew!'

But if he had expected to startle Miss Bates into any admission he was disappointed. Millicent turned to look at him, and having successfully conveyed the impression of not liking what she saw, inquired blandly: 'What did you say, Mr Dowling?'

Larry Dowling flushed and sat back. 'Er — nothing.'

'For which relief, much thanks!' boomed Tyson. 'I am getting bored with this murder. Let us talk about something else.'

'Yes, *do* let's,' said Nigel. 'Murders are *not* precisely one's idea of sparkling dinner-table chit-chat. So gruesomely proletarian. I can never *think* why anyone should want to hear about them.'

Amalfi laughed her lovely throaty laugh, and said: 'Don't be so affected, Nigel darling. Everyone *adores* a good murder. Look at the way they always get into all the headlines and fill the Sunday papers. And what about the way you've been going on about this one? No one else has had a chance to get a word in edgeways!'

She turned to her host and said: 'Tyson, you ought to be entertaining us. If you don't like murders, talk about something else. Anything. Tell us about this house.'

'What about it?' inquired Tyson. 'It was allegedly built about a century and a half ago by a harassed husband whose second wife couldn't get along with the first. But if you want to swot up on it, my late Uncle Barclay wrote an exceptionally tedious book about it which he published at his own expense in the late 1890s and inflicted on his friends. You probably saw one at Gussie's — she has it bound in red morocco and displayed on the piano, to atone for the fact that she's never read it. You'll find several copies lying around here. All the historical and architectural dope down to the last deadly detail. I do not advise it for light reading. But don't let that stop you if you're really interested.'

'I'm not,' said Amalfi. 'Not to that extent, anyway. You are all being very dull tonight, and I want to be flattered and entertained.'

She turned and smiled meltingly at Eduardo, who accepted the invitation with alacrity, and not long afterwards they had all left the dining-room and gone out to drink Turkish coffee on the terrace in front of the drawing-room windows, where Gussie had again demanded the home papers.

Tyson had departed in search of them, and had returned saying that he could not find them, but a few minutes later Nigel had drifted languidly across the terrace with a wrapped package in his hand which he had handed to his employer with an eloquent lift of the eyebrows that had not been lost on at least one member of the party.

The London newspapers had arrived on the same aircraft that had brought the Frosts' guests from Nairobi that morning, and had not been delivered at *Kivulimi* until the late afternoon. The wrapping was still unbroken. 'I thought you said you'd read them?' said Gussie Bingham accusingly.

Tyson affected not to hear her, and removed himself hurriedly to the far side of the terrace where Amalfi Gordon, temporarily deserted, was leaning on the stone balustrade and looking out between the trees to where the moon had laid a shimmering golden carpet across the quiet sea.

'Pleasant, isn't it?' said Tyson, coming to anchor beside her. 'And peaceful. There can't be many places like it left in the world. Or there won't be soon. Progress can be a loutish thing.'

'Don't be pompous and gloomy, darling,' chided Amalfi. 'There are thousands of places just as lovely as this. And as peaceful.'

'That's where you're wrong,' said Tyson, leaning his elbows on the warm stone. 'I've seen a lot of the world. A hell of a lot of it! But there's something special about this island. Something that I haven't met anywhere else. Do you know what is the most familiar sound in Zanzibar? — laughter! Walk through the streets of the little city almost any time of the day or night, and you'll hear it. People laughing. There is a gaiety and good humour about them that is strangely warming to even such a corrugated, corroded and eroded heart as mine, and this is the only place I have yet hit upon where black and white and every shade in between 'em appear to be able to live together in complete friendliness and harmony, with no colour bar. It's a living proof and a practical demonstration that it can be done. They are all, whatever their race or caste or religion, loyal subjects of His Highness the Sultan — may he live for ever! — and they get on together. But it won't last. In the end one of the Jembe kind will manage to destroy it. Yes — there are times when I am prepared to agree with that bigoted old bore, my late Uncle Barclay, that Progress is a lout!'

Amalfi had been picking jasmine buds and smelling them absently, wearing the abstracted smile of one who is not in the least interested in the conversation, but the name 'Jembe' caught her attention, and she dropped the flowers and turned quickly:

'Tyson darling, that reminds me. I'm sorry to go on about this sort of thing, but did you *really* mean that we can none of us leave this house until the police find out who gave that tedious little Arab agitator a dose of poison in Mombasa?'

'God forbid!' said Tyson piously. 'If that were so I might find myself permanently stuck with the lot of you, and I'm not sure that my constitution could stand it. Or yours! No, it's only a question of a day or two, while they make a few inquiries. They might want to ask if any of you by any chance remember seeing someone speaking to him at the airport. Or standing near him. Something like that. Why? Were you thinking of cutting short your visit? I thought you were supposed to be staying with us for at least three weeks.'

Amalfi smiled at him, and reaching up to pull his greying blond beard said: 'But you know quite well that I never do what 'I'm supposed to do, and I never know how long I shall stay anywhere. If I'm enjoying myself madly, I stay, and if I'm not, I move on. It's as simple as that!'

'It must come expensive,' said Tyson.

'Oh, frantically. But I don't *always* have to pay for it myself.'

Tyson bellowed with sudden laughter. 'That's what I like about you, Elf. No deception, is there?'

'*Masses*, darling. You've no idea how much! But not in that way. After all, money *is* rather madly important. Don't you agree?'

'I work for mine,' said Tyson dryly.

'Oh, but so do I. One has to sing for one's supper, you know; and I sing — charmingly!'

'I'll grant you that,' said Tyson with a grin. 'But hasn't it been a bit trying at times? Johnnie Leigh, for instance.'

Amalfi's mermaid eyes clouded. 'Oh but darling — I never can think of money when I marry them. It's always *love*. And it's only later that one—— Oh . . . wakes up to reality.'

'And in the wrong bedroom, with a private inquiry agent hired by your husband taking notes through the transom,' said Tyson cynically. 'Still, you've been lucky in one way. The co-respondent was always noticeably solvent and well able — and more than willing! — to keep you in the mink.'

'Darling!' said Amalfi reproachfully. 'You make it sound as though I were a gold-digger. But I'm not. I'd have married Johnnie even if he hadn't a *sou*!'

'And Robin Gratton? And Chubby?'

'But of *course*! I'm like that. I suddenly feel I *must* have something — that it's the only thing in the world worth having and that once I've got it I shall be happy ever after. And then I'm not. But I adored Chubby. My heart broke when he was killed. It did, really Tyson!'

'Nonsense! You were hardly on speaking terms that last year. And you haven't got a heart, darling. Only a soft mass of emotions. Though I'm not so sure about your head!'

'I'm afraid that's just as soft,' sighed Amalfi regretfully.

'I wonder? Still, you seem to have had your fair share of romance during the last year or two, despite that alleged broken heart. Why don't you bite on the bullet and marry one of them?'

Amalfi laughed. 'What, again? It doesn't seem to take with me, does it?'

'It will one day.'

'Like it has for Lorrie? Perhaps. But how is one to know? I always think I know; and then I find I don't.'

'Try marrying a poor one for a change. You ought to be able to afford it.'

'I don't think I could. One can never really have enough money, can one? All the really heavenly things cost so much. Diamonds and Dior models and holidays in Bermuda.'

'But Chubby must have left you a packet.'

'Not a packet, darling. Unfortunately there turned out to be platoons of dreary aunts and other dim relations that I had never even *heard* of, and it seemed that Chubby was depressingly Clan-minded — worse luck. And then the death duties were *iniquitous*. And anyway, I'm hopeless over money. I always have been. It seems to melt!'

'I'm not surprised; what with diamonds and Dior models and holidays in Bermuda!'

'Yes,' said Amalfi, and sighed deeply. 'That's why it's simpler to fall in love with someone rich. But then I like them to be handsome and charming too, and there's no getting away from it, that kind are limited in number and dreadfully spoilt. They know that they aren't a drug on the market, and they can be difficult.'

'What you mean is that they bite back and won't let themselves be trampled on by any woman for long. And more power to 'em. You know, Elf, I propose to give you some sage advice. You won't be able to go on looking like a luscious slice of peach for ever, and it's time you settled down with a different type.

The kind that'll let you play your favourite game of eating your cake and having it.'

'I don't think I know what you mean, darling.'

'Cut out these playboys with plenty of cash, like young Lash or that slick-smoothie, Eddie. They may be fun, but they'd be hell as husbands for a woman like you. They aren't good at turning the other cheek — or a blind eye! You ought to have learnt that at least by this time. What you need now is a nice kind sugar-daddy of the adoring door-mat type, who will let you get away with murder.'

Amalfi shivered suddenly. '*Ugh!* Darling! What a simile to choose after all that gruesome chatter at dinner!'

'Well, "Make a monkey out of him with impunity", if you like it put that way.'

'Is that what Lorraine did? I wouldn't have said that you were exactly a door-mat type. Or a sugar-daddy!'

'Lorrie,' said Tyson, 'isn't in the least your type. Or only superficially. She's merely incurably romantic. That's her trouble. She'd be perfectly happy married to someone who could offer her a semi-detached and a "daily" — as long as she loved him. You wouldn't be. Now, would you?'

Amalfi gave him a narrowed, slanting look under her long lashes, and there was, all at once, a trace of scorn in her lovely face and a shade of contempt in her voice. 'Darling Tyson. You read us all like a book! So clever.'

'Sarcasm doesn't suit you, Elf. Am I to take it that you are going to take a brief whirl at being a Marchesa? If so, I ought to warn you that Eddie is even more susceptible than you are, and the only reason that he has not totted up a long list of ex-wives, all drawing heavy alimony, is because his grandmother holds the purse strings, and can not only cut off supplies when she chooses, but frequently does. It's a great trial to him; though it doesn't seem to have persuaded him to try work yet. He—— What's the matter? Surely you knew that?'

'No,' said Amalfi shortly. 'I thought——' she stopped and bit her lip, and Tyson laughed.

'Well, don't say later that no one ever warned you! If you've really reached the fatal stage of marrying them younger than yourself, you'd better take Lash Holden. American men put up with a lot more rough stuff from their wives than less idealistic races, and when it comes to the parting of the ways they'll break out into a rash of Old World chivalry and allow themselves to be sued as the erring partner, and milked like goats for iniquitous alimony with never a bleat. But with Eduardo you'd be the one who'd do the paying, if anyone did. His family might have accepted Chubby's widow — though considering the circumstances, I doubt it — but they're likely to kick like cows at those two divorces. And as for that unfortunate business of Douglas—— Well if you'll take my advice, Elf, you'll scrub Eddie and settle for young Lash. That is, if it's not too late.'

Amalfi drew back and regarded him with sudden hostility. 'I don't think,' she said slowly, 'that I am amused any longer. In fact I'm quite sure that I'm not.'

'Because I've told you the truth about yourself and a couple of gilded playboys?'

'No. Because you begin to bore me, darling. And I cannot endure being bored.'

She smiled sweetly at him, her eyes cold, and turned and walked back across the terrace to join the others. And presently Nigel had gone in to switch on the radio-gramophone and turn back the carpet of the drawing-room, and they had all danced: with the exception of Tyson, who could not be bothered, and Millicent Bates, who could not.

Tyson and Millicent had sat side by side on the stone balustrade of the terrace, watching the dancers through the open doors, and Millicent had said moodily: 'I wish you would tell me where you got that secretary of yours, and why. I don't know how a man of your type can stand all that affectation and giggling.'

'He's good at his job,' said Tyson lazily, 'and don't let that affectation fool you. It's fooled a lot of hard-headed businessmen in the publishing line and film racket into thinking that they can pull a fast one, and they've all wound up with headaches, having paid over far more than their original top figure. He deals with all my contracts, and behind that tittering facade he's as cunning and inquisitive as a barrelful of monkeys, and as shrewd as a weasel.'

'I don't doubt it,' said Millicent grimly. 'A nasty type. We had an assistant cashier like that in Market-Lydon. An absolute rotter. I always said that there'd be an ugly scandal one day, and of course there was. You can't trust 'em a yard!'

Tyson chose to be amused, and letting out a roar of laughter he clapped Millicent on the back with a large and hairy hand.

'Bates, you're perfect! You're a collector's piece. But so is Nigel; and I like collector's pieces. From all pale, pink-blooded, pure-souled people, Good Lord, deliver me!'

'That's *your* pose!' snapped Millicent Bates.

'Maybe,' said Tyson, unruffled. 'We all have one. Smoke screens to fool people with. Gussie's is good-nature.'

Millicent stiffened indignantly: 'Pose my foot! Gussie's the kindest creature alive!'

Tyson laughed again, and drained his glass. 'Bates, my Bonnie Brown Owl, I applaud your loyalty while deploring your dishonesty. You cannot have lived with Gussie all these years without knowing that there is nothing she enjoys more than planting a feline barb where she hopes it will hurt most, and then, covered with pretty confusion, pretending that it was just an unfortunate slip of the tongue. It's her favourite parlour sport. You must have found out long ago that Gussie only loves herself. And to forestall you saying "So do you!" I will hasten to say it myself — "And so do I." That may be selfish, but by golly it's sense! Let's face it, Bates, we're not a really pleasant lot, we Frosts. The only one of us who doesn't appear to have had any vices was old Uncle Barclay, and he was a crank! Let's drink confusion to his ghost.'

He got up and walked over to the table with the drinks, and Millicent Bates, following him, put down her empty glass and shook her head. 'No thanks. No more for me. I think I shall go to bed.'

She turned to stare once more at the dancers revolving in the lighted drawing-room: Gussie and Nigel, Dany and Larry Dowling, Amalfi and Lash Holden, Eduardo and Lorraine...

She stood there for perhaps five minutes, watching them with a curious intentness.

'It's very odd,' mused Millicent Bates.

'What is?' inquired Tyson.

'Everything!' said Millicent, and left him.

13

Dany leant wearily against the window-sill of her bedroom and looked out across the treetops to the silver stretch of the sea.

She had come up to her room over an hour ago, intending to go to bed. But once there she found that she was not sleepy. Merely too tired to go to the trouble of undressing, and too dispirited to take any pleasure in the beauty of the night. For it had been neither a pleasant nor a peaceful evening.

Tyson and Millicent Bates had both vanished shortly after ten, and Gussie had quarrelled with Nigel, who had withdrawn in a huff, leaving Dany to deal with the radiogram. Gussie had flounced off in search of her brother, presumably to complain, and Lash, having danced a particularly soulful waltz with Amalfi, had taken her down into the garden — ostensibly to look at the nocturnal flowering Lady-of-the-Night which grew in profusion in a bed some distance from the house.

They had stayed away for so long that Eduardo's southern blood had obviously begun to rise dangerously, and although they had returned separately it was perhaps unfortunate that Lash had been the first to reappear. For there was, unmistakably, a distinct trace of lipstick on his chin.

The Marchese's jealous gaze had not missed it, and his eyes had flashed in a manner that would undoubtedly have brought the house down in the days of the late Rudolph Valentino — a gentleman whom he much resembled. He had spoken a short, hissing phrase in Italian, to which Lash had replied with an even shorter one of strictly Anglo-Saxon origin, and only the agitated intervention of Lorraine had prevented a stirring scene.

Amalfi had not reappeared for some time — part of which, at least, she must have devoted to repairing her make-up. She had pointedly ignored Lash and devoted her attention to soothing Eduardo's lacerated feelings, but she did not appear to be in a good temper.

The only person present who had shown no sign of nerves or temperament was Larry Dowling, and Dany, whose own nerves were uncomfortably taut, was not only duly grateful for it, but despite the fact that there was something about Larry's lazily observant gaze that suggested very little escaped him, even more grateful for the impulse that had made her step-father add him to the house-party. She tried to remind herself that as a journalist — feature writer or no — news was his business, and that the present complicated situation would make entertaining reading for a sensation-hungry public. But it did not seem to weigh against the undoubted fact that she felt safer when Larry was in the room, and more insecure whenever he left it.

She wished that she could bring herself to take the sensible course of retiring to bed, but a raw recollection of the terror of the previous night had made her disinclined for sleep or solitude, and the lights and music, and Larry's strangely reassuring presence, at least provided an illusion of safety. But the long hours spent in an aeroplane had begun to tell on all of them, and by eleven o'clock lethargy had descended on the dancers, and with it a spirit of tolerance.

Nigel came out of his huff and apologized to Gussie, who yawned and informed him that of course she wasn't annoyed with him. She was never annoyed with anyone: even with people who pretended to a knowledge of subjects with which they had only the most superficial acquaintance, and — Oh, dear! but of course she hadn't meant *Nigel*...

Amalfi had shed her hauteur and awarded Lash a forgiving

smile, Eduardo had ceased to simmer, and Lorraine had stopped looking vague and distrait and had begun to sparkle and laugh, and dispense her own particular and potent brand of charm to such good effect that her guests, with the exception of her daughter, had finally departed to bed in the best of tempers.

A bat flitted past the open window and Dany flinched, and was startled to find that so trivial a thing could have the power to make her heart leap and her breath catch. Especially when there was nothing to be afraid of any longer — except the discovery of her identity, which was inevitable anyway. And yet she was still afraid . . .

The night was very quiet and the house very still, and now that the lights had gone out the garden was blue and black and silver only. There were no glints of gold except where the warm reflected glow from her own window touched the top of a jacaranda, and a small orange square, barely visible through the intervening trees, that showed that Lash Holden, in the little guest-house on the seaward corner of the boundary wall, was still awake.

A nightjar cried harshly in the garden below, and Dany's taut nerves leapt to the sudden sound, and she turned impatiently away from the window and looked about her at the strange white-walled room whose high ceiling was almost twenty feet above her head. A room built tall and cool for some lovely lady of the harem in the years before Sultan Saïd had deeded the House of Shade to his friend, Emory Frost — rover, adventurer, black-sheep and soldier-of-fortune.

What had the house seen during its long life? Had there been, as Millicent Bates suggested, 'shady doings' there, and did the rooms remember them? Dany found herself turning quickly to look behind her, as she had done once before in another bedroom in the Airlane in London. But there was nothing behind her except a small cream-and-gilt writing-table on which someone had placed Miss Ada Kitchell's portable typewriter and a solitary book: a solid tome of Victorian vintage that did not look as though it would make entertaining reading.

Dany reached out and picked it up, to discover that it was a musty volume bound in leather that heat and many monsoons had patched with mildew. But despite its age the title was still clearly legible: *The House of Shade* by Barclay Frost.

Dany smiled, remembering Tyson's strictures on the author's style, and dipping into it she found that her step-father's criticisms were fully justified. Barclay's prose was insufferably pedantic, and he had never used one word where half-a-dozen would do instead. Still, it was nice of Lorraine to put it in her room, and she must certainly find time to read some if not all of it.

She was laying it down when she noticed that some inquisitive or would-be helpful servant had opened the typewriter case and had not known how to shut it again. Dany removed the lid in order to set the catches straight, and saw that the machine had also been used, for a fragment of torn cream-laid paper, taken from a shelf on the writing-table, was still in it.

One of the *Kivulimi* servants had obviously been playing with this new and fascinating toy, and Dany could only hope that he had not succeeded in damaging it. She rattled off a line of type that in time-honoured tradition informed all good men that now was the time to come to the aid of the party, and finding that the machine still appeared to function, removed the fragment of paper, dropped it into the waste-paper basket and replaced the cover.

Turning away, she looked at the neatly turned-down bed, but sleep seemed as far from her as ever, and she went instead to the dressing-table, and sitting down in front of it, stared at her face in the glass. Lorraine was right. It was an unattractive hair style and her skin was too warm a tone for red hair.

She removed the spectacles, and reaching for her hairbrush swept the fringe off her forehead, and having brushed out the neat rows of curls that were arranged in bunches on either side of her head, twisted the soft mass into a severe knot at the nape of her neck. Dany's bones were good — as Daniel Ashton's had been — and where a frizzed and fussy style of hair-dressing reduced her to mediocrity, a severe one lent her distinction and a sudden unexpected beauty.

An enormous green and white moth flew in through the open window and added itself to the halo of winged insects that were circling about the electric light, and Dany rose impatiently and, going to the door, snapped off the switch. That should give the tiresome things a chance to find their way out into the moonlight, and she would give them a few minutes to get clear, and then pull the curtains before turning on the light again.

Now that the room was in darkness the night outside seemed almost as bright as day, and she returned to the window to look out once more at the shadowy garden and the wide, shimmering expanse of sea.

Lash's light had vanished and he was presumably asleep. But now that Dany's own light was out she became aware that the window immediately above hers had not yet been darkened, for there was still a warm glow illuminating the jacaranda tree. So Millicent Bates was still awake. And so, it seemed, was somebody else...

A pin-point of light was moving through the shadows in the garden below, and for a moment Dany thought it must be a firefly. Then her ear caught the faint crunch of the crushed shell and coral on the winding paths, and she realized that what she could see was the lighted end of a cigarette, and that someone was walking up through the garden towards the house.

The tiny orange spark was momentarily lost to view behind a screen of hibiscus, to reappear again as a man in a dinner jacket came softly up the nearest flight of steps on to the terrace, and turning along it, vanished round the far corner of the house.

He had looked up at Dany's window as he reached the top

of the steps, and as the moonlight fell on his face she had seen the anxious frown between his brows, and had resisted an impulse to lean out and assure him that she was all right. Though why she should suppose that Larry Dowling was in any way interested in her safety she did not know. It was far more likely that he had merely been strolling in the garden at this late hour because he, like herself, did not feel sleepy.

From somewhere down among the shadowy trees the nightjar cried again. But this time the harsh sound did not make her start, for the thought that Larry was somewhere nearby, and would be spending the night under the same roof, was an astonishingly comforting one. So comforting, that tension and disquiet fell away from her, and all at once she was pleasantly drowsy. She could go to bed now. And to sleep.

Dany's room was the end one on the first floor, above the dining-room and at the top of one of the four flights of stairs that curved upward from the courtyard. A door at one end of her bedroom led at right-angles into a small bathroom that faced west, with beyond it another and larger bathroom belonging to another and larger bedroom that had been given to Gussie Bingham. On the opposite side of her room, and looking out on the same view, was a morning room, and beyond that again a bedroom and a bathroom, the duplicate of her own, which was occupied by Amalfi Gordon.

All the remaining rooms on the first floor — those on the other two sides of the courtyard — were taken up by Tyson and Lorraine, while Nigel, Eduardo, Larry Dowling and Millicent Bates had rooms on the top floor.

'Perhaps not *quite* the thing to do, popping Bates up among all the bachelors,' Lorraine had said. 'But anyone who has ever seen Millicent arrayed for bed — or merely seen Millicent! — would realize that no bachelor is ever likely to cast her so much as a speculative glance, poor girl, so I expect it's all right. I was going to put Ada Kitchell up there — the real one. But

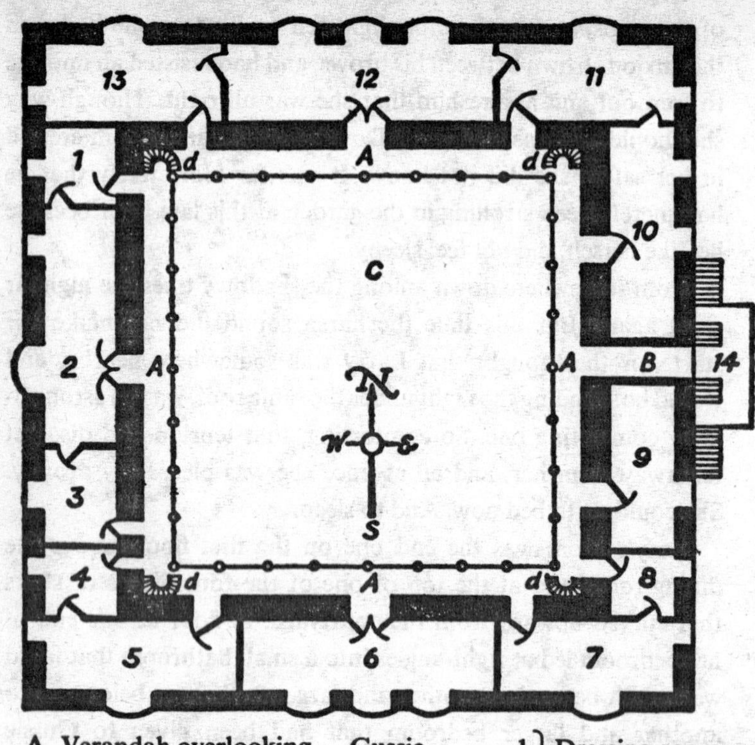

A. Verandah overlooking courtyard

B. Passage to servants' staircase

C. Courtyard

d. Staircase leading up to top floor and down to courtyard

o Pillars at verandah edge

Gussie Bingham's	1	Dressing-room
	2	Bedroom
	3	Bathroom
Dany's	4	Bathroom
	5	Bedroom
	6	Morning-room
Amalfi's	7	Bedroom
	8	Bathroom
	9, 10, 11, 12, 13	Rooms occupied by Tyson and Lorraine
	14	Servants' staircase

that nice Dowling man can have her room instead. He's rather a pet, isn't he?'

Dany caught herself listening for the sound of Larry Dowling's feet on the stone staircase outside her room. But the walls of the House of Shade had been solidly constructed to withstand high temperatures, marauding pirates and tropical hurricanes, and the heavy wooden doors were old and carved and almost sound-proof. She did not know if Larry had returned to his own room or not, but concluded that he must have done so by now, and realized that he would probably have gone up by the servants' staircase on the far side of the house.

A little breeze blew in from the sea, ruffling the leaves in the garden below, and she heard for the first time the song of tropic islands and coral coasts: a sound that is as haunting and as unforgettable as the sigh of wind through pine trees. The dry, whispering rustle of coconut palms.

It was a soothing and pleasant sound and a relief from the stillness and silence that had preceded it, and Dany leant out over the window-sill, listening to it, until another sound made her turn. A curious scraping sound that seemed to come either from the verandah or from the room above her. Probably Millicent dragging a suitcase out from under the bed. Or Larry Dowling, scraping his feet on the stone stair. The breeze blew coolly through the hot room, billowing the mosquito curtains and bringing with it all the lovely scents of the tropic night, and presently Dany heard the clock strike the half hour. Half past twelve. It really was quite time that she got to bed.

She pulled the curtains, shutting out the moonlight and the moths, and had turned to grope her way across the room towards the light-switches by the door when she heard another sound. A curious harsh cry that was followed by a dull thud, and that seemed to come from just outside her door.

Dany stood still, listening, all her drowsiness gone and her pulses once again leaping in panic; until an obvious explanation occurred to her, and she relaxed again. It had only been a nightjar crying in the courtyard, and the wind must have overturned a top-heavy creeper-filled urn at the verandah edge. She smiled ruefully at her own fears, and walking forward in the darkness, felt for the switch.

The light clicked on and the room became safe and bright and comfortable, and there were no shadows. But the breeze had passed and the night was still again, and in that stillness she heard once again, and more distinctly, the sound that she had previously thought might be Millicent moving a suitcase: a soft, slow, unidentified sound that suggested stone moving on stone, and that seemed to come not so much from the room above her as from the verandah outside. It did not last for more than ten counted seconds, but this time it brought a sudden picture into Dany's mind: a picture of someone who was hurt, trying to crawl up the stairs. That cry she had heard — it had not been made by a nightjar, and of course the breeze could not have knocked over one of those heavy stone urns! It had been someone crying out and falling. Larry! ... Supposing it were Larry, tiptoeing up the stairs in the dark so as not to wake her, and losing his footing——

Dany listened at the door, but could hear no further sound. Had Larry been trying to drag himself up the stairs with a sprained ankle, or was he still lying out there in the dark verandah, winded or in pain?

Forgetting caution, she turned the key and jerked open the door.

The moon was not high enough to shine into the well of the courtyard, and Dany could see nothing but darkness except where the light streaming out from her open doorway made a narrow yellow pathway across the coconut matting, and silhouetted a flower-filled stone jar and a single slender pillar against the black emptiness beyond.

There was no chink of light from any other of the many doors that faced each other across the central courtyard, and the night was once again so still that the plop of a goldfish rising at a moth in the pool below was clearly audible in the silence.

Dany spoke in a whisper, afraid of rousing the sleeping house. 'Larry! — Larry, are you there? Is anyone there?'

The whisper made a soft sibilant echo under the high dark roof of the verandah, but no one answered her, and nothing moved. Not even the fish in the pool.

Then another breath of breeze stirred the creepers and flowering shrubs in the stone jars, and as Dany's eyes became accustomed to the darkness the tall lines of pillars with their rounded arches, the dark squares of the doors in the long white-washed wall and the outlines of the stone jars became visible, like a negative in a bath of developing solution. She could make out the long empty stretch of the verandah to her right, but to the left, where it turned sharply at right-angles, the stairs leading to the floor above made a pool of blackness.

She set the door wide and took a hesitant step forward, peering into the shadows. Surely there was something there ...? Someone. An untidy heap, sprawled in the dense shadow below the curve of the stone stairs and so nearly the colour of the matting as to be almost invisible.

Dany ran forward, and stooping above it touched a tousled head that appeared to be twisted at an odd angle. But it was not Larry Dowling. Who then? She caught at the slack shoulders, desperately tugging the heavy shape nearer to the light from the open doorway, and then remembered that the switches of the verandah lights were on the wall near the staircase, and ran to them.

A switch clicked under her shaking fingers, and a sixty-watt bulb enclosed in a hanging lamp of oriental design dispersed the shadows, throwing elaborate fretted patterns across the white wall and the coconut matting. And on Millicent Bates, dressed in pyjamas and an oatmeal-coloured dressing-gown, lying face downwards and very still on the verandah floor.

'Miss Bates!' implored Dany, kneeling beside her and endeavouring to turn her over. 'Miss Bates, are you hurt?'

The foolish question echoed hollowly along the silent verandahs as Millicent Bates's head lolled back from Dany's supporting arm. The breeze had set the lantern swaying, and the fretted lozenges of light shifted and swung and gave an illusion of movement to Millicent's wide, staring eyes. But there was no movement in the dead weight of her slack, heavy body. No movement anywhere except for the swinging, soundless lozenges of light and the flutter of a crumpled piece of paper that stirred in the breeze, flapping like a large pale-coloured moth on the matting.

She's hurt, thought Dany stupidly. Badly hurt ... or she's knocked the wind out of herself. No ... no it can't be just that ... Concussion. Miss Bates had fallen and stunned herself. Those shallow steps with their low, decorative, ridiculously inadequate balustrades—— She must have been coming down them in the dark to see if Gussie were settled in for the night, and slipped and fallen.

Of all the silly things to do, thought Dany frantically. In the *dark*!

The paper fluttered again with a small sound that made her start violently, and she snatched at it, and thrusting it into her pocket, laid Millicent's inert weight back on to the matting, and stood up: trembling but no longer frightened. She must fetch help at once — Gussie Bingham. Tyson——

She ran to Gussie's door and hammered on it, and receiving no answer tried the handle and found that Gussie too had taken the precaution of locking herself in that night. Dany beat on the door and called her by name, and the silent courtyard picked up the sound and echoed it along the lines of arches: 'Mrs Bingham —! *Mrs Bingham ... Mrs Bingham ...*'

A door opened on the adjoining verandah, framing Tyson in a bright square of light.

'What in the name of Beelzebub is the meaning of this infernal din?' roared Tyson, adding his quota to it. 'Who's there? What's up?'

'It's Miss Bates,' called Dany. 'Tyson, *do* come! She's fallen off the staircase, and I think she's concussed herself or — or something. And I can't lift her. She's too heavy.'

The door beside her was thrown open and Gussie Bingham was there, wrapped in a violet silk kimono patterned with wistaria, and with her curling pins inadequately concealed by a turban of lilac tulle.

'Miss Kitchell! Did you want me? What on earth is the matter? Why, Tyson——!'

Tyson charged past her, clad in nothing but a scanty loin cloth of some gaily patterned cotton material, and switching on lights as he went.

Other lights flooded the top-floor verandahs and other heads appeared, peering downwards: Nigel's, Eduardo's, Larry Dowling's . . .

Lorraine ran along the verandah, her little bare feet thrust into absurd feathered mules whose high heels clicked as she ran, and her diaphanous nightgown barely concealed by an equally diaphanous négligée.

But there was nothing that anyone could do. Millicent Bates was dead. She had fallen from somewhere near the top of the staircase on to the stone floor of the verandah, and broken her neck.

14

'I've always said those stairs were dangerous,' shuddered Lorraine, white-faced and shivering. 'Those silly little edges. They aren't rails at all! But I still don't see how she could have done it, even in the dark. You'd think anyone would be *extra* careful in the dark, wouldn't you?'

'I suppose she must have felt faint,' said Tyson. 'In fact that was probably what she was coming down for. To get some aspirin or something off Gussie. Gussie's got their medicine chest in her room.'

'But wouldn't you think she'd have had the sense to just sit down if she felt faint? Really, people are *too* stupid!'

It was obvious from Lorraine's tone that, horrified as she was, she considered Millicent Bates to have been guilty of thoroughly inconsiderate behaviour, and now that the first shock of discovery was over, her emotions leant more to anger than grief.

It was over an hour since Dany had aroused the sleeping household, and they were all in the drawing-room waiting for the arrival of the doctor, an ambulance and the police. All except Gussie — who had succumbed to a fit of hysterics and was now in bed having been given two sedatives and a hot-water bottle — and Nigel Ponting, who had driven in to the town to fetch the doctor and inform the police.

They had carried Millicent's body into Dany's room because it happened to be the nearest, and left it on Dany's bed, where it lay alone, clad in sternly utilitarian pyjamas and an elderly woollen dressing-gown, staring open-mouthed at the ceiling.

Lash had been awakened by the car being backed out of the garage and the flick of headlights across the wall of his room, and seeing the house ablaze with lights, he had put on a dressing-gown and come across to make inquiries.

Amalfi, who had slept through the initial uproar and had been aroused by Gussie's shrieks, had joined the horrified house-party just as Tyson and Larry Dowling were carrying Millicent's limp body into Dany's room. She had behaved with admirable calm, and it was she who had succeeded in putting a stop to Gussie's hysterics by the simple expedient of picking up the jug of drinking water that stood on Dany's bedside table, and flinging the contents in Mrs Bingham's scarlet, screaming face.

Amalfi was now sitting on the sofa, wearing a most becoming confection of peach-coloured satin and lace and looking as poised and sleek and *soignée* as though this was some normal social occasion. She was talking to Lash and sipping black coffee that Lorraine had made in a Cona, but if her composure was genuine, she appeared to be the only one in the room to possess it.

Lash was not even making a pretence of listening to her. He was looking troubled and out of temper, and was apparently more interested in the pattern of the carpet than in anything else, though he occasionally lifted his gaze from it to direct a look of active irritation at Tyson Frost, who was prowling restlessly about the room, looking like some strayed beachcomber from the South Pacific.

Lash, glancing at him and wishing he would stay still, decided that although hair on the chest might be the hallmark of a he-man, too much of it merely suggested that Darwin had been dead right when he attributed the origin of the human species to the ape. There was little to choose between Tyson's torso and a door-mat, and his caged-lion prowl was beginning to get on Lash's nerves. If only the man would sit still for five minutes——! And if only Amalfi would stop talking for ten. His gaze shifted briefly to Dany, and he frowned.

Dany was the only one in the room who was fully dressed, and Lash, noting the fact, and the time, was unreasonably disturbed. Two a.m. And they had all gone off to their several rooms shortly before half past eleven. Yet Dany alone had obviously not been in bed, for she was not only wearing the dress she had worn earlier that evening, but she was still wearing stockings. Which made it seem unlikely that she had merely hurriedly pulled on the dress in preference to coming down in a bathrobe as the others had done. He noticed that she was surreptitiously studying Larry Dowling, and his frown became a scowl.

Dany herself, sitting huddled in the depths of a big armchair and feeling cold and very tired, was wondering how Larry had managed to get back into the house and up to his room in time to change into the pyjamas and dressing-gown he now wore, when she had seen him on the terrace below her window, wearing a dinner jacket, only a short time before she had heard Millicent fall. Or had the interval been longer than she had imagined? How long had she stood near the window looking out into the moonlight after he had left the terrace? Surely not more than ten minutes. Yet Larry certainly had the appearance of one who has been awakened out of a sound sleep, for his hair was rumpled and he yawned at intervals. But despite the yawns there was nothing sleepy about those quiet, observant eyes, and Dany did not believe that he felt in the least drowsy.

Eduardo di Chiago, darkly handsome in scarlet silk pyjamas and a spectacular monogrammed and coroneted dressing-gown, was gallantly assisting Lorraine with the coffee. But he too was noticeably distrait and apt to jump when spoken to, and, like Lash, was obviously finding his host's relentless pacing an acute nervous irritant.

Lorraine, noticing it, said appealingly: 'Tyson darling, *do* sit down! You're making us all nervous. Why don't we all go back to bed?'

'Speaking for myself,' said Tyson, 'because I should have to get up again the minute the doctor and the police arrive. However, there's no reason why the rest of you should stay around. The only people they're likely to want to see are myself and Miss — er — Miss——'

'Kitchell,' supplied Lash with something of a snap.

Tyson turned to scowl at him and said: 'At least there's nothing to stop *you* getting back to bed, so don't let us keep you up. You weren't even here when it happened, and I don't know what the hell you're doing over here anyway.'

'Neither do I,' said Lash morosely. But he made no attempt to move, and once again he looked at Dany. A long, thoughtful and faintly uneasy look.

Amalfi, observing it, turned to follow the direction of his gaze, and her eyes narrowed while her charming, curving mouth was suddenly less charming as the red lips tightened into a line that was almost hard. She had not looked at Dany directly during the last hour, but she looked now.

Dany was sitting in a huddled and childish attitude that should have been ungraceful, but was not, for it revealed the fact that her figure was slim and her legs were long and lovely. She had done something, too, to her hair. Brushed it back and got rid of those distressing curls — and discarded her spectacles. Without them she looked absurdly young. Young enough to make Amalfi disquietingly conscious of her own age, and a crease furrowed her white forehead. She turned back sharply to look at Lash, but Lash was studying the carpet again and appeared to be immersed in his own thoughts which, judging from his expression, were not pleasant.

Eduardo too had looked at Dany: and from Dany to Amalfi Gordon. And his dark eyes were all at once intensely alert and curiously wary. He said abruptly, as though replying to Tyson's question:

'Then I think I go to my bed. You are right. No one will wish to ask me questions, and I feel that it may be I intrude.

This Miss Bates — she has been known to you for many years, perhaps? *Allora* — it is very sad for you. I feel for you so much. You excuse me, Lorraine?'

He kissed her hand, and then Amalfi's — though with less than his usual lover-like gallantry — and having conveyed his sympathy to Tyson in an eloquent look, returned to his own room. But no one else appeared to feel called upon to follow his example; not even Larry Dowling, who could certainly not have considered himself an old friend of the family: and they were all still there when at long last Nigel returned with the doctor and an Indian Chief Inspector of Police.

The proceedings after that had been mercifully brief. The doctor's verdict had confirmed their own, and it was only too easy to see how the accident had occurred.

Miss Bates, descending the staircase in the dark, had either felt faint or misjudged a step and stumbled, and falling over the edge of the balustrade on to the verandah below had broken her neck. It was as simple, and as shocking, as that.

Tyson had done most of the talking and shown them where the body had lain, and Dany had not been called upon to say very much. The doctor had seen Gussie and prescribed rest and, if necessary, another sedative, and he and the Inspector, having assisted in carrying Millicent's body to the waiting ambulance, had expressed their sympathy and left.

The moon was down and in the east the sky was already beginning to grow pale with the first far-away hint of dawn when Dany climbed in under her mosquito-net at last. Her sheets were crumpled and her pillow still bore the impression of Millicent Bates' head. But no one had thought to suggest that she sleep anywhere else, and she was too tired to care very much that she must sleep where Millicent's dead body had lain. Too tired to care very much about anything . . .

She slept so soundly that she did not hear the gentle tap of the house-servant who attempted to bring her a tea tray at eight o'clock, or, an hour later, Lorraine's voice outside her locked door, inquiring if she were awake yet. And it was, finally, Lash who awakened her.

He banged on her bedroom door and went on banging with increasing loudness until she opened it, and when he saw her there, drowsy and bewildered, he said with inexplicable fervour: 'Thank God for that!'

'For what?' asked Dany, blinking at him. 'Is anything the matter?'

'Apparently not,' said Lash, who was looking oddly white and strained. 'But when you didn't come down, and Lorraine said your door was locked and she could get no answer out of you, I thought maybe I'd better come up and make sure.'

'Of what?' inquired Dany, puzzled.

'That you were really only asleep. I guess that lousy business last night was an accident all right, but all the same——'

'Miss Bates——!' gasped Dany, recollection hitting her like a blow in the face. 'I — I'd forgotten. She — Oh, Lash! Oh *poor* Miss Bates. Poor Mrs Bingham ... Is she all right?'

'Mrs Bingham? I guess so. She seems to have recovered enough to eat a fairly hearty breakfast, judging from the tray that went up. How about you? Are you thinking of coming down any time?'

'Of course. Is it late?'

'Just after ten.'

'Ten! Good heavens!'

The door slammed in his face, and a silvery voice from half-way down the verandah said: 'Serenading your secretary, Lash darling?'

Amalfi walked towards him and smiled sweetly up into his face; but above the lovely laughing curve of her mouth her green eyes were cold and steady and held no trace of amusement, and looking down into them Lash was conscious of a sudden sharp sense of shock, as though he had walked unwarily into some solid object in the dark.

He had not known that Amalfi could look like that while smiling like that, and it left him feeling uneasy and strangely unsure of himself. He said defensively, answering her question: 'Strictly in the way of business.'

'Really?' Amalfi's voice was as warmly sweet as her smile. 'And is a lace and nylon wrap her normal working dress? What fun you business men must have!'

She laughed her lovely laugh, and Lash was startled to find himself angry in a way that he had never been angry before.

He looked at Amalfi for a long moment; seeing her as someone he did not know at all, and noticing many things that he had never noticed before: the years that had been so skilfully held at bay; the ice that could glitter in those cool, mermaid eyes and the malice that could speak in that warm caressing voice. The steel that lay concealed behind that charming, irresponsible, childish sweetness ...

Amalfi's long lashes fluttered and dropped, and when they lifted again her eyes were softly appealing and her voice coaxed. 'I'm dreadfully jealous, darling!'

'Are you?' said Lash grimly. 'It must make a nice change.' He turned away from her and went down the curving stair to the courtyard without troubling to see whether she were following or not.

Mr Cardew of the police, his peaceful Sabbath rudely interrupted, called again that morning at the House of Shade, and Tyson took him up to see the scene of the accident.

Mr Cardew commented unfavourably on the extremely inadequate balustrades, pronounced the staircases to be dangerous and suggested that iron rails of a reasonable height should be added at the earliest possible moment, and returned to the city taking Tyson, Dany and Gussie Bingham with him, where there had been certain depressing formalities to be gone through in connection with the death of Millicent Bates.

His office was in a tall, square building, four storeys high and facing the sea, with magnificent carved doors and a clock tower. The Bet-el-Ajaib, the 'House of Wonders'; once a palace built by the famous Sultan, Seyyid Barghash-bin-Saïd, and now doing duty as the Secretariat.

The House of Wonders had been built many years later than the House of Shade, and though on a far larger scale, its design was similar: the rooms with their tiers of verandahs being built about a central courtyard. Except that here the courtyard was not open to the sky, but closed over with a glass roof in the manner of a railway station.

Dany had left Tyson and his sister talking to Mr Cardew, and had gone out to stand on the steps and look out towards the harbour where the clove ship for Pemba lay at anchor, and to gaze at the three ancient guns that stood before the Bet-el-Ajaib: cannon that were stamped with the arms of Portugal, and were part of the booty taken by the Persians at the fall of Ormuz.

She had been tracing the worn inscriptions on the old sun-baked metal when a shadow fell across the cannon, and she looked up to see the Arab who had been on the Nairobi plane with them on the previous day, and whom Nigel had introduced as Seyyid Omar-bin-Sultan.

Seyyid Omar's excellent teeth flashed white in his olive-skinned face, and he bowed and said: 'Good morning, Miss Kitchell. How pleasant to meet you again so soon. You have started your sight-seeing already, I see. Are you admiring our guns? They are very old. Perhaps four hundred years and more.'

'Yes, I know,' said Dany. 'I read about them before I came here. What does that inscription on them say? It's Arabic, isn't it?'

'Persian,' said Seyyid Omar; and traced the graceful characters with one slim brown finger...

'In the Name of God and by the Grace of Mahomed and Ali, convey to the True Believers who have assembled together for

war, the Good Tiding of Success and Victory ... During the reign of Shah Abbas, Sajawi, King of the Earth and of Time, whose Power is ever increasing ...'

His finger slowed and stopped, and he did not read the rest of the long inscription, but looking down at it, repeated in a low voice that held a curious thrill of awe (and perhaps of envy?) that magnificent, arrogant title: *'King of the Earth, and of Time ...'*

'That's wonderful,' said Dany, charmed by the cadence of the words. 'Thank you.'

Seyyid Omar dropped his hand swiftly and smiled at her, and his voice was casual and polite again.

'Yes, that is a fine title, is it not? But there are none to hold it now. Our great days have gone — and our court poets — and who knows when they will return again? But what are you doing alone here, Miss Kitchell? Do you go sight-seeing by yourself?'

'No. I'm afraid I'm not sight-seeing this morning. We — that is Mr Frost and Mrs Bingham and myself, had to come in on — on business.'

'Oh?' Seyyid Omar's expressive brows lifted. 'That sounds dull. I had hoped that your first day in Zanzibar would be more entertaining. I wish that I might offer to show you something of the town, but I myself am also here to keep a business appointment. With the police.'

'The police?' Dany looked startled. 'Why — why so are we. With Mr Cardew.'

'Ah! You too. It is because of the death of an acquaintance of mine, I think? Salim Abeid, who died at Mombasa Airport yesterday. Well, I do not expect that you can give them any more assistance than I can.'

Salim Abeid ... Dany heard the name with a sense of shock, for Millicent's death had pushed that other tragedy into the back of her mind. But now she was reminded of it again; and reminded too that she had seen Salim Abeid talking to this man in the shadow of a wing of the Nairobi West Airport barely an hour before he had died.

'Probably a political murder,' Tyson had said. Jembe had made many enemies among the aristocracy and the rich land-owners — such men, presumably, as Seyyid Omar-bin-Sultan. And Seyyid Omar had been on the same plane . . .

The midday sun that beat down upon the entrance to the House of Wonders was very hot, but a little cold shiver prickled down Dany's spine, and she remembered innumerable stories that she had read of the cruelty of the East: stories stretching from the Arabian Nights down to the recent atrocities of the Mau Mau.

The Isle of Cloves, as its history showed, was not unacquainted with violence and cruelty, and the murder of a rabble-rouser would probably be considered as of little account today as the death of a dozen slaves in the days when the dhows of the slave traders had moored where the little Pemba-bound steamer now lay at anchor, and their crews had tossed out the corpses from among their human cargoes on to those same beaches.

Dany shivered, and Seyyid Omar, observing it, said solicitously: 'It has troubled you. I am sorry that your first morning in our island should be spoiled by such a thing: the death of a man you had probably not even met. Though I believe he was a fellow-passenger of yours from London, was he not?'

The question was asked quite casually and as though it were a matter of no account, but he waited for an answer.

Dany said: 'Yes. But I didn't actually meet him.'

'But Mr Dowling did,' said Seyyid Omar gently. 'And of course your — host's secretary had met him before. Mr Ponting. I am surprised that Mr Cardew should not have wished to see them, rather than you and Mrs Bingham.'

'Oh, but we aren't here about that,' Dany hastened to assure him. 'There was a dreadful accident at *Kivulimi* last night. Mrs

Bingham's companion, Miss Bates, fell from one of the staircases in the dark, and broke her neck.'

'You mean — she is dead?' inquired Seyyid Omar sharply.

'Yes.'

The monosyllable had a flat finality, and suddenly Millicent was dead. Really dead. Until then it had been unreal: a tale that someone had told her and which she had not quite believed. But now it was true...

She heard Seyyid Omar draw in his breath with a little hiss between his teeth. 'That is terrible! I am sorry. I am most sorry. This has been a sad arrival for you indeed. An ill-omened one. I can only hope that it will not give you a dislike of our island and make you wish to leave.'

Dany had no time for a reply, for at that moment Tyson and his sister joined them, and Seyyid Omar offered condolences and sympathy.

They stood in the white glare of the sunlight against a tropical background of flame trees, hard shadows and sauntering white-robed men with ebony faces, and spoke of Millicent: Tyson, burly, bearded and frankly impatient; Gussie looking suddenly ten years older — a lined, shocked, shrunken shadow of the assured and talkative matron of yesterday; Dany with her dyed hair and spectacles, and Seyyid Omar-bin-Sultan, suitably concerned and gravely sympathetic. *Requiem for a British Spinster*...

Seyyid Omar refused an invitation to accompany them to the English Club for lunch, and Tyson, Gussie and Dany returned to the car, and were driven through the narrow streets to a tall old building that fronted the sea and managed to epitomize all that is conveyed by the words 'Outposts of Empire'.

'The doors of all these houses are so lovely,' said Dany, pausing to look back along the white-walled street down which they had come. 'All that carving, and those huge brass spikes.'

'Those were to keep the war elephants from battering in the doors,' said Tyson. 'Useful, as well as ornamental.'

'*Elephants?* What nonsense! You couldn't possibly squeeze an elephant into one of these streets, let alone turn it end on to a door!'

'Yes, there is that,' said Tyson. 'But it's a pretty story all the same. And that really is why Arab doors had those spikes on them once. The days of the war elephants have gone, but the design has persisted. And you're right about the streets. Hell to drive through. In most of 'em, if a car is coming one way and a kitten the other, one of them is going to have to stop. And as this is Zanzibar, it's the car that would give way to the kitten. A pleasant crowd. A very pleasant crowd.'

Nigel joined them at the Club, and they ate a sturdy British meal that made no concessions to the climate, sitting in a huge, echoing, sparsely populated dining-room under the ceaseless whirr of electric fans.

Neither Gussie nor Tyson had much to say, and it fell to Nigel and Dany to sustain some semblance of conversation. But as Nigel was as voluble as ever, Dany's share was mercifully limited to adding an occasional yes or no at reasonable intervals.

Her mind was on other things than Roman society scandals, and she did not perceive their trend until Nigel said: '——the old Marchesa, that's Eduardo's grandmother, pulled *every* string within reach — and has she a reach! And so of course that was *that* as far as poor Eddie was concerned. *Too* frustrating for him. And then darling Lorraine asks him to look up Elf in London, and *here* we go again! Another *grande passion* that is doomed to crack on the same old rocks. Too awful for *both* of them, when you come to think of it.'

'Why?' inquired Dany perfunctorily.

'Oh, but my *dear*! It's obvious. Poor, poor Elf — so romantic and unbusiness-like! Throwing away the substance for an *utter* shadow; did she but know. There she was, all set to bridge the dollar gap by rushing Holden Jnr to the nearest registrar, when who should happen along but Eduardo. All Latin charm, a

Marquis to boot, and apparently *solid* with lire. *Naturally* the poor sweet began to waver. Well, I mean — there *is* a certain glamour about being able to embroider authentic little coronets on one's smalls, and plain "Mrs Holden" doesn't carry *quite* the same simple charm as "the Signora Marchesa di Chiago". Provided the lire and the lovely green-backs balance, of course! But then they don't. Someone really ought to break it to darling Elf.'

'Someone has,' said Tyson briefly, entering the conversation for the first time.

Nigel registered surprise. 'You? Now that *is* a relief — though I did begin to wonder last night if someone hadn't perhaps dropped the *merest* hint. I hope you mean to do the same for poor Eddie. Just a whisper of warning?'

'Eddie,' said Tyson shortly, 'can look after himself.'

Gussie helped herself to a solid wedge of suet pudding, and said: 'What are you two talking about? Warn who about what?'

'Eduardo;' said Nigel, 'about our dear Amalfi. That she may look *stimulatingly* solvent, but that it's all done by mirrors. Or should one be *really* catty, and say *paste*? Excellent imitations of course — she had them made in Paris. But I happen to know that she popped the diamonds and all Chubby's emeralds. The family were furious — my dear, *furious*! But of course there was nothing they could do about it. And after all, one *does* sympathize with the poor sweet. She had every reason to believe that she'd be left madly well off, and it must have been too infuriating to find an absolute regiment of assorted relatives all queueing up for their cut — and getting it! *Too* soul-curdling. One wonders if it was *worth* it? No thanks, I don't feel I could *face* suet pudding. I think I'll try the cheese——'

Millicent was buried late that afternoon, and the entire house-party attended, with the exception of Amalfi, who complained of a headache, and added that in any case she was allergic to funerals.

It was a brief enough service; and to Dany, at least, a tragic one. Not because she had taken any special liking to Miss Bates, who had been almost a stranger to her, but because she could not forget that Millicent Bates had despised all things Oriental and had so disliked the East. Yet now she would never leave it. Alien and alone she must lie in this hot foreign soil, within sound of the surf and the trade winds and the rustling palms, until the Day of Judgement. Poor Miss Bates, who had been so deeply rooted in the life of one small English market town, and who had not wanted to come to Zanzibar.

15

It was a silent and distinctly subdued party who assembled for dinner that night, and afterwards they had gone out to sit on the terrace and made desultory conversation, and no one had suggested dancing.

Amalfi appeared to have recovered from her headache, and in deference to the memory of Miss Bates she wore a deceptively simple dress of black chiffon which lent her a frail and wistful look and made her white skin appear even whiter by contrast.

Both Lorraine and Gussie also wore black. Presumably for the same reason. But as Dany did not possess a black dress (Aunt Harriet having held pronounced views on the unsuitability of black for the young), she had put on the same grey magnolia-appliquéd one that she had worn the previous evening. And it was while Abdurahman, the head houseboy, was clearing away the coffee cups and liqueur glasses, and Nigel was languidly inquiring whether anyone felt like a game of bridge, that she thrust an idle hand into one of the wide pockets that decorated the skirt and touched a crumpled piece of paper.

Dany drew it out and regarded it with faint surprise, wondering how it had got there. It was a half sheet of writing paper, roughly torn along one edge, and flattening out its creases she held it so that the moonlight fell full on it, and read the few typewritten words it bore without at first comprehending their meaning.

May I please speak to you. I am in great trouble, and need advice. Could you be very kind and make it after half-past twelve, as it is rather a private matter, and I do not want other people to know.

My room is underneath yours, and I will wait up. Please come. A.K.

What on earth——? thought Dany, looking at it with wrinkled brows. She turned it over, but there was no more of it. The writer had presumably meant to add something else to it, but had thought better of it and thrown it away. But how had it got into her pocket, and when?

And then, as suddenly and as shockingly as though someone had treated her as Amalfi had treated Gussie's hysterics and thrown a pint of ice-cold water in her face, she remembered——

It was the piece of paper that had fluttered against her skirt when she had knelt above Millicent's body last night, and which she had snatched up and stuffed into her pocket without thinking. But it was more than that. It was proof of murder.

A fragment of conversation from the previous evening repeated itself in her brain as though it were a gramophone playing a record: *'A third what?' 'Murder of course, darling. Things always go in threes ...'* They had gone in threes. There had been a third murder. And an attempt at a fourth — her own. For the note was neither unfinished nor unsigned. It had been written on her typewriter — Miss Kitchell's typewriter — and signed with her initials: Miss Kitchell's initials. And if it had been found——

A clammy mixture of nausea and cold fear engulfed Dany, drowning out the moonlight and the sound of the casual, idle voices. She was caught in a horrible, clinging spider-web, and however much she twisted and turned she could not escape, because there would always be another strand waiting for her ready to wind softly and terrifyingly about her until at last she would be bound and helpless.

Hysteria rose in her, prompting her to leap to her feet and scream and scream, as Gussie had done. To run across the terrace and through the moonlight and out into the white dusty road, and to go on running until she dropped. She fought it down, driving her fingernails into her palms and biting her lip until the blood came. And then a hand came out of the fog and closed over hers. A flesh and blood hand that was firm and real in the midst of miasma and unreality, and that steadied the spinning world and brought it back to some sort of sanity.

The fog cleared and the moonlight was bright again and Lash was standing in front of her; his body a barrier between her and the seven other people on the terrace.

He said: 'Come and take a walk down to the beach. I haven't had the chance of a word with you all day, and there are one or two things that I'd like to go over. You'll excuse us, Lorraine?'

He did not wait for permission, but jerking Dany to her feet he drew her arm through his, and holding it hard against him walked her away across the terrace and down the steps into the ink-black shadows of the tree-filled garden, where he began to talk of business matters and of names that meant nothing to her; continuing to do so as they passed along the shadowy, flower-scented paths, and leaving the garden by a door in the seaward wall, walked down a steep, rocky path to the shore.

The beach was deserted, and nothing moved on it save the quiet tide and a host of ghostly little sand crabs that scuttled to and fro as silently as moths. There were rocks at each end of it: tall rocks of wind-carved, water-worn coral that stood dark against the moon-washed sky and threw sharp-edged shadows on the white sand. But Lash avoided them, and keeping to the open beach stopped near the edge of the tide, where no one could approach unseen and they could not be overheard.

Releasing his grip on Dany's arm he turned her so that she faced him, but he did not lower his voice, or make any attempt to change its pitch, and anyone watching him from the shadows would have supposed him to be merely continuing the conversation he had started in the garden.

'What happened, honey? What was on that paper? Someone write you an anonymous letter?'

Dany held it out to him without words, and saw his face set into harsh and unfamiliar lines as he read it.

After a moment or two he said quite softly: 'Did someone put this in your pocket?'

'No,' said Dany in a whisper. 'I found it last night. It was on the verandah ... by ... near Miss Bates. She must have been holding it when ... I put it in my pocket, and I didn't think of it again until — until just now when I felt it, and took it out, and ... read it.'

Lash was silent for a long time, looking at the piece of paper in his hand, and at last Dany said: 'It does mean — what I think it means, doesn't it?'

'Yes,' said Lash, still softly, and without pretending to misunderstand her: his voice strangely at variance with the ugly grimness of his face and his taut hands.

'What are we going to do? Are you — are you going to tell the police?'

'I don't know. I shall have to figure it out. What did you do with that typewriter? Where is it?'

'In my room.'

'Then this probably wasn't written on it; which may help.'

'But it was,' said Dany with a catch in her voice. 'I thought one of the servants must have been playing with it — the lid wasn't on properly, and there was a bit of paper in it: the other half of that.'

'When was this?' asked Lash sharply.

'Last night, when I went up to bed.'

'Did you touch it?'

'Yes. I tried the typewriter to see if it was all right, and it was, and I took the paper out. It's in the waste-paper basket.'

Lash let out his breath in a little sigh. 'So your fingerprints will be on it. And they're on this too. A nice, neat, slick little fool-proof frame-up! Dear God, what have I let you in for?'

He crushed the piece of paper savagely in one clenched hand

and turned to stare blindly out at the shimmering sea, and Dany saw the muscles along his jaw twitch and tighten. He said, half under his breath and as though he were speaking to himself: 'I ought to have taken you straight to the police — back in London. It might have been a little sticky, but no more than that. Instead of which I have to let you in for a piece of crazy, drunken lunacy that——'

He made a violent despairing gesture, and Dany said quickly: 'Don't, Lash! It wasn't your fault. It was mine for not realizing that you—— Oh, what does it matter? We can go to the police now.'

Lash turned quickly to face her, his eyes blank with bitterness. 'No, we can't. That's the hell of it. We shall have to let the Bates woman's death stay on the books as an accident. There's no other way out.'

'But Lash——'

'There's no "but" about it!' interrupted Lash savagely. 'I may have been behaving like a certifiable moron of late, but I'm still capable of adding two and two together and coming up with the correct answer. That dame was killed because she talked too much; and but for the mercy of Providence, this bit of paper would have been found on her or near her. You'd have been asked to explain it — and a few other things as well! Such as how did the other half of it get into your room if you didn't write it, and what the heck were you doing fully dressed at least an hour after everyone else was in bed? What *were* you doing, by the way? *Were* you waiting for her?'

'Lash!' Dany flinched as though he had struck her.

'I didn't mean "Did you kill her?"' said Lash impatiently. 'Or even "Did you type that note?" Of course you didn't. But did she say anything about dropping in to see you?'

'No.'

'Then why hadn't you been to bed? What had you been doing?'

'Nothing. I just didn't feel sleepy; that was all. I suppose I didn't want to put the light out, and so I kept putting off going to bed. And then I heard a nightjar again, but it wasn't a nightjar——'

Dany shivered, remembering that sound, and said with an effort: 'It was Miss Bates. She must have cried out as she fell. And then I heard a thud . . .'

She told him about that, and about finding Millicent's body and the scrap of paper, and about Larry Dowling, who had been walking in the garden so short a time before.

'Dowling,' said Lash slowly.

He appeared to be turning something over in his mind, and then he shook his head, and abandoning Larry Dowling, said: 'Didn't you hear any other sound at all? No footsteps? Nothing? If someone waited for her to come down those stairs, and then pushed her off them, you'd surely have heard footsteps.'

'No, I didn't. I didn't hear anything else. Just a sort of screech and a thud: I told you. There wasn't any other . . . No. No, I'm wrong. There was another sound. A queer soft grating sort of noise like——' She wrinkled her brows, trying to recall what it was like and put it into words, but gave it up. 'I don't know. But it wasn't footsteps.'

Lash dismissed it with a shrug. 'Let it go. But the fact remains that you were up and dressed, and it wouldn't have looked too good if that note had been found, because it would have helped back up the theory that you wrote it. Which wouldn't have been a criminal thing to have done, and would only have meant that you'd asked Miss Bates to come to see you, and that she'd slipped and fallen while she was on her way down. But the moment you denied having written it the thing would have begun to look screwy, and the chances are that you wouldn't have been believed. They'd have wanted to know why you were denying it when all the evidence supported it; and the next thing you know they'd have found out that you are no more Miss Kitchell than I am, and that you'd skipped out of England on a false passport to avoid a murder rap. It wouldn't have sounded so good, and though maybe you could have talked your way out of one of those situations, I doubt if you could talk yourself out of both. Which is why that accident last night is going to have to stay just the way it is — an accident! Anything else is too darned dangerous. And now the sooner we get rid of this particular piece of poison, the better.'

He took a cigarette lighter out of his pocket, snapped it open and held one corner of the crumpled type-written note to the flame, and Dany said on a gasp: 'Lash you can't — it's evidence!'

'Sure. But it won't be in a minute. And without it that other bit of paper in your room won't mean a thing, and there'll be nothing to connect you with Miss Bates.'

He watched the small scrap of paper that had lured Millicent to her death blacken and curl and burst into flame, and when he could hold it no longer he dropped it and ground the burnt fragments into the sand with his heel. He was silent for a moment or two, scowling down at the small dark depression that his heel had made, and then he said slowly: 'I wish I could take you out of here, but I can't. If we make a break for it, it would only look worse. And yet it's a risk either way. Listen, Dany, I want you to promise me something.'

'What?' inquired Dany in an uncertain voice.

'That you won't ever leave your room at night, for any reason at all. That you'll lock yourself in, and if anyone taps on your door and pushes a note under it asking you to go anywhere, even if it's signed by your mother and written in her own handwriting, you won't even touch it. Give it to me in the morning. And don't go off on any *tête-à-tête* expeditions with anyone — unless it's me! Get it?'

He smiled at her, but it was a smile that did not reach his eyes, and Dany said with a catch in her voice: 'But why should anyone want to harm me? Or try to pin things on me? It was different before — when I had that map or clue or whatever it was. But now it's been stolen. Whoever wanted it has got it. Why doesn't it all stop? Why did anyone have to murder Miss Bates?'

Lash said: 'Because she insisted on telling us that she was in the neighbourhood of this solicitor's house around the time that the guy who rubbed him out would have been on his way in to do the job. That same guy happens to know that you were around too; and he's giving you a strong hint not to talk, or it will be the worse for you! Either that, or he's laying on a useful scapegoat in case he should ever need one. A hell of a lot of guys will do a hell of a lot of lousy things for the sake of three million — take it from me! That's why you're going to watch your step from now on. And I *mean* watch it! We ought to have the cops down on us in a day or two, and after that it's their headache.'

Dany twisted her hands together and said on a sob: 'Lash — I'm frightened.'

'You're not the only one!' retorted Lash with strong feeling. 'I've never been so scared in all my life. I do not relish the idea that one of that bunch back there on the terrace makes a hobby of murder, and I wish I had a gun.'

'But it can't be one of us! It can't be!'

'Don't be silly, Dany. It can't be anyone else. It's one of six people. You, me, Amalfi, Gussie Bingham, the Latin lover or Larry Dowling. Take your choice!'

Dany shivered and Lash reached out suddenly and pulled her into his arms, holding her against him and ruffling the outrageous red curls with his free hand. He said: 'I know, honey. But it'll all be the same in a hundred years.'

Dany made a sobbing and unintelligible remark into his shoulder, and he put his hand under her chin and lifted it. 'What was that one? I didn't get it.'

'I said "be c-careful of my s-spectacles".'

'I never liked them anyway,' said Lash, removing them and kissing her lightly. At least, that is what he had meant it to be, but it did not turn out like that. It began lightly enough, but ended very differently, and when at last he lifted his head he was astounded to find himself feeling breathless and shaken.

'That your first kiss?' he inquired, holding her away from him.

'Yes,' said Dany dazedly; her face bemused and beautiful in the white moonlight. 'How did you know?'

'I get around,' said Lash dryly. 'Well, it's going to be the last for tonight, because if I do that again there's no knowing where we'll end up.'

He stooped and retrieved the spectacles that had fallen unheeded to the ground, and having dusted the sand off them, replaced them carefully.

'And that'll be all for today, Miss Kitchell. I guess we'd better get back to the house and see you safely locked in for the night. And with reference to that last item on the agenda, you might consider letting me have a copy of it tomorrow — in triplicate.'

He walked her back towards the house across the white beach and through the door into the garden, where they encountered Larry Dowling loitering in the shadows by the edge of a shallow pool set about with stone birds and spider lilies. They might have passed without knowing that he was there, except that a reflection moved slightly in the water, and there was a faint smell of cigarette smoke.

Lash had stopped and said: 'di Chiago?' and Larry had moved out into the moonlight and said: 'No. But that was quick of you. It's one of his cigarettes. Can't say I like 'em much: give me gaspers every time. Nice on the beach?'

'Yes, thanks,' said Lash curtly. 'You on your way there?'

'No. Just strolling around,' said Larry. 'Just strolling around.'

Lash said: 'Don't let us stop you,' and went on up the path that led to the terrace.

There were only two people on the terrace: Amalfi and

Eduardo, who appeared to be quarrelling. They broke off on hearing footsteps, and Amalfi said with an edge to her voice: 'Oh, it's you. I hope you had a nice brisk businesslike session and got everything straightened out?'

'We did,' said Lash amiably. 'Thanks for asking.'

Amalfi laughed. 'Gussie was right: you're nothing but an old slave-driver. I really do believe that "Business First" is your motto.'

'The Americans!' said Eduardo. 'So efficient, so ruthless — so eye-on-the-ball. It is wonderful.'

Amalfi said hastily: 'Lorrie said to say good night to you, Lash; she and Gussie both thought they could do with an early night. She wanted to know if you'd like to go along to the fish market tomorrow morning. Gussie wants to see it. She says if she mopes around here she'll go mad, and Lorrie said that if you'd like to tag along you'll have to have breakfast at eight, and there'll be a car going in immediately afterwards. However, I told her I didn't think it sounded at all in your line.'

'Then you thought wrong,' said Lash, still amiably. 'I like fish. Where's Tyson? Is he making an early night of it too?'

'No. He and Nigel are as bad as you. They're doing a bit of work for a change.'

'It won't hurt 'em,' said Lash, and turned to Dany. 'That reminds me: I've got one or two things to do myself. I guess I'd better borrow your typewriter, Ada. I'll go right on up with you now and get it, if that's all right with you?'

'Yes, of course,' said Dany.

She moved towards the door, and Lash was following her when Amalfi spoke softly, addressing no one in particular: 'I do hope this means that Ada's mumps are better?'

16

'I have always considered,' remarked Nigel, holding a delicately scented handkerchief to his nose, 'that a fishmonger's emporium ranks slightly above a morgue, and only a point below a butcher's shop and an abattoir. All those slippery white stomachs and cold coddy eyes glaring at one. *Utterly* emetic. But just look at these colours! *Pure* Roerich. *Do* let's have some of those turquoise-blue fish with coral spots — or what about these heavenly shocking pink ones? You know, this might almost reconcile one to doing the weekly shopping.'

'But can one really *eat* the things?' inquired Gussie, apprehensively eyeing the fish in question. 'Lorraine, you're *surely* not going to buy those pink creatures?'

'Changu, Gussie. They're delicious. Wait until you taste them!'

'Well, if you say so,' said Gussie in a fading voice.

The fish market was a riot of noise and colour, and the variegated and vividly patterned clothing worn by the housewives of a dozen different nationalities was rivalled in both colour and design by the wares they were bargaining for.

It was as though the exotic contents of a tropical aquarium had been emptied onto the crude trestle tables, the floor and the wooden-sided pens and tubs: fish of every conceivable shape and colour, the beautiful jostling the sinister — such things as sting rays, hammer-headed sharks, cuttle fish and octopuses.

Competing with it in the matter of colour, while greatly improving on it in the way of smell, were the stalls of the open market where fruit and grain and vegetables were sold. A glowing, aromatic medley of oranges, limes, bananas, coconuts, cloves and chillies; yams, pawpaws, sweet potatoes, piles of green vegetables and flat wicker baskets full of assorted grains.

'What's that you've been buying?' inquired Lash, coming across Dany standing before a fruit stall with her hands full of greenish-yellow objects.

'Mangoes. I said I only wanted one — just to try. But it seems they don't sell them in ones. Only by the basket, and I couldn't possibly cope with that many. But luckily Seyyid Omar came along, and he—— You do know each other, don't you? This is Seyyid Omar-bin-Sultan; he was on the plane with us.'

'Yeah, I remember,' said Lash, shaking hands. 'I'm very pleased to know you. I'm Lash Holden. I don't think we actually met.'

'You're an American?' said Seyyid Omar.

'That's right. The Country of the Future.'

'Of the present, surely?' corrected Seyyid Omar with a faint smile and a slight emphasis on the noun.

'Maybe,' said Lash lightly, and turned to regard Dany with some suspicion. 'Say, you aren't going to start in eating those things right here, are you?'

'Where else?'

'Well, in your bath, I guess. It looks a messy business. And anyway, you can't possibly eat six mangoes.'

'Just watch me.'

'Not on your sweet life!' said Lash; and arbitrarily confiscated her booty.

Seyyid Omar laughed and said: 'It is plain that Miss Kitchell has not yet tried to eat a mango. A plate and a knife are a help. Will you allow me to lend you one? My house is only a short way from here, and I know that my wife would be very pleased to meet you. If you would accompany me, you may eat your mangoes in more comfort.'

Dany threw a quick look at Lash, and Seyyid Omar, intercepting it, made him a slight smiling bow that included him in the invitation.

'Sure,' said Lash slowly. 'We'd be very pleased to. Here — would you mind holding these for a minute?'

He unloaded the mangoes on Seyyid Omar and strode off across between the stalls to where Nigel was assisting Lorraine in the selection of pineapples, and returned a minute or two later to say that that was O.K. and that the others would be going on to the English Club later in the morning, and would meet them there.

'I will drive you over,' promised Seyyid Omar, and led the way out of the market and towards the harbour.

Seyyid Omar's house was in a narrow street that was a cavern of cool shadows slashed by an occasional hot, hard shaft of sunlight: a huge old Arab house, four storeys high and colour-washed in saffron and blue.

A magnificent brass-studded door with elaborately carved lintels and architraves opened into a stone-paved hall and a central courtyard surrounded by rising tiers of pillared verandahs: a house that was almost a duplicate of Tyson's, though larger.

Seyyid Omar led the way up two flights of stairs to a room on the second floor, where there were latticed windows looking out over the old stone-built town of Zanzibar to where the open sea lay blue and dazzling in the morning sunlight.

A white-robed servant brought sherbet, fruit and cigarettes, and their host's pretty wife instructed Dany in the best way — or the least messy one — of eating a mango.

Seyyide Zuhra-binti-Salem was on first sight a character straight out of the Arabian Nights: Scheherazade herself, or one of Bluebeard's lovely wives. A slender, charming, dark-eyed young woman with blue-black hair and a complexion of pale ivory. It was something of a shock to discover that this enchanting creature not only spoke six languages besides her own, but was entitled, if she so wished, to write the letters B.A. after her name.

It altered all Dany's preconceived notions on the subject of 'ladies of the harem' to find that the young wife of an Arab in Zanzibar was infinitely better educated than herself, or, for that matter, than the majority of European women with whom she had so far come into contact.

It proved to be an entertaining, stimulating and surprising visit; in more ways than one. Time slipped past unnoticed while Zuhra laughed and talked of Oxford and Paris and the Sorbonne, and her husband told them enthralling tales of the island, and volunteered to take them that very afternoon, in the cool of the day, to see the underground wells and the ruins of the haunted palace of Dunga.

Conversation was easy and animated until the subject of the two tragedies that had marred the arrival of Lorraine's guests was raised. It was Lash who had introduced it, and his inquiry as to whether there had been any further developments in relation to the death of Salim Abeid was greeted by an odd little pause. Not long enough to be uncomfortable, but nevertheless definite enough to break the pleasant ease that had prevailed during the last hour and a half.

'Ah,' said Seyyid Omar thoughtfully. 'Jembe — "the thin man".'

He did not reply to the question, but asked one of his own. 'Did you know him?'

'No,' said Lash. 'But he was on the same plane out from London. I understand he was kind of well known in your island. A public character.'

'He wished to be one,' said Seyyid Omar dryly. 'That is not quite the same thing.'

'I take it you knew him?'

'Yes. Slightly.'

Seyyid Omar's expressive brown hands sketched a small deprecatory gesture as though he would have preferred to end the conversation, but Lash did not choose to take the hint. He said: 'Tell us about him. Would you have said that he was a man who made enemies?'

'He was a hireling of Moscow — and of Egypt,' said Zuhra gently.

She disregarded another faint gesture of her husband's as Lash had done, and said: 'Oh, he did not call himself that. He called himself a Democrat — which is Soviet double-talk for the same thing. He wished to found a Single Party in Zanzibar. In other words, a dictatorship. With himself, of course, as the dictator. It was very simple. He had a certain following, for there are, everywhere, dissatisfied, embittered or envious people who get pleasure out of tearing down what they cannot build. And also poor people and unfortunate people and ignorant people, who should be pitied and helped, not exploited — but who are so easy to exploit. Here in Zanzibar we have, perhaps, less of such people than in other places; but enough to cause trouble. He will be no loss.'

Lash said casually, watching the smoke of his cigarette: 'I guess it must have been a political murder. Sounds that way.'

Seyyid Omar shrugged. 'Perhaps. It is always a possibility.'

'But you don't believe it,' said Lash. 'Now I wonder why?'

'I did not say so.'

Lash gave him a slanting look. 'Not in words. Why don't you believe it?'

Seyyid Omar laughed and threw up his hands. 'You are very persistent Mr Holden. Why does the death of Jembe interest you?'

'I guess because it interests your local police to such an extent that I have been requested to stay in Zanzibar for a few days. Just while they make some inquiries. I don't know what that suggests to you, but it suggests quite a few things to me.'

Seyyid Omar rose to replenish Dany's glass, and said lightly: 'Yes, I had heard. I too had an — interview with Mr Cardew yesterday. They seem to think that someone must have stopped to speak to Jembe at the airport, and dropped a pellet in his coffee. Myself, I think it would have taken a brave man or an exceedingly rash one, or else a very stupid one, to do such a thing. Think of the risks of being seen! I cannot believe it was as clumsy as that.' He paused to stub out his cigarette, and added: 'Mr Cardew also told me about the unfortunate tragedy that occurred on the night of your arrival. It must have been very distressing for all of you.'

His face expressed nothing more than polite concern, but there was something in the tone of his voice that made Dany wonder if his linking of those two deaths had been deliberate, and she was conscious of a sudden and urgent sense of unease: as though someone had whispered a warning that she had been unable to catch.

'Nigel Ponting told me in the market this morning,' said Seyyid Omar, 'that she had been with Mr Frost's sister for many years — this Miss Bates. That is sad for Mrs Bingham; to lose a friend and a confidante. Nigel has not been so long with Mr Frost; a few years only, I think; but he could probably tell you more about Jembe than I could. You should ask him. If he does not know he will at least invent something interesting.'

Lash grinned. 'Yeah. You're probably right there. Nigel's a mine of gossip. He ought to be run as a syndicated column. But it's your opinion I'm interested in, not his. You belong here.'

'But is it not one of your sayings that the onlooker sees most of the game?' said Seyyid Omar with a slight smile.

'Meaning that you yourself are right out there with the team?' inquired Lash.

Seyyid Omar laughed and helped himself to another cigarette. He said reflectively, reaching for the match box: 'If you really wish for my opinion, I do not think that Jembe's group were either large enough or important enough to put any other party to the trouble of poisoning him. His was merely a splinter group, and though noisy, a thing of no real weight.'

'Not even worth anyone's while to nip in the bud?' suggested Lash. 'Vested interests, large land-owners and the ruling classes are never very anxious to see the seeds of revolution get sprouting.'

'That is true, of course. But then they never believe it can come to anything. Never. And so they do not even trouble to reach for the weed-killer!'

'You're probably right there,' said Lash. 'Which leaves us with what?'

'For a possible motive for the murder of a man like Jembe?' said Seyyid Omar, striking a match. 'Who can say? Except that as a grave risk was taken, it must have been a strong one. Hate possibly: if it were deep enough and sharp enough. Or money, if it were a large enough sum.'

'Say — three million?' suggested Lash gently.

Seyyid Omar was suddenly very still. So still that he did not seem to breathe, or be aware that he still held a lighted match between his fingers.

It burned down, and he dropped it with a quick gasp of pain and put his foot on the tiny glowing fragment, and Dany stood up hurriedly and said a little breathlessly: 'It must be getting very late. I'm sure we ought to go. What time is it?'

'Just on twelve,' said Lash, rising. 'Yes, I guess we'd better be going. Well, thanks a lot, both of you, for a most enjoyable morning. It's been a great pleasure meeting you, and I hope we'll see more of you. A lot more.'

'I shall call for you this afternoon,' said Seyyid Omar, recovering himself. 'To take you to the wells. And now, if you must go, my car will be waiting below, and the driver will take you to the Club. You will forgive me for not taking you there myself, but I have some things to attend to.'

They took their leave of Zuhra, promising to come again, and went out into the high, shadowed verandah, closing the door behind them. There were no stone jars full of shrubs and creepers here, but in the courtyard below there was a tulip tree and a fountain, and Dany looking down from the verandah edge said: 'Are all the big houses in Zanzibar built like this?'

'To this design?' asked Seyyid Omar. 'No. Very few of them. But it is not surprising that you should ask that, for this house and the one you are living in now were built for the same man, and almost certainly by the same builder. They are probably the oldest houses in Zanzibar. He was a bad character, that old gentleman, but plagued with many wives, so perhaps much may be forgiven him! He came to a bad end, but a richly deserved one — "hoist with his own petard", I think you would say.'

'How?' inquired Dany, intrigued. 'What happened to him?'

'He fell into a trap that he had often laid for others. I will show you. But you must not tell, for it is a secret that very few know. Is that agreed?'

'Yes, of course. It sounds very exciting.'

'I think you will find it so. And instructive.'

Seyyid Omar turned and looked over his shoulder down the length of the verandah, and then down over the balustrade at the storey below. But though they could hear voices and laughter, for the moment there was no one in sight, and he said: 'Quick — while there is no one here.'

He led the way swiftly to the top of the staircase that curved down to the verandah below — a duplicate of the stairs in the House of Shade — and telling them to watch, went to a nearby pillar and stooping down moved something near its base.

There was a slow, soft grating sound; the sound of stone moving on stone; and two of the wide, shallow steps drew back into the wall, leaving a gaping space below the first step so that they were looking down on the stone floor of the verandah, sixteen feet below.

Dany gave a long, helpless gasp that was almost a scream, and Lash caught her by the arm and jerked her back as though he were afraid that she might have walked forward.

Seyyid Omar stooped again, and once more they heard that

soft, rasping scrape, and the yawning gap closed as smoothly as it had opened. The steps were in place once more: solid and seemingly safe, and with nothing to mark them from any other steps.

'It is very ingenious, is it not?' inquired Seyyid Omar softly. 'More so than you would think. Naturally I cannot show you, as it is too dangerous, but when it is open, the first step will tilt when a foot is placed upon it: to ensure that the victim will fall head first, you understand. When that happens the steps go back of their own accord — it is all an ingenious matter of weights and balances — and if it is not done, then one can replace it oneself, as I did. I was sure that you would be interested.'

Lash swung round to stare at him, his mouth a tight line and his grey eyes dangerous, but Seyyid Omar returned his look blandly; the pleasant host, drawing attention to an unusual feature of his house for the entertainment of his guests.

'You will understand,' he said with a smile and a shrug, 'why I do not show many people this. It is always so much safer to keep one's own counsel, do you not think? Shall we go down? You need not be afraid. It is quite safe now.'

He led the way, talking polite trivialities, down the curving stairs to the ground floor and out into the street where a huge white car and an ebony-coloured chauffeur waited to drive them to the English Club.

It was a short enough drive, and during it neither Lash nor Dany spoke, or even looked at each other, and it was not until they were standing in the cool deserted hall of the Club that Lash said tersely: 'Did you move her?'

'Yes. I — I didn't think of that before, but she must have been lying under the staircase when I found her. It was dark and I tried to drag her towards my room. That was why it looked as if — as if——'

'As if she'd fallen over the edge,' finished Lash. 'Well, there's the proof, if we needed it. But at least it couldn't have been pinned on you. You couldn't possibly have known about that devilish booby-trap.'

'Yes, I could,' said Dany, her voice a dry whisper. 'Because I'm Tyson Frost's step-daughter, and it would be difficult to prove that I didn't know. You see, it's sure to be in the book.'

'What book?'

'*The House of Shade*. The one Tyson's uncle wrote. Tyson was talking about it at dinner that night, and he said that there were several copies in the house. There's one in my room. It may have been put there on purpose, so that it would look——'

'Business again?' inquired a charming voice from the staircase, and Amalfi was there: wearing a preposterous rainbow-coloured hat of fringed straw, bought at some shop in Portuguese Street and looking, on Amalfi's golden head, as decorative and enchanting a piece of nonsense as ever came out of Paris.

'No,' said Lash shortly. 'Pleasure. I hope we haven't kept you all waiting?'

'For *hours*, darling! We've all been drinking pints and pints of Pimms. Except Larry, who is being all British-to-the-Backbone on luke-warm beer. Did your fascinating Arab friend introduce you to all the luscious lovelies of his harem? Or don't they have them any more? Nigel says he has a quite ravishing wife, and Eddie's simply pining to meet her. But as it seems that she's got a classical degree, I feel he'd better keep away and keep his illusions.'

Amalfi turned and led the way up to a large high-ceilinged room where the rest of the *Kivulimi* house-party were sitting under whirling electric fans, moodily sipping iced drinks and making no attempt at conversation.

Gussie greeted them with a sombre look and Lorraine with a vague smile, and Nigel said crossly: 'Had I known that you intended to spend the *entire* morning "fraternizing with indigenous personnel" as I believe it is termed among your countrymen, I should have gone home and sent the car back for you. *I* happen to have work to do, even though some people have not. I hope we can go now?'

He sulked the whole way home, but both Dany and Lash had too much on their minds to notice the fact, and Larry Dowling, who was the fourth passenger in their car, took one long reflective look at Dany and also relapsed into silence.

They found Tyson in good spirits but still as averse as ever to discussing any form of business, and on hearing that Lash and Dany were accompanying Seyyid Omar on a sight-seeing expedition that afternoon, he instantly announced that it was a damned good idea and that they could all go: it would give him a pleasant spell of peace and quiet.

'Working, darling?' inquired Lorraine solicitously.

'No. Sleeping! And I shall do it a damn sight better without people chattering and nattering all over the house. Last time Gussie was taken to the wells she was eight — and screamed the place down, as far as I remember! Time she saw 'em again.'

So they had all gone. Lash, Dany and Gussie Bingham in Seyyid Omar's great white car, and Nigel, Amalfi and Larry Dowling in one of the *Kivulimi* cars driven by Eduardo.

They stopped by the roadside in a forest of palms to drink coconut milk from the ripe nuts; explored a copra factory and saw a clove plantation; and leaving the cars in a small dusty side road, followed a narrow, winding track across a no-man's land of scrub and rocks and dried grasses, and came suddenly upon a hole in the ground where a flight of worn stone steps led down into darkness.

'I don't think I like the look of it all,' said Gussie, shuddering and clutching nervously at Dany's arm. 'Suppose we fall into the water and drown in the dark? Hasn't anyone got a torch?'

No one had. But there were matches and cigarette lighters, and Seyyid Omar assured them that there was not the least danger of anyone drowning, and that women from the little village where they had left the cars came here daily to draw water.

The steps led down into a huge underground cave where the light barely penetrated and smooth water-worn rocks sloped sharply downwards towards, not wells, but a spring of water or an underground stream that came up out of the darkness and disappeared again into a black rock tunnel.

Holding cautiously to each other so as not to slip and fall on the rocks, they ventured down to the edge of the spring, their voices echoing strangely through the shadowy vault, and Seyyid Omar told them that the water was supposed to be the continuation of a stream that fed one of the great lakes in Africa, and flowing on far under the sea bed, bubbled up briefly here in Zanzibar; to vanish again into the rock and the Indian Ocean.

'I'm sure it's wildly interesting,' said Amalfi, 'but let's go, shall we? I think it's dark and spooky and altogether rather gruesome, and personally, the sooner I get out of the place the better. What happens if the roof falls in?'

There was an unexpected note of shrillness in her voice, and instantly everyone looked up at the dark curve of rock overhead, and moved closer to each other, their feet slipping on the steep rock-face.

Eduardo said soothingly: 'The roof will not fall in, *cara.* It is only a big cave. There are thousands of such places all over the world. But if it does not please you, we will go at once.'

'Yes, do let's,' said Gussie, shuddering. 'It's giving me claustrophobia.'

Within a few minutes they were out in the open air again. But it was not until two hours later, as the cars drew up before the gateway of the House of Shade, that Dany discovered that the white suede bag that she had carried had been neatly slit open with a sharp knife or a razor blade, and everything in it had gone.

17

'I will see that it is reported at once to the police,' said Seyyid Omar.

He had invited Dany, Lash and Gussie to dine with him at a restaurant in the town, but Gussie having refused on the plea of tiredness they had dropped her at the House of Shade, and driven back to Zanzibar city under a green and lavender sky that was already freckled with pale stars.

'No, for goodness sake, don't!' said Dany hastily. 'The police have had enough of us. Besides, it isn't worth making a fuss about. There was nothing of any value in it. Only a handkerchief and a pair of sunglasses, and a powder compact and a lipstick. That sort of thing. And possibly about eightpence in English pennies!'

'It must have been lifted by one of those picturesque characters in the village near the wells,' said Lash. 'Darned disappointing for him. Though I guess his lady friends will get a load of fun out of smearing themselves with lipstick. It's a shame about the bag, though. I'll get you another one tomorrow. Souvenir of Zanzibar.'

The city by night was very different from what it had been in the heat of the day, for the cooler air had brought all Zanzibar out of doors, and there were gay crowds strolling under the trees in the public gardens and along the sea front, while every roof-top and *baraza* appeared to have its family party.

Music and laughter, the tuneful cry of the coconut seller, and a continual rub-a-dub-dub of drums made a gay, enchanting medley of sound, mingled with the more normal noises of any Eastern city.

'Is it some special day?' asked Dany. 'A feast day, or something?'

'No. What makes you think that?'

'Everyone seems so gay. Listen — can't you hear them? They all sound very happy.'

'It is a happy island,' said Seyyid Omar, smiling. 'And when we feel gay we laugh — or sing; or play the *kinanda* — the mandolin. Or beat a drum. And, as you hear, we feel gay very often. It is a thing worth keeping, I think. Yes — very well worth keeping. But there are times when I become afraid.'

Lash turned his head and regarded him attentively. 'Afraid of what?'

Seyyid Omar slowed the car to a stop under the scented canopy of an Indian cork tree that leaned above a high, white-washed wall, and sat back, resting his slim brown hands upon the wheel: his face faintly illuminated by the dash-board lights.

He said slowly: 'I will be frank with you, Mr Holden. I think that you know something about a sum of money: a very large sum of money that many people have searched for for a great many years, though few have really believed in its existence. That vast legendary treasure that Seyyid Saïd, the first Sultan, was rumoured to have buried at Bet-el-Ras.'

Neither Lash nor Dany made any answer, and Seyyid Omar presumably translated that silence as admission, for after a momentary pause he said: 'I myself did not believe that it had ever existed or was more than a tale or legend. But not so long ago there arose a rumour; a whisper that it was fact and not fiction.'

He shifted a little; a small uneasy movement, and his hands tightened on the wheel. 'There are certain people in this island who need money, a large sum of money, to buy power at the next election. We have an old proverb that says "I will change my religion and the colour of my coat, but thou must pay,' and there are, alas, always votes — too many votes! — that can be bought for cash where they cannot be acquired from conviction. For money will always speak with a louder voice than any politician. One of those who wished to buy power travelled out with you from London, and is now dead. Jembe. But there are others, and they still need money.'

He was silent for a moment or two, and then he gave a quick shrug of his shoulders and drew a cigarette-case from his pocket.

'You do not smoke, I think, Miss Kitchell? You will not mind if we do?'

He offered the case to Lash with a pleasant smile and as the car filled with the fragrant smell of Turkish tobacco, leant back against the seat as though the conversation had been concluded and he had no more to say.

Lash said lightly: 'Then I guess a lot of guys are all set for a sad let-down. Why are you telling us this?'

Seyyid Omar laughed. 'You are not really stupid, Mr Holden, are you.'

It was an assertion, and not a query, and Lash said: 'Not that stupid, anyway! But I don't see what this has got to do with me, or with Miss Kitchell.'

'Don't you? Well, perhaps you are right. All the same, it is just as well to be warned.'

'Warned?' Lash's voice had a sudden sharp edge to it, and Dany felt his lounging body stiffen. 'That's quite often a fighting word where I come from. What exactly are you warning us about? Or have I got it wrong and is this a threat?'

'Ah, no!' Seyyid Omar held up a deprecatory hand. 'You misunderstand me. Why should I threaten? I am merely offering advice.'

'O.K., let's have it.'

'If there is any truth in this legend of the hidden treasure, and should — anyone, have any knowledge of where it may be found, it would, I think, be wise for that person to take such knowledge to His Highness the Sultan, whom God preserve. Or to the police.'

'Why? Because to possess that knowledge is dangerous?'

'That, of course. To be the possessor of such knowledge might prove very dangerous indeed. But there is a much more important, though less personal reason for speaking of it. To prevent it falling into the wrong hands. Such a sum of money can be a dangerous thing when used for evil. And it would be used for evil. Of that you can be sure. There is a curse on it.'

Lash said impatiently: 'You don't mean to tell me that you believe that old wives' tale?'

Seyyid Omar looked at him and laughed. 'So you have heard of it? Yes, I believe it, though you will not. But then you are a young man, Mr Holden, and from a very young country. You still have a great many things to learn — particularly about the East. One of them can be summed up best in words that have been worn threadbare from use, but which cannot be improved upon: "There are more things in heaven and earth," Mr Holden, "than are dreamed of in your philosophy"!'

He turned to Dany with an apologetic smile and said: 'I am sorry, Miss Kitchell. This cannot interest you. We will go on to my Club, where we will talk and drink and you will meet my friends. They will be far more entertaining than I.'

He refused to say anything further on the subject or to answer any questions, and took them to the Arab Club, where they sat out under the stars and spent a pleasant hour. And afterwards they dined on strange foods in a little restaurant in a quiet back street, and then drove to the sea front outside the Sultan's palace, to listen, in company with a light-hearted collection of His Highness's subjects, to the Sultan's band playing — of all things — excerpts from Gilbert and Sullivan and *The Belle of New York*.

The lights were still on and the house-party still up when they arrived back at the House of Shade, for it was barely half past ten. But Seyyid Omar would not come in with them, and watching the tail-lights of his car dwindle and fade Lash had said thoughtfully: 'That guy knows a heck of a lot more than he's telling. A heck of a lot! The question is, who is he really pitching for? Is he on the side of the angels, as he makes out, or is that just a bluff? He wouldn't be the first well-heeled *aristo* to go back on his class and join the fellow-travellers!'

Dany said in a low voice: 'He was talking to that man Jembe at the airport in Nairobi. I saw them.'

'When? Where? You didn't tell me.'

'I didn't think of it. There have been so many other things. Worse things.'

She told him then, and Lash said meditatively: '*Hmm* ... It sounds a screwy set-up all round. Maybe he did the job himself. Slipped this Jembe a slug of cyanide because he's after the number one spot in the Dictator Stakes himself. He may fancy himself as the local Hitler. The Führer of Zanzibar.'

'*"King of the Earth and of Time",*' quoted Dany under her breath.

'What's that?'

Dany flushed and apologized. 'I'm sorry. I was thinking of something. A Persian inscription that he translated for me yesterday. I can imagine him dreaming of being that sort of king — and of restoring that sort of kingdom.'

'And wanting the cash to start it off with. Maybe.'

'But it can't be him. At least, he can't be the one who stole that letter or map or whatever it was off me, because then he'd know where the stuff was, and he doesn't. But he may think I've still got it. Perhaps he even thought I might carry it about with me. I never thought of that!'

'Thought of what? What are you talking about?'

'My bag. You said it must have been slit open by one of the Arabs in the village, but it wasn't. I've been thinking about it, and none of them came within yards of me.'

Lash gave a short laugh and said: 'Listen, honey. If you're thinking that anyone can drive a car with one hand, and at the speed that guy drove, while slitting a passenger's purse and abstracting its contents with the other, you're nuts! And anyway, you weren't even sitting next to him this afternoon. Gussie was.'

'I didn't mean it was done in the car,' said Dany impatiently. 'I told you, I've been thinking. It was all right just before we got to the cave, because I put my sunglasses into it, and I remember stuffing them down on one side of the handkerchief.'

'So what?'

'So there was only one place where anyone could have cut that bag open without my knowing it. In the cave. It was dark in there, and we were all huddled together and grabbing at each other to keep from falling. But there wasn't anyone else down there except — except us.'

Lash stopped abruptly in a patch of pale moonlight and said: 'Are you sure? That it couldn't have happened anywhere else?'

'Yes. Quite sure. That's why I didn't say anything more about it. I was sorry that I'd said anything at all, but I was so surprised when I saw it that the words jumped out. But when I'd thought a bit I realized that it could only have been done while we were in the cave, and that no one who was there would do it just to steal a compact and a lipstick and perhaps a little money. So it must have been someone who wanted something special, and thought that I might carry it with me. It *must* have been!'

'Yes,' said Lash slowly. 'The same bunch again. Six of us who were on the London to Nairobi run, and two who were on the last lap to Zanzibar. Gussie and Elf and Larry Dowling; Nigel and Eduardo and our smooth Arab pal. None of them in the least likely to go in for lifting lipsticks and petty cash. I guess you're right. Someone thinks you've still got it.'

It was a verdict that was to receive swift confirmation.

The remainder of the house-party were playing *vingt-et-un* in the dining-room, but Lash excused himself from joining them and went off to the guest-house, and Dany went up to bed — to discover that in her absence someone had searched her bedroom as thoroughly, though far less untidily, as her room at the Airlane.

Every drawer and cupboard had been gone through, and even the sheets and blankets had been taken off her bed and replaced; though not very neatly. A box of face powder had been probed with a pair of nail scissors and a jar of cleansing cream with a nail file: face tissues had been pulled out of their container and roughly stuffed back again, stockings unrolled and a locked suitcase forced.

'But I haven't *got* it!' said Dany, speaking aloud into the silence as though she were addressing that unknown searcher. The sound of her own voice startled her even more than the evidence of her disarranged possessions, and she turned and ran from the room.

The lights were ablaze in every verandah and in the courtyard, and there were no shadows on the staircases: but she tested every step, her hand pressed to the wall and her heart in her mouth. She could hear voices and laughter from behind the closed door of the dining-room, and she tiptoed past it and out into the quiet garden.

The moonlight and black shadows were not as frightening as the house had been, and she ran lightly along the twisting paths between the flower-beds and the scented bushes of roses, jasmine and Lady-of-the-Night, and skirting the shallow pool with its stone birds, reached the steep flight of narrow steps that led up to the guest-house on the wall.

The lights were on but Lash did not answer her knock, and she opened the door and went in. The little sitting-room appeared to be empty, and supposing Lash to be in the bedroom she was about to call out to him when a sound made her turn sharply.

Lash was standing on the narrow stone window ledge, holding on by the frame, and she could only see his legs and part of his body. The rest of him was outside the window, and he appeared to be attempting to pick a spray of the purple bougainvillaea that hung down over the wall of the house.

He swung himself in again and jumped down on to the floor, brushing dead leaves out of his hair, and said: 'For the love of Mike! — what are you doing here?'

Dany, who had been about to ask almost the same question, abandoned it in favour of more urgent matters. She said breathlessly: 'My room's been searched again. Every bit of it. Like last time, only——'

'Same here,' said Lash briefly. 'Take a look around.'

Dany looked about her and became aware of much the same mild disorder as her own room had contained, and stooping with a cry of dismay she picked up a white fluffy ruin that lay half concealed under the edge of the divan. The late Asbestos; that washable and unburnable cat, his stuffing ruthlessly removed and his green glass eyes stonily reproachful.

'All flesh is grass,' said Lash. 'And all cat's too, judging from the look of it. Yes, someone's frisked this joint in a conscientious manner.'

'Did he get in by the window?'

'I don't know. All I know is that he hasn't missed much. Even my soap has been broken in half to make sure that I hadn't hidden anything in it. Most of the stuff has been put back in place; but not, as you see, very tidily. Here, stand yourself a slug of your step-father's Scotch. At least that has been left alone — I hope!'

He poured out some of the whisky from the bottle that Tyson had left there on the morning of their arrival, and having smelt it, tasted it with extreme caution.

'Seems O.K. No cyanide. At least, not noticeably so. I'd better try it out for effect first. Here's to the witch doctor, deceased, who put a curse on that cash deposit. He certainly knew his onions!'

He drank, and having put down the glass turned to look out

through the open window for a moment or two, and then said: 'Well, I guess this puts one suspect out of court. Pal Omar couldn't have pulled this one. He was with us the whole evening, so he's out. It was one of the others. If only we could find out who knew the trick of that staircase it would help a lot, but there would appear to be at least four copies of that damned book in the house, and you were right about it. It's all there: tucked away back in a musty maze of architectural drawings. It took some finding, but I ran it to earth. Anyone could have stumbled across it and put it to good use.'

He sat down on the window-seat, his reflective gaze still on the moonlit seascape outside, and said slowly: 'I'd like to know more about this Larry Dowling. A lot more. And I'm willing to bet that the cops will too, just as soon as Tyson's letter turns up at Scotland Yard and they move in on us.'

Dany said flatly: 'It isn't Larry. It couldn't possibly be Larry.'

'Why not? There's something phoney about that guy. I've known a good few newspapermen in my time, and he doesn't ring true.'

'But he's not a newspaperman! He's a feature writer. And——'

'What's that got to do with it? He's after a story — Tyson's. So why doesn't he get on with it? If he's done any writing since he arrived, I'm Ernest Hemingway! Then there's Gussie . . .'

Dany subsided suddenly on the divan, nursing the wreck of Asbestos. She said tiredly: 'Yes. I thought of her too. Because she would have known so many things that — that whoever it is must have known. But I don't believe it. I just can't see her climbing fire-escapes and things like that. And she was fond of Millicent.'

'How do you know that? None of us can really know anything much about anyone else. We can only go by what we see. I guess I thought I knew plenty about Elf. I meant to marry her, heaven help me! — and me, I'm an Old World throw-back to my respected Scotch ancestors when it comes to saying "I do." It's not going to mean to me "Until Alimony and the Other Man doth us part". No, I thought I knew more about Elf than any of the other guys had done: that none of them had understood her as I did — all the old routine. That'll show you!'

His laugh held more than a trace of bitterness, and turning his shoulder to the window and the moonlight, he said: 'Millicent Bates may have been rubbed out because she was the active partner in some little scheme of Gussie's. She may have done that job in London, then caught on to it later that Gussie had shot the family lawyer, and taken a poor view of it. And then there's the Latin lover ...'

Lash rose and poured himself another drink, and broke off to remark conversationally: 'Your step-father is one hell of a host. He thinks of everything. Gin, soda-water syphon, bitters, Scotch. Look at 'em all! Say, who does he think I am? It's a libel. Have one?'

Dany shook her head, and he brought his drink across and sat down in an arm-chair facing her; holding the glass between both hands and looking down into the golden liquid intently, as though it were a crystal ball in which he could see the future — or the past.

'The Signore Marchese di Chiago,' said Lash softly. 'Apart from racing cars he has quite a reputation as a fast guy. And a weakness for blondes. He's known Tyson, and your mother, for a good many years, and this isn't his first visit to Zanzibar. He's stayed in this house before. And if there's anything in gossip — largely Nigel's I'll admit! — he's had several affairs of the heart that his family have managed to bring to a grinding halt just short of the altar, and it's a cinch that they'll queer this one too if they can. But maybe this time it's gone deeper. Maybe he's got to have Elf, come hell or high water. She can have that effect on some people. There was one guy — Douglas something — who took a header out of a top storey window when Elf threw him over. But Eduardo isn't the kind that likes taking

"No" for an answer. He comes from a country where a male with a title gets all the breaks, and if he wanted anything badly enough I guess he wouldn't stop at much to get it. But Elf is a strictly cash proposition — from both angles. His and hers. No lire — no Elf. Maybe we haven't paid enough attention to Eduardo and his fiery Southern blood.'

Lash gave the contents of his glass some more practical attention, and lit a cigarette, and Dany watched him anxiously. She wished that she did not feel so frightened, and that she could look at it all as Lash appeared to be doing: as an interesting problem of the 'Who's Got the Button?' variety. But looking about the small room with its silent evidence of an unknown searcher, she was aware of nothing but an acute sense of danger.

This was neither a game nor a nightmare from which she would awake. It was real. It was the springing of a trap that had been set over ninety years ago, and which had caught her when she had called on a prim, elderly, country solicitor to fetch a letter written by a man who had died back in the last century.

Lash said thoughtfully: 'It could be Tyson,' and she came back to the present with a sharp jerk.

'*Tyson?* What are you talking about?'

'This——' said Lash, gesturing with his cigarette at the ill-concealed disorder of the room. 'That——' he indicated the sad remains of Asbestos. 'And your room too. He may have wanted to satisfy himself that one of us hadn't double-crossed him. If you remember, he did once suggest that you might have held on to the contents of that envelope yourself. It could be Tyson. Or Ponting. In fact, why not Ponting? He was in Nairobi. You know, that's quite an idea — except that I guess he'd have made a far neater job of it if this had been his lily-fingered handiwork! He could have been pressed for time, of course, but somehow I can't see that elegant, willowy tulip leaving the place in this sort of mess. If dear Nigel had been conducting "Operation Frisk" I've a strong feeling that we wouldn't have known that anything had been touched. And yet it's got to be someone in the house, who knew that we wouldn't be back for quite a while, and—— Say! Wait a minute!'

He put his glass down and came suddenly to his feet. 'Why didn't I think of that?'

'Of what?' demanded Dany, her voice sharp with anxiety.

'Seyyid Omar! He knew damned well just how long we'd be away. He could even be the original weevil in the woodwork. Yes ... why not? He's a big shot in this island. He'd be the only one who could easily plant his servants — or even his relatives — in the house. And who would know?'

Lash took a quick turn about the room and came back to stand in front of Dany.

'Now look. Supposing he got all his information from a servant in this house — that silent, slippered guy who slides in and out with the coffee and takes the letters to the post. Suppose he can read English after all, and that he read Tyson's letters to this Honeywood, and possibly Lorraine's to you as well, and passed on the information? Omar doesn't go after Emory's letter himself, but he sends a stooge — Jembe — who gets rid of Honeywood but fails to get the goods. Jembe has another try at finding it when he frisks your room at the Airlane, and so he——'

'Steals my passport,' put in Dany. 'But that *can't* be right! What would be the point of stopping me leaving the country?'

'Ah, I've thought of that one: it occurred to me once before. So that you'd mail it. The letter. Who's to say they haven't got a pal planted in the post office here, as well as in the house? It wouldn't be difficult if you were Seyyid Omar. For anyone else, yes. But not for him.'

'I don't think——' began Dany doubtfully.

'No one's asking you to! I'm developing a theory. Now, this Jembe finds that you are on the plane after all — thinly disguised by dyed hair and glasses. So what does he do? He has another shot at stealing the thing in Nairobi, fluffs it, and has to report failure to the boss — our friend Omar, who meets him at Nairobi West. You actually saw 'em talking.'

Dany said: 'Yes. But why should Seyyid Omar want to poison him? It doesn't make sense!'

'I'm not so sure. After all, you've arrived and you've still got the goods. Jembe has shot his bolt and is of no further use — and probably knows too much anyway! So the best thing is to get rid of him and leave the rest to one of these poker-faced guys in white night-gowns who seem to be all over the house, and who would probably skin their grandmothers alive for ten dollars down and ten to follow. For all we know any one of them may easily turn out to have majored in modern languages and picked up a coupla degrees on the side. Who's to tell?'

Dany said: 'Yes ... I suppose so. But you've forgotten something. There are two quite different people in all this. The one — or the ones — who are still trying to find that letter and who think I've still got it, and the one who *has* got it. If Seyyid Omar hasn't got it, who has?'

Lash's face changed and became wholly expressionless. He looked down at the cigarette he held, and after a moment he flipped it away through the open window and said lightly:

'Yes — who? Certainly not our friend the Seyyid, if he was the guy who picked your pocket in the cave and so neatly got us out of the way while one of his tarbooshed minions went through our rooms.'

Dany said: 'But if you really think he's the one behind all this, why did he show us how Miss Bates was killed?'

'To scare us, I guess. Make us lose our nerve — and our heads.'

Lash finished his drink and tossing the empty glass on the sofa, said: 'I think a short talk with your step-father is indicated. I don't think he's got any idea of what a hornet's nest he stirred up, and I intend to bring it home to him — if I have to use a sledge-hammer to do it!'

He looked down at Dany's white face and smiled a little

crookedly. 'It's a helluva mess, honey, but you don't have to lose your nerve.'

'I haven't any left to lose!' admitted Dany ruefully. 'Not an atom!'

Lash laughed and reached down his hands to pull her to her feet.

'Nuts, Miss Kitchell! Momentarily mislaid, perhaps, but never lost. And I don't know if that aunt of yours ever warned you against visiting in bachelor's apartments at this hour of night, but I believe it is frowned upon in the more prudish circles of society. So in about two minutes time I am going to take you back to your room.'

Five minutes later he said reflectively: 'You know something? — This looks as though it might become a habit.'

It was, in fact, just over fifteen minutes later that he finally escorted Dany back to the house.

18

There had been no chance for any private talk with Tyson on the following day, for he had slept late, and then in response to a message delivered to the house, had gone off deep-sea fishing with a friend: a visiting peer who had arrived unexpectedly, and only that morning, in a private yacht.

'Really, *too* exasperating!' complained Nigel. 'We have a positive plethora of work on hand, but will he get down to it? — will he hell! The *rudest* wires from the publisher: one can only hope that the operators can't read English. And he *swore* he'd have a talk with Larry this morning. Have you been able to pin him down to anything yet, Holden?'

'Nope,' said Lash lazily, and turned over on his stomach.

They had all been bathing, and were now basking on the hot white sand on the beach below the house, acquiring what they hoped would be an even tan and not a savage case of sunburn.

'Who's been sending rude cables?' inquired Lash. 'Sounds like my respected Pop.'

'No. Our British publishers. So *testy*,' said Nigel.

Gussie looked up from anointing her legs with sun-tan oil and said: 'I thought you were supposed to be doing some sort of deal with Tyson about the Emory Frost papers, Mr Holden. A business-with-pleasure visit. Though I'm afraid it can't have been very pleasant to ... Oh, dear, I didn't mean to be tactless.'

'You weren't,' Lash assured her. 'And you're dead right about those papers. I am hoping to persuade your brother to sign on the dotted line. If I can get him to sit still that long. But he's a difficult man to pin down, and right now I feel too idle to chase after him.'

'Where's your American hustle?' demanded Gussie with a bright smile.

Lash yawned. 'I guess I shed it somewhere short of Naples — along with my raincoat. Right now I prefer basking to business. But don't worry: I'll get round to it sometime — no kidding. What are we doing the rest of today?'

'Nothing,' said Nigel firmly.

'Swell. That sounds right up my street.'

'Nonsense!' said Gussie briskly. 'We're all going shopping and sight-seeing in the town. It's all arranged. And then we're having tea at the hotel, and Lorraine said something about a moonlight picnic somewhere along the shore.'

'Holy Moses!' murmured Lash devoutly.

'Didn't you, Lorraine?' said Gussie, ignoring the interruption.

'Yes, Gussie dear. But only for anyone who wants to do any of it. You don't have to, you know.'

'I can see no point in coming to a place like Zanzibar if one is going to lie about and sleep all day. One can do that at home.'

'But not on lovely white beaches in the sun,' murmured Amalfi. 'Nigel, why is this sand white instead of yellow?'

'Coral, you pretty ignoramus. And pumice I expect. You know, I found out something totally fascinating the other day. Do you know where all those silly little pumice-stones that you find all along the beaches come from? Krakatoa!'

'And where,' said Eduardo, 'is Krakatoa?'

Nigel shuddered and put a hand over his eyes. 'The educational standards of the drinking classes would appear to be universally and *utterly* inadequate. Krakatoa, my decadent barbarian, was a volcano in the Sunda Straits — that's between Java and Sumatra in case you didn't know — which blew itself to bits in 1883 with a bang that no A-bomb will ever equal. And these are the bits. They bobbed along in the currents and got stranded here.

I can't say I ever used pumice-stone before, but I do now. It *enchants* me to feel that I'm scraping off my ink stains with Krakatoa!'

Eduardo said: 'You ought to write a guide book, you clever little thing, you. Me, I never read them.'

'You, you never read anything if you can help it!' said Nigel crossly.

'Now that is really *very* unjust of you, Mr Ponting,' put in Gussie, wagging an admonitory finger at him. 'And the Marchese was only joking. Why, he was reading all about the house on the very first afternoon we were here. My grandfather's book: *The House of Shade*. Weren't you, now?'

'Was I?' said Eduardo with a shrug of his bronzed shoulders. 'I do not remember. Perhaps I may have picked it up to glance at it. If I did I am quite sure I must have put it down again very, very quickly!'

'Not at all! You are too modest. You were so absorbed in it that you did not even hear me come into the library; and I assure you that there is *nothing* to be ashamed of in being a book-worm. I love a good book myself.'

'The point,' said Nigel, 'is that *The House of Shade* is probably the worst book ever written, and certainly the dullest, and one doubts if any book-lover, worm or otherwise, could bore their way past page two.'

'Then why,' demanded Amalfi petulantly, 'are we boring on about it now? Are you by any chance conducting this shopping and sight-seeing tour this afternoon, Nigel?'

'I am happy to be able to answer promptly,' said Nigel. '*No!* Why? Were you intending to join it?'

'I think so. As long as we don't start until half-past three or fourish. There was a shop in Portuguese Street that had the most divine Indian jewellery, and the man said he'd get in some more to show us today. So Eddie and I rather thought that we'd go along and take another look.'

'Not forgetting Eddie's cheque book,' said Nigel waspishly.

'Nigel darling, you *are* being cross and catty this morning!' complained Lorraine plaintively. 'What's the matter? It's such a lovely day, yet everyone seems to be jumpy and on edge instead of just relaxing peacefully.'

'We are relaxing peacefully,' said Lash, with his eyes shut. 'Just take a look at us.'

'No, you're not. You may look as though you are, but I can feel the atmosphere simply buzzing with jangled nerve ends. I suppose it's all this business of Honeywood and Jembe. And then poor Millicent——'

Gussie Bingham rose abruptly, and snatching up towel, sun-tan oil and sunshade, walked quickly away across the beach and up the short rocky path that led to the door into the garden.

Amalfi sat up, and removing her sun-glasses, said: 'Now you've upset your dear sister-in-law. Too bad. Lorrie darling, be a sweetie and *don't* let's get back onto that subject again.'

'But why be ostriches,' demanded Lorraine, aggrieved.

'Why not? I've nothing against ostriches. In fact I'm all for them if they prefer burying their heads in the sand to poking their beaks into drearily depressing subjects. Are you really taking us in to Zanzibar this afternoon?'

'Yes, if you like. It's Gussie really. She seems to want to keep doing something: so as not to have to think about Millicent, I suppose. Gussie hates being upset. As we're going in, you can all go and sign your names in the visitors' book at the Palace and the Residency. It's rather the done thing.'

'You have my permission to forge mine,' said Lash.

'I shall do no such thing. You'll do it yourself — and like it!'

'O.K., O.K.,' said Lash pacifically. 'Anything you say. I'll go.'

They had all gone. With the exception of Nigel who insisted that he had work to do, and Dany, who had unexpectedly fallen asleep in a hammock in the garden.

'Let her sleep,' said Lorraine, restraining Lash who would have woken her. 'It will do her more good than trailing her around Zanzibar city in this heat, and she doesn't look as though she's had much sleep of late. Nigel can keep an eye on her. She'll be all right. No, Lash! — I won't have her wakened.'

She had spoken with unexpected decision, and taking Lash firmly by the arm, had gone out to the car.

Lorraine had had few opportunities to see her daughter in private after the day of her arrival, for Tyson had warned her against treating Dany with more intimacy than would be due to the secretary of one of her guests. But she had seen her alone in the earlier part of the afternoon, and in the garden: Dany having gone out after luncheon to sit in the hammock, and Lorraine happening to catch sight of her on her way to pick some roses as a peace-offering for Gussie.

'Darling how nice to get you by yourself for a bit,' said Lorraine, abandoning the roses and joining her daughter on the hammock. 'It's so tiresome, never being able to talk to you without looking over my shoulder. I'm afraid all this is being simply horrid for you, baby, but Tyson says it will only be for a day or two, and then the police will sort it all out and we needn't go on pretending that you are the Kitchell woman. Thank goodness!'

She sighed and swung the hammock with one foot, and after a silent interval began a little diffidently: 'Darling ... about Lash——' And then did not seem to know how to go on.

Dany said, startled: 'What about him?'

'You rather like him, don't you, darling?'

Dany blushed to the roots of that distressing dyed hair, and Lorraine, observing the unfortunate colour effect, said abstractedly: 'No — quite the wrong shade for you. It *is* a pity.'

'Mother, what are you talking about?' demanded Dany.

Lorraine threw a hunted look over her shoulder. 'Darling, *don't*! Suppose anyone were to hear you?'

'There isn't anyone anywhere near,' said Dany. 'What were you saying about Lash?'

'Well — I felt perhaps I ought to say something, because it did rather occur to me that you perhaps liked him more than — let's say, than a secretary should. And after all, he is rather an attractive creature, and ...'

She made a slight helpless gesture with one hand, and once again did not finish the sentence.

'And what?' said Dany defensively.

'Well, darling, I happened to go out on to the terrace last night to fetch a magazine I'd left there, and I saw you two coming back to the house. You looked very — friendly.'

Dany said nothing, and Lorraine gave a small unhappy sigh. 'I'm afraid I'm a useless parent,' she said. 'The trouble is, I don't seem to know how to behave like one. But I do feel that as a parent I ought to say something. About Lash, I mean. You do know that he was to have married Elf — Mrs Gordon — don't you?'

'Yes. You told me in your letter. And so did he.'

'Oh, well; that's something.' Lorraine sounded relieved. 'But darling, you will be a little careful, won't you? You see, you've met so few men so far. That's been my fault, I suppose: I've been horribly selfish and not really remembered how quickly time goes. I was always going to be a good mother one day, but you always seemed such a baby. And now suddenly you've grown up. But you don't want to go losing your heart to the first attractive man you meet. In fact it's the greatest possible mistake! It's not that I've got anything against Lash, but ...'

'Which means that you have,' said Dany coldly.

'No, I haven't, baby. Really. It's just that Tyson says he's had a lot of girls, and — well, he simply *adored* Elf, and men do do such silly things on the rebound: snatch at admiration from the nearest person who offers it, to bolster up their wounded egos. It doesn't mean anything. I like Lash, but he's as wild as a hawk and I'm not sure I'd trust him as far as I could throw a grand piano. Elf can manage that type; but when one is young and romantic and naïve, one is apt to take things — and people — at their face value. So — so you will just think a bit, won't you, darling? I mean, you don't have to believe everything he says, just because he's gay and good looking and has a fair share of charm. Take it all——'

'With a pinch of salt?' interrupted Dany bitterly. 'I know!'

'I was going to say "in your stride",' said Lorraine reproachfully. 'But salt will do. After all, it improves so many things, doesn't it darling? Oh — here comes Larry. He's rather a charmer, isn't he. I'm glad we asked him to stay — though Tyson's being a bit sour about him. He says we ought to watch out, because Larry's the type that all women trust on sight and end up falling for, and that all the best bigamists and confidence tricksters have been that kind of man. You know, it's astonishing how catty men can be about each other when — Hullo, Larry. Are you looking for anyone?'

'No,' said Larry, smiling. 'Just looking around. This is a fascinating old place you've got here, Mrs Frost. That wall at the end of the garden is a good ten feet thick if it's an inch. There must have been guard rooms or stables in it once. Were they bricked up?'

'I expect so,' said Lorraine vaguely. 'If you're interested, I'm sure you'll find all about it in old Barclay's book. Are you going to the city with us later on?'

'Certainly; if you'll take me. Is there any chance of your husband joining us?'

'He's meeting us at the hotel for tea,' said Lorraine, rising. She turned and smiled at Dany. 'I'll leave you in possession of the hammock, Miss Kitchell. You ought to put your feet up and have a rest. We shan't be leaving for at least an hour.'

She took Larry Dowling away with her down the winding path between the orange trees and the roses, and Dany watched them go and thought of Lash; and of what he had said only last night about Amalfi Gordon. He had not sounded as though he were still in love with her. But had it just been bitterness and sour grapes?

You don't have to believe everything he says . . .

Was she just 'young and romantic and naïve'? An inexperienced school-girl, taking things and people at their face value? How was one to know? How did one ever learn? The hard way? Had Lash only made love to her because he was snatching at the nearest bit of admiration to soothe his sore ego? Trying to show Amalfi that he did not care?

For the better part of an hour Dany lay in the hammock, staring up at the blue chips of sky through the thick scented canopy of leaves and flowers over her head, her mind so fully occupied with personal problems that she never once thought of Mr Honeywood, or of Jembe, or of Millicent Bates — or of murder. And then, without warning, sleep reached out a light finger and touched her eyes, and she did not even hear Lorraine and Lash when they came in search of her.

It was close on five o'clock when she awoke, and the shadows had lengthened in the garden and the heat had gone from the day. The house was very quiet, but she found Nigel in the drawing-room, sipping China tea and reading a week-old London newspaper.

He dropped the paper on the floor and came to his feet when he saw her, but Dany, glancing down, found her eye caught by familiar words: 'Man Murdered in Market-Lydon.'

Nigel, following the direction of her gaze, laughed and said: 'You have caught me red-handed, Miss Kitchell — soaking myself in crime on the sly. I blush for it. *Too* fish-and-chip. But to tell you the honest truth, after all that sordid chit-chat the other night I felt quite intrigued. That Bates woman went on and *on* about it, until one couldn't help wondering what she was getting at: if *anything*, of course! But one felt, somehow, that there *was* something ... Do sit down and have some tea. Indian or China? The China is divine. Tyson has it sent direct from some aromatic old Mandarin friend in Canton.'

Dany accepted a cup of pale yellowish-green liquid that smelt of dried flowers, and listened a little abstractedly to Nigel's light, melodious voice lilting on and on in a nonstop monologue. It was, she discovered, quite easy to listen to Nigel and think of something else. And then, with shocking suddenness, she was jerked out of her detachment.

'Now *do* tell me,' said Nigel, 'who you *really* are? I won't tell a *soul*. Of course one can *guess*. But it *has* been intriguing me so. Deliciously mystifying!'

Dany gaped at him and dropped her cup.

'Tiens! Tiens!' said Mr Ponting, leaping gracefully to his feet and repairing the damage. 'I *am* sorry. Entirely my fault. But honestly, *dear* Miss Whoeveritis, you simply *couldn't* be Ada Kitchell — not by any stretch of the most *elastic* imagination. And you have no *idea* how flexible mine is!'

Dany said stonily: 'Why couldn't I be?'

'Well darling – your *voice*! Utterly Nancy Mitford. Not a whisper of the New World in it. And what woman *ever* wore spectacles if she didn't need them? Why, those are just plain glass! And — well, not to labour the point, a little blonde bird told me that *actually* there is a rumour flying about to the effect that poor Ada is at this moment incarcerated in the Islington Isolation Hospital with mumps.'

'Mrs Gordon!' said Dany involuntarily. 'I might have known it!'

'Well, frankly, darling, I *do* think that you might. However, don't let it worry you. It probably isn't true, and anyway I won't breathe a syllable. Now do tell me: I'm *dying* to know. *Why?* And of course, *Who?* ... though of course one can make a very accurate little guess at *that* one, can't one?'

'I don't know. Can one?'

'But of course! There is really nothing subtle about our sweet

Lorraine, and when she hurries about the house removing every single photograph of her darling daughter, one *does* tend to ask oneself a few shy little questions. Not that there were *many* photographs. Lorraine is not what one would term *madly* maternal. But there were just one or two. And where are they now? "Gone with the wind that blew through Georgia?" But she forgot that there is a liberally illustrated volume lying around, all about explorations in Central somewhere, which includes a handsome photograph of her first husband; and I fear I was inquisitive enough to take a tiny peek. You really are very like your father, you know. The resemblance was quite remarkable as *soon* as one saw you without those spectacles and that distressing fringe. You forgot them the other night.'

Dany got up and went over to the window, and stood with her back to the room, tugging nervously at the edge of the curtain and staring blindly out at the garden. Her first feeling of panic had subsided, and now she was only conscious of a lessening of tension and a certain degree of relief. Being Miss Kitchell was a strain, and it was going to be very restful to be Dany Ashton again, and to stop pretending — and being frightened. But she wished that Lorraine were here. Or Tyson, or Lash. Someone to advise her as to what she should say and how much she could say.

Had everyone seen through her? Had they all guessed? Not the passport officials at all events! and they were the only ones who really mattered — except for Larry Dowling, who must not guess.

She said: 'Has Mrs Gordon told everyone?'

'About Ada? Oh, I don't think so. She may have whispered something into Eduardo's lovely brown ear, but he won't be in the least interested; and I'm quite *sure* she wouldn't tell anyone else. Not Gussie anyway. And *certainly* not our intrusive Mr Dowling.'

Dany turned quickly. 'Why do you say that? Are you sure?'

'That she wouldn't have twittered to Larry? But my dear, of course not! the man writes for the newspapers, and if he got his predatory little pen on to this, Tyson and your lovely Mum would be distinctly testy, and Amalfi wouldn't like being shown the door at all. You're quite, *quite* safe there. At least, for the time being. I suppose it's all bound to come out sometime or other, but, with any luck, after our scribbling little friend has got his interview — and enough material to libel the lot of us — and left.'

The thought of Mr Larry Dowling appeared to divert Nigel's interest into other channels, for he frowned and said: 'I simply cannot understand what Tyson is playing at. Why doesn't he give the man an interview and a basin full of facts, and send him off? Why ask him to the house and keep him hanging about? — putting him off, and putting him off. Really, *very* vexing. I wish you'd tell me what he's up to. I suppose you know?'

'I don't know anything about Mr Dowling,' said Dany hastily, evading the question.

'And how much do you know about Mr Holden, I wonder?' said Nigel, and gave a malicious, knowing little giggle. His face was both mocking and sly, and Dany said hotly: 'What do you mean?'

Nigel looked at her with his head on one side like some large, sleek, wary bird — a secretary bird. Then he put a finger to his lips and rose swiftly and silently and went quickly and very quietly to the door that led into the hall, and jerked it open.

The whole manoeuvre bore such an exaggerated air of secrecy and stealth that Dany quite expected to see a crouching figure disclosed, kneeling with its ear to the keyhole. But the hall was empty, and having satisfied himself that there was no one there or in the courtyard, Nigel returned to his chair looking slightly self-conscious.

'Forgive the amateur theatricals, but I would *so* much prefer not to be overheard. I take it that you don't really know much about the merry Mr Holden? apart from the usual things — the fact that he was head over heels about the bewitching Amalfi, and got pipped at the post by Eduardo (there ought to be a law against these Latins, don't you agree?). But otherwise, has he spilled the beans? Are you, in the distressing jargon of the age, "hep"?'

Dany said uncertainly: 'I don't know what you mean.'

'Don't you? Hasn't it ever struck you that there is something a little — odd about Lash Holden?'

'No. Why "odd"?'

'Well, "peculiar" if you prefer the word. And don't start jumping down my throat, I beg! As you see, I have been the *soul* of tact, and refrained from probing into *why* you feel it necessary to masquerade as his secretary. But hasn't it ever struck you as odd how *very* conveniently he always turns up at just exactly the right moment? Just like one of those *painfully* competent G-men. Or would it be more accurate to say, like some really expert card-sharp at work? It all looks *so* casual and simple; "Hey presto! — and here's the Ace of Spades; now how on *earth* did it turn up there? *What* an astounding piece of luck!" But is it?'

Dany came back to her chair, but she did not sit down: she held on to the back of it and stared at Nigel, white-faced:

'What are you trying to say?'

'Nothing, darling. I'm merely trying to *hint*. So much safer I always think, don't you? You see, Lashmer Holden, Senior, is a very old friend of Tyson's — an intimate friend, one might say. There isn't anything about Tyson or his house or his affairs that he doesn't know, and he also has the reputation of being one of those forthright characters whose motto is "Never Give a Sucker an Even Break".'

He saw Dany start, and said: 'Why the surprise? What have I said?'

'N-nothing,' stammered Dany. 'It was just that—— What were you saying about Lash's father?'

'Only that Pop Holden is what is technically termed a tough egg. He sticks at nothing and he has of late been edging on to queer street.'

'On to——?'

'Queer Street, darling. Don't be all *ingénue*. I believe he only just squeezed out of being indicted before some committee on a charge of un-American activities. Toying with the Commies. Nothing was ever *proved* you know, so of course one is being *dangerously* libellous even to whisper it. But everyone knew; and I believe it cost him simply thousands of dollars in bribes and what-have-you to keep it out of the courts. We were over there just when it was boiling up, and I believe he tried to borrow off Tyson. *Most* embarrassing. That was why one couldn't help wondering if Tyson hadn't rather naughtily refused to play, and so Junior decided to put the screw on. Very filial, if he did.'

Dany frowned and looked bewildered: 'I really don't know what you're talking about, Nigel, and I think you'd better stop.'

'Blackmail, darling,' explained Nigel, ignoring the request. 'Is that his little game? Has he involved the Daughter-of-the-House in some complicated piece of jiggery-pokery, and is he now telling Step-pop to pay up, or he spills it all to the Press? Tyson's really *very* well supplied with stocks and shares and lovely money, and quite *devoted* to your charming Mum. He'd probably pay and pay. Could it be that, I wonder?'

'No, it couldn't!' said Dany stormily. 'I've never heard such ridiculous nonsense! There isn't a word of truth in it!'

'Now, now, *now*, darling——! Don't get so excitable. You're as bad as Eduardo. Oh well — it was just an idea. But one couldn't help wondering if he didn't have *some* little game on. One is sorry for him, of course. The family name teetering on the edge of the dustbin, the family fortune down the drain, and the glamorous girl-friend (who between you and me must have got wind of the cash deficiency!) abandoning ship for a coroneted Italian cutter. But what is he here for? Just what is he after? That's what I'd like to know. Call me inquisitive if you like — and how right you will be!'

Dany said stiffly: 'You know quite well why he is here.'

'Oh, but you're wrong. I don't. Has he joined the G-men or the F.B.I. perhaps? Is he, if one may be forgiven a winsome little pun, playing International M.I. Fives? Americans are becoming *painfully* Middle-East conscious these days. They can think of nothing else but Spheres of Influence and Rocket Bases. (And women of course — there's still simply *nothing* like a dame! Especially if she looks like Elf!) Or is he playing some sly little game of his own, and if so, what?'

Dany's hands tightened on the chair-back and she said furiously: 'You know perfectly well why he came here! He came to discuss the publication of the Emory Frost papers — and — and for a honeymoon in Zanzibar.'

'That's what *he* says. But the whole question of the Frost papers was discussed *ad nauseam* with his dear Papa less than six months ago in the States. Of course they hadn't been released from the lock-up then, and they might not have been worth publishing. But a couple of letters would have settled the matter. He wasn't invited here, you know. He suggested it himself. And who ever heard of anyone combining a honeymoon with business? Even the most dollar-adoring Yank would shy like a steer at that one. They may worship cash (and who doesn't!) but they are also simply *saturated* with sentiment about such things as Momma and Marriage Bells. That's what makes it all *so* intriguing. Surely you can see that?'

'No!' said Dany stormily. 'I can't. I think you've just got a — a fertile imagination.'

'My dear, *too* right! And at the moment it is positively *fecund.* The wildest conjectures came sprouting out of the soil as soon as I saw the dear boy turning up here minus a honeymoon and plus the phoniest American secretary that it would be possible to conceive in a month of provincial repertory matinees! One was *instantly* reminded of Crippen.'

'*Crippen*? Why? How ...' Dany suddenly discovered that the chair-back was an inadequate support, and releasing it, sat down in the chair instead with a feeling that her legs were made of something that closely resembled half-cooked macaroni.

'*Surely* you've heard of Dr Crippen, dear? He brought off quite a tidy little murder, and then lost his head and skipped out of the country with his secretary, who was faintly disguised as a boy. It popped into my head almost as soon as I saw you. Well, perhaps not *quite* as soon as that, but as soon as I began to feel curious. I confess I was *thrilled.* Delicious shivers all up and down the spine! I said to myself "Now is he escaping from the law, and *where* has he buried the body of poor Ada — the real one?" But that of course was before I'd read the papers.'

Dany said in a brittle, breathless voice: 'What do you mean by that?'

Nigel gave his little tittering laugh and looked down at the newspaper that lay on the floor beside his chair, and then up again at Dany:

'Suppose you tell me that one?'

Dany said jerkily: 'I don't see why I should, but — but I will. If you want to know, Mr Holden happened to be staying at the same hotel as I was in London——'

'So convenient,' murmured Nigel.

'Do you want me to go on?'

'But of course, darling. I am *enthralled.* And I promise I won't interrupt again.'

'His secretary, Miss Kitchell, had developed mumps, and I had — had lost my passport, and hadn't time to get another before the plane left. So he suggested I should use hers. For — for a lark.'

' "Ha-ha"!' said Nigel. '*What* a cut-up the boy is! He must have lots in common with those Northern 'varsity students who think up all the sparkling and sophisticated pranks for the installation of a new Rector. But seriously, darling — *did* she have mumps? Or was it just sleight of hand?'

'I don't——' began Dany.

'The Ace of Spades,' explained Mr Ponting with a trace of impatience. ' *"Hey presto — why,* what *a bit of luck!"* That sort of trick. So simple really; if you know how it's done.'

'But there wasn't any trick about it,' protested Dany. 'Of course she had mumps.'

'How do you know? Because you are a nice, unsophisticated Innocent who believes everything she is told?'

The words were an echo of something else that Dany had heard that day. Lorraine had said almost the same thing. And she too had been talking about Lash——

Nigel said: 'So easy to *say* something like that. And almost as easy, one imagines, to see that you lose your passport! You did say that you'd lost it, didn't you? How — if one may ask another intrusive little question? It isn't a thing one just casually drops on the nearest counter, or leaves in the loo.'

'Well, it was — I mean, I . . .'

Nigel tittered again. 'You seem confused. But it was probably all *too* simple. Like the card trick. You palm one passport, and Hey presto! — here's another! *What* a happy coincidence. See?'

'No, I don't! And I don't believe a word of it. And anyway, why should Lash — Mr Holden — do anything like that? Why bother to bring me here when I was coming anyway?'

Nigel shrugged his shoulders and flung out his hands in an affected gesture: 'Well, darling — I *did* advance a little theory about that, didn't I? But as you trampled on the poor thing *most* harshly, I won't risk making it again. Perhaps he just wanted to keep you under his eye. And why not, indeed? Though I must admit that as the honeymoon was off it was perhaps a *teeny* bit tactless of him to tag along after his ex-love and the new Italian model, and one would have imagined that he would cancel the trip. Oh, well, I expect it will all be as clear as Vichy water one of these days — and equally innocuous. It's much more fun wondering, isn't it? I *adore* mysteries! Have another cup of tea?'

He peered into the tea-pot, clicked his tongue regretfully and announced that there wasn't any and that the hot water was cold. 'Just as well, really, as it's almost drinking time. I'd no *idea* it was so late and I'm dining out tonight with some enchanting Parsees. They serve the most delicious curries, which one can never resist but which play havoc with the digestive juices. Still, better that than eating a picnic meal by moonlight, which is sheer hell. Sandy sausages and mosquito-repellent getting into every glass. I *do* pity you all.'

He rose gracefully. 'Will you forgive me if I leave you to entertain yourself a bit while I hurry off and change? And don't worry, dear Miss Kitchell. Your guilty secret is *quite* safe with me. I promise I won't even drop the teeniest hint to anyone. Cross my heart!'

He retrieved the fallen newspaper, folded it carefully, and tucking it under his arm, tripped away, leaving Dany alone in the empty drawing-room with the tea cups and some most unpleasant thoughts.

19

Lash. *No . . . It isn't possible!* But it was. Unthinkable, but not impossible.

Lash . . . She must speak to him. She would ask him . . .

You don't have to believe everything he says.

But she had believed everything. Why? . . . Because he was Lash, and she had fallen in love with him. Because he was almost the first attractive man she had ever met, and any girl in love for the first time is convinced that this is the real thing — this is for ever. And find that it is neither.

'That your first kiss?' 'Yes, how did you know?' *'I've been around.'*

She hadn't stopped to analyse the significance of that reply, but she did now. It meant that he had made love to a good many other girls: and kissed a good many women. He would know just how to handle them. How to string them along.

She would, she realized, have been perfectly prepared to believe that anyone else might commit murder: Gussie, Seyyid Omar, Eduardo di Chiago, Amalfi Gordon and perhaps even Larry. But not Lash.

She had worked out ways and means and theories, and had heard Lash do so, in the case of other suspects: but it had never occurred to her for one moment that Lash himself might be one. And yet he was surely the most obvious one. He had even pointed it out himself — and she had rejected it: brushed it aside instantly and with impatience.

Was that why he had done so? To ensure that she would reject it? A form of bluff? And yet — he could have done everything ...

Dany dropped her head into her hands, pressing them over her eyes and trying to think back. To think clearly.

His father knew Tyson probably better than anyone else, and Tyson might well have written to him about the discovery he had made among the Frost papers, and also told him what he intended to do. Lash could have gone down to see Mr Honeywood, and been seen by Millicent, who would not have recognized him, or he her — until later.

He had booked a room at the same hotel as Dany, and the rest would have been easy enough to contrive. He might even have been on the fire-escape or the balcony outside her room, and seen her leave it, and walked quietly across the room, and shut the door behind her. Then, taking her own key off the dressing-table, left by the window and come up the stairs, pretending to be the worse for drink.

He would have had plenty of time to search her room while she was waiting in his, and, when he could not find what he was after, to remove her passport and plant that gun. And now that she came to think of it, he had turned up right on cue, when she found it. *'Hey presto and here's the Ace of Spades! now how on earth did it turn up here?' That sort of trick!* ... And it had been Lash's idea that she come with him in the place of Miss Kitchell.

Had Miss Kitchell really had mumps? Or had she merely been informed at the eleventh hour that her presence was not required — because her passport was?

But there had been that night in Nairobi, and the man who had meant to chloroform her. That could not possibly have been Lash. He had been sound asleep on the sofa. No, the whole thing was nonsense! A wild figment of Nigel's jackdaw imagination, that did not stand up to a moment's sober examination.

But ... but there were two people who wanted that letter.

Or two groups of people. One who was still looking for it, and the one who had it. The sealed envelope that bore Emory Frost's initials had been taken out of her coat pocket, the seal broken and the letter abstracted. And it could only have been done by one person — Lash Holden.

'No — no — *no!*' said Dany, aloud and desperately. 'He wouldn't. He didn't. I don't believe it and I won't believe it!'

Who else? whispered a small, remorseless voice in her brain. How else? You don't have to believe everything he says . . .

Dany stood up quickly and began to walk up and down the darkening room, arguing with herself: trying to remember; trying to persuade herself that someone else could have taken it. But there was no way out. No loophole of escape. It had to be Lash.

It was just conceivably possible that a skilful pickpocket could have stolen the whole thing; chiffon scarf and all. But to take it out, remove the letter and return it, was utterly impossible. But Lash could have done it with ease. Either while she was in her bath that morning, or when she had given him her coat to hold on the plane.

'No!' said Dany again, speaking pleadingly into the unheeding silence. But even as she denied it she knew that the answer was 'yes', for she had remembered something else——

Lash standing on the window-sill of his room last night, reaching up into the mass of bougainvillaea that grew above it. Lash's face when she had said: 'If Seyyid Omar hasn't got it, who has?' His face had changed and become blank and expressionless, and he had looked away from her and would not meet her eyes. Yes, Lash had got the letter. She was suddenly and wearily sure of it. He had probably carried it in his pocket, and been startled by the realization that pockets can be picked, when he had seen her ruined handbag, and had decided to find a better hiding place for it.

What did he want it for? If, as Seyyid Omar had said,

there were men in Zanzibar whose ultimate object was a dictatorship under Soviet domination, was Lash a Secret Service man whose task was to prevent this? Or did he want Seyyid Saïd's treasure for himself?

Jembe ... Millicent Bates ... It could have been Jembe who had meant to search her room at Nairobi, and Lash could have known it, or guessed it. Millicent had said that she never forgot a face, and Lash had said that she had died because she talked too much. Lash's father almost certainly possessed a copy of *The House of Shade*, and the note that had lured Millicent to her death had been written on Ada Kitchell's typewriter.

'A rakish heel who could hook the average woman with the ease of a confidence trickster getting to work on a frustrated small-town spinster ...' Someone had said that — about Lash. Was she, Dany, a frustrated small-town spinster? Lorraine too had suggested that she was young and inexperienced and naïve — and too romantic! — and Nigel had begged her not to be so *ingénue*. So perhaps she was all those things.

A tear crept down Dany's white cheek and she brushed it away impatiently. Crying would not help her, but there was at least one thing that would. She could make sure. She could go to the guest-house and look for Emory Frost's letter. Not now, because it was getting late and the others would be back soon. But as soon as another opportunity offered and she was certain of Lash being out of the way.

The cars returned not five minutes later, and as Dany had no desire to see or speak to anyone at the moment, she ran up to her room and locked the door, and only opened it when Lorraine knocked on it to ask if she were all right, and had she had a good sleep?

'You know, darling,' said Lorraine worriedly, observing her daughter with some anxiety, 'you're looking very washed out. Or perhaps it's that hair. I really do think we should——'

'Mother,' interrupted Dany tersely, 'did Tyson ever write to

Lash's father about that letter of Emory Frost's? The one I fetched from Mr Honeywood?'

'Darling, I've no idea. He may have done — they've always been such bosom buddies. Why?'

'Nothing,' said Dany quickly. 'I only wondered if — if anyone else knew about it.'

'I don't think so. Except of course that someone must have known, mustn't they? Really, it's all very worrying and upsetting, and I often wish — Oh, well — don't let's talk about it.'

She sat down on the dressing-table stool, and looking at her charming reflection said: 'I look a mess. I wonder if there's time for a bath before we start off on this picnic? No, I suppose not. We didn't mean to be back so late, but Tyson brought a friend of Elf's along to the hotel. It seems he flew to Mombasa only the day after you, and joined George Wallingborne's yacht, and they got here late last night. Tyson's been out fishing with them. A man called Yardley, Sir Ambrose Yardley. And if you ask me, he's only come here because of Elf. He should have been doing something or other in Khartoum, but he only stayed there about a day and a half, and followed her down here. I suppose I should have asked him back to the house: he was angling for it. But Eduardo was being rather rude and silly about the whole thing, and I really felt that I could not cope with any more dramas. And anyway, we're all lunching with them tomorrow.'

She dabbed her face absently with some of Dany's powder, rubbed it off again, and rose with a sigh.

'Don't put on anything too nice darling, because we're having a picnic supper on the beach. Tyson's idea. He's gone all Boy Scout and wants to build a drift-wood fire and fry sausages. *Ugh!* I can't think of anything much less alluring, but he's feeling energetic and all hearty-and-outdoor. Don't be too long, will you baby?'

The sky was rose-pink and apricot with sunset and the house was full of shadows by the time Dany returned to the drawing-room. She had expected to find the entire house-party assembled there, but there were only two people in the room: two people standing so close together that for a moment, in the dim light, they had looked like one.

They moved quickly away from each other as they heard the soft sound of Dany's sandalled feet on the thin Oriental rugs, and Amalfi Gordon came towards her, her face and her slender figure dark against the wash of sunset that burned beyond the french windows. She passed Dany without speaking, and went out of the room and across the darkening hall, her high heels clicking on the polished stone.

Lash said: 'Why the old-fashioned look, bambina? Did you think you'd walked in on a Grand Reconciliation scene? Because if you did, you've got it wrong. I'm not as polygamous as I look.'

Dany said coldly: 'I can't see that it is anything to do with me if you feel like hugging Mrs Gordon.'

'Now wait a minute! I was not hugging her!'

'No? Well that's what it looked like to me. Where has everyone else got to?'

'I don't know, and I can't say I care. Tell me what you've been doing with yourself all the afternoon? I didn't like the idea of leaving you on your own, but Lorraine said to let you sleep, and that Nigel would keep an eye on you. Did he?'

'Yes,' said Dany briefly.

She turned to leave the room and Lash came quickly after her and caught her arm. 'What's the matter, honey? You aren't really sore at me, are you? Look, I can explain——'

'Can you?' said Dany bleakly. 'But then I don't have to believe your explanations, do I?'

Lash's fingers tightened painfully on her arm and he jerked her round to face him, and then released her abruptly as someone came quietly through the open door behind her.

'Hullo,' said Larry Dowling, his casual, pleasant voice in marked contrast to the quietness with which he had moved. 'Am I late? Where is everyone?'

'In the garden, I guess. Why don't you go and look for them?' snapped Lash.

'Yes, let's,' said Dany thankfully. 'I'll come with you, Larry.'

She caught at his arm and they went out past Lash through the french windows and on to the terrace, where they were joined a few minutes later by Gussie and Tyson.

Dany had hoped to find some opportunity to speak privately to her step-father, but it was obvious that she was not going to get it tonight. Tyson had spent a strenuous day fishing and drinking, but it did not appear to have exhausted his energy. He herded his guests down to the shore and along the wet sands in the last of the sunset, and having selected a suitable spot in a little bay less than a quarter of a mile from the *Kivulimi* beach, set them to collect drift-wood for a fire.

'He gets these hearty fits at intervals,' explained Lorraine in a resigned aside. 'Very exhausting while they last, but fortunately they don't last long. You shall all have a lovely smoked salmon and caviar meal tomorrow to make up for it. But I do think this view is rather heavenly, don't you? Look at those fantastic rocks. And that dhow out there — isn't it enchanting? I wonder where it's bound for? Hejaz or Samakhand . . .'

Gussie said tartly: 'They'd have some difficulty in navigating her there, unless she's amphibious!'

'Oh, I didn't mean literally. Her cargo, perhaps. But those are such lovely names.'

As the sunset faded and the sky turned from pink to lilac, lavender and green, the firelight gained strength and lit up the weird shapes of the coral rocks and the fronds of pandanus as though they had been stage scenery. And presently the moon rose, lifting into the quiet sky like some enchanted Chinese lantern and filling the night with magic.

The sausages, as Nigel had predicted, were both sandy and underdone; but honour and Tyson being satisfied, Lorraine had produced an excellent selection of cold foods that had been carried down to the beach by one of the house-servants. And later, when the remains had been carried back again, they played what she called 'suitable moonlight music' on a portable gramophone, and explored along the shore.

Tyson and Lash went off armed with flashlights and fish spears to peer into the rock pools further down the beach, and Dany, watching them go, suddenly made up her mind that this was as good an opportunity as any to visit the guest-house. They would obviously be occupied for at least half an hour, and it would not take her much more than ten minutes to get back to the house, where there would be only the servants, who at this hour would have retired to their own quarters. She would be back again before anyone had troubled to notice that she had gone, and she could not endure the thought of another night — or even another hour — without knowing.

Gussie was discussing cookery with Lorraine, while Larry Dowling was lying on his stomach on the sand and putting records on the gramophone, and Amalfi and Eduardo had strolled away along the beach in the wake of Lash and Tyson. It would be quite easy.

Dany stood up, brushing off sand, and went across to murmur in her mother's ear, and Lorraine said vaguely: 'Yes, of course. But why not just behind a rock, darling? There are lots about.'

Dany withdrew, flushed and indignant, and once out of range of the dying firelight began to walk quickly, hurrying without running, until at last she reached the rocks that bounded one end of the *Kivulimi* beach, where she paused briefly to look back. But she could no longer see the glow of the drift-wood fire or any of her fellow picnickers, and the only thing that moved in the moonlit world were the ghostly little crabs, the lazy, lapping tide, a soft breeze and the lateen sail of an idling dhow.

Once on the far side of the rocks the *Kivulimi* beach lay before her, quiet and deserted, and Dany ran across the white, open sand and up the short rock path to the door in the garden wall.

The heavy wooden door with its flaking paint and iron nail heads creaked as it opened, and the sound was suddenly daunting. Dany stood still under the stone archway, listening intently, but she could hear nothing more than the soft breathing of a little breeze that whispered among the leaves of the garden and rustled the palm fronds.

There were no lights on in the house, but the white-washed walls and the window-panes caught and reflected the moonlight so that it gave the impression of being brightly lit and awake and watchful. An impression so strong that for a moment Dany found herself wondering if it was still looking seaward, as it had in a past century, for the sails of ships — merchant ships, pirate ships, whaling ships, ships from Oman and the dhows of the slave traders. *Then I'll go sailing far, off to Zanzibar …*

Dany caught her breath in a small sob, and looking resolutely away, turned to follow a path between the orange trees, skirting the pool and keeping parallel to the wall until she reached the flight of steps that led up to the guest-house.

The top of the wall was bright with moonlight, but the steps were in black shadow, and Dany was half-way up them when she heard the gate creak again.

She froze where she stood; listening with every nerve strained and alert for the soft crunch of crushed shell and coral that would tell her that she had been followed. But it did not come, and as the gentle breeze lifted the fringe on her forehead she remembered that she had left the gate open, and the breeze would have swung it on its hinges. And turning again she ran up the remaining steps, careless of noise and only aware of the necessity for speed.

The guest-house too was in darkness, and Dany turned the handle of the door, and pushing it open, felt for the switch.

The light seemed startlingly garish after the cool white night outside, and she turned it off again; realizing that she did not need it, for it was not here that she meant to search. She did not even glance about the room, but went straight to the window and looked out and up.

The bougainvillaea swung down from the roof edge in a mass of blossom whose colour had been almost lost in the moonlight, and it was not going to be nearly as easy as she had thought to stand on the narrow window-ledge and reach up.

The wall itself was built up on a little rocky cliff, and there was a drop of at least thirty feet from the window-ledge on to more rocks. Looking down on them Dany felt a cold qualm of vertigo, but it was too late to draw back, and she might not get a chance like this again.

She set her teeth, and having climbed cautiously on to the narrow ledge, holding desperately to the wooden frame, found that the worst part was turning round to face the wall. But once that was accomplished the worst was over, and with her back to the horrifying drop below her she found that she could look up into the mass of creeper above her with comparative ease.

She reached up and felt among the leaves, but could find nothing; and then her wrist touched a round edge of stone. There was a gutter some distance above the window; a narrow curve of stone, choked with dust and dead leaves and jutting out a few inches from the wall in the shadow of the overhanging creeper.

Dany found that she could just reach into it, and probing with shrinking fingers, fearful of snakes or spiders, she touched something that was not a dead leaf. And knew with a dreadful, sinking despair that she had been right. It was Lash who had taken the letter.

She drew it out from its hiding place and looked at it in the moonlight. A man's white linen handkerchief wrapped neatly about something that could only be a small folded piece of paper.

She felt a little sick and oddly light-headed, and for a moment she swayed against the wall, pressing her cheek against the rough stone, and afraid of falling. Her left hand, gripping the window-pane, felt cramped and numb, and she knew that she must make the effort to get down and back into the room while she had the power to do so. She could not stand here, silhouetted against the lamp light, where anyone passing on the beach below could look up and see her.

She bent her head and her knees, and sliding her left hand down the frame, stepped down on to the low window-seat.

And it was only then, looking down at her scarlet linen sandals on the gaily coloured cretonne cover of the window-seat, that she remembered that she had turned out the light only a few minutes ago. But it was on now.

Dany stood quite still: unable to move or breathe. Unable even to lift her head.

Then someone had seen her leave, and had followed her. Someone had come up the steps and into the guest-house; but standing on the window-ledge with the rustling of the creeper in her ears she had not heard them. And in the shock of finding the thing that Lash had hidden she had not even noticed that the light had been switched on, or known that someone was standing in the doorway, watching her...

She lifted her head very slowly and stiffly, as though fear had frozen her muscles, and looked into the cold eyes that were watching her from across the room.

20

'There now! I *knew* you'd lead me to it if I gave you the chance,' said Nigel Ponting in a self-congratulatory tone. 'Really, *too* simple.'

He tripped across the room and held out a thin, elegant hand. A hand as curved and predatory as the claw of a bird of prey.

'That's a good girl.'

He twitched the handkerchief from between her nerveless fingers and unwrapped it, disclosing a small folded square of yellowed paper which he opened and favoured with a smiling, comprehensive glance. 'Yes, indeed. The goods — as advertised. How very satisfactory! And now, darling, if you'll just stay right where you are——'

Dany shrank back and clutched at the sides of the window as he came towards her. 'Nigel — what are you going to do? You can't tell them! Not yet. He — there must be some explanation. He must be — be in the F.B.I., or something like that. You said so yourself! He *couldn't* be a murderer. He couldn't! Don't tell anyone. Give him a chance to explain first. Or — or to get away ...'

'What *are* you babbling about, dear girl?' inquired Nigel. 'Don't tell who what? Give who a chance to explain?'

'Lash. Oh, I know he took it, and I suppose it looks bad, but it can't be. And even if it were, I don't want the police to get him, whatever he's done! Nigel, please——!'

Nigel stared at her for a long moment, and then burst out laughing. 'My dear girl——! Oh, this is *too* delicious! Do you mean to say that you still haven't got it? Well, well! don't they teach you anything at these expensive schools? Perhaps it's a pity to disillusion you. But why not? It isn't your American dreamboat whom the police would want to interview. Alas, no. It would be yours truly — Nigel P.'

'*You?* But you can't — It couldn't be——'

'Oh, but it could. It was! I read that peculiar document of Emory Frost's (your respected step-father is not aware that I possess a duplicate key to his locked box!) and also the letters to Honeywood. Even — I blush for it — your mother's to you. It was all laughably simple. Then all I had to do was to ask for a holiday, slip off to Kenya, and get a dear friend to flip me across to Egypt where there are simply *dozens* of nasty men who will do anything to annoy the Great White Raj.'

'Egypt——' repeated Dany in a dazed, foolish whisper. 'But Mr Honeywood wasn't——'

'Tch! Tch!' said Nigel reprovingly. 'You don't really suppose I stayed there, do you? No, they merely fixed me up with the necessary papers and popped me on to the plane for Naples, where I was met by a fascinating character; quite unscrupulous and *madly* talented. He used to be top make-up man in a film company before the war — and *what* a loss to the trade! You simply wouldn't have recognized me boarding the London plane a couple of hours later. I made a ravishing Signora. Too *chic!* I wasn't *nearly* so alluring on the return journey; but perhaps just as well, as we had some *rather* impressionable Oriental potentates on board. Direct to Cairo that time: and by a different line of course — you've no idea how efficient the whole set-up is! The staff work was quite beyond praise. As slick as a Sputnik. One was *most* impressed.'

A sudden hysterical wave of relief swept over Dany, drowning all other considerations. 'Then it wasn't Lash! It was you — it was you!'

Her knees buckled under her and she collapsed on to the window-seat, weak with tears and laughter.

'Of course it was,' said Nigel with a trace of impatience. 'Who else would be likely to know everything that went on in this house? And the whole affair would have gone off swimmingly if only you'd done what you were told. Really, *very* tiresome of you! I had it all worked out. Honeywood knew me, and he'd have had the packet ready and handed it over like a lamb when I explained that Tyson had sent me for it because you couldn't come. But you had to change the time and go and see the old fool in the morning instead, and mess everything up. So vexing and unnecessary.'

He frowned at the recollection, and then his face cleared and he laughed. 'Ah well——! "All's well that ends well". And now, darling, as we haven't got all night——'

Dany scrubbed her eyes with the back of her hand and looked up. And then, suddenly, terror was back. A crawling, icy terror that widened her eyes until they were dark pools in her white face.

She had been too stunned by shock and relief to take in more than a fraction of what Nigel had said, but now, staring up at him, she realized that he had been saying things that he would never have said unless ... unless ...

Her mouth was so dry that it was an effort to speak at all, and when the words came they were only a harsh whisper:

'What ... are you going ... to do?'

'Only give you one little push,' said Nigel gaily. 'It's a thirty-foot drop, and on to rocks, so it ought to do even better than that cunning little staircase trick. And Holden will be able to tell them just exactly how it happened. You were standing on the sill to reach into his private *cache* and you must have slipped and fallen. Like this——'

His hands caught her, forcing her back over the low sill, and then the dreadful numbness left her and she began to fight, twisting and clawing. But the ledge was low and her back was to the uncurtained window, and there was nothing to grasp at but wood and stone.

Her finger-nails scraped and broke and her screams were no more than harsh, gasping breaths: she was no match for Nigel's five-foot-nine of lean bone and muscle, and those thin white hands, that had once felt so limp, were astonishingly strong and curiously smooth — as though they were encased in silk. They gripped her shoulders, pulled her forward and then jerked her head back violently against one side of the window embrasure so that it hit the stone and stunned her.

A savage pain seemed to slice its way through her skull: coloured lights shot before her eyes, and the strength went out of her. She heard Nigel's little giggling laugh, but it seemed to come from a long way off, and to be cut off suddenly and sharply. And then the grip on her shoulders relaxed and she was falling... Falling down miles of echoing darkness from the window ... No, not the window... Down a well. An underground well. Deep and cold and black, where there was black deep water in which she would drown...

The water filled her eyes and nose and mouth, choking her, and something burned her throat and choked her afresh. She struck out wildly, struggling to swim and to keep her head above water, and her hand touched something and clutched at it frantically.

A voice that hurt her head abominably said: '*Hi!* — look out! Let go of my ear!' And she opened her eyes with an enormous effort and found herself looking up at Larry Dowling.

Mr Dowling, who also appeared to have been in swimming, was tenderly massaging the side of his head and holding a dripping water jug, the contents of which he had evidently poured lavishly over Dany.

She stared up at him, blinking the water out of her eyes and wondering why he was there and where she was. Nothing made any sense except that, somehow, he had saved her from drowning.

'Are you all right?' inquired Larry Dowling anxiously.

Dany attempted to give the matter her consideration, and after a moment said childishly: 'I'm wet.'

'I'll say you are!' said Mr Dowling fervently, taking the words in an uncomplimentary sense. 'You must be mad! Going off like that on your own when——'

'You're wet too. Did you jump in with all your clothes on?'

'I fell into that bloody bird-bath — that's why I didn't get here a lot sooner. I'm sorry about that. But at least you're not dead. It was a near thing though — *phew*!'

He took out a sopping handkerchief and mopped his wet forehead and Dany said: 'I think I'm going to be sick.'

'Here——! don't do that,' said Mr Dowling, alarmed. 'Try another swig of this.'

He reached for a bottle that had been standing on the floor beside him, and lifting Dany's head poured a liberal quantity of some fiery liquid down her throat.

Dany gasped and choked, but the stuff warmed her stomach and helped to dull the excruciating pain in her head. Larry Dowling, having laid her back, took a long pull at the bottle himself and said: 'Gosh, I needed that!'

He put it down, and lifting Dany, carried her over to the divan and lowered her on to it carefully. 'Are you feeling any better?'

'I don't know. What happened? Was I going to drown?'

'Drown? No. He was stuffing you through the window, and in one more minute—— However, don't let's think of that. Can you stand up?'

'Who was stuffing me through a window? I don't know what you're — *Nigel*!'

Dany attempted to rise and once again a blinding wave of pain and nausea lashed out at her.

'Here, take it easy,' urged Larry Dowling anxiously. He sat down beside her and put a dripping arm about her, supporting her.

Dany leant against his wet shoulder and said without opening her eyes: 'Where is he?'

'Over there,' said Larry briefly. 'It's all right. He won't move for hours — if ever. I cracked him over the head with a bottle of gin.'

Dany forced open her eyes again and saw for the first time that Nigel's limp body was lying face downwards on the floor near the window. She could not see his face, but there was a lump on the back of his head the size of a healthy orange, and his hands were joined behind him by links of metal.

She said slowly and stupidly: 'Handcuffs. Where did you get them?'

Larry Dowling looked slightly embarrassed. 'As a matter of fact, I thought at one time I'd have to use them on you.'

'On *me*?'

'Yes. I've been tailing you for days, young woman. And a tedious dance you've led me. You actually bumped into me once in London — rushing out of the dining-room at the Airlane. I was afraid you might recognize me next day, but you didn't.'

'*Tailing* me? To get a story? But you're——'

'Only a simple cop, I'm afraid. I'm sorry if it's a disappointment to you. We were going to grab you in London, and then, what with one thing and another, it seemed a better scheme to see where you went and what you led us to. The M.I.5 boys had a few ideas of their own on the whole situation, and wanted us to play it their way. So we radioed all the proper people to let you through on that borrowed passport, and I was sent along to find out what I could.'

'Oh,' said Dany; and added after a pause for thought: 'Lash isn't going to like that.'

'Lash has got a lot of explaining to do,' said Larry Dowling.

'I have, have I?' said a furious voice from the doorway. 'Well let me tell you that it's nothing to the explaining you're going to have to do!'

Dany said: 'Lash—— Oh, Lash!'

'I'll deal with you later,' said Lash savagely. 'When I've taken care of this double-crossing ten-cent Romeo of yours!'

He covered the distance between them in two hasty strides, and before the startled Mr Dowling had even grasped the implications of his remarks he had thrust Dany to one side, gripped her rescuer by the collar, jerked him to his feet and slugged him scientifically on the jaw.

Mr Dowling went down for the count and Dany started to laugh, burst into overwrought tears, and quite suddenly slid off the divan on to the floor in a dead faint. Making it three in all.

Lorraine was saying: '... raw beef steak. It's the only thing. I put it on Tyson once when he got into an argument with some men in San Francisco, and it worked *wonders*. Didn't it, darling?'

'Yes,' said a resonant voice. 'I ate it. And where do you think you're going to get raw beef steak at this hour of the night, I'd like to know?'

Dany winced and opened her eyes. She was lying in her own bedroom and there seemed to be a lot of people in it. Lorraine, Tyson, Gussie Bingham ... She tried to turn her head, but finding that it was too painful, gave up the attempt and lay still.

At least she was not wet any longer, for someone had removed her drenched clothes and put her into a nightgown. She wondered if anyone had removed Larry's, which had been a good deal wetter, and she must have made an attempt to inquire, for suddenly they were all leaning over her, looking at her anxiously, and Lorraine was saying: 'Darling, how do you feel?'

Tyson said: 'Now don't go trying to sit up. Much better to lie still. Get some brandy into her.'

'I think Mr Holden gave her some,' said Gussie.

'Nonsense! How could he? She wasn't conscious. Here, Dany——'

Dany attempted a feeble protest, but to no avail, and Tyson, having dealt efficiently with the matter, laid her back on the pillows and said bracingly: 'Now you'll feel better!'

'Do you, baby?' inquired Lorraine anxiously, holding both her hands. 'Lash has taken one of the cars in to fetch a doctor and the police and medicines and things, and they'll be here soon, and then you'll be all right.'

Dany said: 'I'm all right now. Where's Larry? He saved me.'

'I know, darling. *Bless* him! If it hadn't been for him—— Oh, don't let's think of it. It's too awful!'

'It was Nigel.'

'Yes, darling. We know.'

'Ought to have known from the beginning,' growled Tyson, sitting down moodily on the end of her bed. 'No one else could have possibly known every dam' thing there was to be known. I suppose he took the letters off Abdurahman and said he'd post 'em. And he'd met old Honeywood, so he thought it would be quite easy. Turn up just before you, get the letter and then shoot him. And while you were being held up and questioned he'd be off and away.'

'But *how*?' said Gussie. 'How could he possibly be in England? He was in Kenya!'

Tyson said: 'Obviously he flew out. If you're in that camp, nothing is too difficult.'

'In what camp? What are you talking about?'

'The Reds, of course. Dowling is being a bit cagey about it, but it's obvious that the police, or M.I.5, or some of those cloak-and-dagger boys, had a line on him. And on this Zanzibar business.'

'What Zanzibar business?'

'An under-cover revolutionary movement that has recently

been started in this island. Dowling says that Nigel's always been in it up to his neck. He's one of the really fervent kind, and those are always more dangerous than the ones who are merely after the cash rewards. He was behind Jembe's party: working to turn the island into a hot little Soviet stronghold. Get rid of British influence, then the Sultan, start a "Democratic" republic — and up with the red flag! And the next step would have been to slap an iron curtain round it, and use it as a spring-board for all sorts of merry Russian ballets. But they needed money to buy votes and supporters and get the thing really moving, and when that paper of old Emory's turned up it seemed they'd got it.'

'But they hadn't got it!' protested Gussie.

'Don't be unintelligent, Gussie! They meant to get it. They thought it was more or less in the bag. All they had to do was to get that envelope off Honeywood. And since Nigel was the obvious person to get it, they arranged to send him home and get him back again — presumably by means of some flourishing and very well organized under-cover route. And then Dany spoilt the whole show by jumping the gun.'

Gussie said: 'It's all very confusing. And I still don't understand what this Jembe was doing in England, anyway.'

'At a guess, because the Reds have never learnt to trust one another a yard, and I imagine that he was sent to keep an eye on Nigel. But Nigel failed to get the goods off Honeywood, so he put Jembe on to trying to find it — that is the supposition, anyway — and to planting that gun and pinching her passport for good measure. To ensure that the police would be kept busy suspecting her for a bit, so that she'd probably end by posting off the letter.'

'*Too* silly,' said Lorraine. 'Once he knew she had it, he ought to have just let her bring it out with her, and found some way of getting it off her here.'

'Ah, but he couldn't travel out with her — and Jembe could!

Nigel would have had to nip back to Kenya in order to meet the plane at Nairobi, and I imagine he didn't trust Jembe. Probably thought that if Jembe got his hooks on it, while on his own, he'd stick to it and leave the Revolution to chase itself round the block. Dowling says that Jembe was obviously trailing Dany too, and so knew quite well who she was, and it seems that either he or Nigel had another crack at getting the letter in Nairobi. As a result of which, that blasted young idiot, Lash, got the wind up and swiped it.'

'Why?' croaked Dany.

'Oh, hullo kid. You feeling better? Have some more brandy,' said Tyson. 'Do you good.'

'Do you really think she ought to, darling? inquired Lorraine anxiously.

'Why not? Look how much better she's looking already. Drink it up, child.'

Dany drank, blinked, and said: 'Why did Lash take it?'

'Because he's an interfering, impertinent, insolent young son-of-a—— Well, let it go. He didn't like the set-up and thought it was a dangerous thing for you to have. Thought you'd be safer without it.'

'Why didn't ... he ... give it ... you,' said Dany slowly and carefully.

'Says he wanted to know a hell of a lot more about things before he did. Didn't trust me or anyone else with a sum like that at stake. Blast his impertinence!'

Gussie said in a hard voice: 'And Millicent? Why does Mr Dowling think that Nigel did that?'

'Probably because he was afraid that she really might have spotted him. He was officially supposed to be in Kenya, so what had he been doing mucking about in Kent? He'd actually read *The House of Shade*, which is more than I have — I've never been able to struggle further than page six — so getting rid of Millicent was easy.'

'And I suppose he killed Jembe too,' said Gussie with a shudder.

'Probably. If he talks, we may know. However, Dowling appears to have landed him such a crack that there's an even chance he won't. Can't think why he couldn't have used the siphon. Sheer waste of gin.'

'Tyson, how *can* you!' said Lorraine, releasing her daughter's hands and straightening up indignantly. 'Why, it saved Dany's life!'

'She'd have been saved quite as effectively by soda water,' said Tyson. 'Or better still, a bullet! Can't think why he didn't shoot.'

'Because of Dany, of course! He was afraid he'd hit her. He told you that.'

'So he did. Well, just as well he was there. Very lucky he saw her slip away.'

'Did he know that it was Nigel all the time?' inquired Gussie.

'I don't think so. But he had a few shrewd suspicions. It seems that parts of Kent were fairly misty on the morning that Honeywood was killed, and one or two trains ran late in consequence. Dowling says that Nigel mentioned that mist twice; though as it was only localized, and there was no mention of it on the news or in the papers, how did he know a thing like that — unless he was there? But Dowling didn't know that Nigel was hoping to needle Dany into leading him to Emory's letter, and he very nearly didn't get there in time because——Oh, there you are, Dowling. How's the jaw?'

'Swell,' said Larry Dowling bitterly, '— if I may borrow an Americanism from the donor. By this time tomorrow I shan't even be able to talk.'

'Or see out of your left eye,' said Tyson. 'The boy would appear to pack a punishing left. But I still can't see why he should have thought——'

'Neither can I,' said Larry. 'Considering that I happen to be a loving husband and an indulgent father. How are you feeling, Miss Ashton?'

'Drunk,' said Dany. 'You all will keep on giving me brandy and whisky and things.'

She held out her hands to him. 'I'm sorry about your face, Larry. And — and thank you so very much. For everything.'

Her voice broke and her eyes filled with weak tears, and Larry sat down on the edge of the bed and took her hands in his.

'You haven't anything to thank me for. If I'd had the sense to look where I was going I'd have got that pro-Red so-and-so before he started any rough stuff. But because I didn't, I expect your head is a good deal worse than my jaw; so you're not really even with me yet!'

Gussie, who had been standing by the window, said: 'Here are the cars. This will be the police. Or the doctor.'

'And Holden,' said Larry Dowling, hastily releasing Dany and rising to his feet: 'Time I went. I'm not taking any chances on being found holding your hands again and getting another crack on the jaw. That boy is too impetuous by half. See you tomorrow.'

He went out, leaving the door ajar behind him, and they heard footsteps running up the stairs and then Lash's voice on the verandah outside. 'You here again?'

'And very well chaperoned,' said Larry, 'so you can keep your hands in your pockets! Have you brought the doctor?'

'Of course. I also gave him your letter.'

'Thanks. Where is he now?'

'Ministering to that murderous louse, who has apparently surfaced — worse luck!'

'Good: I'll send him up to see Miss Ashton as soon as he's finished down there.'

Larry's footsteps retreated and Dany sat up dizzily as the door opened and Lash came in.

He paid no attention at all to Lorraine, Gussie or Tyson, but came straight across to the bed and took Dany into his arms.

'Don't mind us,' remarked Tyson caustically.

'I don't,' said Lash, '— much.'

He turned his head to look over his shoulder at Lorraine, and said: 'The doc will be up here as soon as he's through with Ponting, and after that, if I know doctors, he'll throw me out on my ear. So I'd be deeply obliged if you'd all scram.'

'Of course, dear,' said Lorraine. 'Come on Gussie. Tyson——' The door closed behind them.

Dany said: 'Lash, you aren't a G-man, are you? I thought you might be — or a murderer — because you'd taken that letter, and Nigel said—— And I knew I ought to hate you if you were a murderer, but I couldn't — and I'm so glad you're not a G-man! I didn't want you to be, and I'm so sorry. Lash, I'm sorry — so sorry——'

Lash said: 'All right, honey, all right. You're sorry. For Pete's sake, how much brandy did they give you?'

'Lots,' said Dany. 'Lots and lots and lots. Firs' Larry, then you, then Tyson... It's good for you. I shouldn't have listened to Nigel. Lash, you will forgive me, won't you? because I couldn't bear it if you didn't... I couldn't bear it——'

'This is just about where we came in,' said Lash. 'Only it was me last time. It's a judgement on me! Darling, you're plastered! All right, I'll forgive you — but after this if I ever catch you drinking anything stronger than a chocolate-soda, so help me, I'll take a strap to you! Darling — my darling — *my darling*...'

The African police-constable on guard saluted smartly and ushered Mr Dowling into a small ground-floor room leading off the central courtyard, where the window shutters were further reinforced by iron grille work and the doors were stout. A room that was, oddly enough, the self-same one to which Tyson's grandfather, Rory Frost, had brought his share of Sultan Saïd's treasure for temporary safe-keeping on a wild, rainy night over ninety-five years ago. No one now alive was aware of this; yet, strangely, a superstition survived that the room was, for some obscure reason, a place of ill-omen: which perhaps accounted for the fact that until an hour or so ago it has been kept locked and unfurnished.

Now, however, having been hastily denuded of dust and innumerable spiders-webs, it contained a heavy brass bedstead, a couple of cane armchairs loosely covered in faded chintz, a bed-side table, and an ornate, marble-topped Victorian wash-hand-stand complete with an imposing array of flower-patterned china utensils. It also contained — in addition to the doctor — Nigel Ponting and Mr Cardew: the former lying prone upon the bed with his right wrist securely handcuffed to a brass bedpost, while the latter, who had arrived at the House of Shade in response to an urgent telephone call from Larry Dowling, occupied one of the cane chairs, pad and pencil at the ready.

Mr Dowling noted with approval that the doctor had wasted no time. The wet towel that some amateur hand had hastily wound about the secretary's head, in the manner of an untidy turban, had been removed, together with his coat, and a shirt sleeve that had been rolled back disclosed the mark of a recent injection on Nigel's bare arm. An empty syringe lay on the bed-side table, and Nigel's eyes were open. He was muttering to himself, and watching someone whom he could see, but the others could not, moving about the room.

'Is it going to work, Doc?' inquired Superintendent Cardew in an undertone.

'I don't know,' returned the doctor shortly. 'I've never had occasion to use it before. And, if it does, I don't guarantee that you'll get the truth. It's more likely to be a load of old rubbish or else pure fantasy. And, what's more, I'm not at all sure that this business isn't illegal and that I won't wind up finding my-self struck off the Medical Register!'

'Nonsense. Besides, if anyone hears of it — and they won't —

you can always say that you were only carrying out the orders of the police, and put the blame on us. We're used to that.'

'And how!' endorsed Larry feelingly. Adding a trifle anxiously that he hoped that the quality and volume of the sound was going to improve, because at present he could not make out a word that the prisoner was saying.

'Give him time,' urged the doctor, busy replacing the discarded turban with an elaborate and highly professional bandage. 'You can't expect that stuff to act with the speed of light.'

Larry sighed, and pulling up the vacant chair, seated himself gingerly in its creaking depths, produced his own notebook and pencil, and sat waiting to take down anything relevant that the prisoner might say.

Mr Ponting continued to mutter unintelligibly and the doctor, having completed the bandage to his satisfaction and felt his patient's pulse again, picked up the syringe and wrapped it in a square of surgical gauze. He was stowing it away in his bag with some ostentation — as if to forestall any request from the guardians of the law for a further injection of the drug he had been asked to administer — when Nigel Ponting began to talk: aloud and clearly ...

'... There is no proof,' declared Nigel, addressing the unseen person whose movements he had been watching, and who was now apparently standing at the foot of the bed. 'I've been too clever for them. There isn't an atom of proof, and they'll never think of looking under Tyson's floorboards for that duplicate key ... Right under his nose! And of course for any serious work I always took care to wear gloves — that pair of silk ones to match my skin that Don had specially made for me in Cairo. They've proved invaluable. There'll be no prints on the stair mechanism, or anywhere else. They teach you to cover your tracks, as you know. They're very insistent about that. Old Honeywood never noticed the gloves even though it was mid morning. Though of course it was a grey day, and I have to admit that the mist was a bonus — one might almost call it providential — if one believed in Providence, which luckily I don't...

'A pity it wasn't thicker ... If it had been, that Bates woman would never have recognized me — silly bitch! *I never forget a face!* That really was bad luck. Hers not mine. Tiresome, beady-eyed old busy-body! I certainly didn't remember hers. But of course after that I had to get rid of her as quickly as possible ... I must tell you about that. It was laughably easy and I really do pride myself on it ... It was a stroke of genius. All I had to do was type an urgent little note on the Ashton girl's typewriter, push it under Bates's door, set the stair trap and wait for her to fall into it. Which of course she did — *plunk*!

'... Yes. Terrible about Jembe — I don't know how I'm going to manage without him. I wonder who did it? We shall have to find out. I suppose the police will have searched his luggage. Let's hope he was careful: his type so often aren't ... too conceited. It's our weakest link. Oh, well, I shall have to find a replacement. It shouldn't be difficult — three million will buy almost anything! ... We could swing the elections for a fraction of that. It's after we've done it that the trouble will start. I know we need islands and that this one is the best one to begin on ... but the snag is going to be the Zanzibaris. They're too damned easy-going. They'll have to be educated ... taught to kill. And to hate. That's the important thing. Hate ... to hate ... to hate. And after that ...'

The harsh, unfamiliar voice, that contained no trace of those high-pitched and carefully cultivated fluting tones that had been part of a successful disguise for so long, talked on and on, while the horrified doctor (who had been more than half inclined to take all he had been told about Ponting with a large helping of salt) frowned and fussed and muttered oaths that were certainly not Hippocratic, and Messrs Cardew and Dowling scribbled swiftly, filling page after page of their official notebooks. Jotting down names that would later be identified and their owners traced, together with dates and details that were to prove damning...

When at last the hoarse voice slurred to a stop, the doctor — having declared that the performance was over and that the prisoner would now sleep for several hours — departed upstairs to see what he could do for Miss Ashton, and Mr Cardew mopped his brow with a pocket handkerchief and announced that he would be jiggered.

'If you'd told me that, and I hadn't heard it with my own ears, I wouldn't have believed a word of it,' confessed Mr Cardew. 'And, whatever the Doc's reservations are about using that drug, there was nothing phoney about that performance! If ever anything came straight from the horse's mouth, that did! But I didn't follow that stuff about the three million that's going to give Jembe's dupes a walk-over in the elections, and turn Zanzibar into a Communist paradise and a base for Russian spy-rockets and atom-subs and all the rest of it. Whose three million?'

'Tyson's grandfather's,' said Larry. 'The old reprobate reportedly stashed away roughly that amount as his share of Sultan Saïd's treasure, which he and a subsequent Sultan, Majid, somehow got their hooks on. And all this murder and mayhem was apparently sparked off by a map that shows where he hid it. It seems to have turned into a nasty adult version of that popular children's party game, "Hunt-the-slipper", and to date three people — if one can count "the thin man" as one of them — have been murdered for the sake of that map.'

'Who's got it now?'

'Mr Frost, I imagine. Unless it's still on the floor of young Holden's room in the guest annex. I forgot to ask.'

'Do you think they'll find it? — the loot, I mean.'

'I expect so. That is, if it's still there. It may not be. But if it is, at least it won't be going to swell the coffers of some local Dictator and his Commissars, and their home-picked brand of the K.G.B.'

'No, thank God! Well, Dowling, now that that's over, I'll be off to dig the Resident out of bed and see what can be done to ensure that this murderous fellow-traveller gets sent back under guard to stand trial at the Old Bailey. And a very good night to you!' The door banged behind him.

'Some hope!' sighed Larry sadly. And resigned himself to spending what remained of the night in a creaking and far from comfortable cane armchair.

Postscript from 'Kivulimi'.

... it sounds to me a very dull place for a honeymoon, baby. Though I do see that you both felt you'd had enough of romantic places for a bit. It's a pity we didn't buy you a mackintosh and some sensible shoes, but anyway, I expect you can get them there, and I'm sure you're both having a heavenly time, even if you are only on parole or bail or something. And by the way, Larry said to remind you that if you don't turn up in London on the right date and the right time he'll have you both arrested and never speak to you again. So you won't go all starry-eyed and forget, will you darling? (Tyson says that if I'm referring to your husband, I mean pie-eyed. But of course I don't.)

I think we've got rid of the police at last, which is a blessing (except for darling Larry. I wish he could have stayed) and we had a bit of drama over Elf. I expect you saw the announcement in the papers. She's going to marry Sir Ambrose Yardley. She says that Tyson advised her to marry someone like that. Very naughty of him, as of course Eduardo was simply heart*broken, and we had the most exhausting scenes — and right on top of everything else: I can't tell you! Still, they've both gone, and if I know Eddie, he's already in love with someone else.*

Everything else seems to have been sorted out, except for the Jembe business. I don't suppose we shall ever know about that, but it seems that Nigel didn't do it, and Tyson says he's quite sure that Seyyid Omar did. He was dining with us here the other night and mentioned that Jembe suffered from air sickness, or nerves or something, and that he'd given him something to take for it. And then he looked at Tyson with that bland smile of his and said: 'Like your revered uncle, one does what one can.' And then they both drank Barclay's health. Really — men! *How could they? When one thinks of all that lovely money. Oh I forgot you wouldn't know about that — I must tell you——*

It wasn't nearly as easy as they thought to find it, the treasure I mean, because of course Tyson's father had bricked up all those walls. (*Tyson says he was always messing up the place with improvements.*) *And when we got there at last, all we found was a rather pompous letter from Barclay. It was a bit difficult to read, as it had got damp, but we read it and it seems that the silly old man had come on the gold when he was poking about in the foundations for material for that boring book of his, and believe it or not, he had carried it all out, bit by bit and night after night, and dumped it into the sea from one of those little fishing carracks, about a mile offshore.* Really, *darling!*

He said money in a place like Zanzibar was a source of evil, because all it led to was Progress; and he was against progress, because it seldom led to happiness, and more often only meant hideous buildings, ugly factories, dirty railway yards and noisy motor cars, and things like strikes, lockouts and exploitation. He preferred coconuts, cloves and charm.

Tyson says it's rather like a story called 'The Treasure and the Law', but I don't think I can have read it. By the way, he's sending Lash a copy of The House of Shade *as a sort of extra wedding present, and he says if the first one's a boy you'd better call him Barclay, because in his opinion there can't be too many of them.*

Tyson doesn't seem to think much of Progress either. He says it was a good idea, but that it's got out of hand.

Well, darling——

Death in the Andamans

In fond memory
of
'Fudge'
(Rosemary Cosgrave)
and the Islands

'The isle is full of noises . . .'

The Tempest

AUTHOR'S NOTE

This story was roughed out during a wild and stormy afternoon towards the end of the long-ago thirties, on a tiny island in the southern waters of the Bay of Bengal.

I happened to be there because a great friend and fellow art student, to whom this book is dedicated, had accompanied her parents to this far-flung bit of Empire when her father was appointed Chief Commissioner of the Andaman Islands. Shortly after her arrival in Port Blair she had written inviting me to come out and spend the winter with them: an irresistible invitation that would have had to be resisted had it arrived any earlier, since my art had not been paying very well and I could not possibly have afforded the fare. But as luck would have it I had recently put away my paint-brushes and tried my hand at writing instead, and to my stunned surprise a children's book and my first novel, a crime story, had both been accepted for publication. What was more, an advance had been paid on them!

The sum involved was, by today's standards, incredibly meagre. But it seemed vast at a time when a return tourist-class passage by sea, from England to India and back again, cost only £40 (which is less than $50 at the present rate of exchange), and suddenly I was rich! I hastily bought a one-way ticket to Calcutta, where I eventually boarded a little steamer, the S.S. *Maharaja*, that called once a month at the Andamans, and four days later landed at Port Blair and was taken by launch to Ross — an island about the size of a postage stamp that guarded the entrance to the harbour and was topped by Government House, the residence of the Chief Commissioner.

The largest building in Port Blair was a pink, Moorish-style jail; for the main island had been used for almost a century as a convict settlement, and more than two thirds of the local population, many of them Burmese, were either convicted murderers serving life sentences, or the descendants of murderers — this last because 'lifers' were allowed out after serving a year or two in the jail, permitted, if they wished, to send for their wives and families, given a hut and a plot of land and encouraged to settle. Even the majority of house-servants and gardeners on Ross, including those in Government House, were 'lifers': and a nicer lot of people I have seldom met! But the house itself was another matter . . .

It was a disturbingly creepy place. What my Scottish grandfather would have termed 'unchancy'. And if ever there was a haunted house it was this one. The incident at the beginning of this book happened to me exactly as I have described it, except that the figure I saw was not a European but a malevolent little Burman armed with a *kriss* — the wicked Burmese knife that has a wavy-edged blade. Other and equally peculiar things happened in that house: but that, as they say, is another story. The settings, however, and many of the incidents in this book, are real.

There actually was a picnic party at Mount Harriet on Christmas Eve, and there was also a British Navy cruiser visiting Port Blair. We saw the storm coming up, and ran for it, and a few of us managed to get back to Ross on the ferry: though I still don't know how we made it! Once back, we were cut off from the rest of Port Blair, and from everywhere else for that matter, for the best part of a week. The various Christmas festivities that we had planned were literally washed out, and by mid-afternoon on Boxing Day there was still a horrific sea running and every jetty in Port Blair had been smashed flat. But since the worst of the hurricane appeared to have passed, Fudge and I fought our way around Ross, ending up at the deserted Club, where we sat sipping gimlets* and staring glumly at the damp patches on the ballroom floor and the wilting decorations that we had put up so gaily only three days before.

Perhaps because I had just written a crime novel I remarked idly that the present situation would be a gift to a would-be murderer. No doctor on the island, no police, only a handful of the detachment of British troops, no telephone lines operating and no link at all with the main island, and despite the gale, the temperature and humidity so high that any corpse would have to be buried in double-quick time — and probably without a coffin at that! To which Fudge replied cheerfully: 'You know, that's quite an idea! Who shall we kill?'

We spent the next half hour or so happily plotting a murder, limiting our characters to the number of British marooned on Ross, minus Fudge's mother, Lady Cosgrave, because we decided that our fictional Chief Commissioner had better be a widower with a stepdaughter, and plus two naval officers who had, in fact, been members of the picnic party on Mount Harriet, but had managed to make it back to their ship by the skin of their teeth. And since our real-life cast seemed much too average and humdrum, we derived considerable amusement from endowing them all with looks, characters, colouring and quirks that the originals did not possess.

All in all it proved a very entertaining way of passing a long, wet afternoon. But it did not occur to me to make any use of it, because I had gone back to painting again. I never gave it another thought until a year later, by which time my mother and I were in Persia — or Iran, if you insist, though I prefer the old name. (A 'Persian' carpet or a 'Persian' poem sounds far more attractive than an 'Iranian' one any day.)

*A popular short drink in the days of the Raj, consisting of gin, ice and a dollop of Rose's lime juice, plus a dash of bitters (optional). These, too, would appear to have vanished along with the Empire.

The Second World War had broken out that autumn, so sightseeing and sketching were not encouraged — particularly sketching! — and time was hanging a bit heavy on my hands. It was the period known as the 'phoney war', and there being little else to do I decided to try my hand at writing another crime novel, using the plot that Fudge and I had concocted in the Andamans. Which I did: though by the time I finished it I was unable to get the manuscript home to my British publishers, owing to the fact that by then the war was no longer in the least 'phoney'. And it was not until a long time later that it appeared in print in England under the title of *Night on the Island.*

This is how a tale that was invented during an idle afternoon on a tiny, storm-bound island in the Bay of Bengal came to be written in Persia, in a small town on the banks of the Shatt-al-Arab, called Khurramshah, which not so long ago was reduced to rubble in the fighting between Iran and Iraq. Sadly, Ross had long since predeceased it; falling a victim to Japanese bombing that demolished Government House and its ghosts, together with every other building on the island — including the little club-house where this story began.

I am told that the jungle has taken over Ross and that no one goes there any more. But that nowadays there is a modern hotel for tourists at Corbyn's Cove. Time and the Tourist march on!

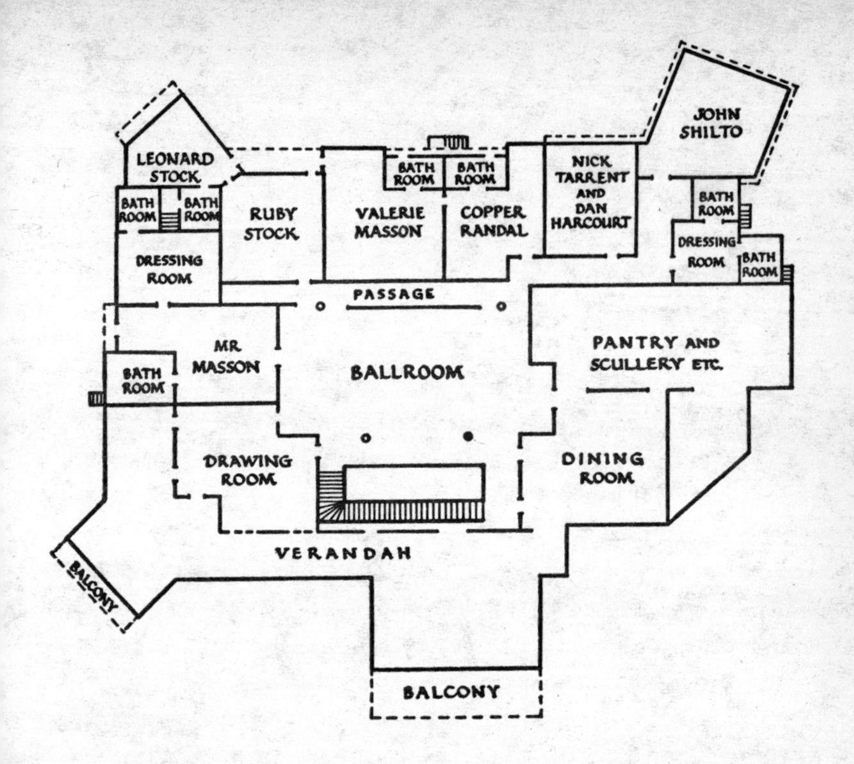

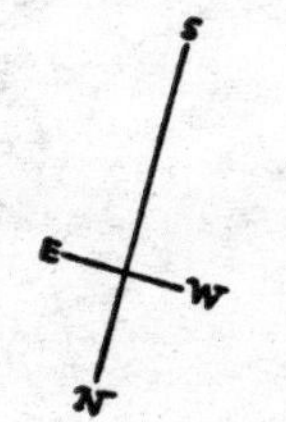

PLAN OF FIRST FLOOR,
GOVERNMENT HOUSE,
ROSS

1

Something bumped lightly against the side of her bed and Copper Randal, awakening with a start, was astonished to find that her heart was racing.

For a moment or two she lay staring into the darkness and listening. Trying to identify what it was that had woken her so abruptly. And why she should be afraid? But apart from the monotonous swish of the electric fan blades overhead there was no sound in the silent house, and the hot, windless night was so still that she could hear the frightened pounding of her heart. Then somewhere in the room a floorboard creaked . . .

Every nerve in her body seemed to jerk in response to that small, stealthy sound and suddenly her heart was no longer in her breast but had jumped into her throat and was constricting it so that she could barely breathe. She had to force herself to sit up and ease one hand out from under the close-tucked mosquito netting, moving very cautiously, and grope for the switch of her bedside light. She heard it click as she pressed it, but no comforting light sprang up to banish the darkness.

This, thought Copper, swerving abruptly from panic to impatience, is absurd! She rubbed her eyes with the back of her other hand and pressed the switch a second time. But with no better result. Yet there had been nothing wrong with the lamp when she turned it off, so either the bulb had given out during the night, which seemed unlikely, or else . . . Or else I'm dreaming this, she thought uneasily.

The idea was a preposterous one, but nevertheless she pinched herself to make sure that she was awake, and reassured on that point, pressed the switch a third time. Nothing. Then the bulb must have . . . It was at this point that irritation changed swiftly back into panic as she remembered the yards of flex that lay across the uncarpeted floor and connected the lamp on her bedside table to a plug on the far side of the room. Supposing someone — something — had passed by her bed and tripped over the flex, jerking the plug from its socket? She had done that herself more than once, so there was no reason to suppose——

'Stop it!' Copper scolded herself in a furious whisper: 'You're behaving like a lunatic! And what's more, if you sit here in the dark for just one more minute, you'll end up screaming the house down. So get going!' Thus adjured she took a deep breath and summoning up all her courage, pushed up the mosquito netting and slid out of bed.

The smooth, polished floorboards felt pleasantly cool to her bare feet as she groped her way across to the switch by the bathroom door, and finding it, pressed down the little metal knob with a feeling of profound relief.

Once again a switch clicked beneath her unsteady fingers, and this time a light came on. But it was not the bright, warm comforting one she had expected. Instead, a queer, greenish, phosphorescent glow filled the room, and aware of a movement beside her, she turned sharply and saw, standing so close to her that without moving she could have touched him, the figure of a little wizened man in a suit of soiled white drill.

Copper shrank back, both hands at her throat and her mouth dry with terror. But the intruder did not move. In that dim light his blanched face glimmered like that of a drowned man coming up out of deep water, and she could see that his wrinkled features were set in an expression of malignant fury: a blind, unseeing rage that did not appear to be directed at her, for the unfocused eyes stared past her at someone or something else. But there was no one else, and the whole house was still. So still that the silence and the queer greenish light seemed part of one another, and Time had stopped and was standing behind her, waiting . . .

I ought to scream, thought Copper numbly; Val's only in the next room. I've only got to scream—— She opened her mouth but no sound came from her dry throat, and the green light began to flicker and grow dim. It was going out and she would be left alone in the dark with . . . with . . .

And then at last she screamed. And, astonishingly, woke to find herself in her bed, shivering among the pillows, with the last echoes of her own strangled shriek in her ears.

A light snapped on in the next room and seconds later a dark-haired girl in pink cotton pyjamas, newly aroused from sleep, burst through the curtained archway that separated the two bedrooms, calling out encouragingly that she was coming and what on *earth* was the matter?

'N–nothing,' quavered Copper through chattering teeth. 'Only a nightmare. But a perfectly beastly one! I still can't believe . . .' She reached out a trembling hand and switched on her own light, apologizing confusedly for making such an appalling din: 'I didn't mean . . . I was going . . . I *am* sorry I woke you, but I thought he — it—— And then the light started to go and—— Oh Val, am I glad to see you! D'you mind staying around and talking to me for a bit until I've simmered down and unscrambled myself? Bless you——!'

She lifted her mosquito net and Valerie crept in underneath it and having annexed a pillow and made herself comfortable at the foot of the bed, observed crisply that any talking to be done had better be done, pronto, by Copper. 'Have you any *idea* what a ghastly noise you were making? It sounded like an entire glee club of love-lorn tom cats yowling on a rooftop. What in heaven's name were you dreaming about?'

'I'm not too sure that I was dreaming,' confessed Copper with a shudder. 'In fact I actually pinched myself just to make sure I wasn't: and it hurt, too.'

'Tell!' ordered Valerie, and composed herself to listen while Copper embarked hesitantly on an account of the peculiar happenings of the last fifteen minutes or so, ending defensively: 'It was *real*, Val! Right up to the time that I switched on the light by the bathroom door, I could have sworn I was awake and that it was all really happening. It was far more of a shock to find myself waking up in bed than it would have been to find myself being murdered!'

'*Hmm.* I'd say that the trouble with you,' diagnosed Valerie sapiently, 'was either too many of those curried prawns at the Club last night, or else you've been letting the fact that you are living on a sort of Devil's Island — anyway, a penal settlement — get on your nerves.'

'The latter, probably.' Copper relaxed and lay back on her pillow, watching the whirling, white-painted blades of the electric fan flicking swift shadows across the high ceiling, and presently she said slowly: 'It's a bit difficult to explain, but don't you think there must be something a little out of kilter . . . something unchancy . . . about the Andamans? Just think of it, Val. In this particular bit of the Islands almost three quarters of the population, including most of your father's house-servants, are convicted murderers serving a life sentence. They've all killed someone. Surely that must have *some* effect on a place — any place? Murderers being sent here year after year? All those dead people whose lives they took . . . the atmosphere must get choked up with them like – like static. Or wireless waves, or – or something——' She hesitated and then laughed a little shamefacedly. 'I'm sorry. I don't seem able to explain it very well.'

'Try not to think about it,' advised Valerie practically. 'Otherwise you'll be waking me up nightly dreaming that you're being murdered by convicts or haunted by the ghosts of their victims, and I'm not sure that I could take any more of that scarifying "woman wailing for her demon lover" stuff. It scared me rigid.'

'Don't worry, I'm not likely to have a dream like that twice, touch wood!' said Copper, reaching up to rap the nearest mosquito pole with her knuckles. 'And anyway, it wasn't a convict I was dreaming about. Unless there are any European convicts here. Are there?'

'No, of course not. What did he look like?'

'Rather like a rat. If you can imagine a rat with wrinkles and a lot of grey, wispy hair. A mean, vindictive sort of face. He wasn't much taller than I am, and he was wearing a grubby white suit and a big ring with a red stone set in it. You've no idea how terribly solid and detailed it all was. I saw him so clearly that I could draw a picture of him; and it wasn't like a dream at all. It was *real*. Horridly real! I was here, in this room. And I not only felt that switch click, I heard it. The only unreal thing was the light being green.' She shivered again, and turning her head, sat up in sudden astonishment and said: 'Why, it's morning!'

The clear pale light of dawn had seeped unnoticed into the room as they talked, dimming the electric bulbs to a wan yellow glow. Copper slid out from under the mosquito net, and crossing to the windows drew back the curtains: 'It must be getting on for six. I don't know why, but I thought it was the middle of the night.' She leant out over the window-sill, sniffing the faint dawn breeze that whispered through the mango trees on the far side of the lawn, and said: 'It's going to be a marvellous day, Val. Come and look.'

Valerie snapped off the bedside lamp and joined her, and the two girls knelt on the low window-seat to watch the growing light deepen over the sea and stretch along the ruled edge of the far horizon.

Below them lay a wide strip of lawn bordered on the far side by mango, pyinma and casuarina trees that overlooked the grass tennis-courts, a tangled rose garden and two tall, feathery clusters of bamboo. Beyond this the ground sloped down to the beach so steeply that the clear, glassy water that shivered to a lace of foam about the dark shelves of rock appeared to lie almost directly below the house, and only the tops of the tall coconut palms that fringed the shores of the little island could be seen from the upper windows. Sky, sea and the level stretch of lawn seemed to be fashioned from Lalique glass, so still and smooth and serene they were: the still, smooth serenity that presages a perfect Indian Ocean day.

The fronds of the coconut palms swayed gently to a breath of scented air that wandered across the garden and ruffled Valerie's dark hair, and she stretched a pair of sunburnt arms above her head and sighed gratefully. 'So cool! And yet in another hour it will be hot and sticky again. A curse upon this climate.'

'That's because you've been here too long. You're blasé,' said Copper, her eyes on the glowing horizon: 'After that endless London fog and rain and drizzle, I don't believe I could ever have too much sun, however hot and sticky.'

'You wait!' retorted Valerie. 'I may have been in the Islands too long, but you haven't been here long enough. Two more months of the Andamans and you'll be thinking longingly of expeditions to the North Pole!'

Valerie Masson, born Valerie Ann Knight, was the stepdaughter of Sir Lionel Masson, Chief Commissioner of the Andamans. A childless man, Sir Lionel had been a widower for close upon seventeen years; during which time he had paid school bills and written cheques at frequent intervals but, since his visits to England had been infrequent, had seen little or nothing of this stepdaughter who had taken his name. He knew that the child was well looked after in the home of a couple of devoted aunts, and his only anxiety on her behalf (in the rare intervals in which he thought of her at all) was the fear that in all probability she was being badly spoiled.

His appointment as Chief Commissioner to the Andamans had coincided with Valerie's nineteenth birthday, and it had suddenly occurred to him that he not only possessed a grown-up step-daughter, but that it might be both pleasant and convenient to install a hostess in the big, sprawling house on Ross. The idea was well received. Valerie had welcomed it with enthusiasm and for the past two years had kept house for her stepfather, played hostess at Government House, and enjoyed herself considerably. Which last was not to be wondered at, for although she could lay no particular claim to beauty, her dark hair grew in a deep widow's peak above an endearingly freckled face in which a pair of disturbing green eyes were set charmingly atilt, and these assets, combined with an inexhaustible supply of good humour, had worked havoc with the susceptibilities of the male population of Port Blair.

Her present house-guest, Miss Randal — Caroline Olivia Phoebe Elizabeth by baptism but invariably known, from an obvious combination of initials, as 'Copper' — had been her best friend since their early schooldays, and at about the time that Valerie was setting sail for the Andamans, Copper had been reluctantly embarking upon the infinitely more prosaic venture of earning her living as a shorthand typist in the city of London.

For two drab years she had drawn a weekly pay cheque from Messrs Hudnut and Addison Limited, Glass and China Merchants, whose gaunt and grimy premises were situated in that unlovely section of London known as the Elephant and Castle. The weekly pay cheque had been incredibly meagre, and at times it had needed all Copper's ingenuity, coupled with incorrigible optimism, to make both ends meet and life seem at all worth supporting. 'But someday,' said Copper, reassuring herself, 'something exciting is *bound* to happen!'

Pending that day she continued to hammer out an endless succession of letters beginning 'Dear Sir — In reply to yours of the 15th ult.', to eat her meals off clammy, marble-topped tables in A.B.C. teashops, and to keep a weather-eye fixed on the horizon in ever-hopeful anticipation of the sails of Adventure. And then, three months previously, that sail had lifted over the skyline in the form of a small and totally unexpected legacy left her by a black-sheep uncle long lost sight of in the wilds of the Belgian Congo.

A slightly dazed Copper had handed in her resignation to Messrs Hudnut and Addison Limited, cabled her acceptance of a long-standing invitation of Valerie's to visit the Islands, and having indulged in an orgy of shopping, booked a passage to Calcutta, where she had boarded the S.S. *Maharaja* — the little steamer which is virtually the only link between the Andamans and the outside world. Four days later she had leaned over the deck rail, awed and enchanted, as the ship sailed past emerald hills and palm-fringed beaches, to drop anchor in the green, island-strewn harbour of Port Blair.

That had been nearly three weeks ago. Three weeks of glitteringly blue days and incredibly lovely star-splashed nights. She had bathed in the clear jade breakers of Forster Bay and Corbyn's Cove, fished in translucent waters above branching sprays of coral from the decks of the little steam launch *Jarawa*, and picnicked under palm trees that rustled to the song of the Trade Winds.

It was all so different from that other world of fog and rain, strap-hanging, shorthand and crowded rush-hour buses, that she sometimes felt that she must have dreamed it all. Or that this was the dream, and presently she would awake to find herself back once more in the cheerless, gas-lit lodgings off the Fulham Road. But no: this was real. This wonderful, colourful world. Copper drew a deep breath of utter contentment and leant her head against the window-frame.

Beside her, Valerie who had also fallen silent, was leaning out of the window, her head cocked a little on one side as though she were listening to something. There was a curious intentness about her that communicated itself to Copper, so that presently she too found herself listening: straining her ears to catch some untoward sound from the quiet garden below. But she could hear nothing but the hush of the glassy sea against the rocks, and after a minute or two she said uneasily: 'What is it, Val?'

'The birds. I've only just noticed it. Listen——'

'What birds? I can't hear any.'

'That's just it. They always make a terrific racket at this hour of the morning. I wonder what's come over them today?'

Copper leant out beside her, frowning. Every morning since her arrival in the Islands she had been awakened by a clamorous chorus of birds: unfamiliar tropical birds. Parrots, parakeets, mynas, sunbirds, orioles, paradise fly-catchers, shouting together in a joyous greeting to the dawn. But today, for the first time, no birds were singing. 'I expect they've migrated, or something,' said Copper lightly. 'Look at that sky, Val! Isn't it gorgeous?'

The cool, pearly sheen of dawn had warmed in the East to a blaze of vivid rose that deepened along the horizon's edge to a bar of living, glowing scarlet, and bathed the still sea and the dreaming islands in an uncanny, sunset radiance.

'*"Red sky at morning"*,' said Valerie uneasily. 'I do hope to goodness this doesn't mean a storm. It would be too sickening, right at the beginning of Christmas week.'

'Good heavens,' exclaimed Copper blankly, 'I'd quite forgotten. Of course — this is Christmas Eve. Somehow it doesn't seem possible. I feel as if I'd left Christmas behind at the other side of the world. Well, one thing's certain: there won't be any snow here! And of *course* there isn't going to be a storm. There isn't a cloud in the sky.'

'I know — but I still don't like the look of it.'

'Nonsense! It's wonderful. It's like a transformation scene in a pantomime.'

As they watched, the fiery glow faded from the quiet sky and the sun leapt above the horizon and flashed dazzling swords of light through the diamond air. Hard shadows streaked the lawns, and the house awoke to a subdued bustle of early morning activity.

The new day was full of sounds: the low, hushing, interminable murmur of the sea; the sigh of a wandering breeze among the grey-green casuarina boughs; a distant hum and clatter from the servants' quarters; and the dry click and rustle of the bamboos.

'Be not afeard; the isle is full of noises, Sounds and sweet airs, that give delight, and hurt not,' quoted Copper, who had once played Miranda to Valerie's Ferdinand in a sixth-form production of *The Tempest.*

She had been thinking of the contrast between the darkness and terror of the past night and the shining glory of the morning when Caliban's charmed, immortal lines slipped into her mind, and she had repeated them almost without knowing it: speaking them as though they were an assurance of safety and a spell against evil, and so softly that the words were barely audible. But Valerie's ear had caught them, for she said with an unexpected trace of sharpness: 'That's all very well, but speaking for myself I'm distinctly afeard, and at the moment I'd say Keats was more on the ball than Caliban!'

'*Keats?* Why Keats?'

'"La Belle Dame sans Merci". That place by a lake, where "no birds sing". Well, there are still none singing here this morning and I don't like it — or that red sky either! I don't like it one *bit!*'

Copper stared at her: and puzzled by her uncharacteristic vehemence, turned to lean out of the window again and listen intently. But Valerie was right. The isle was still full of noises. But in its gardens no bird sang.

2

The Andaman Islands, green, fairy-like, enchanted, lie some hundred miles off the Burmese coast in the blue waters of the Bay of Bengal. Legend, with some support by science, tells that their hills and valleys were once part of a great range of mountains that extended from Burma to Sumatra, but that the wickedness of the inhabitants angered Mavia Tomala, the great chief, who caused a cataclysm which separated the land into over two hundred islands, and marooned them for ever in the Bay of Bengal.

For close on a hundred years a small part of the Andamans had been used by the Government of India as a penal settlement. The only important harbour, Port Blair, lies on the south-east coast of South Andaman, with its harbour guarded from the sea by the tiny triangular islet of Ross, the administrative headquarters of the Islands.

Ross covers less than a mile in area, and into its narrow confines are packed over forty buildings that include a clubhouse, barracks, two churches, a hospital and a native bazaar. Topping this heterogeneous collection of dwellings, and set among green gardens, stands the residence of the Chief Commissioner: a long, rambling two-storeyed building that for some forgotten reason is known in the Islands as 'Government House', and whose windows look down on roofs and tree-tops and out to sea where the lovely, lost islands stray away on either hand to the far horizon like a flight of exotic butterflies.

On this particular Christmas Eve morning the Massons and Miss

Randal were breakfasting as usual in the dining-room of Government House. It was not yet nine o'clock but the day was unusually hot and close for the time of year, and the electric fans were whirring at full speed as Valerie filled in the details of the day's programme — an all-day picnic to the top of Mount Harriet followed by a large dinner party at Government House — to an inattentive audience.

The Chief Commissioner, normally an amiable though somewhat absentminded man, was frowning over a letter that had arrived half an hour earlier with a batch of official correspondence, and which he had already read at least twice, while Copper's gaze had strayed to the open windows that looked out across the harbour mouth to the pink, Moorish-looking walls of the cellular jail and the little town that some homesick Scot had named Aberdeen, which lies facing Ross on the mainland of Port Blair. A 'mainland' that is in fact only the largest of the Islands, though always referred to by the inhabitants by the more imposing title.

To the right of the town the land curves in a green arc between Aberdeen and North Point, embracing Phoenix Bay with its boats and steam-launches and lighters rocking gently in the blue swell; tiny Chatham Island with its sawmills and piled timber; Hopetown jetty where, in 1872, a Viceroy of India was murdered; and rising up behind it, on the far side of the bay, the green, gracious slope of Mount Harriet.

For once, however, Copper was not alive to the exotic beauty of the view, her attention at that moment being centred upon the slim, gleaming lines of a cruiser that lay at anchor far up the reaches of the harbour.

His Majesty's Ship *Sapphire* was paying a fortnight's visit to the Andamans; to the delight of the British denizens of Port Blair, for the problems of an enclosed society are many. It becomes difficult to infuse much enthusiasm into entertaining when every dinner, dance, bridge party or picnic must of necessity be made up of combinations and permutations of fifteen or twenty people, all of whom have lived cheek by jowl for months past — often for years — and whose individual interests and topics of conversation have become so well known that any form of social gathering is apt to become a routine performance. Which explains why the arrival of H.M.S. *Sapphire* had been welcomed with relief as well as pleasure.

Copper's thoughts, however, were not concerned with the *Sapphire* either as a social saviour or a decorative addition to the scattered collection of seagoing craft reflecting themselves in the pellucid waters of the bay. To her the cruiser existed solely as the ship which numbered among its company of officers and men, one Nicholas Tarrent R.N.

There was a certain electric quality about Nick Tarrent that had nothing whatever to do with his undoubted good looks, for possessing it a plain man or an ugly one would have been equally attractive, and Copper had been in love with him for precisely eight days, seven hours and forty-two minutes. In other words from the moment she had first set eyes on him, two hours after the arrival of H.M.S. *Sapphire* in Port Blair.

' — and some of them,' continued Valerie, 'want to sail from here to Hopetown jetty, where a lorry will meet them and take them up to the top of Mount Harriet. Charles had the boats brought across from Chatham last night so that they can start from the Club pier. The rest of us will take the ferry to Aberdeen and then go on by car. Harriet is only just across the other side of the bay, and I don't suppose it's more than two or three miles from here as the crow flies. But to get to it by road it's over thirty miles and — Copper! you're not listening.'

'I'm sorry,' apologized Copper in some confusion. 'I was looking at the view. It's fascinating.'

'Yes, I know: but if I'd realized you'd be able to see him at this range I'd have had the blinds drawn. Really, Coppy, you might *pretend* to take some interest. Here have I been going over all the arrangements for your benefit, and you haven't bothered to listen to a word. If you could just stop thinking about Nick Tarrent for five minutes, I'd be deeply grateful!'

Copper had the grace to blush, and Valerie laughed and said contritely: 'I'm sorry, Coppy. That was abominably rude and scratchy of me. I can't think why I should be feeling so jumpy and cross this morning. I suppose it's the heat. I shall be glad when we reach Mount Harriet: it's always much cooler up there.'

'It does seem to be a lot hotter today, doesn't it?' said Copper, relieved at the change of subject. 'Or perhaps it's just because it's so still? There doesn't seem to be a breath of air. Who's coming on this picnic?'

'Almost everyone. They're all finding their way there under their own steam. Rendezvous about twelve to twelve-thirty, at the top. You and I are going with Charles.'

'Who's Nick going with?'

'He's sailing over. He and Dan Harcourt and Ted Norton are taking one of the boats, and Hamish is going in another with Ronnie and Rosamund Purvis, and I think George Beamish is supposed to be taking that gloomy girlfriend of his, Amabel, in the third. Mr Hurridge is having a lorry sent to meet them at Crown Point jetty, so they ought to fetch up at Mount Harriet a good bit ahead of us. Except that there's no breeze today.'

'And what about *dear* Mrs Stock? I suppose she'll be there — worse luck!'

'Don't be catty, Coppy!'

'Why not? I enjoy being catty about Ruby. I heard her telling Nick in a honey-sweet voice at the Withers's barbecue that it was "*such* a pity that dear Copper gave the impression of being just a *tiny* bit insipid, because *actually* the girl was really terribly, *terribly* efficient — a complete blue-stocking in fact — she used to hold a *dreadfully* responsible executive post in London"!'

Valerie laughed. 'Dear Ruby! She probably still believes that old story that men are terrified of intelligent women.'

'And in nine cases out of ten, how right she is,' commented Copper gloomily.

'Perhaps. But at a guess I'd say that Nick is the tenth; if that's any comfort to you. As for Ruby, she hasn't a brain in her head.'

'She doesn't appear to need them! You have to admit that she has what it takes. And I suppose she *is* rather attractive in an overblown "Queen of Calcutta" way; what with that black hair and those enormous eyes — not to mention her vital statistics. What really defeats me is how she ever came to marry someone as depressingly ineffectual as poor Leonard. Whenever I see them together I catch myself wondering why on earth she did it? I suppose he must have had *something* that she wanted: though I can't imagine what! Leonard always reminds me of one of those agitated little sand-crabs that pop up out of holes at low tide, and nip back again when they see you looking. An apologetic sand-crab. He ought by rights to have married someone like Rosamund Purvis; they'd have made a marvellous pair — not an ounce of guts or sex-appeal between them. Then Ruby could have married Ronnie, which would have been far more suitable all round.'

'I expect,' said Valerie thoughtfully, 'that Ruby considered one person with sex-appeal in a family to be quite enough. She seems to be allergic to competition.'

'Unless she is promoting it,' observed Copper tartly. 'Anyway, I still don't see why she has to go after Nick when she already seems to have every other available male in the Islands lashed to her chariot wheels — with the solitary exception of your Charles.'

'She collects them,' explained Valerie, helping herself to more coffee, ' — the way some people collect stamps or matchboxes or Old Masters.'

'So it would appear,' said Copper crossly. 'And I can't think why her husband stands for it.'

'Oh, *Leonard*——! He doesn't count. And anyway, I don't suppose he notices it by this time. Or minds any more.'

'Perhaps not. But I should have thought Rosamund Purvis would. It can't be pleasant to see your husband dancing attendance on someone else's wife. Though if it comes to that, I suppose she's used to it, too. In fact her dear Ronnie and Leonard's Ruby are two of a kind; except that with Ronnie it's Old Mistresses! Oh dear — why am I being so bitchy and bad-tempered? What's the *matter* with us today, Val? We must have got out of the wrong sides of our beds this morning. I'm feeling all edgy and irritable. Not at all the right spirit for Christmas Eve. Or any other eve, for that matter! *"Peace on Earth, Goodwill toward Men"* — and Women, I suppose: which presumably includes Ruby Stock. When are we due to start off on this expedition?'

'Just as soon as you finish that mango. I told Charles we'd meet him at the Club not later than a quarter to ten, so we'd better get a move on.'

The Chief Commissioner, who had heard nothing of this conversation, folded up the single sheet of paper that had been engrossing his attention, returned it to its envelope and rose from the table: 'If you will excuse me,' he said, 'I have some work to do. By the way, Valerie, do you want the launch this evening?'

'No thank you, Dad. We'll catch the six-thirty ferry. We shall have to get back early if Copper and I are to change and then decorate the table and see that everything is set for the party.'

The Chief Commissioner groaned. 'Good lord, I'd forgotten that we had a dinner party here tonight. I take it this means that I shall not get to bed until after midnight? Oh well, I suppose one cannot avoid one's social obligations at Christmas time.'

He turned away from the table, and then paused and turned back: 'By the way, I forgot to mention that I have had a cable from the Captain to say that the *Maharaja* has been delayed and will not be in until late on Boxing Day.'

'Oh, *Dad*! Oh, no! — that means no Christmas mail.'

'I'm afraid so,' murmured the Chief Commissioner mildly. 'Well, it can't be helped.' He removed himself from the dining-room, Kioh, the Siamese cat, stalking sedately at his heels. And fifteen minutes later his stepdaughter and her guest left the house and walked down the short, steep, sunlit road to the Club, where Valerie's fiancé, Charles Corbet-Carr, senior subaltern of the detachment at present occupying the military barracks on Ross, was waiting for them.

Charles, a tall, fair young man of a type frequently described by female novelists as 'clean-limbed', possessed a pair of startlingly blue eyes and a sense of humour that was at present prompting him to model his conversation upon the only reading provided by the Calvert Library: an institution that would appear to have been last stocked during the frivolous twenties by a fervent admirer of such characters as Bertie Wooster, Berry and Co., and 'Bones of the River'.

Apart from this temporary aberration, Copper had no fault to find with him, and she grinned at him affectionately as he came quickly down the Club steps, kissed his betrothed, and spoke in an urgent undertone: 'There is a slug in our salad, honey. John Shilto, no less. He came over on the lumber boat this morning. I gather he's staying with old Hurridge for Christmas and wasn't expected until this evening, but as his host and everyone else is off on this picnic I more or less had to ask the old basket to come along too. You don't mind, do you? I couldn't very well leave him here *"alone and palely loitering"* for the entire day — Christmas Eve and all.'

'No, of course not, darling. I can bear it. But he'll have to sit in the back among all the bottles and—— Hello, Mr Shilto.' She went into the Club ahead of them to greet a heavily built hulk of a man who rose out of a wicker chair at her approach, and Copper, recognizing what she termed 'Val's Social-Poise Voice', realized that Valerie did not like Mr Shilto. Well, she needn't worry, thought Copper bleakly, I'm the one who will have to sit in the back of the car and make polite conversation with him . . .

Valerie was saying: 'It's been a long time since you were last over here. We never seem to see you at the Club these days. You won't have met Miss Randal . . . Copper, this is Mr Shilto. He owns one of the largest coconut plantations in the Islands. You must get him to take you over it one day.'

'I shall be delighted,' said Mr Shilto extending a damp, fleshy hand. 'I hope you mean to make a long stay, Miss Randal? What do you think of our Islands?'

Why *must* people always ask that question? thought Copper with a touch of exasperation: like reporters! Aloud she said: 'I think they are beautiful.'

Charles ordered lemon squashes which arrived in tall, frosted glasses, clinking with ice and borne by a slant-eyed Burmese 'boy' who wore a wide length of vivid cerise cloth wound closely about his body, a short white jacket and a headscarf of salmon pink into the folds of which he had tucked a white frangipani flower. But while the others talked, Copper sat silent; sipping her drink and gazing out of the Club windows at the sunlight sparkling and splintering against the glassy surface of the bay, and thinking that she had never before understood the true meaning of colour. Where the water was deepest it was ultramarine, shading to a pure, vivid emerald in the shallows, with bars of lilac and lavender betraying the hidden reefs. And across the bay Mount Harriet rose up from the ranks of coconut palms in a riot of green, every shade of it — rich, tangled, tropical — against a sky like a sapphire shield . . .

A ship's hooter sounded twice from the Ross jetty, and Charles said: 'There goes the five-minutes signal,' and reached for his sun-helmet. Copper gulped down the icy contents of her glass and stood up, and they went out into the hot, blinding sunlight across the baked lawns under the gold mohur trees and past the little summer-house that is built out from the sea wall of the Club, and whose floor covers half the deep, dim tank where the turtles intended (though seldom used) for Government House dinner parties swim languidly in the gloom, to the small wooden jetty where the little steam-ferry jerked at her moorings as though impatient to be off. But with her foot on the gangplank, Copper checked and turned to stare across the harbour, puzzled and uneasy.

Far out in the bay and moving towards the foot of Mount Harriet, three small white triangles showed bright against the shimmering blue. But it was not the sight of the distant boats that had arrested her attention and brought a sharp return of the strange disquiet that had possessed her earlier that morning.

'A lousy day for sailing,' commented Charles, following the direction of her gaze. 'They must be rowing — there isn't a breath of wind. Well, rather them than me! What's up, Coppy? Anything the matter? Got a tummy-ache or something?'

'The birds . . .' said Copper confusedly. 'Why have the birds all gone? There were none in the garden this morning. And – and look——! There are no gulls in the harbour. There have always been gulls before . . . and birds . . . Do you suppose——?'

She shivered suddenly, aware of a curious feeling of tension and foreboding in the hot stillness of the morning and the fact that there were no gulls in the harbour. Though why their absence should worry her she could not have explained. Did birds know things that humans did not? Had the airless, breathless day sent them some warning that grosser senses were unable to comprehend, and had they obeyed it and——

Valerie said from behind her: 'What are you dithering about, Coppy? Do get a move on, you're holding everybody up.'

Copper started as though she had been awakened from a dream, and uttering a hasty apology, ran up the gangplank and on to the ferry.

3

'*Caterpillars* as big as that? How interesting,' said Copper; managing with considerable difficulty to turn a yawn into a bright social smile and wishing that Mr Shilto would not talk so much. She wanted to give all her attention to the queer, wild, fascinating country that was flicking past them as the big car whirled along the winding thirty-mile road to Mount Harriet, but there had been no stopping Mr Shilto ...

Valerie was sitting beside Charles, who was driving, and Copper and Mr Shilto had been packed into the back of the car among a large assortment of bottles containing gin, beer, cider, gingerbeer, orange squash, soda water, and yet more beer.

The bottles clicked and clinked against each other as the car swung to the sharp bends in the road and John Shilto tried to find a more comfortable position for his feet.

He was a fat man who, had it not been for his height, would have appeared gross, and in spite of the burning suns of many years in the Islands his face had the unpleasantly pasty appearance of some plant that has grown in the dark. His narrow eyes, set between puffs of pale flesh, were too close together and markedly shrewd and calculating, while his conversation (which for the past ten miles had been concerned with the destructive activities of the coconut caterpillars) was as unprepossessing as his person.

Copper, who cared little for caterpillars, coconut or otherwise, once again allowed her attention to wander as the car swung into a green tunnel of shade. Giant trees arched overhead, their large, queerly shaped, exotic leaves blocking out every vestige of sunlight, while on either side of the road the dense tropical forest leant forward as though it were only waiting until the breeze of their passing had died away, before slipping forward to close over the road once more.

'Annihilating all that's made To a green thought in a green shade,' thought Copper: and wondered how Andrew Marvell could have known about tropical forests? Ferns and long-tangled creepers clung to the branches overhead or swung down in looping festoons, the tree trunks were garlanded with sprays of small white orchids, and here and there an occasional Red Bombway tree, its leaves flaming in an autumnal glory of scarlet, patched the shadowed forest with a festive fire and reminded her that this was Christmas Eve . . .

The car slid suddenly out of cool greenness into the bright sunlight of a small clearing that contained a tiny huddle of palm-thatched native huts, lime trees and banana palms. Here the forest had been forced to retreat a few reluctant paces and stood back — a towering wall of impenetrable shadow that seemed to stare down with hostility at that small, courageous attempt at civilization within its borders. A thin, flashing, emerald flight of parakeets flew screaming across the clearing, and from the edge of the forest a great slate-grey iguana — direct descendant of the dragon of fairy-tale — turned its scaly head as the car swung into a long, straight strip of roadway that ran through the star-patterned shadows of a coconut plantation.

It was at this point that Copper was abruptly awakened to a renewed sense of social shortcoming by the fact that Mr Shilto had at last fallen silent. She had the uncomfortable impression that he had stopped rather suddenly and in the middle of a sentence, and she turned hurriedly towards him with a bright smile which she hoped might be taken for intelligent interest. But Mr Shilto was no longer aware of her . . .

He was staring at the road ahead with an expression that was as plainly readable as it was startling. Rage, fury and fear were written large across his pallid features, and Copper had barely assimilated this surprising fact when he shrank into the extreme corner of the seat, pressing himself back until his head touched the hood, as though he were trying to keep out of sight.

I wonder who he thinks might see him and why it should matter if they did? thought Copper, intrigued by this peculiar manoeuvre. She said without thinking: 'Is this your plantation, Mr Shilto?' — and almost immediately remembered that Valerie had once pointed out the vast acres of palms beyond East Point as the Shilto plantation.

Mr Shilto did not reply and it was obvious that he did not even know that she had spoken. His eyes were warily intent on the white road and the straggling ranks of palm trees, and Copper saw him pass the tip of his tongue over his thick lips as though they were dry. She was about to repeat her question when her attention was suddenly diverted by a favourite and forcible oath from Charles: *'Godfrey-and-Daniels-blast-iron-furnaces-from-Hull!'* howled Charles passionately; and jerked the car to a sudden stop.

'Anything the matter? Or are you just tired of driving?' inquired Copper.

'Engine's red hot,' replied Charles briefly, climbing out into the road and stretching his long legs. He threw up the sides of the bonnet and gingerly unscrewed the radiator cap, and pushing back his sun-helmet drew the back of his hand across his damp forehead and swore fervently.

'What's up, darling?' asked Valerie, joining him in the road.

'Believe it or not,' said Charles bitterly, 'those sinkminded saboteurs at the garage have apparently omitted the trifling precaution of filling her up with water. *Mea culpa!* — I should have checked up. She's bone-dry, and we shall have to push the brute. Thank God we're on a bit of a slope here and Ferrers's bungalow is only about a quarter of a mile further on. We'll be able to get water there.'

Mr Shilto, who had not yet spoken, shot out of his seat at speed of light, and stumbling into the road stood in the harsh sunlight, his pasty face no longer pale but patched with a rich shade of puce, and spoke shrilly and with inexplicable violence: 'Oh no you don't! I'm damned if I'll——'

He checked abruptly and appeared to recollect himself. The angry flush faded from his cheeks and he licked his dry lips again and spoke as though speech had become an effort: 'I mean — what I mean is — well, surely it would be simpler to walk back and fetch water from that spring we passed a few moments ago?'

'Using what for a bucket?' demanded Charles reasonably. 'And anyway that was over a mile back, and it shouldn't take us more than five minutes to roll this wretched vehicle down to Ferrers's bungalow. There's no need for you to go in.'

Valerie laid a hand on John Shilto's arm and said in a placatory voice: 'Charles is right, you know. It's the only thing to do. We're late as it is, and everyone else has probably arrived at Harriet by now. They'll be madly thirsty in this heat, and we've got all the drinks!'

The big man's flickering gaze shifted from Valerie to Charles and back again, and he forced a smile: 'Yes – yes, of course. I had only thought that it might be easier if — I mean . . .' He appeared to be unable to finish the sentence and Charles turned away and released the brake.

After the first few yards the car rolled along with comparatively little propulsion, gathering momentum until it was hardly necessary to do more than guide it, and presently they reached a wooden bridge over a muddy tidal stream fringed with mangrove, where Charles brought it to a stop.

A small side road, barely more than a rough track, branched off to the left among the columns of the palm trunks and led to a long, low, island-built bungalow which presented a forlorn and dilapidated appearance, as though it were slowly rotting from neglect, and a slovenly Burmese servant came down the pathway from the house and spoke in the vernacular to Charles, who said: 'Here, Val — you understand a bit of this language, don't you? What's he saying?'

'He says that Ferrers isn't here,' translated Valerie.

'What's that?' Mr Shilto, who had been keeping to the far side of the car, came out of hiding and addressed the servant in his own tongue, and after a moment turned to his companions with an expression of sullen ill-temper and said brusquely: 'Yes, that's right. This is one of the house-boys. He says that the Stocks stopped off here half an hour ago and that they've taken Ferrers on with them to Mount Harriet. Well if that's the case, you can count me out of this damned picnic, and that's flat.' He sat down abruptly on the dusty running-board, and pushing back his hat, leaned against the car door with the air of one who does not intend to move for some considerable time.

Copper, a bewildered spectator of the scene, saw Charles's mouth tighten and realized that he was keeping his temper with difficulty. His voice, however, remained calm and unruffled: 'Please yourself, of course. But I don't know how you propose to get back. I doubt if there'll be anyone passing here in the right direction to give you a lift. And Val and Copper and I have to get on; and that right speedily.'

'Of course,' put in Valerie sweetly, 'you can always walk. It can't be more than ten or twelve miles back to Rungal, and you could probably get a lift in a lorry from there.'

Mr Shilto appeared to digest the truth of these statements with considerable distaste, and after a moment or two he rose reluctantly from the running-board and said he would go up to the house and write a chit that one of the servants could take to the nearest telephone, asking for a call to be put through for a taxi: observing in conclusion that if Ferrers had gone to Mount Harriet for the day, he could wait here until it arrived.

'Good idea,' approved Valerie. '*Do* hurry and get that water, Charles darling.'

The two men turned and went up the path to the bungalow, followed by the house-boy, and Copper said explosively: 'Well I'm——! What on earth was all that about, Val? Construe, please.'

'Guilty conscience, I imagine,' said Valerie with a short laugh. 'I don't suppose he ever uses this road himself, so he'd probably forgotten that our shortest way to Mount Harriet is through Ferrers's plantation. If he *had* thought of it, he'd never have agreed to come.'

'But *why*, for heaven's sake? Come on, Val — tell!'

'Possibly for fear that Ferrers might take a pot-shot at him as he passed? — he's quite capable of it! In fact he's publicly announced his intention of murdering John Shilto on more than one occasion.'

Valerie sat down on the low rail of the bridge and Copper perched alongside her. A sour smell of mangrove mud hung on the humid air and below them huge, gaudily coloured butterflies dipped and drifted lazily over the slimy banks and the ugly, crawling, tentacle-like roots of the mangrove trees that the receding tide from the mile-distant sea had left uncovered.

'It's a longish story,' began Valerie, tilting her hat over her freckled nose to shade her eyes from the glare, 'and no one really knows the true ins and outs of it. The local gossips have collected the odd fact here and there and averaged the rest, so I don't swear by all of it. Anyway, Ferrers Shilto — the owner of that decrepit shack over there — is John Shilto's first cousin and only living relative, and a good many years ago, John, who was doing fairly well with a coconut plantation out here, apparently needed some ready-money badly and couldn't lay his hands on it.

'He eventually hit on the brilliant scheme of persuading Ferrers, who was living in some peaceful spot like Ponder's End on the interest of a smallish capital, to come out to the Andamans and make a fortune. He wrote home to say that there was a super plantation going dirt cheap in the Islands, its owner having made his pile and wishing to retire, and that he would have bought it himself except for the fact that he was already making such a packet on his own that he had decided to be magnanimous and let dear cousin Ferrers in on the ground floor.'

Valerie paused to flick a fallen leaf at a big scarlet dragon-fly that was sunning itself on a mangrove root, and said thoughtfully: 'I suppose Ferrers must always have had a yearning for romance in spite of — or because of? — Ponder's End. And perhaps John Shilto knew it, and so knew that he'd fall for the plantation scheme. Anyway, to cut a long story short, Ferrers swallowed it hook, line and sinker and could hardly wait to hand over his little capital to cousin John and come rushing out East to become a millionaire planter and live on a coral island. That was about fifteen years ago and old history by now. But I gather that it didn't take Ferrers more than fifteen days — or possibly fifteen hours — to find out that he'd been badly swindled, or that the rich planter off whom he had bought the plantation was in reality dear cousin John himself.'

'But what's the matter with it?' demanded Copper. 'It looks all right to me.'

'Well, for a start, over half of it is water. The plantation was supposed to cover about five hundred acres, but when Ferrers got out here he discovered that at least half of that was taken up by a tidal lagoon. You can't see it from here. It's right over there, about half a mile from the house, and a thin strip of the plantation cuts it off from the sea except for a narrow channel; which makes it technically part of the property. As for the palms, they may look all right but they hardly ever bear, because of the creeks which run through the plantation. Coconuts won't thrive properly near mangrove mud, you see.'

'What a filthy trick!' exploded Copper, straightening up with an indignant jerk that almost precipitated her into the muddy waters flowing sluggishly eight feet below. 'Why, it's no better than stealing! I can't understand why any of you even *speak* to that man!'

'It's difficult not to, in a community as small as this one,' said Valerie with a wry smile. 'Yes, it was a pretty rotten bit of dirty dealing. But then some people seem to be born into the world to be swindled, and poor Ferrers is obviously a Grade-A example. No one but an utter mug would have paid over their entire capital without having a searching look at the goods first.'

'He obviously trusted his cousin not to let him down!' said Copper indignantly.

'I suppose he did,' agreed Valerie. 'Anyway, he wouldn't have known if it was a good proposition or not even if he had come out and looked at it. You don't stand much chance of becoming an expert on coconuts in Ponder's End, and I expect John wrote merrily of copra and oil and "raw nuts" and so on, and it all sounded most impressive. Anyway, Ferrers came. And he's been here ever since. You see, he didn't have the money to get back, and of course no one out here would ever buy the place off him. It's the original White Elephant.'

'And that was more than fifteen years ago,' said Copper slowly. 'Oh, poor Ferrers!'

'He makes just enough to live on,' said Valerie, 'and I dare say he would be as happy here as in some dull little semi-detached villa, if it wasn't for his rage at being done down. He never forgets it for half a second. He and John haven't spoken for years, and I imagine they don't catch sight of each other more than they can help.'

'A bit difficult in Port Blair, surely?' commented Copper: 'I should have thought that it was next to impossible to avoid anyone in a community consisting of a handful of people all living practically in each other's backyards. How do they manage it? Wear blinkers?'

'Well, it is a bit tricky,' confessed Valerie, 'but of course we all help. They don't go about much, and no one ever asks them to the same parties. When John is present you steer the conversation off coconuts, mangrove and Ferrers, and when Ferrers is around you do the same of coconuts, mangrove and John. Quite simple, really.'

'Haven't they ever met by mistake?'

'Only once, I believe. Some muddle over the Government House garden party, about two Chief Commissioners back. Everyone is asked to those sort of crushes of course, but usually neither Shilto, or only one, turns up. On this occasion they evidently both thought the other had refused, so unfortunately they both turned up. I believe there was a most impressive scene. Insults fairly ricocheted around, and in the end Ferrers had to be forcibly removed by half the guests while the other half sat on John's head. It gave Port Blair a topic of conversation for months afterwards, and is still occasionally resurrected by the "old guard" at deadly parties when everything else has given out.'

'It sounds very exhilarating,' observed Copper, 'I wish I'd seen it. But I still can't understand why, when they know what a swindler he is, anyone ever invites John Shilto to anything!'

'My poor dear! In these islands if you once started cutting people off your visiting-list because you disapprove of things they've done or said in what is humorously termed their "private lives", you'd have an extremely sticky time with your entertaining. Now I'm being cynical and catty, so I'd better stop.'

'Ferrers Shilto,' said Copper thoughtfully, 'was on the *Maharaja* with me when I came down from Calcutta. What was he doing in Calcutta if he never leaves the Islands?'

'Oh, you've met the little man, have you? I think he goes up about once a year to see to the business end of what few nuts he does manage to sell.'

'I didn't actually meet him,' said Copper. 'All I saw of him was the top of his pith hat when he came on board. But I saw his luggage. Very aged Gladstone bags. The Captain said he was seasick, but as the sea was like a mill-pond most of the way I was vaguely curious.'

'Probably the after-effects of a terrific yearly jag?' suggested

Valerie. 'For all we know, Ferrers may have hidden depths. What *do* you suppose has happened to Charles? He's had time to fetch enough water to fill a swimming-pool by now. Let's go and—— Oh, here he is. What *have* you been doing, darling?'

'Drinking Ferrers's beer,' said Charles, sloshing water out of a battered bucket into the radiator. 'And now that both I and this hellish vehicle have received adequate liquid treatment, I propose that we set forth on our travels again. Get in you two.'

'What about Mr Shilto?' inquired Valerie, complying. 'Has he sent for a taxi, or is he going to try the alternative solution, and hike?'

'God knows!' said Charles cheerfully. 'I did not pause to ask. Ferrers's back premises stink like a sewer, so I was not disposed to linger. I've no idea what the little man is using to manure his plantation — decayed octopi and sea-slug, at a guess. The pong is fearsome. John Shilto went out to investigate, and I left him to it. It will do him no harm to be asphyxiated. Let's go——'

He pressed the self-starter and released the brake; and as he did so John Shilto came rapidly down the path between the palm trees, and breaking into a run, reached the car just as it began to move. His face was curiously flushed and he seemed to be labouring under the stress of some powerful emotion, for his pale eyes glittered with ill-suppressed excitement and his breathing was hurried and uneven.

He jerked open the rear door of the car and tumbled in beside Copper, and having settled himself back and slammed the door, said breathlessly: 'I've changed my mind. I think after all that I ought to come with you.'

He wiped the sweat off his face, and becoming aware that his three companions were staring at him with unconcealed astonishment, forced a rattle of singularly mirthless laughter.

'I – I have been thinking,' he said. 'About Ferrers, you know. It is really high time that we buried the hatchet — high time! The — ah, misunderstanding between us may have been partly my fault, and if so it is only right that I should try and make amends. We must shake hands and let bygones be bygones. He is my only relative — first cousins and all that. Blood is thicker than water and it is not right that—— Yes, yes, we must certainly see if we cannot make a fresh start . . . shake hands . . . After all, we must not forget that today is Christmas Eve, and *"The Better the Day, the Better the Deed"* — eh?'

Mr Shilto paused expectantly as though for comment.

'Oh — er — quite,' said Charles inadequately.

He released the clutch with unintentional abruptness, and the car shot forward down the sun-dappled road that leads to Mount Harriet.

4

Mount Harriet, the highest point in the Islands, was the hot-weather resort of the officials from Aberdeen and Ross, and the Christmas Eve picnic was an annual affair that took place in the grounds of the deserted summer-time Government House that crowned the flat-topped peak.

Charles brought the car to a standstill on the weed-grown drive, and Ronnie Purvis, the Forest Officer, a slimly built man in a spotless white yachting-suit, pulled open the door and greeted Copper with practised charm: 'At last, my lovely one! I'd begun to think you weren't coming and that my day was going to be ruined. But you're certainly worth waiting for. You look good enough to eat, and I don't know how you do it! Come and hold my hand . . .'

Copper descended from the car and said firmly: 'I don't feel like holding anyone's hand in this heat thank you, Ronnie. All that I'm interested in at the moment is a cold drink. And the colder, the better! Hullo, Amabel — did you have a good trip over?'

'No,' replied the damsel addressed: 'There wasn't any wind, so George had to row and he got blisters. They'll probably go septic. It just goes to show, doesn't it?'

Miss Amabel Withers, daughter of the Port Officer, was a plump, stolid maiden with a quite remarkable bent for pessimism, and her concluding remark, which might have been taken to mean anything from a comment on the weather to a reflection on the uncertainty of human existence, was a favourite observation that did not require an answer.

Copper turned to grin at the blistered George, a freckle-faced subaltern who was unaccountably enamoured of young Miss Withers, and said: 'Bad luck, George. Still, it may not actually come to gangrene, and if it should, we can always amputate. I can't think why any of you were mad enough to take out a boat on a day when there isn't . . .'

She broke off, leaving the sentence unfinished, for at that moment a tall man who had been lying in a patch of shade at the far side of the lawn stood up and lifted a hand in greeting and, as always at the sight of Nick Tarrent, Copper's heart gave a little lurch. Abandoning her sentence, together with George Beamish and the importunate Mr Purvis, she went straight across the lawn to him. And it was not until she was within a yard of him that she realized that he was not alone, or that a long, green wicker chair stood in the same patch of shadow, and in it, stretched at full length and wearing a scarlet linen dress that exactly matched her lipstick and the varnish on her long, pointed nails, languorous and seductive as a harem favourite, lay Ruby Stock . . .

Mrs Leonard Stock was a striking-looking woman of what is usually termed 'uncertain age', who might well have been accounted a beauty had her face not been spoiled for that accolade by an expression of discontent that had been worn for so long that it had eventually become an integral part of her features. But few critics would have found fault with her admirable figure and shining, blue-black hair, her great pansy-brown eyes and the smooth golden texture of her sun-browned skin. As the beautiful daughter of a subordinate in India's Post and Telegraphs Department, Ruby had been born and brought up in that country, and after completing her education at a convent school in the south of India, become the reigning belle among her set in Midnapore. But from the first, she had been both ambitious and consumed by envy of all those of a higher social status than herself, and that envy drove her like a spur until it became the mainspring of her being. Some day, she vowed, she would be the equal of any of the supercilious wives of high officials to whose dinner parties and lunches she was not invited. And with this end in view she had married Leonard Stock, son of an English country parson, who occupied a minor post in the Indian Civil Service.

Leonard was not earning anything approaching the pay that several other suitors of the dashing Ruby De Castres could offer, but for all that he was considered among her set to be a good match. First and foremost because he was what Anglo-India refers to, snobbishly, as a 'Sahib', and secondly, because rumour had it that although his present position in the Civil Service was a modest one, he would go far.

Rumour, however, as is frequently the case, had been misinformed. Leonard Stock was a pleasant enough little man, amiable, friendly, and unassuming, but totally incapable of firmness or decision — as Ruby De Castres, now Ruby Stock, was to discover within a few brief months of her marriage. Facing the fact that her husband would never rise to any heights if he remained in Midnapore, she had urged him to accept a position in the administration of the Andamans when that opportunity had offered. And so the Stocks had come to the Islands, and at first all had been more than well with them.

Here no echo of her past life had penetrated, and Ruby manufactured, with that facility of invention and superfluous falsehood that is so frequently the hallmark of her type, a father who was a retired Lieutenant-Colonel, an ancestral estate in Ireland, and a Spanish great-grandmother. She entertained lavishly, and to her Leonard's anxious remonstrances over their steadily mounting bills, merely retorted that it was necessary for them to keep up their position if he was ever to get on in the world. And when the four years' tenure of his post in the Islands was up, she persuaded him to apply for an extension.

The move was a fatal one, and he knew it. But he was too weak to resist, for Ruby answered his half-hearted protests with tears and temper, and eventually he gave in. With the result that his post in India, to which he could have returned, was filled. Other men moved up to close the gap, and now he must either continue to ask for and obtain extensions, or find himself out of a job. That had been sixteen years ago; and the Stocks were still in the Islands . . .

Beautiful, ambitious Ruby, the erstwhile belle of Midnapore, was now a soured and embittered woman who clung to her fading charms with despairing tenacity as being her only defence against the dragging monotony of her existence. And since women were few in the Islands, there had always been some man, often several, tied to her apron-strings. The pursuance of 'affairs' had become the sole interest of her shallow, childless life, and as a result of this she looked upon every other woman in the light of a possible rival.

Until the arrival of Valerie, Mrs Stock had possessed no serious competitor in Port Blair, and she had resented the girl's youth and distinction with an acid inward bitterness and an outward display of gushing friendliness. But Valerie had not proved the rival she had feared, for her instant annexation by Charles Corbet-Carr had made her impervious to the attentions of all other men. Copper Randal, however, posed a definite threat.

Ruby had decided on sight to add Nick to the 'chain-gang', as Port Blair was wont to refer, ribaldly, to Mrs Stock's admirers. But from the first it was painfully apparent that the option, if any, on Nick Tarrent's affections was held by that newly arrived tow-headed chit from Government House. Wherefore Mrs Stock's greeting of the aforementioned chit was characteristic——

'What on earth kept you, darling?' (Ruby had read somewhere that people in fashionable social circles constantly referred to each other as 'darling'.) 'No — don't tell me, I can guess. You had a puncture! Such a romantic road, isn't it? I expect John Shilto is completely *épris* by now! Quite a catch my dear, I assure you. Dear me, how useful punctures are! I wonder how people did without them before there were cars?'

The tinkling laugh that accompanied this pleasantry was not untinged with malice, and Copper's smoke-blue eyes widened into an expression of child-like innocence: 'Well, of course you'd know, Mrs Stock,' she countered sweetly.

'*Game, set and match*, I think!' murmured Nick to his immortal soul. Aloud he said briskly: 'Hullo, Copper. You're abominably late. I gather you brought the drinks with you — and about time too! I could do with one. And I'm sure Ruby could too. Let's go and collect them.' He took Copper firmly by the arm and walked her rapidly away across the lawn before Mrs Stock had time to reply.

'Oh dear, that was *beastly* of me,' said Copper remorsefully. 'But she did ask for it! All the same, we shouldn't have just walked off and left her.'

'Thanks,' said Nick grimly, 'but I had no desire to act as referee at a cat-fight. You are too quick on the uptake for one so young. It shocks me. It also appeared to shock poor Ruby considerably. Shall I mix you a gin sling, or would you rather have shandy?'

'Shandy, please. The box with all the gingerbeer and the rest of the soft drinks is still in the car, I think.'

'Here it is,' said Leonard Stock, appearing beside them with a bottle-filled packing-case. 'Where shall I put it? Good-morning, Miss Randal.'

'Dump it somewhere in the shade,' advised Nick. 'Here, let me help you.'

'Don't bother, I can manage.' Mr Stock deposited his burden in the shadow of a group of flame trees and hunted through the bottles for one containing gingerbeer: 'Shandy, I think you said. We might make a large jug of it. I could do with some myself. It really has been a very trying morning. Quite exceptionally airless. I had hoped that there would be a breeze up here; one can usually count on it. But there does not seem to be a breath of wind anywhere today.' He fumbled in his pockets for a handkerchief, and having wiped the palms of his hands, dabbed ineffectually at the sweat that trickled down his face and neck.

'Hullo, Leonard,' said Valerie, joining them. 'You're looking very hot and bothered. And so you should be! — what's all this we hear about you bringing Ferrers Shilto along to join the glad throng?'

Mr Stock threw a hunted look over his shoulder and said in an agitated undertone: 'Yes, I – I'm afraid we did. But how *were* we to know? You see, the padre and Mrs Dobbie brought us in their car, and as they wanted to ask Ferrers about bringing some bedding — he's staying with them for Christmas you know — we stopped at his bungalow, and . . . Well, it seemed only neighbourly to ask him to come on with us to the picnic, for of course we had no notion that John would be here. *None!* It really is *most* awkward.'

'You're telling us!' said Charles, accepting a glass of Mr Stock's shandy. 'In fact, here we go now. Stand by for fireworks! The cousins Shilto, Copper. Grand reunion scene in three sharp explosions. That's Ferrers in the beachcomber get-up: the skinny little shrimp with his back to us and seething fury in every line of it.'

The phrase was descriptive, for there was a tense and quivering animosity about the wizened figure in the stained and crumpled suit of drill who faced John Shilto's confident advance, and a sudden silence descended upon the company as the older man came to a stop before his cousin and held out a large, fleshy hand. Perhaps because of it, his voice when he spoke sounded unnaturally loud and forced: 'Well, well! This is a surprise!' said Mr Shilto with spurious heartiness. 'I must admit that I didn't bargain on running into you here, old man. But as we have met, what about taking this opportunity to call bygones bygones? Eh?'

His laugh rang as loud and forced as his voice, but it appeared that Ferrers Shilto was either short-sighted or else that he did not intend to take his cousin's proffered hand, for he did not move. The silence deepened and drew out until it seemed to acquire a solid entity of its own, and once again John Shilto's heavy features became mottled by a dark, ugly tide of colour. He dropped his hand but managed, with a palpable effort, to retain the semblance of a smile: 'Oh, come on, old man, be a sport! After all, it's Christmas, you know. *"Peace and Goodwill".*'

Ferrers Shilto laughed — a shrill, cackling, almost hysterical sound — and said, astonishingly: 'So you've found out, have you? I wonder how you managed it? Well a hell of a lot of good may it do you!'

The words, meaningless as they appeared to the openly listening bystanders, evidently possessed a meaning for John Shilto. And afterwards Copper was to remember the way in which both colour and smile had been wiped off his face as though with a sponge, leaving it pasty white and raw with rage. To remember, too, the hot, bright sunlight and the dappled shadows, the silent group of people, and the strange, fleeting look that she had surprised on one other face . . .

John Shilto put up a fumbling and uncertain hand and tugged at his collar as though it were too tight for him, then turning abruptly, he walked away across the lawn with a curious stumbling tread.

Hurried and somewhat guilty conversation broke out again as the spectators of the recent drama awoke to a belated sense of social shortcomings. But as Ferrers Shilto turned on his heel, Valerie heard Copper draw in her breath in a short hard gasp and saw her stiffen as though the sight of the little man's face had given her a violent shock. 'What's the matter, Coppy?' she asked sharply: 'You look as if you'd seen a ghost.'

'I believe I have,' said Copper huskily.

She forced an uncertain laugh and said in a voice that was not entirely under control: 'Don't look so alarmed, Val. I'm not mental. At least I don't think I am. But — that nightmare I had. I know it sounds fantastic, but the man I saw in it was Ferrers Shilto!'

A period of deep, warm, post-luncheon peace had descended upon Mount Harriet.

Those members of the picnic party who had failed to secure one of the coveted beds in the house had disposed themselves for slumber on rugs and cushions in various shady corners of the garden, and Valerie, Copper, Charles and Nick, beaten by a short head in the race for the comforting though restricted shade of the fig trees on the eastern edge of the lawn, had retired with all the rugs they could muster to the lorry.

This capacious and utilitarian vehicle, the property of the Public Works Department, was ordinarily employed in carrying loads of gravel or stone for road repairs, but had on this occasion been borrowed to transport half the party from Hopetown jetty to Mount Harriet. Traces of its workaday occupation still lingered between the boards and littered the corners, but failed to discommode the four who, climbing in over the tail-board, spread rugs and cushions upon the dusty floor and settled down to a peaceful afternoon's siesta.

'This is bliss,' said Charles drowsily. 'Wake me up in time for a late-ish tea, someone. And let us pray that no hearty friends get bitten with the idea of going down to bathe and drive off with us, like last time!' He settled himself comfortably on his back on the floorboards and closed his eyes: only to open them a moment later as footsteps crunched the gravel outside and some unseen person approached the lorry and, pausing beside it, laid a hand on the edge of the tail-board.

Copper opened her mouth to speak, but stopped at a grimace from Charles. *'Ronnie!'* mouthed Charles silently; and indicated by dumb show that if Mr Purvis discovered their occupation of the vehicle he would undoubtedly add himself to their party. Whereupon the four lay quiet and made a creditable attempt to cease breathing, and after a moment or two the hand was withdrawn and the footsteps moved away in the direction of the house.

'Saved!' sighed Charles. 'That tedious Romeo would have pressed in and talked the entire afternoon.'

'It wasn't Ronnie,' announced Copper, peering through a crack in the side of the lorry. 'It was the Shilto cousin — Ferrers.'

'That's odd,' said Valerie. 'I thought it was Ronnie, too. I wonder why? What do you suppose Ferrers is doing wandering around loose? I'd rather hoped that after the Big Scene the padre would put a leash on him. Charles, do you suppose——?'

'No, I don't!' said Charles firmly. 'I see no evil, I hear no evil and I speak no evil. Not at the moment, anyway. I am suffering from post-prandial torpor and I intend to slumber. So pipe down, light-of-my-life, and let us have not only peace but quiet.'

The lorry had been parked in the shade of the house, and presently a faint, unexpectedly cold breeze stole across the garden, cooling the clogging warmth of the afternoon to a more pleasant temperature. A drowsy silence fell, in which Charles snored gently and a wandering bluebottle investigated Nick's unconscious chin . . .

Afterwards not one of them could be quite certain at what point they had awakened. But awakened they were, all four of them. And by the time they had arrived at full consciousness they had overheard sufficient to make them realize that this was no time to rise and disclose themselves. Therefore they lay still, concealed by the high wooden sides of the lorry, while a scant yard away the cousins Shilto exchanged words of an uncousinly nature.

Piecing together, in the light of after-events, what they could remember of that conversation, it appeared that John Shilto had offered to buy back his cousin's plantation at more than twice the price he had originally received for it; giving, as a reason for this astounding gesture, his desire to put an end to the old quarrel between them. This offer Ferrers was in the process of rejecting with every indication of scorn and loathing when the occupants of the lorry awoke to the fact that they were involuntarily eavesdropping on a private conversation.

' — and if,' announced Ferrers Shilto, concluding a speech generously interlarded with expressions of a distressingly personal and opprobrious character, 'you imagine for one minute that I am going to be had for a mug twice over by a crook like you, you can think again! You could offer me *forty* times the sum you swindled out of me for that stinking, rat-ridden, pestilential plantation, and I wouldn't take it! And what's more I shall make my will tomorrow — just to be sure that you never get your hands on it! No, my beloved cousin, this is where I get my own back at last. That plantation is mine. Every single, slimy acre of it, wet or dry. And if you so much as set foot on it, I'll have my servants thrash you off it!'

His voice rose until it cracked hysterically, and the elder Shilto, with one parting vitriolic epithet, turned on his heel and retired from the field of battle.

Presently Ferrers too departed, and Charles, having made a cautious survey, announced that the coast was clear. 'An exhilarating interlude, wasn't it? Teeming with drama, passion, human interest and mystery. The works! I enjoyed it immensely. What sort of dirty work do you suppose our John is up to now? Or have we witnessed a miracle and is he a genuine victim of remorse and the Christmas spirit? A sort of latter-day Scrooge? Somehow, I doubt it.'

'What about *"speaking no evil"* now?' inquired Valerie.

'Ah, but that was when I was feeling somnolent and well fed. As I am now no longer either, I am only too willing to believe the worst of everyone. So let us dismiss the case of Shilto versus

Shilto and concentrate instead on getting some tea before my disposition deteriorates still further. Hand me down those rugs, my love.'

They walked round the side of the house, and passing under the creeper-clad porch, crossed to the far end of the lawn to where the remainder of the party were grouped about a well-covered tablecloth spread in the shade of the frangipani trees.

'Come and talk to me for a change, Copper,' invited Ronnie Purvis. 'There's room for a small one this end. Move over, Hurridge, and let us grab this damsel off the Navy. Have some sandwiches: the damp ones are cucumber and the mangled and messy ones are jam.'

'Cucumber, please,' decided Copper, inserting her slim person between the nattily yachting-suited figure of Ronnie Purvis and the large, khaki-clad bulk of Mr Albert Hurridge, the Deputy Commissioner. She was guiltily aware that her preoccupation with Nick Tarrent had had the effect of making her completely uninterested in every other person on the Islands with the exception of Valerie and Charles, and seized now with a temporary fit of remorse, she listened patiently to the Deputy Commissioner's incredibly dull and anecdotal conversation, bore equally patiently with the stereotyped flirtatiousness of that self-satisfied lady-killer Mr Ronald Purvis, and did her best, though without much success, to include his silent, faded wife in the conversation.

Ronnie Purvis was a member of that well-known genus, the compulsive philanderer, who imagines that his job in life is to brighten it for every woman he meets. Inordinately vain, he was possessed of a vain man's cheap attraction, and no one had ever quite understood how he had come to marry poor, dull, faded Rosamund Purvis. For if Mrs Purvis had ever had any claims to prettiness, the heat and fevers of the tropics had shrivelled them away long ago, and at thirty she succeeded in looking a good ten years older than her husband's bronzed and athletic thirty-six.

People were apt to refer to Mr Purvis as 'poor, dear Ronnie', and to add that it was a tragedy that he should be tied to that limp, uninteresting woman. Few would have believed the truth: that Rosamund Purvis had been a Bachelor of Arts at twenty-two, and one of the most brilliant students of her year at Oxford. A dazzling future was prophesied for her; and then, a year later, she had met Ronald Purvis, home on leave from India, fallen helplessly in love with him, and married him. That had been seven years ago, and the loneliness of forest camps, the damp, sticky, cloying heat of the Andamans, the birth and death of two successive children, and her husband's eternal philandering, had combined to turn the once-pretty and intelligent woman into the colourless nonentity that Port Blair knew as 'Poor, dear Ronnie's dreary wife'.

Meanwhile poor, dear Ronnie continued to flirt desperately with any and every girl he met, and to explain to them in turn, in sad, brave tones, how little his wife understood him — a phrase only too often in use, and which can generally be taken to mean that, on the contrary, she understands him only too well. He also continued, at thirty-six, to look as young as he had at twenty-five, and to conduct those of his flirtations which progressed into 'affairs', with unblushing openness in his wife's house.

'I can't think why on earth she stands it,' Charles had once said to Valerie: 'If I was in that woman's shoes, I'd clear out and leave him to his messy little affairs. She's got no guts.'

'Perhaps she's in love with him?' suggested Valerie.

'Rats!' retorted Charles inelegantly.

But as it happened, Valerie had been right. Rosamund Purvis despised her husband and bitterly resented his infidelities. But she still loved him, and so she stayed with him: tired, disillusioned, middle-aged at thirty, knowing herself an object of pity and contempt to the settlement . . .

Ronnie, however, was not having his customary success at the present moment. Valerie he had failed to impress from the first, and her subsequent engagement to Charles Corbet-Carr had effectually put a stop to any romantic adventures he may have anticipated in that direction. In the position of Public Boyfriend Number One, Mr Purvis had worked systematically through the present scanty female population of Ross and Aberdeen, and was suffering from the pangs of acute boredom at the time the *Maharaja* had docked at Chatham, bearing on board Miss Caroline Randal.

One look at the new importation and Ronnie decided that the gods had indeed been kind to him, and calling up all his well-worn stock-in-trade of charm, boyishness, impudence and romantic technique had confidently advanced to conquer.

But alas for high hopes! H.M.S. *Sapphire* and Lieutenant Nicholas Tarrent had between them effectively ruined the merry season of Christmas as far as Mr Purvis was concerned. And since he was not accustomed to competition, the spectacle of Nick Tarrent cheerfully monopolizing the new importation had done much toward souring his otherwise cheerful disposition: though little towards lowering his self-esteem, and Copper found herself parrying his ardent advances throughout the meal, while one half of her mind was engaged in actively disliking Ruby Stock and wondering what she could be saying to Nick that necessitated her draping herself across one of his shoulders?

5

'. . . Jarawas,' said Mr Hurridge.

'I beg your pardon?' said Copper, suddenly realizing that the Deputy Commissioner was once again in full spate.

'Jarawas,' repeated Mr Hurridge impressively. 'I do not think you fully realize the fact that we are all actually sitting in Jarawa country at this very moment.'

He observed Copper's look of blank incomprehension and said in a slightly injured tone: 'I do not believe you have been listening to one word that I have said, Miss Randal.'

'I'm sorry,' apologized Copper. 'I'm afraid I was thinking of something else. What were you saying?'

'I was speaking of the Jarawas,' said Mr Hurridge with dignity. 'They are a tribe of aborigines that inhabit parts of these islands.'

'I thought they were called Andamanese,' said Copper brightly.

'No, no. The Jarawas are entirely distinct from the Andamanese: they are quite untameable little people who live in the forests, and no one has ever managed to learn their language or become friendly with them. They use bows and arrows and shoot on sight, and they are as wild today as they were when Marco Polo first wrote of the Islands.'

Mr Hurridge, now well away, launched into a long and pompous account of raids made on outlying settlements and lonely forest outposts by the savage little men, and of the impossibility of successful expeditions against them owing to the denseness of the wild jungle in which they lived. Mount Harriet itself, said Mr Hurridge, was well inside Jarawa country, and a dozen paces beyond the far edge of that smooth lawn would take one into the Jarawa jungles——

'We could all be murdered at any minute,' said Amabel Withers with automatic pessimism: 'It just goes to show, doesn't it?'

'Don't let 'em scare you, Copper,' cut in Ronnie Purvis. 'The Jarawas have hardly ever been known to come near this end of the island. And anyway they only kill for food or iron, or water in dry years; never for fun.'

'If that's supposed to cheer me up,' said Copper with a shiver, 'it doesn't. I thought this place was supposed to be nice and peaceful; no wild animals, not many snakes, and nice friendly Andamanese. Now I shall have heart failure whenever I hear a twig snap. Come and hold my hand, Mr Norton: I'm going to peer over the hedge at this Jarawa country, and I feel I should like some police protection.'

The tea party broke up and wandered across the lawn, and presently Valerie had taken Copper into the house and shown her a sight that was to remain clear in her memory for the rest of her life. They had mounted the staircase side by side and turned into a wide, glassed-in verandah that ran round three sides of the top storey of the house, where Valerie had pushed open a window and said, *'There——!'* And Copper had found herself gazing down at what must surely be one of the loveliest views in the world.

Far below her the Islands lay scattered over a glassy sea that was so still and smooth and shining that the wandering currents showed like paper streamers straggling across a ballroom floor after a carnival night when the dancing is over and the dancers have gone. The air had cooled with the approach of evening and the Islands were no longer veiled by a shimmering heat-haze, but clear-cut and colourful: lilac and lavender, blue and green and gold in the tropic evening——

'Keats must have dreamed of this view,' said Copper. 'These

are his *"magic casements, opening on the foam—Of perilous seas, in faery lands forlorn".'*

'Y–es,' agreed Valerie hesitantly. 'But there are times when I wonder if the magic is white or black?'

'Why do you say that?' asked Copper curiously.

'I don't know. Only — well, sometimes there is a queer sort of feeling about the Islands. Oh, not in the way you meant last night. But – but they seem so out of this world. As though civilization and the twentieth century had only made a little scratch on the surface, and underneath they were still strange and . . . And *"forlorn"* and *"perilous"*, I suppose! I believe that if one lived here for too long they might do odd things to one. To one's character, I mean. Change it, and make it different and—— Oh, I can't explain. I'm probably talking nonsense. You know, it's odd, but all day I've had a queer feeling; rather as though I were an overwound watch-spring wondering what happens when the breaking-point is reached? A loud, twanging noise perhaps, and all my nice, orderly, civilized little ideas flying in every direction in a gloriously crude and uninhibited manner. Now I *am* talking nonsense!'

'No,' said Copper slowly. 'I think I know what you mean. Everyone seems to be feeling a bit edgy today. I know I am! I was even driven to exchanging a catty scratch with La Stock. And then there were the Shiltos snarling at each other, and even Mrs Purvis got quite crisp when Amabel Withers started on yet another of those gloomy anecdotes about local characters who have been drowned or eaten by sharks or caught by an octopus.'

'I expect it's the heat,' said Valerie with a sigh. 'We haven't had any rain for days. A really good shower, and we shall all return to normal — tempers included. *Don't do that, Coppy!* You'll stain your arms!'

Copper, who had leant far out over the window-ledge, drew back sharply. 'Don't do what? Heavens above! — what on earth is it?'

'Sorry,' apologized Valerie. 'I should have warned you. It's some red stuff they stain all the outside woodwork with. We've even got it all over our house on Ross. I believe it's earth-oil, or something of the sort. It's an appalling nuisance because it comes off on everything.'

'It does indeed!' commented Copper acidly, scrubbing her vividly coloured elbows with an inadequate handkerchief.

'No one warned me either,' said Valerie with a grin, 'and I well remember an awful occasion when ... Good grief! *Look over there!* Hi! — Hamish!' She leant out of the window and yelled down to Captain Rattigan, the earnest and ginger-headed officer in command of the military detachment on Ross who was standing on the drive below: '*Hamish!* — there's a hell of a storm coming up! You sailing people had better get going pretty quickly if you don't want to get caught in it. *Hurry!*'

Copper turned and saw, far to the south-east, a low band of tawny-coloured darkness that lay along the horizon. It had a hard black edge to it, as straight as though it had been drawn with a ruler, and above it an ugly, ochrous stain was spreading upwards into the evening sky.

'But it's *miles* away,' she protested. 'It could miss us altogether. Or fizzle out before it gets here.'

'Perhaps,' said Valerie shortly: 'But I don't like the look of it at all. Come on, we'd better go down.' She turned and ran for the garden, where a discussion was already in progress as to who should sail home and who go by car.

George Beamish and Amabel Withers, Ted Norton of the police and Surgeon-Lieutenant Dan Harcourt of H.M.S. *Sapphire* having elected to return by road, Hamish was busy collecting substitute yachtsmen, and Copper arrived in excellent time to see Mrs Stock take playful possession of Nick Tarrent's arm and demand to be taken back with him in Dan Harcourt's place: 'And don't try and put me off, Nick!' she announced gaily, smiling up into his eyes and wagging a roguish and admonitory finger.

'I'm not a bit afraid of storms and I just *adore* sailing! And you needn't pretend that you are taking anyone else, because Dan has only this minute decided to drive back. Haven't you, Dan?'

'Dear Ruby!' murmured Charles gently.

Hamish's voice made itself plaintively audible above the general babel: 'Then that's fixed, is it? Stock, and I are taking one boat, Ronnie and Rosamund and Ferrers another, and Tarrent and Ruby and Shilto will take the third. All right?'

'Cautious chap, Nick,' commented Charles: 'Bang goes Ruby's tête-à-tête!'

Copper laughed and unaccountably felt her heart grow several degrees lighter. She would not have admitted even to herself quite how apprehensive she was becoming of Mrs Stock's determined and mature attractions. The eight yachtsmen packed themselves into the lorry and departed, while the remainder of the party set about collecting rugs and picnic-baskets in a leisurely manner. They would take less time to return by road than those who were sailing back across the bay, and since the majority of them intended to catch the six-thirty ferry from Aberdeen to Ross they could allow themselves another half hour on Harriet.

The conversation turned naturally to Home — for this was Christmas Eve and the acute nostalgia of the Exile for familiar scenes and the years that have been and will return no more, seized achingly on the little group under the frangipani trees. Memories of other Christmases. Of holly and mistletoe, mince pies and carol singers. Even Copper was conscious of a brief pang of homesickness, and for a fleeting moment Nick, Valerie and Charles, the green islands and the enchanted sea grew dim and unreal, and she was a child again, climbing on to a nursery chair to hang gay, glass balls on a Christmas tree . . .

She shook herself as though to be rid of the memory, and having helped to stow the last of the rugs in the cars, strolled to the far edge of the lawn where the breeze which had strengthened at the approach of sunset blew her ash-blond hair into a tangled halo about her head. Below and to her left on the quiet sea off North Bay a tiny white sailing-boat was moving sluggishly towards Ross. It was too far out to be one belonging to the Mount Harriet party, and Copper imagined it must be Valerie's father returning from a peaceful and private afternoon's sailing. She watched it idly for a few moments, and then as her eyes strayed beyond it, stiffened suddenly to alarmed attention.

They heard her calling from the far side of the pepper trees, but the breeze took the words away, blurring them to unintelligible sounds. 'What do you suppose she wants?' inquired Valerie: 'Charles darling, do have a good look round and see that we haven't left anything.'

Copper reappeared suddenly, running across the lawn, and said breathlessly: 'Come and look at this!' She dragged Valerie at a run to the far side of the garden, the others following more slowly: 'Look!' said Copper, still agitated. They looked in silence; gazing in the direction of her pointing finger to where H.M.S. *Sapphire*, no longer at her moorings, steamed slowly out of the harbour, her bows set to the open sea. 'They've gone!' said Copper blankly.

'No, he hasn't,' said Valerie, correctly translating the thought: 'There hasn't been nearly time for the dinghies to do more than get clear of Hopetown jetty. That is, if they've even started yet, which I doubt — what with Ruby insisting on helping to get the sail up!'

Copper's strained attitude relaxed and she laughed a little unsteadily as Charles said: 'Let's ask Dan,' and turned about to hail Dan Harcourt, who was strolling towards them across the lawn. 'Come and take a last, lingering look at your departing home, Doc. Were you by any chance aware that your mess-mates were proposing to light out and leave you marooned?'

Dan Harcourt glanced along Valerie's pointing finger and his jaw dropped. 'Great Scott! Why — what on earth——?'

'We don't know,' said Copper. 'Don't you know anything about it either?'

'No. There must be something up: someone staging a riot in some insalubrious coastal spot, and the Navy ordered to show the flag for moral effect.'

He grinned suddenly and largely: 'I say, what a bit of luck for me getting left behind! Sickening for all the other poor types having to spend Christmas striking warlike attitudes. I bet they're cursing! Nick will have missed it too: pretty lucky for both of——' The sentence broke off in a little shiver that made his teeth chatter.

Copper swung round sharply and he laughed and said: 'Sorry. Goose walked over my grave. Hadn't we better get going if we're going to catch the ferry?'

They piled into the three cars and left Mount Harriet behind them. And at no point during the drive down the steep hill road did one of them think to look back to where, behind them, that ominous belt of tawny darkness grew and broadened with uncanny swiftness, blotting out the brightness of the quiet evening sky.

Barely had the last car passed through the gates and rounded the first bend of the jungle road when the new-found silence of the deserted house was again disturbed. This time by the bell in the small telephone box in the corner of the verandah by the dining-room door. The phone rang shrilly, its urgent metallic cry echoing eerily through the silent house.

It rang for perhaps five minutes, and then ceased. And silence flowed back and closed over Mount Harriet like a quiet cloud.

6

'It's getting very dark,' said Copper. 'Are we going to miss the ferry?'

Valerie leant forward and peered at the dashboard clock. 'No, we're all right. We've got nearly half an hour yet and it shouldn't take us more than twenty minutes from here.'

'Um,' said Copper dubiously. 'I've never yet been on a picnic with you and Charles when we haven't missed the ferry.'

Charles said: *'Pessimist!'* but applied his foot with more force to the accelerator and took the next bend at fifty.

'Why is everything such a queer yellow colour?' persisted Copper restlessly. 'You ought to switch on the headlights, Charles. You'll run off the road in a minute — it squiggles so.'

'Look, who's driving this car?' demanded Charles. 'You or me?'

Copper apologized hastily and leant out to look back at the sky between the double wall of trees behind them. They heard her catch her breath in a harsh gasp, and Dan Harcourt, who was returning with them in place of John Shilto, leant out in turn and whistled expressively. 'Great Caesar's Ghost——! Here, step on it, Charles, or inside another five minutes we're going to be overhauled by the father and mother of a storm!'

Above and ahead of them the sky was still clear and serene, but behind them it had turned to a leaden pall of darkness against which the tangled mass of the jungle and the tall tops of coconut palms stood black and motionless, and not a leaf stirred. Even the ferns and orchids and the long, delicate festoons of creeper that swung down from every overhanging branch hung so still that they appeared to be rigid, and the rattling swiftness of the ancient car seemed the only sound in all the breathless, waiting islands.

Charles tilted the driving-mirror so as to give himself a view of the lowering sky behind him, and said: '*Crippen!* We're going to be lucky if we beat this! Hold on to your hats, and we'll see if we can knock sixty out of this galloping bedstead.'

He switched on the headlights as they bucketed out of a side-turning and swung left with a screech of tortured tyres into a long, straight stretch of road lined with shadowy coconut palms. But the storm was overhauling them with relentless swiftness, and by now more than half the sky was darkened by it and the far hills had been blotted out. '*Hurry*, Charles!' implored Valerie.

'It's no good telling me to hurry,' retorted Charles with something of a snap: 'Address your admonitions to this blasted mousetrap! — she's bursting her stays as it is, and even if we could by some miracle kick another five miles an hour out of her, she'd fall to pieces in the process!'

'This *would* happen on Christmas Eve!' mourned Valerie. 'Charles, do you think the others will hold the ferry for us? We were the last to leave and we've got the worst car, so the Dobbies and George and Amabel and Co. are bound to have arrived by now.'

Charles said: 'You forget they've got to decant Hurridge and Ted Norton first. We'll probably be at the jetty as soon as they are. *Listen!* . . . What's that?'

For some minutes past they had been vaguely aware of a curious humming sound that was barely audible above the noise of the car. But now, suddenly, it deepened until it sounded like the croon of wind through telegraph wires, and grew steadily in volume until the whole island seemed to vibrate to it as the fabric of a church will tremble to the low tones of an organ.

Charles shouted: 'Hold everything — here she comes!' And even as he spoke, the storm was upon them.

It hit the breathless immobility of the evening with the impact of a sixteen-inch shell. Shattering the brooding stillness into a thousand tortured fragments as the wind leapt upon the island; shaking it, savaging it, tearing it as though it were a terrier with a rat: bending the tall trunks of the coconut palms as though they had been saplings, and lashing them to and fro in a wild confusion.

Trails of jungle creeper, ripped from their airy moorings, leaves, twigs and orchids, fragments of branches and startled insects whirled across the windscreen of the car and tangled themselves about the radiator as the car rocked and bucketed onwards, keeping to the crown of the road with difficulty. Valerie could see Charles's lips forming wicked words on discovering that the windscreen-wiper was out of order, and she groped for some cotton waste and leant out, the wind whipping her hair across her eyes. The car lurched to a standstill as Charles applied the brake and dragged her back into her seat with a relentless hand. '—! —!' yelled Charles; his words completely unintelligible against the roar of the wind. He snatched the cotton waste from her and performed the operation himself.

Valerie was aware of Copper shouting something in her ear as the car bounded forward again: *'Nick!'* shouted Copper, white-faced with terror: *'The boats! They'll be out in this!'*

Dan Harcourt, who had caught a word or two above the fiendish flapping and rattling of the aged car and the whining howl of the wind, yelled back reassuringly that they'd be all right and had probably got in about a quarter of an hour ago, and ...

Valerie turned sharply to look at him. In the reflected glow of the headlights his face betrayed nothing but confidence, but having sailed more than once with him during the past week she knew that Dan must be very well aware of the time it would take to sail from Hopetown to Ross with a fair wind. And there had been no breath of wind for half an hour before the storm ... They can't possibly be more than half-way by now, she thought with panic: and shrank back against her seat as the first swollen drops of rain splashed heavily against the windscreen.

Copper had never imagined such rain. It came down like a river in full spate. A heavy, opaque curtain of water that descended on them out of the inky sky with the terrifying suggestion of a tidal wave, blotting out the road before them so that they appeared to be driving into a shifting, liquid wall. The aged car leaked profusely from a dozen points, and by the time they reached the outskirts of Aberdeen bazaar its four passengers presented the damp and bedraggled appearance of survivors from a shipwreck.

There was a brief lull in the storm as they arrived at the jetty where they found four occupants of the other two carloads, the Reverend Dobbie and his wife, and Amabel and her George, grouped in an unhappy huddle in the iron-roofed shelter on the quay. The other two members of the party, Ted Norton and Deputy-Commissioner Hurridge, being resident on Aberdeen were mercifully exempt from braving the stormy strip of harbour water in an attempt to return to Ross, and though Amabel also lived on Aberdeen, she had been invited to several Christmas parties on Ross and would be putting up for a couple of nights with the Purvises.

As the Ford drew up under cover of the shed, a bearded Sikh in a dripping mackintosh cape came forward and presented a damp envelope to Charles, who ran his eye down the single sheet of paper and said: 'It's from Amabel's father. Mr Withers says we'd better not attempt to cross over to Ross unless there is a lull. He says he phoned to Harriet to try and stop the others sailing, but as it took ages to get through, he missed us, and that we'd better park ourselves on him and Mr Hurridge for the night.'

'Oh *no*! Charles,' protested Valerie. 'We're giving a party tonight. We *must* get back! The worst is over — it's not blowing nearly so hard now. Do let's go, *please*!'

'We'll put it to the vote,' decided Charles, climbing reluctantly out of the driving-seat and joining the group in the shed: 'Who's for going, and who's for staying?'

After a few moments of animated discussion it was unanimously decided to risk the crossing and dispense with Mr Hurridge's hospitality. 'Come on then,' urged Charles, 'let's make a dash for it. We can't get much wetter than we are already!' And plunging out of the shelter of the shed they fled along the open jetty to where the ferry heaved and shrieked at her moorings.

It needed the combined threats, orders and pleadings of the eight would-be passengers to induce the native crew to attempt the trip, for the wind still howled through the narrow straits between Aberdeen and Ross, and the driven rain, lashing downwards at an acute angle, ricocheted off the heaving waters in a sheet of steel. But since the fury of the rain had temporarily beaten the sea into comparative submission, they cast off hastily: the clumsy craft backing reluctantly away from the jetty and rolling like an elderly and drunken duck.

Copper never forgot the twenty minutes that followed. A dozen times it seemed that they must be swamped or driven back on the jagged teeth of the rocks off the jail point as the labouring ferry heeled over to the wind. *'Hell!'* said Charles after the first five minutes. 'We never ought to have done this. I'd no earthly right to let you come.'

'I expect we'll be swept out to sea,' pronounced Amabel gloomily. 'It just goes to show, doesn't it?'

'Don't be absurd!' snapped Valerie. But it was a disturbing thought, and more than one of the passengers conjured up an unpleasantly vivid mental picture of the ferry being swept through the harbour mouth and out into the angry, desolate leagues of ocean beyond Ross; though neither George nor Copper were among their number — George being occupied with the welfare of his Amabel, and Copper with visions of Nick Tarrent being drowned in the bay, dashed upon the rocks of North Point, or possibly eaten by sharks.

Amabel, struck by a melancholy association of ideas, did not improve matters by suddenly embarking at the top of her voice on a gruesome story of several private soldiers who, long ago, while trying to row from Aberdeen to Ross upon a stormy night were swept out to sea and finally thrown upon the beach of Havelock, a tiny island many miles down the coast. Their boat being smashed upon the rocks and starvation looming imminent, one of their number had attempted the desperate swim between Havelock and Ross to fetch help. But the distance between the two islands being anything from fifteen to twenty miles of shark-infested sea, it is not surprising that he was never seen again; or that having scoured the coasts, the rescue party that eventually landed upon Havelock should find the survivors dead of thirst and starvation, with the details of their tragedy scratched upon a sun-dried scrap of paper.

'— and there's a tablet in the Ross church to the one who tried to get help. You can see it next time you go there,' added Amabel. 'I expect the sharks got him. Or perhaps barracudas; they're worse than sharks. A dreadful thing to happen, I always think.'

Her fellow-passengers eyed her with distaste, and it was obvious from their bleak expressions that including the padre and with the exception of George, they could all of them have thought up several equally dreadful things that they would have liked to happen, immediately, to Miss Withers. Presently Valerie began to turn a delicate and unbecoming shade of green, and Copper shut her eyes and began to think more kindly of drowning. The Reverend Dobbie embarked on a mental recitation of the 'Prayer for Those at Sea', and Charles said: 'By God, we've made it!' as the ferry crashed inexpertly against the pontoon off Ross jetty . . .

Five minutes later, soaked and shaken, they were safe ashore and being packed into the three big Government House rick-shaws, known on the island as 'buggies' — a survival of the days when they were drawn by ponies — that had been waiting under the shelter of the sheds by the jetty, Valerie and Copper to return to Government House, the pale silent Amabel, with George trotting alongside, to the Purvises', the Dobbies to the Vicarage, and Charles and Dan, on foot, to Charles's quarters in the Mess.

But half an hour later there was still no news of the boats, the telephone wires were down and the ferry, having broken its moorings, had made the perilous trip to Chatham and succeeded in reaching anchorage there.

Sir Lionel Masson, who had returned, wet and disinclined for conversation, some few minutes after the arrival of his daughter, had had a hot bath and changed, and on hearing that the telephone had ceased functioning, had donned a mackintosh and gone out into the streaming darkness to get what information he could, while his daughter and her friend, dry and newly clothed though still somewhat damp as to hair, made a gloomy pretence of decorating the dinner table with crackers and artificial holly.

'I can't think why we're doing this,' said Valerie, looping a tinsel ribbon half-heartedly between the tall silver candlesticks. 'I don't imagine that more than three people will turn up, as the forest-launch is sure to land the sailing crowd on Chatham when it's rounded them up, and they'll never get the ferry or anything else across here tonight.'

Copper turned away without answering, and for perhaps the tenth time in as many minutes crossed to the windows and attempted to peer through their rain-streaked surface into the wet darkness beyond. The big clock in the lower hall struck eight as she flattened her nose against a pane, and presently she cupped her hands about her eyes to shut out the light from the room, for she thought she had caught the faint flicker of a rickshaw lamp gleaming through the wild darkness below the house where the drive wound up through an avenue of tossing flame trees. The gleam showed again, more distinctly this time, and a rickshaw drew out from the shelter of the trees.

Valerie dumped a heap of gaudily coloured crackers on to the dining-table and said: '*"Sister Anne, Sister Anne, do you see anyone coming?"*'

'Yes . . . I think it must be your father coming back. There's a rickshaw coming up the drive. Let's go down.'

They ran across the ballroom which formed the upper hall of the house, and down the stairs to the front door, arriving anxious and breathless as a rickshaw drew up under the wide, covered porch and Sir Lionel descended from it, shaking the wet off his coat. 'They've got back,' he stated briefly in answer to Valerie's urgent query. But there was that in his face which gave her a sudden stab of renewed anxiety. Something horrid has happened, she thought. Aloud she said: 'Come upstairs and tell us about it while I mix you a drink, Dad. And do take off that sopping coat. You'll catch an appalling cold.' She preceded him upstairs to the big glassed-in verandah that was furnished as a lounge, and mixed him a stiff brandy and soda as he sank tiredly into an easy chair.

He sat silent for several minutes, watching the bubbles rise through the amber liquid to burst at the glass's rim, until at last Copper said, sharply anxious: 'What's happened? Are they all safe?' and Sir Lionel appeared to pull himself together. He drank off half the contents of the tumbler before replying and then spoke heavily.

'They were in the water for well over half an hour and the forest-launch had the devil of a time finding them. Apparently all three dinghies were swamped in the first five minutes, but fortunately they were all within yards of each other when it happened — which was just as well, for if they'd been some distance apart, the launch might have been hours rounding them up. They were picked up just this side of North Bay and were landed here. Some of them will be along in a moment. I came on ahead to tell you.'

He paused for a moment, his eyes once again following the streaming line of bubbles in his glass, and suddenly he looked very old and tired. At last: 'They didn't find them all,' he said. 'Ferrers Shilto was missing.'

Valerie drew in her breath sharply. 'You mean he was drowned?'

'Not necessarily. He may have been swept away from the others and caught in a current, and managed to get ashore on North Bay. Or even somewhere on the Aberdeen side.'

Valerie said: 'But you don't think it's likely. And – and anyway, there are sharks,' she added with a shudder.

'Don't!' besought Copper. 'What about the others, Sir Lionel?'

The Commissioner turned to her with relief: 'Oh, they're all right — except for Mrs Stock, who seems to be suffering from shock more than exposure. She was rather hysterical, I'm afraid. I have arranged for John Shilto and Tarrent and that young doctor off the ship — what is his name? Oh yes, Harcourt — to sleep here tonight. I hope we have enough bedding. Of course the whole affair is disgraceful. There was a stupid bungle at the wireless station. We should have had a storm warning this morning, and instead of that it was only received about four-thirty. But luckily ships in this harbour have to keep up a reasonable head of steam: otherwise that cruiser would never have got clear in time. As it was, she cut it rather fine.'

'Why did she have to go out?' demanded Copper. 'I thought ships tried to get *in* to harbours in a storm?'

'Not this one. There is not enough deep water. And far too many rocks. Besides, this is only the beginning of the storm. There's a lot more to come, and if the *Sapphire* had stayed here she would have been driven on the rocks like the old *Enterprise*. Her only chance was to make for the open sea and——' He broke off as voices sounded from the lower hall, and putting down his unfinished drink rose and walked over to the banisters.

Mr Stock, oozing water like a leaking sponge, was coming up the stairs, rain squelching from his soaked shoes on to the polished treads and leaving little gleaming puddles at his every step. He checked his ascent on seeing the Commissioner, and stood looking upwards from the well of the stairs, one hand clutching the banisters and the light from the hall below him blackly silhouetting his weedy figure.

'Well, Stock?' inquired the Commissioner.

Mr Stock shuffled his feet and cleared his throat nervously. As ever there was about him a faint, servile suggestion of cringing, as in a habitually ill-treated mongrel dog, but in the present instance it appeared more apparent than usual.

'Well, what is it?' The Commissioner's voice was unexpectedly tinged with nervous exasperation: 'Have they found him?'

'Yes — er — no. You mean Ferrers Shilto? No. I only came to inquire if you would be so good as to give my wife a bed for the night. You see — er — our roof has gone.'

'Your *what*?'

Mr Stock let go of the banister, swayed dangerously, and clutched at it again to steady himself: 'Our roof. The storm — the storm has blown away a large portion of it, and part of the house is quite — er — quite uninhabitable. So I thought that if you would very kindly allow Ruby — my wife — to sleep here tonight ... I — she suffers severely from insomnia you know, and she says that her fear of the rest of the roof falling would aggravate it. So I thought ...' His voice trailed away and his teeth chattered with cold and fatigue.

Valerie said: 'Why, of *course* we can! Can't we, Dad? And of course you must sleep here too, Leonard. You two can share the big spare room and Nick and Dan can double up in the other one, and we'll make up a bed for Mr Shilto in the turret room.'

Mr Stock muttered profuse thanks, refused a drink, and stumbled out into the night leaving behind him a snail-like trail of dampness. 'Poor little man,' said Copper. 'He looks simply green. It must be a particularly nasty jar after capsizing in a storm and being in the water for hours, to arrive home and find no roof on your house.'

'Not to mention a wife in the last stages of hysteria!' said Valerie. 'If there is one thing dear Ruby really revels in it's a spot of drama, and I bet she'll extract the last ounce of it from the present situation or die in the attempt. Poor Leonard! Come and help me get the rooms ready, Coppy.'

7

Government House was a large, old, two-storeyed and rather gloomy building, full of bats and curious echoes. At sundown the bats swooped through the tall, dim rooms, and once the lights were lit a host of little semi-transparent lizards would appear out of holes and crannies in the high ceilings, to pursue with shrill chirruping cries the moths and night-flying insects that were attracted in by the lamps.

The ground floor was entirely taken up by offices and a guard room, and a wide, shallow-stepped staircase led from the entrance hall to the living rooms above. The upper storey of the house centred about the ballroom; a huge, dim room with a floor of polished boards, into which the staircase emerged, and from which almost every other room in the house led off. A wide, glassed-in verandah ran the length of the house and along part of one end, cutting off most of the light from the drawing-room which was, for this reason, seldom used except by night, and behind the ballroom, separated from it by a couple of pillars and a small section of wall that formed a sketchy passageway, were five bedrooms; one of which, the turret room, was normally used as a morning-room, but was now being pressed into service again as a bedroom for Mr Shilto.

Valerie collected an armful of sheets and pillow-cases from the linen cupboard and set about preparing for the unexpected influx of guests. 'I expect the mattresses are all damp and that everyone will get pneumonia,' she said lightly, 'but there isn't time to air them. Come on, Coppy; it's no use trying to dodge those bats. They'll never hit you, anyway!'

'That's what you think! But then you're used to them, and I'm not. You know, Val, there really is something very odd about this house. It's quite cheerful in the daylight, but have you ever noticed how – how *unfriendly* it gets the moment the sun goes down? And at night it's sometimes positively hostile. Or am I being over-imaginative?'

Valerie straightened up from tucking in a blanket and said slowly, 'No. Even I have noticed it sometimes, and I wouldn't call myself particularly imaginative. Perhaps it's because most of the walls are hollow. Those funny things like portholes, half-way up some of them, are something to do with ventilation I believe. But it means that bats and rats and lizards, and goodness only knows what else, can get between them and run about inside and make odd noises. And then draughts blow through them and make even odder ones. Not to mention several families of wild cats who live in the roof and creep about overhead at night!'

'Perhaps it's that,' said Copper doubtfully. 'That, and the fact that most of the rooms have no doors, but only those funny little swinging shutters across the middle instead. They may stop people seeing into a large part of the room, but you can't lock them. And even if you could, anything and anyone could get in underneath them just as easily as the bats fly in over the top of them.'

'Oh well, nothing is ever likely to come in,' said Valerie comfortably. 'Although I must say it would be nice to be able to shut a door on oneself at night. But then I'm used to it by now, and this "no doors" system does help to keep the place cool. It lets every scrap of breeze there is blow right through the house. And you mustn't worry about this being an unfriendly sort of house at night, Coppy, because it's much too well guarded.'

That last was certainly true, for the house had a guard from the British Detachment on duty day and night, as well as a permanent guard of Indian Police. Every bathroom in the house had a small outside staircase leading to the ground for the use of servants and sweepers, and at night one of the police guard slept at the foot of each staircase, while as an additional precaution, electric lights burned from dusk to dawn in the garden; one at each corner of the house. But Copper did not feel capable of explaining that the sense of unease that the house gave her was in no way connected with anything that might make its way in from outside, but rather with an almost tangible unfriendliness that the big rooms held in themselves.

They had barely finished making the beds when Mrs Stock arrived, muffled in a dripping mackintosh and supported by the anxious Leonard. Valerie led the way into the spare bedroom, and Mrs Stock, waving aside Copper's proffered arm, tottered across the room and collapsed in a damp heap upon one of the newly made beds. 'Leave me alone!' she commanded fretfully. 'I don't want *anything*. I only want to go to bed. And don't *fuss* me, Leonard! I shall be quite all right if I'm left alone!'

A belated remnant of social poise returned to her, and she turned to Valerie: 'So good of you to have me, dear. I don't know *what* I should have done. The house is in *ruins*, and Leonard has done nothing . . . and after that terrible, *terrible* experience . . .! I shall never be the same again. Never! No — I'd rather have dinner in bed. *Please go!*' This last was nearer an order than a request, and Copper and Valerie, murmuring helpful suggestions about sending in hot soup and brandy, backed hastily out of the room.

'That's odd,' commented Valerie, surprised. 'I imagined that we were in for the dramatic story of her sufferings, told in minute detail. Oh well, I expect we shall get it tomorrow.'

'There's Nick,' cried Copper suddenly, hearing a voice in the lower hall. She ran across the ballroom and leant over the banisters, listening.

The stairhead posts in the upper hall had been carved by some long-dead Burmese convict, once an artist at the bloodstained court of Thebaw, into the form of gigantic slant-eyed faces with wide, grinning mouths, like the masks of Burmese devil-dancers, one of which, at the top of the stairs, Valerie had christened 'Hindenburg'. Copper had slipped one arm about it as she peered below, and Nick Tarrent, standing in the lower hall, glanced up and for a brief second suffered a savage shock of fear, for it seemed to him as he looked upward into Copper's white, anxious face that someone stood beside her. Someone whose dark, malignant features peered out of the shadows over her shoulder and grinned in evil anticipation.

The impression was so vivid that he had opened his mouth to cry a warning when he realized that the lurking terror was nothing more than a carved block of Burmese teak. But the momentary stab of fear had shown in his face, and Copper's voice held an added edge of alarm: 'Nick! — are you all right?'

Nick's relief made him laugh. 'Yes, of course. A bit damp, but still in possession of life and limb. Charles took us along to his quarters to have a bath and a change. Luckily he and I are about the same size. Dan shoved himself comfortably into a suit of George's, but you should see old Shilto! — every button and seam working overtime.'

'Where's Charles?' inquired Valerie, joining Copper by the banisters.

'Just arriving. In fact, here's the rearguard now. George and I got off to a flying start.'

Charles, Dan Harcourt, John Shilto and Hamish Rattigan, followed shortly afterwards by the Purvises and Amabel, came in from the wet, wild night, and mounting the stairs, joined Valerie and Copper in the verandah where drinks and salted nuts had been set out. 'The Dobbies aren't coming,' announced Charles 'Mrs Dobbie is still feeling seasick. They sent their apologies.'

The verandah looked cheerful enough with its gay, chintz-covered chairs and sofas. But outside the rain lashed savagely against the big glass windows that closed it in, while sudden vicious gusts of wind rattled at the hinges and wailed about the house; moaning, whispering, tapping to be let in; screaming like a host of banshees or sighing like a small, lost, lonely ghost . . .

Valerie stopped mixing short drinks and put down the cocktail-shaker with a thump: 'This is too miserable for words,' she said. 'Charles, help me move these things into the drawing-room. The further away we are from the wind and the windows, the cosier we'll be. All those black, wet panes of glass give me the shivers.'

Charles and John Shilto carried the table of drinks between them, and the party moved gratefully into the more cheerful atmosphere of the drawing-room where the sound of rain and wind was less obtrusive. But Copper laid a hand on Nick's sleeve and stopped him as he was about to follow them: 'Nick . . . what happened? We were terribly worried about you.'

'We?' inquired Nick with the ghost of a grin.

'I,' corrected Copper gravely. 'We were only half-way home when the storm hit us, and I was convinced you'd be drowned.'

'Your conviction was shared,' said Nick lightly. 'To tell you the truth, Coppy, I thought we were done for, and I still can't make out how we all managed to get away with it.'

'Not all,' said Copper with a shiver.

'You mean Ferrers? Oh, he'll be all right. Probably been picked up by now, if he hasn't swum ashore.'

His tone was light enough, but he avoided Copper's eyes and she flushed resentfully: 'Don't talk to me as if I was in the kindergarten, Nick! You know he hasn't got a chance, don't you?'

Nick shrugged his shoulders. 'Well — yes. I'm afraid he's done for all right, poor devil. God, what a jolly Christmas Eve!'

'Tell me what happened to you,' commanded Copper, perching

on the arm of a verandah chair and clasping her hands about her knees.

Nick hesitated for a moment and jerked his shoulders uncomfortably as if to shrug off an unpleasant memory. Then, 'It was the queerest thing I've ever experienced,' he said. 'We heard it coming. It made a noise like an express train in a tunnel, rushing towards us; very faint at first, but getting nearer and quicker and louder. And then it hit us as though it were something solid made of reinforced concrete. We hadn't time to think and barely time to get the sail down. It caught us broadside on and just flattened us out. One minute we were pegging along in a flat calm, and the next second we were in the water with all hell let loose round us . . .

'We tried to count heads, and as far as I know everyone was O.K. Then the rain arrived, and after that you couldn't see your hand in front of your face. The boats kept bumping into each other, bottom-side up, and the sky was pitch black and the rain ricocheted off the water in a boiling fury. There wasn't anything to do but just hang on like grim death. I don't know where everyone else had got to, but I managed to get Ruby astride the keel of my boat, and I think someone else was hanging on to the other end, though I've no idea who it was. And there we stuck for what seemed like an hour or so, until the forest-launch bumped into us and nearly slaughtered the lot of us.'

'But hadn't you all drifted apart by then?' inquired Copper.

'Oddly enough, no. I'd an idea that we'd be picked up at opposite sides of the bay, but I gather we weren't more than twenty feet apart when the launch found us. Though even then Hamish's boat took a bit of finding; we must have passed her a dozen times without spotting her. It was only when we'd got everyone on board that we realized Ferrers was missing.'

'But didn't anyone see him go?'

Nick gave a short, mirthless laugh. 'No. And it's not surprising, with three boats all barging about in the smother and everyone concentrating on sticking like a limpet to the nearest bit of woodwork. Ronnie Purvis says he thought he was on the end of my boat, but the chap on the launch says he thinks he only pulled in Ruby and myself and that there wasn't a third person with us. So you can see how easy it would have been to lose sight of Ferrers.'

Copper shivered, and said: 'He probably got caught under the boat when it turned over, and never came up at all.'

Nick shook his head. 'He came up all right, because he was one of the first people I remember seeing when I came to the surface. He was hanging on to the next boat, and I remember noticing, in the silly way that one does notice unimportant trifles in moments of stress, that he was wearing a clumsy great garnet ring about the size of a sixpence. His boat bumped into ours just before the rain came, and he was holding on to the centre-board with one hand. I thought for a minute that he'd cut himself. And then I saw that it wasn't blood but a red stone.'

'What wasn't blood?' inquired an interested voice from behind them.

Nick turned swiftly and smiled into Valerie's inquiring face: 'Nothing, Val. Just idle chatter.'

Valerie said: 'Then for Pete's sake come and chatter in the drawing-room! The party is being very sticky, and I can't imagine why anyone turned up. I know if I'd spent an hour or so being soaked in the bay I'd have insisted on going straight to bed. Even Rosamund is looking a bit on edge, and everyone else is frankly bad-tempered. So come in and pull your weight. Hullo, here's Dad.'

'I'm sorry to be so late,' said Sir Lionel, entering upon Valerie's words: 'I'm afraid, Val, that none of your other guests will be able to get here. The ferry can't run, and Norton has gone back with the forest-launch, so he won't be here either.'

'That's all right,' said Valerie. 'I realized that no one else would be able to make it. We were really only waiting for you and Dr Vicarjee and Truda and Frank.'

Vicarjee was the Bengali doctor, Miss Truda Gidney the matron and only European nurse in the small hospital on Ross, and Frank Benton the Commissioner's personal assistant.

'In that case,' said Sir Lionel, 'we can go into dinner, because Vicarjee and Benton went out shooting together and are stranded in Aberdeen and can't get back, and Miss Gidney sent a message to say that both hospital ayahs had leave today and are in the same predicament, so she doesn't think she should leave.'

'Poor old Truda,' said Valerie. 'I wouldn't have her conscience for the world. Fancy having to spend a night like this in an empty hospital, without even a patient to keep you company? No one's sick just now, so she might just as well have come. But I can see her point. Well, if no one else is coming, we may as well go into dinner. Come on, Rosamund, you must be starving.'

She took Mrs Purvis's arm and led the way into the dining-room.

8

Dinner that night was not a cheerful meal. There had not been time to order the removal of the superfluous chairs or to rearrange the seating, and the vacant places lent a gloomy air to the long, gaily-decorated table.

Valerie had ruefully bidden her guests to disregard the place cards and to sit where they liked, and the depleted Christmas Eve party huddled together at one end of the table, sitting close to each other as though in need of mutual comfort and support. But in spite of the artificial sprays of holly, the glittering strings of tinsel and the mounds of gaily-coloured crackers that lay piled on the white cloth, a proper Christmas spirit was noticeably lacking, and conversation plodded heavily through a bog of social trivialities with frequent halts in miry patches of silence.

If only, thought Valerie despairingly for at least the fourth time during the meal, Leonard wouldn't break every silence by saying brightly, *'It must be twenty past — an angel's passing!'*... I wonder who invented that idiotic saying anyway? If he says it again I shall scream! She sighed heavily, and pushed a piece of plum pudding around her plate with a moody fork, while somewhere behind her in the shadowy depths of the ballroom a monotonous little *drip, drip, drip,* told her that the rain had discovered a weak joint in the armour of the roof tiles, and that the first of a series of small, gleaming pools was in process of forming on the polished wood floors of the living rooms.

The house leaked abominably in wet weather, and Valerie thought resentfully of the array of bowls and pails that would presently litter the floors and lie in wait to entrap the feet of the unwary, and beckoned reluctantly over her shoulder to a servant who padded forward on noiseless feet and having received a low-voiced order vanished in the direction of the pantry. Presently the dull drip of water on wood changed to the small, metallic *plink* of water dripping into an enamelled bowl, and on the far side of the table Copper abandoned her methodical manufacture of bread pellets and lifted her head sharply: 'Listen — the leaks have started. Now I suppose we shall have to go to bed in a swamp. I wonder if Kadera has remembered to move my bed? The last time it rained, a vindictive leak dripped right on to my pillow and I dreamt I was bathing — and woke up to find that I was.'

Valerie laughed and turned to Mr Shilto who was sitting on her right: 'Is your house as bad as this one, Mr Shilto? The last time it rained we had so many leaks that we might just as well have been living under a sieve.'

But her effort at making light conversation fell on stony ground, for Mr Shilto, who had been staring with blank fixity into the darkness beyond the candlelit table, neither turned his head nor shifted his gaze, and Valerie realized suddenly that he had not spoken since the beginning of the meal and did not know she had spoken to him now. I suppose he's bound to be a bit distrait, she thought, curbing an unexpectedly strong feeling of irritation, after all, his cousin has just been drowned, and even though they were on bad terms with each other, sudden death is always pretty shocking.

Not, she had to admit, that there was anything to suggest shock in John Shilto's pale, puffy face. It wore, if anything, a look of gloating excitement, and it flashed into her mind that he had at that moment an odd look of Kioh, her stepfather's Siamese cat, when she was stalking a bird or a lizard. Becoming aware that she was staring at him, fascinated, she spoke hurriedly and at random: 'The last time it rained, there were so many leaks that we ran out of pails and basins and had to start on the cups and saucers. The

P.W.D. are always promising to get it put right, but you know how it is with them. They talk a lot, but nothing *ever* happens!'

Mr Shilto did not reply, but the brief spell of embarrassed silence that followed his failure to respond to his hostess's social efforts was broken with unexpected violence by the repetition of her last statement. Rosamund Purvis, subdued, unemotional Rosamund, who had sat throughout the meal in a silence that had been unobtrusive because she was seldom other than silent, spoke in a queer, high-pitched voice that somehow gave the impression that it did not belong to her:

'*But nothing ever happens!*' she said. And suddenly, shockingly, threw back her head and laughed: a shrill, uncomfortable laugh that held no suggestion of mirth, but was purely hysterical.

'*Rosamund!*' Ronnie Purvis's voice cut across the discordant sound but did not check it.

'*Nothing ever happens,*' gasped Mrs Purvis. '*Ha! Ha! Ha!* That's funny! That's very funny. Nothing ever happens!'

She rocked to and fro, her hands clutching the tablecloth in front of her while the tears of her uncomfortable mirth wet her faded cheeks and Dan Harcourt, standing up swiftly, crossed to the sideboard and poured out a glass of water: the others sitting in stunned silence.

'Stop that, Rosamund!' commanded Ronnie Purvis furiously. 'Stop it at once! You're making an exhibition of yourself!' He jumped to his feet and started towards his wife, but Valerie and Copper were before him. Between them they took the still laughing Mrs Purvis by her arms and lifted her almost bodily from her chair. 'We'll leave the men to their drinks,' said Valerie composedly: 'Come on, Rosamund, let's go and have our coffee in the drawing-room.'

Mrs Purvis's mirth subsided as suddenly as it had arisen. She looked round dazedly at the startled circle of faces, and her own pale features flushed painfully: 'I'm sorry,' she said uncertainly. 'I – I thought . . . It seemed funny; nothing happening——'

'So it is,' said Valerie lightly. 'Dad, don't let them stay swapping stories too long. Come on, Amabel.'

But as though the incident had not been sufficiently unpleasant in itself, young Miss Withers took it upon herself at this juncture to add a further touch of discomfort to the evening's festivities. She rose slowly to her feet, her round cheek bulging with some concealed sweetmeat, and let her prominent blue eyes travel about the table. 'There are thirteen of us,' she announced with gloomy relish. 'It's funny we didn't notice before that we'd sat down thirteen.'

A smile of satisfaction illumined her round, pink face, and she added smugly: 'Well anyway, I'm all right. I didn't get up first, so I shan't be the one who'll die.'

With which pleasing reflection she selected a second lump of coconut ice and trailed away in the wake of Valerie, Copper and Mrs Purvis.

Dan Harcourt, entering the drawing-room some twenty minutes later, noticed with interest that during that interval Mrs Purvis had borrowed some rouge and applied it with an amateur hand. Also that the two uneven patches of pink that now decorated her cheeks merely served to emphasize rather than to conceal the shocking pallor of her face and draw attention to the nervous twitching of her colourless mouth. What on earth's the matter with the woman? he wondered uneasily; she looks as though she was working up for a bad nervous breakdown and I only hope to God she doesn't have it here and now!

There appeared to be some justification for this fear, for Mrs Purvis, who had been discussing a forthcoming tennis tournament when the men entered, faltered on seeing them and ceased speaking, leaving a sentence cut short in mid-air. Furthermore, during the next half-hour, while Valerie served coffee and the conversation became general, she sat silent and rigid; occupying herself with a frightened, furtive scrutiny of her fellow-guests that did not pass entirely unobserved, for Copper's interest too was caught and held by that odd, secretive inspection of Rosamund's . . .

Nick was talking about Calcutta where the *Sapphire* had been before her arrival in Port Blair: 'We thought we were going to be there for Christmas week,' he said, 'and there was a certain amount of sourness when we were suddenly slung off here instead. I remember being fairly outspoken on the subject myself. I'd spent a short leave in Calcutta not long before: stayed at the Grand Hotel, which was a welcome change from stewing on the equator in a two-by-four cabin, and I thought I'd repeat the performance for Christmas. But all things considered this is a decided improvement in programme; hurricanes or no hurricanes. Come on, Copper! take an interest in my laborious social chatter will you, or Stock and Hamish will rope us in to play bridge. They've got that predatory Culbertson gleam in their eye and I refuse to be victimized. Try and look absorbed and interested, there's a good girl.'

Copper said in an undertone: 'Nick — look at Mrs Purvis.'

'Why? At the moment I prefer to look at you.'

'No, seriously Nick. There's something very odd about her tonight.'

'Cotton stockings and a touch of *la grippe*, at a guess,' suggested Nick. Copper ignored the flippancy and continued as though he had not spoken: '. . . she's got something on her mind, and if it didn't seem so absurd, I'd say she was frightened of someone in the room but hadn't quite made up her mind which one. She keeps looking at everyone in turn as if she was trying to work something out. It's – it's almost as though she were playing *"Is it you? . . . Is it you? . . . Is it you?"*'

Nick flung a cursory glance at Mrs Purvis and said: 'Come off it, Coppy! She's merely had a bit of a shock — what with being tipped into the harbour and then this Ferrers business. You'd be a bit jumpy yourself if you'd been in her shoes.'

'Watch her,' urged Copper, low-voiced, 'and *then* tell me that she's only "a bit jumpy".'

Nick obediently hitched himself round in his chair and did as he was commanded, and after a moment or two his expression changed from resignation to reluctant interest.

Rosamund Purvis was sitting on the extreme edge of her chair, her thin, clever hands clenched together in her lap and tense rigidity in every line of her nondescript figure. She was sitting so still that her very immobility served to draw attention to her flickering gaze, for though she did not turn her head, her hazel eyes, wide as a frightened cat's, darted warily, continuously, searchingly, from face to face in an oddly questioning, oddly disturbing scrutiny. And it was only after watching her for several minutes that Nick noticed something which had escaped Copper's attention: that Mrs Purvis's disturbing scrutiny did not extend to the entire party, but only to certain members of it. Those members who had made up the sailing party.

He was in the process of digesting this curious fact when Dan Harcourt came up behind them and Copper turned her head and spoke in an undertone: 'Dan, what's biting Rosamund Purvis? Look at her . . .'

'I've been doing so,' said Dan, leaning on the back of Copper's chair and continuing to watch Mrs Purvis with detached, professional interest: 'She looks,' he said musingly, 'as though she was wondering who had buried the body.'

'Cheerful couple, aren't you?' observed Nick irritably. 'Copper has just been propounding a similar enlivening theory. Well, you're a doctor, Pills — why don't you take some action? Advise the woman to take a couple of aspirins and shove off home before she springs another of those Ghoulish-Laughter scenes on us. I'm not sure I could take it twice in one evening.'

Copper said seriously, addressing Dan, 'Nick thinks she's only edgy because of being upset in the storm. But it doesn't look like ordinary edginess to me. She looks — *frightened* . . .'

'So frightened,' agreed Dan Harcourt thoughtfully, 'that if anyone came up behind her just now and touched her on the shoulder, she'd probably go off like a bomb and scream the roof off.'

The words were barely out of his mouth when the correctness of that belief was unexpectedly proved. Kioh, the Siamese cat, her tail twitching gently like a miniature panther, appeared in the doorway behind Mrs Purvis's chair and having glanced about the room with slanting china-blue eyes, leapt lightly on to the arm of the chair, brushing against Mrs Purvis's bare shoulder. A split second later the languor of that apathetic gathering was as effectively shattered as though a bomb had indeed fallen in its midst, and Valerie's ill-fated dinner party came to an abrupt and shattering close.

Mrs Purvis was on her feet, screaming.

She did not even look to see what had touched her, but stood there for perhaps the space of ten seconds, her eyes starting from her head in stark and horrifying terror and her mouth wide open. Then, before any of her startled audience could collect their scattered wits or move towards her, she crumpled at the knees like a rag doll and fell forward on to the polished floor in a dead faint.

9

'W*hy did I leave my little back room in Blooms-bur-ree, Where I could live on a pound a week in lux-ur-ee?'* crooned Copper gently, applying cold cream to her nose some two hours later.

Valerie laughed.

'I'm afraid it does look like being a pretty mildewed Christmas for you,' she apologized. 'Today couldn't very well have had a stickier finish, and tomorrow looks like being as bad — if not worse.'

'Well, at least it hasn't been dull,' said Copper, reaching for the hairbrush. 'In fact it's been packed with brisk incident. But I'm glad it's over. A few more fireworks from Rosamund and I swear I'd have started screaming myself.'

'Wasn't it hellish?' sighed Valerie. 'Poor Dad! I bet it put years on him. He was talking stamps with Hamish when Rosamund exploded, and he rose out of his chair like a rocketing pheasant and his spectacles fell off, and Leonard trod on them.'

She began to giggle, and Copper, catching the infection, said unsteadily: 'You missed the high spot of the evening. George was clutching a glass of fruit cup that he'd just collected for Amabel, and when Rosamund yelled he nearly jumped out of his skin and the fruit cup went all over Amabel. She was simply soaked, and that new georgette dress of hers immediately shrunk up like a bashful snail — it was on the tight side to begin with, and you know how that stuff shrinks when it's wet! What with a few slices of banana nestling coyly in her hair and a strip of lemon peel hanging round one ear, she looked incredibly abandoned and rakish, and when George tried to pick them off she slapped him. Poor George! I'm afraid his faith in women has received a nasty crack.'

Valerie leant her head against a mosquito pole and gave way to immoderate mirth, and presently, mopping her eyes and striving to recover her composure, observed that it was not a *bit* nice of them to collapse into giggles like that, as it was simply horrid at the time, even though it might seem funny now. 'I thought poor Rosamund was never coming round. However, she seemed all right by the time they removed her. Dan and Charles went along with her to the hospital while Ronnie went down to fetch her night things.'

'The hospital is much the best place for her,' said Copper firmly. 'Besides, it'll give Truda something to fuss over if she really hasn't any patients at the moment. Funny, the way Rosamund refused flatly to go back to her own house. You'd have thought she'd much rather go home instead of insisting on being taken off to sleep in a ward under Truda's eye.'

'Thank goodness she did!' sighed Valerie, 'I was scared stiff she was going to stay here. I simply *had* to ask her, but I was madly grateful when she held out for the hospital. She'd evidently made up her mind to go there or go off her head, and if she'd stayed here I'd have gone off mine! One hysterical female in the house is more than enough, and Rosamund's yells have evidently brought dear Ruby to the verge of a nervous breakdown. I bet the miserable Leonard is in for a hell of a night!'

'*"We don't have much money,"*' quoted Copper flippantly, '*"but we do see life!"* What did they do with Amabel, Val? I lost sight of her in the general flurry after she'd taken that crack at George. Surely they haven't let her go back to the Purvis mansion unchaperoned?'

'Good heavens, no! She's gone along to the hospital with Rosamund, which leaves Ronnie abandoned by his entire harem. Rosamund clung to her like a demented limpet and refused to move without her; though whether from a well-founded mistrust of Ronnie, or because she finds something very sedative and soothing about Amabel, I don't know. Anyway they have both trailed off to Truda's tender care.'

'I wish I'd known that Dan had gone up to the hospital with them,' said Copper. 'I'd have told him to bring back some form of sedative for Ruby. Chloroform, for preference!'

'Oh gosh!' gasped Valerie, giving way to a renewed attack of mirth: 'I *did* enjoy that part of the evening's fun and games! I shall never forget all your faces when she came bursting out of her bedroom on top of Rosamund's big scene, and rushed into the drawing-room like Sarah Bernhardt in pink pyjamas.'

'I didn't notice her pyjamas,' confessed Copper. 'Her dressing-gown was what got me. I might have known that she'd have one like a film vamp's, all yards of train and acres of pink satin edged with marabou trimming. The minute I saw it I knew it was only a question of seconds before somebody fell over it, what with every-one dashing about being helpful, and of course it *would* be the wretched George.'

'I wonder which hurt most?' mused Valerie. 'The smack in the eye he got from Amabel, or the crack on the jaw he got from Ruby? They both sounded pretty crisp.'

'Oh, *poor* George,' gasped Copper: 'It's a shame to laugh! But it *was* funny. At least I thought it was funny until she tripped over her own train and collapsed on to Nick, and then I admit my sense of humour wilted a bit.'

'Personally, I was extremely grateful, because if it had been anyone but Nick the confusion would have been ten times worse. I thought he dealt with her in a masterly manner. "The Silent Service" for ever! Charles, for instance, would probably have felt it his duty to prop her on a sofa and fetch brandy or salts or something, but Nick simply slung her up as if she'd been a sack of coals and dumped her back in her bedroom with, as far as I can make out, instructions to stay there and put a sock in it. She was so astonished she stopped squealing at once and didn't move out of her room again. Which you must admit was no ordinary achievement.'

'I suppose so,' agreed Copper doubtfully. She sat silent for a few moments, slowly removing cold cream with a wad of pink tissue and frowning at her reflection in the mirror, and presently observed thoughtfully: 'Dan says he has a hell of a temper. Ruby was gushing about Nick at that Corbyn's picnic, and Dan told her that if she'd ever had the wrong side of Nick's tongue she'd realize that skinning was preferable. It's funny, because I should have thought he was too lazy.' She rose, yawning. 'I suppose we ought to go to bed. I'm dead tired. What's the time, Val?'

'Nearly midnight. In a few minutes it'll be Christmas Day. Somehow it doesn't seem possible, does it?'

'No,' said Copper, pulling out the edge of her mosquito net and scrambling into bed, 'but I don't see why it shouldn't. It's odd how one always associates Christmas with snow and icicles and holly, when the first Christmas Day belongs to a little hot town in the East with palm trees and camels and flat-roofed houses.'

'Well I must admit I like the Frost-and-Carol idea best,' confessed Valerie. 'And as for Christmas morning without a stocking, it's a mere hollow mockery to me. But this wretched *Maharaja* having let us down with a thump, there won't be any stockings tomorrow: or many presents either.'

She stopped and lifted her head, listening. The clock in the lower hall was striking midnight, and they kept silence until the last chime died away in the darkness.

'Merry Christmas, Val.'

'Merry Christmas, Coppy darling — and good-night.' Valerie slid off the bed and tucked in Copper's mosquito net for her, and switching off the light vanished through the curtained doorway into her own room. A few minutes later her own light winked out and the house settled down under the blanket of the stormy darkness.

The wind still blew in a half gale, and above the steady drumming of the rain Copper could hear the muffled clamour of the sea raging furiously about the tiny island. There was a certain sullen rhythm in that sound which at any other time might have been soothing, but tonight, mingled with the desolate, wolf-pack howl of the wind and the remorseless thunder of the rain, it held something sinister, and the thought that had been kept at bay all the evening rose as a clear picture before Copper's mental eye; held relentlessly before her by the roar of the breakers.

Somewhere out in that cold, malignant sea, Ferrers Shilto's wizened body must be being dragged and battered by wind and tide; swung and tossed between black, hissing hills of water; pounded in a roaring maelstrom of foam upon the jagged coral reefs of forgotten beaches, or swept out in the close clasp of the currents into that lonely, landless sea that stretched away and away to the South Pole——

Copper dropped into an uneasy sleep . . .

She was standing among the coconut trees on the shore of North Bay in a high wind that tore through the palm fronds and drove the steel-grey seas in upon the rocks at her feet. Something glimmered whitely among that welter of foam: something now half-seen, now hidden by the flung spume. It came nearer — larger — clearer . . . and as the wind blew louder, it shook itself clear of the grey sea, and Ferrers Shilto came walking up out of the bay. Water ran from his soaked garments and streamed in wind-blown rivulets from his shock of grey hair, and a band of seaweed that had caught about his skinny throat fluttered in the wind as though he wore a curiously woven scarf. His small, wrinkled face wore an expression of almost ludicrous astonishment, and as he came nearer, Copper saw that he held his left hand against his breast, and that from between the spread fingers protruded the handle of a knife.

There seemed nothing unnatural in the fact that he should walk up out of the sea, even though she knew that he had been drowned; and fear did not touch her until her eyes fell on the knife. But with the sight of that shining handle the blind panic of nightmare swept down upon her, freezing her, so that she could neither move nor scream. Ferrers's wide, incredulous eyes came nearer and nearer, and there was blood upon his hand: a single splash of scarlet. He was so near her that the wet, wind-blown strand of weed about his throat touched her face . . . And Copper awoke, shuddering with terror, to find a cold drip of water from yet another leak in her ceiling trickling down her cheek . . .

The storm seemed to have blown itself out, though not the rain, and she pulled up her mosquito net and switched on the light. Slow, gleaming drops were forming and falling from the ceiling immediately overhead. She looked about her bedroom in shivering exasperation, and having fetched a soap-dish and the tooth-glass from the bathroom, pushed her bed to one side of the latest leak, threw out her wet pillow, and placing the soap-dish and the tooth-glass where they would do most good, climbed back into bed and switched off the light. But this time she could not go to sleep. The horror of her recent dream, coupled with the necessity for action in the matter of leaks, had awakened her too thoroughly, and sleep had receded beyond recall.

The air inside her shuttered room was warm and damp and heavy, and the swish of the fan blades seemed barely to disturb it. And now that the wind had dropped the house was very quiet. It was still raining, but only very lightly, and after the recent clamour of the gale the silence was an almost tangible thing; emphasized rather than broken by the sound of the sea, whose muffled thunder seemed only to provide a background to the hush that had fallen with the falling of the wind. Yet there was no quality of restfulness in the silence, but rather one of suspense and waiting; as though the storm, far from blowing itself out, had merely called a brief halt in which to collect its forces for a renewed attack. Inside the darkened house the stillness was full of little sounds. Tiny, tinkling sounds in a dozen different keys, caused by water dripping into a varied assortment of bowls and basins. A sudden crack of wood as a piece of furniture contracted, the thin keening of mosquitoes, the flitter of a bat's wings in the darkness and the light patter of rain on the roof. And after a time Copper became aware that there was someone else besides herself who could not sleep that night. Someone who came quietly up the staircase and crossed the dark ballroom floor.

She heard the tread of the top step creak and felt the slight vibration of the floorboards as someone went past her door towards the turret room. It'll be one of the house servants going round to see that everything's all right, she thought.

A moment later the noiseless footsteps returned, and although she still could not hear them, the familiar vibration of the floorboards told her that the night wanderer had passed her door again. It occurred to her that it might be Kioh on the prowl, but she dismissed the idea almost immediately, for though Kioh was addicted to night prowling, the pressure of her velvet paws was not sufficient to betray her passing in this particular manner.

The unknown promenader returned across the ballroom once more: this time from the direction of the drawing-room for Copper heard the creak of the loose board just outside the drawing-room door. And inexplicably, with that sound the house began to fill with fear.

Fear crept in upon it like the noiseless advance of the monsoon mists across the wet forests, until it pervaded every nook and corner of the dark rooms. Fear blinked from behind the wet, glimmering window-panes, whispered in the rustling patter of the rain and dried Copper's mouth as she shrank back against her pillows, staring into the darkness with eyes that were wide with unreasoning panic. She could hear the beating of her own heart like an urgent, frantic drum in her breast. A drum that seemed to prevent her breathing as she strained her ears to catch a nearer sound. There was a second loose board in the passage to the right of her room, and she was waiting to hear it creak . . .

When at last it did so, she pulled herself together with an effort and reached for the switch of the bedside lamp. But with her finger upon it she hesitated; checked by the unpleasant thought that with a light in her room she would be clearly visible to anyone standing in the darkened hall outside.

Her hand dropped and she sat listening; rigidly erect beneath her shrouding mosquito net and struggling desperately with that rising tide of terror. A distant rumble of thunder blended with the sound of the breaking seas, but the silent walker did not return, and suddenly she could bear it no longer. She slid out of bed and groped her way across the room to the curtained doorway that separated her room from Valerie's, moving very warily for fear of making a sound and agonizingly aware of the pitfalls presented by the various objects that had been set to catch the drips. And when in spite of her caution her foot encountered the cold enamel rim of the soap-dish, it was all she could do to keep from crying out.

'For God's sake pull yourself together!' Copper told herself frantically. 'You're behaving like a hysterical schoolgirl, and you ought to be ashamed of yourself!' But reason failed to make a stand against the fear that filled the dark house, numbing her body and whispering to her imagination that if she continued to walk forward in the darkness, her outstretched, groping hands would not touch the friendly, swaying curtains or the solid wall, but a face — a wet face with a band of seaweed bound like a scarf about its skinny throat.

Copper's own throat stiffened with that fear, and she found she had to force herself forward as though her body was a machine which would no longer obey her will. And then she had reached the curtains, and was through them and dragging at Valerie's mosquito net.

Valerie had been asleep. But few people sleep very deeply in the Andamans, and she was awake almost before Copper's fingers touched her shoulder. She sat up and reached for the electric light switch, and a comforting yellow radiance illumined Copper's white face and the hanging folds of mosquito netting. 'What's the matter, Coppy? Been having another nightmare?'

'There's someone walking about the house.' Copper's whisper was unsteady in spite of her efforts to control it, and Valerie turned swiftly to face the door into the ballroom and listened for a moment or two. But except for the light patter of the rain, the swish of fan blades and the little chorus of drips from the leaking roof, the house was silent.

'Nonsense! No one would be trotting about the place at this hour. You know Dad doesn't let the house servants come upstairs at night and that Iman Din always sleeps down in the hall at the foot of the staircase. Besides, who on earth would be likely to want to perambulate around on a night like this? I expect it was bats. Or Kioh.'

'It *wasn't*,' insisted Copper, shivering uncontrollably. 'There *was* someone in the hall ... they were walking around in the dark. I felt the floor shake. You know how it does when anyone crosses the ballroom. And those two loose boards — the one outside the drawing-room and the one in the passage — I heard them creak.'

'Probably Ruby wanting a drink or a biscuit.'

'Then why go along the passage or into the drawing-room for it? And why walk up and down? Whoever it was out there has crossed the ballroom at least three times.'

'You've been having another nightmare,' accused Valerie. 'Own up, Coppy!'

Copper flushed guiltily, remembering her unpleasantly vivid dream of Ferrers Shilto's return from the sea. But since she had no intention of admitting to that at the present moment, she ignored the accusation and said stubbornly: 'It wasn't bats and its wasn't Kioh, and I wasn't asleep. Someone has been walking about the house ... *And what's more*,' she added, her voice dropping again to a whisper, '*they're still there* — look at Kioh!'

The Siamese cat had evidently been curled up asleep in the cushioned seat of Valerie's big armchair, for there was a betraying hollow that marked where her sleek, small body had rested. But something — perhaps Copper's entry — had disturbed her, and now she was standing upon the floor in front of the chair, facing the door that led into the ballroom.

The doors between the bedrooms and the ballroom were of the type that Copper had previously criticized: two swinging shutters, such as one sees in the taprooms of public houses and railway refreshment rooms, that spanned the centre of the door space, and closed with a latch, leaving a few feet of open space above and below. These half-doors were wide enough to stop anyone outside from seeing more than the extreme upper section of the wall and part of the floor of the bedrooms; and conversely to prevent anyone inside seeing into the ballroom, even by daylight. But cats can see in the dark; and Kioh, from the floor, had an uninterrupted view of the room — and of someone, or something, who was moving about there.

Her short, sleek, cream-coloured coat was no longer smooth but roughened where the hairs had lifted along her back, and she had crouched a little; her black tail twitching and her china blue eyes glaring fixedly at something that Copper and Valerie could not see. They watched her head turn slowly as her gaze followed someone who moved in the darkness beyond the door, and Valerie cleared her throat, which had suddenly become constricted, and raising her voice called out: '*Kaun-hai?* . . . Who's there?' There was no reply, but once again there came the familiar tremor of the floorboards as someone crossed the ballroom.

Kioh's black, pricked ears flattened and she began to growl softly in her throat — a small, oddly unnerving sound. Then step by step, and still growling, she backed away from the door until she had reached the safe harbourage of Valerie's bed.

'That's funny,' said Valerie, unaware that she too was speaking in a whisper, 'she's usually a most truculent animal.' She reached down to stroke the crouching shape, and the cat, whose eyes were still fixed on the doorway, seemed to explode at her touch as though it had been a small charge of dynamite, and whirling about, spitting and snarling, it streaked across the room to vanish behind the wardrobe . . .

'Oh my God!' gasped Copper. 'I believe I've bitten my heart in half — it jumped into my mouth and now it's in pieces. For heaven's sake let's go out and turn up the ballroom lights and see who's there. I can't stand this!'

'All right,' said Valerie shakily. 'But I didn't hear anything. I'm sure it's only bats.'

'Bats my foot!' retorted Copper forcefully. 'You don't have to hear! You can *feel*. If you don't believe me——' Before Valerie could stop her, she had reached over and switched off the light.

'Copper!'

'Ssh. Listen.'

They had not long to wait. There was no sound, but after a few moments they felt again that soft vibration of the floorboards, and presently, following it, there came the faint, unmistakable creak of the loose board by the drawing-room door.

'*Now* do you believe me?'

'Yes. There's someone prowling about the rooms. Turn the light on, Coppy, I'm going to see who it is.' Once again the bedside lamp made a friendly pool of light in the room, and Valerie said: 'We'd better put something on. If it's one of the servants, we can't go skittering about in our nightgowns.'

She found that she was still speaking in a whisper and was unreasonably annoyed by the discovery; but somehow she could not bring herself to speak aloud. She flung Copper a gaily striped wrap of towelling, and slipping her own arms into a silk dressing-gown, tightened its belt about her slim waist with a savage jerk as though it gave her courage, and added, still whispering: 'I expect we'll find it's only Ruby giving her insomnia an airing.'

'Well, Ruby or no Ruby,' said Copper, 'I'm taking a golf club with me. I admit I'd be happier with a poker, but a steel-shafted mashie makes me feel almost as good.'

Valerie reached wordlessly for the niblick and Copper was suddenly seized with inconvenient mirth: 'Oh g–gosh! we must look such f–fools! And I can't think why I'm laughing, because it isn't really a bit f–funny and I'm scared to death!'

'So am I,' admitted Valerie, 'but I shall have hysterics if I sit here any longer. I was all right until Kioh made that hellish noise, but that finished me. Come on, Coppy, and for heaven's sake hold my hand!'

Holding firmly to each other with one hand and clutching a golf club apiece with the other, they tiptoed over to the doorway. The main electric light switch for the bedroom was just inside the door, and Valerie turned it on, flooding the room with harsh light. Then pushing apart the swinging shutters, they braced themselves and stepped into the darkness.

To reach the switches for the ballroom involved walking a few yards down the passage to the left of the door. But the light streaming from Valerie's bedroom was sufficient to guide them, and a few seconds later a flood of light wiped out the lurking shadows in the ballroom.

There was no one there, and gaining confidence, they crossed the end of the ballroom and turned on the lights in the dining-room where the long, polished table, cleared of its glittering decorations, gleamed like a strip of dark water. 'Nothing here,' said Valerie, speaking aloud for the first time in ten minutes. But even as she spoke something moved swiftly in the shadow behind them, and they whirled round, white-faced.

Nicholas Tarrent, clad in pyjamas and a dressing-gown, stood scowling at them from the edge of the dining-room.

'Oh God, Nick, you gave me such a fright!' gasped Valerie.

'Nothing to what you've given me! What the hell do you two think you're doing, wandering about at this hour of the night? Brushing up your approach shots?'

Valerie and Copper, who had been endeavouring to conceal their possession of a couple of steel-shafted clubs, had the grace to blush. 'As a matter of fact,' confessed Copper, already slightly ashamed of her recent fears, 'we thought we heard someone walking about the house, so we came out to see who it was. We didn't know it was you.'

'*Me?* Why, you wretched golfing maniacs, I've only this moment torn myself from my bed. I heard someone prowling about, and when lights started springing up all over the house I thought I'd better come and investigate in case someone had been taken ill.'

'Do you usually conduct an investigation round a sick bed with a squash racquet?' inquired Copper accusingly.

Nick laughed. 'You've got me there. I'd forgotten I was still clutching the damn thing. As a matter of fact it was the only weapon within reach, and between you and me, I felt happier with something in my fist. You two ruddy little night-birds have been giving me the cold creeps, tiptoeing around in the dark.'

Valerie and Copper exchanged a swift look. 'In the *dark*?' said Copper.

Valerie turned to Nick: 'Had you heard us for long, before the lights went on?'

'Well, hardly *heard* you. But I felt the floor vibrate every time you passed. And there are a couple of loose boards around: I heard them creak once or twice and I was beginning to think that this would bear looking into when the lights went up. So I came out to see what was up.'

'Then there *was* someone out here!' said Valerie. 'It wasn't us, Nick. We heard the boards too. And Kioh saw something in the ballroom. She stood and watched it moving, and it got on our nerves. So we came out to see who it was.'

They had all been talking in undertones to avoid arousing the rest of the house, but now Copper's voice sharpened: 'Well, what are we going to do? We all heard someone moving about, and unless we make certain that there is no one hiding up here, I for one shan't sleep another wink.'

'All right. Have it your own way,' said Nick. 'Come on. Keep your eyes on the ball and don't press.'

Picking their way among the assortment of bowls and basins set to catch the leaks they made their way across the ballroom into the drawing-room, through the wide, glassed-in verandah and back past the dining-room again. They searched the pantry and the larder and along the passage to the turret room, and opened the doors of the nearby bathroom and the small room beside it. They looked behind and under sofas and chairs, bookcases and cupboards, made certain that all the doors and windows that led out of the house, or on to the two balconies that opened off the closed verandah, were locked, and by the time they returned to the ballroom they had searched the top storey of the house as thoroughly as was possible without entering the bedrooms occupied by Valerie's father, the Stocks, or John Shilto.

Sir Lionel's room and the turret room where John Shilto slept were the only two bedrooms in the house possessed of an orthodox door, and as their doors were closed it was unlikely that anyone other than the owners would have passed through them. The bedroom occupied by the Stocks, which lay beyond Valerie's, closed with the usual ineffectual swing shutters, but a faint, rhythmic sound of snoring suggested that at least one of the occupants was sound asleep.

To make their rounds complete, and more for form's sake than anything else, they looked into Nick's room — this with extreme caution to avoid disturbing the peaceful slumbers of Dan Harcourt — and went through the girls' bedrooms before ending up in the ballroom once more. But with the exception of Kioh, whom they flushed from under Valerie's window-seat, still hostile and inclined to spit, they had found nothing and no one. 'Well I hope everyone's satisfied,' said Nick shortly, his finger on the switch of the ballroom lights. 'Unless it was your father, Val, or Shilto or one of the Stocks, it was bats or the wind. Or too much plum pudding! Take your choice.'

'The last, I expect,' admitted Valerie, yawning. 'Plus a touch of Rosamund Purvis's hysterics thrown in. Well, thanks for your support, Nick. I'm sorry we spoilt your beauty sleep. Come on, Coppy — bed, I think.' She switched off the lights and they turned to go back to their own rooms. But they had barely taken more than a couple of paces into the darkness when they heard Copper gasp.

There had been so much stark fear in that small sound that Nick flung out an arm and caught her against him. 'What is it, Copper?' His voice was sharply peremptory. 'Someone brushed past me,' quavered Copper in a dry whisper. 'They almost touched me — Nick, *listen*!'

All three stood still: and heard, in that stillness, clearly and unmistakably, the creak of the loose board by the drawing-room door, and felt the tremor of the floorboards beneath their feet . . .

'This is ridiculous!' said Nick furiously. He thrust Copper away and took a quick stride back to the switches, and once again the ballroom was flooded with light. But there was no one there, and beyond it the drawing-room doors yawned black and empty.

'Iman Din will be in the hall downstairs,' quavered Valerie. 'He's supposed to stay awake, but he always falls asleep and someone may have passed him. Let's go and wake him up.'

They went quickly over to the banisters, and turning on the lights above the staircase, looked down into the well of the hall.

But Iman Din, the old, white-whiskered *chaprassi** who slept at the foot of the hall stairs by night, was not asleep. He was standing by the bottom step of the staircase, looking up at them as they leaned over the carved banister rail above him, and he did not look as though he had been recently awakened from sleep,

*Office messenger.

but rather as though he had been standing there, listening, for some considerable time.

'Well, I'm damned!' said Nick explosively. 'The old coot must have heard us pottering round hunting burglars, and he hasn't even raised a finger to help us or to find out what all the activity was about. Useful sort of guardian for our slumbers. Ask him if anyone has passed him, Val.'

Valerie leant over the banisters and spoke to the old man in Urdu. He answered her in the same tongue, and Copper saw her start and jerk back, frowning.

'What does he say, Val?'

'Nothing; only some nonsense.' Valerie was plainly disturbed and not a little angry.

Nick said: 'The point is, could anyone have come up those stairs tonight without that whiskered Methuselah spotting them?'

The old man shifted his gaze to Nick, and spoke in slow, accented English: 'Who should enter? The Sahib sees that the door is barred' — he gestured with a claw-like hand towards the massive front door with its heavy iron bolts. They caught a glimmer of light from the guard room through the glass panes of the side door, and heard the sentry on duty ground the butt of his rifle on the stone flags outside.

'Don't beg the question,' snapped Nick. 'Could anyone have come up these stairs since Harcourt Sahib came home?'

'Assuredly,' said the old man gravely. He turned again to Valerie and spoke swiftly in the vernacular.

Nick began to lose his temper. The hands of the hall clock pointed to a quarter to three; he had had very little sleep and his experience in the storm had not been pleasant. Above all, Copper's panic had awakened something in him that he had as yet not stopped to analyse. 'See here,' said Nick dangerously, 'if I find that you or your pals have been trying any funny stuff in the house tonight, I'll come down and wring your neck. First you say that the door is barred and no one can come in, and then that someone could have come up these stairs. Well, there was someone up here five minutes ago, and you're coming up to help find out just who it was!'

'The Sahib is angry,' said Iman Din gravely. 'He does not understand. But I will show that no *man* passed this way.' He started to mount the shallow stairs, and Valerie gripped Nick's arm: 'No,' she said breathlessly. 'No, let's go back to bed, Nick. We've looked through the rooms once. Go back, Iman Din.'

'Rubbish,' said Nick curtly. 'Come on up. And you two clear off to bed. Iman Din and I will scoop in this sleepwalker.'

Iman Din, continuing his ascent, put his foot upon the top step of the staircase, and, as always, it creaked sharply.

'There!' said Copper. 'That's the first sound I heard. Somebody *did* come up these stairs.'

'Of course there was someone up here! And I believe this old devil knows who it was. What did he say to you, Val?'

'Nothing. Just native rubbish.'

Nick caught her by the shoulder, and swung her round to face him. 'Well, let's hear it. You're being damned irritating, Val, and for two pins I'd smack you. Odd as it may seem I could do with some sleep. But as long as people are going to perambulate up and down the hall the minute the lights are out, I can't see myself getting any. Come on, out with it.'

'Oh, very well,' snapped Valerie. 'If it's any help to you, he says it's a ghost.'

There was a short and pregnant silence. Then: 'Ghost, my Aunt Fanny!' said Nick angrily. 'No ghost could make the floor vibrate like that, or weigh enough to make those boards creak. Don't be a mug, Val!'

Iman Din's wise old eyes travelled from one to another of the three faces before him, and then past them to the doorway of the darkened drawing-room. He let his breath out in a little sigh and said: 'The Sahib says one pressed upon the board which speaks. Look, and I will show——'

He led the way into the ballroom, and stopped before the open doorway. 'Will the Sahib walk through?' Nick complied, frowning. There was no sound, and Copper said: 'Of course it didn't creak that time. He didn't tread on it. He stepped over it.'

'And why so, Miss-sahib?'

'Because of the water, of course——' began Copper; and stopped, catching her breath sharply. For she had suddenly seen what the old man had seen before her . . . There had been a leak in the roof just above the drawing-room door, and a spreading pool of water saturated the floorboards. But when the three of them had searched the house the lights, as now, had been on, and because they could see they had avoided the various bowls that dotted the floor and stepped across the wet patches. But someone walking in the dark would not have seen that wet stain, and so would have walked into it instead of over it. And the board would have creaked under their feet. Yet it was not this that had driven the blood from Copper's face. She had, in the same instant, seen something else. Something they could all see now——

'Ah!' said Iman Din. 'Now the Sahib understands. When a foot is placed upon that board it speaks in the darkness. But the wood is wet — the Sahib sees how wet. Yet no mark leads beyond it, though the floor is polished!'

Copper and Valerie started back from the gleaming stain and stared at the smooth, polished floorboards. Nick did not speak, but he placed his foot squarely upon that wet space, which creaked beneath his tread, and walked back to join them.

There was no need for words.

Four clear damp footmarks patched the strip of floor that he had walked across.

'The Sahib sees,' said Iman Din softly. He drew a sudden, hissing breath between his yellowed teeth, and flung out a skinny, pointing hand: *'Look there, Sahib! There — where the storm returns!'*

The three whirled about to stare where his gnarled forefinger pointed across the darkened drawing-room to the verandah beyond. And as they looked a vivid flash of lightning bathed the inky sky beyond the expanse of window-panes in a livid radiance that silhouetted, for a fraction of a second, the figure of a man who stood in the angle of the dark verandah. A small, wizened figure who appeared to be wearing about his neck a ragged scarf, the ends of which fluttered out upon the draught.

With a sob of pure terror, Copper flung herself frantically at Nick, burying her face against his shoulder. 'What — who is it?' quavered Valerie, gripping his arm. Nick shook himself free and raced across the drawing-room and into the verandah.

It took him a full minute to find the verandah switch, and it was a further two or three minutes before he returned, walking slowly across the drawing-room, his hands deep in the pockets of his dressing-gown and a puzzled frown between his brows.

Valerie and Copper had vanished, but the old *chaprassi* stood where he had left him, silent and motionless.

'You saw it, Iman Din. What—— Who was it?'

'Sahib,' said Iman Din, 'it is One who returns, seeking vengeance.'

10

'*Christians awake, salute the happy morn!*' carolled Charles, entering the breakfast room. 'Sorry I'm late, sir. Happy Christmas, darling — and here's your present. I know you chose it yourself, but let's have expressions of rapturous surprise, just for the look of it. Morning, everyone. Happy Christmas!'

Valerie had invited Charles to have breakfast with them on Christmas morning, but the storm was responsible for the unusually large assembly in the dining-room, and Charles alone appeared to be in good spirits.

John Shilto, looking if possible even more pasty as to colouring and morose as to expression than usual, was helping himself to kidneys and bacon and ignoring the timid conversational efforts of Leonard Stock. Mrs Stock, who had recovered sufficiently to put in an appearance, was seated, freshly rouged and curled, between Nick and Dan Harcourt, while Sir Lionel, a man who preferred to eat his breakfast in a ritual silence occupied by the perusal of three-weeks-old newspapers, was moodily sipping coffee and turning at frequent intervals to glance at the clock as though help might be forthcoming from the blandly unemotional dial. He had responded without animation to Valerie's kiss and her 'Merry Christmas, Dad' and made no attempt to return the conventional greeting.

He's probably got the right idea, thought Copper, avoiding Nick's eye and helping herself to grapenuts. It certainly can't be called 'merry' at the moment!

Copper was suffering a reaction from the night's alarms;

though curiously enough it was not the remembrance of the mysterious prowler that was disturbing her. The terrors of the dark hours seemed less alarming and even a little foolish by the cold light of morning, compared with her own frantic clinging to Nick, and Copper flushed angrily at the memory of her fear-stricken abandonment. And more than angrily at the recollection of Nick's treatment of it. He pulled me off him as if I'd been a nasty type of leech, she thought resentfully, and he probably thinks I did it on purpose; like Ruby, clinging round his neck like a ton of chewing-gum last night — and then I do exactly the same thing a few hours later! I expect, decided Copper forlornly, that he's used to it.

Breakfast was an even less pleasant meal than dinner had been the night before, and with the exception of Charles, no one made the slightest effort to improve it. They ate for the most part in silence, and at the conclusion of the meal dispersed without hilarity: to assemble an hour later in the hall, coated, hatted, gloved, in possession of prayer books and (it is to be hoped) armed with collection money.

Packing themselves under the waterproof protection of the waiting buggies they covered the few hundred yards that separated Government House from the little English church on Ross where, owing to the violence of the storm and the fact that the ferry was unable to run, the Reverend Dobbie's Christmas Day congregation had been reduced to a minimum. Mrs Dobbie had done her best to ornament the altar and chancel in a manner she considered suitable to the season, but the sprays of oleander and wilting branches of casuarina had formed a sorry substitute for holly and evergreen, and the church was very dark, for the doors and windows had been tightly shuttered against the stormy day. But no shutters could keep out the draughts, and the candle flames swayed and flickered, streaming out at right angles to their wicks like small, shining flags, while the timeworn carols sounded thin and strange as they rose in unequal competition with the beating of the rain and the howl of the wind.

'O come, all ye faithful, Joyful and triumphant . . .' Copper's voice supported Valerie's against the tuneless but determined baritone of Hamish Rattigan, who occupied the pew immediately behind them, and it occurred to her, with no sense of regret, that a year ago she had sung that same carol in one of London's loveliest churches. There had been hundreds of candles like drifts of golden stars, holly and Christmas roses, a glittering Christmas tree and a world-famous choir: high, pure, boys' voices, with the deeper tones of the men like tolling bells. And in her heart an echoing waste of loneliness and vague, unformulated longings.

And now once more it was Christmas Day, and the four walls of the little dim church with its wheezy harmonium and meagre congregation contained the whole of Copper's heart's desire, while outside the walls, in spite of rain and wind, hurricane and recent death, lay all Romance — a hundred coral-reefed islands scattered over a jade and sapphire sea. Life, Beauty and Adventure: and Nicholas Tarrent, that as yet unknown quantity . . . who had probably got at least a dozen wives in every port, did one but know! thought Copper, taking herself firmly in hand. At which point in her meditations she discovered that the carol having been concluded, the congregation, with the exception of herself, were again seated, and from his place on the opposite side of the aisle the subject of her reverie was endeavouring to draw her attention to the fact.

Copper sat down hurriedly and for the next fifteen minutes endeavoured to fix her attention on the Reverend Dobbie's almost inaudible address.

The afternoon continued as wet and wild as the morning, but towards four o'clock the storm showed signs of having blown itself out at last. The wind had dropped again and the rain died away into a light drizzle, and by the time that the house party, whose numbers had been augmented by the addition of several extra guests, collected in the verandah for tea and Christmas cake, the clouds had lifted and Mount Harriet stood out blackly against a sullen grey sky.

'Let's go for a walk around the island,' suggested Valerie. 'It really does look as though the worst is over, and I'd like to see how much damage has been done.'

'A considerable amount, I fear,' said the Chief Commissioner, joining the group in the verandah and helping himself to an egg sandwich: 'In fact, I'm afraid that you will all have to make up your minds to being marooned on Ross for several days. The hurricane has smashed the jetties and the pier into matchwood, and until something can be done about that no boat can reach us. What is still more annoying is the fact that the telephone wires have gone, and I am told that until this sea goes down there is no chance of repairing them. So for the time being we are completely cut off.'

'But what about our milk and butter, and things like that?' demanded Valerie, dismayed.

'We must make the best of it, my dear. There should be plenty of tinned milk in the house, and we can do without butter and fresh meat for a few days. At least we are in our own homes, instead of being stranded on the wrong side of the bay like Dr Vicarjee and Frank Burton, who, I am afraid, will have to resign themselves to staying in Aberdeen for some days to come.'

'But what about the dance at the Club and—— Oh, damn! damn, *damn*!'

'Cheer up, Val,' comforted Charles. 'That's life, that was. Don't let's spend the rest of the day in gloom. Action is indicated. Remember that this is Christmas Day, and as the padre has already pointed out, the motto for the moment is *"Peace on Earth, and Goodwill towards Men"* — which means me. You girls go and shove a mac on and come for a walk. It will do your tempers good.'

The wind might have dropped, but it had by no means disappeared. It was still blowing in steadily from the south-east

— driving the grey seas on to the rocks and the sea-wall of Ross as though with each crashing onslaught it must engulf the tiny island — as Nick, Copper, Valerie and Charles walked arm-in-arm down the steep roadway from the Residency to the jetty and the Club.

Behind them, with her escort, came Mrs Stock, who appeared to have recovered both her looks and her spirits. She showed little sign of the collapse that had followed her ordeal of the previous day, and had temporarily transferred her attention from Nick to Dan Harcourt, to whose arm she now clung, uttering little feminine shrieks and cries as the wind dragged at her skirts and fluttered the ends of the gay silk scarf that she had tied becomingly about her carefully waved head. Leonard Stock had not accompanied the party, but Hamish, her faithful adorer, had possession of her left arm, while George and Ronnie, the latter unusually taciturn, completed her entourage. The rear of the procession was brought up by Amabel and John Shilto, neither of whom appeared to be enjoying the other's society.

Amabel's nose was suspiciously pink and her eyes noticeably swollen, and her thoughts ran in continuous and gloomy circles: Why did I have to slap George like that? Not that he didn't deserve it. He did. But it was all Mrs Purvis's fault, behaving like a stupid — a stupid—— Amabel's vocabulary failed to produce a sufficiently withering adjective with which to qualify the extreme stupidity of Rosamund Purvis whose regrettable display of lung power had blasted Amabel's young life. I wish I were dead, thought Amabel bleakly, then perhaps George would be sorry!

The storm had left a trail of ruin across the little island. Trunks of fallen palm trees, rent from their inadequate moorings or snapped off like broken broomsticks, lay across the paths and tilted drunkenly down the slopes. Leaves, twigs and flowers, stripped from trees and creepers, carpeted the ground and festooned the broken telephone and electric light wires. Coconuts lay smashed upon the roadways, and even now an occasional nut would fall with a thud, bespattering the earth with milky fluid or bouncing unbroken on to the rocks, to be snatched away by the mountainous seas that still crashed upon the broken fragments of Ross jetty, deluging the causeway in clouds of spray and tossing an untidy litter of wreckage over the Club lawn.

The small summer-house that overhung one end of the turtle tank was now roofless, and the water in the tank was higher than Valerie had ever seen it before as she leant over the edge, peering into its murky depths. A huge dim shape flickered for a moment in the heaving darkness of the shadowed water below her and a horny head emerged for a brief second, regarded her with an austere eye, and withdrew abruptly. Valerie laughed and said: 'If this sea keeps up it may break down the wall, and then you'll all escape. Good luck, chums! Charles, what about walking round Barrack Point to watch the waves? They're gorgeous after a storm.'

The wind met them as they rounded the point, and they paused, entranced, to watch the terrible masses of the steel-grey seas driving down upon the island to crash on to the jagged rocks below the sea-wall in a maelstrom of foam. 'Do let's go down to the beach,' begged Copper. 'It'll look much more exciting from there.'

'There isn't any beach we can go down to,' pointed out Nick. 'And if you think I'm going to let you climb down on to those rocks, you can think again. You'd be dragged off them and swept out to sea inside five minutes. Use some sense!'

'I don't mean here,' said Copper. 'I meant farther along, where the sea-wall stops. Even at high tide there is still a strip of sand there that isn't covered. Look — I'll show you.'

The small curving beach below the house was protected by two natural breakwaters of rock, and they had little difficulty in scrambling down the steep slope between the palm trees and reaching the narrow strip of sand. And as Copper had predicted, the towering waves that swept down upon the island appeared doubly awe-inspiring when seen from the level of the shore. Like dark hills of water that mounted higher and higher as they neared the shore, their crests and flanks streaked with livid bars of foam, to curl over at last and crash down into acres of boiling surf.

'Imagine being wrecked in a sea like that,' shuddered Copper. 'You wouldn't stand a chance. There can't be a lifeboat in the world that could get through it. I'm not surprised that the *Sapphire* ran for her life!'

'Wonder where the old girl's got to?' murmured Dan Harcourt disrespectfully, screwing up his eyes against the stinging salt-laden wind and peering out to sea: 'I don't suppose she's far off. Except that there isn't a harbour worth mentioning around here, so she may have made for the coast. Anyway, I'll bet the boys are all feeling pea-green and peculiar.'

'What would have happened if they hadn't left Port Blair?' inquired Copper, interested.

'The same thing that happened to the old *Enterprise*,' said Ronnie Purvis: *'Smasho!'*

'Why? What happened to it?'

'Oh, don't you know?' Amabel, who could be counted upon to know the details of any disaster, brightened up a trifle and added her voice to the conversation: 'They had come here on a visit, like the *Sapphire*; only of course it was years and years ago — 1891, I think — and a storm got up before they could leave harbour and they got driven on to the rocks off South Point. Ever so many of them were drowned, and there's a tablet to them in the church. Didn't you notice it?'

'No,' said Copper shortly. 'I'm thankful to say I did not!'

But Amabel was not to be deflected from the recital of disaster: 'Well, it's there; and the new *Enterprise* presented the ring of bells in the church steeple in memory of them. At low tide you can still see the boilers of the old *Enterprise* on the rocks off South Point, all covered with barnacles. We sail round them sometimes when we go fishing. I suppose the tide carried the rest of the ship out to sea when it broke up, but these were too heavy. Fancy all those people drowning so close to the shore. It just goes to show, doesn't it?'

'Show what?' inquired Copper irritably. Amabel's story had spoilt her enjoyment in the sight of the thundering seas, and what had seemed so splendid a spectacle a few minutes ago, now appeared sinister and cruel and strangely menacing. All those people, going to their deaths so close to that same shore, in that same cold, savage sea . . .

'The natives say,' continued Amabel, determined to extract the last ounce of gruesomeness from her story, 'that when there's a storm the noise the tide makes coming over those boilers is the voices of the drowned men among the rocks calling for help, and that on stormy nights you can see their faces coming up through the water like . . .' She was interrupted by a sudden gasping cry from Mrs Stock, and broke off, staring: 'What's the matter?'

Mrs Stock, still retaining her grip upon Dan and Hamish, was peering intently at the waves, her head a little thrust forward. She flushed at the inquiry, and laughed a little uncertainly. 'It's funny,' she said, 'but for a minute I thought I saw a face looking at me from out of a wave, just before it broke. I suppose that story about the drowned men of the *Enterprise* is making me see things. But it looked so real that it gave me quite a nasty shock. It was just out there——' She released Hamish's arm to point with a vermilion-tipped finger: 'In the second line of waves. I expect it was one of those seal things. A dugong.'

'A dugong?' exclaimed Copper, thrilled. 'You mean one of those creatures that people used to think were mermaids? Where! . . . Where!'

They all turned with her to stare into the grey, crashing seas, their eyes confused by blown spray and distracted by bobbing wreckage. *'There!'* said Valerie suddenly. 'I believe I saw something over to the right. No, it isn't — it's only half a coconut!'

'No, it's not,' said Copper. 'It's – it's—— *What is it, Nick?*'

The cold ridge of water that was towering to its fall raced in upon the shore, and from beneath its curling crest, pale and glimmering against the dark wall of water and whiter than the boiling foam, there peered a face——

Mrs Stock screamed at the top of her voice as the wave, crashing in spray, surged up the beach and flung its burden at their feet. Ferrers Shilto had returned.

'Don't look, dear!' said Nick sharply. He caught Copper by the shoulder and swung her around forcibly. But Copper had seen, as they had all seen . . .

He lay on his back where the tide had flung him, his feet in the creaming froth of foam and flotsam, his eyes wide open and his face, unmarked by the jagged coral rocks, wearing an expression of almost ludicrous astonishment. His left hand lay across his chest and something glinted redly: a single splash of scarlet.

'There's blood on it!' sobbed Copper. She wrenched herself from Nick's hold and faced the thing that lay on the beach. But the foam of the next wave dragged at its feet, disturbing the limp figure so that its hand fell away from its breast and lay palm down on the sand. And there was no blood. Only the red blotch of the big garnet that winked and glowed from the clumsy bronze ring on Ferrers Shilto's finger.

Nick said: 'Get these women away, George. Purvis, you'd better get up to the hospital and collect a stretcher. Go on, Copper darling. You and Val see to those two women. George will go with you.' Copper turned obediently, and taking the shivering Amabel by the arm, dragged her away up the steep grassy slope above the beach, followed by George and Valerie almost carrying the now completely hysterical Ruby between them.

The noise of their departure died away among the palm trunks, and on the beach Nick, Charles and Hamish lifted the limp, wizened body. There was a small pinkish stain where the head had lain, but as Dan Harcourt stooped above it the lash of another wave obliterated it, and he straightened, frowning, and followed to where they laid the dead man above the reach of the waves.

John Shilto had made no move to help them, and now he stood motionless beside the bedraggled object that had been his cousin, staring down at it with a curiously unpleasant expression on his pasty features. I believe the bastard's actually *gloating!* thought Nick disgustedly. And turning away, he took out a cigarette and lit it, shielding the match flame from the wind with his cupped hands, and leant back against a palm tree to wait for Ronnie Purvis and the stretcher.

Charles and Hamish followed his example, but Dan Harcourt remained beside the body, staring down at it with an intent expression that suggested, strongly, a terrier at a rat hole. Presently he went down upon his knees and examined the widened pupils of the staring sightless eyes, and then, carefully and minutely, the fingers of both lax hands. The big garnet winked redly as it turned, and he let the cold hand fall and came to his feet again, brushing the sand off his knees.

Charles said: 'It's odd that he hasn't been smashed up at all: you'd have thought all those rocks and reefs would have battered him to bits.'

'Tide,' said John Shilto curtly, speaking for the first time. 'It must have pulled him out of the harbour mouth clear of the rocks. And, as you see, when it turned it landed him back at the one place where there is a clear strip of sand. The current pulls in strongly towards this beach and most of the big wreckage gets flung up here.'

'Oh yes?' said Hamish without interest, and looked anxiously at his watch. They had left the house just before five but now it was well past six o'clock, and aided by the thick blanket of the storm-clouds the swift tropic darkness was closing in on them: 'I wish Ronnie would get a move on,' he said uneasily. 'It'll be dark before he gets back.'

'It's all right,' said Charles, 'here he is now — with young Dutt and a couple of troops, plus stretcher. They must have run most of the way.'

'Truda is behaving like a lunatic,' panted Ronnie Purvis, sliding down the bank on to the narrow strip of beach: 'She says that she won't have the body in the hospital because she's there by herself — except for my wife, who for some goddam reason won't leave, and backs her up. If we insist, we'll have them both in hysterics. What the hell are we going to do? It'll be dark inside fifteen minutes and we can't bury him until tomorrow. We've got to park him somewhere for the night.'

'What about the church?' suggested Hamish, prompted by some hazy notion of lying-in-state. Ronnie Purvis gave a short laugh. 'Can you see Mrs Padre standing for it? Or half the old women in the place, for that matter! No. We've got to get him under cover somewhere. But I'm damned if I know where.'

'If I might make suggestion,' said Dr Vicarjee's young assistant in his soft, imperfect English, 'there is Guest House. It is empty and very seldom used. For many months now no one is using.'

'That's the ticket!' said Mr Purvis with relief. 'Well done, Dutt. Only outside visitors are ever put up in that moth-eaten dump, and they won't ever hear that it's been used as a morgue. If we planted him anywhere else you'd find people refusing to live in the house afterwards. Right, then. Take him along to the Guest House, will you.'

Hamish said: 'I'll go along too, just to see it's O.K. I suppose you'll have to make some sort of examination, Dutt, now that Vicarjee is marooned on the mainland?'

Dan Harcourt took a swift step forward as though he would have spoken, but he evidently changed his mind, for he checked and turned away without speaking, and Charles said: 'See you later then, Hamish; I gather we are both attending a Christmas party up at the house. We've certainly had a jolly day for it! Come on, Nick.'

They turned together and made off in the gathering darkness

towards the house whose already lighted windows gleamed through the trees above them, and John Shilto, with one last, long stare at the sheeted figure being lifted on to the stretcher, turned on his heel and followed them.

11

If the Christmas Eve party had been a failure, the dinner party on Christmas night could definitely be classed, in the hostess's phraseology, as a total frost.

Mrs Stock had taken to her bed, but there had been no question of cancelling the party, for with the house full of guests the table was bound to be fairly crowded. And as Valerie said, one or two more were not likely to add or detract from the general gloom, so if she had to give a dinner party at all she might as well have Charles there to hold her hand under the table and help her through it.

Whether Charles fulfilled the first of these conditions was a matter only known to himself and Valerie, and as he happened to be left-handed the matter was in doubt. But in spite of his best efforts at cheerfulness and his fiancée's valiant support, the conversation at dinner was barely more than spasmodic. Copper looked white and on edge, while Nick was for once strangely taciturn.

Nick had problems of his own to contend with. The sight of Copper's distress had not only disturbed him but made him explicably angry: a combination of emotions that caused him considerable irritation, since he was not yet sure of his own feelings towards her. She appealed to him in a way that no woman had ever done before — and a good many women had held a temporary appeal for Nick Tarrent. But Copper was something different. There were times when he would have liked to snatch her up in his arms and kiss her so that she could not breathe, and others when he would have liked to pick her up and throw her into the sea — though whether from a sense of irritation with her or himself, or a desire to be free from her disturbing hold on his heart, he did not know. Nor was he at all sure that he wished to find out . . .

Seated on Nick's left, John Shilto was eating oysters in a manner which caused the majority of his fellow-guests to wish that he would extend his habitual silence to his consumption of food, and beyond him sat Dan Harcourt, absent-mindedly manufacturing bread pills and gazing thoughtfully into space. Valerie, looking drained and tired, was keeping up a desultory conversation with Leonard Stock and Ronnie Purvis, while beyond them Amabel and George sat side by side in a state of congealed gloom and unconcealed misery.

Silly idiots! thought Copper bleakly: they've only got to say two words and they'd be sobbing on each other's necks inside half a minute. I wonder why it's so difficult to say 'I'm sorry?' . . . I wonder why you can't ever be really sensible about the people you care for most? I wonder why I should have dreamt that Ferrers had been stabbed? — everything else was the same, but there wasn't a knife . . .

Her thoughts, back again in that frightening groove, sheered away from it violently, and she turned feverishly to the silent Hamish. 'I had no idea that there were oysters in these waters, Hamish. Do you ever find pearls in them, or are the pearl kind different?'

'Eh?' said Captain Rattigan, waking abruptly from his sombre meditations. The demon of jealousy was gnawing painfully at Hamish's vitals, for although his goddess could do no wrong in his infatuated eyes, Ruby's attentions to Surgeon-Lieutenant Harcourt that afternoon had been more than marked. And almost more than Hamish felt himself able to bear. He had not heard Copper's question and she repeated it.

'Oh — er — yes,' said Hamish, 'I don't think so.'

Charles, nobly following this lead, said: 'I believe there are a lot of oysters around, but the local fishermen are too lazy to go out and dive for them. They prefer hanging over the jetty with a piece of string and a hook and hoping for the best.'

'Last year, one of them went to sleep and fell in,' said Amabel, offering her contribution to the conversational gaiety: 'And he was drowned. Like Ferrers.'

There was a brief silence, during which her fellow-guests regarded young Miss Withers with varying degrees of emotion, and then Sir Lionel said absently, reaching for the salt: 'That reminds me, I had a letter from Ferrers only a day or two ago asking me if . . . the red pepper, please, thank you . . . but I never had time to answer it, and now the poor fellow is dead. Very sad.'

'Yes, indeed,' agreed Leonard Stock unhappily. 'I cannot really feel responsible, but Ruby says——'

'Responsible?' The Chief Commissioner looked startled. 'Responsible for what?'

'Well . . . er . . . You see, Ruby thinks — that is . . . Well, what I mean is, I suppose it *was* partly our fault; in a way. If only we hadn't happened to stop off at Ferrers's bungalow yesterday this would never have occurred. It was most unfortunate. But it was really *not* my fault. Mrs Dobbie wanted to ask him about bringing some bedding, and I don't see how I could have . . . But Ruby says——'

Sir Lionel said impatiently: 'I cannot see what you are worrying about, Stock. Or why you or your wife should feel in any way responsible for something that was only an unfortunate accident. It might have happened to anyone.'

'That's exactly what I said. "But, my dear," I said, "it might even have been *you*! Or any of us." But Ruby seems to think . . .'

'That it's all your fault,' finished Valerie shortly. Mr Stock flushed and said incoherently: 'Yes — no. No! I'm sure she . . . I didn't mean . . . You mustn't think——' He gestured agitatedly with his oyster fork.

Copper murmured something that sounded suspiciously like

'apologetic sand-crab' and Valerie threw her a repressive look and said hurriedly: 'What was Ferrers writing to you about, Dad?'

'What's that?'

'The letter. You said that Ferrers had written to you.'

'Did I? Oh yes. Well I do not think we want to go on talking about poor Ferrers this evening. It cannot be pleasant for Mr Shilto.'

John Shilto grinned at him sardonically from across the table, and said: 'I beg that you won't let my feelings concern you, Sir Lionel. Naturally my cousin's death was a great shock to me, but we were hardly on such friendly terms as to make it a mortal blow. And as for this letter, since it is probably the last that Ferrers ever wrote, I am of course——'

But Copper did not allow him to finish, for she too did not wish to speak of Ferrers Shilto; or to be reminded of that pallid face with the astonished eyes. And seized with a sudden and uncontrollable horror of the subject, she said violently: 'Sir Lionel is right. We don't want to talk about him. Surely we can talk about something else? — anything else!'

'Attagirl, Coppy!' approved Charles, seconding the motion. 'What shall we try instead? Let's all decide whom we dislike most and then talk about them. There's nothing like a bit of mutual loathing to draw people together. *"Peace on Earth, Goodwill towards Men!"* What about George? We can probably all find something lousy to say about George. Wake up, George! You are about to be thrown to the lions.'

Copper laughed and had the grace to look ashamed of herself, but the dinner party, finding Charles's guide to conversation a useful one, settled happily down to reviling Europe's least-liked public character, and Ferrers Shilto was temporarily forgotten. But only temporarily . . . The girls had barely left the table to return to the far verandah for coffee when a soft-footed servant announced that Dr Dutt was below and wished to speak to the Commissioner.

'Send him up,' said Sir Lionel, busy with the port; and two minutes later the slim figure of Dr Vicarjee's young assistant entered the dining-room. There were raindrops on his coat and his shoes left damp patches upon the floorboards. 'What is it, Dutt?' inquired Sir Lionel. 'You look pretty wet. Have some hot coffee?'

'Thanking you, but no, sir. I am come only to ask leave for burial of corpse. I have myself held inspection and signed certificate of death, in regretted absence of Dr Vicarjee. Climate here is most humid and corpse should be interred tomorrow morning at latest, with your order.'

Dan Harcourt stirred suddenly in his chair and leant forward across the table. 'Isn't it usual, sir,' he inquired of the Chief Commissioner, 'for two doctors to sign a death certificate?'

Dr Dutt interrupted, bristling slightly: 'That has already been done. Oah yess — I know all procedures. Matron, Miss Gidney, who is lady doctor, has also signed, so all is in order.'

'Yes, yes. Of course, that is quite sufficient.' Sir Lionel did not like being bothered by what he considered unnecessary red tape. 'He had better be buried as early as possible tomorrow morning. I will see that the padre is notified. By the way, Shilto, your cousin was not an R.C. by any chance? No . . . I thought not. Then I will notify Mr Dobbie. I will write the order now.'

He rose to leave the table, and Dan Harcourt pushed back his chair and stood up. 'Forgive me butting in, sir, but — er — could I, as a matter of interest, have a look at the body? I'm a doctor myself and I might be able to help Dr Dutt with his examination.'

'Already the examination has been performed,' said Dr Dutt stiffly, indignation quivering in every line of his slim figure.

'But——'

Sir Lionel turned irritably upon this pushing young man. A surgeon-lieutenant, was he? Well, possibly that meant some kind of a doctor on a ship, but not on shore. 'It seems to me to be quite unnecessary, Mr Harcourt,' he said coldly. 'Come, Dutt.'

Dan flushed and stepped back: Sir Lionel was right. It was no business of his and he had invited that snub. All the same . . . He watched Sir Lionel and young Dutt leave the room, and having finished his drink, went off to play card games in the drawing-room. But the party spirit was lamentably lacking that Christmas night, and it was barely ten-thirty when Valerie stacked the cards and voted for bed. 'It's been such a mildewed day that the sooner we finish it the better,' she said. 'Charles darling, will you and Hamish see that Amabel gets safely up to the hospital? I suppose she *is* still parking there with Rosamund?'

'What about making George see her home?' suggested Charles. 'Then they'll be able to stage a reconciliation on the way, which will ease the present situation a lot. After all, they couldn't very well do the entire trip in stodgy silence. Or could they?'

'Could they not!' sighed Valerie. 'They managed to sit out an entire meal side by side without uttering a twitter. Besides, you know what a fat-head Amabel is. She'd never bring herself to speak a kind word; not with several buggy-men two feet off her and a police orderly trotting along behind.'

Charles said: 'No, I suppose not. I'd forgotten it was raining. I had pictured them wandering hospital-wards, hand in hand, and forgiving each other nobly by the reservoir. However, I do not propose to get soaked to the skin because George has had a tiff with his girlfriend. He can darn well take her back himself, reconciliation or no reconciliation. I'm for bed. Come on round behind this useful screen where Leonard can't see us, and kiss me good-night. I have had a trying day and I need a spot of cherishing.'

Ten minutes later the last of the guests had departed, and those left behind in Government House had turned out the lights and gone to bed. Christmas Day was over; although Christmas night had still an hour to run . . .

The hall clock struck eleven, and silence flowed in upon the darkened rooms. Outside, a cold sea-mist drifted in from the south to creep across the garden and engulf the quiet house, muffling the guard-lights and blotting out the tall trees, and at the edge of the verandah roof, above the sentry's box, the rain collected in a little pool which presently overflowed in a thin, steady trickle on to the flags below.

'Gawd! what an 'ole!' sighed the sentry bleakly. 'A Merry Christmas — I *don't* think!'

Dan Harcourt had retired to the bedroom he shared with Nick, but he did not undress.

He stood by the window, his hands deep in his pockets, and looked out into the thickening mist beyond the strip of lawn below him, whistling softly between his teeth and frowning into the night.

Nick, who appeared to be in a singularly unpleasant mood, donned a pair of cerulean pyjamas — previously the property of Mr Charles Corbet-Carr — and having morosely requested him to stop that depressing noise and get to bed, climbed in under his own mosquito net and lay down with his back to the light. But Dan made no move to comply with either of these suggestions. His thoughts were fully occupied, and it is doubtful if he was even aware that Nick had spoken, for he continued his tuneless whistling and it was at least fifteen minutes later that he broke off to say abruptly: 'Look here, Nick, I'm in a bit of a quandary and I'd like your advice.'

Receiving no answer he turned from the window and came over to Nick's bed. But Nick had fallen asleep.

For a moment or two Dan debated the wisdom of waking him up, but it seemed an unkindness to do so, and abandoning the idea he switched off the lights and returned to his own bed: but not to sleep. Instead, he lit a cigarette, and getting in under the mosquito net lay down fully clothed and stared up into the darkness where the electric fan blades swished softly in the warm, damp air. It was a pity about Nick. He would have liked to talk the thing over with him. But Nick was obviously dead tired and would probably, if awakened, be more blasphemous than helpful . . .

Dan shifted uneasily on the sheets. What was he to do? Was it any business of his to interfere? After all, but for an accident he himself would not have been marooned on Ross. And but for a freak of the tides Ferrers Shilto's body would have been battered to pieces upon the jagged coral reefs, or else carried miles out to sea and far down the coasts before being thrown ashore. In either case, all that was left would, if found, have been buried hurriedly and without question, and taking that into consideration, was it any business of his, Dan Harcourt's, to meddle with the affair? There was an old and wise adage to the effect that it is always safer to let sleeping dogs lie.

But if it was murder . . .?

If it was murder there was also another saying, one that was probably equally true in practice, to the effect that a man who kills and gets away with it will live to kill again: and again . . .

And if it isn't murder, thought Dan, it's something so damn peculiar that I shall need a personal demonstration before I believe in it. No, that little man never died by drowning. I've seen men who've died that way, and I'll swear he didn't. But no one is going to believe that unless I can prove it. As for that young snip of an assistant, Dutt, he wouldn't know the difference between a corpse and a case of concussion! I'll bet he never even conducted the sketchiest of examinations — he'd consider it a waste of time. On the strength of the fact that a man is reported to have fallen into the sea on Tuesday and his body gets washed ashore on Wednesday, he would cheerfully have signed a dozen documents certifying death by drowning without so much as taking a second look. While as for that woman up at the hospital who wouldn't even let 'em dump the body there, I'll bet she signed without laying eyes on it!

Dan turned restlessly in the hot darkness while his cigarette burned out between his fingers. They were burying Ferrers Shilto in the morning — early in the morning, Sir Lionel had said. Therefore if he intended to do anything about it he must do so now, since it would be useless to voice suspicions once Ferrers's body was six feet underground. He dropped the burned-out stub of his cigarette on to the floor and lit a fresh one; the yellow flare of the match illuminating for a brief moment his brown, boyish face and the frown between his narrowed eyes. It flickered out in the darkness and he lay back and reviewed the situation once more . . .

Nick had said that the boats had been about half-way home when the storm struck them, which meant that they had foundered in the widest part of the bay and in deep water. There were no rocks within a considerable distance of them, and Nick had seen Ferrers clinging to one of the upturned boats some minutes after they had capsized. That did away with any theory that he might have been hit on the head and killed in the process of capsizing by the mast or the boat itself. Or that he had met his death among the rocks. No one, again quoting Nick, could have managed to swim to the shore in that sea, let alone a frail middle-aged man of negligible physique, such as the late Ferrers Shilto.

Then how——?

There's nothing for it, thought Dan resignedly, but to go down and see for myself. If I don't, I shall worry about it to the end of my days. And if ever I hear that anyone else from these islands has been drowned or otherwise reported accidentally dead, I shall wonder if it really was an accident — and feel like a murderer myself.

He slid off his bed and tossed his cigarette out of the window where it described a thin glowing arc and disappeared into the mist, and having groped about for an overcoat, remembered with irritation that his own was on board the *Sapphire* and by this time probably in the Nicobars, and that he had neglected to borrow one. It would mean getting wet, but resigning himself to the inevitable he turned up the collar of his dinner-jacket — one of George's — and having collected a torch from the dressing-table, paused to remove his shoes. There was no point in awakening the entire household!

The clock in the hall struck the quarter to midnight as he tiptoed across the silent ballroom and descended the stairs to the hall where old Iman Din lay stretched upon his thin mattress, his turban on the floor beside him and a cloth draped across his face, sound asleep. It is to be feared that Iman Din, although a Muslim and therefore, theoretically, a teetotaller, had also been celebrating Christmas, and had fallen from grace to the extent of imbibing toddy in the Ross bazaar. As a result, his slumbers were particularly sound and his rhythmic snores did not cease when Dan Harcourt stepped over his recumbent body, and replacing his own shoes drew the bolts of the front door.

But with his hand upon the door-latch, Dan stopped and turned back, for hanging on the hall hatstand was a mackintosh cape with a hood of the type worn by the guards and orderlies in wet weather. 'Just what the doctor ordered!' thought Dan; and carefully removing it from its peg he fastened it about his own shoulders, pulled the hood over his head, and thus protected against the rain opened the front door and stepped out into the wet night.

The sentry, yawning in his box, challenged him as he passed, and Dan stopped and came across to him: 'I'm just going out for a breather. Too damned stuffy in the house and I can't sleep. I hope it's all right?'

'Certainly, sir.' The sentry's wooden countenance relaxed into a grin and became human: 'Wish I could join yer, sir! Fair feeds me up, standin' about 'ere—— Christmas night an' all!'

Dan laughed, and pulled out a half-empty packet of Goldflake. 'Tough luck. Have a cigarette.'

'Not allowed to smoke on duty, sir,' said the sentry wistfully, averting his eyes from the betraying stub that glowed two feet away among the wet flowerpots where he had thrown it upon hearing approaching footsteps.

'Keep 'em until you get off,' advised Dan. He pressed the packet into the sentry's grateful hand.

'Thank you, sir. Much obliged. Good-night, sir.'

'Good-night.' Dan turned away, and with no warning premonition of danger to send him back to the safety of his room, walked down the steep pathway and disappeared into the cold embrace of the mists.

The Guest House on Ross was a large, two-storeyed building of dismal aspect, standing just below the grounds of the Chief Commissioner's house at the top of the steep road that led up from the pier and the jetty. It had at that date remained empty for some considerable time, and was only used when auditors and such-like governmental wildfowl descended upon the Islands. The *chowkidar**, as is the custom of such people, was sound asleep with his blanket pulled well over his head, there was no sign of a police guard, and there appeared to be no one to dispute Dan's entrance.

The outer doors were locked, but it did not take him long to find a window whose latch he could force, nor, having once entered the house, to discover which room was doing duty as a temporary morgue.

They had laid the body of Ferrers Shilto on a trestle table in what must have been the living-room, wrapped in a tarpaulin sheet from which slow drops of brine oozed to fall on to the uncarpeted boards beneath and stray away in thin trickles, so that in that dim, empty room the dark blot of the makeshift catafalque had the appearance of a spider crouched in the centre of a web. Dust lay in a thick layer underfoot except where the feet of Dutt and the stretcher-bearers had disturbed it, and in

* Nightwatchman.

that wide space of shadows the beam of Dan's pocket torch made a lonely pool of light, before whose wan glow the darkness retreated a few reluctant paces.

Outside the house the rain trickled from the eaves and gutters of the roof, and wisps of sea-fog pressed against the black, winking window-panes like white faces peering in from the night. But inside the air was dank and heavy, and there was no sound to break the silence save the monotonous *drip*, *drip*, *drip* of sea-water from the still shape under the tarpaulin.

A bat that had been roosting on the gaunt frame of the electric fan swooped down with a rustle of leathery wings and fluttered about Dan's head, and he struck up at it involuntarily with his torch. As he did so, the torch slipped from his grasp, and striking the floor, went out, leaving him in a darkness that was so complete as to seem solid.

After a few minutes of blasphemous but ineffectual groping he remembered he had a box of matches in his pocket, and struck one. The hiss and splutter of its lighting sounded astonishingly loud in the silent room, and by its small flame he saw his torch lying near the open door. But as he reached it the match burnt out, and in the brief moment of dark before his fingers closed upon the cold metal, he thought that he heard something, or someone, move in the blackness beyond the doorway.

Pressing the switch of the torch he found to his intense relief that the bulb had not been broken, for once more a yellow beam of light beat back the shadows, and he flashed it about the room and through the doorways. But there was no one there, and except for himself and the dead man the house appeared to be empty. Nevertheless, he found to his disgust that his hands were shaking and that his breathing had quickened as though he had been running.

Of all the damned nonsense! thought Dan savagely: I'm getting as bad as that screaming woman Ruby Whatsername. Astonishing how an empty house at night can give one the jitters! Psychological,

I suppose—— He steadied himself with an effort and walked up to the rickety trestle table and its quiet occupant. And it was only then that he saw that the coverings of tarpaulin had been roughly stitched about the body. Evidently they intended to bury it like this if no coffin could be produced in time. Dan fumbled in his pocket, and producing a small penknife, ripped out the coarse stitches and drew back the impromptu shroud.

The stiff folds of tarpaulin fell back with a curious crackling sound and Ferrers Shilto's white face, still wearing that look of incredulous astonishment, gazed up at him, wide-eyed. And suddenly all nervousness left Dan Harcourt and he was once again a doctor, cool and impersonal, and this thing on the table before him was merely part of a doctor's job. He slipped off the heavy mackintosh cape he wore, and turning back the cuffs of his dinner-jacket, bent over the table and began his examination. It did not take him long.

It was perhaps five minutes later that he straightened up with a long-drawn sigh and pulled down his cuffs again. He had seen everything that he had wanted to see, and knew everything that he had wanted to know.

He heard no sound, nor did he see the shadow that moved in the shadows behind him. But suddenly and inexplicably he was aware of danger. Some sixth sense, stronger than reason, rang an imperative alarm bell in his brain, calling on him to turn.

A board creaked behind him and he spun round . . .

An hour later the sentry outside Government House saw a caped and hooded figure walk rapidly up the path towards the house. It nodded a brief greeting to him as it passed, but did not speak, and the sentry, mellowed by illicit cigarettes, followed the dim figure with a grateful gaze.

'I 'ope 'e's enjoyed 'is little stroll,' mused Private Alfred Reginald Weekes: '*Er-iaw-ooh!* Gawd! I couldn't 'arf do with a bit of shut-eye!'

He heard the front door close softly, and then the sounds of bolts being gently pressed home.

Inside the house the clock struck half past one.

12

'Val, come here a minute. What do you make of this?'

Valerie, on her way to breakfast, paused beside Copper who was thoughtfully examining the intricate carving of the stairhead.

'What is it? Oh, a moth. No, it isn't; it's only a bit of that pink feather stuff off Ruby's dressing-gown.'

'I know,' said Copper. 'But what is it doing here? She never came past here last night. That is, not unless she was prowling around after we'd all gone to bed.'

'What would she want to prowl here for?' asked Valerie reasonably, 'she's got everything she wants in her own rooms.' She reached out, and removing the small scrap of pink swansdown stood for a moment turning it between her fingers and frowning. 'Perhaps she was only taking her insomnia for an airing. Unless, of course, she was——' Valerie broke off abruptly, and turning away said: 'Come on, Coppy, or the eggs will be stone cold. Good-morning, Nick.'

' 'Morning, Val. Hullo, Coppy. Have either of you seen Dan?'

'Not yet,' said Valerie, preceding him into the dining-room. 'Why?'

'He wasn't in his bed when I woke up, and he appears to have neglected his ablutions this morning.'

'You'd probably been snoring and he was only too glad to get out,' suggested Copper lightly. 'Good-morning, everyone.' She seated herself at the table and poured out a cup of coffee: 'I expect you'll find he's gone for a walk to get up an appetite for breakfast.'

'What — in this weather? Not bloody likely! The fog's so thick you could cut slices out of it with a spoon. And being of a charitable and Christian disposition, I will ignore your first and offensive suggestion.'

Valerie said: 'I'll get one of the servants to hunt him up and tell him that breakfast's ready.' She called a *khidmatgar** and gave a brief order in the vernacular.

'How's your wife this morning, Mr Stock?' inquired Copper. 'I hope she had a good night?'

'What's that?' Leonard Stock, who had been surreptitiously endeavouring to read the back of the Reuters news-sheet that was engaging the Chief Commissioner's attention, jumped guiltily and dropped his pince-nez into his coffee.

'I said that I hoped that your wife had slept well,' said Copper distinctly.

'Oh yes. Oh yes, quite well, thank you,' replied Mr Stock, fishing around in his coffee cup with a teaspoon. 'We both passed an excellent night, all things considered.'

'I only asked,' said Copper mendaciously, 'because Valerie thought that she heard sounds from your room last night, and wondered if your wife had wanted anything.'

Mr Stock looked slightly taken aback: 'From our room? I'm sure she must have been mistaken. Ruby would certainly have called out to me if she had wanted anything in the night.'

'*Called out* to you?' inquired Copper, puzzled.

Leonard Stock flushed pinkly, and abandoning his ineffectual fishing operations with his teaspoon, retrieved his dripping pince-nez with his fingers and gave a little nervous laugh.

'You see — Ruby prefers a room to herself. She says that I — er — that I occasionally — er — snore. And as she is a very light sleeper and suffers terribly from insomnia, I have had to remove my bed into the dressing-room, which has a proper door, so that she can shut it — the door between the rooms I mean — and not

* Waiter.

be disturbed. I'm afraid that I myself am a somewhat sound sleeper, but I am sure I would have heard her if she'd got up in the night, because in order to get to the bathroom she would have had to pass through my——' He stopped abruptly, and crimsoned as violently as though he had been guilty of unspeakable vulgarity, but Copper's attention had evidently wandered. She was engaged in spreading marmalade on her toast and thinking deeply ...

The guest rooms occupied by the Stocks were next to Valerie's, the tiny verandah outside being shared by both rooms, and beyond the bedroom was a large dressing-room which corresponded, on a smaller scale, with the turret room at the opposite end of the house — now occupied by John Shilto. The bathroom led off from this, and as a heavy teak door separated the dressing-room from the bedroom, it was unlikely that Leonard Stock would have heard any but a fairly loud movement from his wife's room once the door was closed between them. Which meant that it would have been perfectly simple for Ruby to slip out of her room into the ballroom without her husband being any the wiser, and if it was true that he snored, she had only to listen for that sound to make sure that he was asleep before moving.

A dark and quite unfounded suspicion of John Shilto slid into Copper's mind; to be instantly rejected. She harboured no illusions as to Mrs Stock's standard of morality, having been regaled with too much local scandal by the island gossips, who had been only too delighted with the opportunity of unloading their choicest titbits on to the newcomer. But John Shilto was not a type likely to appeal to any woman; even one of Mrs Stock's man-collecting proclivities!

Copper glanced across to where he sat silent and morose eating scrambled eggs at the far side of the table. There were heavy dark pouches under his eyes that she did not remember having noticed before, and he looked unshaven and ill and as though he had passed a sleepless night. He's rather like something that's grown up in a cellar, thought Copper; and decided that whatever Ruby Stock had had in mind last night, it could not have been John Shilto!

Another and far more unpleasant thought struck her, and she turned sharply to look at Nick; and was as instantly ashamed of herself. I *am* a toad! thought Copper in sudden contrition, ashamed of her own suspicions: I must have a low, mean, horrid sort of mind. But what *was* Ruby doing, creeping about the house last night? Leonard is right. If she'd wanted anything reasonable she'd have woken up the entire house rather than move a finger to get it herself! And she was barefoot too — she must have been. Those silly feather slippers of hers would have made an awful racket, clicking across the ballroom; and if . . .

Copper twisted a little sideways in her chair and surreptitiously studied Nick's attractive profile with anxious eyes. Of course it's nonsense! she thought ruefully. I suppose it's only because I'm jealous of that woman that I think of these things. I *am* jealous of her: I suppose I'd be jealous of anyone who looked at him like that. Even Val . . . Even *Amabel*—— Oh dear!

She sighed a small unhappy sigh. After all, what — apart from the fact that she was in love with him — did she know about Nick Tarrent? Less than nothing! And anyway, he and John Shilto were not the only other men in the house: there still remained Sir Lionel and Dan Harcourt. Sir Lionel naturally did not count. But how about Dan? Ruby had certainly been very charming to Dan on the previous day, and he had not shown himself unwilling to be charmed. What was it that Nick had just said about him? Something about his having got up early and gone for a walk? It seemed an odd thing to do on such a morning, for although the rain had stopped, the fog had thickened until it pressed about the house and the island like a muffling pall of grey cotton-wool.

Copper helped herself to more toast as a red-uniformed *chaprassi* advanced noiselessly to Valerie's side and spoke in an undertone.

'*What's* that?' Valerie's voice was sharp.

The man shrugged his shoulders, and sketched a gesture with his brown hands.

'But it's absurd!' Valerie turned to her stepfather: 'He says that they've looked everywhere, but they can't find Dan Harcourt. The orderlies say no one has left the house this morning, and the servants say he isn't anywhere inside it. Dad, hadn't we better send someone out to look for him? He must have gone out by one of the servants' staircases without being seen, and got lost in this mist.'

Nick pushed back his chair and rose to his feet. 'In that case, we'd better go and round him up at once. With a fog like this he might well walk off the edge of a breakwater. Anyone coming with me?'

'I'll come,' said Valerie.

'Nonsense!' snapped Sir Lionel irritably. 'I imagine that young man is perfectly capable of looking after himself, and I object to any of you careering round the island in this fog. I expect he went off to the Mess and is having his breakfast down there.'

Valerie stared at her stepfather in some surprise. It was unlike him to be irritable with her, and she noticed suddenly that he was looking old and rather ill, and suffered a pang of conscience; realizing that she had been too wrapped up in Charles of late to pay much attention to his well-being. 'What's the matter, Dad?' she inquired. 'You're looking a bit off colour this morning.'

'There is nothing whatever the matter with me,' said Sir Lionel coldly. 'I merely stated — I will repeat it if you wish — that I would rather you did not go wandering round the island in this weather.' He gathered up the typewritten news-sheets, and disregarding Valerie's hurt and astonished face, left the dining-room.

'He's quite right,' consoled Copper swiftly. 'There's no sense in all of us breaking our necks hunting up Dan. I'll bet he's with Charles. Let's ring up the Mess.'

They excused themselves and left the table, but Copper, looking back from the edge of the ballroom, surprised a curious look upon Mr Shilto's unalluring countenance. He had turned in his chair and was looking towards the windows, and for a moment she thought that he was laughing. It was gone in a moment, but the impression remained that the fat, bulky shoulders in the ill-fitting linen coat had been jerking and quivering with suppressed mirth.

Nick, who had gone to his room for a coat, returned across the ballroom, frowning blackly.

'Look here,' said Nick abruptly, 'I've just found something damned odd: I don't know why I didn't notice it before, but Dan's own clothes are in the bedroom, so he must still be wearing that borrowed dinner-jacket. And his bed has been slept on but not in. I'm going down to make inquiries.'

He turned on his heel, and taking the staircase three steps at a time, flung out of the front door and vanished into the mist. To return five minutes later, with the scowl still on his face——

'I can't understand what Dan's up to. I've been talking to the sentry and the police orderlies, and they still stick to it that no one left the house this morning. Not that that means much! In this fog I expect he could easily slide out by one of the back staircases without being spotted. But what does sound a bit odd is that one of the sentries swears that he left the house about twelve o'clock last night — said he couldn't sleep or something and was going to take a stroll around — and didn't come back until about an hour and a half later . . .

'That old fool in the hall was sound asleep of course and never heard him either time, but the sentry says he remembers that Dan shut the door behind him "very quiet like" when he came back, so I don't suppose he wanted to advertise his return. Anyway, one thing they all swear to is that he didn't go out a second time, and that bearer of yours — blast him — says he didn't notice whether the Sahib was in his bed or not when he brought the morning tea, because the mosquito nets were down. I'm told that a police guard sleeps at the foot of every outside staircase all night, so Dan couldn't very well have gone out again until daylight without falling over someone. What the *blazes* do you suppose he's up to?'

'Val's just phoning Charles to find if he's down at the Mess,' said Copper: 'the Ross wire has been fixed, thank heaven.'

As she spoke, Valerie came out of the verandah where she had been telephoning, looking both worried and annoyed: 'No,' she said shortly in reply to Nick's query, 'he's not there. *Or* up at the hospital — or down at the Club either. Of course there's still the barracks and Ronnie Purvis. I couldn't get hold of Ronnie. His man said he was out, and didn't appear to know if anyone else had been to the house or not. Oh dear! as if there wasn't enough fuss and unpleasantness without Dan playing the fool!'

'Dan's no fool,' said Nick curtly, 'and if he isn't here it's because he's got a very good reason for being elsewhere! Either that or the silly ass has fallen over something in this bloody fog. Well, there's only one thing to do and that's round up a search-party: I'm off to co-opt Charles and Hamish and anyone else I can get hold of.'

He swung round and bumped into the Chief Commissioner who had been making for the staircase followed by Leonard Stock and Mr Shilto. '*Blast* — I beg your pardon, sir. I——' He stopped suddenly, checked by the sight of their formal attire.

'Valerie, my dear,' said Sir Lionel, 'we are just off to attend poor Ferrers's funeral. I thought that we should excuse you from coming as it is such a wretched day.'

'Oh,' said Valerie blankly, 'I'd forgotten. No, I don't think Copper and I will go, if you don't mind, Mr Shilto?'

'I? But of course not, Miss Valerie. I know that your sympathy will be with us, and that is as valuable a tribute as your presence.' John Shilto grinned maliciously and passed on down the staircase in the wake of Sir Lionel. But they did not reach the hall.

There was a sudden commotion outside the front door, and a dishevelled, unrecognizable figure thrust past the guard and flung itself up the stairs to stop, panting for breath and clinging to the banisters, before the Chief Commissioner.

It was young Dr Dutt, who had apparently run up the steep path to the house, for his gasping words were unintelligible and he appeared to be labouring under the stress of some violent emotion.

The Chief Commissioner, becoming indignantly aware of the curious faces of the orderlies and servants in the hall below, grasped the young man firmly by the arm and propelled him forcibly up the stairs and into the drawing-room. 'Now,' said Sir Lionel, thrusting him into the nearest armchair, 'take your time, and try to get your breath. Stock, will you please fetch a glass of water?'

Leonard vanished obediently, and the young doctor, acting upon the Chief Commissioner's advice, abandoned his attempts at speech, and concentrated upon regaining his breath.

There was something startling about his appearance as well as his sudden arrival. The slim, dapper, self-satisfied figure of the previous night had disappeared, and in its place sat a frantic-eyed youth with disordered hair and clothing. His shoes and trousers were splashed with the mud of the wet roads, and looking at him Copper experienced a premonition of disaster so violent that for a moment it turned her giddy and sick.

It must have shown in her face, for Nick's hand shot out and caught her wrist. He held it for perhaps the space of four seconds, and then dropped it with a little encouraging shake; and perhaps it was that more than anything within herself that held her steady during the moments that followed. For Dr Dutt had recovered his breath.

He gulped down a few mouthfuls of water and stood up, holding tightly to the back of his chair, and though his voice was still breathless and jerky and his English had become more dislocated than ever, his story, which he insisted in relating in strict sequence, was only too clear . . .

He had, he told them, been able to raise a makeshift coffin for the corpse of Ferrers Shilto, and with four men to carry it had repaired to the Guest House some twenty minutes ago for the purpose of coffining the body. But when they removed it from the trestle table on which it rested, they had discovered to their annoyance that owing to the bulkiness of the tarpaulin which had been sewn about it, the coffin lid could not be made to close. There had been nothing for it but to remove the tarpaulin, and after sending out for a knife to rip out the twine with which it was stitched, they presently uncovered the body . . .

Dr Dutt paused to swallow convulsively and renew his grip upon the chair back, his starting eyes once more visualizing the full horror of that moment.

'Well, go on,' snapped Sir Lionel tartly. 'What was the trouble? Don't tell me he wasn't dead after all!'

Dr Dutt licked his dry lips and his eyes turned slowly to Sir Lionel's, and from there to each face in that silent circle.

'I am warn before I open,' he said, his voice barely more than a harsh whisper: 'My hand — it is wet. And when I look upon it, it is blood. But do I warn? No! I think I am cutting myself on knife. Then the cover is remove, and – and there is not Mr Shilto, but the gentleman who speak to me last night and say, "I also am doctor." And – and he is dead!'

'God!' said Nick in a queer whisper. *'Dan——!'*

He swung round and ran from the room, and they heard his feet on the stairs, and then the crash of the front door as it slammed shut behind him.

13

'Dan!' said Valerie in a small, choking voice. 'Oh, it isn't true! I don't believe it. It can't *possibly* be true.'

Dr Dutt turned to her almost gratefully: 'That is what I speak to myself. I say: "It is not true. Here is much witchcraft!" But the other fellows they are seeing too. They are very poor, ignorant men, but they say: "Here is not Shilto Sahib, but the young Sahib from the large ship. It is evil magic!" and they are fearful and they run away. Then I myself run here with great speed to tell of this terrible calamity.'

Sir Lionel, who had not moved or spoken, let his breath out in a long sigh and said in a curiously halting voice: 'You are certain of this? That it is Surgeon-Lieutenant Harcourt?'

'How can I mistake? Twice I have seen him!'

'And – and you are sure that he is — dead?'

'Most certainly. He is dead as door-nail. There is no doubt.'

'But *how*?' inquired Leonard Stock shrilly, his stunned face a curious greenish white. He took a stumbling step forward and clutched at the young assistant's arm, shaking it violently: 'It's absurd, man! You must be mistaken! A man can't die and then go off and sew himself up in sacking afterwards. It doesn't make *sense*!'

'Don't be absurd, Stock!' snapped Sir Lionel. 'Is it likely he'd sew himself up? Pull yourself together!'

'Then – then you think it is — *murder*?' gasped Mr Stock in a half-whisper, his eyes flaring with a sudden stark terror.

'*Murder?* What the devil are you talking about? Why should it be murder? I imagine that the young fool went down to take a look at the body last night and probably stumbled or met with some accident in the dark, and broke his neck. You know what our local people are like. Always terrified to report any accident for fear that they will be held responsible for it. It's more than likely that a native guard or that fool of a *chowkidar* found him, and realizing that he was dead, got into a panic and hit on the idea of sewing him into Ferrers's piece of canvas in the hope that he'd be buried without anyone being the wiser.'

John Shilto gave vent to a sudden bark of laughter: a shocking and unexpected sound. 'It's a good theory,' he said, 'but it won't wash. Why hide one body at the expense of landing yourself with the other?'

'I'm afraid I don't follow you,' said Sir Lionel stiffly.

Dr Dutt said: 'But Mr Shilto he is right, yess! Two bodies are not present. There is only Mister Harcourt.'

'What's that?' Sir Lionel swung round to face John Shilto. 'You say that Ferrers's body has been removed?'

'Oh, no I didn't,' contradicted Mr Shilto blandly. 'I merely arrived at the obvious, and apparently correct conclusion, that it has been removed. Harcourt was a slim man, but in spite of that he was a good deal larger than my late-lamented cousin, and although the thickness of a tarpaulin shroud might have accounted for the rather larger appearance of the corpse, it could never for a moment have been expected to disguise two corpses as one. And if, as I imagine, the substitution of the bodies was intended to conceal the fact of Harcourt's death, it stands to reason that the previous occupant of the tarpaulin must first have been removed.'

'Do you mean to tell me,' demanded Leonard Stock, his voice shrill and quivering with shock, 'that except for the accident of the coffin lid being unable to close, young Harcourt would have been buried as your cousin and nobody would ever have known?'

'You follow me like a shadow,' grinned John Shilto derisively. 'I mean just that.'

The Chief Commissioner turned on him angrily: 'This is no joking matter, Shilto! We are wasting valuable time. I suggest we go down to the Guest House immediately. And the sooner we get the police on to this, the better.'

Mr Shilto gave another bark of mirthless laughter: 'The police? A fat lot of good they're going to be to us while they're all stranded over on Aberdeen! We haven't a single police official here on Ross; and until this sea goes down, and the jetty is repaired, they have as much hope of reaching us as if we were surrounded by a hundred miles of open sea. What's more, with the telephone line to Aberdeen gone, and this fog, we have no possible means of communicating with them.'

Sir Lionel looked at him with a curiously narrowed gaze. 'Yes, of course,' he said slowly. 'I had forgotten that. I suppose, to a murderer, it would be a useful circumstance.' He turned to Dr Dutt: 'You have not told us yet how Surgeon-Lieutenant Harcourt met his death.'

Dr Dutt's lower jaw dropped noticeably, and he shuffled his feet uncomfortably: 'I – I regret, sir, to have made no note as yet. The man he is dead, so I do not pause for examination but come hastily to inform yourself.'

'Then in that case, the sooner we get down to the Guest House and find out, the better!'

The Chief Commissioner turned abruptly to the door, and followed by Mr Shilto, Leonard Stock and Dr Dutt, passed down the hall stairs and out into the fog.

As the sound of their footsteps died away, Copper said in a muffled voice: 'I think . . . I think I'm going to be sick.' Her face and voice fully confirmed this statement, and Valerie, jerking herself out of her own horror-stricken immobility, grabbed her by the arm and rushed her out of the room.

'Feeling better now?' she inquired some ten minutes later.

'Yes,' gasped Copper, rising rather shakily from the bed where she had flung herself after putting her recent threat into execution. 'I can't think why I should behave like this. Idiotic of me. I do apologize.' She walked unsteadily over to the windows, and subsiding on to the broad window-seat unlatched them and flung them wide, letting in a cool drift of mist-laden air.

Valerie left the room, and returned a few minutes later carrying two small glasses: 'Brandy,' she announced. 'I think we'd better try it. It may pull us together.'

Copper accepted a glass and drank the contents with a wry face: '*Ugh* — beastly stuff; it always reminds me of being extremely seasick on the Dover–Calais boat. However, I do feel slightly better. How about you?'

'Oh, I'm all right, but—— Oh, Coppy, isn't it ghastly! Poor Dan . . . and only last night he was alive, and——'

'Don't!' said Copper violently. 'If we start thinking of it like that we shall go to pieces and start behaving like Ruby and Rosamund. Don't let's go over it all again: I can't bear it! Let's talk about something else instead. No, of course we can't really do that. But couldn't we try and see if there isn't something we could do about it? Then we could at least think of it as a sort of cold-blooded problem, like a crossword puzzle or a cypher.'

Valerie said: 'We can try, anyway. I'm all for doing something. Let's – let's be really female and start by ordering ourselves a cup of tea.' She rang the bell and gave a brief order to the house-boy who answered it, and as the door closed behind him Copper said abruptly: 'Val, I've got an idea. No one has told Ruby yet, have they? About Dan, I mean?'

'I don't think so. No, of course they haven't. They all went straight from the drawing-room to the Guest House. Why?'

'I thought it might be a good idea if we went along and broke the news, just . . . just to see how she takes it.'

Valerie looked puzzled. 'What are you getting at? She'll only have hysterics again. You know what she's like. And frankly, I don't think I could bear another of her scenes just now. She was doing her alluring best with Dan yesterday, and the minute she hears this she'll be able to convince herself that he adored her, and dramatize herself accordingly.'

'I wonder?' said Copper thoughtfully. 'Val, I've been thinking. She must have been creeping about the house last night. Have you any ideas as to what she was up to?'

'Yes,' said Valerie promptly, 'I think she was probably after——' She stopped abruptly, and flushed.

'— Nick,' finished Copper.

'Well, yes,' admitted Valerie uncomfortably. 'Bitchy of me of course, and I've no evidence. But then she *is* a bit of a man-chaser as well as being very attractive in an opulent Serpent-of-the-Nile sort of way, and frankly, I couldn't see any reason for her to be prowling about the house at night, and without her slippers — you've no idea the fuss she makes about possible scorpions — unless she'd staged an assignation with someone. Sorry!'

'Don't apologize,' said Copper sadly: 'I'm a cat myself where Nick is concerned — a hell-cat, I suppose! I thought the same thing until I remembered that he wasn't the only man in the house.'

'You mean it might have been Dan?'

Copper nodded. 'But that's not what I'm getting at. Listen, Val, suppose we were both wrong and it wasn't anything like that? Suppose she knows something? Heaven knows what and I've no idea why she should know anything. But you must admit it's a little odd that she should be prowling about last night of all nights. She could have heard something!'

'Perhaps,' admitted Valerie after some thought. 'Anyway, it's worth trying even if we *do* have to cope with another bout of hysterics! If there really was any connection between her night prowlings and Dan's, she may give herself away when she hears that he's dead.'

'That's why I'd like to be there to see how she takes the news,' said Copper. 'And if we wait until Leonard gets back he'll get in with it first. So what about it?'

'Right! Come on — let's go now.'

They found Mrs Stock sitting up in bed, attired in the same pink satin garment whose abundant supply of marabou-trimming had betrayed her wanderings on the previous night. She was engaged in applying scarlet lacquer to her finger-nails, and though she appeared placid enough, Copper wondered if her unusual high colour did not owe more to rouge than to the natural bloom of which she was so inordinately proud. If there were dark circles below her eyes they had been carefully disguised with cream and powder, and she certainly did not give the impression of having passed a wakeful night.

She greeted the two girls languidly and then, with more energy, inquired fretfully why she had not been informed earlier that Ferrers Shilto's funeral was to take place that morning? 'Of course, I might have known that Leonard wouldn't tell me. He never tells me *anything*! But I do think, Valerie dear, that you at least might have let me know. Shaken as I feel after that shocking occurrence yesterday, it was my duty to attend — if only out of respect for poor Ferrers.'

'You needn't worry,' said Valerie, 'it's been postponed.'

'What's that?' Mrs Stock sat up quickly, scenting mysteries. 'You don't say so! . . . Oh—' she sank back against the pillows: 'the weather, I suppose. But I expect the fog will clear by lunchtime and they'll have it in the afternoon. I wonder, Valerie dear, if you would send down to my house for my hat-box? I shall need a black hat. The *ciré* straw, perhaps——'

Valerie interrupted firmly. 'I'm afraid the funeral won't be this afternoon either, Ruby. You see, when they went to put Ferrers's body in the coffin, they found that it had disappeared.'

'*Disappeared!* But what——?'

'There was a body there all right. But it wasn't Ferrers's body.

It – it was Dan Harcourt's, and he was dead. Someone killed him last night and put him there instead.'

If they had wanted a reaction from Mrs Stock, they got it. But it was an entirely different reaction from the one they had expected, for Ruby neither screamed nor indulged in the emotional hysterics with which she had greeted the appearance of Ferrers's corpse on the previous day. She merely stared at Valerie in appalled silence, while every vestige of colour drained slowly out of her face until it was no longer a face but a grey clay mask, crudely patched with staring blotches of vivid pink rouge and gashed with scarlet lipstick.

She tried to speak, but though for a moment or two her lips moved soundlessly, no words came, and then quite suddenly she toppled sideways in a dead faint. 'Now we've done it!' gasped Valerie. 'For heaven's sake come and help, Coppy. Fetch some water, or brandy, or something!'

'Shove her head over the side of the bed,' suggested Copper anxiously. 'It'll bring the blood back to it.'

This treatment, though crude, proved remarkably effective, and a few moments later Mrs Stock was lying back among her pillows, white and shaken, but once more in full possession of her faculties. In very full possession, it appeared, for she neither wept nor dramatized. She accepted an offer of brandy, and having gulped down a few fiery mouthfuls, lay still for a while; staring fixedly ahead of her as though she were remembering something — and making it fit . . .

She seemed to have forgotten that Valerie and Copper were in the room, but at last her enormous eyes turned to them and her lips twisted into the semblance of a smile. 'You really should be more careful, Valerie dear,' she said huskily. 'My nerves are not strong, and bad news always affects me more than it does other people. Such shocking news, too! If you don't mind, I think I should like to be quite quiet for a little; to give myself a chance to recover. You won't mind?'

'No,' said Valerie awkwardly. 'No, of course not. I'm so sorry.

Are you sure you wouldn't like one of us to stay with you? I don't like leaving you like this.'

'I assure you I am perfectly all right,' snapped Mrs Stock with a sudden return of vigour: 'All I need is a little peace and quiet.'

Valerie and Copper, murmuring apologies, backed out thankfully and fled back across the ballroom to the safety of a verandah sofa.

'Well, what do we make of that?' inquired Valerie dropping down among the sofa cushions. 'Have we got anywhere or haven't we? I was scared stiff for a moment: I thought we'd given her a heart attack. Do you really think she knows anything about Dan?'

'No. At least, it's obvious that she didn't know a thing about him being dead. She may be a good actress, but I'm quite sure she isn't as good as all that. It gave her a ghastly shock.'

'It certainly seemed to,' admitted Valerie doubtfully. 'But you're wrong about one thing. I've seen her act in amateur shows, and believe me, she is darned good.'

Copper looked thoughtful: 'You mean the whole thing may have been an act?'

'No — not really. I don't believe even Sarah Bernhardt could have made herself turn that horrid colour. She got a terrific shock all right. But there may have been several reasons for it besides the obvious one. If you ask me, I think that something happened last night that she didn't quite know what to make of, but that the minute she heard our story, it – it made sense.'

'I see,' said Copper slowly. 'And her faint needn't have been a real one, but only to give her time to think and to pull herself together?'

'Well, you saw how quickly she came out of it! And how she flung us out of her room as soon as she could. Believe me, that alone is more than peculiar, because if there is one thing that Ruby enjoys more than another it's an audience, and this sort of thing should have been meat and drink to her. The fact that she didn't want to say or hear anything more about it is reasonably good proof, to anyone who knows her, that she either suspects something or thinks she knows something.'

Copper stared reflectively out into the fog beyond the wet window-panes and bit at the tip of one finger and presently she said: 'You know, there's something we've both rather taken for granted. We've both decided that Dan was murdered. But there may be something in your father's theory about someone finding his body and getting scared stiff of being accused of killing him. After all, who on earth would want to kill Dan? — and why?'

'Perhaps we'll know now,' said Valerie, turning her head to listen: 'Isn't that someone coming up the drive at last?' They heard the front door bang and steps ascending the stairs, and then Charles and Nick came into view and joined them in the verandah just as a *khidmatgar* appeared bearing a laden tea-tray.

'I forgot that we'd ordered tea,' said Valerie. 'Would you two like some, or would you prefer something stronger?'

'I could do with a stiff brandy and soda myself,' said Charles. 'Same for you, Nick?'

Nick, who was looking white and grim, answered with a brief affirmative. He lit himself a cigarette from the box on the writing-table, and Copper, watching him, saw that his hands were shaking. Perhaps he was aware of it himself, for he flicked the match into the ash-tray and thrust his hands into his pockets.

Valerie poured out tea, and a minute or two later a house-servant appeared with brandy and soda.

'I needed that,' said Nick, putting down a half-empty glass. He dropped into an armchair and stared bleakly ahead of him into the dim ballroom beyond the dark, carved head of 'Hindenburg', and Valerie said tensely: 'Tell us what happened.'

Nick finished the contents of his glass before replying, and then said curtly: 'He was murdered, of course.'

He heard Copper draw in her breath in a little hard gasp, and turned towards her, his voice suddenly gentle: 'It's all right, Coppy. He can't have known a thing about it. He was hit on the side of the head, and as far as we can tell, it must have killed him instantly.'

Nick did not think it necessary to add that the killer had also taken other precautions to ensure that his victim should suffer no resurrection this side of the grave. He did not like to think of what had been done to Dan.

Charles said savagely: 'Curse this bloody storm! If only the sea would go down we might be able to do something. But as there isn't a decent doctor, or a single police official in the place, it looks very much as if the bastard who killed him is going to get away with it.'

'Why should you think that?' inquired Copper sharply.

'My dear girl, it's obvious! Dr Vicarjee would have been able to give us a lot of valuable information — as, for instance, how long Dan has been dead. But since poor Dutt is in such a flat spin that it's no good going by anything he says, we haven't much idea when it happened. Then there are fingerprints and footmarks and — oh, probably a whole cartload of clues lying about that would mean something to the police. But by the time anyone from the mainland can land on this damned island the case will be stale. Wind, weather, damp and decay will have successfully wiped out or disguised a dozen possible clues, and the murderer will have had lots of time to think things over and, if he *has* made any mistakes, to see that they are rectified. No, I imagine it's the first few hours that must count most in a murder case, and the hell of it is that there's no one here who can do anything!'

'There are four of us,' said Copper shortly.

'And a hell of a lot of good . . .' Charles broke off and scowled thoughtfully into space for several minutes, and then said slowly: 'At least it would give us something better to do than sitting around twiddling our thumbs and cursing.'

Nick walked over to the window, and staring out into the wall of fog that blotted out the world about them but could not silence the thunder of the sullen sea that kept them prisoners, said bitterly: 'Listen to that! It may not go down for days. So if we've got to wait until it does, and until the jetty is mended, we may just as well fill in the time by playing detectives. If the police were here we should merely be a bloody nuisance to them. But as they aren't, I don't suppose we can do much harm. Or good either, if it comes to that! But it will at least be an improvement on trying to make bright conversation or kicking the furniture. And I only hope,' he added viciously, 'that if we ever manage to get our hands on the bloody-minded bastard who murdered Dan, that the police will keep off Ross for long enough to make him look upon hanging as a merciful release!'

'I'll drink to that,' said Charles and tossed off the contents of his tumbler: '*Omne tulit punctum qui miscuit utile dulci — He has carried every vote who has combined the useful with the pleasing.* And as that is about the only Latin tag I remember, it's just as well it's appropriate. We are with you, Inspector Tarrent. Where do we start?'

'With the sentry, I think. He appears to be the last person, with the exception of the murderer, to see Dan alive.'

'Right. And after that I suggest we take another and closer look at the Guest House and the grounds. I don't imagine anyone else has done that yet. Val, you'd better see if you can get anything more out of the servants, and Copper can make herself useful by wandering round the house with a magnifying glass. You never know, there might possibly be a stray clue lying around.'

'I shouldn't recognize one if I saw it,' said Copper bleakly. 'But at least it will help pass the time. Come on, Val. See you two later.'

She put down her untasted cup, shivered, and walked away down the long, dim verandah.

14

A search of the house failed to produce anything resembling a clue, and after a fruitless half-hour Valerie suggested that they try making notes instead, and arming herself with a writing-block, pencils and a notebook, retired with Copper to a quiet corner of the verandah.

'If we both write down every single thing that's happened during the last two or three days, we may spot something that will give us a lead. It always seems to work in books.'

'Only when there is a private detective with a brain like a buzz-saw to spot the clue,' observed Copper sceptically. 'Where are you going to start? The picnic on Mount Harriet, or the day the *Sapphire* arrived?'

'Neither,' said Valerie. 'I've had a better idea. We'll put down the name of anyone who could possibly have had anything to do with it, and then write under each name anything we can remember of what they have said or done in the past few days and nights. What about that?'

'It sounds a pretty hopeless task,' said Copper doubtfully, 'but I suppose we'd better start somewhere. Are we going to cancel out the idea of it having been done by one of the natives? Because if not, it means making a list of everyone on the island. And that isn't possible.'

Valerie chewed the end of her pencil, and after an interval of frowning thought, said: 'I think we can safely wash out the native population. You see, I've lived here long enough to know something of these people and I'm positive, in my own mind, that unless it was the work of a lunatic no islander would have killed a man with whom he had no quarrel. But when Dan was off the ship he was with us, so we know that he can't have had any trouble with the natives, and no lunatic would ever have substituted Dan's body for Ferrers's — or even *thought* of it!'

'That still leaves the British troops,' said Copper, 'and there are a good many of them.'

'Yes, I'd thought of that. We shall have to get Charles and George and Hamish to question them. But there are only about half a dozen of them here on Ross, because all the rest of them were picnicking out at Corbyn's Cove on Christmas Eve and are stuck in Aberdeen by the storm. And in any case, except for the sentry, none of them would have been out of barracks at that time of night, so I think we can fairly safely wash them out too.'

'But that only leaves *us*!' said Copper, appalled. 'Our party, I mean. Val, it can't *possibly* be one of us. It's too fantastic.'

'Fantastic or not, we may as well try and simplify matters by seeing if we can prove that it *wasn't* one of us. That ought to narrow the field a bit, if nothing else.'

'Oh, all right. Here goes, then. Let's start with Ruby. We've got a lot that we can write under her name.'

'RUBY STOCK,' said Valerie, writing it down in block capitals. 'I'd better give her a couple of pages. John Shilto next. I can't think up anything against him at the moment except that he gives me the shivers. Who else?'

'It's no good working on those lines,' said Copper impatiently. 'We must put everyone down, regardless of whether we've anything against them or not. For all we know, almost anyone may be capable of murder if the provocation is sufficient. And I don't suppose the storm helped!'

'What do you mean by that?'

'Only that we were all a bit on edge before it broke. Don't you remember saying yourself that you felt like an overwound watch-spring? Suppose there was someone else who felt like that, and who reached the breaking-point that you described so graphically? Came sort of morally unstuck——?'

'You mean, went mad?' demanded Valerie.

'Not exactly; except that anyone who killed Dan *must* have been mad. I'm not quite sure what I do mean.'

'Oh, all right, let it go. I suggest we put down all the names in alphabetical order, starting with Amabel.'

Despite the horrors of the morning, the vision of Amabel in the role of a murderess reduced the amateur detectives to hysterical mirth. 'It's awful of us to laugh,' said Copper, dabbing her eyes with the corner of the window curtain, 'but that's done me more good than six brandies-and-sodas. Odd what a stimulant a good girlish giggle can be. Where were we? We've put down Ruby and John Shilto and Amabel. Then there's Ronnie Purvis and Rosamund — something against both of them by the way! — and Leonard Stock, George Beamish, Hamish Rattigan and Dr Dutt.'

Copper reached for the list, and after a moment's deliberation wrote down five more names: Sir Lionel's, Valerie's, Charles's, Nick Tarrent's, and finally, her own.

'Two more,' said Valerie, looking over her shoulder. 'In spite of my recent strictures on locals and troops, I feel that we should add the sentry and Iman Din.'

Copper flung down her pencil. 'Look, if we are going to include people like that we may as well give up at once! It's hopeless. At this rate we may as well suspect the padre.'

'That's an idea,' said Valerie calmly. She picked up the pencil and wrote MRS DOBBIE, MR DOBBIE, TRUDA GIDNEY, and had the pencil removed from her hand by Copper, who added a neat cross underneath the last name.

'What's that for?' demanded Valerie.

'X. "The Unknown Quantity". That's to allow for its having been done by one of the locals for some senseless reason that we would know nothing about.'

Valerie put her hand to her head. 'I shall go mad! Let's drop the whole idea, and try working out Einstein's theory of relativity instead.'

'Cheer up,' comforted Copper. 'I admit it looks pretty hopeless, but that's only because we haven't got anything to go on yet.'

'You're telling me! Let's open a few more windows. I feel that a bit of cold air might clear the brain.'

She flung open the window next to her and leant out across the wet sill, breathing in the thick, mist-laden air. The rain had stopped and the wind had fallen, but the surge of the tide about the grey island still rose like the clamour of an angry mob.

'I wonder why the sea hasn't gone down? It must be the swell from a big storm further south. Sometimes a storm that has missed us by hundreds of miles will send colossal breakers rolling in with hardly a breath of . . . Copper! Quick — come here!'

Copper dropped notebook and pencil and leant out beside her.

'Look!' Valerie pointed to her left where, by leaning out of the window, they could see the corner of the house where Leonard Stock's dressing-room on the first floor jutted out into the mist.

There was a shadowy figure standing against one of the pillars of the ground-floor verandah among the pots of palms and ferns that were massed at the verandah edge: a not unusual sight, since guards, orderlies, *chaprassis* and servants were in more or less constant circulation on ordinary days, though they were less in evidence in wet weather. But it was the attitude of the figure that had attracted Valerie's attention, for it stood pressed against the pillar as though hiding from someone or something beyond the turn of the house. And even as they watched, a police orderly came into view and it dodged round to the far side of the pillar; to reappear after a cautious interval when the man had passed.

A breath of wind thinned the mist for a brief moment, and Valerie caught her breath: '*Ruby!* Come on, Coppy!'

Copper needed no second invitation, and a minute or so later both girls were creeping down the small wooden staircase outside

Copper's bathroom and had reached the garden, where they stopped, momentarily at a loss, for Mrs Stock — if the skulking figure among the palm pots had been Mrs Stock — had vanished. '*Damn!*' whispered Valerie. 'What do we—— No, there she is! By the orchid trees . . .' The dim figure showed for a brief second beyond the canna beds, making for the shelter of a group of trees upon whose rough bark Valerie had been attempting to grow orchids: 'We'll have to make a dash for it. Thank God for this fog . . . we may be able to get clear of the house without being spotted by one of the guards.'

Footsteps crunched the gravel as she spoke, and the two girls shrank back under the scanty cover of the stairway. But the orderly passed without seeing them, and a moment later they were across the lawn and safely swallowed up by the mist, and though they had lost sight of the quarry, her trail was plain upon the wet grass: 'Lucky she wears such high heels,' said Copper in a whisper.

The small betraying pits in the soaked ground led them across the back of the tennis courts to where the ground fell away steeply on to the road that encircled the island, and below it, to the rocks and the sea. Nothing grew on the slopes below the garden save a few scattered coconut palms, and the sea-mist was not thick enough to blot out a hurrying figure that showed dimly ahead of them: 'It's Ruby all right,' confirmed Valerie. 'What on earth is she up to? Do you suppose she's making for the hospital by the beach road?'

'What about catching up with her and trying a bit of third degree?' suggested Copper, who favoured direct action. But Valerie shook her head regretfully. 'What's the good? She'd have some story or other: probably that she was taking a walk to calm her nerves. No, we must just stick to her heels and see if we can find out what she's up to.'

Despite the mist, this was not as easy as it sounded, for Mrs Stock was continually stopping to look behind her, and with only the inadequate shelter of a few palm trunks upon the steep slopes, the watchers had a bad time of it. She was obviously making for the narrow roadway that curls round Ross, but when she reached it she did not, as they had confidently expected, turn along it, but crossed it and plunged downwards to the beach. 'Val, you don't think that she – that she did it herself?' gasped Copper, white-faced. 'She couldn't be going to do something stupid?'

'You mean commit suicide? Not Ruby!' said Valerie scornfully. 'But all the same she's up to something pretty queer. Come on, now's our chance.' She broke into a run, and together they fled down the slope and across the road to where a group of palm trees leant out from its edge, overlooking ground that fell away almost sheer to the rocks and the angry sea.

Once off the road, their quarry had become hidden from anyone above it by the steepness of the slope, but from the shelter of the palm trunks they could see her again, almost directly below them. She was making for the huge, piled rocks that formed a natural breakwater at one end of the little beach upon which the sea had given up Ferrers Shilto the previous evening. And since there was no cover below the road, and she could now no longer move out of their range of vision — unless of course Copper's dark suspicion proved correct! — they flattened themselves against the smooth wet boles of the palm trees by the road's edge and watched her slither down the last few feet of grass and clamber on to the rocks.

The tide was out, and only a breath of wind blew in from the south, stirring but not dispersing the ghostly veils of mist. But the piled rocks were wet and glistening with spray from the huge, smooth-backed rollers that swung in from the misty sea, and Copper shivered as she watched. There seemed to her more menace in the endless, towering advance of that gigantic swell, than in all the shrieking savagery of the gale-hounded seas on the previous evening, but it did not appear to disconcert the shadowy figure on the rocks below.

Mrs Stock, stumbling and slipping on the wet, treacherous surfaces, was making her way to where the sea engulfed them, and Valerie said suddenly: 'I – I think we'd better shout.' She opened her mouth to do so, but Copper's fingers clenched about her arm and checked her, for below them Ruby had stopped——

She stood upon a flat-topped rock, silhouetted dimly against the grey seas and the flung spray, and appeared to fumble at her breast. Then of a sudden they saw her arm come up and back, and then quickly forward as she flung some unseen object far out into the boiling waters beyond the rocks.

A moment later she had turned, and was retracing her steps.

'This is where we move, I think,' muttered Valerie, and they turned together and fled back up the steep path to the shelter of the trees beyond the tennis-courts, where they waited, panting, until some minutes later Mrs Stock hurried past them to pause behind the orchid trees, and seizing a favourable opportunity, slip across the gap between the trees and the house and vanish up the back staircase that led to the tiny landing off which both her bathroom and Valerie's opened.

The amateur detectives, following her example, reached their own rooms, damp and breathless but unobserved, some five minutes later. In which they were luckier than they knew, for while they had been making lists of suspects and shadowing Mrs Stock, the entire population of Ross had been roused to hunt for the missing body of Ferrers Shilto, and search-parties had been scouring the island. This at Nick's suggestion; though the majority of the searchers were convinced that it was a waste of time.

'Sheer idiocy!' had been John Shilto's verdict. 'Surely it's obvious that whoever wanted to get rid of the body would simply have dumped it into the sea? It's probably miles down the coast by now!'

'I disagree,' snapped Nick. 'The sea handed it back once. And quite apart from that, there's something else that you haven't taken into consideration. At what point in this island, with a sea like this running, could a body have been dumped into deep water? The answer is: *None!*'

Here he had been unexpectedly backed up by Leonard Stock. 'You see, sir,' Mr Stock explained apologetically to the Chief Commissioner, 'the jetty has been completely destroyed, and so has the pier.'

'No, I am afraid I don't see,' said the Chief Commissioner shortly. 'Perhaps you would be good enough to explain.'

'Look here,' cut in Nick brusquely, 'you saw the sort of sea that was running last night — and for that matter is still running? Well, add to that the fact that the tide is now out, which means that it turned about seven this morning. Q.E.D., it must have been coming in about the time the killer would have been trying to get rid of the body, since it stands to reason he wouldn't wait until daylight. Well, what's going to happen to anything that you chuck into that sort of sea from anywhere on this damned island? It's going to get thrown back at you inside five seconds! And if you want to prove the truth of that, all you've got to do is to take a walk round Ross and see for yourself...

'Had the pier or the jetty been standing, there might have been a chance of weighting the body and pushing it off from the furthest point of either in the hope — not very reliable even then — of the current swinging it clear of the island. But as Stock has just pointed out, there is now no jetty. Therefore the body is still somewhere on this island, and I've a strong hunch that when we find it we'll also find the answer to one or two rather pressing questions!'

'The most pressing being why anyone should have taken the trouble to switch the corpses,' said Charles thoughtfully. 'If you have to dispose of one body by chucking it into the sea, why not chuck in the chap you have just murdered, instead of going in for all this elaborate substitution business?'

'I imagine a small matter of weight was the main reason,' said

Nick: 'Dan can't have been more than four or five inches taller than the original corpse, but he was considerably heftier. Whoever killed him would trust to luck that Dutt and his helpers, lifting that bundle of tarpaulin from the table, would not notice that fact. But the extra two or three stone of dead weight would have made a hell of a lot of difference to anyone hauling the body single-handed down to the shore. And there's another thing——

'Once Dan was safely buried as Ferrers, if Ferrers's body had ever happened to turn up again, it would almost certainly be unrecognizable and would be written off as the corpse of some unknown chap off a passing ship. Whereas if Dan's body had turned up, however much damage the fishes had done it might still have been obvious to an expert that far from having been accidentally drowned, he had been deliberately and nastily murdered! I can clearly see why the bodies were exchanged. And I am also prepared to bet that the original corpse is still somewhere on this island!'

The Chief Commissioner had been forced to admit the common sense of these statements, and fifteen minutes later the hunt had been organized and was in full cry.

Copper and Valerie, returning from shadowing Mrs Stock, had missed running into a section of the search-party by a narrow margin.

15

The two girls had lunched alone, for the Commissioner had sent word that he, Nick, Stock and John Shilto would be having something to eat at the Mess.

Mrs Stock had had a tray sent in to her room, and shortly after half past one Sir Lionel had returned to the house, where he had held an informal inquiry into the morning's proceedings. Copper and Valerie had not been required to attend, and they had sat in uneasy silence in the verandah above, listening anxiously to the murmur of voices while the slow minutes crawled past and the fog pressed against the window-panes and crept into the quiet house.

At long last the office door had opened, and they heard Leonard Stock's voice in the hall below, anxious and protesting: 'I feel sure there must be some mistake. Perhaps when Dr Vicarjee is back his verdict will be – will be different . . .'

'There is *no* difference, I am telling you!' — Dutt's voice, shrill and indignant—— 'All the facts they are plain. As plain as pike-staffs! It is murder! Miss Gidney, she is agreeing too. You will ask her, please. If it is as you say, that the man he is drowned, then there will be water in his lungs. But there is not water. None. It is murder!'

Valerie got up suddenly and ran to call down over the banisters: 'Leonard — what *is* all this? Who are you all talking about? What's happened?'

'Oh . . . er . . . ah——' The question appeared to have taken Mr Stock by surprise. 'I did not realize that you were there.

Perhaps I should not have said — that is——' Dr Dutt's agitated voice cut hurriedly across Leonard's stammered incoherencies: 'You will excuse, please. I go now. There is much work.' The front door banged behind him, and after a moment or two there was a sound of reluctant footsteps ascending the staircase, and Leonard Stock came into view.

He smiled nervously at Copper, and having directed a hunted look at Valerie, observed hopefully that it was still very foggy and that he had never known such unseasonable weather: 'Almost chilly, is it not? In all my years in the Islands, and I think I can safely say that I am the oldest inhabitant . . . well, hardly *inhabitant*, I suppose; after all, there must be people here who . . . what I mean is I really do not think that I can recall such freakish weather . . . there is no other word for it. I——'

Here Valerie, who had no intention of being sidetracked on to a discussion of the weather, cut through Mr Stock's nervous spate of words as unceremoniously as Dr Dutt had done: 'Who were you talking about just now, Leonard? Who wasn't drowned?'

'Well . . . er . . . um . . . Ferrers,' said Leonard unhappily, and cleared his throat with a small embarrassed cough.

'Ferrers!' Valerie's white face seemed to turn whiter. 'But that's nonsense! Of course he was drowned. Why we all saw him, and — *Leonard!* . . . Have they found him?'

'Er — yes. I'm afraid so. I mean—— Well, Dutt and Miss Gidney have performed some sort of an — er — an autopsy, and Dutt has advanced the theory that Ferrers too — was er — was in fact — er — um——' Leonard's thin bony hands sketched a fluttering futile gesture and Copper caught her breath and said huskily: 'Murdered!'

Leonard turned towards her with an expression of relief: 'Yes. Yes, that is what it amounts to. But Dutt must have made a mistake. He is — um — not a very efficient young man as — er — yet. Perhaps when he has had more experience . . . But I feel sure that once the sea has gone down and the jetty has been repaired and – and Dr Vicarjee has been able to return, we shall find that it is all a — um — a mare's nest. It has to be. Anything else is unthinkable. After all, who would want to murder Ferrers?'

'John!' said Copper before she could stop herself. And was instantly appalled at what she had said.

Leonard Stock appeared equally horrified. His nervous, over-bright eyes widened in dismay and he threw a quick, frightened glance over his shoulder in the direction of the staircase and the hall below. '*Ssh!* He might hear you! No, no *really*, Miss Randal, you should not — what I mean is——' Leonard became entangled once more in a maze of half-sentences, and Copper said ruefully: 'I'm sorry. It was a beastly thing to say and I didn't really mean it. But I couldn't help remembering that scene at the Mount Harriet picnic.'

'Oh, I know; I quite see. And you will have heard, of course, that they did not get on at all well — the Shiltos, I mean. But *fratricide*! Or – or what amounts to it. Oh no! . . . unthinkable. You may be quite sure, as I am, that poor Dutt has made a mistake. When Dr Vicarjee returns we shall discover that Ferrers was drowned after all, and then everything will be all right.'

'All *right*?' repeated Valerie, looking at him with a mixture of amazement and contempt. 'How can it be all right when Dan—— Oh, it's all awful and horrible and unbelievable! It doesn't seem *possible* that any of it can really have happened.'

'Yes, yes,' agreed Mr Stock earnestly. 'Terrible. Quite terrible! I do feel for you. Such a very unpleasant shock. I shall not enjoy having to break it to poor Ruby. I have not yet dared — er — I mean, I did not like—— Well, the truth is that poor Ruby is particularly sensitive to — er — shock. Her nerves, you know. But I suppose she will have to know sometime. There is no point in putting it off. And yet I must own——'

Valerie said quickly: 'You don't have to worry, Leonard. She knows. I told her myself.'

Some of the nervous tension seemed to leave Leonard's meagre body and he relaxed visibly. 'Oh. Then I need not — um . . . I do hope she was not too upset?'

'I'm afraid she was, rather.'

'Oh. Oh dear. Then I suppose I had better go and see how she is. She will have been expecting me, but I really could not get away before. There were so many things . . . and then your father . . .' His voice trailed away and stopped, and Valerie said encouragingly: 'No, of course you couldn't get away. Ruby will realize that. It's been a horrible day for everybody.'

Leonard smiled wanly, and bracing his thin shoulders, turned and went away across the dim expanse of the ballroom, his shoes squeaking dolefully on the polished boards, and presently they heard him tapping nervously on his wife's door. It opened and closed again, and Valerie said: 'Poor Leonard! I'm afraid he's in for a bad half-hour. And what'll you bet that before dear Ruby is through with him she'll have managed to make out that it's all his fault and that he is personally responsible for the whole thing, and Leonard, poor toadstool, will be apologizing for it. I can't think how he stands it.'

But Copper was not interested in Leonard Stock's matrimonial troubles, and she had not been thinking of him. Only of what he had said. She spoke in a half-whisper, as though she were addressing herself rather than Valerie: '*Murder——!* He said that Ferrers was murdered too. Then that was why! Dan must have known . . .' She shivered suddenly and violently; and once again a door banged in the hall below and there was a sound of footsteps on the stairs. But this time it was Charles and Nick: Charles for once grave and unsmiling, and Nick looking drawn and grim and exhausted.

Charles said briefly, cutting short Valerie's anxious questions: 'We can't talk here. We'd better all go down to the Mess.' And turning abruptly on his heel he led the way back to the hall and out into the clammy embrace of a fog that seemed to grow thicker by the minute.

Mist filled the long, tree-shaded drive with a dense shifting greyness that smelt as dank as a sea cave uncovered by a spring tide, and when at last the Mess loomed out of it as a dark, dimly seen shape and Charles pushed open the front door, the fog came in with them and eddied about the silent hall.

Charles's quarters, which lay on the far side of the ante-room, consisted of a small bathroom and a large, white-washed and somewhat untidy bed-sitting room decorated with several photographs of Valerie, some depressing school and regimental groups and a clutter of golf clubs and fishing-tackle. 'Hardly the Ritz,' said Charles, ushering in his guests, 'but at least it's reasonably private. And there are quite a few things that have come up for discussion.' He closed the door behind him, and Nick sat down and said tiredly and without preamble: 'We found Ferrers's body, and Dutt says that he was murdered.'

'I know,' said Valerie with a shudder. 'Leonard told us. But he seems to think that Dutt must have made a mistake.'

Nick shook his head. 'Not a chance, I'm afraid. We've been checking back over that half hour in the bay in some detail, and one thing is quite clear: Ferrers Shilto survived the overturning of the boats. I can swear to that myself, because I caught sight of him clinging to the keel of one that bumped into ours, and there was nothing much the matter with him then. But sometime just after that — or it may have been any time during the half hour that we were all in the drink — someone smashed in the back of his head.'

Copper gave a swiftly suppressed exclamation, and Nick turned his head sharply towards her. 'What is it, Coppy?'

'Nothing,' said Copper hastily. 'I only wondered — I mean, how could anyone tell it was murder — a blow on the back of the head? It sounds as if it could easily have happened by accident.'

'This particular blow,' said Nick grimly, 'was given with the end of a tiller. The tillers on those boats are the kind that have a metal-bound slot at one end that fits over the top of the rudder, and the wound on the back of Ferrers's head was made by someone holding the handle of a tiller and hitting him damned hard with the slotted end. There's no mistake about that; the imprint is quite clear. It wasn't spotted before because his hair hid the mark and the blood had been washed off by the sea.'

'But I still don't see why it couldn't——' began Copper.

'Listen, sweetheart,' interrupted Charles briskly, 'the end of the tiller that killed Ferrers is usually attached to the rudder. Therefore it could only have come in contact with his skull once it had come unshipped. If it had been floating round loose and a wave had knocked it against his head, the very most it could have done would have been to leave a bit of a bruise. Instead of which it hit him with enough force to smash in his skull, and also produced a hell of a bruise — and a lot of swelling, which apart from anything else, appears to prove that it was done before and not after death. Now perhaps we can go on? . . . Good! Nick, I think we'd better have a bit of recapping from you. Just to get the record straight.'

'All right.' Nick leant back in his chair and frowned at the ceiling as though arranging his thoughts, and presently he said slowly: 'On Christmas Day — that is, yesterday — we went for a walk round the island at about five o'clock, and very unfortunately for the murderer, Ferrers's body turned up. Even more unfortunately for him, it had escaped being mutilated by fish or reefs, and Dan, who was a doctor, was on the spot. We don't know enough to do more than guess at this bit, but it's pretty obvious that something made Dan suspect that Ferrers had not died by drowning . . . And if I hadn't been a triple-distilled idiot,' added Nick with sudden bitterness, 'I'd have realized that he suspected it from his subsequent behaviour.'

'That applies to all of us,' said Copper quickly.

Nick threw her the ghost of a grin and stubbed out his half-smoked cigarette, grinding it down in the ash-tray with a viciousness that betrayed the state of his nerves. He lit another, and said: 'Dan apparently saw enough on the beach yesterday evening to make him suspect that this wasn't a plain case of drowning, and I can only suppose that he didn't say anything then and there because it wasn't his job to cut in on the local medico. But of course it's quite obvious that that young ass of an assistant is as much use as a sick headache, and could barely be trusted to tell the difference between scarlet fever and heat rash. I gather he barely looked at Ferrers's body other than to see it shoved into the Guest House and sewn up in canvas. And I suppose one can hardly blame him. After all, in justice to young Dutt, it seemed a perfectly clear case to all of us! — except to Dan, who as far as we can make out must have slipped down to the Guest House late last night to take another look at the corpse. And here we stop guessing for a bit and come to the sentry's evidence. Charles can tell you about that. The sentry was one of his chaps and he did most of the talking.'

Charles leant an elbow on the shelf above the fireplace and took up the tale: 'Weekes, the chap on sentry duty, says that Dan came out of the house just before midnight last night. It was raining a bit and he was wearing one of the orderlies' mackintosh capes: they found a smear of blood on it . . .' Charles's voice was suddenly uncertain, and he jerked his shoulders uncomfortably and hurried on: 'The sentry challenged him, and Dan said he couldn't sleep and was going to take a stroll, gave the chap a packet of cigarettes, and pushed off. That sounds all right as far as it goes, but here comes the rub: Weekes swears blind that Dan returned about an hour and a half later, nodded to him, popped into the house and bolted the door behind him. He says he heard the hall clock strike half past one immediately afterwards. Now if he is right, how did Dan get out again, and why?'

'Obvious,' said Copper briefly. 'It wasn't Dan.'

'Don't talk tripe, Coppy. The sentry swears——'

'I don't care *what* the sentry swears! It's so obvious, it simply *screams* at you! You said Dan was wearing one of the orderlies' capes. Well, they have a big hood that goes right over your head and——'

Nick said: 'Charles, you and I should see a brain specialist. Of course that's it! Dan goes down to the Guest House to take a look at the body, and while he's there he's caught at it and murdered. We know that he was killed there, for there were stains on the floor that had been wiped up; but not quite well enough. The murderer substitutes Dan's body for Ferrers', takes Ferrers's body off and hides it, and having cleared away all traces of his dirty work puts on the mackintosh cape, and with the hood pulled well over his head, walks calmly back to the house.'

Charles said: 'I ought to have a nurse. Of course. It is, as my grandmother's cook used to say, "As plain as the nose on me face".'

'And,' pointed out Copper, 'I notice that the sentry didn't say that Dan actually spoke to him when he came back.'

'That's right,' said Charles. 'He didn't speak. And I don't know if it has struck anyone else, but it seems to me to point to two things. The first being that whoever returned to the house inside that mackintosh was not only the murderer, but someone who must have watched Dan leave and listened to his conversation with the sentry. Otherwise how did he know that he could return to the house without being challenged?'

'But —' Valerie's voice shook — 'but that would mean that the murderer was someone in the house!' In spite of her recent suspicions concerning Mrs Stock, the idea that a double murderer might actually be a member of the household was incredibly and horribly shocking. 'Not necessarily,' said Nick. 'It would have been obvious to anyone that to get to the Guest House Dan must have passed the sentry. Therefore it was a fair gamble that the sentry would pass him in again without comment.'

'But Nick — if it wasn't someone from the house, why should they come back again?' 'Alibi,' said Nick shortly. 'Muddy the trail. And a very sound idea too, because if Dan had failed to come back, it's quite on the cards that the sentry would have become uneasy and reported the fact sometime last night. There would probably have been a search within an hour or two of the murder, and then heaven knows what might not have come to light. So Dan *has* to return, because with luck Ferrers will have been buried before any serious attention is given to the fact that he is missing.'

Valerie said unhappily: 'I do hope to goodness you're right. It would be too awful if it had to be someone in the house. But . . .'

'Of course I'm right. That's the hell of it. It widens the field too much. If we could only be certain that the man who impersonated Dan did *not* get out of the house again, we'd be able to narrow down our list of suspects considerably. As it is, the only solid fact that we seem to have got out of all this is that Dan died sometime between midnight and one o'clock. And I'm not sure that that's much help.'

'Yes, it is,' said Charles. 'Because it adds a bit of support to your theory that the chap who came home at one-thirty got out again.'

'How do you make that out?'

'Well, it's really all a matter of timing, isn't it? Dan leaves the house about midnight, chats to the sentry, and shoves off to the Guest House — say at five minutes to twelve. Allow a good few minutes for getting down there, and more for finding a way in — and by the way we found a ground-floor window with a broken catch so presumably he got in by that. We can't tell whether he had time to take a look at Ferrers, or if he was murdered before he had the chance. But I imagine he couldn't have been killed much before twelve-thirty: which gives the murderer just about an hour in which to kill Dan, swop his body with Ferrers's, sew it up again in the tarpaulin, hide Ferrers's body, clear up the blood on the floor and get back to the house again. Can't be done!'

'Why not?' inquired Copper. 'If he worked quickly, surely it's perfectly possible?'

'Possible. But damned unlikely! Nick didn't tell you where we found Ferrers's body. I'm afraid this is going to put you off the soup at the next Guildhall banquet you are invited to attend, but as a matter of fact it was found very cunningly stowed away in the turtle tank.'

'Ugh!' said Valerie, shuddering. 'What a place to hide it in. Of course it would float and anyone looking in would have seen it.'

'You're wrong there,' said Charles. 'It was, in fact, very neatly done. And if it hadn't been for the — er — unusual behaviour of the turtles, it might not have been spotted for days. You know that summer-house thing that is built out over the top of half the tank?'

'Of course.'

'Well, the body had been carried round the outer wall of the tank on the seaward side of the summer-house, and lowered into the darkest corner of the tank behind the pillar that supports the floor. It was hanging there by a rope that had been tied under its arms and then fastened to the crossbeams. An ingenious job which must have taken quite a bit of doing in the dark.'

'For goodness sake, why there?' asked Copper breathlessly. 'Of all silly places!'

'Not so silly,' said Nick dryly. 'It would have been a damned good hiding-place if it hadn't been for the turtles, because since it's right on the bay, the minute the sea went down all the killer had to do was to get there after dark, haul up the body, tie a weight to it and push it off the end of the Club breakwater at the turn of the tide. As for Dan, who would not have been seriously missed or searched for until after the funeral, he would be presumed to have taken a toss in the mist and fallen into the sea.'

'Then what we've really got to find out,' said Copper slowly, 'is not who killed Dan, but who killed Ferrers. And then we've got the answer to both.'

'That's about it. The reason for Dan's murder is obvious: he was killed because he discovered, or suspected, that Ferrers had been murdered. What we need now is a motive for the killing of Ferrers.'

'Mount Harriet!' said three voices simultaneously.

'You mean that conversation we overheard at the picnic? Yes: I think that's fairly obvious. So I suggest our first suspect goes down as Mr John Shilto.'

Valerie said: 'Listen, Nick — I don't know about you, but I shall soon be getting hopelessly muddled. This morning Coppy and I decided that we must have some method in our madness, so we made a list of possible suspects so that we could enter up everything "for" or "against" each person. Let's stick to it.'

'Good scheme,' approved Charles. 'Produce your suspects.' Copper handed over the list that they had compiled earlier in the day, and Nick and Charles read it with some amusement. 'Can't you see Amabel spreading death and destruction with a tiller?' grinned Charles.

'The same thought gave us the one laugh of a mildewed morning,' admitted Valerie. 'But Copper said there was no use making a list of suspects unless we put down everyone and then started eliminating by proof to narrow it down.'

Nick said: 'Copper is right. When it comes to murder you can't start by saying, "I'm sure so-and-so can't have done it, he's got such a stupid face," or "Of course she didn't do it! she's got such an angelic disposition." You've got to suspect everyone.'

'We have,' admitted Copper frankly. 'You'll find your own name on the list.'

Nick gave a short and rather bitter laugh. 'Well, why not? You don't really know much about me, do you?'

'No,' said Copper in an oddly uncertain voice: 'That's why I put your name down.'

Nick swung round to face her, his eyes suddenly narrow and angry, but she would not meet his gaze, and after a moment he turned his attention to the notebook in his hand. 'Fortunately,' he stated curtly, 'in spite of Copper's theories we can cut this list down by half. Pencil please, Charles.'

'Why?' inquired Copper indignantly as Charles reached for a pencil from his writing-desk and tossed it across.

'Because, my dear girl,' said Nick acidly, 'we have already decided that although there were two murders, there is only one murderer. Therefore, as Ferrers was killed during the time that the sailing party spent in the water on Christmas Eve, it stands to reason that only a member of that party could have done it. Which brings the suspects down by half. We can now eliminate you, Valerie, Charles and the Commissioner as a start. Amabel and George are out of it too, and the padre and Mrs Dobbie and the sentry. Also "X". The "unknown quantity" I presume, Copper?'

'Yes,' said Copper defensively: 'I thought it might have been one of the natives. But there were none on the boats, of course.'

'That still leaves us with a pretty large list of suspects,' said Valerie despondently.

Charles said: 'Only five. That's a lot better than fifteen!'

'Five?' Valerie rose from the bed and went to lean over Nick's shoulder: 'You mean seven!'

'Look, darling,' began Charles patiently, 'we've already agreed that the man who masqueraded as Dan last night was the murderer, and if so——'

'What makes you so sure it was a man?' cut in Valerie quickly.

'My dear Val!'

'She's quite right,' said Copper. 'We can't be sure. It could just as easily have been a woman. Those capes come down well below the knee, and they're so bulky that you couldn't be certain of the size — or the height! — of anybody wearing one, because the peaked hood would give an impression of height. And anyway I'll bet the sentry barely looked at the person who passed. He would have been so sure it was Dan that his eye would have been blind to details.'

Nick said: 'They're right, of course, Charles. We can't rule out the possibility of its having been a woman.'

'Have it your own way,' said Charles. 'Keep 'em on the list. But as it's half past four and I need refreshment, I propose to call a short interval. Or do I mean "adjourn the court"? Val darling, phone your father that you and Copper will be out to tea: then we can carry on these bloodcurdling discussions after we have fortified the inner man.'

He tucked her hand under his arm and they went out to organize tea and telephone Government House.

16

There was a brief interval of curiously strained silence after they had left the room, and then Nick said pleasantly: 'So you think my name should be included among the suspects, do you, Copper? May I ask why?'

'Certainly you may,' replied Copper lightly. 'Always providing you don't expect an answer.'

A spark leapt to life in Nick's grey eyes for a swift unreadable moment, and then he laughed and lay back in his chair. 'Take it that I'd merely appreciate one, then. Do I get it?'

Copper considered him for a long moment. His dark hair was unusually smooth and the eyes that held hers were once again narrowed and lazy. But she saw too, and with a tremor of disquiet, that in spite of his indolent posture and the suggestion of a smile that curved his mouth, there was something about him — some tenseness of line — that suggested wariness.

'I've already told you why,' said Copper defensively. 'Until we can eliminate by proof, we must include everyone.'

Nick said very softly: 'But that isn't what you meant in my case, is it, Copper?'

'No,' said Copper after a moment, in an oddly brittle voice: 'No. You were right when you said we didn't know anything about you. We don't.'

'And therefore I am probably capable of murder?' suggested Nick ironically. 'Very instructive!'

Copper stiffened and her eyes were suddenly both reckless and angry. 'Do you want me to go on?' she inquired crisply.

'Of course. I'm all for hearing your candid opinion of me.'

'It's not a question,' said Copper coldly, 'of my opinion of you, candid or otherwise. I thought we had already decided — I think you were the one to point it out? — that the murderer of Ferrers Shilto and Dan must be one of seven people. And as you are one of those seven I had supposed, from your question, that you'd like a disinterested opinion on the possibility of suspicion resting on you. Apparently you don't.'

'I accept the correction,' said Nick gravely. 'I shall be more than grateful for a — disinterested opinion.'

Copper got up abruptly, and moving to the window stood looking out into the mist with her back to him and her fingers playing restlessly with the window-latch. The slow seconds ticked away to the tune of the fog-dew dripping from the roof-edge outside, and at last, and without turning, she said in a deliberately cool and conversational voice: 'You were the only one who knew Dan Harcourt before he came to the Islands, and for all we know there may have been some quarrel between you that we know nothing about. They — the police — will think of that. You may have had a dozen reasons for hating Dan.'

'Thanks,' said Nick, without sarcasm. 'You are right. It's just as well to get a "disinterested" opinion' (once again he stressed the word slightly) 'on how people are likely to regard one when it's a case of looking for a murderer. Go on.'

Copper said haltingly: 'I know it sounds rude and – and beastly, but I thought you'd better see——'

'Oh, don't apologize!' interrupted Nick. 'It's very interesting. What about Ferrers? Where does he fit into my murderous schemes?' Copper turned abruptly to face him. The knuckles of her clenched hands showed white and her voice had a defiant edge to it: 'I have no idea——'

'You surprise me!' murmured Nick.

' — why you should murder a man whom you had only met

that day. But then it is always possible that you had met him before. Say about a month ago?'

'Meaning what?' inquired Nick softly.

'Meaning . . . just that!'

Copper turned away again and stared blindly out at the drifting mist. Her anger had vanished as suddenly as it had come, but something else had taken its place: an indefinable and disquieting tension. And when at last she spoke, it was without turning her head, and in a voice so low as to be barely audible: 'Ferrers Shilto,' said Copper, 'used to go to Calcutta on business once a year, travelling on the *Maharaja*. I know when he was last there, because he was on board with me when I arrived here. And I know that he had stayed at the Grand Hotel because I saw the labels on his luggage; you couldn't miss them. I know, too, that during the time he was there the *Sapphire* was on a visit to Calcutta, and you told me yourself that you had stayed——' Her voice failed her and she turned stiffly to face him.

Nick was sitting quite still. A faint curl of smoke drifted from the cigarette between his fingers, but there was no other movement in the quiet room, and Copper saw with a tightening of the heart that a queer little change had come over his face. It was so slight as to be barely perceptible — yet it was there. He had made no motion of surprise or denial, but the lines of his mouth had become fixed and his grey eyes coldly angry, and presently he said: 'Thank you for defining my position so clearly. Perhaps you'd like to know that your surmise is correct. I did meet Ferrers Shilto in Calcutta.'

He made no attempt to qualify that terse statement, and Copper drew her breath in a small, hard gasp, and feeling her knees suddenly go weak, sat down abruptly on the end of Charles's bed.

Nick came to his feet in one swift unexpected movement, and crossing the space between them in two strides, caught her by the shoulders and jerked her to her feet. She made an instinctive movement to wrench herself away, but the grip of his hard fingers on her shoulders held her rigid, and she abandoned the attempt to free herself as useless and undignified.

Releasing his hold on one shoulder he caught her chin in his free hand, and jerking her head up to meet his gaze, laughed down at her small startled face and wide apprehensive eyes. 'I should never have given you credit for such a vivid and unpleasant imagination, darling. Seriously, do you think that I may have done it?' His voice sharpened suddenly: *'Answer me, Copper!'*

'It isn't a question of what I think,' said Copper stiffly. 'I have only pointed out that you *could* have done it.'

The fingers about her chin tightened convulsively, but he said coolly enough: 'You haven't answered my question.'

Copper's lips closed in a stubborn line and she stared at him in silence, suddenly as angry as he was. A minute ticked by. Sixty seconds that seemed as long as an hour — or a day. Then, 'That's all I wanted to know,' said Nick dryly. 'So you think I might even be a murderer, do you, Copper? Well, has it occurred to you yet that if I were capable of committing two murders, I might be equally capable of committing a third? After all, you appear to be the only one who has spotted any connection between myself and Ferrers Shilto.'

The warm strong fingers about her chin relaxed their grip and slid downwards to close gently about her throat, but Copper did not move. She stood as though frozen between anger and fear. A fear that held no considerations for her own safety, but was nonetheless real for that.

It was, of course, absurd to think of Nick in connection with murder, and it would be a mis-statement to say that she had dismissed the idea. It being impossible to dismiss an idea that has never for a moment been entertained. But it had occurred to her that the authorities might well consider Nick as a possible suspect, and her imagination, stimulated by anxiety for him, had instantly presented her with several uncomfortable lines of thought: including an unfortunate recollection of his late sojourn in Calcutta. She had blurted out the results of her anxious meditations from a vague feeling that she must warn him that he might be regarded with suspicion, and she had expected him to laugh at her. But he had not laughed. He had merely been angry. Couldn't he *see* . . .?

The fingers about her throat tightened steadily, and suddenly Copper became aware of the blood drumming in her ears. She opened her mouth to cry out, but found that she could make no sound. And in the next instant Nick bent his head and kissed her parted lips, long and deliberately.

A moment later the door was flung open behind them and Charles's voice said: 'What on earth are you two waiting for? A gong? Come along and have some tea. Val's made enough toast for sixty.'

Nick's hand dropped to his side, and Copper stepped back — both hands to her throat and her heart beating jerkily.

Nick swung round with a laugh: 'As usual, Charles, you arrive in the nick of time — no pun intended. I was about to commit my third murder.'

'Don't let me stop you,' said Charles.

'Copper here,' explained Nick lightly, 'has just been proving, with a wealth of damnatory detail, that I could easily be the local murderer. What are you going to do about it, Charles?'

'Nothing!' said Charles firmly. 'I'm sorry, Coppy: you're probably dead right, but as he is a good deal larger than I am, I shall prudently ignore it and . . .' He stepped back hurriedly as Copper brushed past him into the ante-room, her chin high and her cheeks scarlet.

'Hullo!' said Charles, recovering his balance and disentangling his feet from among a collection of carelessly placed fishing-tackle. 'The lady seems annoyed. Have I put a foot into it somewhere?'

'Both, I imagine,' said Nick with unexpected bitterness. 'And practically everywhere. Copper's dead serious about this question of my having committed the local crimes. She almost convinced *me*!' He laughed shortly, and Charles echoed the laugh; and then remembering Copper's face as she had passed him, stopped laughing and frowned. 'Do you mean to say,' he demanded incredulously, 'that you think that Copper thinks——? Of all the unmitigated drivel! Why, the girl thinks you're——*Ahem!*'

Charles pulled up abruptly on the brink of betraying certain strictly private confidences imparted to him by Valerie, and Nick said curiously: 'Thinks I'm what?'

'Oh, er — I forget. But if you ask me, she's merely been trying to take the mickey out of you. You oughtn't to buy it. Come and have some tea: Val's collected enough to feed a school treat.'

They ate toast and Christmas cake in the ante-room of the Mess, and afterwards, when the cups and plates had been cleared away, Valerie wrote steadily in the notebook and was presently able to announce that she had put down a rough outline of the happenings of the last two days, and that it was time they got back to work. 'Where were we?' inquired Charles.

'Narrowing down the suspects. And now I suggest that we give each of the seven members of the sailing party a page apiece and put down any evidence we can think of, for or against, under each name. Here they are: JOHN SHILTO, RONNIE PURVIS, LEONARD STOCK, HAMISH RATTIGAN, ROSAMUND PURVIS, RUBY STOCK and NICHOLAS TARRENT. And I should think we could cross off at least three of those straight away, wouldn't you?'

Nick said curtly: 'No, don't cut any of them. Who was the first on the list? John Shilto, wasn't it? Well, what have we got against him?'

'Easy!' said three voices.

'All right. One at a time. Come on, Copper. You'd make the best counsel for the prosecution.'

'I've already prosecuted one case this afternoon,' said Copper coldly. 'Charles can take this one.'

'Right,' said Charles, nothing loth. He lifted his tea cup: 'Here's to logic; never sell her short! To begin with, John doesn't — I mean didn't — hit it off with Ferrers. Everyone in the Islands knows that. However, coming down to more concrete evidence, we all overheard a couple of pretty crisp scenes between them on the day of the Harriet picnic, so I think that can go down on his charge-sheet as a start.'

'That's all very well,' said Valerie, scribbling hard, 'but was it enough of a scene to make John want to murder Ferrers?'

'Judging from what I know of John Shilto, easily! But whether it was enough to make him actually *do* the deed is another matter.'

'Yes, it would help a lot if we knew what was behind that row at Mount Harriet.'

Copper said: 'I think I've got an idea.'

'Another one?' murmured Nick, lifting an eyebrow.

'Yes!' snapped Copper dangerously. 'Another one. Any objection?'

'None at all. I was merely expressing admiration.'

Valerie glanced up sharply from the notebook on her lap and looked inquiringly from Copper's face to Nick's. Her brows drew together in a puzzled frown and she said quickly: 'What's your idea, Coppy?'

Copper jerked her gaze angrily away from Nick's mocking eyes, and collecting her thoughts with an effort, said: 'You remember how anxious Mr Shilto was that we shouldn't stop at his cousin's bungalow for water, and how furious he was when he heard that the Dobbies had taken Ferrers on to the picnic?'

'Do we not!' said Charles. 'Said he wasn't going on with us if Ferrers was going to be there, and after making a fatuous fuss about it, suddenly changed his mind and came with us after all.'

'That's just it,' said Copper. 'It was too sudden. And I don't believe for one minute that any change of heart or Christmas spirit was responsible for it. I believe he must have seen something or heard something that made him change his mind about coming.'

'Such as what?' said Valerie.

'I don't know. But he might have seen that the plantation was doing very much better than he had ever imagined it could, and realized that his cousin was on the verge of making it pay at last.'

'And decided to stage a big reconciliation scene and buy it back before Ferrers realized that it was on the upgrade? Yes, I suppose there's something in that. Did he go into the house, Charles?'

Charles considered the point and shook his head. 'I don't think so. He strolled around a bit at the back, but as I thought he wasn't coming with us, I left him to it. And anyway the place smelt like a sewer, so I didn't linger.'

'Oh well, it's a sound idea, Copper. Has anyone else got any more theories on the subject of Public Suspect Number One?'

'I have,' said Valerie. 'You can call it feminine intuition if you like, because I've got no proof. But I'm prepared to bet my entire allowance for the next two years, against Amabel's bridge winnings, that John was delighted about Ferrers's death. He's been going about in a sort of nasty gloating trance ever since.'

'And I'll endorse that,' said Copper.

Charles sighed. 'Righto,' he said. 'Enter two dollops of feminine intuition on the debit side. Anything more? . . . No? All right, account closed for the moment. Nick will please sum up.'

Nick lay back in his chair and stared meditatively at the ceiling again, and presently he said: 'Will this do? Points against John Shilto. One: he had a long-standing quarrel with his cousin, which culminates in a hell of a row a few hours before the murder. Two: he could easily have murdered Ferrers during the storm. (Against that one, so could any of the other six suspects.) Then, if he *was* the murderer, he would instantly have spotted Dan's unhealthy interest in the corpse, and a guilty conscience would have given him the clue to it——

'His room was at the end of the passage, next to the one Dan and I were in, and he might have heard Dan leave. Or again, he might have been waiting in the ballroom for fear he should do so. In which case, of course, he would have watched Dan go out and wouldn't need to be told where he was going. He collects a weapon, follows him to the Guest House and kills him . . .

'The problem then is how to get rid of the body, and the answer is right under his nose — together with a ball of twine and an outsize cobbler's needle! He sews Dan into the tarpaulin, carries Ferrers down to the Club breakwater where he discovers that it's no good trying to chuck him into the sea again, and hits on the idea of dumping him in the turtle tank. Having done that, all he has to do is to throw the weapon into the sea, put on Dan's mackintosh cape and get back to the house. That's all, I think.'

Copper said: 'Can I add something, please? It – it was only an idea of mine, but when Dan was discovered to be missing and we were all getting a little worried about it, I thought that Mr Shilto seemed to be amused.'

'In that case,' said Nick, 'we'd better add another Maltese Cross, indicating adverse feminine intuition, to the charge-sheet. Anybody got anything else to add? No? Well I have. Write it down, Val. When it was suggested that a search be made for Ferrers's body, Shilto was against it, tooth and nail. Said it was a complete waste of time, and sundry other things, and when I insisted, barged out of the room in a hell of a temper, spitting with wrath. Altogether a pretty peculiar demonstration; and with the discovery of Ferrers's body and the added discovery that he had been murdered, it begins to look even more peculiar. Well, that's about all I think. Who's next on the list?'

Valerie flicked over a page of the notebook: 'Romeo Purvis. Anyone got anything to say about Ronnie? . . . No?'

'What? Not even a Maltese Cross?' gibed Nick. 'Lucky devil!'

'I've got something,' said Valerie, 'and Copper can vouch for it that it isn't just something I've thought up recently, but something

I noticed at the time. When Rosamund made that silly scene on Christmas Eve, Ronnie was scared out of his wits. It's not much, but I'm prepared to swear to it. I told Copper about it at the time.'

'Yes,' endorsed Copper, 'and you were dead right, because when she yelled the place down later that evening, Ronnie was scared again. And not for her sake, either.'

'Oh God!' sighed Charles. '*More* feminine intuition!'

Valerie threw a sofa cushion at him and said: 'One more crack like that from you, my own, and I'll throw my engagement ring after it!'

'Is that a promise?' inquired Charles eagerly.

'No. It's an awful warning. So close down, Charles darling, unless you want a two carat diamond in your eye. To return to Suspect Number Two — anything else? No? Very well, Ronald Purvis — no evidence. Go on, Charles, make a case out of that.'

Charles sat up indignantly: 'Good Lord, why me? Give me an easier one for heaven's sake. Oh well——' He subsided gloomily, and cleared his throat: 'In the prisoner's favour: no reason for killing Ferrers Shilto.'

'No *known* reason,' corrected Valerie. 'For all we know he may have had half a dozen.'

'So might Amabel!' retorted Charles with some asperity. 'Are you conducting this prosecution or am I? Then leave me the floor, my love. Where was I? Oh yes. Against the prisoner: as a member of the sailing party he had the opportunity of killing Ferrers Shilto. For the prisoner: so, apparently, had six other people.'

He brooded for a moment or two, and then added: 'From that point on, if Ronnie is our murderer, all that Nick said about John Shilto can equally well apply to him. He spots Dan's interest in the corpse and hangs about outside the house to make sure that he doesn't make a move towards further investigation. Sees Dan come out, hears him speak to the sentry, follows him down to the

Guest House, kills him, disposes of the bodies and returns to the house disguised as Dan in order to delay the search for him until the supposed Ferrers is well and truly underground. After which he slides out of the house by a back door and trots off home. And that appears to be all. M'Lud, the case rests!'

He threw himself back in his chair and closed his eyes with ostentation.

Valerie said: 'That's all very well, darling, but you haven't suggested any reason why he should have killed Ferrers in the first place.'

'Don't be silly, sweetheart! He can't possibly have had any reason for doing such a thing. *Ergo*, he did not kill Ferrers. I was merely endeavouring to show that *had* he done anything so fantastic, he could also have killed Dan. Who's next?'

'Leonard Stock,' said Valerie, turning a page. 'Anyone got anything to say about Leonard? No? All right: you take over, Coppy.'

Copper said: 'In the absence of any concrete evidence, I plump for Leonard Stock as the murderer. First, because he's the most unlikely person, and as anyone who has ever read a murder story knows, it's always the most unlikely person who turns out to have done the deed — and fifty thousand authors can't be wrong.'

'I suppose,' drawled Nick, 'that, acting on that assumption, you would unhesitatingly have nominated Amabel if she had been in the running for the Suspect Stakes?'

'Then you suppose wrong!' snapped Copper. 'I should have known Amabel couldn't possibly have done it even if I'd found her standing over the corpse with a bludgeon in one hand and blood all over her! I should merely be convinced that she'd just turned up, at the wrong moment as usual, and picked up the weapon out of mere cow-like curiosity. But I do *not* know that Leonard couldn't have done it. It seems to me that he stands as good a chance as anyone of being the murderer. Because——'

She hesitated for a moment, as though doubtful as to how her next observation would be received, and then continued in a tone of some diffidence: 'Have any of you ever noticed that Ronnie Purvis wears a cornelian signet ring on his left hand?'

It was obvious that her question had not only taken her hearers by surprise, but that its connection with the subject under discussion completely eluded them. Valerie's forehead wrinkled in a puzzled frown, and she said: 'Yes, but I don't see . . .'

'I think I do,' said Nick abruptly. 'She means that someone might have seen a hand and thought——'

He broke off without finishing the sentence, and Copper turned to look at him for a moment. It gave her a queer stab of uneasiness to find that Nick should instantly know what she implied by what she had not said. She looked away again swiftly, and turned to Valerie: 'I – I was thinking of Ferrers,' she said uncertainly. 'He wore a garnet ring on his left hand, and in the rain it might have been mistaken for Ronnie's. They were both red, you see.'

'But I still don't——'

Nick said: 'Shut up, Val!'

'Supposing——' Copper was choosing her words with some difficulty, 'supposing that during the storm somebody wearing a red ring had caught at the same boat that Leonard was holding on to? I know Nick said that the rain and spray had reduced visibility to a matter of inches, but Leonard might have seen a hand where he couldn't see a face. He could have thought that the hand belonged to Ronnie, and taken a crack at the owner.'

Charles sat up with some violence: 'But damn it, Coppy, why the hell should Stock want to murder——' He stopped, and then said more slowly: 'You mean — Ruby? I get you. *Hmm!*' He fidgeted restlessly with his cigarette-case for a moment and said at last: 'Yes, I suppose there might be something in it. But supposing you're right about that? I'm not saying that Stock hadn't damned good reason for wanting to do in Ronnie Purvis, but why only Ronnie? God knows I don't want to cast nasturtiums at dear Ruby, but what is Ronnie among so many?'

'Perhaps the proverbial last straw? You must admit it was a pretty blatant straw.'

'Oh, I'll admit that,' said Charles impatiently. 'More like a haystack, if you ask me. But unless rumour lies more than ordinarily blackly, there have been a good many haystacks of that kind in poor old Leonard's matrimonial meadow. Also — forgive me for pointing it out — hadn't one of the members of our jury rather — er — usurped the limelight of late?'

'You mean Nick,' supplied Copper before anyone else could speak. 'Of course. But that might be an added reason in favour of killing Ronnie, because it would provide an alibi. You see,' she added with a touch of malice, 'Leonard would know perfectly well that the minute the *Sapphire* left, Ronnie would move back into favour again.'

Charles shifted uncomfortably: 'Well, as a matter of fact, Coppy, my charmer, I meant you. Ronnie has rather turned from his old allegiance since your arrival on the scene.'

Copper intercepted Nick's amused glance, and flushed hotly, and Nick said: 'Nice to know that as a professional homebreaker I'm in such good company.'

'Charles is quite right,' interrupted Valerie hastily, frowning at Nick. 'I can't see why, if Leonard was feeling murderous on Ruby's account, he should have reached the breaking-point at a time when the Ronnie affair, from both his and Ruby's angle, had taken a bit of a back seat.'

Copper said: 'Because he may never have had an opportunity before. I mean a chance of doing Ronnie in without getting hanged for it. And then the storm may have provided the chance he had been looking for.'

'Oh well, I suppose we'd better put it down as a remotely possible motive,' sighed Valerie. 'LEONARD STOCK. Opportunity: same as everyone else. Motive: Ruby. Bumped off

Ferrers in mistake for Ronnie. Rest of the case same as the other two. On the debit side: Copper says he's done it because he's the most unlikely person, and because he thought he was writing off Ronnie because of Ruby. Anyone got anything for the credit column?'

Nick said: 'Yes. You can put me down for the defence. Copper's theory may or may not hold water, but here's something that holds gallons. Has it occurred to anyone that Leonard Stock stands about two foot two in his bedsocks and is about the weediest little specimen, with the possible exception of the late Ferrers Shilto, in the entire Islands? I'm well aware that even the most miserable misfit can wang a man over the head with a marlinspike or a hammer or what-have-you. But it would take a considerable quantity of sheer solid guts and muscle to drag a dead body single-handed from the Guest House to the turtle tank. And it must have taken wrists of iron to carry it round the narrow wall of the tank and hang it from that crossbeam under the floor of the summer-house.

'Fourthly, fifthly and sixthly, the entire performance plainly called for quick thinking, cool-headedness and a packet of nerve. And though I hate to cast cold water on Copper's fresh young enthusiasms, even if Stock possesses the necessary mental qualifications, he quite obviously hasn't the physical ones. So I think we can safely count him out as not being of the stuff that murderers are made of.'

'And of course you'd know about that,' said Copper sweetly.

'Look here, you two!' snapped Valerie in sudden exasperation, 'if you feel you must scratch at each other, you can do it later. Just try and remember that this is serious!'

Nick laughed. 'See what your acidity has let us in for, Copper darling? A public reprimand, no less! That's the stuff, Val. *"Order in court!"* Well, what's the verdict on Leonard? Guilty or not guilty?'

Valerie said: 'I'm not going to put anyone down as either guilty or innocent without positive proof.'

'Oh, all right,' sighed Nick. 'Charles, be a Boy Scout and pour a stiffish whisky into the nearest glass and merely disturb it slightly with soda . . . . My blessings on you. Here's to crime!' He drank deeply. 'Next prisoner, please.'

'Hamish,' said Valerie. 'Come on, Charles.'

'Oh, no you don't!' said Charles. 'I've done my stuff on Ronnie. This is your headache, young Portia.'

Valerie shook her head determinedly. 'Sorry. I'm saving myself for Ruby — we've got several lines on her that you haven't heard about yet.'

'Oh, my God!' moaned Charles. 'You women! You cats! You scratchy little hell-cats!'

'I like that!' said Valerie indignantly. 'Here have you and Nick been pointing out half a dozen damning details in connection with John Shilto, Ronnie and Leonard, and did I once rise up and accuse you of being catty?'

'If you two,' drawled Nick gently, 'have a bone to pick, I have it on good authority that there is a Frigidaire in the pantry.'

Charles laughed. 'He's got you there, Val. All right. I withdraw. I apologize. I grovel. Anything, in fact, for a quiet life. I will even, in the interests of peace and justice, strive to make out a case against that old Angora rabbit, Mr Rattigan to wit.'

Clutching a whisky and soda in one hand and his brow in the other, Charles collapsed into the depths of his armchair and brooded deeply, but after several minutes he announced himself defeated: 'It's no good. In spite of remorselessly racking the brain, I can't think up a single damn thing against the old cloth-head. Apart from the fact that he is a prominent member of our Ruby's chain-gang, there is no blot upon his blameless copy-book. And as he doesn't wear a ruby on his left hand, he couldn't even have been killed in mistake for—— Oh, that's the wrong way round isn't it?'

Charles took a deep draught from his glass and gazed wildly about the room as though seeking inspiration from the walls and ceiling. 'Go on,' commanded Valerie remorselessly. 'You must do better than that. What sort of thing do you think might madden Hamish to the point of murder?'

'Unpolished buttons,' said Charles promptly. 'The old egg nearly busts himself with fury if he spots one of our chaps sporting a button or a belt-buckle that you can't actually see to shave in. He may look like a fluffy form of rabbit, but when he does lose his temper — happily only about once quarterly — he doesn't skimp it. Frankly speaking, Hell pops and strong men take cover.'

Valerie frowned, wrinkled the end of her nose, and entered: 'Debit: Temper' on the charge-sheet. 'It's not much,' she said doubtfully. 'Couldn't you improve on it a bit? Rack the brain a bit more, Charles. Did anything happen on the Harriet picnic that might have made him lose his temper?'

'That's no good,' said Nick impatiently. 'Half a dozen things might have done that. Ants in the mince pies for instance. It's got to be something that would make him lose his hair with Ferrers.'

'I've got it!' said Charles suddenly. 'See Copper's brilliant theory re: Leonard, and apply same without loss of time to Hamish. God will, I trust, forgive me for grossly maligning the poor guffin, but as I have already had occasion to point out, anything for a quiet life. Does that let me out?'

Valerie said doubtfully: 'Well I see what you mean, and if it's the best you can do——'

'Best I can do!' exploded Charles. 'Isn't that just like a woman? Copper produces a half-baked theory to the effect that that little pip-squeak, Leonard, may have wanged Ferrers in mistake for Ronnie, basing this incredible fabrication of a fevered imagination upon the tottering foundation of a brace of Woolworth rings. It is received with all solemnity. But when I suggest that it might apply equally well to Hamish, what happens? Do I receive a share of the applause? Not on your life! I am instantly reviled. I resign. I throw in my half-dozen towels — two bath, two face and two mat. Will someone please hand me the brandy. I intend to get tight.'

'It's all right, darling,' said Valerie soothingly. 'You're perfectly right, of course. It was very clever of you to think of it. You mean that if Ruby had pitched Hamish a yarn about Ronnie pestering her with improper advances, he might try taking a club to Ronnie?'

'That *was* the idea,' admitted Charles with dignity. 'The poor poop is plain cuckoo about her. She's probably the first woman he's ever fallen for, so he's beyond the reach of reason where she's concerned. I believe she could even wheedle him into thinking lightly of the "Glorious Regiment", let alone mere murder!'

'Rubbish!' said Nick shortly. 'Look here, Val — and you too, Charles — it's about time we stopped fabricating unnecessary fairy tales. I admit I don't know much about Rattigan. But you do. Do you honestly mean to tell me that you think that if Ruby Stock had pitched a "persecution" yarn to him, he'd rush off and try and murder Purvis? Not on your life! He'd haul him off by the scruff of his neck and knock him down with all due ceremony behind the squash court!'

Valerie nodded reluctant agreement: 'You're right, of course, Nick. Which effectively disposes of Hamish. Anyone got anything to add before I close the score? No? Right: then that brings us to Ruby.'

17

Valerie drew a deep breath: 'Now listen you two — this is really serious. Copper and I have a few solid clues for you to work on.'

She proceeded to describe in detail Copper's discovery of the fragment of swansdown on the stairhead, together with Mrs Stock's reception of the news of Dan's murder and her surreptitious errand to the rocks. 'It was all rather frightening,' she concluded, 'and I'm leaving it to you to decide if you think there could be anything in it, and if so, what. You see — ' her voice broke unexpectedly and she shivered. 'You see she – she must have been near the staircase last night. And – and the murderer must have come up those stairs——'

The sentence dwindled into a whisper of pure terror, and in an instant Charles was out of his chair and had caught both her hands in his. 'I know one thing!' said Charles violently, 'and that is that until this thing is solved I'm sleeping at your house, even if I have to take a mattress and camp on the ballroom floor. It's all right, Val! Don't look like that, sweetheart. There's nothing to be scared of at the moment — Army and Navy both in attendance. And now shall we exchange a passionate kiss here, or in the pantry?'

Valerie's taut nerves relaxed and she laughed tremulously. 'I'm sorry. I do apologize. A momentary spasm of panic brought on by suddenly realizing that Copper and I were probably sleeping in the same house with an honest-to-God murderer last night.'

Charles dropped a swift kiss on to his fiancée's head, and seating himself on the arm of her chair remarked: 'After which brief but affecting interlude, let us return to La Stock. You say you found a chunk of her pink trimmings decorating the stair-head? Well, that presumably means that she was out and about sometime during the night — but not necessarily at half past one. And anyway, it stands to reason that she can't be the murderer if she was parading about the place in forty yards of pink satin profusely decorated with feather frillings. It doesn't make sense.'

'Why not?' demanded Valerie. 'She might have heard Dan cross the hall and followed to see where he was going. And if she saw him put on the mackintosh cape and go out, she could have run back, changed into something more suitable, sneaked out by the back and rushed down to the Guest House. And I would also like to remind you that Ruby weighs around nine stone seven, stands about five foot nine inches in her stockings, and swings a pretty good golf club and tennis racket. So far as mere muscle goes, I imagine that she would be more than equal to dealing with Ferrers, dead or alive!'

Charles whistled gently through his teeth and abstractedly wound a lock of Valerie's hair about one finger: 'Perhaps. But all the same, I don't believe it. And that's not merely because I can't help jibbing at the idea of a woman having done the job, for I imagine that when it comes right down to bedrock, most women are more capable of murder than the average man. But for all that I don't believe it was Ruby. And you can put that down on the charge-sheet as a large blot, signifying male intuition as opposed to female.'

Valerie jerked her head away impatiently and said: 'I don't care how many intuitions you've got about her. They don't alter the fact that she was prowling about the house last night sometime between eleven and half past one, because that bit of swansdown on Hindenburg proves it.'

Nick abandoned his indolent pose and sat up abruptly: 'By jove! I wonder if she was the person that the sentry saw in the office?'

'What's that?' Both girls turned on him simultaneously.

'Forgot to tell you,' said Nick. 'The sentry produced another piece of information this afternoon. He said he'd seen the Commissioner mucking about in the office as he passed the window when coming on duty last night. I've forgotten how he came to mention it, but it was rather odd because the Commissioner denies having been near the office after nine o'clock. He cross-questioned the sentry, and the man said that as he walked down the verandah past the office window he saw there was a light on inside, and as there was a gap in the curtains, glanced in as he went past and saw someone standing by the desk . . .

'He assumed that it was the Commissioner working late; which was a fairly usual occurrence. But when we got down to brass tacks it turned out that the light came from a small green-shaded reading-lamp on the desk and that all he actually saw was the silhouette of someone bending over the desk. And when asked to describe what it looked like, he couldn't swear to any detail of the figure: said he'd only given it a casual glance and was so certain that it was the Commissioner that he hadn't bothered to think any more about it.'

Valerie said: 'You mean it might have been Ruby?'

'It's possible. If you think for a minute, one thing is bound to strike you. Why should the sentry have been so positive that the person in the office was your stepfather? He couldn't explain it himself, but it's fairly obvious that whoever it was or wasn't, it was a European, and that one fact, in the snapshot view he had between the curtains by the shaded light of the reading-lamp, impressed itself on his mind without his realizing it. And if a European, then naturally Sir Lionel: one's brain often unconsciously betrays one's eye, and vice versa. But it could just as easily have been a woman wearing a coat.'

'I see,' said Valerie thoughtfully. 'Ruby might have come to the top of the stairs to see if it was possible to get down unseen, and spotted that old Iman Din was out of play and that the coast was clear. If there was anything in the office that she wanted, she'd be certain to go back to her room and swop that dressing-gown affair for a coat. She's got a heavy brown tweed one, cut like a man's overcoat.'

'Then that may be the solution,' said Nick. 'Probably nothing much in it except another "Possible", to add to a growing list of "Possibles" without a single "Probable" to cheer them up.'

Valerie said: 'But what on earth would Ruby want out of the office? If it *was* Ruby?'

'Heaven knows. Your stepfather went through the entire room with a small-tooth comb, but he said there was not only nothing missing, but that nothing had been moved. So I'm afraid the incident isn't much use to us, except as providing a possible solution for Mrs Stock's night wanderings.'

Charles said: 'What about her day wanderings, comrade? That trip of hers to the rocks smells rather strongly of kippers to me. After all, we haven't yet found the weapon that was used to kill Dan. What about that as a solution to her proceedings?'

'You mean she was disposing of the evidence?' put in Valerie. 'It did look rather like that, but — surely the weapon that killed Dan must have been pretty solid?'

Nick said: 'A club, or a coal hammer or something of that description. Yes; I see your point. Even with the mist, and at that range, you would have been able to see it if what she chucked into the sea had been anything hefty.'

'We didn't see anything at all,' said Valerie. 'And what's more, I believe that she carried the thing she threw away stuffed down the front of her frock, and it stands to reason that she couldn't shove a hammer or a kitchen poker down there without it being pretty noticeable if anyone had stopped her.'

Nick uttered a sound between a laugh and a groan and pushed his hands through his hair so that it was ruffled again. 'God forbid that I should ever meddle with a job like this again! What we need is Scotland Yard and the Ten Best Brains of Britain to cope with this bloody jig-saw puzzle. And I — heaven forgive me! — had an idea that if we dug about we might with luck come across something that would give us a lead. But I didn't bargain for half a hundred separate leads. Let's go and tackle that woman about it at once and see what she's got to say.'

'No!' said Valerie firmly. 'That would be fatal. If we try and bounce her into anything she'll only deny it hotly. Copper and I will wait for a suitable opportunity, and try and lure her into having a girlish chat when she is slightly less hysterical.'

'All right. Then let's get on with the three-ring circus. Who's next?'

'Rosamund Purvis. Take over, Nick.'

'Nothing doing. It takes a woman to prosecute a woman. Take her yourself.'

Valerie chewed the end of her pencil for a moment or two, and then wrote once again in the notebook. 'How will this do?' she inquired. 'ROSAMUND PURVIS. Opportunity: same as everyone else. Motive: possibly the same one as Copper suggested for Leonard, and Charles for Hamish — "Mistaken Identity", i.e. she killed Ferrers in mistake for Ronnie. Goodness knows she must have wanted to do it pretty often. He treats her abominably, and——'

'You know,' interrupted Nick wearily, 'that theory of Copper's struck me as pretty far-fetched the first time I heard it — though I will admit that it did seem to be just within the realms of the remotely possible. But with every repetition it appears less and less so. For heaven's sake let's scrap it for the moment and try another.'

'But I can't think of another,' complained Valerie plaintively. 'I must say I'm inclined to agree with you. But if you can think up any reason why Rosamund would want to murder Ferrers, you're a better man than I am Gunga Din and you can darn well take over the prosecution yourself!'

Nick said irritably: 'It's no earthly good asking me to supply reasons. Damn it all, Val, I've only been on this flaming island a little over a week, so it's hardly likely that I'd know much about the character and private lives of the local inhabitants. All I know is that this ring theory is so thin it's transparent!'

Copper turned swiftly to face him: 'Is it?' she said tersely. 'Then perhaps this may thicken it a bit. Do you remember the afternoon of the Mount Harriet picnic, just after lunch, when we four were in the lorry and someone came up and put a hand on the edge of it?'

'What's that got to do with it?' inquired Charles impatiently: 'Of course we remember. It was Ronnie, and—— No, by God, it wasn't! It was Ferrers!'

Copper threw Nick a brief, triumphant glance and turned to Charles: 'What made you so sure at first that it was Ronnie, Charles?'

Charles considered the question, wrinkling his nose thoughtfully. 'Damned if I know,' he admitted. 'But now that you come to mention it, I did think it was him, and I was surprised when it turned out to be Ferrers. I certainly can't remember noticing any ring, but that could have had something to do with my jumping to the conclusion that Passionate Purvis was in our midst.'

'Of course it had,' said Copper. 'Not many Englishmen wear rings, and the ones that do usually wear plain gold signet rings. But Ronnie wore a ring with a large red stone set in it, and so did Ferrers. And you are so used to seeing Ronnie's ring that your subconscious mind registered *Ronnie* when you saw a man's hand with a red ring on it. And don't tell me I'm wrong, because I know I'm not!'

'Don't worry,' said Charles, 'I lack the necessary nerve to contradict you. And I daresay you're right. In which case I suppose these series of ring-theories must remain on the books for the present; which appears to thicken the general fog to no ordinary extent.'

'I don't see why it should,' said Valerie obstinately.

Charles moaned and closed his eyes: '*O Woman! in our hours of ease!* Listen, my love, think! — ponder! — consider for a brief moment! If we retain this ring business, it would appear that the whole island is swarming with people who were panting to massacre Ronnie, and that the elimination of the late unlamented Ferrers was due to a mere slip of the spanner. It seems to me to add endless vistas of sinister conjecture to a landscape already overstocked with sinister vistas.'

He drank deeply and subsided on to the sofa, and Valerie said: 'Oh well, let's leave it for the moment and get on with the case against Rosamund. For the prosecution: she plays a good game of tennis and is the best swimmer in the Islands, bar none, so she could have coped with the problem of disposing of Ferrers's body without much difficulty. Then there was definitely something extremely queer behind that display of nerves on Christmas Eve. She was scared to death.'

'She was,' agreed Nick. 'And on thinking back on her behaviour that night, I would like to advance a theory of my own that could account for it. It seems to me just possible that she saw Ferrers die.'

'But you——'

'*Ssh!* — don't interrupt. Let us suppose, for the sake of argument, that she was holding on to the same boat as Ferrers, and saw just enough to realize that someone beyond him had deliberately cracked him over the head? If that were so, the chances are that she would have let go her hold in a panic, and swum around in the smother until forced to grab hold of a boat that she probably hoped was not the one she had originally been attached to. After that there'd have been no point in her saying anything. Unless she knew who had done the hitting, which is unlikely. I think it was Copper who remarked that same evening that Mrs Purvis appeared to be playing a peculiar game of *"Is it you? — Is it you? — Is it you?"* with herself. Which could support the theory that she was aware, even then, that Ferrers had not been drowned but murdered. It would also account for her subsequent behaviour.'

'Um,' said Valerie thoughtfully. 'It does seem to fit. That is, if she didn't do the job herself and wasn't wondering who, if anyone, had seen her do it?'

'For the defence,' said Copper, taking over: 'she wasn't on the beach when Ferrers's body turned up, and neither was she at the Christmas Day dinner party. Therefore she couldn't have known of Dan's interest in the corpse.'

Valerie said: 'Against that we have Amabel and Dutt and Ronnie and Truda. All, or any of them, could have told her something. And even if she hadn't heard any details, if she was the murderer she'd be scared to death at hearing that the corpse of her victim had turned up, and be pretty restless until the body was safely buried. She could easily have got out of the hospital that night, and perhaps gone to the Guest House to assure herself that the murder hadn't been discovered, and found Dan there.'

'Hell!' groaned Charles. 'Then that's six of them who could have done it. Oh well, we might as well make a good job of it and prove that they all did it. Who's next for the electric chair?'

'Nick,' said Valerie, and laughed. She appeared to be the only one amused. Charles was watching Nick over the rim of his glass, and Nick was watching Copper. Copper kept her eyes on the tips of her shoes and said nothing, and Valerie, suddenly aware of tension, looked up from her notebook and glanced from one to another of the three still faces. She opened her mouth, and then closed it again without speaking.

Nick said dryly: 'Well, Copper?'

He saw Copper's fingers clench themselves together in her lap, but apart from that slight movement she might not have been aware that he had spoken.

'Why this magnanimity, sweet? I can take it, we murderers are tough. Produce your evidence, Coppy. Even if Val and Charles don't see eye to eye with you about it, it's as good as that signet-ring stuff any day!'

Charles saw Copper's chin come up with a jerk, and rushed in where angels might justifiably have feared to tread: 'Yes, come on young Sherlock. Spill the sinister beans and put us out of our misery. Then we can tear up all those appalling notes that Val has been preparing for the purpose of spreading confusion and despair, and fall on Nick in a body. I shall direct operations from behind the bookcase, and you and Val can do the actual arresting. After which we can bury him behind the squash court, and go off to dinner secure in the righteous conviction that we have faithfully administered the King's Justice.'

'I haven't anything to say on Nick's behalf,' said Copper in a small cold voice. 'Either for or against. To misquote him, "It takes a thief to — "' she checked a little ostentatiously. ' — I mean, it takes a man to prosecute a man. You can take it over, Charles.'

For a brief moment the knuckles of Nick's hands showed white, and then he laughed and relaxed once more in his chair. Valerie gave Copper a puzzled look, and then turned back to Charles: 'Last prisoner, darling. Take over the charge-sheet, and after that you can come up to the house and I'll make you a mint julep and hold your hand on the drawing-room sofa.'

'A clear case of bribery and corruption,' sighed Charles. 'But then I have always been a weak character. Oh, all right. Prisoner at the Bar, did you or did you not, on the afternoon of December the twenty-fourth, either of intent, or under the impression that you were slugging Mr Ronald Purvis, cause the decease of one Ferrers Shilto?'

'Objection!' said Nick. 'I appeal to the court. That's a leading question.'

Valerie said: 'Objection sustained. Get on with it, Charles.'

'All right — all right. Don't rush me! Case for the prosecution: that the said Nicholas Tarrent, being a member of the sailing party, had full and ample opportunity for slugging the said Ferrers Shilto. Moreover he possesses the physical ability, together with the necessary nerve, guts, brains and what-have-you, to carry out the task to a successful conclusion. Added to which is the damning fact that he shared a room with the second victim, and therefore would certainly have been aware of his suspicions regarding the corpse of the said Ferrers Shilto——

'In fact,' said Charles, reverting to plain English, 'for all we know, Dan may have spilt the beans to him and told him that he proposed to have a look at the corpse. In which case he would have had plenty of time to plan the whole thing before leaving the house: murder of Dan, disposal of Ferrers, the entire works. I will even withdraw my previous assertion that the job couldn't have been carried out inside an hour and a half. Given quick thinking, it could probably have been done in that time and with a few minutes to spare.'

Nick said: 'A bit more of this and I shall burst into tears and confess all. Go on, Charles. You're doing fine.'

'Matter of fact,' confessed the counsel for the prosecution, 'that about cleans me out of ideas. You see there's the small matter of motive. Just between the two of us and strictly in confidence, what *was* your motive?'

'Objection!' murmured Nick.

'Oh yes, of course. Leading question, an' all that. It's no good, Val, you'll have to enter "No Motive" on the prisoner's charge-sheet. And that, thank God, can go in reference to Ronnie as well as Ferrers, for if anyone had mentioned the word "ring" again I should have screamed aloud and burst a blood-vessel. You can put down that, as far as we know, the prisoner Tarrent had no quarrel and very small acquaintance with Mr Ronald Purvis. Was not sentimentally smitten by Mrs Ruby Stock, and had only laid eyes on Mr Ferrers Shilto a couple of hours or so before the murder. Otherwise all things are equal. Can I stop now?'

'You can,' said Nick. 'And I may say that my case in your hands, as compared with Copper's, is as a bucket of whitewash to a truck-load of coal.'

Charles hitched himself round in his chair and regarded Copper with interest. 'You mean she's suppressing evidence, do you? Well, far be it from me to discourage her. In fact if anyone else has any more evidence against anyone, I'd be everlastingly grateful if they would tie a brick to it and drop it in the harbour. I have had just about as much of it as I can stand in one day, and my brain is reeling. It appears to have been conclusively proved that there are not one, but seven murderers or potential murderers loose upon Ross, and I shall therefore retire to bed tonight wearing a bullet-proof vest under my pyjamas and clutching a loaded shot-gun in either hand. Amateur detectives and intending sleep-walkers, please note!'

Valerie laughed, and turning in her chair slid a hand under his arm. 'Thank God our late librarian didn't have a yen for Ethel M. Dell! I don't think I could have borne a stern, square-jawed hero in this situation. Thank you, darling. Your act has been terrific, and for about the first time in weeks I've really appreciated it.'

'It was rather good, wasn't it?' agreed Charles complacently. 'What the dramatic critics would have termed "a fine, sustained performance".'

'If you don't watch it,' observed Copper crisply, 'you'll wake up one fine morning and find that you're talking like that naturally.'

'But I am,' said Charles. 'I do! I find it's a thing that grows on one — like boils. But not to worry. A good strong dose of Hemingway will eliminate the germs.'

'Try Anouilh, darling,' advised Valerie. 'And now listen — I'm going to read out everything I've written this afternoon, and after that I suggest we clear out and go for a quick walk round the island before it's dark. But before I start reading we'll have a five-minute silence during which I want everyone to go over as much as they can remember of the last two days, starting with the Mount Harriet picnic. And if they can think of any incident, however tiny, that strikes them as odd or unusual, to produce it for inspection. Ready?'

The minutes ticked themselves away in a deep silence.

'Time's up! What are you frowning over, Coppy? Thought of something?'

'Yes,' said Copper doubtfully, 'but — I know you'll think I'm mad, because it's something that I can't catch hold of. I can only remember that something happened at the picnic that was odd. I can't even remember anything about it, except that something that day made me think "That's queer!" But perhaps I'll remember it later. Anyway, it couldn't have been very important.'

'Shove down a question mark, Val,' ordered Charles. 'Here's a red pencil — catch! Copper may think of it later. And now, if that's all, I suggest we get on with the reading.'

Valerie returned to her chair, and picking up the notebook, added a large red question mark to the record. 'Now,' she said, 'I'm going to read straight through everything we've written down here, and I want you to please concentrate, and if anything strikes you as particularly important to make a note of it. Here goes——!'

She sat down and began to read in a clear emotionless voice while her audience sat silent and absorbed. Charles moved to switch on the light above her head, for it was getting too dark to see, and once during the reading Copper caught her breath in a small gasp and stiffened in her chair. The movement was as slight as the sound, but Nick turned his head sharply, and saw that her face was very white and her eyes wide and terrified.

'That's all,' concluded Valerie. 'Has anyone got anything to add to it?'

Two heads were shaken.

'Did anything strike anyone as being of particular importance?'

Nick glanced sideways at Copper and saw her fingers tighten convulsively upon the arm of her chair. But she did not speak;

though neither did she shake her head in denial as he and Charles had done.

'Then that's that!' said Valerie, shutting the notebook with a bang. 'And now let's rush out and get some exercise. It's still horribly misty, but a change of air will do us all good.'

She tossed the notebook into a corner of the window-seat, sublimely unaware of how close one twist to its tangled reasoning would have brought them to the truth.

18

It was almost dark when they left the Mess to take a brisk walk around Ross, and the tiny island was still close-lapped in a mist which veiled the last of the lingering daylight.

The faint breeze that had arisen earlier in the day had died with the approach of night, and except for the ceaseless thunder of the surf, which from long familiarity had become barely noticeable, an almost uncanny silence brooded over the island. Not a leaf rustled or a twig stirred, and they could hear the fog-dew dripping from the hibiscus hedges and the gold mohur trees.

For a while the four walked in silence, their footsteps in unison though their thoughts were widely divergent.

Charles, his arm tucked through Valerie's, was thinking of what she had said when she had thanked him for 'putting on an act'. She had thought it was only for her sake and Copper's that he had done his best to keep their discussions on as light a level as possible. But it had also been for his own, because he had not dared let himself look too closely at the picture of Valerie — his own Valerie — lying asleep in that darkened house while a murderer fresh from his killing crept in from the mists of the grey island and barred the door behind him. For beyond that thought lay the knowledge that tonight she would once again pass the dark hours in the same house.

Registering a mental vow to act upon his recently expressed intention of spending the night at Government House, Charles tightened his hold on her arm and Valerie returned the pressure fervently: though she herself had not been thinking of the dark present, but of some golden, hoped-for future when she and Charles were married . . .

Nick, walking between her and Copper, his hands in his pockets and his long, loose stride restricted to their shorter steps, was thinking confusedly of the past. Of Calcutta, and of Ferrers Shilto's face against the background of a corridor in the Grand Hotel. He had looked like a frightened, vicious rat — a cornered rat. Who could ever have supposed that they would meet again, and so soon? And how was Copper going to regard the Calcutta incident? Nick had never yet cared what others might think of his actions, but then Copper was not 'others' . . . His mouth twisted wryly and he scowled into the gathering dusk.

Beside him, her blond head bent and her slim shoulders a little hunched as though against an imaginary wind, the subject of his thoughts walked with her eyes fixed upon the wet road. And for once — perhaps for the first time for over a week — she was not thinking exclusively of Nicholas Tarrent.

Copper was re-living an apparently trivial incident that had occurred two days before, and hearing again a single line from the notebook that was lying discarded on the window-seat in the ante-room of the empty Mess. An incident and a statement that contradicted each other. Had *no* one else noticed it? Would no one else remember it? Would Valerie? She longed desperately to tell Nick; to beg for his advice and reassurance. But Nick had suddenly become a stranger; and he, too, had got something to hide. Perhaps they all had? Even Charles — even Valerie . . .!

Why had Nick been so angry with her for pointing out that he might lie under suspicion of murder? Admittedly, she had wanted to hurt him. She had tormented herself with the knowledge that he must, in the past, have attracted more than his fair share of fluttering feminine adulation, and she resented bitterly the recurring suspicion that she might appear to him as just another infatuated little idiot who took his casual attentions as proof of something more serious, and entirely non-existent.

Nick, she had thought, would probably expect her to believe that although the rest of the island might be under suspicion, he alone could do no wrong in her too openly admiring eyes, and she had therefore decided to show him that he meant no more to her than any other member of that fatal sailing party. But the result of her ill-advised disclosures had been to turn Nick from a friend into a stranger from whom she could not ask for help. And even if she could do so, would she dare risk it? Dan had been a friend of Nick's, and Nick might——Copper's hunted brain returned helplessly to its original groove and started on the same round once more, like a caged mouse on a wheel.

Silent and preoccupied, the four walked down the dim deserted roads past the hospital and the little bazaar whose doors, close-shuttered against the damp sea-mist, still showed friendly chinks of yellow lamplight in the growing darkness. On a clear night they would have seen the sprinkled lights of Aberdeen across the narrow strip of heaving waters that separated Ross from the mainland. But tonight the mist lay thick upon the yeasty seas, and as they looked into that blank, shifting wall they might have been isolated by hundreds of miles of empty ocean.

They passed the sheds that stood behind the jetty, where their footsteps, muffled until now by the wet ground, suddenly rang loud, and came out by the little bandstand that had once, long ago, been a centre of social life in the glittering tropic evenings, though no band had played there for many a long year. Beyond it their feet left the crushed coral of the roadway and encountered the yielding sponginess of rain-soaked grass as they crossed the Club lawn, beyond which the breakers still sent up ghostly fountains of spray.

A small dark building at the edge of the lawn, barely discernible in the dusk, sent a cold shiver down the spine of more than one of the four who passed it, and instinctively they drew closer together: remembering that sometime last night, in the misty rain-spattered darkness, someone had carried Ferrers Shilto's body to that same small building, and that for more than twelve hours afterwards it had hung there in the blackness above the shadowy tank, while the turtles snapped and splashed in the storm-clouded water below and Dan lay dead in the Guest House.

As if by mutual consent they turned simultaneously and walked quickly across the lawn to where a yellow glow from the Club windows gleamed comfortably through the mist. But apart from the barman and a Burmese waiter there was no one there but Ronnie Purvis, whom they found aimlessly flicking over the pages of a nine-weeks-old illustrated London weekly at one end of the deserted ballroom, and who was plainly the worse for drink.

Apparently he had been there for several hours, imbibing steadily, and had long since passed the convivial stage and the subsequent quarrelsome one, and Nick, eyeing him with detached interest, wondered if this was a usual procedure with him or whether he had merely set himself to get drunk as a relief from other and grimmer realities.

Charles, who knew him better, did not even wonder. Ronnie was a frequent victim of what he himself termed 'one over the eight', but he seldom if ever went in for really hard drinking; and then never alone. Mr Purvis was a man who liked company with his whisky, and rather than drink alone would normally have combed the island for a companion. Yet tonight he had been deliberately drowning something in drink. And it was certainly not sorrow. Funk, diagnosed Charles dispassionately: the fellow's scared stiff about something and has been trying the effects of Dutch Courage. Now I wonder what the hell he's so frightened of?

That Mr Purvis was frightened was as patently and disturbingly plain to everyone in the room as the fact that he was drunk. His usually bronzed features (Ronnie subscribed to the popular theory that 'all handsome men are slightly sunburnt') were a curious putty colour, his hands so unsteady that the leaves of the periodical he held shook as though they were in a wind, while his eyes were as wide and glaring as a frightened cat's, and any unexpected sound or movement caused him to start violently.

There was something about his obvious terror that was infectious, for Nick could see its reflection in Valerie's face. He saw, too, that the fear which had been in Copper's eyes ever since Valerie had read through the contents of the notebook had deepened to something still and panic-stricken, and rising abruptly, he crossed the ballroom floor and switched on every light in the big room. An action that at least had the effect of dispelling the lurking shadows, though it failed to add much cheerfulness to the scene.

The Club had been decorated in honour of the Christmas festivities with branches of casuarina intertwined with strings of fairy-lights, but the branches were already wilted and sad-looking, and the flood of light seemed only to intensify the dreariness of the empty, damp-stained dance floor and make it seem larger and blanker and more deserted than before.

Charles ordered a round of drinks which were brought by the slant-eyed, soft-footed Burmese boy, who materialized noiselessly out of the shadows beyond the ballroom. But alcohol did little towards raising anyone's spirits. Ronnie Purvis was beyond making even an effort at conversation, and though Charles and Valerie struggled valiantly, their efforts to dissipate the general gloom were markedly unsuccessful.

Copper was making a pretence at reading an out-of-date copy of the *National Geographic* magazine, but Nick, who was watching her without appearing to do so, saw that although she turned a page at regular intervals her eyes were fixed and her gaze unmoving and he was unpleasantly reminded of Rosamund Purvis, and Dan's voice saying something to the effect that he believed if someone came up behind her and touched her on the shoulder, she'd scream the roof off. The same, decided Nick, might well be said of Copper at that moment: except that Copper wouldn't scream — she wasn't, thank God, the screaming kind. But she might easily faint . . .

Outside the Club the sullen swell crashed monotonously against the stone and concrete of the sea-wall, and occasionally a larger wave, more powerful than its fellows, would fling up an arc of spray to rattle against the ballroom windows, causing Ronnie Purvis to start violently with every repetition of the sound.

Charles put down his unfinished drink and rose abruptly: 'Come on, let's get out of here. Leave that beastly lemon drink of yours, Val; you can get another one up at the house. I've had enough of this.'

His companions rose with alacrity, and Ronnie stumbled to his feet, his mouth twitching. 'I – I think I'll come with you,' he said thickly. 'G–gloomy hole this. R–rotten Club. M–mind if I walk up with you as f–far as my bungalow?' He clawed at Charles's arm as though he was afraid of being refused and as if some special terror lay in having to walk, alone, the few hundred yards that stretched between the Club and his front door.

'Of course not,' said Charles impatiently, disengaging his coat-sleeve from Ronnie's clutching fingers: 'Put down that drink and come along.' He turned on his heel, and Mr Purvis, interpreting these instructions according to his own desires, paused to swallow what whisky remained in his glass before running unsteadily after him.

The air outside felt almost cold after the stuffy closeness of the atmosphere inside the Club, and though night had fallen there was still no breath of wind, and the light rain that was sifting down upon the island barely stirred the leaves beneath its silent fingers. It powdered Valerie's dark hair with stars and turned Copper's pale gold head to silver, and made a glimmering haze about the lamps that lined the roads between the dim sentinel columns of the coconut palms.

They dropped Ronnie Purvis at his bungalow, though it was patently obvious that he would have greatly preferred to accompany them to Government House. 'Can't go home alone,' mumbled Ronnie, swaying dangerously and clutching at a lamp-post to steady himself: 'That's what they're waiting for . . . Ge' me alone, so they c'n shoot me. Shtole m'revolver. S'gone. Looked everywhere.'

'What's that?' said Charles sharply. 'Did you say your revolver had been stolen?'

'Not shtolen . . . taken; so's I carn s–shoot 'em first!'

'Listen, Ronnie,' said Charles urgently. 'If you've lost your revolver you'd better go and look for it, and if you can't find it, you'd better report it!'

'Not losht. Just gone. No one in the housh . . . all 'lone. Lesh all have a lil' drink'n be merry — f'r t'morrer we die!'

Ronnie's bungalow was in darkness except for a gleam of light from the servants' quarters, and Valerie remembered suddenly that as both Rosamund and Amabel were up at the hospital, he would be alone in the empty house. Bare charity suggested that she should at least offer him dinner that night. But she could not bring herself to do so, because his drunken terror reacted too unpleasantly upon her own taut nerves. Refusing his invitations and cutting short their goodbyes she dragged at Charles's arm, and they turned hurriedly away, leaving Mr Purvis standing in the pool of light from the nearest lamp, swaying on his feet and casting desperate, terrified glances into the darkness beyond.

Valerie said in a low, breathless voice: 'Did you see — I only noticed it when we were standing under the lamp — he isn't wearing his ring.'

'Yes,' said Charles thoughtfully, 'I noticed. It almost begins to look as though there may be something in that theory of Copper's after all, doesn't it?'

'You mean you think that Ferrers *was* killed in mistake for Ronnie?'

'No. But I think that that possibility has suddenly occured to Ronnie!'

'But why?'

'Why not? It occurred to Copper. Besides, do you ever remember his not wearing that ring before? He even wears it when he's bathing!'

Nobody answered him. They walked on in silence and at the top of the ascent passed the Guest House: its outline barely discernible through the misty darkness and its windows glinting secretively through the screen of wet leaves, reflecting the glow from the nearest lamp like the eyes of animals caught in the headlights of a car.

Copper turned her head away from it as they passed, but she could not turn away the picture that rose before her mind's eye: the picture of Dan Harcourt walking under those wet branches and through that rusty gate to meet his death. And all at once it seemed to her that there was no safety anywhere in all that misty, marooned island: not out in the wet night, nor in the lighted house above them. She found that her heart was hammering in her throat, and fought down a frantic impulse to turn about and run back down the road they had climbed. But there was nowhere to run to. No safety, no security, no haven . . .

They turned through the stone-pillared gates of Government House and walked up the curving drive under the dark, dripping branches of the flame trees, and they were half-way up when a dim figure materialized out of the mist ahead of them. It proved to be Leonard Stock, on his way down to his house to collect a few more of his wife's belongings.

Leonard was nervous and talkative, and like Ronnie Purvis, inclined to throw quick, darting glances behind him. And Valerie, catching herself doing the same thing, wondered if everyone on the island was equally on edge? She supposed that they must be. It would have made little material difference to their situation if they had been able to communicate by telephone or signal with Aberdeen, but somehow the feeling of being completely cut off — marooned and locked in with murder — was a particularly horrible one. Like being shut into a dark room which you knew to be empty, and then, close beside you, hearing someone breathe . . .

Mr Stock was obviously infected with the same feeling; and even more obviously, intensely disliked the task his wife had set him of going down to his empty, darkened house to fetch some probably useless trifle which she could easily have done without. Valerie, who felt sorry for him but thought him a fool to put up with his wife's shenanigans, inquired what everyone had been doing that afternoon? 'I'm afraid I've been neglecting my guests rather badly. How is Ruby? And Mr Shilto?'

'Ruby is still a little exhausted, I fear. She decided to remain in bed. Shilto's been in his room most of the afternoon, and I'm afraid I've hardly seen him. He came down to the office and borrowed a typewriter and some foolscap, so I imagine he's been getting down to some work.'

Valerie said: 'I hope Dad got my message about not coming back for tea? He was busy when I rang up.'

'Yes. We were making a thorough search of the office,' explained Mr Stock. 'You see, I had a theory that something might be missing, because one of the sentries thought he saw a light in the office shortly before midnight last night, and as your father denied being there, I — we, were afraid that perhaps some unauthorized person had come down after the rest of the household were in bed and – and removed something from it.'

'And have they?'

'Oh no, there's nothing missing, except——' Mr Stock stopped abruptly and looked sly and a little malicious.

'Then there *is* something missing! Do tell us!'

Mr Stock made a pretence of wavering, but it was obvious that he had some special tit-bit of information that he was bursting to impart. 'I – I don't think Sir Lionel——' He hesitated, fingering his lip, and having glanced nervously over his shoulder, lowered his voice and said: 'You won't let it go any further, will you? I don't suppose it matters very much if you four hear of it, but I should never really have allowed you to get it out of me.'

Nick's mouth twitched at this interpretation of Leonard's

obvious desire to impart information, but Valerie said impatiently: 'Go on. What was it?'

'The letter!' said Mr Stock in a conspiratorial whisper. 'The letter that Ferrers wrote to your father, which he did not have time to answer. It's been stolen. I'm quite sure of it.'

'Why? Did Dad tell you so?'

'Oh dear me, no. He merely asked me if I had seen an envelope addressed in Ferrers's writing, and when I said I had not, he said it was of no importance: no importance whatever. He was very positive about it.'

'Then I don't suppose it was,' said Valerie shortly.

'It must have been, for if it were not, why should he be so anxious to find it? And he *was* anxious. Oh, indeed he was. You see I — er — happened to return unexpectedly to the office and found your father had opened all the drawers once more and was going through the letters again, though we had already gone through them with the *greatest* care only half an hour before. He was talking to himself too — you know how he sometimes does when he is worried — and I distinctly heard him say, *"But it should be here: I know I left it here!"* He was not at all pleased when he saw me: really quite rude. I don't think I have ever been spoken to like . . . But I am positive that there was no letter there in Ferrers's writing. Positive! One cannot mistake it. Besides, he always used that cheap violet-coloured bazaar ink. It is the greatest pity that I did not — er — I mean . . . Um, I — er — I suppose that none of you have seen it? Or – or would know what it was about?'

'No,' said Valerie curtly.

Leonard flushed and his eyes darted from face to face in an apparently uncomfortable realization of having said far too much. But somewhere behind them there lurked an avid curiosity and an odd glint of panic — or was it malice?

There followed a brief, uncomfortable pause that was broken by Valerie: 'Don't let us keep you,' she said coldly. 'I'm sure you must have a lot to do, and Ruby will be wondering what has happened to you.'

Mr Stock, encountering her freezing glance, lost himself in a maze of half-sentences, and backing away, scuttled off down the dark leafy tunnel of the drive, and Charles, watching him go, said: 'I wonder what it is that he thinks he knows? Did you see his face? He looked like a cat that has scoffed the canary.'

Nick turned to peer into the misty darkness that had swallowed up the slight figure of their late companion, and said thoughtfully: 'I think that the sooner we take another look at that notebook of Val's, the better. However, this is neither the time nor the place to stand around arguing, and I'm getting damnably damp. Let's get indoors.'

They found the big house ablaze with lights, as though the servants too had caught the prevailing unease and with the coming of darkness had attempted to hold fear at bay by turning on every lamp in the place. But light alone had no power to banish the fear that pervaded it: a fear that whispered in the swish of the bats' wings, the chirruping of the little gecko lizards and every creak of floorboard or furniture, and lurked in the shadow of every curtain and behind each half-opened door.

There was no sign of Sir Lionel Masson, John Shilto or Ruby Stock, and the big house was uncannily quiet. Charles sent down to the Mess for the discarded notebook, and while they were waiting for it Valerie ordered drinks to be served in the verandah. She was annoyed to find herself talking in something approaching a whisper, and even more annoyed, on raising her voice, to discover that it had acquired a slight tendency to tremble.

The air in the verandah smelt stale and faintly musty, and she crossed to the french windows that led on to the small balcony beyond the drawing-room and threw them open. The frangipani tree in the garden below was in bloom, and its pungent perfume, intensified by night and the light fall of rain, drifted in from the misty darkness; cloyingly sweet and unpleasantly reminiscent, thought Valerie, shivering, of the heavy scent of hot-house flowers at an expensive funeral.

She banged the window to again; bringing down a pattering shower of raindrops from the bridal-creeper that grew thickly above the balcony and jarring from its foothold one of the little gecko lizards which had been crawling across the high ceiling in pursuit of a moth. It fell with a small sharp *plop* at Copper's feet, and Nick saw every vestige of colour wiped from her face and her teeth clench hard upon her lower lip to stop herself from screaming.

He stood up swiftly, and reaching her in two quick strides, caught her by the elbows and jerked her to her feet, and before she could speak had propelled her firmly into the drawing-room and pushed her down into an armchair at the far side of the room. Leaning over her, a hand on each of the chair arms so that she could not rise or escape, he said in a low voice: 'What is it, Coppy? What are you frightened of? Tell me, darling.'

Copper's eyes, dark with fear, clung to his as a drowning man to a spar, but she only shook her head dumbly.

'Why won't you tell me? Is it because you're afraid that I may have had something to do with all this?'

Her eyes did not move from his, and he felt her mind stumble and recover itself. She wet her lips with the tip of her tongue and spoke with a manifest effort. 'No,' she said in a dry, halting whisper. 'No. It's — nothing to do with you.'

'Then tell me what's the matter?'

'I — can't,' said Copper, twisting her hands together. 'There – there isn't anything to tell. Really there isn't. I – I'm only feeling a bit on edge . . . like everyone else.' She essayed a stiff little smile that twisted her lips but did not reach her frightened eyes, and the taut lines about Nick's mouth softened suddenly.

'You're a rotten bad liar, Coppy darling, and just at the moment you couldn't deceive a blind baby. Of *course* you're on edge; we all are. I'm not in too good a shape myself. Look——'

He held out a hand for inspection, and she saw that it was not quite steady.

Nick replaced it on the arm of her chair and smiled down at her. 'You see? We've all got the jitters, dear — and with reason. We should be supermen if we hadn't. But it takes more than that to explain why you should have them so badly that a silly little incident like that lizard coming adrift could bring you to within an ace of screaming the roof off.'

'I — it didn't,' denied Copper uncertainly. 'You're imagining things.'

'Am I?' He jerked a clean handkerchief from his breast pocket and with a swift, unexpected movement, leant forward and touched it to her lips. She pulled back with a startled gasp and Nick held out the handkerchief. The white linen was marked with a small scarlet stain.

'Think that's imagination?' he inquired gently. 'It's no good stalling, Copper. You're not scared in the way the rest of us are scared. Or even as that chap Purvis is — which in his case I imagine to be equal parts of alcohol, bad conscience and terror of being the next victim. An hour or so ago you were no more on edge than Charles or Valerie or myself. But you spotted something that frightened you when Val read out the contents of that damned notebook, didn't you? *Didn't you, Coppy!* You either thought of something, or remembered something, that frightened you badly. And you've been thinking of it ever since and twisting and turning it over in your head to see if it fits.'

'No!' said Copper breathlessly. *'No!'*

'It's true. And what's more, you're still frightened! You're frightened now. What is it, sweet? Tell me——'

'I . . . I . . . can't,' said Copper with difficulty.

Nick's hands tightened upon the arms of her chair, and his mouth hardened. 'You mean you won't.'

Copper's voice was barely audible: *'I – I daren't!'*

Nick straightened up and put his hands in his pockets. 'I

apologize,' he said curtly. 'I should have remembered that I'm a suspect myself.' Copper flung out a beseeching hand, but he stepped back and turned off the light. 'I think this is where we get back to playing detectives,' he said. 'Here's the citizen who went for the notebook.'

Charles and Valerie called from the verandah, and Copper rose unsteadily from her chair and walked past him to join them.

19

'Here's the fatal volume,' said Charles. 'Now let's see if our newest clue fits in anywhere. The disappearing letter. What do you suppose was in it?'

'We can always ask,' said Valerie. 'In fact I'll go and hunt up Dad now and find out.'

'You do that, honey. It may turn out to be just what we need. And believe me, one really solid lead would be like manna in the wilderness at this moment!' Valerie rose, but was forestalled by one of the house-servants who arrived on the verandah with a message from her stepfather.

Sir Lionel, it transpired, had gone down to see Mr Dobbie — presumably about the burial of both Ferrers Shilto and Dan Harcourt — and had accepted an invitation to stay on for supper: he might not be back until late and Valerie was not to stay up for him.

'Well, that's that,' said Charles. 'Never mind, we can always ask him tomorrow. And I don't suppose that it will turn out to be of any interest, anyway.'

Nick said shortly: 'There I don't agree. If Leonard's guess is right, and someone has swiped it, then it means it contained something of more than ordinary interest. And if it really is missing, it's an even bet that we know who's got it. John Shilto!'

'Why?' demanded Valerie. 'I don't see why it *has* to be him?'

'Use your wits, Val! That "next-of-kin" business. We've already decided that John Shilto changed his mind about coming on to the Harriet picnic because of something that he saw or heard while he was at Ferrers's house, and we all heard him offer to buy back the plantation.'

'We also,' added Charles, 'heard Ferrers turn down that offer extremely nastily. So nastily, in fact, that John's chances of inheriting anything in the sweet-by-and-by could have been profitably swapped for a peanut. But as Ferrers died intestate, John presumably inherits anything there is going. Which could turn out to be plenty. For all we know, copra is due for a rise. Or perhaps Ferrers had found a method of draining his plantation, or fertilizing it, that was making the nuts grow like mad. He may have written to your father to say that he was expecting a bumper crop and wanted extra facilities for exporting the stuff. Something on those lines.'

'Y–es,' said Valerie doubtfully. 'But I still don't see why John Shilto would want to steal the letter. After all, since it had already been read he couldn't hush it up, so why else would he want it?'

'Curiosity?' suggested Nick. 'Or possibly a guilty conscience? He may have wanted to check up on what his cousin had been writing to the Commissioner about, so that he'd know how much of the gaff had been blown.'

Charles said impatiently: 'This is all guess-work. I suggest we try something a bit more practical for a change, and I have a proposal to make.' He rubbed his chin and frowned thoughtfully in the direction of the darkened drawing-room, and after a moment stood up, and crossing swiftly and silently to the door that led into it, peered inside. He stood there for several minutes, listening and letting his gaze wander about the room, before returning to his chair.

'What's the matter, darling?' inquired Valerie with an uncertain laugh. 'Making sure that there are no murderers under the sofas?'

Charles did not echo her bantering tone. 'I thought I heard something move in the drawing-room,' he said slowly. 'Probably only bats or a lizard — or Kioh. But it seems to me that we've all been talking too much and too audibly. So if you will kindly cluster round a bit closer, I propose to lower the old voice a bit. Now listen: what I have to propose is this. You girls, by fair means or foul, must lure the Shilto out here and keep him entertained, while Nick and I go through his room with a magnifying glass and a small-tooth comb.'

Valerie shot out a hand and caught at his sleeve. 'Don't be absurd, Charles! What on earth do you expect to find there?'

'Nothing,' admitted Charles frankly. 'But hope, we are told, springs eternal in the human breast, and you never know what might not turn up. With luck, Ferrers's letter!'

There was a brief silence, and then Valerie rose briskly to her feet: 'All right. But while you're doing it, Copper can try her hand at vamping John Shilto and I'll see if I can't get something out of Ruby.'

Charles said: 'That's my little Mata Hari! And look, Copper, for God's sake keep the Shilto in play for at least half an hour. Or twenty minutes will do, but that's the absolute deadline. We'll wait in Nick's room until you've got the man away, and then sneak in. And for all our sakes don't let him come nipping back to relieve nature or anything, or we're sunk.'

'I'll do my best,' said Copper doubtfully, 'but I can't exactly detain him by force, you know.'

'Nonsense! Sit on his head. Or throw a faint — or take him off to see your etchings. Use your imagination, girl!'

'You two,' put in Valerie firmly, 'will have to do the job as quickly as you possibly can. And if the worst comes to the worst and he does come back while you're still there, you'll both have to hop out by one of the windows.'

'Thanks,' said Nick grimly. 'A mere drop of twenty feet or so — to say nothing of the possibility of landing on the head of some luckless sentry.'

Valerie laughed. 'It's all right, Nick,' she consoled. 'I wasn't suggesting that you should choose suicide as an alternative to capture. There's a ledge about two feet wide that runs round the outside of the turret room and almost joins up with the balcony outside your room. You can easily get back to your own balcony from it. At least, it's easy by day, though it'll probably be a bit messy by night.'

'I dislike the word "messy",' said Nick. 'It suggests a spade-and-bucket case: *"The driver took a little knife and scraped him off the wheel."* Only in our case it would be the path, or possibly a sentry.'

'It's all right, my timorous mariner,' Charles reassured him: 'She doesn't mean that kind of mess. It's your gent's natty suiting that is doomed to suffer mortal injury. They stain all the outside woodwork here with some red muck that "comes off on you something lovely". Which means that if Copper fails to freeze on to old Shilto for the requisite time limit, we shall either have to go home in Val's pyjamas, or remain in hiding until she can get our suits back from the cleaners. However, these are the grim risks that stare every amateur detective nastily in the eye, so let us give them the cut direct. *"Lay on, Macduff!"* — *"Once more into the breach, dear friends, once more!"* — *"Excelsior!"*'

'For Pete's sake stop being so bloody *Boy's Own*!' snapped Nick, exasperated.

It was some fifteen minutes later that Valerie joined Mr Shilto and Copper in the verandah, and a single look was enough to inform Copper that one assignment at least had proved unsuccessful.

Valerie shook her head in answer to an interrogatory eyebrow, and for the next quarter of an hour assisted in plying Mr Shilto with drink and conversation. Which proved to be a trying ordeal in more ways than one, since Mr Shilto, like Ronnie Purvis, had also been bolstering up his spirits with strong drink. Though unlike Mr Purvis, it had had the effect of making him disconcertingly boisterous, for he talked loudly and disjointedly, punctuating his remarks with frequent bursts of foolish laughter. The minutes seemed to crawl like hours, but at long last Charles and Nick reappeared and Mr Shilto finished the remainder of the brandy and removed himself.

'Any luck?' demanded Valerie in a feverish whisper. 'I had none with Ruby. At the first hint of the subject she closed up like a hysterical clam and almost threw me out of the room. What happened to you two? You were away for *hours*. We thought you were *never* coming!'

'It took a bit of time,' said Charles, 'because we made a pretty thorough search. But it was worth it. Look!' He pulled a piece of crumpled paper out of his pocket and handed it over.

Valerie straightened out its creases, and her eyes widened in a face that had become suddenly colourless. For it was an envelope, addressed in cheap violet ink and in a curious spidery handwriting that she had occasionally seen before, to——

Sir Lionel Masson, C.S.I., C.I.E., C.B.E.,
Government House,
Ross.

The writing was Ferrers Shilto's, but the envelope was empty.

20

'— and when they were found,' concluded that indefatigable pessimist, Miss Amabel Withers, 'they were all dead.'

'We have all heard that story at least six times, Amabel!' snapped Valerie with unwonted irritation, 'and if you could possibly keep off the more morbid stories in the Islands' repertoire for this one evening, I'm sure we should all be profoundly grateful.'

Amabel's snub nose glowed pinkly — a distressing habit it acquired when its owner was in any way upset — and her somewhat cowlike eyes filled with tears. Valerie was smitten with sudden compunction: 'I'm sorry, Amabel. I'm a pig. Pay no attention to my beastly snappishness. But if we *could* keep off stories of Battle, Murder and Sudden Death just for tonight, it would be a help.'

Once more they were all seated about the long dining-room table, and Amabel had come over from the hospital for dinner. She had reported that Rosamund Purvis, though by now completely recovered from the 'nervous breakdown' brought on by the accident to the sailing party, had decided to remain at the hospital to keep Truda company. 'You see,' explained Amabel with a characteristic lack of tact, 'Truda couldn't come because she thinks that the hospital cook, who is ill, may be going to die, and Rosamund wouldn't come because she said she'd rather be in hospital with six dead cooks than in a house with one live murderer.'

Her observation had been received in virulent silence, and

Valerie, gallantly suppressing a strong impulse towards violence, had managed to turn the conversation to the non-arrival of the S.S. *Maharaja*. But with doubtful results.

'I shouldn't wonder,' offered Amabel with a touch of animation, 'if it hadn't been wrecked. I expect a storm like that could easily turn a ship right over.'

Comment being useless: 'Valerie, my dear,' said the Commissioner, 'I think we had better go in to dinner,' and they had finished their drinks hurriedly and trooped into the dining-room; a silent party temporarily united by a common desire to lay violent hands upon Miss Withers.

During the meal Amabel, who had drunk two cocktails of Charles's devising, with fatal results, had excelled herself. Possibly the unusual silence of the remainder of the house-party was partly responsible for this, since few of them felt equal to manufacturing social conversation, and there was not one among them who did not have his or her own disturbed and secret thoughts. Wherefore Amabel droned on unchecked, and but for the subject-matter of her conversation they might all have welcomed her excessive volubility. But struck by a melancholy association of ideas, stories of murder, mystery, and death by drowning tripped off her tongue in unceasing and morbid procession.

Valerie had endured all these with exemplary patience. But a repetition of the story that Amabel had told on the ferry during the storm on Christmas Eve was too much for her, and had finally provoked her to acid comment. Her belated outburst effectively checked the flow of horrors for the remainder of the evening, but failed to dispel the gloom that their recital had cast over Amabel's fellow-diners, who with one consent hurried over the remainder of the meal and left the table before the arrival of the coffee and liqueurs.

Valerie and Copper left Miss Withers and the men to their own devices, and went off to see Mrs Stock, who had changed rooms with her husband and was now sitting up in bed in the small dressing-room, sipping Ovaltine, with the pink feathered wrap dragged carelessly about her shoulders.

She looked tired and hag-ridden and as though she had suddenly aged ten years, and Valerie noticed with a slight sensation of shock that for the first time since she had known her Mrs Stock had no make-up on her face. Without it, her skin showed coarse and colourless and marked with fine lines about the eyes and mouth, and the fact that she was a middle-aged woman was suddenly and startlingly apparent.

Her hair tangled about her head in disordered black wisps which served to accentuate the pallor of her face, and though she greeted the two girls apathetically, Copper saw that her eyes, like Ronnie's and her husband's and Mr Shilto's, were never still, but darted incessant, uneasy glances about the small room. 'I found I couldn't sleep in the larger one,' she said in reply to Valerie's inquiry about her change of room: 'There were so many bats, and one can't keep them out. And anyway, I am never really comfortable at night in a big room. I think a small bedroom is so much more – more cosy, don't you?'

Valerie, remembering Ruby's own house and her conversion of its largest room — originally the living-room — into her bedroom, had some difficulty in concealing her surprise at this statement. 'Er — yes,' she agreed hastily: 'I suppose so. I hadn't really thought much about it. I suppose they build the rooms large for coolness. I do hope you won't find this one stuffy? There's no wind just now. Would you like me to open one of the windows for you?'

'No!' said Mrs Stock with unexpected violence, clutching at Valerie's arm as though to restrain her if necessary by force: *'No!'* She subsided suddenly at the sight of the girls' astonished faces, and forced a smile. 'I – I'll open it myself later when I put the lights out. I do so dislike all those beetles and moths and insects flying in.'

Valerie, refraining from the obvious comment that the mosquito net would effectively prevent them from becoming a nuisance, stayed talking for a few more minutes, and then said good-night.

'I wonder,' said Mrs Stock, 'if you'd give Leonard a message from me? Would you mind telling him that as I'm feeling particularly tired, I'm going to try and get to sleep at once, and that as I don't want to be disturbed I have put his washing things on the chest of drawers in the next room. I'm sure that John Shilto won't mind letting him share his bathroom just for tonight.'

'Of course. Are you quite sure there's nothing else we can do for you?'

'No. No, nothing at all, thank you. Good-night. And please close that door as you go out.'

Valerie and Copper withdrew thankfully, shutting the door of the dressing-room behind them, and they were half-way across the big bedroom — now Leonard's — when a sound stopped them, and they looked back at the closed door of the room they had just left. From the other side of it came the unmistakable sound of a key being turned in the lock, followed by the rasp of bolts pressed home into their sockets. Mrs Stock, it appeared, was barricading herself in for the night.

'I wonder what she's up to inside there?' said Valerie thoughtfully. 'I wonder if——' She frowned speculatively at the teak panels of the closed door, and then turned on her heel again: 'Come on, Coppy. Let's go and rescue Amabel before there's another murder. I should hate to see Charles arrested for homicide, however justifiable.'

But when they rejoined the remainder of the party in the drawing-room, Miss Withers was no longer talking. She was sitting huddled up in a corner of the sofa and complained of a headache. Amabel was unused to alcohol, even in its mildest form, and those pre-dinner cocktails were having after-effects. The Commissioner had vanished, and Charles, Nick, and Mr Shilto, grouped about the empty fireplace, were discussing fishing with a noticeable lack of animation, while Leonard Stock, who was occupying a lonely seat by the bookcase, was yawning over a tattered copy of *Country Life*, and struggling to keep his eyes open.

Valerie paused beside him and delivered his wife's message, which was received without comment: evidently Mr Stock was only too used to being inconvenienced by his Ruby.

On a sudden impulse, which she was afterwards unable to account for, she lowered her voice, and with her eyes on the group by the fireplace added the brief information that they had discovered the envelope of the missing letter in John Shilto's room: 'So you see, Leonard, you were right about it having been taken from the office. But I don't expect Father ever thought of it when he said there was nothing missing.'

Looking down, she surprised an expression of what she could only describe as utter shock in Leonard's pale eyes. It was gone again in a moment, but the little man was obviously shaken: '*John Shilto!*' he said in an uncertain whisper. 'It isn't possible! I thought——' He pulled himself up short. 'I mean, what possible reason could he have had for wanting that letter? There must be some mistake. Yes of course that's it, a mistake . . .'

He babbled on for a full minute, but Valerie received the impression that he was talking at random to cover up some deeper sense of shock or surprise than was conveyed by his words, and she was suddenly angry with herself for having spoken. She cut short his low-voiced incoherencies, and excusing herself, crossed to the far side of the room where Copper was idly turning the pages of a photograph album.

'I rather think I've made an ass of myself,' she confided in a rueful undertone. 'I lost my head and told Leonard that we'd found the envelope of that letter in John Shilto's room, and it seemed to shake him to the core. He's quite obviously got a theory of his own about all this, and it doesn't include John Shilto. Or it didn't, up to five minutes ago! You don't think he *really* knows something, do you? Ought we to ask him, because . . .'

'No, *don't!*' interrupted Copper quickly. 'I mean — he – he could only be guessing, and we're all doing that. Don't let's——' She broke off at the approach of Amabel, and said with some relief: 'Hullo, Amabel, come and play mah-jong, or Slam or something.'

'I dode thig I will, thag you. I thig I'b going to ged one of my colds,' confided Amabel in dismal tones. 'They always start with a headache. Id cabe on suddenly with the puddig.'

Valerie, lending a suitably sympathetic ear, suppressed a giggle with difficulty and said: 'Let's leave the men to talk fish, and see if we can find some aspirin for your head. And when you've taken it, Charles can see you home. You'll be much better off in bed if you're sickening for a cold. Coming with us, Copper?' The three girls withdrew unobtrusively and went off in search of restoratives for Amabel.

'Dad's got something much better than aspirin,' said Valerie. 'It's a sort of powder stuff in a capsule, and it acts twice as quickly. I'm not sure I couldn't do with one myself, to steady the nerves a bit! We'll go and hunt through his medicine cupboard.' She pushed open the door into Sir Lionel's bedroom, switched on the light, and followed by Amabel, vanished through a doorway to the right which led into her father's dressing-room. Copper could hear the chink of bottles as they hunted through the medicine cupboard, but instead of following them she paused instead by the open french windows that gave on to a small creeper-covered balcony overlooking the garden.

Below her in the misty darkness one of the guard lights that remained on all night gave out a dim radiance that touched the creepers with faint gold, illuminating a cataract of scented blossoms that foamed across the wooden balustrade and fell in tangled profusion to the ground. And struck by a sudden thought, Copper walked out on to the wet balcony and peered downwards.

But by that faint light it was impossible to tell if the thick masses of creeper had been torn or misplaced.

A breath of wind stirred the mists into ghostly eddies about the old house, and she shivered and turned back again to the comfort of the lighted room.

Sir Lionel's bedroom was large and bare and furnished only with a handful of necessities: a cupboard, a narrow bed with a small table beside it, a larger writing-table and a single chair. There were no pictures or ornaments, but a recent photograph of Valerie shared a double leather frame on the writing-table with an older and more faded one of a woman who must have been her mother, for the resemblance between the two faces was remarkable. Copper reached out instinctively, and picking up the frame, examined them with interest. And she was replacing it when something slipped from between the photograph and the back of the frame, and fell upon the table. A sheet of paper covered in thin, spidery writing in cheap, violet-coloured ink. Ferrers's letter . . .

Copper stared at it with a feeling as of cold fingers closing about her heart. It was torn in one place, and it had been badly crumpled, but here and there a few words stood out staringly.

. . . should be most grateful if you could give me some idea as to what the law is on such matters. The lagoon is undoubtedly my property, and therefore anything that it contains is presumably mine, but . . . would prefer to have some official ruling as to where I stand before getting in touch with dealers . . . acquired an aqualung in Calcutta, and the results have been surprising . . . As you will realize, I cannot risk . . . legal angle must be assured . . .

Pearls——! So that was it! Not the plantation — the lagoon. He had stumbled upon a pearl bed, and—— Why, of course! She herself had asked a question about pearl oysters just before Sir Lionel had spoken of the letter from Ferrers. That should have told her! It had been the mention of oysters that had reminded him of Ferrers; not Amabel's reference to a fisherman who had been drowned. And she herself had put an end to the conversation because she had not wanted to be reminded of that sodden, shrivelled little corpse that the sea had flung ashore.

Pearls ... John Shilto must have known. That smell that Charles had complained of at the back of Ferrers's bungalow: oysters of course. Oysters rotting in the sun ...

A voice from the adjoining dressing-room said encouragingly: 'That's right. Swallow it whole. Now in a few minutes you'll feel a lot better.' Copper returned to the present with a start, and thrusting the letter hurriedly back into its hiding-place, turned quickly to face Valerie and Amabel as they re-entered the bedroom.

Returning with them to the drawing-room it was a shock to discover that the fishing story with which Charles had been regaling the company when they left was still in progress, for she felt as though they had been away an hour. But a glance at the clock revealed that they had been absent for barely eight minutes.

Leonard Stock had given up the unequal struggle and departed to bed, and Charles evidently took their reappearance as a signal for breaking up the party, for abandoning his salmon in midstream he jumped up and offered his escort to Amabel as the lesser of two evils — the greater being the continued company of Mr John Shilto.

'I dode thig you need bother,' said Amabel flatly. 'I'b going back in a rigshaw, and one of the orderlies will come along, adyway.'

'Then just let's make sure you get off,' urged Charles, a thought tactlessly. 'Hullo, Copper old girl. You look as if you'd seen a ghost. What's up?'

'Nothing,' said Copper stiffly. 'I'm – I'm a little tired.' And then somehow Nick was standing between her and the inquiring glances that Charles's comment had provoked. 'Same here,' he said lightly. 'Bed for everyone, I think.'

The house-party trooped yawning into the hall, and Nick put a cup into Copper's cold hand and closed her nerveless fingers about it, holding them there with a strong warm clasp. 'It's only black coffee,' he said in an undertone, 'but it's hot. Be a good child and get it down. It'll pull you together.'

Copper essayed a shadow of a smile and drank obediently, her teeth chattering against the rim of the cup.

The others were saying their goodbyes at the head of the stairs by the time she had finished, and Nick took the empty cup from her hand and followed her into the hall. John Shilto departed unsteadily for his room and Charles and Valerie went down into the front hall to see Amabel into her rickshaw. But when Copper would have followed them, Nick put a restraining hand on her arm. He leant against the banisters, his shoulder to the carved stairhead and his eyes on the group in the hall below, and spoke without turning his head: 'What's happened, Copper?'

'I found the letter,' said Copper in a strained whisper.

'The devil you have! Where?'

'In Sir Lionel's room. It was hidden behind a photograph in a leather frame. I – I picked the frame up, and the letter fell out.'

Nick continued to lounge against the banister rail and to watch the departure of Amabel with apparent interest, but his voice compensated for his lack of gesture: 'Take a pull on yourself, darling. It's pretty obvious that whoever took it wouldn't want it found on or near him, but at the same time didn't want it destroyed. And the Commissioner's room would be about the best hiding-place in the house, for no one would think of searching for it there — least of all Sir Lionel! — and when it's wanted again whoever put it there has only to wait until Sir Lionel is safe in his office, and sneak in and collect it.'

'I suppose so,' said Copper in a steadier voice. 'I don't really know why finding it should have scared me so much. It's – it's all this secrecy, I suppose. Everyone having something to hide.'

'Even I,' agreed Nick ironically. 'Tough luck, Coppy! I wonder what dark secret young Amabel is concealing behind that guiltless countenance? And if it comes to that, what are you?'

Copper was saved the necessity of answering by the return of Valerie and Charles.

'*Dear* Amabel!' said Charles, mounting the stairs. 'How I love that girl! Her forebears must have driven a flourishing trade in the undertaking business, and I imagine that Burke and Hare figure pretty prominently in the Withers family tree.' He draped himself limply about the stairhead and added: 'You don't think that we could have been on the wrong track over this murderer business, do you? I mean after this evening's performance I wouldn't put it past Amabel to have pulled off the job herself for the sole purpose of adding another snappy anecdote to her collection of Morgue Memories.'

Nick was not amused. He said tersely: 'Has she gone? Good. Then if the coast is clear, let's get back to the drawing-room for a bit. This spot is a damn sight too public and Copper has got something to tell us.'

They returned to the empty drawing-room where Charles helped himself to a generous nightcap and Copper related her discovery of the letter. And its contents.

'*Pearls!*' said Valerie breathlessly. 'Gosh!'

'Gosh is right,' agreed Nick. 'Pearls. Or in other words, dollars and cents and the pound sterling. Some people might even consider them worth murdering for.'

Charles said grimly: 'Some person quite obviously has!' He finished his drink and put down the empty glass with a thump. 'Well, it's a comfort to have something solid to go on at last, after an entire afternoon devoted to floundering around in a sea of woolly conjecture. That ring theory of Copper's about everyone intending to take a crack at Romeo Purvis and copping old Ferrers by mistake, has been sticking in my gullet. As a motive, it appeared to my limited brain pure dishwash. But here at last we have a good, solid motive for any number of murders. Offered a sufficient quantity of gleaming globules as an inducement, I might very well try my hand at a little light murdering myself.'

He turned about and indicated Valerie with a wave of his hand: 'Just cast your eye over there. The small whatnot which, if you look closely, you will observe pinned to my loved one's bosom, was reluctantly donated by myself to mark her last birthday, and set me back a matter of forty-five quid. And what does this bauble consist of? Three — count 'em — three under-sized lemon pips which the jeweller who stung me with them insisted were pearls of genuine and not Japanese manufacture, mounted in roughly ten bob's worth of gold. Therefore, by a simple process of calculation — and deducting fifteen quid as an absolute maximum for mounting and making — those three miser-able blobs of tallow are worth just about ten pounds apiece, and are barely visible at a distance of two yards. It therefore stands to reason that a pint-size mug of passably decent pips would probably net something in the neighbourhood of fifteen to twenty thousand pounds. Am I right?'

'Just about,' concurred Nick. 'So how's that for a motive for murder?'

'It will do to go on with,' said Charles.

'Then – then it *was* John Shilto!' Valerie spoke in a half-whis-per. 'But how did he find out?'

Charles gave a short laugh. 'Probably smelt a rat — or rather a load of rotting oysters — when he went up to the bungalow that morning. You can't open a live oyster nearly as easily as a dead one, so it saves time to let 'em die in the sun and then start in looking for pearls. He probably did a snoop round the back premises to see what in the name of Sodom and Gomorrah Ferrers was using to manure his plantation with, and stumbled across the shells. I know he's been to Ceylon, so he may well have seen the pearl fisheries there, and tumbled to the fact that those shells did not merely mean that Ferrers enjoyed eating oysters.'

Nick frowned thoughtfully into the black night beyond the

window-panes, and said slowly: 'Yes. I think it looks more and more as though it must be John Shilto. But I don't think we can just scrub the possibility of its having been someone else.'

'I agree. And I'm not.'

'Oh, nonsense, Charles,' said Valerie impatiently. 'Of course it can't be anyone else! Where would anyone else come in? Ronnie, for instance?'

'Same place as everyone else, I imagine! Ronnie could probably do with a bucketful of pearls.'

'Who couldn't?' asked Nick. 'I don't mind telling you that I could do with them myself. And by the way, Copper, you can now add another black mark to my charge-sheet. If I remember rightly it was only the absence of any motive that stumped you: apart from that you could probably have made out an excellent case against me.'

Copper did not answer, but Valerie, seeing her wince, rushed hotly to her defence: 'That isn't in the least amusing, Nick! If Copper ever suggested that there might be a case against you it was quite obviously to warn you that, outside of ourselves, you might be considered by some other people to be equally suspect with the rest of the sailing party — and that you should be prepared to face the fact!'

Nick grinned and said without irony: 'Accept my apologies, Val: there will be no more acidity in court. But returning to Purvis, I doubt if he's got the nerve to commit murder. Though if it comes to that, I don't believe that the Stocks have either! On the other hand, it seems to me to stand out a mile that both Ruby and Leonard know something — or think they know something. A rather dangerous state of affairs, I should have thought, with a murderer around. So I think that at this point a talk with dear Ruby might be profitable, for if that woman really *was* peering over the banisters some time during the night watches, the chances are that she can make a pretty shrewd guess at the identity of the murderer.'

'Um,' said Charles. 'Possibly. On the other hand, if Ruby thinks that she knows who did it, why the hell is she keeping her mouth shut?'

Nick shrugged. 'You have me there,' he confessed. 'I could probably dream up half-a-dozen fairly plausible reasons, given time, but the only ones that occur to me at the moment seem a bit flimsy. However you might consider these: sheer panic; the inability to produce any concrete proof beyond her own word which, unsupported, might be insufficient to secure a verdict. Or black terror for fear that she might be the next victim on the list if she admitted to any knowledge of the murder.'

Charles produced a sound uncommonly like a snort. 'B——! I mean, rubbish! Do you mean to say she couldn't pick a time when she was surrounded by a mass of citizens, and then blow the gaff? Of course she could! She's only got to get in a huddle with a few of the local inhabitants, and then say, "There is your murderer! Grab him!"'

'But suppose she wasn't believed?' said Copper in a low voice. 'Supposing it was someone – someone . . .' Her voice trailed off into a whisper as Charles swung round to face her: 'Supposing it was who, Coppy?'

'I – I don't know,' said Copper uncertainly. 'Just — anyone. I mean, supposing she didn't know for certain, but – but only——' Once again her voice failed, and she stopped.

'Only what?'

Copper did not reply, and Nick's eyes narrowed speculatively as he watched her. But Valerie, who did not appear to have noticed her hesitation, said with a sigh: 'I'm afraid all those laborious notes I made this afternoon are going to need re-writing, now that we've got hold of this pearl motive. What about getting our hands on Ferrers's letter? We could do that easily, because the parent is still working like a beaver down in the office, poor pet.'

Nick shook his head. 'I wouldn't, if I were you. You see now that we know where it is, it seems to me a good scheme to leave it severely alone and tell no one, but merely keep an unobtrusive watch on that door tomorrow and see who goes to fetch it. Presumably whoever put it there has some reason for wanting it back; otherwise he'd have destroyed it.'

'Which is not quite so easy as it sounds,' commented Charles. 'Torn up scraps of paper can be collected and read. See Crime Club. Also traces of burnt paper, in a house where a paper is missing, are apt to wear a suspicious look. However, just between you and me, what about shelving the entire question until tomorrow? My head is reeling with a varied and malignant collection of clues, motives and suspicious acts, and unless I am much mistaken, a collapse into complete lunacy is imminent. Let's talk about the weather instead.'

He drank deeply, and turned to Valerie. 'By the way, Star-of-my-soul, what alibi did you hand your respected parent to account for my spending the night here? He murmured something to me about the state of the Mess roof, to which, being unprepared, I had no adequate comeback.'

'I *am* sorry,' apologized Valerie guiltily. 'I should have warned you. I knew Dad would say it was all nonsense if I said I'd asked you to stay here because I was afraid there might be a murderer in the house, so I told him that the storm had broken the Mess roof and your room wasn't fit to sleep in.'

Charles exhaled noisily: 'And what,' he inquired, 'do I say when he comes down tomorrow to view the damage? Just that it was all a hearty little joke? Or that I've just that minute mended it with glue and stamp paper?'

Valerie laughed, and reached out to ruffle his hair. 'It's all right, darling, you know he never goes near the Mess if he can help it. And anyway, it achieved its object. You *are* sleeping here.'

'Not yet,' said Charles. 'But I intend to — and that right speedily!' He drained his glass and stood up. 'Bed, I think, is indicated. And lots of it.'

One by one the lights snapped out until, except for one in the lower hall, the big house was in darkness. And twenty minutes later Copper and Valerie, tucked inside their respective mosquito nets and with their beds tonight placed side by side in Valerie's room, heard Sir Lionel's footsteps mount the stairs and cross the ballroom. Valerie called out a good-night, and a moment after his answer they heard his door shut.

'Night, Val.'

'Night, Coppy. Sleep well.' Valerie slid an arm out from under her mosquito net and switched off the little bedside lamp that stood on a table between them, and darkness and quiet swept down upon the room, broken only by the flitter of a bat's wing and the whisper of the fan blades cutting into the warm damp air. But presently she spoke again, her voice an anxious undertone: 'I'm glad Charles is here tonight. But – but I wish he wasn't sleeping in Dan's bed . . .'

Copper did not reply, and supposing her to be asleep, Valerie turned on her side, tucked one arm under her pillow, and went to sleep.

21

Copper was not asleep. And as the dark hours dragged on, sleep receded further and further from her tired brain.

The house was so still. So deathly still that after a time she realized that the rain must have stopped because she could no longer hear the soft drip of water from the gutters at the roof edge. Even the sea had quietened at long last, and the distant roar of the breakers had softened to a lower key; a soft, drowsy note, like the purr of a giant cat. But the isle was still full of noises, and the apparent stillness was, as ever, made up of a hundred small sounds which welded together made up the sum total of silence, and Copper's taut nerves separated each sound from its fellows.

Every unexplained creak or patter, every whisper of a bat's wing or tap of a night-flying beetle against a window-pane — even the familiar sound of the hall clock striking the slow passing of the hours — made her pulses leap with terror; and when a nightjar cried harshly in the garden her heart seemed to jump into her throat and she found herself clutching at her bedclothes with frantic fingers to keep herself from screaming.

She tried not to think of Dan and Ferrers — and death. Or of any of the horrible happenings of the last three days and the sheer terror of the night between Christmas Eve and Christmas Day. But it proved to be beyond her powers, for her weary mind betrayed her and took her stubbornly back over every hour of those long hours and through every detail of those grim little notes that Valerie had written down in her sprawling, schoolgirl hand. And with every recollection her fear mounted.

They had been mad — mad and stupid and conceited — to imagine for one moment that they could help to unravel this ugly, bloodstained tangle. Their interference and probing could not possibly help . . . but it might well end by placing every one of them in terrible danger, for someone who had already killed twice might, if sufficiently frightened, kill again.

Supposing that unknown killer were to grow suspicious of them? Of their actions, their inquisitive interest, their questions — and begin to fear that between them they might stumble upon the truth? The prospect was too frightening to contemplate. Yet it was impossible not to ask questions. Not to guess — and be afraid.

What was Nick hiding? What was Ronnie afraid of? Why had John Shilto drunk so steadily that evening and talked so disjointedly and wildly? What had frightened Rosamund Purvis and why had Ruby changed her room and locked and bolted herself into it that night? Why hadn't Dan told anyone of his suspicions regarding the death of Ferrers Shilto, and why had the news about the finding of the envelope in John Shilto's room come as such a shock to Leonard Stock?

The questions shifted and jostled through Copper's aching brain like pieces of a jig-saw puzzle, and it seemed to her that they lacked only the addition of one key piece to fall swiftly and easily into place. And suddenly it was borne in on her, with inexplicable conviction, that the clue to the whole murderous tangle lay concealed behind that final question mark in Valerie's notebook. A red question mark that stood for a trivial incident at the Mount Harriet picnic that had struck her as odd. If only she could recall what it was, the pieces of the puzzle would fit together and the answer to all their questions would be found in the completed picture.

But she could not remember. Try as she would it eluded the grasp of her tired brain, and she turned back wearily to the long procession of information and conjecture that lay between the covers of the notebook, pressing her palms against her aching forehead as she added up the sum of whys and whats and whens. But the only answer that presented itself was too frightening to be faced, and she shied away from it as though it were something tangible that must be avoided at all costs.

Her hunted mind turned desperately to Nick. But with no sense of relief, since Nick, like everyone else, was hiding something: and that in itself was as terrifying to her as the actual fact of Dan's murder, for the core of her terror lay not in any fear that Nick might be implicated in the crimes, but in the fear that he might possess some vital piece of information that was of danger to the murderer, and for the suppression of which he must be silenced. As Dan had been silenced . . .

Copper sat up in bed, clasping her hands about her knees and staring into the darkness. Tomorrow she must warn Nick — she must warn them all — that in meddling with this affair they were playing not so much with fire as with high explosive. She felt a little sick at the remembrance that it was she herself who was mainly responsible for their activities, since it was she who had suggested that they try and help track down Dan's murderer. But Dan was dead. Nothing that they could do would alter that fact or bring him to life again, but their continued meddling could easily lead to another death on the island. Tomorrow, before it was too late, she must make the others see this.

Before it was too late . . .? All at once it was as though a cold finger had reached out of the darkness and touched her, stilling the beat of her heart: for suddenly, sickeningly, she remembered Ronnie's missing revolver.

How could she have forgotten it? How could *any* of them have forgotten it? Why hadn't they realized its deadly significance? Ronnie had been so drunk, and they had been impatient of his alcoholic babblings and anxious to get away. And then Valerie had startled them with the remark that he was no longer wearing his ring, and a few moments later they had met Leonard Stock, whose news about the missing letter had sidetracked them on to Ferrers. Sidetracked them when all the time here, surely, was proof that a third murder was not only contemplated, but already planned.

Copper gripped her hands together and tried to think what she must do.

In the morning, as soon as it was light, she would wake Charles and Nick, and after that there must be no rest for anyone on the island until that revolver was found. Thank God the heavy sea swell seemed to be running itself out at last, and perhaps tomorrow they would be able to establish communication with the mainland. The arrival of Dr Vicarjee and Benton, the P.A., of Ted Norton and his police, and of Mr Hurridge, the Deputy Commissioner, would lighten the tension on Ross to a considerable extent.

Copper sighed wearily and laid her aching head against her knees, and as she did so something touched her arm very softly, and once again her heart seemed to stop beating. The next moment she realized that it was only her mosquito net which had billowed inwards, stirred by a draught from the open windows. A breeze had at last arisen to disturb the stillness of the mist-laden air, and outside in the garden it rustled the leaves of the mango trees, set the dry stems of the bamboo clusters clicking together, and passed in a cooling breath through the darkened rooms.

The hall clock struck two, and in the stillness that succeeded its metallic chime, Copper thought she heard a floorboard creak somewhere in the silent house. And instantly she was terrifyingly alert: waiting, with every nerve taut, for the faint vibration that would betray the passing of anyone ... of anything ... through the ballroom. But she could not have told whether it came or not, for as she waited another puff of breeze, stronger than the last, billowed her mosquito net again and shook the iron rods that supported it. When it had passed, though she continued to strain her ears for any further sound from the ballroom, none came, and after a few minutes she lay back on her pillows and tried to relax.

A faint measure of ease returned to her, probably due more to nervous exhaustion than to anything else, and a blessed drowsiness began to steal over her, drugging her brain. Tomorrow, thought Copper sleepily. Tomorrow I must tell Nick ... the revolver ... it isn't safe ... Tomorrow ...

It was then that she heard the shot.

The crashing reverberations of that violent sound shattered the silence into a hundred savage echoes that seemed to fill the house and give no indication of direction. It was followed by a frozen moment of utter stillness; and then the house was full of noises.

Copper was half out of bed, struggling frantically to free herself from the clinging folds of mosquito netting, when the light snapped on and Valerie was standing beside her, clutching at her, her face blanched and even her voice drained of blood: *'What was it?'*

'Ronnie's revolver!' sobbed Copper in a harsh, choking whisper. And free of the mosquito net she snatched up her dressing-gown, and without pausing to put it on or to consider what danger she might be running into, tore herself free of Valerie's clinging fingers and ran out into the passage.

There was a blaze of light in Nick's room, and as she reached the doorway someone running out collided violently with her flying figure.

'Nick!' said Copper in a breathless sob, *'oh, Nick!'* The next instant she was lifted off her feet and held so closely that she could hardly breathe. Her own arms were tight about his neck, and she was sobbing in hard, dry gasps.

'Are you all right?' Nick's voice was harsh with fear, and he held Copper as though he would never let her go.

'I thought you'd been killed,' she sobbed. 'I thought he'd killed you!'

Nick kissed her hard and savagely, holding her close. Lights were flashing on in room after room and the house seemed full of people in pyjamas and dressing-gowns, and noisy with fear-filled voices. Charles, whom the shot had barely awakened, came blundering out into the passage and crashed into them. 'Left, I think,' he said breathlessly, and Nick thrust Copper away from him, and the two men raced along the passage towards the turret room, Valerie and Copper at their heels.

The turret room was in darkness, and for a blasphemous minute Charles groped for the electric light switch and called John Shilto by name. Then there was a click, and the lights flashed up, and Charles said: 'Damned if he isn't asleep — or drunk!' for they could see the bed with its close-tucked mosquito netting, and through its shrouding whiteness, the dark bulk of the body that lay on it.

But John Shilto was not drunk. He was not even asleep.

Something was dripping from the bed on to the smooth uncarpeted floor, and each slow drop fell with a monotonous little splash into the small, grinning pool that had already formed beside the bed and was spreading sluggishly along the joins of the floorboards.

Nick tore out the mosquito net with a savage hand, and after one swift look, dropped it and spun round: 'Get out of here, Copper,' he ordered curtly. 'You too, Val! You can't do anything. He's dead.'

Neither girl moved. It seemed as though they had lost the power to do so. Then, suddenly, the Commissioner was in the room, and Leonard Stock, his feet thrust hastily into tennis shoes and wearing a vividly patterned dressing-gown that looked as though it must belong to his wife.

Orderlies, *chaprassis* and one of the sentries were thronging the entrance to the turret room, and of all the household only Ruby Stock appeared to be conspicuous by her absence.

The Commissioner pushed past Valerie and strode to the bed. 'What is it?' he demanded. 'What happened? *Good God!*' His voice cracked harshly as he swept the mosquito net aside.

There was a sudden frozen silence in the crowded room, broken only by the slow splash of falling blood, and for a moment it seemed as though the house itself were holding its breath from horror.

John Shilto was very dead. Where his head had been there was now only something blotched and shapeless and dripping. One lax hand lay outside the sheet, its fingers loosely clasped about the barrel of a heavy service revolver, a bullet from which had so recently and violently awakened the house. There was a faint reek of cordite in the air, and pinned neatly to one corner of the pillow was a folded sheet of foolscap. '*Suicide*, by God!' breathed the Commissioner. He stretched out a hand towards the revolver and Nick said sharply: 'Don't touch it — fingerprints!'

But he was too late. Sir Lionel's fingers had already closed about it, and he swung round and glared at Nick: 'Don't talk such damned nonsense! Who else's fingerprints should there be on it, other than his own?'

'At a guess, Purvis's,' said Charles.

'*Purvis!* Then how the devil——? Here, Stock, you'd better take charge of it for the moment.'

Leonard Stock stepped back hurriedly, treading on the toes of an inquisitive house-servant who, taken unawares, yelped sharply.

'I——? Oh, er — of course. Certainly.' He accepted the weapon reluctantly, as though afraid that it might explode in his hand, and held it as far away from him as possible, eyeing it unhappily, while Sir Lionel, having ordered servants and orderlies from the room, turned back to the bed. 'And now — ' began the Commissioner. But he was not allowed to finish, for Charles cut unceremoniously across his sentence: 'Val darling, you and Copper clear out, will you? At once, please.'

'No,' said Copper in a taut voice. 'I'm not going until I know why he did it. If – if he did it. Why hasn't someone read that paper?'

Sir Lionel swung round with a muffled exclamation and ripped the folded paper from its fastening. It proved to consist of a single closely typed sheet of foolscap with the final signature in a bold sprawling hand. He glanced swiftly through it, and then, very deliberately, read it aloud:

I, John Chalmers Shilto, being of sound health and in my right mind, have decided to put an end to my life. The circumstances which have brought about this decision are as follows:

The estrangement between my cousin, the late Ferrers Shilto, and myself is common property, but few have realized how bitter it has been. I do not propose to weary others with an account of our private dispute. It is enough for them to know that the bitterness of years culminated, on Christmas Eve, in a difference of opinion, on a private matter, which convinced me that the Islands were not large enough to accommodate both my cousin Ferrers and myself. I therefore decided upon his removal.

Fate played into my hands, and during the storm on the evening of the same day, my cousin and I shared for a few moments a hold upon the same upturned boat. At the moment at which we overturned I had grasped at, and still retained, the tiller of my boat. It made an excellent weapon. I struck my cousin on the back of the head and I believe that he must have died immediately. A few moments later another boat bumped into mine, and I left mine and clung to it. The visibility was so poor throughout that I do not believe anyone noticed the exchange, for it was next to impossible to see who was one's neighbour, and I should not have recognized my own cousin except for a ring he wore upon the hand with which he had grasped the keel beside me. No one noticed his absence, and it was not discovered until we were taken aboard the forest-launch nearly half an hour later, when it was naturally assumed that he had been drowned.

However, an unlucky freak of the tides returned his body, undamaged, to Ross; and by an even more unlucky accident,

Surgeon-Lieutenant Harcourt was present on that occasion. He saw what Dutt missed, and unfortunately for himself went down to the Guest House on the night of December 25th in order to verify his suspicions.

But since he had already displayed them too clearly I was prepared for some such action on his part. I managed to get clear of the house without being seen, and followed him to the Guest House, where I killed him.

I sincerely regretted having to perform this act, but I had no choice in the matter. It was a case of my life or his, and I preferred, not unnaturally I think, that it should be his. But once again I was unlucky, for the lack of a few inches in the size of the coffin destroyed what I flatter myself was a well-thought-out plan of action.

Since then I have had to realize that the chances of discovery are increasing hourly, and that to diminish them, I should have to kill again. I may say that I enjoyed killing Ferrers, but the elimination of young Harcourt was distasteful to me, and any further killing — perhaps, of necessity, even women — would not only be distasteful, but would also add to the risk of discovery. Life under these conditions would not be worth living, and so I have decided to cut the Gordian knot of a situation that has grown too complicated for me. My regards and apologies.

John Chalmers Shilto

There was a brief silence after Sir Lionel had finished reading, and the page of foolscap crackled harshly as he refolded it. He said heavily: 'I think we had better send for a doctor. Dutt will have to do.'

Charles took Valerie's arm and propelled her towards the door. 'You and Copper had better go back to bed, darling.'

Valerie said beseechingly: 'We can't, Charles — you know we can't!'

'All right then, go and sit in the verandah. I'll come along as soon as I can. Here, Leonard' — he grabbed Mr Stock by one gaily-coloured sleeve — 'be a good scout and take these two kids off to the verandah. And just see that they don't start having hysterics. It's all right, Val, Leonard will keep you company and I'll be along in a few minutes.'

He hustled the two girls out of the room, and Mr Stock followed with grateful alacrity.

22

'I don't believe it!' said Copper, breaking a long silence.

The three of them were sitting in that part of the verandah that lay beyond the drawing-room, for as though by mutual consent they had come as far as possible from the thing that lay in the turret room.

Ten minutes had passed since Charles had ordered them from the room, and for ten minutes they had not spoken. True, Mr Stock had made an abortive attempt at conversation, but the blank and unresponsive stares of his two charges had caused him to drop the idea and he had taken instead to tapping a nervous little tattoo on the arm of his chair.

Valerie turned her blank gaze from the dark window-panes and asked listlessly: 'What don't you believe?'

'I don't believe he killed himself.'

'What's that?' Valerie sat up with a jerk, staring at her, and then relaxed again. 'Oh, don't be ridiculous, Coppy,' she said wearily. 'It's quite obvious that no one else could have done it. Besides, what about that letter?'

'That's just what I mean. Would you have thought that he'd write like that? I mean, express himself in that way?'

Valerie shrugged her shoulders. 'It was a bit pedantic, but then I imagine that writing one's Last Will and Testament, so to speak, would be inclined to make one go a bit legal and pompous. What do you think, Leonard?'

Mr Stock, who was looking grey and strained, started slightly on being addressed, and thought for a moment. 'Yes, I think perhaps you are right,' he admitted cautiously. 'And then, too, anyone contemplating suicide cannot really be considered normal; although they are probably quite sane. So it is not to be expected that they would write a normal letter. I imagine that the majority of suicide notes are either hysterical or dramatized, and the slightly pedantic phrasing of poor Shilto's letter was probably the latter.'

'*Poor* Shilto!' said Valerie violently. 'A low-down, cold-blooded cowardly murderer! He at least had the excuse of a quarrel with Ferrers, but he killed Dan just to save his own beastly skin. Poor *Dan*——!' Her voice broke.

Mr Stock shuffled his feet uncomfortably and murmured something about *'De mortuis'*, and Copper said: 'Personally, I'd consider the saving of one's own skin a much better reason for committing murder than a mere difference of opinion. And that's another reason why I don't believe he did it. We overheard part of that second quarrel, and however much they spat at each other it didn't seem—— Oh, I don't know!' She sighed impatiently and turned to stare out into the darkness.

'What's that?' inquired Mr Stock eagerly. 'You actually heard the Shiltos quarrelling on another occasion?'

'Yes,' said Copper, and repeated, verbatim, what she could remember of the dispute, while Valerie peered apprehensively into the shadows of the darkened drawing-room beyond them and Leonard Stock looked interested and malicious and, finally, disappointed. When she had finished he shook his head and said: 'No, I agree it does not seem enough by itself to have driven Shilto to committing murder. It is a great pity, of course, that you didn't hear more. But you must not forget the years of enmity behind it. Taking that into account, I think his act is understandable — though hardly forgivable.'

Copper turned to stare at him in frank contempt. The bathos of the phrase 'hardly forgivable' applied to an act of deliberate and cold-blooded murder struck her as little short of ludicrous, and even managed to bring a wry smile to Valerie's weary mouth.

The three of them were sitting in a solitary pool of light thrown from a heavy bronze standard-lamp; for although most of the lights in the rest of the house were burning, the drawing-room and the verandah had been in darkness save for the standard-lamp. But the small pool of light in which they sat seemed to form a charmed circle in the dark verandah, holding them safe from the shadows of the rooms beyond and the grim, quiet figure that lay hideously illumined in the turret room at the far side of the house.

Copper shifted her gaze from Leonard's restless fingers to the comforting immobility of the huge bronze dragons, fashioned by some long-dead Burmese craftsman, that writhed in frozen fury about the massive base of the curiously wrought standard that had once held high an incense burner in some forgotten temple, and was now relegated to the lowly task of bearing a couple of electric bulbs. And as her eyes followed the curves and twists of the metal, her mind traced again the tortuous curves and twists of recent events.

She had forgotten her earlier terror and her resolve not to meddle further in this murderous business, for John Shilto's letter should have completed a pattern; but it had not done so. There was still something missing. The key piece of the jig-saw puzzle——

She lifted her head and spoke abruptly: 'I don't understand why he didn't give the reason for that quarrel with Ferrers. If he'd decided to kill himself, surely there was no reason why he shouldn't speak of it? He didn't strike me in the least as a man who would mind washing dirty linen in public. Especially if it was Ferrers's dirty linen.'

Valerie said impatiently: 'Are you still harping on the idea that it wasn't suicide? Because if that's one of your reasons for thinking it wasn't, it's a poor one. I can't see why he should have made his statement longer than it was. If he'd started out to put down all the whys and wherefores and ins and outs of his quarrel with Ferrers, he'd probably never have had time to shoot himself before he was caught.'

'Yes, I realize that,' said Copper, stirring restlessly. 'But all the same I can't help feeling that there's a catch somewhere. He — well, he didn't seem to me the type of man who'd ever kill himself. Anyway, not until he was actually cornered.'

She pressed her hands to her aching temples, thinking again of the thing that had haunted her ever since Valerie had read through the contents of the notebook: a picture and a statement that contradicted each other. Nick had said that only seven people could lie under suspicion of killing Ferrers Shilto, because only seven were out in the bay with him when he was murdered. But Copper, looking down on the bay from Mount Harriet barely twenty minutes after Ferrers and those seven had left, had seen a sail. A tiny, white triangle against the expanse of opalescent water below her, that could not have belonged to any of the three boats that had left from Crown Point jetty . . .

Leonard Stock cleared his throat apologetically. 'If I may make a suggestion,' he said hesitantly, 'are you not making rather a mistake in — er — perspective?'

'I don't think I know what you mean?'

'Well — er — even supposing that it was unlikely that a man of Shilto's temperament would shoot himself, surely, in this case, it is even more unlikely that anyone else did? I imagine you were asleep when the shot was actually fired, and therefore——'

'I wasn't,' interrupted Copper. 'I was awake.'

'Oh. Then that will probably help to prove my point. May I ask what you did when you heard it?'

'Jumped out of bed,' said Copper.

'And ran out *immediately*?' — there was a slight emphasis on the last word.

'Well, almost immediately. You see I forgot about the mosquito net, and I got myself tangled up in it.'

'Then how long was it, would you say, between the firing of

the shot and the time it took you to reach the door of your room?'

Copper considered for a moment. 'Not much more than a minute, I imagine. I didn't even stop to put on my dressing-gown. I just grabbed it up and streaked for the door.'

'Did you meet anyone in the passage?'

'Only Nick — and Charles.'

'No, I mean coming away from the turret room.'

'No,' said Copper slowly, 'I didn't. But it was dark except for the light from our room and Nick's.'

Valerie said: 'It's no use, Copper. I can see what Leonard's getting at, even if you can't. And he's quite right. There simply would not have been time for anyone else to fire that shot and get clear of the room before we all came rushing in. No one would have dared risk it, because the chances of someone being awake and running out in time to cut off their retreat would have been too great.

'And if you're going to suggest that it might have been someone who got in from outside, *don't*! Once the shot was fired, sentries and guards would have been dashing around the house, and the risk of trying to pop out of a window would have been terrific. And quite apart from that, it would need another Douglas Fairbanks to take a jump of about twenty feet on to a gravel path and then get up and dodge a gang of sentries!'

Copper looked unconvinced, and Leonard Stock cleared his throat again and said diffidently: 'You see, it's the time factor. To fire the shot and then pin a paper to the pillow, tuck in the mosquito net again and get out of the room and down the passage, and be out of sight before anyone arrived, would not, I think, have been possible.'

'No,' said Valerie positively. 'Of course not. So shut up, Coppy.'

Copper did not answer, and Valerie saw that she had shrunk back into the far corner of the sofa, and that her slim figure was all at once curiously rigid, while her eyes were staring into the shadows beyond them as though she had seen something move in the darkened drawing-room.

'What is it, Coppy?' asked Valerie sharply. 'What are you—— Oh, it's only Kioh.'

The lithe form of the Siamese cat advanced into the pool of light, purring amiably, and rubbed against Copper's ankles, and Copper bent forward to stroke the dark head with a hand that was noticeably shaking. Valerie saw her pass her tongue over her lips as though they were dry, and presently she straightened up a little stiffly and said in a voice that in spite of her struggle to control it was more than a little unsteady: 'I – I saw her move, and – and it gave me a fright. I'm afraid I must be going to pieces. Nerves or something, I suppose.' She looked across at Mr Stock and essayed a stiff little smile: 'Cats are creepy things, aren't they? Would you be very kind and move the lamp to the other side of your chair so that it throws some light into the drawing-room?'

'I'll switch on the ones in the drawing-room if you like,' offered Mr Stock, rising hopefully.

'*No!* No, don't go in there! It – it feels cosier sitting in just this little patch. The house seems so huge and empty when all the lights are on——'

'Now, now, we mustn't let ourselves get nervy, you know!' said Mr Stock with an attempt at roguishness. 'There, is that better?' He placed the lamp so that its light penetrated into part of the darkened drawing-room and thinned the close-packed shadows.

'Thank you,' said Copper shakily. 'You're very kind.'

A pulse was hammering in her throat and her eyes were wide and frozen as she stared into the shadows beyond the reach of the lamp. But behind their fixed gaze her mind was working frantically. She knew now who had murdered Ferrers and killed Dan Harcourt. And who, a short half-hour ago, had shot John Shilto.

The question mark in Valerie's notebook was no longer a query but the key piece to the jig-saw puzzle; and with it, as she had known it would, the other pieces had fallen into place. But there was still another and more difficult problem to face. How could she prove it? What could she do? For the moment, at least, she could do nothing. She must wait until Nick came, and tell him everything. Nick would know what to do . . .

And then, suddenly and horribly, her heart seemed to leave her breast and jump chokingly to her throat. For Valerie was speaking: 'Good heavens, Leonard! You've got blood on your hands! You must have touched him! *Ugh*, how beastly!'

Leonard Stock looked down quickly at the palms of his hands, and his eyes widened as he looked. For the lamp-light that fell on them showed them smeared and blotched with red. But it was not blood . . .

Copper was on her feet and had flung out a frantic hand in a desperate attempt to check Valerie's next words, but she was too late: 'No, it's not blood. It's only that stain off the woodwork of the balcony. Why, Leonard, you're covered with it! Where on earth have you——'

Then she stopped, and in the frozen moment that followed there sprang into her dilated eyes, fully fledged, the implication that hung on those words. Valerie stood up slowly, staring at him, her mouth dry and her hands shaking.

'You!' she said in a whisper. *'It was you!'*

Leonard Stock let out a long breath like a sigh and rose to his feet, stretching himself. And it was as though a harmless, dried-up twig had suddenly uncoiled and shown itself to be not a fragment of dead wood, but a live and poisonous snake.

'Yes,' he said very softly — almost complacently, and as though he were speaking a thought aloud rather than answering a question. 'Yes. It was I.'

'It isn't true!' said Valerie in a choked whisper. 'It can't be true. You're only making fun of us, aren't you?'

'No,' sighed Leonard Stock. 'I would deny it if it were not for the fact that I made a slip just now. My very first slip — and a bad one. It was extremely careless of me, but I hoped that it would pass unnoticed. However, I'm afraid Miss Randal is sharper than one gave her credit for being. A pity.'

He chuckled. It was a remarkably unpleasant sound.

'Yes,' said Copper steadily. 'I did see it. It was a great pity.' Her eyes did not leave his face, but her ears were straining for the sound of voices that would tell her that Nick and Charles were coming.

'For *you*, I fear,' said Mr Stock with another cold little chuckle. 'Much as I regret the necessity, I can clearly see that I shall now have to add two more — er — perhaps I had better say *"eliminations"* to my list.'

Valerie's fingers closed over Copper's arm: 'Scream, Coppy!' she said breathlessly.

'No!' said Copper sharply: and Valerie's own scream died unuttered. She had forgotten that Leonard still held Ronnie Purvis's revolver. 'Very wise of you,' grinned Mr Stock.

The lamp-light glinted wickedly along the barrel of the weapon he held in his hand, and the realization of their complete helplessness swept over Copper in a sickening wave. Beyond the stretch of the dark verandah there was a continuous coming and going of hurrying figures between the hall and the turret room. But none of them had entered the verandah. And since neither she nor Valerie could call out, for all the help they could give they might as well have been a mile away. Would Nick and Charles *never* come?

Crowding close on the heels of that thought came the blinding fear that when they did so, the cornered little maniac before her might be goaded into killing from sheer terror. Copper had no knowledge of firearms, but she possessed a hazy idea that a service revolver contained several bullets — was it six? Only one had been used for the murder of John Shilto, which meant that five remained. One for herself, one for Valerie. Still three left. Charles . . . *Nick!*

Cold panic took possession of her brain: to be ousted by colder logic. Her taut muscles suddenly relaxed and she said quite steadily: 'May I sit down? If I don't, I think I shall fall, and that might make rather a noise.'

Mr Stock grinned. 'Of course. Very sensible of you. You too, my dear.' He gestured with the gun barrel at Valerie, who obeyed him; moving as stiffly as though she were a jointed doll, her dilated eyes still fixed upon the weapon in his hand. 'Closer together, please. Thank you.'

Copper saw his eyes leave them for a brief instant and flicker towards the ballroom from where they could hear the sound of voices as a *chaprassi* called down instructions to someone in the hall below. Then his gaze came back again to the two girls, and slid from them to the windows behind them.

'It's no good,' said Copper quietly and very distinctly. 'You know quite well you can't kill us. You daren't fire that revolver because of the noise. And if you tried hitting either of us over the head, the other one would scream the place down and you'd have lost your last chance of escape.'

Leonard Stock nodded in grave agreement. 'You're an intelligent young woman. Yes, I had just reached the same conclusion myself. *Hmm.*' He shifted his weight from one foot to the other with a little rocking movement and squinted down at the weapon in his hand, and after a moment or two he said: 'I'll tell you what I propose to do instead . . .

'I propose, presently, to walk out of this house. And if I should hear any cries or sounds of pursuit I shall shoot the first person I see after that; and probably the next four as well, as this admirable weapon still contains five bullets. Therefore, unless either of you prefers to have the blood of several innocent persons on your head, you will watch me go without screaming or calling for help, and you will also refrain from raising an alarm for at least half an hour afterwards. Have I made myself quite clear?'

Valerie and Copper nodded wordlessly.

'In that case,' said Mr Stock, 'I will wait until Dutt's arrival, which will ensure the removal of most of the household from the hall to the turret room and give me a clear field. It will also allow me a few more moments in your company, so if those two somewhat thoughtless swains of yours should join us, I am sure you would not be so foolish as to arouse their suspicions. May I add that I am an excellent shot?'

He returned the weapon to the pocket of his dressing-gown, and to Copper's bewilderment, re-seated himself and lit a cigarette.

'Valerie, my dear,' he said smoothly. 'I am very much afraid that I shall have to trouble you. I do not really think I should leave the house in these garments, so perhaps you would be so good as to go to my room and fetch me the pair of stout walking shoes you will find there? Also the flannel trousers and the tweed coat, both of which are hanging over the back of a chair, and my shirt, hat and raincoat...

'You will please do this without being seen. A simple matter if you keep in the shadow and select a time when someone is not actually passing through the ballroom. I will ask you to be as quick as possible, and warn you, in case you have forgotten, that if I get suspicious at the length of time you are away, or if you return in company with anyone else, the consequences will be most unpleasant for your young friend here.'

'I won't go!' said Valerie in a dry whisper.

'Go on, Val,' said Copper evenly. 'It's all right. He won't shoot unless he is cornered, and if you do as he asks you'll at least lessen the chances of his shooting Charles or Nick.'

'Your friend has grasped the situation admirably,' approved Leonard Stock. 'I advise you to do the same.'

Valerie stood up uncertainly. 'All right,' she said shakily. 'I'll do it.' She turned away and, fear lending wings to her feet, ran through the doorway into the drawing-room and vanished into the shadows.

Copper sat tensed and waiting, and with every second that dragged by she saw Leonard Stock's face become more strained and his eyes more wary. Watching him, she wondered how she had ever thought his face was characterless or weak, for in the yellow lamp-light it looked neither. And all at once she knew why. That curious flickering light that seemed to burn behind the pale eyes was suddenly revealed for what it was: a consuming desire for revenge. And with that knowledge cold panic clutched once more at her hammering heart. Weak he had been, possibly characterless. But now he was neither, for hatred had given him both strength and character.

She wondered how long the spark of revolt had been smouldering in his heart. And what had suddenly caused it to flare up and consume him? . . . Had it been the storm? What long years of disappointment and lost opportunity, of snubs from social and official superiors and incessant nagging and bullying by an overbearing wife, lay behind the sudden metamorphosis of a small, diffident man into the merciless and cold-blooded little killer who had already murdered three men, and was perfectly capable of putting a shot through her head should Valerie fail to keep to the letter of his instructions?

His sudden pedantic turn of speech. Was that too a sign of hate? What he himself had described as 'dramatization'? He was acting — even the nonchalance of his present pose was acted — but his pale eyes remained tense and watchful, and as the moments ticked by and Valerie did not return, Copper saw his hand move stealthily towards his pocket, and in spite of the close atmosphere of the verandah she was suddenly ice cold . . . What did it feel like — being shot? A cold bead of sweat ran down her forehead and smeared her cheek: and then Valerie was back again, light-footed and breathing in quick gasps, her arms laden with clothing.

'Ah!' said Leonard Stock on a short sigh. 'I was beginning to think that you had been stupid. Sit down beside your friend, please.'

He slipped out of the dressing-gown and began to clothe himself; drawing on the garments over his pyjamas, swiftly but without undue haste. And as he dressed he talked in a low, precise voice that made his words seem like so many drops of ice water.

'Yes,' he said, 'it is strange how in spite of exercising the greatest caution one can yet make such unpardonable slips. Throughout this affair I have made no mistake which might have been avoided. I think I put the case clearly in that typescript that I pinned to poor Shilto's pillow. The discovery of Harcourt's body, owing to the unexpected production of a coffin that proved to be a few inches too small, was a quite unavoidable accident. But the plan for the elimination of John Shilto appeared to contain no flaws. I thought it all out very carefully from every angle and down to the last detail, though the broad outline was of course childishly simple . . .

'I had only to walk from my room to his, and after pinning the letter to his pillow (he was fortunately drunk enough to be sleeping soundly) shoot him, allow myself a margin of roughly fifteen to twenty seconds to complete the scene, and then step out of the window. This admirably patterned dressing-gown of my wife's served as an excellent camouflage to anyone looking up from below, but the mist proved even more valuable.

'The moment those two young men in the next room had run out into the passage nothing was more simple than to enter their room from the balcony, and walking through it, pick my time and join those who were crowding into the turret room. But I forgot that damnable stain, and I followed it up by the almost worse slip of forgetting about the mosquito net. I congratulate you on spotting that, my dear. You did, didn't you?'

'Yes,' said Copper steadily. 'Valerie and Charles and I were the only other people in the room when Nick pulled out the mosquito net to look at Mr Shilto. No one else could have known that it wasn't like that when we found him. Unless it wasn't suicide, but murder. And then only the murderer could have known.'

'Ah, yes. It was regrettably careless of me. A bad slip.'

'There was another one,' said Copper conversationally, her voice unstrained but her eyes intent. 'Not exactly a slip, but a useful clue.'

'You surprise me,' murmured Mr Stock, stooping to lace his shoes — the revolver beside his foot and within easy reach of his swiftly moving fingers. 'I had imagined that outside those two glaring examples I was blameless.'

Copper said: 'On the day of the Mount Harriet picnic I saw you carry a packing-case full of bottles from the car to the far side of the lawn, single-handed; and I remember being surprised. Then later, when we decided that you couldn't be the murderer because you hadn't the strength, I had forgotten about it and could only remember that something had happened that afternoon that had struck me as a little peculiar. I couldn't even connect it with anyone in particular. But when you made the slip about the mosquito net, and I realized that you must have been in John Shilto's room before we were, I thought: "It's impossible, because whoever shot him must have killed the other two, and he isn't strong enough." And then quite suddenly I remembered the box of bottles, and so I asked you to move the lamp, to make sure. It takes two of the servants to lift that lamp, yet you lifted it easily.'

Mr Stock straightened up and laughed his little bloodless laugh: 'Clever!' he approved. 'Very clever of you. Yes, I once wanted to be a gymnastic instructor at a private school; before I came out to India. But Ruby thought athletics of that description were undignified, and so I gave it up. But I used to practise in secret. I've never missed doing a few press-ups every morning.'

His thin lips stretched to show his teeth, and the sheer concentrated malignancy of that smile chilled Copper's blood and made her shrink back involuntarily. But Leonard Stock was not thinking of her ... *'Ruby!'* he said softly, and his lean fingers tightened convulsively about the weapon he held. '*Dear* Ruby! I'd put a shot through her head before I go, except that she'll hate this worse than death! I think she suspects even now. For the first time in her life she's frightened — and of me!'

It was plain that he was no longer addressing Copper, but speaking his thoughts aloud: 'Seventeen years I've put up with her. Seventeen years from my life——! And for a good many of them I've been planning how I'd kill her. It's been my one recreation — planning the details of her murder. But this was better. Who would have supposed that that little rat Ferrers would stumble on a pearl bed? If we hadn't stopped at his bungalow that day I might never have found out. It must have been in that tidal lagoon behind the house. He'd left the shells to rot in the sun — the fool!'

Once again, and too late, Copper remembered something. A look she had seen on Leonard's face when the Shilto cousins had met at Mount Harriet. Yes, he had known even then; and had realized in that moment that John Shilto also knew . . .!

But he was still speaking, and now his voice held a note of injury and bewilderment: 'I didn't mean to kill him. It wasn't my fault. It was the storm. I'd felt queer all day — keyed up and on edge — and when it broke, something seemed to snap. He was beside me, and suddenly it came to me that if I killed him I could get the pearls. Freedom and money. Freedom from these damned Islands — freedom from Ruby! With the pearls, I could walk out — disappear . . .

'So I killed him. Harcourt was a mistake — his mistake, not mine. And as it seemed that John Shilto had also found out about the pearls, I realized that he would have to go too. Besides, it was useful to have those two murders pinned on someone else. And then for the whole thing to fall to pieces over a smear of red wood-stain and a slip of the tongue!'

Leonard Stock jerked back his head and laughed: so suddenly

and so shrilly that involuntarily Copper started to her feet. In a flash the barrel of the revolver was levelled at her breast, held in a perfectly steady hand. 'No tricks, my dear,' urged Leonard Stock.

He reached behind him, and picking up his raincoat struggled into it; changing the revolver from his right hand to his left and back again in the process. There were voices from the direction of the hall, and he said: 'Ah, that will be Dutt arriving. Yes, he is going to the turret room, so I shall be able to leave without attracting undue attention. May I remind you both not to go rushing to your friends with this story until I have had ample time to get clear of the island? Say half an hour?'

'Are you mad?' interrupted Valerie breathless: 'You're marooned on this island like the rest of us!'

'Oh, dear me, no.' Leonard Stock laughed with genuine amusement. 'You forget that I always keep my own boat in the old swimming-bath. And after the discovery of Harcourt's body I took the precaution of provisioning her — just in case of accidents. This is no weather to be setting out in a sailing boat, I will admit. But she has a good engine, and luckily the sea appears to have fallen considerably, so I shouldn't do too badly. Half an hour should see me well off the premises. So remember, no immediate hue and cry if you wish to avoid further bloodshed.'

He wagged the heavy revolver at them with a grim joviality, and grinned maliciously. 'Well — *au revoir*, my dears. I trust we shall not meet again, but one can never——'

He stopped suddenly. There were voices in the ballroom, but this time it was Charles. Charles and Nick.

Copper swayed sickeningly and caught at the arm of the sofa to steady herself. She saw Leonard Stock slip the heavy revolver into the pocket of his raincoat, but his hand still kept a grip on it and she knew that his unshaking finger was still upon the trigger.

He did not again remind them that at least one life, if not all their lives, depended upon their behaviour during the next few moments. Perhaps he knew that they needed no reminder. He began to speak in his usual rather diffident voice, and they saw, with a fresh stab of fear, that his face had once more become weak and characterless and rather foolish, as though he had drawn a mask over that other face whose owner had murdered three men.

Valerie gave a hysterical laugh and said: 'And I once said that story about Jekyll and Hyde was far-fetched! One lives and learns.'

'What's that about Jekyll and Hyde?' inquired Charles. And then he and Nick were standing beside them: real and solid and alive in an unreal world.

Nick looked sharply from Copper to Valerie and said: 'You two look pretty done up. A stiff brandy all round would about suit the case I think.'

'Suits me all right,' said Charles. 'God! What a night! Hello, Leonard, old man, what are you all togged up for? If you're thinking of fetching Dutt, you're too late. He arrived a few minutes ago and they're all poring over the body again. So we beat it.'

'Er — as a matter of fact,' fluttered Mr Stock, 'Ruby is a bit upset, and she says she cannot go to sleep again without some tablets which she sometimes has to take, which are unfortunately down at our house. I said that I would slip down and fetch them — it won't take me a moment.'

'Jeepers, these wives!' said Charles. 'Who wouldn't be a bachelor?'

Copper attempted a laugh. 'That's a nice thing to say in front of your future wife, Charles. Are we going to get those drinks or aren't we?'

'Of course. Come on.' They moved off down the verandah, Leonard Stock walking a little behind them, and paused at the top of the stairs. 'I think I should appreciate that drink more when I come back,' said Mr Stock.

'We'll save you one,' promised Charles. 'Don't go breaking your neck in the dark.'

'I shall do my best to avoid it,' said Mr Stock primly. 'Good-night.'

He began to descend the stairs slowly and rather stiffly. And as he did so, Sir Lionel Masson came quickly across the ballroom: 'Hullo, Stock — where are you off to?' He did not wait for an answer, but hurried on in a preoccupied voice: 'By the way, that revolver of Purvis's — I'd better take charge of it.' He held out a hand, and Mr Stock stopped upon the staircase and made his fourth and final mistake.

Had he said 'I put it in your room,' or any similar lie, the events of that night might have had a very different ending. But some instinct of obedience betrayed him, and mechanically he had begun to draw the revolver from his pocket. A split second later he had recognized the error. But by then it was too late, for the Commissioner had seen it.

'Thanks,' he said. 'I'll see Purvis about it in the morning. It's quite disgraceful that he should not have kept it locked up.'

Mr Stock did not move, and Nick took a step forward as though to take the gun. But as he did so Copper moved quickly and stood between him and the figure on the staircase below, her cold fingers clinging to his. She could see rage, uncertainty and cunning contending together in the eyes of the shrivelled little killer in the raincoat, from whose features the mask had once more slipped to show the face of murder. Then the Commissioner had brushed past her, and descending the few steps that lay between them, held out his hand.

With a curious little sigh, Mr Stock drew out the revolver. He looked once more into the faces above him, and was silent for a long moment. Then suddenly and unexpectedly he laughed, a loud, shrill peal of laughter; his lips drawn back from his teeth in a curiously animal grimace. And startled by the sudden shrillness of that sound, Kioh, who had followed at the Commissioner's heels, spat indignantly, and bounding forward, streaked between his feet and down the stairs . . .

It was all over in a moment, before anyone could move or cry out.

Leonard Stock, taken unawares, stepped backwards and missed his footing. Instinctively, his hands came up and his finger must have tightened upon the trigger, for as he fell there was a blinding flash and a crashing detonation, and his body tumbled backwards down the shallow steps and came to rest at the turn of the staircase, where it quivered once, and then lay still.

The bullet had entered under his chin and come out at the back of his head, and he was dead long before they reached him.

23

It was a glorious day. The pearly sheen of morning had melted before the shimmering sunlight of midday, and beyond the curving sands of North Corbyn's the sea was an expanse of smooth, translucent turquoise that stretched away, island-dotted, to the far horizon, where it met and merged into the blue of a cloudless sky.

Valerie and Copper, accompanied by Nick and Charles, had boarded the little fishing-launch *Jarawa*, and complete with bathing-suits and picnic-baskets had anchored off North Corbyn's to spend a day of alternate sun- and sea-bathing.

The Commissioner had been deeply thankful to see them leave. He hoped that they would be able to put out of their minds, if only for that day, the horror and confusion of the night on which John Shilto and Leonard Stock had died; though he doubted if he himself would be able to do so. It had taken some little time to get a coherent account of the events preceding Leonard's death from his overwrought stepdaughter and her friend, and at first he had not believed them. In fact it was not until dawn had broken that an inspection of the sailing boat in the disused swimming-bath, and a long and harrowing interview with Stock's wife, had finally convinced him that a murderer had indeed paid for his crimes by becoming his own executioner.

Two crowded and grimly unpleasant days, full of endless inquiry and discussion, had followed. The bodies of Ferrers, Dan, John Shilto and Leonard Stock had been buried, and though the mists still clung thick about the tiny island, the sea had fallen and communication with the mainland had at last been restored.

Sir Lionel had made an abortive attempt to keep Valerie and Copper in bed, but they had rebelled against staying there and had wandered about the house and the fog-shrouded island looking worn and hollow-eyed; flatly refusing to discuss any aspect of the recent murders and starting violently at every unexpected sound. But on the third day the sun had risen into a cloudless sky, the mists had melted with the dawn, and the harassed Commissioner had instructed his stepdaughter and her friends to remove themselves off the island and to stay off it for as long as possible.

'And if I so much as see a *flicker* of you before dinner,' said Sir Lionel, 'I shall give the whole lot of you seven days' hard labour. So now you know! You can have the *Jarawa* for the day and go out fishing or picnicking or bathing. And now get out and leave me to my labours.' He kissed Valerie, and hustled them firmly out of the house.

The Islands, new-washed by storm and mist and drenched in sunlight, appeared greener and lovelier than ever before, and there were lime trees in blossom in the jungle behind North Corbyn's. Huge, gaudily painted butterflies lilted to and fro on the windless air, the sands of the long white beach were wet and firm underfoot, and the sea that had recently raged so wildly was now as flat as a looking-glass, its water crystal-clear and patched with lavender and lilac where the reefs of coral patterned the sea-floor.

The *Jarawa* had anchored as close to the beach as possible, and its four passengers had waded ashore with the baskets and bathing-towels on their heads to spend the morning swimming and sun-bathing. Afterwards they had eaten a picnic lunch under a tree that spread its branches far over the sands, before settling down to a prolonged and peaceful siesta: from which Copper had been the first to wake, aroused in the late afternoon by the crying of a gull overhead.

Propping herself on one elbow she had looked out across the

beach at the tranquil sea, and found it hard to believe that barely a week ago it had risen up in a shrieking frenzy to lash out at the Islands, smashing and tearing. For by now the waves and the wind had already swept away most of the traces of their recent rage, and save for a few prostrate coconut palms and the unusually large number of shells that strewed the sand, there was little visible evidence of those wild days and nights. 'Except on Ross,' thought Copper soberly. There were four new graves on that little island to mark forever the passing of the great storm.

For the first time since that terrifying night when John Shilto had died and Leonard Stock had become his own executioner, she found herself able to think of it all calmly and with a certain amount of detachment; and after a while, with curiosity. And apparently Valerie too had been awakened by the gull, and her thoughts must have been moving on the same lines, for she turned on her elbow and her voice broke the drowsy afternoon silence: 'Charles——'

'Mm?'

'Charles, how did everything happen? I mean about Leonard, and the Shiltos and everything. Did you ever find out?'

'Ask me some other time,' murmured Charles into the hat that he had tilted well over his nose.

'I don't want to know another time. I want to know now. I haven't wanted to know before, because I felt that if anyone so much as *mentioned* the grisly subject to me, I'd go off the deep end. But getting away from Ross, and all this heavenly sun and peacefulness, has been like a tonic, and I suddenly feel sane again — and full of curiosity.'

'I, on the contrary,' said Charles, 'am full of food and drink, and I require repose and not conversation as an aid to digestion.'

Valerie consulted her wrist-watch: 'You've had more than two hours, and you've got the digestion of an ostrich. So wake up and tell us all about everything or I shall point you out to a few hermit crabs.'

Charles groaned and turned his back on her: 'Ask Nick. He knows much more about it than I do.'

'Nick is included of course. We want lots of information from both of you: don't we, Coppy?'

Copper nodded. 'I didn't feel I wanted to know before,' she admitted, 'but I do now. I suppose it's because this place is such heaven that battle, murder and sudden death seem unreal and not so very important by contrast. Sort of "turnip-lanternish", if you know what I mean. Whereas back on Ross, even on a day like this, it all still seems far too real and frightening, and the turnip-lantern isn't merely two inches of candle and a hollowed-out pumpkin, but a real and rather horrible ghost.'

Nick tilted his hat back from his eyes and grinned at her. 'And you think that hearing all about the whys and wherefores would help to lay the ghost. Is that it?'

'No,' said Copper after a brief pause. 'I don't think anything but lots of time, or perhaps lots of happiness, will lay this particular ghost for any of us. But knowing something about the whys and wherefores will make it less frightening.'

Nick sat up and brushed the sand out of his hair, and propping his back against a conveniently curving tree root, lit a cigarette and said: 'Fair enough. Wake up, Charles, a voice cries, *"sleep no more!"* In this case, two voices. So let conciliation be your policy.'

'Hell!' moaned Charles, propping himself on a reluctant elbow and reaching for the beer. 'All right. Which bit of the recent unpleasantness do you two harridans require me to elucidate?'

'We don't want a "bit",' said Valerie. 'We want chapter and verse, right from the very beginning.'

Charles imbibed half a glass of beer and ruminated, and presently he said: 'Remember that sort of lagoon that was part of the "plantation" which John Shilto palmed off on to Ferrers? Well, it turns out to be simply crawling with pearl oysters.'

'Do you mean to say that all these years it's been right under——'

'Look,' said Charles, 'if you propose to interrupt this enthralling narrative with girlish cries, I shall return to my slumbers. You confuse me. Where was I? Oh yes. Well somehow or other, we shall never be certain how, Ferrers discovered the fact that though half his plantation was worth about fourpence ha'penny, the other half was probably worth, at a conservative estimate, about a million sterling.'

'Gosh!' said Valerie, awed. 'I didn't think there was that much money in the world!'

Charles grinned. 'It is a pretty good slice, isn't it? A pity we didn't do a bit of paddling there ourselves. Imagine old Ferrers's fury on realizing that he'd spent fifteen or sixteen years in a state of extreme poverty and simmering rage, while all the time a film star's salary was sitting in his backyard, only needing a bathing-suit and a bucket to be collected. I'll bet that thought did something towards tingeing his cup of joy with cascara!

'Well, to continue with the saga, the little man popped over to Ross, borrowed the *Encyclopaedia Britannica* off the padre, and read up everything he could find under the expression "Pearls". He then took to spending half his time in a bathing-suit in the lagoon, and evidently hauled up a goodish few shells, which he spread around in the sun behind his house until the flesh rotted and he could open them and dig in the debris — which accounts for the appalling stink that was hanging about the place. He must have collected more than a hundred fair-sized pearls this way, but he realized that he was only touching the fringe of the matter. To get at the real boodle he needed a diver. Or better still, a diving-suit. So one day he packed his toothbrush, pocketed his pint of pearls, and made tracks for Calcutta.'

'Of course!' said Copper. 'What a fool I am! I wondered, when Val first told me about him, how he'd managed to put up at the Grand if he was so poverty-stricken. I suppose he sold the pearls?'

'That is the supposition, my sweet. Anyway, he managed to

bring back a complete diver's suiting with him, and he couldn't have swapped *that* for a sandwich! He got going with it, and business boomed. He hauled up bucketloads of shell and the plantation began to smell like a sewer. And here the first fly mixed itself up in the ointment. Someone, it was quite obvious, was shortly going to ask questions about this extraneous perfumery. And when they did, where exactly did he stand in the eyes of the law? Had he complete and legal right to the produce of his pond, or would the Board of Agriculture and Fisheries, or some similar collection of bewhiskered bandits, sneak up on him and collar two thirds of the loot? It was certainly a problem, and after a bit of brooding he wrote off to the Commissioner and popped the question — disguising the reason for this request with some merry tale about an argument with a friend in Calcutta.'

Valerie laughed. 'I shouldn't have given the little man credit for so much imagination,' she commented.

'Oh, he had a certain amount of brain under that thatch,' said Charles. 'And this brings us to Christmas Eve: *"Noel! Noel!"*

'On Christmas Eve we stop at Ferrers's bungalow to get water, and John Shilto smells a rat — or, let us be accurate, about a ton of rotting oysters. I smelt it too, and it meant nothing more than nasty stink to C. Corbet-Carr. But John Shilto had been to Ceylon, and the odds are that he's smelt that smell before. This bit is only guess-work of course, but I imagine he snooped around and stumbled on the truth. Not the complete truth, but only half of it — probably due to the fact that Ferrers had a passion for oysters, and as his servants were a slovenly crew, there were certain to be a goodish few shells permanently cluttering up his backyards. But "pearl" shell is a bit different. And John Shilto spots that difference all right!

'Placing two and two together and adding them up to a total of six, he erroneously decides that Ferrers *hasn't* spotted it; and legging it down the path after us, pitches that yarn about the soothing effects of Christmas and how he yearns to clasp his cousin by the hand — which is not surprising, considering that to all intents and purposes the hand contains a fistful of pearls! But alas for day-dreams, Ferrers not only knows the difference between edible and pearl oysters, but he is sitting on both his hands and has every intention of continuing to do so.'

Valerie said: 'Yes, that bit seems all right. But it wasn't John who killed Ferrers. It was Leonard. How on earth did Leonard get on to it?'

'Cast your mind back, my angel,' urged Charles. 'Remember when we stopped at Ferrers's bungalow his boy told us that the Stocks had been in and had taken him on with them? The Stocks had the Dobbies on board, and Ferrers was coming to Ross to spend a couple of nights with them. Behold the peculiar workings of Fate! Mrs Dobbie wishes to shove in some inquiry about bedding — is he bringing his own or isn't he? — and it is a hot day and Ruby wants a lemon squash. So they all troop up to the bungalow where, according to Ruby, they find Ferrers in high spirits . . .

'They suggest that he comes on to the picnic with them and goes back with them to Ross afterwards. The idea is well received, and while he's packing a toothbrush, Leonard, who was always a bit of a snooper, takes a stroll round the back of the house to see if Ferrers is using a school of stranded whales to manure his plantation — which is what it smells like. Here he stumbles across a quantity of pearl shells, but they only appear to indicate that Ferrers likes oysters. And it is not until he pokes his nose into the shed behind the house that his brain begins to buzz a bit. You see, there was a diving-suit in that shed.'

'How do you know all this?' demanded Valerie.

'Ferrers's Burmese house-boy saw him rubber-necking around. And here Ruby takes up the tale. She says that Leonard came back looking rather excited, and as Ferrers was still absent and they were tired of waiting, they popped into his room to assist with the packing. Apparently they walked in without knocking and caught the master of the house on his hands and knees, with the matting rolled back from a corner of the floor——

'Leonard's arch inquiry as to whether he was looking for something produced a quite unaccountable explosion of wrath, and for a brief space high words buzzed briskly to and fro. Then Ruby appears to have suggested acidly that from the fuss he was making anyone would suppose he had something to hide, which pungent truth seems to have brought him to his senses, and he apologized all round and mumbled something about having seen a scorpion. He put back the matting and something rolled out of it. Ruby says she saw her husband put his foot on it, and when Ferrers's back was turned, pick it up and put it in his pocket. She meant to ask him about it afterwards but forgot. However we now know that it was a pearl, and that Leonard, who was no fool, was also putting two and two together, and unlike John Shilto, totting them up to the correct total.'

Valerie shifted restlessly: 'Do you mean to say,' she demanded, 'that Ferrers went off to Harriet leaving a lot of pearls lying around the house?'

'They weren't lying around. They were very neatly stowed away under a loose floorboard. And he wasn't looking for a pearl that he'd dropped. He can't have known that he'd dropped one. He was merely stowing away the swag, and the one Leonard picked up was just sheer bad luck as far as Ferrers was concerned.'

'And for that matter,' interrupted Copper, 'as far as Dan and John Shilto and Leonard himself were concerned.'

'Well, yes. If you care to look at it that way,' admitted Charles. 'Now let's think. What comes after that? Oh yes. Quarrel between the cousins Shilto and departure of sailing party.' He turned to Nick, who was meditatively blowing smoke rings at the chips of blue sky that gleamed through the network of green leaves overhead, and said: 'As a member of the sailing party, Mr Tarrent will now take over. *En avant, mon brave* — the floor is yours.'

Nick blew another smoke ring and said: 'You already know what happened when the storm hit us, and since we now have an accurate account of the murder, typed by Stock himself for the purpose of shoving the blame off on Shilto, we know how he spotted that his next-door neighbour was Ferrers — which proves that there was some sense in Copper's ring theory after all! The idea of knocking Ferrers on the head probably jumped into his mind then and there.

'He had been steering his boat and was still clutching the tiller, which had come adrift when they turned turtle. He wanged Ferrers over the back of the head with it, causing an impacted fracture which laid him out in one. Ferrers vanished abruptly, and Leonard decided that murder was child's play. But he hadn't seen that there was somebody on the other side of Ferrers — Rosamund Purvis!

'It's not surprising that he didn't spot her, for her head was a good deal nearer the water than Leonard's because she was holding on to the rudder, and she herself saw very little; what with smashing rain and splashed-up sea, and that howling wind. *But she saw enough to realize that someone had been deliberately murdered within two feet of her!*'

'Of course!' said Valerie suddenly. 'We ought to have realized from the way she behaved that something more than ordinarily nasty had happened. She was much too sensible and stolid a person to have reached that pitch of hysteria over a sailing spill and the fact that one of the party, whom she disliked, had been drowned.'

Nick flicked the stub of his cigarette at an inquisitive hermit crab, and leant back with his hands behind his head: 'I agree. But we can now understand why the poor woman was so worked up. You see, she knew that Ferrers hadn't been drowned. She knew he'd been murdered for she had actually seen it done: he'd been killed within a foot of her. But she had no idea who had done it! She says that she let go of that boat as though it was red hot, and after a few minutes crashed into what she hoped was another one. After that of course it was no use saying anything, as having once let go of the original boat, she had no means of finding out who else had been on it.'

'But what about Ronnie?' asked Valerie. 'Why was he so scared? Don't tell me *he* saw it done too!'

'No. He didn't see it done, but he got hold of the weapon.'

'The tiller? But I thought Leonard threw it away?'

'He did, but being wood it floated, and some time later it biffed into Ronnie, who grabbed it. The sea was getting rougher by this time and he was afraid of being washed off his boat, so he stuck the tiller through his braces with some hazy idea that it might help to keep him afloat if he lost his hold.

'It was still there when the forest-launch picked him up, and he says he hauled it out and dropped it on the floor of the cabin, and it wasn't until about half an hour later, when they'd given up the hunt for Ferrers and were heading home, that something about it caught his eye. There was a band of metal about the business end of that tiller, and something had got wedged between it and the wood. The sea had washed off all traces of blood, but it hadn't been able to dislodge that bit of flesh and a tuft of grey hair.'

'Ugh!' shuddered Valerie. 'How beastly!'

'Yes, it gave Ronnie a bit of a jar too. He picked the thing up to take a closer look at it and discovered that there not only *was* a ragged scrap of flesh and grey hairs wedged between the wood and the metal, but it was quite out of the question that it could have got there by accident. By that I mean the tiller could easily have biffed into someone while floating around loose, but unless it had been applied with a considerable amount of beef behind it, that scrap of flesh could not possibly have got wedged so far down the crack . . .

'Even then, the idea of deliberate murder didn't enter his head. He says he was too shaken up to think straight, and his immediate feeling being one of disgust, he heaved the tiller overboard. But after a bit, when his brain began to function, he started putting two and two together. With the result that at the dinner party that night there were actually three people present who knew that a murder had been committed: the one who had done it, and the two who knew that it *had* been done, and how, but had no idea who had pulled it off.'

'Hence Rosamund's acute attack of St Vitus's Dance,' put in Charles. 'Not a particularly comfortable feeling, having to sit around in a party one member of which you know to be a murderer, but without the least idea which one it is. I don't wonder she was a bit jumpy. Or Ronnie either! If I'd been in their shoes I should have locked myself in my own room and refused to move without a strong police guard. I rather imagine — though of course Ronnie denies it hotly — that his dear wife's firework-display made him suspect that she'd done in Ferrers herself.'

Valerie said: 'And I suppose Rosamund will also deny that she ever thought Ronnie did? Of course it's obvious she did from the way she insisted on going off to the hospital and wouldn't stay with us or go back with him. At least she could be certain that Truda hadn't done it!'

A brief silence followed on Valerie's last words, for they were thinking, all four of them, of the same thing. The dark hours that followed Rosamund's departure.

'How do you explain that?' asked Valerie at length. It was not necessary to ask what she was referring to.

'There isn't any explanation,' said Nick slowly. 'Unless you're prepared to accept Iman Din's.'

'You mean,' said Valerie with a shiver, 'that – that it *was* Ferrers who came back that night?'

'God knows,' said Nick. 'I'm not prepared to swear to it one way or another. It may only have been an optical illusion due to the lightning, and the noises may have been made by cats or bats or rats. On the other hand, after a brief stay in these islands I'm prepared to believe almost anything. And then of course there is always that time-worn remark of the late William Shakespeare's: *"There are more things in heaven and earth, Horatio, Than are dreamt of in your philosophy"* — and that goes for Copper's nightmares too! So let's leave it at that, shall we?'

'Yes, *do*,' said Charles cordially. 'And here I too propose to leave you and take one last, long, lingering splash into the sea before giving my attention to tea. Anyone coming with me? Right! I'll race you for the last marron glacé!'

The four rose simultaneously and raced down the beach into the water.

'I,' said Copper, shaking salt water out of her eyes, 'am going to get tea ready while you finish the story. Go on, Charles.'

Charles ceased rubbing his head with Valerie's towel, and looked indignant. 'Good Lord, Coppy, you don't want to hear any more, do you? I thought I had successfully glutted your appetite for meticulous detail.'

'Don't be silly, Charles! Of course you've got to finish it. Go on.' Copper vanished round the back of the tree where they had built a little fire of driftwood, while Charles took up the tale once more.

'We now come,' said Charles resignedly, 'to Christmas Day and the reappearance of Ferrers. Which you must admit was a shocking bit of bad luck for Leonard — Ferrers being washed up on that particular beach. Practically anywhere else, and he'd have arrived so badly bashed up by rocks that neither Dan nor anyone else would have spotted anything odd about him. But as it was, there were probably several things that made Dan brood a bit. What was it Vicarjee said, Nick?'

'Oh, just that a drowned man usually goes a sort of bluish colour, and as I remember, Ferrers was anything but blue. And that there should have been froth round his mouth and nose — or anyway inside his mouth, and something peculiar about "washerwoman's hands" that I didn't quite follow. Anyway, there were evidently enough signs missing to make Dan wonder if the man really had been drowned. He can't have spotted the crack on the back of the head, because he never turned the body over; and it wasn't easy to spot unless you were looking for it, for twenty-four hours in the water had washed it clean, and that mop of hair covered it up fairly thoroughly. But I suppose the more he thought about it, the more certain he became that there was something fishy about the whole thing, and — well you know the rest. He pushed off to see for himself...

'Here Leonard Stock reappears on the scene, and we are back again at guess-work. But this is what seems to have happened. Leonard must have got a nasty jar when Ferrers's body was reported to be present and correct, but a much nastier one when Val's father mentioned during dinner that night that he'd had a letter from Ferrers — possibly on the subject of pearls. As far as we can make out he must have slipped out that night and gone down to the office to hunt for it, but failed to find it. For the simple reason that John Shilto had got there first. In fact he was probably on his way back from the office when he saw Dan cross the ballroom, and realized what he was up to.

'After that he presumably slid back to his room, pulled a pair of pants on over his pyjamas, shoved on a raincoat, and left by the back staircase that leads out of his bathroom. He must have calmly stepped over the Indian guard, who, it now appears, was asleep for the greater part of the night with his mackintosh over his head.'

'What *I* don't understand,' said Copper, appearing abruptly from behind the tree with her eyes watering from the effects of wood smoke, 'is why Ruby didn't hear him; considering that he had to go through her room to get to the ballroom and the office.'

'Because, my sweet,' said Charles, 'Ruby's reported insomnia is pure baloney. She apparently sleeps like the proverbial log, and the insomnia racket was merely another method of annoying

Leonard and making a fuss over herself. In other words, it was a complete myth and Leonard knew it, though he found it convenient to play up to her sometimes. You remember how he told us the next day how badly Ruby had slept? Well, as it happened, though he wasn't aware of it, he was right for once.

'Ruby wasn't sleeping so well that night, and she *did* hear Leonard go out. *And* come back again! It puzzled her considerably. So much, in fact, that she didn't immediately rise up and inquire what the heck he meant by it, but after a bit of broöding got out of bed and went into his room to institute inquiries. He wasn't there, and what's more, the back door from his bathroom was open.

'Being Ruby, she seems to have jumped to the conclusion that he was carrying on with some woman, and she put on her dressing-gown and went out into the ballroom to investigate. I cannot suppose that she ever *really* expected to find either of you two holding her husband's hand in the verandah, but anyway she evidently had a good snoop round, and after leaving a chunk of feathers as a souvenir on Hindenburg, got back to her room and found there was still no Leonard.

'It was just about then that she began to get nervous. There was something a bit sinister in this silent popping to and fro, and she wondered if Leonard was beginning to suffer from softening of the brain? She says that she must have stayed awake for nearly an hour, waiting for him, and it was during that time that it occurred to her to go through his pockets and see if they didn't contain some betraying note suggestive of a rendezvous. She found something all right! Knotted into a corner of his handkerchief was a pearl.

'It was evidently a pretty good line in pearls, and to Ruby, "money talks". She seems to have had quite a chat with it that night, and the upshot was that she lay doggo and didn't see her husband again until after you two had broken the news about Dan.'

Valerie looked bewildered: 'But – but why did she behave so oddly when she heard about it? Copper and I thought that she must either have done it herself or seen it done. She very nearly had a fit!'

'Use your brain, my small angel. Put yourself in her place. She has been wondering what on earth her husband could have been up to on the previous night, and suddenly she hears that at just about the time that he was out and about, a murder was committed. I don't wonder she had a fit. If I'd been in her shoes, I'd have had a dozen. She obviously jumped to the instant — and perfectly correct — conclusion that her husband had done it——

'You know, I feel we all owe Ruby an apology if we've ever spoken slightingly of her brain. She's got brains all right — the cunning kind. Having flung you two out, she ties a wet towel round her head and thinks things over. Why was Dan killed? What was he doing in the Guest House? Why has Ferrers's body disappeared? The answers that we missed, she got in one. And the pearl gave her the clue to the murderer of Ferrers. Oh, she's clever all right, is our Ruby!'

Valerie said: 'Then it was the pearl that she threw away? Why?'

'Because she lost her nerve. She had no idea how many people knew about those pearls, or how long it would be before everyone knew and the motive for the murder begin to look obvious. She wasn't taking any risk of being mixed up in it herself, so she took that pearl and heaved it into the sea. And it must have broken her heart to do it. About a hundred and fifty quid in the ash can!'

'But what about John Shilto?' asked Copper. 'Why did he go about grinning to himself in that revolting manner? And why did he borrow that typewriter?'

'Taking your questions in order,' said Charles, 'he had good reason to be pleased with himself. He discovers that Ferrers is on to a fortune in pearls, and when he tries to get in on it, is told to go and boil his head. A few hours later Ferrers is dead and he, John, is the next of kin. As to your second question, Shilto senior, just to make assurance doubly sure, borrows a typewriter for the praiseworthy purpose of forging a will, purporting to be Ferrers's, leaving all his worldly goods to cousin John in the hope that he will forgive and forget. It was an extremely touching document, and in spite of the solemnity of the occasion we all laughed like a row of buckets when we read it. It was found in his coat pocket, and I imagine the main reason for his pinching that letter from the office was because he needed a signature to forge from.'

'What did we pack the tea in?' demanded Copper, reappearing for the second time: 'How did the letter get into Sir Lionel's room?'

'In that thing like an aluminium soap-dish,' said Valerie. 'Yes, how did it get there, Charles?'

'I expect one of the *khidmatgars* shoved it in with a spoon—— Oh, you mean the letter? Well, your father too evidently had his suspicions about John Shilto. He'd lent him his bathing-wrap to wear as a dressing-gown — that striped towelling one.'

Valerie said: 'Charles, what *are* you babbling about? What on earth has a bathing-wrap got to do with all this?'

'Only that there was a thread of striped towelling caught on the broken edge of the office desk that morning. That's why, when he found the letter was missing, your father didn't say anything for fear of putting Shilto on his guard. But he watched his opportunity and sneaked into the turret room later that day where, sure enough, he unearthed the letter. He left the envelope where he found it, and took the letter away to go through it later and try to discover why it had been pinched; hoping Shilto wouldn't spot that it had been removed. Result — we find the envelope in Shilto's room, and Copper finds the letter in your father's. Dense fog of confusion all round.

'As for John, if his fate hadn't already been decided upon before, it was definitely sealed when you told Leonard that the letter — you didn't say "envelope only" — had been discovered in John's room. Leonard didn't know exactly what Ferrers had written in that letter, but he guessed that it would be enough to put John Shilto on to the right track as regards the pearl bed, and shortly afterwards he pushed off to his house. Presumably in order to compose and type that "confession" and to plan out any odd details.

'He'd already pinched Ronnie's revolver; I suppose the discovery of Dan's body made him realize that he might at any moment have to pin the murders on someone else, and what better way of doing it than a third murder, dressed up to look like suicide? He went down to his own house at about a quarter to ten, taking an orderly with him for the look of the thing, and was away more than two hours, for it was roughly about midnight when he got back. And then of course Ruby played right into his hands.

'She was certain that he was the murderer, and she was scared to death. Here was a man whom she'd bullied and brow-beaten for years, and now he had killed two men in cold blood. She was in mortal terror for her own life, and she changed her room so that she could lock herself in for the night. But even then she daren't sleep, and although she heard the shot and the general uproar afterwards, she didn't stir from her room until morning.

'Well, that's about all that's new. The rest is pretty well what Leonard told you himself. Shilto had drunk too much and was out like a light, so it was money for jam. All that Leonard had to do was just stroll in about two a.m., switch on the small bedside light, pull out the mosquito net, pin that "confession" to the pillow, and, wearing a glove of Ruby's on his right hand, put the muzzle of the revolver to Shilto's head and pull the trigger . . .

'The moment the shot was fired he put the thing in Shilto's hand and closed his fingers round it, tucked in the mosquito net, snapped off the light and stepped out of the window. The whole thing can't have taken more than ten or fifteen seconds, and he knew he could count on a margin of at least half a minute after the firing of the shot. He'd even chosen his costume with care. That jazz-patterned thing of Ruby's was a perfect camouflage against the criss-cross patterns of the woodwork and the tree shadows on the wall. But he forgot about the mosquito net, and worst of all he forgot about that red stuff on the outside woodwork. Anything else you want to know?'

'Yes,' said Valerie promptly: 'What about Ronnie? Why was he in such a hopeless panic that last evening?'

Charles chuckled. 'Ah, that was Amabel! You see, two murders on two successive days had been too much for Ronnie's nervous system. He hadn't an inkling as to why they had been done, and then Amabel-the-Ever-Bright, by some curious fluke, produced the same theory that had already occurred to Copper.

'She made some fatuous remark about his ring while Ronnie was up at the hospital that afternoon, and then, remembering that Ferrers had also worn one, offered the suggestion that perhaps red rings were bad luck, and he might be killed too. A typically Amabelish remark, which might have passed over his head if she hadn't followed it up by adding that perhaps the murderer had mixed him up with Ferrers?

'At the time, Ronnie apparently laughed it off, because it sounded so ludicrously far-fetched that only Amabel's unfaltering determination to take the worst possible view of everything could have thought it up. But after a bit he began to wonder if perhaps there mightn't be something in it? He couldn't imagine why anyone — even John — should bother to kill Ferrers, and the thought that perhaps someone had meant to take a crack at him instead gave him no ordinary jar. And when on top of this he discovered, around five-thirtyish, that his revolver had taken unto itself legs, he went straight off the deep end and drank about half a bottle of whisky, neat. After that, there being no more alcohol in the house, he pushed off to continue the good work at the Club. Which is where we came on the scene.'

'I see,' said Valerie thoughtfully. 'Poor Ronnie! It shows he realizes that he's not all that popular if he could think up several reasons why someone should want to kill him.'

'Do him a lot of good,' said Charles callously. 'Nasty little philanderer! With any luck it will have given him such a heck of a jolt that he'll turn over a whole tree full of new leaves, and blossom into a Perfect Husband. In which case, if I may coin a phrase, *"Good will have come out of Evil"*.'

A meditative silence fell upon the group under the big tree, in which they could hear the friendly bubble of a boiling kettle and the snap and crackle of flames. 'Tea!' announced Copper, appearing round the tree trunk with an outsize teapot, her cheeks flushed from the fire.

24

The sun dipped below the rim of the horizon as they packed up the picnic-baskets and strolled back along the shore to the anchored *Jarawa.*

The retreating tide had transformed the wet sands into a curving silver mirror that reflected the colours that flooded the pale sea and pearly sky in waves of wonder. The far islands had lost their look of shimmering transparency and become silhouettes of violet velvet against the opal sea, and a dimness had crept over the flaming green of the jungle-clad hills; softening and blurring it with a blue, grape-like bloom.

Sky and sea turned slowly from shell-pink to primrose and gold, and then to lavender and green. And a full moon rose through the twilight above the quiet glassy floor as the little *Jarawa* throbbed her way home across the darkening sea past dim romantic shores and lonely reefs uncovered by the retreating tide, towards the tiny island of Ross that was already pricked with pin-points of light. Presently in the gathering twilight a single star gleamed palely; to be joined before long by another, and another, until the dim bowl of the sky was sequined with them: their brilliance dimmed by the growing glow of the moon.

Nick, lying prone upon the roof of the launch and following up a private train of thought, said: 'My ship gets in tomorrow.'

He did not add that it also left on the morrow, and that this was therefore his last evening in the Islands, for they already knew that.

For a moment no one answered him, and then Valerie said:

'Let's not go home. Let's take our supper to Corbyn's Cove. It's such a heavenly moon, and it's going to be a heavenly night.'

Charles gave his unqualified approval, and then observed, more practically, that they would have to return to Ross for food. 'All right,' agreed Valerie. 'We'll collect some from the Club, and ring up from there for a car to meet us at Aberdeen, and phone Dad and tell him we shan't be in to dinner. Then we shan't waste any time.'

'My practical Penelope!' murmured Charles approvingly. 'What an organizer the little woman will make! With her at my side, a Field Marshal's baton is as good as in my pants pocket.'

He relapsed into a contented silence which was broken by Copper's suggestion that they should add George and Amabel to the party. 'Heaven forbid!' said Charles, sitting up in alarm. 'I have no wish to spend the evening refereeing. Romance is what I yearn for; moonlight and tropic shores to delight the eye, and some of the more soupy and sentimental recordings of Bing Crosby to soothe the ear — plus caviare and Guinness to stay the inner man. An evening with Amabel and George in their present humour can only lead to high words and indigestion.'

Copper laughed, but stuck to her point with unexpected stubbornness.

'Oh, let 'em come, Charles,' said Nick lazily. 'Can't you see that Copper's gone all sentimental? She wants to try her fine Italian hand at playing Cupid, or Providence, or something of the sort, and reunite two sundered hearts. Isn't that right, Coppy?'

Copper flushed and frowned. 'You're too acute, Mr Tarrent, but I suppose you're right.'

'Of course I'm right. And I agree with you. Left to themselves, those two fat-heads will spend the remainder of George's term of penal servitude drooping about the island like a couple of bereaved earwigs and avoiding each other's eye. But if we plant them on a nice strip of moonlit beach, and then sneak off and leave them to it, they'll be publishing the banns by the time we get them home. I defy anyone to resist a night like this.'

Copper gave him an odd sideways look, but made no comment, and Charles said: 'Oh, all right. Let us sacrifice ourselves on the Altar of Romance. It can only lead to our being stung for an expensive plated fish-slice and/or toast-rack apiece, but what of it? *"It is a far, far better thing that we do now, than we have ever done before,"* — or words to that effect. Hullo, here we are!' The *Jarawa* bumped alongside the rough-and-ready structure that temporarily replaced the damaged jetty, and the picnickers disembarked.

An hour later, packed into the same aged Ford that had taken them up to Mount Harriet on that fateful Christmas Eve picnic, they were speeding along the moon-drenched road to Corbyn's Cove.

Nick, who was driving, had Copper and Amabel and an assortment of biscuit tins beside him, while Valerie, George and Charles shared the back seat in company with the picnic-basket, a variety of bottles and several travelling rugs. And it was, as Valerie had predicted, a heavenly night.

Moonlight striped the road with lines of white satin between the ebony shadows of the tree trunks, the air was warm and still and heavy with the scent of flowers, and the lovely, curving bay of Corbyn's Cove was a silver arc fringed with tall palms that leaned out across the sands, cutting clear patterns against the moon-washed sky and barring the sands with shadows, 'sable on argent'.

A gramophone provided undemanding music while a picnic supper was eaten on the dry sand in front of the palm-thatched bathing-huts, and though the records that had been borrowed at random from the Club proved to consist solely of dance-music, played by popular bands and sung by crooners, the slurred sweetness of the trite melodies that drifted out across the white beach and the glimmering bay were transmuted by the wizardry of the night into pure magic.

'George, dear,' begged Valerie charmingly, at the conclusion of the meal, 'would you be a darling and see if I brought a torch in the pocket of the car? It doesn't matter if it isn't there.'

George trotted off obediently, and having dispatched Amabel to the water's edge with a pile of dishes to be washed, the remaining four members of the party removed themselves hurriedly from the scene.

'Phew!' gasped Valerie, flinging herself down panting and breathless on a bank of sand at the far end of the beach. 'I haven't run like that since the days when for my sins I played right wing in the school hockey team! I wonder what Amabel will do when she finds we've left her to it?'

'You mean,' corrected Charles, 'when she finds that we've left her to George. Well, if she has a spark of intelligence — which I doubt — she will fling herself into his arms and say, "George darling, if you will only forgive me, I'll never touch fruit cup again!" But judging from what I know of the young dim-wit, she'll give her famous imitation of an underdone doughnut instead. And the same, I fear, will apply to George.'

Copper, who had been lying on her back gazing up at the moon, sat up and brushed the sand out of her hair. 'I will bet you ten rupees,' she said, 'that by the time we get back they will be closely entwined and rapturously forgiving each other. Any takers?'

Charles looked up at the moon and down the long curve of the beach, and finally out at the silver sea and the tiny black shape that was Snake Island. Somewhere behind them a frangipani tree was spilling its sweetness on the warn night air, and the sea murmured drowsily among the rocks of the point. Charles sighed. 'No,' he said. 'No takers. I believe Nick was right, and that to resist a night like this is beyond the power of mortal man — or mortal woman either. It isn't merely romantic, it *is* Romance; and with a capital R. Val, my star, hold my hand. I am inspired.' He breathed deeply and wriggled down on to his spine.

'Copper,' said Nick abruptly, 'do you mind if I return to this murder business for a moment?'

'Not particularly. Why?'

'Something that's been puzzling me. What was it you thought of that scared you so badly when Val was reading through the notes in the Mess?'

Copper did not answer, and after a short interval of oddly embarrassing silence Nick repeated his question. 'It was nothing important,' said Copper in a restrained voice.

'I'll tell you what it was,' said Valerie surprisingly.

'*Val!* But you don't——'

'Yes, I do. She thought Dad might have done it,' said Valerie calmly. 'Didn't you, Coppy?'

'Good God!' said Charles. 'Sir Lionel? *Why*, for Pete's sake?'

'Well I – I remembered the sail. There was someone else sailing in the harbour, and when we got home they told us that Sir Lionel had been out. You see all the time we'd been saying that there could only be seven suspects, because only seven other people were out in the bay when Ferrers was killed. But there were eight; and Sir Lionel was the eighth.'

'I see,' said Nick soberly. 'Poor Coppy! A nasty thought to take to bed with you. Why wouldn't you tell me?'

'I – I suppose I was afraid you'd — do something. And he was Val's father and—— Oh, I don't know. I was scared silly. I worked it all out how he could have done it, and I thought perhaps that explained why Ronnie, who obviously knew something, wouldn't tell; because he wouldn't be believed. Then when I found the letter, I nearly went crazy. Val, I do apologize: I must have been crackers!'

'Nonsense, darling. It was very intelligent of you. You notice that the fat-head by my side never spotted the significance of that other sail? I did though, and it gave me a few nasty moments. But then it was different for me, because of course I *knew* he couldn't possibly have done it. Charles, darling, may I use your arm as a pillow?'

'Certainly, my sweet. All that I have is yours — even after that last dirty crack at my expense. Nick, chuck me over a cigarette. Thanks.'

They settled themselves comfortably in a row with their backs to a tide-driven bank of sand, looking out across the shining sea in a silence deep with content, while the soft murmur of the waves and the monotonous trilling of the cicadas among the trees on the hillside behind them sang a song more sweet than that of any night club crooner.

'Does anyone remember,' said Nick, breaking a long and peaceful silence, 'what Copper said this afternoon about only a lot of time, or a lot of happiness, laying the ghost of the late unpleasantness on Ross?'

'Umm,' said three voices, in drowsy affirmative. 'Why?'

'I have been brooding,' said Nick, 'upon the latter half of that remark.'

He relapsed into silence.

'Well?' inquired Valerie curiously.

'Well, what?'

'Well, go on.'

'Oh — only that the second proviso appears to me to be more attractive than the first. I don't think I particularly want to wait until I'm middle-aged before I stop waking up with nightmares and dreaming I'm back among the murderers.'

Valerie laughed softly. 'In that case, why not try the second method?'

Nick twisted round to face her. 'Then I take it that you agree with Copper as to its reliability? I wouldn't like to go in for it, only to find myself still haunted by grim spectres.'

'Speaking for myself,' said Valerie, 'the remedy has my fullest approval. And in partnership with this slumbering object on my right, I propose to put it to the test in the near future. Signed: Valerie Anne Masson.'

'What about you, Charles? Do you endorse this damsel's view?'

'I'll endorse anything tonight,' said Charles. 'You only have to show me the dotted line.'

Nick said: 'Oh well — in that case——' He lay back against the sandbank and clasped his hands behind his head.

'*"He either fears his fate too much, Or his deserts are small"*—' quoted Valerie wickedly.

'What's that? Oh, of course; Jamie Graham. *"That puts it not unto the touch, To win or lose it all."* I wonder. Copper?'

'Yes?'

'Will you marry me?'

'*What!*'

Three figures out of the four were no longer prone, but sitting bolt upright. Nick continued to lie on his back and gaze at the moon.

'*What* did you say?' demanded Copper.

'You 'erd!' said Charles.

'I asked you if you'd marry me,' repeated Nick obligingly.

'Oh!' said Copper.

'Charles,' said Valerie firmly, 'I think this is where you and I fade rapidly away behind a palm tree.'

'Not on your life, my sweet! I am intensely interested. Besides, we men must stick together. How do I know that Nick won't shortly be needing my shoulder to sob on or my services as Best Man? Go on, Coppy; a fair answer to a fair question. We hang upon your words.'

'Don't be absurd!' flashed Valerie, jumping to her feet. 'Nick, you ought to be ashamed of yourself!'

'Don't go,' said Copper surprisingly. 'I think I may need a bit of support too.'

'Of course she does,' approved Charles. 'Sit down, Val, my treasure. Go on, Coppy. I demand on behalf of my client that he shall be put out of his misery. A plain straightforward Yes or No, Miss Randal.'

'I think,' said Copper thoughtfully, 'that there are one or two questions I'd like to ask first.'

'Oh, that's all right,' said Charles, 'the man's stiff with money, if you're wondering if he can keep you in Chocky-Bix. In fact, his yearly income, quite apart from the salary donated to him by a benign Government, is of such proportions as to make my own not-too-miserable pittance look like a trouser button in the collection plate. My advice to you is grab him quickly before he regains his senses, because——'

He subsided abruptly with his mouth full of sand.

'That'll hold him for a bit,' said Valerie serenely. 'Go on, Coppy. What is it you want to know?'

Copper turned to look down upon Mr Tarrent's recumbent figure: 'Nick——'

'Darling?'

'Did you mean to ask me that question tonight?'

'No,' said Nick unhesitatingly. 'To be frank, I had every intention of leaving without asking it.'

'I thought so,' nodded Copper. 'Then why didn't you?'

'Because I found that I had no alternative between that and living out a ghost-haunted existence.'

'Don't!' said Copper sharply. 'I wasn't being funny. I want the real reason.'

'Neither was I. And that is the real reason. I wasn't referring to Leonard's victims, sweet. The ghost would have been yours, and I should have been persistently haunted by the fact that I'd once seen the Real Thing, and failed to grab it.'

'Love-fifteen to my client,' said Charles, spitting out sand.

'Shut up, Charles!' said Valerie.

Copper said gravely: 'Why were you so angry that afternoon in the Mess?'

Nick did not answer for a few minutes, and in the clear moonlight Copper saw the shadow of a frown etch itself between his eyebrows. Presently he said: 'I wasn't only angry. I was blind furious, if you want to know. You had thought up so many things against me that I believed you really thought I might have done it. And it hit me pretty hard to realize that I ranked so low in your estimation that you could even suspect me of murdering one of my own friends. I was so damned angry I could cheerfully have strangled you!'

Copper said: 'I was only trying to warn you.'

'I know. Though I have my suspicions of that *"only"*. I believe you intended it as a slap in the eye as well. Didn't you?'

Copper flushed, but she was too honest to beg the question. 'Yes.'

Nick laughed shortly. 'Well, you succeeded all right. I've seldom had a worse one. Any more questions?'

'Two more. When did you meet Ferrers Shilto before, and why did you keep quiet about it?'

Charles sat up again with some violence. 'Do you mean to tell me,' he demanded, 'that you've been concealing a skeleton in your closet all this time? Good God! — if I'd known you were holding out on us I'd have arrested you without a qualm!'

'I'm sure you would,' said Nick dryly. 'Perhaps that was what I was afraid of. How did you know, Coppy?'

'I told you. I saw the labels on Ferrers's luggage, and you told me yourself where you'd been staying. The times fitted. But it was just a shot in the dark — that you might have met him. And when I saw that it had gone home, and you wouldn't explain, I was frightened.'

'May I ask you something before I answer this? Why do you want to know?'

Copper considered the question for a moment.

'Partly curiosity, I suppose. But mostly because it's the only missing piece of the story. I know everything else except that, and once it's explained, the story is complete.'

'The same,' said Charles, 'goes for me — with the accent heavily on the curiosity. Produce your skeleton.'

Nick pulled out another cigarette and lit it with some deliberation before replying. Then he lay back again, and looking up at the black patterns of the palm fronds against the moonlit sky, spoke in a voice that was entirely without expression — slowly, as though he were choosing his words: 'I met Ferrers Shilto while I was in Calcutta. We were both stopping at the same hotel. I — there was a friend of mine in Calcutta; a woman. She was attractive and popular and — married . . .

'To cut out a lot of unnecessary narrative, she was seen leaving my room at four o'clock one morning by the late unlamented Ferrers. He happened, unfortunately, to be occupying the room opposite mine, and recognized the lady. She and her husband were very well known. Next morning he went round to her house and tried his hand at a little light blackmail. He may have been finding it difficult to get cash down for the pearls — I don't know. Anyway he had no success, for the lady, doubtless remembering the masterly tactics of the late Duke of Wellington under similar circumstances, replied that he could publish and be damned, since it would be a case of her word against his.

'If he'd had the sense to leave it there, he might have got off scot-free. But he came to me and suggested that I might find it advisable to pay up. Disregarding the old school tie, and elderly as he was, I tore him into small shreds and threw the remains into the street. I also told the Manager that he had been attempting to blackmail me, and as he hadn't paid his bill, he was requested not to return. And — that's about all. I had no idea where he came from or where he had gone to, and it gave me no ordinary jolt to find him on the lawn at Mount Harriet. My only consolation is that it must have given him a much worse one!'

Nick stopped speaking, but he did not look at Copper.

'Um,' said Charles thoughtfully. 'A bit tricky for you all round.'

'Damnably,' agreed Nick. 'I hope now you appreciate my reasons for suppressing that information.'

'Like hell I do! I wouldn't like it to be widely known that I'd been recently threatened with a particularly nasty form of blackmail and had soundly beaten up the blackmailer, who was later discovered murdered. People might begin putting two and two together and making the answer thirteen.'

'Exactly,' agreed Nick. 'And after all, except for Dan I was the only stranger in your midst and, as Copper kindly pointed out, no one really knew anything about me. In addition to that, there appeared to be no motive for the thing. *"Cui bono?"* is apt to be shouted a bit after a murder, and I imagine *"the victim of blackmail"* is as good an answer as any. So I kept my mouth shut and hoped for the best; both for my own sake and——'

He stopped abruptly and frowned.

'You mean Copper,' said Charles, '— it's no good kicking me, Val, my sweet. We all know what he means. It's quite obvious to one and all that half the reason he kept his mouth shut was because he was afraid Copper would give him the bird on receipt of said information. Isn't that right, old man?'

Nick remained silent, and after a moment or two Copper said: 'Were you in love with her?'

He did not reply for so long that Valerie began to think that he had either not heard the question, or did not intend answering it. But Nick had both heard it and realized that it must be answered. Only he dared not answer it quickly or thoughtlessly. Instinct warned him that if he said 'No,' he would lose Copper. Only the truth would serve him now. But what exactly was the truth? *Had* he been in love with that electric, red-haired lady? Certainly she had been very fascinating, and he had been quite willing to be fascinated. Even more certainly, she had ended by falling in love with him. But for himself the attachment had never gone very deep, and despite her obvious wish for something more serious, had remained no more than a surface affair of froth and sparkle.

Even that fatal four a.m. visit had been no more than a mild indiscretion. They had been to a dance at the Saturday Club, and afterwards had driven to Tollygunge to bathe. Judith had offered to drive him home, and on dropping him at the hotel had invited herself in for a drink. It was late and he had been sleepy. Too sleepy to be sensible, and not sleepy enough to appear ungallant. Judith had stayed for fifteen minutes, during which time he had yawned at least fifteen separate times. She had laughed, and told him that his manners were abominable, kissed him in the middle of the fifteenth yawn, sighed, and left him — to walk straight into Ferrers Shilto who was returning after an equally late night.

But would Copper believe that? Nick had never cared before what anyone believed of him, but now ... Copper's question was still waiting.

He said slowly: 'I was very fond of her. She was beautiful and intelligent and amusing; and a good companion. Perhaps if you'd asked me that question a week or so ago, I might have said "Yes", because I didn't know then what being in love meant.'

Copper said: 'What does it mean?'

'I'll answer that one,' said Charles firmly. 'Shut up, Nick! I arrived at the same fence a few months ago, and so I knew the answer before you did. He means, Coppy, that even though he had no intention of getting engaged or married, or otherwise entangled, and had firmly intended to dodge it or die in the attempt, he has discovered — probably with disgust — that the light of Reason has been put out and that he has been forced, against every prompting of intelligence, common sense and will-power, to chuck himself and his future at your feet, because he knows that unless you can be persuaded to pick them up, neither the one nor the other will ever be of any value to him again.'

Charles paused for a brief moment, and lifting Valerie's hand, touched it lightly to his check and continued more slowly: 'He knows, too, that even if you won't pick them up, the fact that you once touched them will be the only really worth-while thing that ever happened to them.'

Copper said: 'Is that what it means, Nick?'

'Yes,' said Nick. 'It means, too, that even if you turn me down and I never see you again, I shall still go on loving you.'

'The whole thing in a nutshell!' said Charles. 'A masterly summing up, combining sentiment, sincerity and a touch of pathos with a manly independence of spirit. Come on, Caroline Olivia, the court awaits your verdict. Make it snappy!'

Copper sighed and looked up at the moon. 'But Charles darling, I can't rush into this. How do I know that I should like spending half my life in places like Malta and Gibraltar and Jamaica and Java and Plymouth and——'

'Listen!' interrupted Charles firmly. 'Arithmetic, and not Geography, should be the key-note when selecting a suitable mate. My client possesses large quantities of cash, cleanliness and charm, so let us have no more of this waffling. Do you or do you not take this man for better or for worse? My advice is a hurried affirmative before the offer is withdrawn.'

'Do I, Val?' asked Copper.

'I think so, dear,' said Valerie tranquilly.

'The casting vote,' sighed Copper. 'The Ayes have it.'

'Val,' said Nick, 'would you mind removing your property further up the beach? In about ten seconds I propose to kiss this girl with considerable fervour, and I should prefer to do so without helpful instructions from Charles.'

'Darling,' said Charles, 'the man is an ungrateful polyp, and I deeply regret having tendered him my valuable advice during the recent crisis. However, there is an excellent clump of palms on our left, where, under the cover of darkness, I can get engaged to you all over again. Let us withdraw the hem of our garment.'

They drifted away down the moonlit beach.

Mr Hurridge, Deputy Commissioner and confirmed bachelor, had driven out to Corbyn's Cove to smoke an after-dinner cigar and meditate upon the recent dark happenings on Ross.

He would have to write a report. Several reports in fact. It was all very terrible — dreadful! A shocking affair. His deepest sympathy went out to all on Ross who had endured those days and nights of terror: in particular the young people, over whose youthful lives this dark affair would cast an ineradicable shadow. He pictured them sitting in the Commissioner's house, silent and subdued; awed by their recent contact with swift and violent death. Graver, older . . . I wonder, thought Mr Hurridge, if it would be considered indelicate if I were to arrange a picnic — say next week? A little soon after these recent bereavements perhaps, but I feel that they should not be allowed to mope.

He had been somewhat taken aback, on arrival at the Cove, to find the Ford parked among the palm trunks, but had decided that it must be Mrs Stock — come to be alone with her shame and sorrow.

Mr Hurridge could observe no lonely figure walking by the sad seashore, but on approaching the bathing-huts with the intention of seating himself on one of the wooden benches that stood outside, he became aware of voices and paused involuntarily. The conversation was hardly edifying:

'It was all my fault, darling!'

'No it wasn't; it was mine, darling!'

'Oh no, darling! I was horrid!'

'You weren't horrid, darling!'

'Anyway, it was really all that horrid Rosamund's fault — it just goes to show, doesn't it?'

'Then you do forgive me?'

'Oh George!'

'Oh Amabel!'

Mr Hurridge averted his head and hurried past. He was profoundly shocked. It seemed — under the circumstances — little short of indelicate that young Amabel Withers and George Beamish should drive out to Corbyn's Cove with no better object than to indulge in sentimental reconciliations, when after all . . .

He slowed his steps and made for a patch of shadow where a fallen palm trunk, victim of the recent storm, offered an inviting seat.

It was, alas, already occupied.

'We'll be married as soon as I can get home. That'll be about April. Oh Val, darling — only four months!'

'Oh Charles! Oh bliss!'

Mr Hurridge felt like an elderly maiden-lady who has discovered a burglar under the bed.

It was indecent! It was outrageous! Was *Murder* — three murders no less, not to mention one accidental though well-deserved death! — a matter of so little moment that the young people of Ross could thus ebulliently discuss love up and down the Islands?

'Disgusting!' said Mr Hurridge, and coughed with loud disapproval.

He decided to pause for meditation and a quick cigar upon the sandbank at the far end of the beach. But it was not to be. Mr Hurridge's luck was out and Romance was definitely in.

'There's still one thing I forgot to ask you. Do you love me, Coppy?'

'Oh Nick!'

'Oh *damn!*' said Mr Hurridge.

He wheeled about, tripped over a piece of driftwood, dropped his unlighted cigar upon the sand, stooped to retrieve it and was sharply bitten by a crab, and abandoning it, departed blasphemously down the beach — a misogynist for life.

As Amabel would doubtless have said, 'It just goes to show, doesn't it?'

Death in Kashmir

For
GOFF
and the delectable valley.
With all my love

CONTENTS

'Who has not heard of the- - - - -
vale of Cashmere . . . ?'

Thomas Moore, *Lalla-Rookh*

AUTHOR'S NOTE

When I first began to write murder mysteries — 'whodunits' — I would try to write at least two thousand words every day: Sundays excepted. If I managed to exceed that, I would credit the extra number to a day on which I knew that some unavoidable official duty or social engagement would prevent me writing at all. It was my way of keeping track of the length of each chapter and controlling the overall length of the book, and at the end of each day I would make a note against the date of the number of words I had written and considered worth keeping. Which is why I have on record the exact day and date on which I first met my future husband, Goff Hamilton, then a Lieutenant in that famous Frontier Force Regiment, the Corps of Guides.

It was on a Monday morning and the date was 2 June 1941, and I happened at that time to be living in Srinagar, the capital city of Kashmir, which is one of the loveliest countries in the world. Goff, who was up on short leave, fishing, had called in to give me a letter that he had promised a mutual friend to deliver by hand. I presume I wrote something that day, since I was actually at work on my daily quota when he arrived. But there is no entry against that date — or against a long string of dates that followed.

The manuscript stopped there, halfway through a chapter. Because what with getting married, having two children, working for the WVS and also for a propaganda magazine, and living in a state of perpetual panic for fear that Goff would not get back alive from Burma, there was no time to spare for writing novels.

It was not until the war was over and the British had quit India, the Raj become no more than a memory and Goff and I and the children were in Scotland, living in an army quarter in Glasgow and finding it difficult to make ends meet, that I remembered that I could write, and decided that it was high time I gave the family budget a helping hand.

I therefore dug out that dog-eared and dilapidated student's pad in which I had begun a book that I had tentatively entitled *There's a Moon Tonight*, and read the two and a half chapters I had written during that long-ago springtime in Kashmir.

It didn't read too badly, so I updated it to the last months of the Raj instead of the first year of the war, and when I had finished it, posted it in some trepidation to a well-known firm of literary agents in London, who fortunately for me, liked it. I was summoned to London, where I was handed over to one of their staff, a Mr Scott, who was considered the most suitable person to deal with my work on the grounds that he himself 'knew a bit about India'. He turned out to be the Paul Scott who had already written three books with an Indian setting, and would one day write *The Raj Quartet* and *Staying On*, and as he became a great friend of mine, my luck was clearly in that day. I hope that it stays in, so that readers will enjoy this story of a world that is gone and of a country that remains beautiful beyond words, despite mankind's compulsive and indefatigable efforts to destroy what is beautiful!

I would also like to mention here that having recently seen the TV versions of Paul's *Jewel in the Crown* and my own *Far Pavilions*, and been constantly irritated by hearing almost every Indian word mispronounced (some even in several different ways!), I have decided to let any readers who may be interested learn, by way of a guide which follows, the pronunciation that my characters would have used in *their* day. In some cases no syllable is accented, in others the syllable on which the accent falls will be in italic type, and the rest in roman. The spelling will be strictly phonetic because too many words were not pronounced as they were spelt, e.g. *marg* (meadow), though spelt with an 'a', was pronounced *murg*! And so on . . . Thus leading to considerable confusion!

PRONUNCIATION GUIDE

The right-hand column shows how each word should be pronounced: the stress is on the italicized syllable(s).

Apharwat	Apper-waat
Banihal	Bunny-harl
Baramulla	Bara-*mooler*
Bulaki	Bull-*ar*-ki
bunnia	bun-nia
chaprassi	ch'*prassi*
chenar	ch'*nar*
Chota Nagim	*Choter* N'geem
chowkidar	*chowk*-e-dar
Dāl	Darl
feringhi	fer-*ung*-ghi
ghat	gaut
Gulmarg	Gul-*murg* (Gul rhymes with pull)
Hari Parbat	Hurry *Purr*-but
Hazratbal	*Huz*-raatbaal
Jhelum	*Gee*-lum
khansamah	khan-*sah*-ma
khidmatgar	kit-ma-gar
Khilanmarg	Killan-murg
maidan	*my*-darn
mānji	*maan*-jee
marg	murg
memsahib	*mem*-sarb

Nagim Bagh	N'geem Barg
Nedou	*Nee*-doo
pashmina	*push*-mina
Peshawar	P'shower
Rawalpindi	R'l'*pindi*
sahib	sarb
shikara	shic-*karra*
Srinagar	Sr'in-*nugger*
Takht-i-Suliman	Tucked-e-*Sul*-eman
Tanmarg	Tun-*murg*
tonga	*tong*-ah

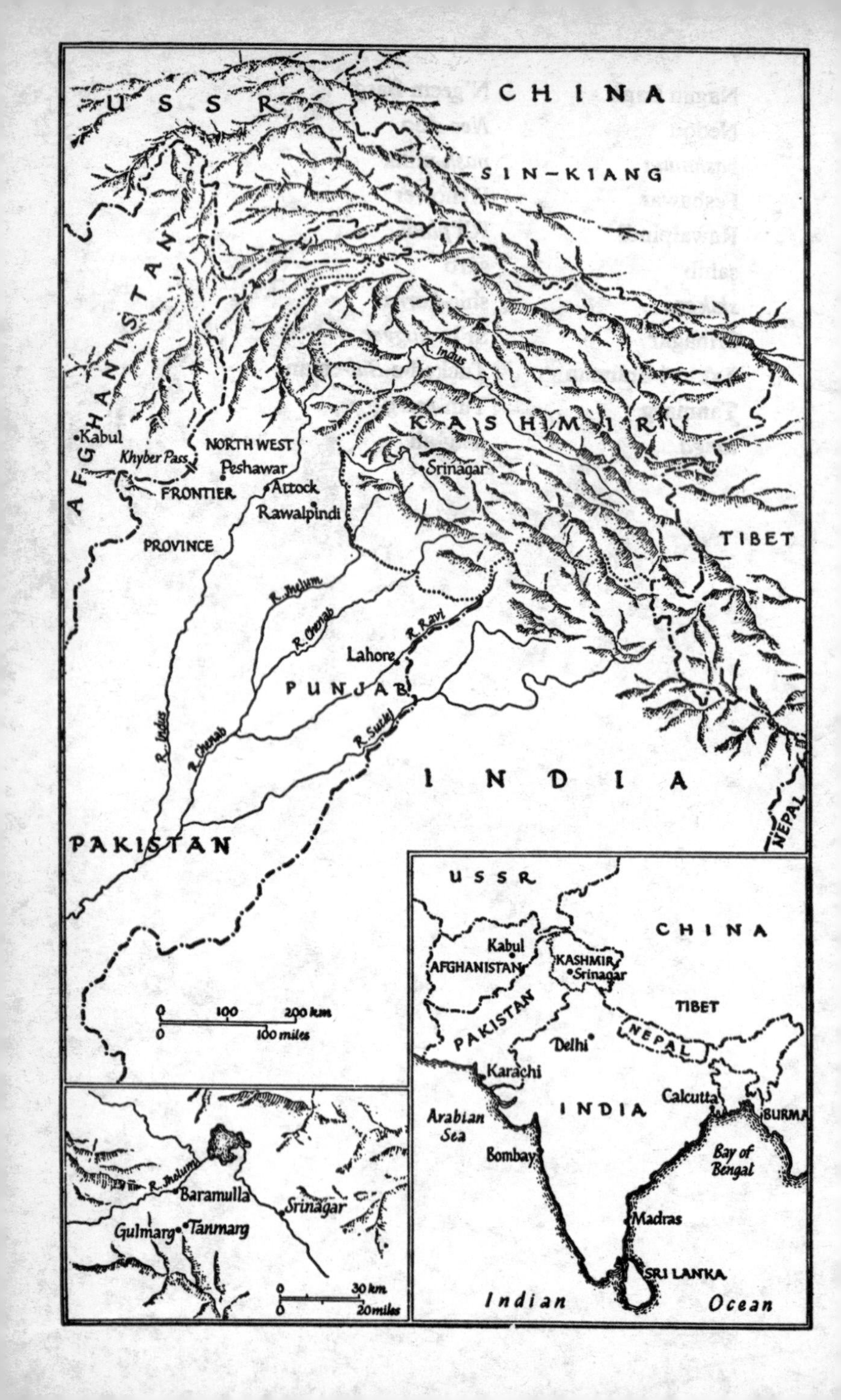

U S S R
CHINA
SIN-KIANG
AFGHANISTAN
R. Indus
KASHMIR
Kabul
Khyber Pass
NORTH WEST
Peshawar
FRONTIER
Attock
Rawalpindi
Srinagar
PROVINCE
TIBET
R. Jhelum
R. Chenab
R. Ravi
Lahore
PUNJAB
R. Sutlej
R. Indus
R. Chenab
INDIA
NEPAL
PAKISTAN
0 100 200 km
0 100 miles
R. Jhelum
Baramulla
Srinagar
Gulmarg
Tanmarg
0 30 km
0 20 miles
USSR
CHINA
Kabul
AFGHANISTAN
KASHMIR
Srinagar
PAKISTAN
TIBET
Delhi
NEPAL
Karachi
Calcutta
Arabian Sea
INDIA
BURMA
Bombay
Bay of Bengal
Madras
SRI LANKA
Indian Ocean

Part I

GULMARG

'The white peaks ward the passes, as of yore,
The wind sweeps o'er the wastes of Khorasan; –
But thou and I go thitherward no more.'

Laurence Hope, *Yasin Khan*

1

Afterwards Sarah could never be quite sure whether it was the moonlight or that soft, furtive sound that had awakened her. The room that except for the dim and comforting flicker of a dying fire had been dark when she fell asleep was now full of a cold, gleaming light. And suddenly she was awake . . . and listening.

It was scarcely more than a breath of sound, coming from somewhere outside the rough pinewood walls that divided that isolated wing of the rambling hotel into separate suites. A faint, irregular rasping, made audible only by the intense, frozen silence of the moonlit night.

A rat, thought Sarah, relaxing with a small sigh of relief. It was absurd that so small a thing should have jerked her out of sleep and into such tense and total wakefulness. Her nerves must be getting out of hand. Or perhaps the height had something to do with it? The hotel stood over eight thousand feet above sea-level, and Mrs Matthews had said——

Mrs Matthews! Sarah's wandering thoughts checked with a sickening jar as though she had walked into a stone wall in the dark.

How was it that awakening in that cold night she had been able, even for a few minutes, to forget about Mrs Matthews?

Less than a week ago, in the first days of January, Sarah Parrish and some thirty-odd skiing enthusiasts from all parts of India had arrived up in Gulmarg, that cluster of log cabins that lies in a green cup among the mountains of the Pir Panjal, more than three thousand feet above the fabled 'Vale of Kashmir'. They had come to attend what was, for most of them, their last meeting of the Ski Club of India. For this was 1947, and the date for India's independence — the end of the Raj and the departure of the British — had been set for the following year.

Beautiful mountain-locked Kashmir was one of India's many semi-independent princely states which, by treaty, were in effect 'protectorates' of the Government of India, ruled over by hereditary Maharajahs, Nawabs, Rajas or Ranas who were 'advised' by a British Resident. And though access to this particular State was not easy, since it is walled in on every side by high mountains, it has been regarded for centuries as an ideal hot-weather retreat from the burning plains — the Great Moguls, in their day, making the journey on elephants, horses or in palanquins.

The British had followed where the Moguls led, and made it one of their favourite playgrounds. But because the State would not permit them to buy or own land in Kashmir, they had taken to spending their holidays there in houseboats on its lovely lakes, in tents among the pines and deodars, or in rented log cabins in Gulmarg, which is little more than a grassy bowl among the mountains that overlook the main valley. A bowl that some homesick Briton (presumably a Scotsman?) converted into a series of admirable golf-courses, and which during the winter and early spring is blanketed deep in snow.

Every year, during this latter period, the Ski Club of India would hold one or more of its meetings in Gulmarg. And on these occasions the rambling, snow-bound, summer hotel would be opened to accommodate members and their friends. This year had been no exception, and anyone and everyone who could possibly manage to get there had done so. The weather had been perfect and the party a gay one: until, with shocking suddenness, tragedy had struck.

Mrs Matthews — grey-haired, sociable, delightful — had been picked up dead from among the snow-covered boulders near the foot of the Blue Run.

She had not been missed until late afternoon on the previous day, as dusk was falling and the skiers converging on the welcoming lights of the hotel — straggling up from the nursery slopes, or down from the snowfields of Khilanmarg that lie high above Gulmarg, where the pine forests end. Even then it had been supposed that she was in her room.

She was there now. They had brought her back to it and laid her on the bed, and Sarah wondered, with a little prickling of the scalp, if the comparative warmth of the narrow, pineboard room had been sufficient to thaw the dreadful stiffness from those frozen, contorted limbs.

A terrified coolie, bringing firewood to the hotel, had stumbled upon that sprawling figure in the dusk, and Sarah had seen her carried in: a grotesque jumble of widespread arms and legs that could not be bent or decently straightened.

Sarah had liked Mrs Matthews — everyone liked Mrs Matthews — and the unexpected sight of that rigid corpse had filled her with such shuddering nausea that, unable to face the prospect of food, she had retired early and supperless to bed and had taken a long time to fall asleep. Now all at once she was wide awake; and with little prospect of dropping off again while her room remained bright with moonlight, and that faint rasping sound frayed at her nerves.

Strange that there should be rats up here in winter, with the snow lying deep for so many months and the huts shuttered and deserted. Hadn't she once read somewhere that they could not stand extreme cold? Perhaps Kashmiri rats were different ... Sarah tossed and turned restlessly, and wondered irritably what had possessed her to draw back the curtains? At the time, it had seemed pleasant to lie and look out at the snow and the night sky, but she should have realized that sooner or later the moon would shine into the verandah and reach the window of her room.

Earlier in the evening, because the atmosphere of her small bedroom had seemed close and stuffy after the crisp night air outside, she had half opened her bathroom window and left wide the communicating door between the two rooms. But the logs that had blazed in the fireplace a few hours ago were now only a handful of grey ash, and the room was very cold.

The prospect of getting out of bed in order to draw the curtains and close the bathroom window was not a pleasant one and Sarah shivered at the thought. Yet now, in addition to feeling cold, she was also beginning to feel hungry and regret foregoing her supper, and there was a tin of biscuits on the bathroom shelf. She could fetch a handful and close the window and the bedroom curtains at the same time. Reaching out a reluctant hand for the fur coat that was doing duty as an extra blanket, she huddled it about her shoulders and slid out of bed. Her soft, sheep-skin slippers were ice-cold to her shrinking toes, but they made no sound as she crossed the room and went through the open doorway into the bathroom.

The small, wooden-walled suites in this wing of the hotel were all alike, each consisting of a bed-sitting room, plus a narrow, primitive bathroom, the back door of which opened onto two or three shallow wooden steps that led down to a path used only by those hotel servants whose duty it was to clean the bathrooms or to carry up hot water for the small tin bathtubs.

Sarah did not bother to switch on the light, for the open window allowed the cold glimmer of moonlight on snow to fill the unlit bathroom with a pale glow that was more than enough to see by. But she had taken no more than two steps when she stopped short, listening to that barely audible sound that she had supposed to be the gnawing of a rat. It was clearer now — and it could not possibly be a rat, because rats did not gnaw metal. Sarah stood quite still, holding her breath and straining to hear. There it was again! So soft a sound that had it not been for her opened door and window she would never have heard it. The stealthy rasp of a file on metal.

This time it was followed by the faint rattle of a window-frame;

though there was no breath of wind. And suddenly she realized what it meant. Someone outside was trying, with infinite caution, to file through the fastening of a window. Not her own, for that stood open. Whose, then?

The room to her left was unoccupied, and since the one immediately beyond it belonged to Major McKay of the Indian Medical Service, who held strong views on the value of fresh air and boasted of sleeping with every window wide in all weathers, it could not be either of those. The room on her right was occupied by a Miss Rushton, a girl in her mid-twenties, while in the one beyond it, between Miss Rushton's room and one occupied by a Colonel Gidney, lay the body of Mrs Matthews.

Sarah shivered at the thought of that locked room and its silent occupant, and clenching her teeth to stop them chattering, moved cautiously forward until, standing flat against the wall, she could peer out obliquely from her half-opened window. A wide bar of shadow lay across the slope and the path below, but beyond it the snow sparkled brilliantly in the moonlight, thinning the shadows with reflected light so that she could see quite clearly the rickety wooden steps that led up to Janet Rushton's bathroom door.

There was someone standing just beyond those steps: a shapeless figure whose hands, showing dark against the weather-bleached woodwork, were busy at the level of Miss Rushton's window. There was also a metal object lying on the window-sill — she could see it gleam in the reflected moonlight. A jemmy, perhaps? or some improvised crowbar?

Sarah's immediate reaction was one of pure rage. Mrs Matthews not twelve hours dead, and already some ghoulish coolie from the village, or a dishonest hotel servant, was breaking in to steal the dead woman's belongings! Because of course it must be that, and the would-be thief had merely mistaken the window, since Janet Rushton, the girl in the next room, wore no jewellery and appeared to have brought little more than a change of skiing clothes and slacks with her. Which made it highly unlikely that anyone bent on random theft would take the trouble to file through the catch of her window. Particularly when she, Sarah — an obviously more profitable victim! — had obligingly left hers wide open!

She decided to shout and bang upon the window, confident that this would be more than enough to scare any thief away. But even as she opened her mouth to carry out this laudable intention, the figure turned its head and her shout died unuttered: for it had no face . . .

For a moment it seemed to Sarah that her heart stopped beating. Then in the next second she realized that she was looking at someone who was wearing a mask: a hood of some drab material that completely covered the wearer's head and neck, and had holes cut in it for eyes. In almost the same instant she realized that the object lying upon the window-sill, so near to those purposeful hands, was a gun. And all at once she was afraid. Afraid as she had never been before in her short twenty-two years of life.

This was no ordinary thief. No pilfering Kashmiri would wear a mask or carry firearms. Besides, of what use were such precautions against a dead woman? Then it *must* be Miss Rushton's room that was his objective——

Sarah backed away from the window inch by inch and regained her bedroom. Her breath was coming short as though she had been running, and it seemed to her as though the thudding of her heart must be as audible as drumbeats in the silence. Janet Rushton . . . she must warn Janet . . . Her cold fingers fumbled with the handle of the verandah door and managed to turn it. I mustn't run, she thought: I must go quietly. I mustn't make a noise . . . She forced herself to ease open the door slowly so that it made no sound.

The narrow wooden verandah that ran the length of the wing was bright with moonlight, and outside it a sea of snow glistened like polished silver, blotched by the dark bulk of the main hotel buildings. In front the ground fell steeply away until it reached the

more or less level ground of the golf-course and the *maidan*,*
beyond which it swept upward again to meet the inky shadows of the deodar forests and the cold brilliance of the night sky.

It had snowed for half an hour or so earlier in the night. Snow lay thick upon the verandah rails, and a powdering of blown crystals covered the wooden floorboards with a thin, brittle carpet that crunched crisply under Sarah's slippers. The small sound seemed terrifyingly loud in the frozen quiet of that silent, sleeping world: 'Loud enough to wake the dead' ... the phrase slipped unbidden into her mind, and the picture it conjured up did nothing to lessen her tension.

She reached Janet Rushton's door and turned the handle; only to find that the door was locked. But either Miss Rushton was already awake or she was an exceptionally light sleeper, for Sarah heard a swift rustle from inside the room as though someone had sat up suddenly in bed. She tapped softly, urgently, upon the rough wooden panel of the door, and still there was no reply; but as though disturbed by the sound, an overhanging mass of snow at the edge of the roof detached itself and fell with a sighing *flump* into the snowdrift below the verandah rails, setting her heart racing again. And in a fresh access of panic she grasped the door handle and rattled it urgently.

There was a swift movement from inside the room, and after a moment a voice breathed: *'Who is it?'*

'It's me — Sarah Parrish!' whispered Sarah in ungrammatical frenzy: 'Open the door. Quick! *Oh hurry!*'

She heard a bolt withdrawn and the click of a key turned in the lock, and the door opened a few inches; a narrow slit of blackness in the moon-flooded verandah. Janet Rushton's voice, curiously taut and breathless, said: 'What is it? What do you want?'

'Hush!' begged Sarah urgently. 'Don't make a noise! There's someone trying to get in through your bathroom window. You've

* An open space in or near a town, a parade-ground.

got to get out of there, quickly. He may be in by now! I saw him — it ...'

Janet Rushton still did not speak and Sarah, exasperation suddenly mingling with her panic, thrust with all her strength against the close-held door and stepped over the threshold.

A hand gripped her arm and jerked her forward into darkness, and she heard the door close behind her and the rasp of a bolt shot home. *'Don't move!'* whispered a voice beside her – a voice she would never have recognized as belonging to the gay and gregarious Miss Rushton — and the next instant something cold and hard was pressed against the side of her neck. Something that there could be no mistaking. A small, ice-cold ring of metal.

Sarah stood quite still, rigid with shock, while in the darkness a hand went over her body with a swift and frightening efficiency. There was a short gasp, as if of relief; then: 'Now tell me what you want,' said the harsh whisper.

Sarah touched her dry lips with her tongue: 'I've told you. There's someone trying to get in by your bathroom window. For heaven's sake stop playing the fool and let's get out of here!'

The cold rim of metal did not move, but in the moment of silence that followed there came a faint and unidentifiable sound from somewhere outside the building, and suddenly the cold pressure was withdrawn. There was a swift movement in the darkness beside her, and Sarah was alone. She heard a door open and the sound of someone stumbling against a chair in the dark bathroom, and turning, groped her way to the electric light switch and pressed it down.

The harsh yellow light of a single shaded bulb revealed a counterpart of the bare wooden walls and shabby, utilitarian furniture of her own room. It shone down upon the narrow tumbled bed and struck sparks from the edges of a pair of skates that lay upon the floor, lit up the slim lines of the skis that leant against the cupboard, and glinted wickedly along the short polished barrel of the weapon in Janet Rushton's hand ...

Sarah's eyes, narrowed against the sudden light, lifted slowly from the small, ugly weapon to the face of the girl who stood in the bathroom doorway, watching her.

Janet Rushton was an attractive girl of the healthy, outdoor variety, whose chief claim to good looks lay in fresh colouring and abundant curly blond hair rather than in any regularity of feature. But there was no vestige of prettiness in the face that stared back at Sarah above the gleaming barrel of the little automatic. The blue eyes were hard and unwavering in a face so white and haggard with fear and desperation as to be almost unrecognizable.

She came forward into the room, drawing the door shut behind her with her free hand without turning her gaze from Sarah's, and said softly: 'There *was* someone there: the window-catch has been filed through and there are marks in the snow. But whoever it was must have heard us and gone. What happened? Who was it?'

'How on earth should I know?' demanded Sarah heatedly. She had been more shaken than she would have thought possible, and her receding panic was rapidly being replaced by wrath: 'I went into my bathroom to get some biscuits, and I heard a noise outside. I'd already heard it, and I thought at first it was a rat; but it was someone trying to open your window, and . . .'

'Who was it?' interrupted Miss Rushton in a harsh whisper

'I've just told you! I haven't any idea!'

'Was it a man or a woman?'

'Why, a —' Sarah checked, brows wrinkled, and after a moment's thought said slowly: 'A man, I suppose. I don't really know.'

'You don't *know*? But that's absurd! It's almost as bright as day outside.'

'Yes, I know. But you see he — it — was in the shadows and close against the wall. Anyway it never occurred to me that it could be a woman. I thought it was some coolie or a hotel thief, who meant to burgle Mrs Matthews' room and had mistaken the window.'

'Why should you think that?' The question was sharp with suspicion.

'What else should I think?' snapped Sarah, exasperated. 'No one is likely to raise much fuss if half Mrs Matthews' possessions are stolen, because the chances are that no one will be able to say what's missing. You can't tell me that any ordinary sneak-thief is going to take the trouble to break in at your window when mine is already open. Of *course* I thought it was Mrs Matthews' room he was after! I was just going to shout and scare him off, when ... when ...' Sarah shivered so violently that her teeth chattered.

'When what? Why didn't you?'

'He — it — turned its head, and it hadn't got a face.' Sarah shivered again. 'I mean, it was wearing a sort of tightly fitting hood with holes for its eyes, and it had a gun. I – I knew then that – that it couldn't be some ordinary little thief, and I was scared out of my wits. All I could think of was to get you out of your room before that creature got in. And,' concluded Sarah stormily, exasperation and wrath overcoming her once more, 'all I got for my pains was a gun jabbed into me!'

Janet Rushton gave a sharp sigh and dropped the gun into the pocket of the windbreaker coat she wore over her pyjamas. She said uncertainly: 'I – I'm most awfully sorry. It was terribly stupid of me. I'm afraid I lost my head. But I ... you startled me. I'm always nervous in this country — especially in a hotel. It makes me feel safer having a gun, and I——'

'Oh, rubbish!' interrupted Sarah tersely. 'You aren't the nervous kind; I've seen you ski! There's something very peculiar about all this, and I don't like it. What's going on?'

A slow flush rose in Miss Rushton's white face, and faded again, leaving it if possible paler than before, and all at once Sarah was smitten with compunction: the girl looked so exhausted and desperate. Her anger ebbed away and she smiled unexpectedly into the drawn face: 'I'm sorry. I didn't mean to be cross and scratchy, and I don't want to do any of this "fools rushing in where angels fear to tread" stuff, but it's beginning to look to me as though you're in some kind of a jam. Are you? Because if you'd like any help, here I am. I've got quite a good shoulder for crying on, and a bottle of aspirin and a tin of salts in the next room. Just state your preference. We aim to please.'

She was relieved to see an answering smile replace the look of tension upon Miss Rushton's face. 'That's nice of you — considering the hysterical reception I gave you,' conceded Janet in a more normal voice. 'Thank you for coming in as you did. I can't apologize enough for treating you like that, but you see I've – I've been rather worried lately. Oh, it's only a purely personal matter — but ... Well, I suppose I've been letting it get on my nerves a bit. I was half asleep when I got out of bed, and I didn't realize who you were when you came bursting into my room in the dark. It was a bit unnerving, you know. I ... I don't know what you must think of me.'

Her voice seemed suddenly to fail her, and she took a few jerky steps to the nearest chair, and sitting down abruptly, as though her legs could no longer support her, helped herself to a cigarette from a box on the table beside her and looked vaguely about her for a light.

Sarah handed her the box of matches that stood on the chimney-piece, and said lightly: 'You lie very badly, you know. Still, if that's your story, you stick to it. I'm going to make up the fire and wait here while you smoke that cigarette, and after that, if you're feeling any better, I'll get back to my own room.'

She turned to the task of stacking pine chips and fir cones from the wood-box onto the still faintly glowing embers in the fireplace, and blew them into a blaze while Miss Rushton lit the cigarette with uncertain fingers and smoked it in silence.

Sarah added some dry, aromatic deodar logs to the fire and sat back on her heels: 'There. That'll blaze up beautifully in a minute or two. It's a pity we haven't got a kettle. I'd like to go all girlish and make a pot of tea.'

Janet made no comment. She had been watching Sarah make up the fire: studying her intently. Now she stubbed out the end of her cigarette in the ashtray on the table, and getting to her feet, walked over to the fireplace and stood leaning against the chimney-piece, staring down at the bright leaping flames. Presently she said abruptly: 'Why did you think I was lying?'

Sarah leaned back against the side of an armchair and looked up at her with a disarming smile. 'I didn't think. I knew.'

'What do you mean?'

'Do you really want to know?'

'Yes, of course.'

'Well, I'm not exactly an idiot, and as you've already pointed out, it's almost as bright as day outside — and you took a good long look at me through the crack of that door! Half asleep, my foot! You knew exactly who you were shoving that gun into, and — well, I'm curious. That's all.'

The pale face above her flushed painfully in the glancing firelight, and Sarah said contritely: 'That was rude of me. I'm sorry. You don't have to tell me anything if you don't want to, and if you're feeling better now I'll go back to bed. At least this business should give everyone a laugh at breakfast!'

She stood up and held out her hand: 'Good-night.'

Janet Rushton looked from the outstretched hand to Sarah's face, and turning away to pull up the small chintz-covered armchair, she sat down again and said haltingly: 'Don't go just yet ... please! I – I'd be very grateful if you'd stay a little longer and just ... just talk to me until I feel a bit less fraught. You don't know what a relief it would be to sit back and listen to someone else, instead of sitting here by myself and – and thinking about ... Besides, after that thief scare, I couldn't feel less like sleeping. So if you could stay for a bit ... ?'

'Of course,' agreed Sarah cheerfully, resuming her seat on the floor and clasping her arms about her knees. 'What would you like me to talk about?'

'Yourself, I think.' Janet's voice, which had been noticeably quiet, returned to its normal pitch, and Sarah automatically raised her own to match it.

'Story of my life? *"Me"*, by me. Mankind's favourite topic! All right. I'm afraid it's not wildly enthralling, but such as it is, you shall have it. Let's see ... Well, to begin with, like most of us I'm a mixture of England–Ireland–Scotland–and–Wales, which nowadays adds up to "British" to save time. But I was born in Cairo of all places, because Dad was in the Foreign Service and he and Mother happened to be posted there at the time. I even have a vague recollection of being carried round the Pyramids, sitting in front of Mother on the back of a camel. I suppose I was about three then, and ... But perhaps you've been to Egypt?'

'Not yet. It's one of the places I've always meant to visit one day — ever since I heard about Tutankhamun's tomb when I was in primary school.'

'I mean to go back there too, one day. To see all the things I missed. I remember a lot more about Rome, because I was older when Dad was posted there, and I still haven't forgotten all my Italian — or any of the other languages I picked up at the various schools that "Foreign Service children" go to. It was a marvellous life for a child. I can't think of a better one, and I only wish ... Oh well, I don't suppose that any of the places I remember will ever again be quite the same as they were before the war. Just as Vienna was never the same after the First World War! *"Babylon the great is fallen, is fallen ..."*' Sarah sighed and dropped her chin onto her clasped hands.

'You were lucky,' observed Janet. 'My father was in the Indian Army, so like most "children of the Raj", I and my brothers got shipped back home at a very early age, to be "educated". A lot earlier for Tony and John and Jamie than for me. After that we only saw our parents about once every two years until our school-days were over and we came back here again. Didn't you ever go to a boarding-school in England?'

'Yes. But not until I was fourteen. That was because ... Well, my parents were due to go to America, and they were taking me with them, like they always did. But it – it was the year the war broke out. We'd been on holiday in England that summer, and we sailed on the *Athenia* at the beginning of September.'

'The *Athenia*? But wasn't she——?' Janet stopped abruptly and Sarah nodded.

'Yes. She was torpedoed the day after war was declared, and ... and my parents went down with her. There weren't enough life-boats, you see.'

A log burst into flame and the fire blazed up and crackled merrily. Janet said: 'I'm sorry,' and Sarah gave a sharp little sigh.

'So am I. It seemed such a ... such a pointless waste. They were both so ... Oh well, that's how I finished my schooldays in a boarding-school in Hampshire; because Dad had managed to pitch me into a lifeboat with a lot of other children, and we all got back safe and seasick to England, where I was scooped in by my grandparents and eventually sent to Gran's old school. It got bombed twice while I was there, and the first time we moved into two wings of someone's Stately Home, and when that went too, into a clutch of Nissen huts that were a lot warmer. Then, as soon as I struck seventeen, I left and joined the WRAFs. I was de-mobbed last year, and as I wanted to see our Vanishing Empire before it vanished for keeps, I jumped at the chance when my Aunt Alice suggested that I come out and spend a few months with them in Peshawar.'

'What made you come up to Gulmarg?'

'Why, skiing of course! What else? We always went skiing during winter and spring holidays before the war, and I was given my first pair of skis before I was five. So when the Creeds told me about this meeting, and offered to give me a lift in their car, up and back, I couldn't resist it. I was afraid I might have forgotten how to ski, but thank goodness it seems to be one of those things that you don't forget — like riding a bicycle.'

'Who are your aunt and uncle?' asked Janet.

'The Addingtons. Aunt Alice is mother's eldest sister, and Uncle Jack's commanding the Peshawar Brigade at the moment. You've probably met them.'

'Yes,' said Janet slowly, 'they were up here last year. I wondered why your name rang a faint bell — it was your uncle, of course. I sat next to him at a dinner party last year and he mentioned you. It seems you had a good war record.'

'No more than anyone else in the Women's Services,' said Sarah with a laugh: 'That's just Uncle Jack blowing the family trumpet. He didn't do too badly himself, what with a bar to his DSO after Alamein, and another in Burma. I only got the usual service medal.'

'Plus a commission in record time,' observed Janet thoughtfully.

Sarah blushed vividly. 'Well ... yes. And, as that more or less concludes our broadcast from Radio Parrish, I'd better be going. That is, if you're feeling a bit less fraught?'

'I think I am,' conceded Janet, 'but if you're prepared to stay a little longer I'd like to tell you something. I don't suppose I should, but in the circumstances it seems preferable to letting you go on being curious — and possibly "giving everyone a laugh" with the story of this business tonight. Besides, God knows I need help — you were right about that.'

Sarah gave her a puzzled look, and abandoning her intention of leaving, settled back to wait with a curious mixture of expectancy and apprehension. But Janet seemed in no hurry to begin. Instead, she turned her head and looked searchingly about her as though to make sure that there was no third person in the small room, and Sarah's gaze, following hers, lingered upon the door that led into the darkened bathroom, across which lay the long shadows of the tall, polished skis. The heavy curtains over the windows hung still and smooth in the firelight, and the painted parchment lampshade cast a circular shadow upon the wooden ceiling. The silence in the small room was all at once oppressive, and Sarah had the sudden and disturbing fancy that the cold silent night and the frozen snowdrifts had crept closer about the outer walls to listen.

The flames whispered and flickered in the silence and a drop of moisture fell down the chimney and hissed upon the glowing logs.

Miss Rushton rose stiffly and crossing to the bathroom door opened it to reach in and switch on the light. Closing it again, she stood for a moment looking at it thoughtfully, and Sarah, watching her, remembered that her own bathroom door could only be fastened with a drop-latch fitted with a flimsy catch from the bedroom side, although the opposite side was fitted with a bolt. Janet Rushton dropped the latch into place and came back to her chair: 'I'm going to tell you this,' she said softly, 'because — well, partly because I've got to tell you something and I'm too dog-tired to think up a lie that would hold water. And partly because in case anything happens to me I should like someone to know.'

She stopped as though that explained everything, and Sarah said sharply: 'What do you mean? What could happen to you?'

'I might die — like Cousin Hilda.'

'*Cousin Hilda?* ... Oh, you mean Mrs Matthews? I'd forgotten she was a relation of yours; no wonder you're feeling upset. It was a ghastly thing to happen. But there's no need to be morbid about it. After all, it was an accident that could only happen once in a blue moon.'

'It wasn't an accident,' said Janet Rushton quietly and quite definitely.

'What on earth do you mean?'

'I mean that Mrs Matthews was murdered.'

The night and the silence and the brooding snowdrifts seemed to take a soft step closer and breathe about the isolated wing of the dark hotel, and the little flames that rustled about the deodar logs whispered ... *murdered ... murdered ... murdered.*

'That's ridiculous!' exclaimed Sarah indignantly. 'Major McKay's a doctor, and he said it was an accident. He said that she must have slipped on that rotten snow and hit her head on those rocks as she fell.'

Yet, unaccountably, she did not believe her own words. There had been something about Janet Rushton's incredible, unemotional statement that carried conviction in the face of all sane judgement and reasoning.

'I know what they said. But they're wrong. I know she was murdered. You see, we had been afraid of this for some time.'

'We?'

'Mrs Matthews and I.'

'But – but . . . Oh, I know she was your cousin, but *really*, Janet!'

'As a matter of fact, she wasn't related to me at all. That was only camouflage.'

Sarah came to her feet in one swift movement. 'I think,' she said evenly, 'that you must be over . . . a bit over-imaginative.'

Janet Rushton smiled a little wryly. 'Why didn't you say "over-dramatizing yourself"?' she asked. 'It was what you were going to say, wasn't it? No: I'm not over-dramatizing myself. I only wish to God I were!' Her voice broke on the last word and the fingers of her clasped hands twisted convulsively together. 'I'm sorry: I thought you wanted to help. But I can quite see how far-fetched and Horror-Comic all this must sound to you. If it's any comfort to you, it sounds pretty crazy to me, so I don't know why on earth I should have expected you to believe it. I ought to have had more sense.'

'But I do — I mean, I can't . . . Oh, *hell!*' sighed Sarah despairingly, subsiding once more onto the hearthrug. 'I'm the one who ought to be saying, "I'm sorry", not you. And I really am sorry. I suppose I thought for a moment that you must be making fun of me just to see how much I'd swallow, and I reacted by doing a Queen Victoria: the *"We are not amused"* line. Can I change that instead to "Go on, convince me"? Please, Janet. I mean it.'

Janet's attempt at a smile was not entirely successful, but the nod that accompanied it satisfied Sarah, who smiled back at her warmly. But that brief check had evidently served to reawaken the older girl's sense of caution, for she stayed silent for an appreciable interval; sitting very still and apparently listening, though as far as Sarah could hear there was no sound from outside the room, and only the flutter and purr of flames and the occasional crackle of a burning log from inside it. Nevertheless, Miss Rushton continued to listen, and presently she rose to her feet, and crossing over to the outer door, switched off the light, and drawing back the bolt with her left hand (the right one, Sarah noted, was hidden in the pocket that held the little automatic) eased open the door.

The flood of moonlight that lay along the verandah had narrowed as the moon moved up the sky, but the long, snow-powdered arcade with its fringe of glittering icicles hanging from the roof-edge above was silent and deserted, and the only marks upon it were the prints of Sarah's footsteps.

Janet stood in the doorway for a moment or two, looking about her and listening to that silence. Then, stepping back, she closed and bolted the door, switched on the light again, and having checked the window fastenings and made sure that the curtains were closely drawn, looked across at Sarah and said very softly: 'You won't mind if I turn on the radio, will you? Cousin Hilda and I used to use it whenever we wanted to talk in a place where we could be overheard, so I know all the available stations backwards, and one of them puts on a discussion group around this time of night — or at least, that's what it sounds like. I've no idea where it comes from or what language they're talking, but voices make a better cover than music. So if you don't mind . . .'

She stooped to remove a small battery radio set from a chest of drawers that stood against the wooden wall between the door and the window, and placing it on top, adjusted the knobs and switched it on, releasing an excitable babble of voices that would have done credit to a family of Neapolitan fisherfolk enjoying a domestic row.

The volume, however, while not sufficient to disturb the

slumbers of any fellow-guests further down the verandah, was more than enough to prevent anyone outside the room from separating the lowered voices of Miss Rushton and her visitor from the medley of masculine and feminine chit-chat and the incessant whine and crackle of static.

'I see what you mean!' commented Sarah, automatically keeping her voice below the level of the invisible disputers: 'Well, go on with what you were telling me. I'm all ears.'

Janet returned to her chair, and leaning forward, elbows on knees, to warm her hands at the fire, said carefully, as though choosing her words: 'You must have heard of the Secret Service, though I imagine it never occurred to you that very ordinary people like Cousin Hilda — Mrs Matthews — and myself could belong to it. No!' as Sarah made a startled movement and seemed about to speak, 'let me finish. People like us — like me — are only small fry. Our job is just to collect information: odds and ends of rumour and talk and gossip that can seem meaningless by themselves, but when added to other scraps collected by other people can — may — mean a great deal. Well, some months ago the department we work for picked up a . . .'

She paused, apparently searching for a word that would not commit her too far, and finally selected an ambiguous one: 'A trail——'

2

Sitting by the fire with her sensible, schoolgirlish hands spread out to the blaze, and speaking in a carefully controlled voice that was pitched to reach no further than Sarah's ears, Janet Rushton told how she had been sent to Kashmir to contact and take her orders from a Mrs Matthews, who, since it might cause comment if an unmarried girl were to live alone, would pose as a relative so that the small houseboat on the Dāl Lake near Srinagar, that had already been taken in Janet's name, could be moored next to Mrs Matthews' much larger one. How between them they had found out what they had been sent to find out: only to discover with horror that it was no more than the tip of a submerged and deadly iceberg whose presence no one had even suspected ...

The situation was not one that they were equipped to deal with, and the enormity of the lurking menace had made it neccessary for them to pass on the details of their discoveries to someone in higher authority: yet their orders specifically forbade them to make any move to leave the State without the permission of their department. Since none of their various Kashmiri contacts operated at a sufficiently high level to be entrusted with such potentially lethal and unstable dynamite, Mrs Matthews had sent off the equivalent of a 'Mayday' call for help — though she was well aware that it would not be easy for anyone of their own nationality, or any non-Kashmiri for that matter, to arrive in Srinagar and get in touch with them without being noticed and talked about: for the simple reason that by then the year was drawing to a close.

The hordes of summer visitors had all left long ago, and the fact that she and Janet had been able to remain without exciting remark was because both had a talent for sketching in water-colours, and November happens to be among the loveliest of months in the valley. For it is then that the snowline moves down-ward to meet the forests, the chenar trees put on every shade of red from vermilion to crimson, and willows, poplars and chestnuts blaze yellow and gold.

As painters, this annual transformation scene had provided them with an impeccable reason for staying on when all the other visitors had left. Just as it had previously given them an admirable excuse not only to drive, ride, walk or be paddled in a *shikara** to any spot they cared to see, but to fall into casual conversation with innumerable strangers who would pause to watch the artists at work, linger to ask questions and offer advice, and finally squat down beside them to talk. An end that had, according to Janet, played no small part in their selection for this particular assign-ment.

It was during this period, when the last of the leaves were falling, that Mrs Matthews had sent off that 'Mayday' call and sat back to wait for the help that she assured the anxious Janet would not be long in arriving. But four days later the *Civil and Military Gazette*, one of India's best-known daily newspapers, had carried a small paragraph reporting the accidental death of a Major Brett who had apparently fallen from his carriage on the Frontier Express, *en route* to Rawalpindi: 'Foul play was not suspected, and the police were satisfied that the unfortunate man had at some time during the night, and while still half asleep, opened the side door of the carriage in mistake for the bathroom door . . .'

The accident was clearly not considered important enough to rate the front page, and had been tucked away on an inner one among a rag-bag of assorted news. But according to Janet, Mrs

* A flat-bottomed, canopied punt.

Matthews had read and re-read it, looking uncharacteristically shocked and upset.

'I'd never seen her look like that before,' said Janet. 'She was always so calm and good-tempered ... even at the worst times. I asked her if he'd been a friend of hers, and she said no, she'd only met him once: he'd been in the room while she was being given her orders. But she couldn't help wondering if he had been on his way to meet us, because she didn't believe the accident story. He wasn't the kind to make that sort of silly mistake.'

'But surely, if the police——?' began Sarah breathlessly.

'If one of – of our people dies in an accident, we let it go at that. Officially, anyway. That may sound callous, but it's a lot safer all round than asking a flock of questions that can only lead to embarrassing answers. Cousin Hil — Mrs Matthews — said we mustn't worry, because if he *had* been the one, and on his way here, someone else would be sent instead. But – but I worried. I couldn't help thinking that if it wasn't an accident, and he'd been killed to stop him coming here, then – then the people who did it might know about us. And that if anything were to happen to us, no one would ever know what – what we knew.'

When the last leaves had fallen and cat-ice began to form on the lakes, the two of them had abandoned their houseboats and moved into Nedou's Hotel in Srinagar, to wait with ever-increasing anxiety for an answer to that urgent call for help. Knowing only too well that with every day that passed it would become more and more dangerous for anyone to answer it, because at that season of the year no casual visitor in their right mind cares to undertake the long, cold and frequently hazardous journey along the winding mountain roads that lead to the valley. Not unless they have a very good reason for doing so — one that leaps to the eye or is easily explained! Though even then such rare wildfowl are apt to be conspicuous.

One such reason accounted for Mrs Matthews and her young cousin being able to take up residence, and without causing so much as a raised eyebrow, in the almost empty hotel where, apart from the suites occupied by a few elderly permanent residents living on their pensions, only a handful of rooms were kept open for the use of occasional visitors. The fact that both women were skiing enthusiasts.

Like the watercolour sketching, this had been a point that had not been overlooked by their employers; and Gulmarg, the little summer resort that had become one of the favourite playgrounds of the Raj and the chief meeting-place of the Ski Club of India, lay within easy reach of Srinagar — a car drive of twenty-four miles to the village of Tanmarg on the insteps of the mountains, followed by a four-mile ride on the back of a sure-footed hill pony up the steep and stony bridlepath that zig-zags upward through the forest, bringing the visitor to the shallow bowl of Gulmarg which lies in the lap of the tall ridge of Apharwat.

Both women had brought their skis with them, and everyone in the hotel was soon aware that they had skied in Europe before the war, and on several occasions since then at meetings of the Ski Club in Gulmarg, whenever there had been sufficient members to make it worthwhile opening the snow-bound hotel for ten days or so. 'You don't find people coming up here to ski on their own,' explained Janet, 'because it isn't worth opening it for just two or three people. And skiing on the level ground in the valley isn't much sport.'

Two days after they had moved into the hotel in Srinagar, and while they were becoming seriously worried over the lack of response to their 'Mayday' signal, a violent snowstorm had swept in from the north; blocking the passes, closing the Banihal route and both the Murree and Abbottabad roads into the valley, and ensuring that no plane could cross the mountains to land on Srinagar's still somewhat makeshift airfield. Telephone, telegraph and power lines fell before the onslaught of wind and snow, blacking out all Kashmir and isolating it from the outside world for more than a week. And even when it was over, the sky remained dark and threatening, with stormclouds hiding the high peaks, the airfield blanketed in drifts ten to twenty feet deep, the city snow-bound and avalanches threatening the toiling gangs of coolies who fought to clear the winding road through the mountains beyond Baramulla. The Banihal route could not even be attempted and was to remain closed for several weeks.

The first bus to struggle through brought sacks of mail, and Janet and Mrs Matthews had ski'd over to the post office on the Bund to collect their letters. They had also volunteered to fetch the rest of the hotel mail, and it was only after they had distributed this that they had time to open their own, most of which consisted of Christmas cards. The rest was of no interest except to the recipient, but one envelope — posted unsealed in the manner of printed circulars — contained a ten-page Christmas catalogue issued by a well-known store in Rawalpindi.

Mrs Matthews, to whom this had been addressed, glanced through it and left it open on the writing-table in her room for the remainder of the day, where the room bearer and any hotel servant whose duties brought him there — not to mention the odd resident who dropped in for a drink and a chat — had ample opportunity to see it, and to leaf through it if they wished. But later that night, when the majority of guests were safely in bed and the curtains were close drawn, she had removed from her small paperback library of favourite books that accompanied her everywhere, Stella Gibbons' *Cold Comfort Farm*; and with its help decoded the message that the Christmas catalogue contained——

'She told me about it next morning while we were skiing on the Takht,' said Janet. 'The man who had fallen from the Frontier Express *had* been on his way up to see us. But it didn't necessarily mean that the opposition had connected him with us, so we were not to worry. Someone else would be arriving as soon as possible and would identify himself in the usual manner. Cousin Hilda said he'd be arriving that day, because if the mail bus had got through it meant that the Murree–Baramulla road was passable, and that judging from the date on the envelope, the catalogue had been posted in Rawalpindi just over a week ago. He must obviously have been snowed up in some Dâk bungalow on the road.'

She stopped and fell silent for a space; staring bleakly into the leaping flames, until at last Sarah said in an uncertain whisper: 'Didn't he come?'

Janet dragged her thoughts back from whatever unpleasant paths they had been wandering along, and said: 'Yes. He came. His name was Ajit Dulab and he was one of the best game shots in the country. And one of the best polo players, too. He was supposed to be up here to see if he could bag a snow-leopard — they get driven down to the lower hills by bad weather. The State put him up in one of the Maharajah's Guest Houses, and a senior official gave a cocktail party for him to which we were all asked. To cut a long story short, he managed to arrange a meeting with Cousin Hilda — she was going to give him a skiing lesson — and she told him everything. And the next day he said the weather was too bad for shooting, so he bought a couple of snow-leopard skins at a shop on the Bund, and left.'

'Then what are you worrying about?' asked Sarah. 'It's his headache now, not yours!'

'He never got back,' said Janet in a hoarse whisper.

'You mean ... you mean he was *murdered*?' gasped Sarah.

'I don't know! I suppose it could have been an accident. Just – just bad luck. That road can be very dangerous; cars and buses and lorries are always going over the edge. There are so many places where the mountainside drops straight down below it for several hundred feet into the gorge where the river runs — and no one gets out of that alive. Apparently his car was swept over by an avalanche.'

Sarah released her breath in an audible sigh of relief and said: 'Then it *must* have been an accident!'

'Perhaps. But avalanches can be started by people, and someone could have been waiting ... it could have been done on purpose.

If only we could have been sure that it was an accident we'd have felt... well, better, I suppose. But we weren't sure. We didn't even know, afterwards, if someone else had been sent up here or not. Perhaps someone was, and didn't make it either... like – like the other two.'

'Do you mean you had to sit here and wait and do nothing?' demanded Sarah, astounded. 'Haven't you got a radio transmitter, or a receiving set, or anything like that? I should have thought——'

'Small, portable transmitters,' interrupted Janet shortly, 'not only don't work well among mountains, but transmissions can be picked up by people they're not intended for. And worse still, traced! It would have taken no time at all for word to get around that someone was transmitting in code from the valley, and then the hunt would have been up — and the game with it!'

'Oh. Yes, I see. But surely you could have telephoned?' said Sarah — intrigued by this glimpse of the mechanics of spying, but puzzled by the slowness and elaboration. 'The lines must have been mended by then. Or why not just send off a telegram?'

'In *India*?' said Janet scornfully. 'Just how long have you been out here?'

'Only a month and a bit,' admitted Sarah. 'Why?'

'Well for your information, there is no such thing as a secure telephone in all India — let alone in Kashmir! The Viceroy and the C-in-C and the Director of Central Intelligence, and one or two other bigwigs, probably have a scrambler apiece; but no one else would be able to get their hands on one. Certainly not in a Native State! The lines go through endless telephone exchanges and can be tapped almost anywhere by a child of two. As for telegrams, they get passed from hand to hand and everyone reads them — see *Kim!*'

'But if they were in code?'

'Codes,' retorted Janet impatiently, 'are the worst give-aways of all, because except for very brief ones that sound like sense — and boring sense at that! — a message in code instantly focuses attention and curiosity, and plenty of suspicion, on both the sender and the receiver. In our business no one writes down anything. Unless . . .' she hesitated, and for a brief interval her gaze seemed to leave Sarah and turn inward again to some disturbing mental picture that her words had conjured up; and when she finished the sentence it was in a completely different tone, and almost inaudible: '. . . unless we *have* to — if there's time.'

Another icy little prickle ran down Sarah's spine, and goaded by it, she said with a trace of tartness: 'But the message Mrs Matthews got in Srinagar must have been in code. The Christmas catalogue.'

'Yes, that's true. But since it came through the post, it got held up for a good many days by the storm — like that man who came up to see us. And no one could have read anything different into it, or even realized that there was anything else to read, except the person it was addressed to. Because only that person would have the key. A different key each time! It's almost the only code in the world that's impossible to crack, because nothing's written down, and you go by numbers — and the words are in another book. But unfortunately it doesn't work except for fairly short messages, because it isn't just *any* numbers. And what we had to say needed a lot of words and explanation.'

'It all sounds appallingly complicated to me,' observed Sarah disapprovingly.

'So is learning to walk a tightrope over Niagara, I imagine! Or finding one's way across the Gobi Desert. And this is worse than either. In the end we got another message, in much the same way as the other one. It told us to move up to Gulmarg for the Ski Club Meeting, and that the agent who would contact us here would be a skier. And also how we could meet him without anyone knowing.'

It had sounded a pretty good idea, said Janet. Skiing in Gulmarg, in her opinion, being an infinitely better reason for coming to Kashmir in winter than trying to bag a snow-leopard. But the brief message had concluded with a single, dreaded word that in their tabloid dictionary stood for 'Watch out — you have obviously been spotted!' It had shaken Janet badly, for despite the suspicions that had been raised by the deaths of those two agents, she had persuaded herself that the second was almost certainly due to a genuine accident, and that if the first was not, there was no need to suppose that the killers had any suspicion as to whom the victim was travelling to meet. But now one small word had destroyed all that . . .

'I was so sure we were safe,' whispered Janet. 'I didn't believe that anyone could possibly suspect a middle-aged, gossipy widow who liked to paint and knit and go to coffee parties and whist drives, or a girl who played golf and tennis and went out sketching, and danced and picnicked with subalterns up on leave. But I suppose we must have made a slip somewhere . . . Or else someone has turned traitor: that – that does happen . . .'

Her voice broke and died out, and she swallowed convulsively as though her mouth had suddenly become dry. Once again her hunted gaze travelled swiftly and furtively about the little room — to the crackling radio, the closed, blank doors and the windows where the faded curtains hung still and undisturbed. And when she spoke again it was still in a whisper.

'After that message came, I was afraid . . . terribly afraid. Mrs Matthews wasn't. She was wonderful. But she took extra care. She carried a gun everywhere, and she made me carry one. She saw to it that our doors and windows were locked and barred at night, and that we didn't eat or drink out of any dish or jug that someone else hadn't helped themselves from first. I'd have given anything, then, to leave. But we had to wait for the one who was to meet us here. We *had* to. But he still hasn't come, and now Cousin Hilda is dead; and I'm afraid . . . *I'm afraid!*'

Sarah reached out a steadying hand and said with an attempt at calm good sense that she was far from feeling: 'Now you know you don't mean that. That's just hysteria.'

Janet Rushton jerked back in her chair and said angrily: 'You don't believe me! You think I'm either mad or imaginative, don't you? *Don't you?*'

'Actually,' said Sarah slowly, 'I don't. Though heaven alone knows why I don't! But I do think you are exaggerating the situation a little. Major McKay is an Army Doctor and both he and Dr Leonard say that Mrs Matthews' death was an accident. So for all you know it *may* have been just that. An unlucky accident.'

Janet Rushton's laugh was not a pleasant sound as she brushed Sarah's hand off her knee: 'Listen, my poor innocent, I may be frightened, but I'm not a fool. My nerve may have cracked a bit, but my brain hasn't — yet! I've already told you that Mrs Matthews carried a gun. Well it wasn't on her when she was found, and there could only be one reason for removing it. The murder had to look like an accident, and if there had been a loaded automatic on her it would have raised doubts in even the woolliest of minds; not to mention giving rise to a lot of awkward questions. People, even middled-aged widows, do not usually carry loaded weapons unless they are afraid of something.'

Sarah said: 'Couldn't it have dropped out into the snow when she fell? Or perhaps the coolie who found her may have stolen it?'

'She wore it in a little holster under her arm — like I do in the daytime — and someone must have searched her body to find it. No coolie would have touched a corpse found under these circumstances, because he would have been too afraid of being accused of having something to do with her death. And even supposing a coolie *had* tried to rob the body, do you suppose for one moment that he would have gone to the trouble of removing the holster as well? It would have been easy enough to slip out the gun, but it can't have been so easy to remove the holster and the sling. It must either have been cut away or her ski-coat taken off and replaced, which could only have been done while her body was still warm, because afterwards she — it——'

'I know,' said Sarah hastily, 'I saw them bring her in. But how do you know the gun wasn't there when they found her? Major McKay may have taken charge of it.'

'Because,' Janet's voice was once more barely audible, and she shivered uncontrollably, 'I found her at about four o'clock. Before the coolie did.'

'You!'

'Yes. I – I was worried. I hadn't seen her since dinnertime the night before, because when I went to her room after breakfast she'd already left and the room servant said she'd gone off with the Khilanmarg party. So it wasn't until you and Reggie Craddock and the Coply twins came back early from Khilan, and said you hadn't seen her, that I began to get really worried. I went out to look for her myself. I don't know why I went straight to the gully ... except that Reggie had warned us that the snow there was dangerous, and I was afraid that——' Janet left the sentence open, and then finished abruptly: 'Anyway, I found her.'

'But —' whispered Sarah breathlessly, 'but that must have been long before that coolie found her! Why didn't you fetch somebody?'

'What was the use? She was dead. She had been dead for hours. Even I could see that. Besides, I couldn't afford to have my name brought into it, so I came back to the hotel by a different route and said nothing — it had begun to snow again by then, so I knew that my tracks would be covered.'

Sarah said sharply: 'What are you going to do now? Why don't you go to the police?'

'The *police*?' said Janet scornfully. 'Of course I can't go to the police! What would I tell them? Give away the results of months of work and planning, and ruin everything at the eleventh hour? Or say I "just had a feeling" that it wasn't an accident — and be told that I'm a hysterical female for my pains? No. There isn't anything I can do but wait.'

'Wait?' repeated Sarah incredulously. 'Wait for what, for heaven's sake?'

'I've told you. We have to meet someone here. I can't go until he comes. Mrs Matthews is dead, but I know all that she knew. And I have to pass it on to the right person. After that, like you said, it's somebody else's pigeon and not ours — mine — any longer.'

Sarah wanted to say 'suppose he doesn't come?' but stopped herself in time: it seemed an unnecessarily cruel remark in the face of the girl's desperate fear. She said instead:

'Why don't you take a chance and write it down for once — the important part — and risk posting it? Yes, I *know* you said that agents in your department don't put anything in writing because letters can go astray or be stolen and cyphers can be decoded. But it also seems,' she finished crisply, 'that agents can be killed!'

'Yes,' said Janet Rushton slowly. 'Agents can be killed. That was why I didn't believe you when you came to my door tonight. I thought it was a trap. That you had come to kill me.'

'You *what!*'

'Why not? If anyone had told you a few hours ago that I was a Secret Service agent, would you have believed them?'

'Well . . .'

'Of course you wouldn't! Because I don't look like your idea of a Secret Service agent.'

'Yes, I suppose so. I see. No wonder you pulled a gun on me! I thought you must have gone mad; or else I had.'

'I know,' said Janet wearily. 'I realized that if you weren't one of — *them* — then I would have done something that was going to be appallingly difficult to explain away. But I had to do it, because the other risk was so much greater.'

'How do you mean? What other risk?'

'If you had been one of them and I had hesitated for fear you might not be, I should have had no second chance. It was better to risk letting myself in for a lot of awkward questions and complicated lying than to risk that. You see, it's not just my own life that's at stake. It's far more important than that. Now that Mrs Matthews is dead I'm the only person who knows what she knew. I was never any more than a sort of second string to her. She gave me all my orders. But now I'm on my own and I've got to keep alive. I've *got* to! I can't let her down. I can't let it all be lost.'

The tired, passionate voice cracked queerly on the last word and after a moment Sarah said curiously: 'What made you decide that I was on the level?'

Janet Rushton smiled wanly. 'Oh, partly intuition I suppose, but mostly simple arithmetic.'

'I don't understand.'

'Don't you? It's very easy. You hadn't any weapon on you and you had told me the truth — there *had* been someone at the window: someone who must have been there quite a while, for they had made a very neat job of filing through that catch. Well, if you weren't on the level you wouldn't have warned me.'

'Oh I don't know,' said Sarah with a smile. 'I might have planted him there as a sort of decoy duck.'

'Yes. I thought of that too. You learn to think of most things in this job. But that didn't add up either. If you had planted someone at that window you could only have done it to provide an alibi: an excuse for getting in or for getting me out, supposing I had refused to open the door to you. Your reasoning could have been that before letting you in I might run to the bathroom window and check up on whether you were speaking the truth, and then, convinced of your *bona fides* by a sight of the decoy duck, I would of course have opened the door.'

'Then what makes you think —' began Sarah.

'I didn't go to the window first,' interrupted Janet. 'I made certain instead that you had no weapon on you; and by the time I got to the window, whoever had been there had heard us and gone. It did occur to me then that possibly it was a plot: not to kill me, but to gain my confidence. But if it had been that, then it was an entirely pointless gilding of the lily for your decoy to take on a long, cold and exceedingly tricky job on my window merely to provide an alibi, when the briefest demonstration would have served the same purpose equally well.'

'I see,' said Sarah slowly; and shivered. 'You seem to have it all worked out. And — just for the record of course — I am on the level, you know.'

'I know,' said Janet, with an odd inflexion in her voice. She raised her tired, hunted eyes from a contemplation of the glowing logs in the small brick fireplace, and gave Sarah a long and curiously calculating look.

The logs fell together with a little crash and a sudden spurt of flame, and Sarah stood up slowly and said: 'What is it you want me to do?'

Something taut and watchful in Janet Rushton's face relaxed, and she said: 'You're certainly not stupid.'

'Not particularly. You wouldn't have told me all this merely in order to stop me chattering at the breakfast table. If that was all you were after, you'd have fallen back on the complicated lying. You were weighing it up all the time I was telling you the story of my life, weren't you? I'm quite sure you could have thought up a convincing explanation for me, but you decided to tell the truth instead. There had to be a reason for that.'

'There is. The reason is that I'm – I'm desperate. I'm in a corner, and so I'll have to take a chance.'

'And you're taking it on me. Is that it?'

'Yes. You appear to have a reasonable amount of intelligence, and you couldn't have done well in the WRAF, or been such a good skier, without a fair amount of physical courage. And I need help. Will you help me?'

Sarah held out her hand. 'Shake,' she said gravely; and smiled.

The other girl's fingers, cold and tense, closed tightly over hers for a brief moment. 'Thank you,' said Janet with real gratitude, and getting up from her chair she crossed to the writing-table, pulled open a drawer, and taking out an envelope and a fountain-pen returned with them to Sarah.

'If my luck's in,' she said, 'you may not have to do anything. In fact, I hope to God you won't! But just – just in case, I'd like to have your address on this, and to know that if you should ever get it you'll do something about it. I'm not sure what, but I shall have to leave that to you, and I've a feeling that you won't let me down.'

'I'll try not to,' replied Sarah soberly. 'But why *my* name? Surely——'

'I daren't put anyone else's. *I daren't!* Because it could give that person away. But you're different. You're not one of us and you don't know anything. You are only someone I met skiing, so it's just possible that this will get to you without trouble if – if anything should happen to me.'

'Nothing's going to happen to you,' said Sarah firmly. She took the proffered envelope, noting as she did so that it was sealed, and though not empty, did not contain very much — certainly not more than one or at the most two sheets of thin writing-paper. And accepting the pen, she scribbled her name and address on the envelope and returned it.

Janet stood weighing it thoughtfully in her hand, and when she spoke again it was so softly that Sarah could barely catch the words and had the impression that she was talking to herself:

'The next problem is going to be getting this safely locked up when no one else is around, which isn't going to be easy if I'm being watched. Unless ... Yes, that would do. I can take it down with me tomorrow——' She gave a small, brisk nod, as though in confirmation of some plan, and thrust the sealed envelope into her pocket. 'And now,' said Janet in her normal voice, 'I think you'd better get back to your own room.'

'Are you quite sure you'll be all right?' asked Sarah uneasily. 'After all, that window's open now, and a child could deal with the door-latch. I'll stay if you like. Suppose he — it — whoever it was — comes back?'

'Don't worry,' said Janet. 'No one is in the least likely to have a second try tonight. The lights are enough to advertise the fact that I'm awake and ready, and I shall leave the bathroom light on and wedge a chair under that door handle.'

'Well, if you're certain it's OK,' said Sarah doubtfully. 'Anyway, promise me that if you hear any unexplained noises you'll bang on the wall and yell.'

'I promise,' said Janet with a pale smile.

She crossed to the door, and drawing back the bolt opened it cautiously and glanced rapidly up and down the deserted verandah before turning back to Sarah. 'It was nice of you to come,' she said awkwardly. 'I – I can't tell you how grateful I am.'

'Nonsense,' said Sarah lightly. 'I was meant to come. Predestination or whatever it's called. Fate, I suppose: *"There's a divinity that shapes our ends, rough-hew them as we may,"* and all that. Good-night, dear.'

The door closed softly behind her, and once more she heard the click of the key turning in the lock and the muffled rasp of the bolts as they were pressed home. A few seconds later the radio was switched off and the night was quiet again.

Sarah stood for a moment looking about her, her back to the door. After the comparative warmth of the firelit room the verandah was an icy cavern of pale shadow that stretched emptily away past closed, secretive doors and shuttered windows. The white, glistening waste of snow lay piled all about the rough wooden walls and hung thick and heavy upon the low roofs, blotting out the sharp angles of the buildings and drawing soft, curved lines against the frosty sky.

Far away across the *marg** a tree cracked sharply with the sound of a distant pistol shot, as its sap froze inside the rough bark. The

* A meadow. In this case all the open grassy spaces of the three golf-courses were known collectively as the *marg* and the polo-ground as the *maidan*.

thin sound, a pinprick in the silence, echoed faintly round the bowl of the sleeping *marg*, and Sarah, who had moved towards her own door, checked sharply. But it was not that faint sound which had stopped her.

The moon had risen higher into the night sky and half the verandah now lay in shadow. Only a narrow bar of cold white light remained at its edge, fretted with the sharp pattern thrown by the verandah railings. But in the reflected light from the wastes of snow beyond the railings, Sarah could see quite clearly on the film of white snowflakes that lay upon the verandah floor the prints of her own fur-lined slippers.

But there was now another set of footprints upon that pale and fragile carpet. The footprints of someone who had walked on tiptoe down the deserted verandah and paused outside Janet Rushton's door...

3

The sight of those footmarks was more shocking to Sarah than anything that Janet had told her, and as she stared down at them she felt as though she had been abruptly and violently propelled out of a make-believe world into one of chilling reality. For though it would not be true to say that she had disbelieved Janet, she had consciously allowed for a certain amount of exaggeration due to the effects of sorrow, fear and shock. Now, suddenly, it had become real to her. Because the proof was here before her eyes.

Her first instinctive reaction was to warn Janet. But even as her hand went out to knock once again on that door, she checked and turned back to look down again at those betraying prints. Whoever had made them had clearly not stayed listening very long; which meant that they had not been able to hear anything and been forced to retreat, disappointed. And since Janet had suspected that there might be an attempt to eavesdrop, and had guarded against it — and had also, in Sarah's opinion, endured enough for one night! — there seemed little point in bursting in on her a second time merely to tell her that she had been right.

There was, of course, something far more useful that she herself could do: follow that line of prints and find out where they led to! But even from here she could see that they had entered the verandah by way of the three stone steps at the far end, and left again the same way. And since the possibility that whoever made them might be lurking somewhere among the black shadows cast by the end of the hotel wing, waiting to see if anyone would do just that, was too daunting to be faced, Sarah fled back to her own room, and once safely inside it locked and bolted herself in.

After all the alarums and excursions of the past hour she had not expected to be able to fall asleep again. But here the experience gained during the war years, when she had learned to make use of every opportunity to snatch what sleep she could between air-raids or the departure and return of home-based bombers and fighters, stood her in good stead.

Her eyes had already closed and she was almost asleep, when it occurred to her that the second set of footprints, like her own, had been made by a woman . . .

It was at breakfast next morning that Reggie Craddock, the Secretary of the Ski Club, made his announcement.

He referred briefly to the tragic death of Mrs Matthews, and to his own previous warning that the Blue Run was unsafe for skiing. The snow, said Reggie Craddock, was rotten in places, and due to the thawing of a stream, most of the track was ice and very dangerous. No one, under any circumstances, was to ski in or near the run for the remaining four days of the Spring Meeting, and anyone found doing so would be automatically suspended from membership of the Club. He added the bald information that Mrs Matthews' body was being taken down to Srinagar that day for burial, and sat down with evident relief as a babble of low-toned conversation broke out around the tables.

Sarah glanced across the dining-room to where Janet Rushton's blond head gleamed in the brilliant morning sunlight that streamed through the snow-fringed window-panes. Janet's face showed no visible traces of her last night's panic, and Sarah, noting that she was wearing a dark tweed coat and skirt in place of her usual ski-suit, presumed that she would be accompanying her supposed cousin's coffin down to Srinagar and attending the funeral there. At the moment she was talking to Hugo Creed — a large and jovial character, built on generous lines, who was temporarily on the non-skiing list owing to an unfortunate altercation with a tree on Red Run.

Janet had been commiserating with him and Major Creed had evidently said something that amused her, for her laughter came clearly across the room, and hearing it, Sarah was tempted to wonder if the happenings of the previous night had not been a particularly vivid nightmare, or the product of a feverish imagination? But though she might possibly have been able to discount Janet's story, she could not forget those clear, betraying prints on the snow-powdered floor of the verandah.

Later that morning, on her way to the post office to send off a letter to her Aunt Alice, she had stopped to look behind her more than once, haunted by an uncomfortable feeling that she was being followed. But except for a few distant figures stumbling upon the nursery slopes below the hotel, the shimmering sweep of the snow-blanketed *marg* was empty and glittering in the clear sunlight that was thawing the snow to a soft slush under her skis. And there were fewer skiers than usual, since several of the older members had accompanied Janet down to Srinagar, from where they would return after a post-funeral luncheon at Nedou's Hotel.

She was on her way back from the post office when she saw the Creeds, who were watching a beginners' class on the nursery slopes, and went over to join them. She had known them in Peshawar and been driven up to Kashmir in their car, and despite a considerable disparity in their ages, Mrs Creed (Antonia by baptism, but 'Fudge' to her many friends) had beome a particular friend of hers.

'Hello, Hugo,' hailed Sarah, coming to anchor beside them: 'Why isn't Fudge pushing you around in a bath chair? I thought you were supposed to be on a bed of sickness?'

'Not quite, my child,' said Hugo comfortably, closing his eyes against the sun-glare. 'No bones broken, or anything like that. A mere matter of bruisery. I'm as stiff as an old boot, and Fudge has been rubbing me with pints of embrocation, with the result that I smell like a sewer. You can wind me from five hundred yards, but I am becoming hourly more supple.'

He brushed away some melting snow from the bench he was seated upon, clearing a space for Sarah: 'Come and sit down. I know of few more invigorating pastimes than watching one's fellow-man earnestly endeavouring to remain upright while sliding down a snow slope of one-in-one with six feet of planking strapped to his boots. Take that one, for instance: observe the exaggerated caution of his advance. Now he's off — that's the stuff! — now he's gaining speed — his skis are crossing — now he's dropped a stick—— Wait for it! ... *Magnificent!* The purler of a lifetime. I have no doubt that Messrs Metro-Goldwyn-Mayer would have paid him thousands to record it for a custard-pie comedy, and we get it all free. ***Bravo, sir! Bravo, indeed!***'

'*Do* shut up, Hugo!' begged Fudge. 'Don't laugh at him Sarah! It only encourages him. That's Major McKay. Reggie says he'll never make a skier, but he will try; he spends hours on the nursery slopes. He's looking simply furious, poor dear, and spitting out snow.'

'And doubtless a few teeth as well,' said Hugo, interested. 'Did I ever look like that when I was learning to ski, Fudge?'

'Worse,' said Fudge, 'far worse. Like Henry VIII doing the splits.'

'I resent the comparison,' said Hugo with dignity. 'Anyway, you have got your numbers wrong. Henry certainly, but not eight. Five, I think. Or whichever one Laurence Olivier recently introduced to the public. Many people commented at the time upon his close resemblance to myself. "Larry old boy," they said, "or is it Hugo?" Quite embarrassing it became. Cease giggling, Sarah. It does not become you.'

'I'm sorry,' said Sarah laughing, 'but I've often wondered who you reminded me of, and of course it's Henry VIII.'

'There!' said Fudge triumphantly, 'What did I say? Thank you, Sarah.'

'It's a plot,' sighed Hugo. 'But I forgive you, Sarah. You're so pretty. When I have sent this harridan of mine to the block, may I hope that you will step into the vacancy thus created? No security of tenure, of course.'

'I'll think it over,' promised Sarah. 'Are you two coming on the Khilan party tomorrow?'

'I'm coming,' said Fudge. 'Hugo won't be able to make it, worse luck, but I am deserting him for the night. I wouldn't miss my last chance of a night at the ski-hut for anything.'

'There's wifely devotion for you,' observed Hugo sadly. 'Does she forego her selfish pleasures to stay and anoint my creaking joints with yet more embrocation? Not on your life! She leaves me cold and rushes off to ski with snakes-in-the-grass like old Reggie. Hello, Reggie. Rounded up your numbers for the hut tomorrow?'

'Yes,' said Reggie Craddock, panting up the slope below them, his skis slithering and skidding on the slushing surface. 'Hell take this sun! The bally place is a bog. If this thaw keeps up, goodbye to our last four days skiing.'

'Never mind,' comforted Hugo. 'You can all have a jolly time tobogganing on the slopes with the hotel tea-trays. Nice, clean, boyish fun. Who's for the hut tomorrow?'

The ski-hut stood on the snow slopes of Khilanmarg, which is the long plateau, high above the bowl of Gulmarg, where the tree-line ends and the forests run out at the foot of Apharwat, the tall bare ridge of mountain, seamed with gullies, that rises above it for another fourteen thousand feet. Khilanmarg, the Meadow of Goats, is well named, for in summer it provides a grazing ground for flocks of goats and sheep who crop the grassy levels and scramble about on the rocks and the steep slopes of the mountainside above. But in winter the snow turns it into perfect skiing ground, and it was a practice of the Ski Club members to go up in parties to Khilanmarg and sleep the night in the ski-hut, which gave them more skiing time on the following day, since it eliminated the long pull up through the forest paths from Gulmarg, fifteen hundred feet below.

Reggie said: 'Quite a goodish crowd staying the night, and some only coming up for the day. Fourteen of us for the hut I reckon. Let's see, there's Sarah here, and Fudge of course, and the Coply twins. And Mir Khan and Ian Kelly, and those two birds from Calcutta — what are their names? Thingummy and Something.'

'Thinley and Somerville,' prompted Fudge.

'Yes, that's it. And myself of course, and Meril Forbes and the Curtis girl, and Helen and Johnnie Warrender. That's the lot I think.'

'Oh, dear! Is Helen really coming?'

'So she says. Why?'

'Nothing, only——'

'Miaow!' interjected Hugo.

'I wasn't going to say anything!' protested Fudge indignantly.

'I'm sure you weren't. I know how dearly you love Helen.'

'Now who's being catty? *Miaow* yourself! But I won't pretend she doesn't madden me. She's like – like——'

'Quite,' said Hugo. 'Biscuit crumbs in the bed. You need say no more.'

Sarah, who had been checking names on her fingers, said suddenly: 'But that makes thirteen, not fourteen. You'll have to rake in someone else, Reggie. You can't take up a party of thirteen. It would be unlucky.'

'It was fourteen when I made out the lists,' said Reggie, 'I must have forgotten someone.'

'Me,' said Hugo sadly.

'Of course. *Damn!*'

'Don't apologize,' said Hugo with a gracious wave of his hand.

'I wasn't. I was just wondering who to rake in to take your place.'

'It can't be done. There's only one of me: the country carries no spares. I am what *Fifi et Cie* would doubtless label an "Exclusive Model".'

'I wish you wouldn't chatter so much,' said Reggie irritably. 'I can't think straight while you babble. Do you suppose we could get Tomlin to take your place?'

'He's sprained his wrist.'

'Curse, so he has. What about Stevenson?'

'He's umpiring the beginners' race tomorrow.'

'Oh well, I expect we shall raise someone. Anyway, I'm not superstitious myself, and if Fudge and Sarah will refrain from commenting on the fact, I don't suppose anyone else will think of counting heads. Sarah can keep her fingers crossed and drape charms round her neck if it really worries her.'

'Sound common sense,' approved Hugo. '*"A Solomon come to judgement!"* If you can bring yourself to believe that certain things are unlucky, you must also be able to believe that certain other things are lucky. So if you see my dear wife plodding up to Khilan tomorrow, Reggie, festooned with horseshoes, bristling with white heather, and clutching a four-leaved clover in one hand and an outsize log of wood in the other, you will know that she is merely taking suitable precautions against disaster.'

'There's the lunch gong,' said Reggie. 'I think I'll push off. Good Lord — look at McKay! Golly what a toss! It's a wonder they don't break their necks, isn't it? Has he been doing that sort of thing all morning?'

'Without ceasing,' replied Hugo. 'It's very nearly perpetual motion. Still, it provides the bystanders with a lot of good, clean fun, and if his rugged bulldog spirit forbids him to chuck the whole idea and take up ballroom dancing instead, he will undoubtedly succeed in breaking his neck in the near future, ruining a perfectly good pair of skis in the process. Then we can all have a jolly laugh and you can put the nursery slopes out of bounds.'

'Considering Mrs Matthews is being buried today, I don't think that's a particularly funny remark,' observed Reggie Craddock frostily.

'Oh God!' said Hugh. '*"We are not amused!"* Sorry, sorry, sorry. Lead me lunchwards, Fudge, before I put my foot in it further. Coming, Sarah?'

The rest of the day passed without incident, and watching Janet Rushton at supper that evening Sarah decided that she was either a remarkably good actress, or had allowed the shock of finding Mrs Matthews' body to exaggerate her fears.

That night there were no unusual sounds from the other side of the thin wooden wall of her bedroom; but Sarah found herself unable to sleep, for the deathly silence of the previous night was broken now by a soft chorus of drips from the thawing snow on the roof, falling with a stealthy, monotonous patter into the piled snowdrifts below the verandah rail, pitting them with small, dark, ice-fringed holes. There was a breeze too: a faint uneasy breath of wind that sighed and whispered along the dark verandahs and under the snow-laden eaves, and combed through the black deodar forests behind the hotel with a sound like far-off surf.

An hour or two after midnight it died away and frost drew a silent finger along the rooftops; checking the thaw and re-hanging fantastic fringes of icicles from every gutter and ledge. Silence flowed back across the *marg*, and Sarah slept at last. To be awakened by a discreet tap upon the door and the arrival of her morning tea.

Bulaki, her down-country bearer, reported that it had snowed in the early hours of the morning and that the hotel's Kashmiri servants said that bad weather was coming. He looked cold and unhappy, and his dark face appeared blue and pinched and as woeful as a monkey's. He inquired between chattering teeth if it was still the Miss-sahib's intention to spend the next night in the Khilanmarg ski-hut, and on receiving a confirmatory answer observed darkly that no good would come of it.

The ski-hut, said Bulaki, was damp and insecure. It was also a place of evil omen, for had not the first ski-hut been buried by an avalanche — and with no less than three young sahibs within it at the time? He himself had spoken with a man who had helped to dig out the bodies of those same sahibs, and ... At which point Sarah had cut him short with some haste, and having repeated her intention to spend the night in the Khilanmarg hut, requested him to pack what she would need for the expedition while she was at breakfast.

Twenty minutes later she stepped out into the snow-powdered verandah and descended the hill to the dining-room, which was situated in a large block some distance below the wing in which she slept. The hotel buildings lay scattered over the top and sides of a steep little hill that rises out of the centre of the shallow bowl in the mountains that is Gulmarg — the 'Meadow of Roses'. A bowl that in summer is one vast, green golf-course, walled about by forests of pine and deodar and chestnut, and dotted and encircled by innumerable little log huts that bear a strong resemblance to those of a mining camp in any cowboy film.

Despite Bulaki's warnings of bad weather it was a glorious morning. The sun had not yet reached into the bowl of Gulmarg, but it lit up the mountain tops that rose above it and glittered upon Sunrise Peak in a dazzle of light. Breakfast was a hurried meal, and immediately after it some twenty or so members of the Ski Club packed their rucksacks with sandwiches and Thermos flasks, and strapping on their skis set off on the long climb through the pine forests up to the open snowfields of Khilanmarg.

The day had been all too short, and with the lengthening shadows of evening a chill had crept over the snowfields, and those of the party who were returning to the hotel drained the last drops of tea from their Thermos flasks, ate the last crumbs of cake, and buckled on their skis for the homeward run. One by one their small figures, dark against the rosy-tinted snow, and dwarfed by the lowering bulk of Apharwat whose steep sides rise up from the gentle slopes of Khilanmarg, swooped away across the sparkling levels to vanish among the shadows of the pine woods.

Sarah, who had been skiing in Christmas Gully with Ian Kelly and the Coply twins, paused on the ridge of the Gully to watch the nightly miracle of the sunset. 'Isn't it wonderful!' she said on a breath of rapture.

A girl's voice spoke from behind her: 'Yes, it is pretty good, isn't it? Like a transformation scene in a pantomime — not quite real.'

Sarah turned sharply to find Janet Rushton leaning upon her ski-sticks at the rim of the Gully and looking down to where a spangle of lights pinpricked the distant cup of purple shadows that was Gulmarg.

'Hello!' said Sarah, surprised. 'I didn't know you were staying up here for the night. I suppose you've taken Hugo's place? The fourteenth man.'

'Yes. I couldn't resist it. I didn't mean to stay, but Reggie brought pressure to bear. 'Said the party might develop the jitters if they discovered they were thirteen. Load of old rubbish really; and anyway, his efforts have been wasted.'

'But you're staying?'

'Yes; I said I would. Besides — well anyway it's too late now. The others have gone and it would only cause comment if I insisted on rushing after them on my own.'

'Why? What's happened?'

'Nothing much, except that Evadne Curtis has developed tummy trouble or cold feet or something, and I've just heard that she decided to go back to the hotel after all, and those two, Thinley and Whatsisname, have gone down with her. She comes from their part of the world and it appears that both of them are rivals for her hand. So naturally neither of them was going to let her go with the other. All very understandable, but it means we're now only eleven and I needn't have said I'd fill in for Hugo, after all. Oh well——!'

Sarah was conscious of a sudden wave of relief. She had

watched the small dark figures of the homeward-bound skiers vanish among the pine woods with a feeling of heavy foreboding that she had not wished to analyse, but which she now realized had its roots in the fear that somewhere down in that rapidly darkening hollow far below, death lay in wait for Janet; death tiptoeing along the silent, snow-powdered verandahs of the old hotel, or lurking among the shadows at the foot of Blue Run. But now Janet would not be there. She was here, and safe; far above the shadows of the black, watching trees and the secretive wooden walls of the old hotel. Here in a clean, fresh, frosty world. Safe . . .

Sarah laughed aloud in sheer relief. 'Come on,' she said, 'race you to the hut.'

She was a good skier; but Janet was an excellent one, and drawing ahead effortlessly she arrived with a swish of flung snow at the hut a full sixty seconds ahead of Sarah, who found her leaning against the far corner of it and dusting the snow off her suit. Her gaze was on the dim hollow far below them, and her face in the waning light was once again strained and anxious.

She said abruptly and in an undertone: 'I shouldn't have stayed up here. It's too great a risk. I've been a fool. I should have gone back with the others.'

'Risk?' repeated Sarah sharply. 'What do you mean? What risk is there in staying up here?'

'It's not that,' said Janet. 'It's . . . oh well, perhaps it doesn't matter.' She turned to glance up at the steep slope of the mountain-side that rose behind the small hut, and at the clear star-pricked sky above it, and added with apparent inconsequence: 'Anyway, there's a moon tonight.'

A tangle of dark figures shot past them in a flurry of snow to collapse in a confused heap before the hut door. 'Get your skis out of my hair, Alec!' demanded Ian Kelly. 'Where are the others, Sarah?'

'Some of them have arrived and some of them are just arriving,' said Sarah. 'Hello, Reggie. Where have you been?'

Reggie Craddock and his two companions, a tall slim Indian with a face that would have graced a Greek coin, and Meril Forbes, a thin sandy-haired girl with pale eyes and a multitude of freckles, came round the side of the hut and joined the group by the door.

'Up to the top of Gujar Gully,' said Reggie, unstrapping his skis. 'By the way, you all know each other, don't you? Miss Forbes, and Mir — I can't remember all your names, Mir.'

The tall Indian laughed. 'One is sufficient. But we have all met before.'

'Speaking for myself, very painfully,' said Ian Kelly. 'I cannoned into Mir coming down Red Run two years ago and I'm still black and blue. Where did you learn to ski, Mir? Up here?'

'No, in Austria, and then in Italy. I had not skied up here before that year. It is good snow.'

'Best in the world!' asserted that loyal Secretary of the Ski Club, Reggie Craddock. 'By the way, I'm thinking of doing a run to the Frozen Lakes tomorrow morning. Five-thirty start. Anyone coming with me? What about you, Janet?'

'No thanks. Too much of a slog. I feel like idling for a change.'

'I will go,' said Mir Khan, 'and so will Ian. It will do him good. He is putting on weight. Two years ago he was a gazelle — a fawn!'

'Ah youth! youth!' sighed Mr Kelly. 'I was young then — at least nineteen. All right, I'll martyr myself. Coming with us, Sarah?'

'I'll think about it,' said Sarah. 'Come on, Janet, let's see if anyone's got the lamps lit and the stove going. I'm frozen.'

The door closed behind them and within minutes the last gleam of daylight faded from off the mountain tops. Stars glittered frostily in the cold sky, and far away, beyond the towering peak of Nanga Parbat, a flicker of lightning licked along the ranges. But overhead the sky was clear and cloudless, and paling to the first pallid glow of the rising moon.

The interior of the ski-hut was partitioned into three sections: a living-room with a men's dormitory leading off from it to the left and a women's dormitory to the right. A double tier of bunks ran round three sides of each dormitory wall; fourteen bunks to each room, with an additional three bunks in the living-room in case of need. But the days when the ski-hut could be filled to capacity had gone, and Reggie Craddock had been both surprised and pleased at being able to muster the handful who now replaced the thirty-one of earlier years.

Fudge Creed, who was engaged in drying socks at the iron stove that stood in the middle of the women's half, welcomed Sarah and Janet with enthusiasm, and dropping her voice to a feverish whisper said: 'My dears! Thank heavens you've come: another ten minutes and I should have sunk through the floor. I never realized before how lowly are my antecedents, and how few, if any, of the right people I know. I don't believe there is a single peer whom I can call by his first name — let alone his nickname!'

Janet burst out laughing and looked at once younger and less anxious. 'Helen, I suppose! Where is she?'

'Having her skis waxed next door.'

'I thought I heard female voices from the men's side as we came through. All most reprehensible!'

'Ssh!' warned Sarah. 'Here comes your little chum.' But it was not Helen Warrender who pushed open the door and entered, but Meril Forbes: a colourless young woman in every meaning of the word, who despite an over-abundance of freckles might have been quite pretty had it not been for the hunted expression she habitually wore. Meril had the misfortune to be an orphan and to possess, as her sole relative and guardian, an elderly and autocratic aunt who lived more or less permanently in Kashmir. If she had ever possessed any character or will of her own, it had long ago been submerged in the strong waters of her aunt's personality, for Lady Candera was one of those domineering old ladies who employ outspokenness to the point of rudeness as a form of social power politics, and are feared and deferred to in consequence.

'Hello, Meril,' said Janet, sitting down on the floor before the stove, and tugging off her boots. 'Glad to see you were able to come up for the meeting after all. I thought I heard something of your not being able to make it. What happened? Aunt Ena suffer a change of heart?'

Meril's face flushed faintly under its powdering of freckles. 'Something like that,' she admitted. 'First she said she wouldn't hear of it, and then suddenly she told me I could go.'

'If I were you, I'd take a chopper to the old pest,' advised Janet candidly. 'No jury would convict. You've got a sweet, kind nature, Meril; that's your trouble. What you need is to get roaring drunk and recite the Declaration of Independence to your aged aunt.'

Meril Forbes smiled wanly. 'She's been very good to me on the whole, you know. I mean, if it hadn't been for her, I should have had nobody. She's done a lot for me.'

'Oh well,' said Janet, getting up, 'as long as you feel like that about it. What do you suppose there is for supper? I've had nothing but some sandwiches since breakfast.'

'I can tell you,' said Fudge, with some satisfaction: 'Mutton broth and stew. Both good — I made 'em. Lots of coffee — me again. And lemon cheese-cakes sent up by the hotel. What do you suppose I've been doing while you three were frivolling around the snow-slopes with your boy-friends? Cooking the supper — that's wot!'

'Bless you. I had visions of having to do it myself. Let's go and knock the stuffing out of it without delay.'

The remainder of the party were already gathered about the stove in the living-room, sipping cautiously at a weird concoction of hot rum, lemon, and various other mysterious ingredients procured and manufactured by Johnnie Warrender.

'Ah — *les* girls!' exclaimed Johnnie, waving a steaming glass. 'Come and try a snort of this, darlings. Just the thing to keep out the cold. A "Hell's Belle" — that's what they're called. Jolly good name, too, hell's bells!' He laughed uproariously. It was evident that Johnnie was already 'well on the way' — a not unusual condition for him. Sarah accepted a glass and retired with it to the farther end of the room where she sat sipping it gingerly and observing her fellow-guests with interest; in particular, Johnnie's wife, Helen, who was talking to Mir Khan and Reggie Craddock.

The other women in the party were wearing slacks and woollen pullovers, as were the men. But Helen Warrender, alone of the party, had brought a more exotic change of clothes for the occasion: a smartly draped wool dress, low-necked and short-sleeved, in a vivid shade of emerald green. Her silk-clad legs ended in green shoes with rhinestone buckles, and there were a pair of large rhinestone clips at the neck of her dress, and matching ones on her ears.

This was another woman who, like Meril, could have been pretty, perhaps even beautiful, if her face had not been marred by its expression: in her case one of chronic boredom and discontent that no amount of cleverly applied make-up could conceal. A lavish use of lipstick failed to disguise the bitterness of the sullen mouth or the downward droop of its corners, while the glittering, scarlet nail-polish that she favoured only seemed to emphasize the restlessness of the hands that fidgeted ceaselessly with an endless chain of cigarettes lit one from the other, and thrown away half smoked.

All in all, decided Sarah, Mrs Warrender struck a strident and incongruous note in the rough-and-ready surroundings of the ski-hut. A note as artificial and out of place as the rhinestone ornaments that twinkled and flashed in the smoky light from the kerosene lamps.

The room was very hot, and the waves of heat from the crude iron stove, allied to the thick haze of cigarette smoke, the babble of voices and the fumes of Johnnie's 'Hell's Belle', combined to make Sarah very sleepy, and as soon as possible after the meal, although it was still barely past nine o'clock she retired, yawning, to her bunk.

The others were not long in following her example, for they had risen early and it had been a long and healthily tiring day. Moreover, the best skiing tomorrow would be before breakfast while the snow was still crisp and dry from the night frost. By ten o'clock the last oil lamp had been extinguished and the ski-hut was dark and quiet.

It must have been an hour before midnight when Sarah awoke, for the moon was well clear of the heights above Khilanmarg, and its cold clear light, intensified by the glittering wastes of snow, lent a queer luminous quality to the darkness in the little ski-hut.

She lay still for a minute or two, gazing out at the shadowy, unfamiliar outlines of the narrow room with its dimly seen tier of bunks, and listening to the muffled and rhythmical rumble of snores proceeding from the other side of the partition, where Mr Reginald Craddock was presumably sleeping on his back. A wandering breath of wind from Apharwat soughed under the snow-hung eaves and whispered its way across the empty white levels, and down in the pine forest a branch cracked sharply, breaking under the weight of snow.

A moment later that distant sound was repeated from somewhere inside the hut. And of a sudden the darkness thinned, and Sarah found herself looking at the clear outlines of the little iron stove which less than an instant before had been a dark blur. A second later she realized why this was so: someone had opened the hut door.

For a moment or two she lay still, listening. But beyond that sudden creak of a hinge there was no further sound, and she sat up cautiously and peered out over the edge of her bunk.

There was only one entrance to the ski-hut, and that was by the door that led into the living-room. But the inner door between the women's side and the living-room was open; and so also was the outer door of the hut, for the living-room was bright with moonlight and by its reflected glow Sarah could just see the faintly snoring bundle in the next bunk that was Meril Forbes.

The bunk beyond it was Janet's, but it was empty, and the reflected light from the open doorway of the room beyond showed the tumbled blankets and glinted faintly on the sides of the little stove. And suddenly, horribly, Sarah remembered again that line of footprints on the empty verandah, and the way the light had glinted along the barrel of the little automatic in Janet Rushton's hand ...

The next moment she was out of bed and thrusting her feet into her ski-boots. Pulling her heavy coat off the bunk, she dragged it about her shoulders, and was at the door and across the living-room, and looking out into the night. Something moved against the wall of the ski-hut, and as a shadow blotted the gleaming brightness of the snow she said, *'Janet!'* in a gasp of relief.

The shadow checked, and Janet's voice said in a sharp whisper: 'Sarah! What on earth are you doing out here? Get back at once before you catch pneumonia!'

'I heard the door creak when you went out,' explained Sarah between chattering teeth. 'It woke me up, and when I looked out of my bunk and saw you weren't there I was afraid something had happened.'

She wriggled her arms into the sleeves of her coat, and buttoning it up about her stepped out into the snow, and as an after-thought, turned and very quietly closed the door: there was no necessity to wake others in the hut. The hinge creaked faintly again, and the latch fell into place with a soft click.

Janet Rushton was leaning against the wall of the hut, strapping on her skis. She was fully clothed and wore a neat dark skiing cap tied over her yellow curls, and a thick woollen muffler about her throat. She sang softly, just under her breath, as she tugged at the stiff straps and buckles: an old tune that Sarah had heard the dance bands play on the radio and at dances in wartime England — how long ago?

'The moonlight and the moon,
And every gay and lovely tune that's played for you,
Were made for you.
The Summer and the Spring,
And that golden wedding ring,
Were only made for you,'

sang Miss Rushton.

She fastened the last strap, and straightening up, pulled on a pair of fur-lined skiing-gloves and picked up her ski-sticks. In the clear moonlight Sarah could see that her eyes were sparkling and she looked young and gay again, and as if a heavy load had been lifted from her shoulders.

'What are you up to?' demanded Sarah. 'What's happened, Janet? Where are you going?' Her whisper was sharp in the stillness.

'Hush! You'll wake the others. Come over here.' The snow crunched crisply under their feet as they moved out into the moonlight and away from the shadows of the ski-hut.

Janet said: 'He's come, Sarah. He's come at last. Now everything will be all right and tomorrow I can go away from these horrible mountains and be free again. Look over there!'

She caught Sarah's arm and pointed with one gloved hand to where, far below them, the moonlight filled the bowl of Gulmarg with milky light.

'What?' whispered Sarah. 'I can't see anything.'

'There, among the trees, to the left of the Gap.'

On the far side of Gulmarg, from among the furry blanket of the distant tree-tops that showed iron-grey in the moonlight, a single speck of light glowed like a minute red star in a stormy sky. A pinpoint of warmth in the immensity of the cold, moonlit world that lay spread out before them.

'I can see a speck of light, if that's what you mean,' whispered Sarah. 'A red light.'

'Yes, that's it. We've been waiting for that light for days. Ever since we came up here one or other of us would watch for it every night, and I'd begun to think it would *never* come. That's partly why I decided to stay the night up here — to tempt my luck. I knew that if it did I could see it from here just as well as from my room at the hotel. Perhaps better.'

Sarah said: 'But what are you going to do? You can't go down there now.'

'Of course I can. I'm a good skier. Better than almost anyone here. I can get there in under half an hour.'

'Don't be absurd!' They had been speaking in whispers, but Sarah's voice rose perilously: 'You'd never find your way through that forest by night.'

'*Ssh!* You'll wake somebody. I'm not going that way: I'm going down Slalom Hill and the Blue Run. Reggie Craddock did it in ten minutes and I can do it in eight. After that I'll cut straight across the *marg*. Say another twenty minutes at most.'

'Janet, you're mad. You can't do it! And you can't go by Blue Run. You heard what Reggie said about it — and – and——'

Janet laughed softly, her breath a white mist on the still air. 'It's all right, Sarah. Don't look so horrified. I'll keep to the edge of the run, and I know the route like the back of my hand. Don't worry, there won't be a murderer waiting for me down there at this time of night, and I'll be back long before morning. If I'm not — if I'm delayed, I'll go straight back to the hotel instead and pretend I got up early for the run down. Tell the others that, will you, if I'm not back in time?'

Sarah said: 'I can't let you go like this. Something — anything — might happen! Look, if you'll wait just a minute while I get my skis and put on a few clothes, I'll come with you.'

'No. You're a grand girl Sarah, but you're not a good enough skier. You'd probably break your neck on that run, and that would hold me up.' She smiled at Sarah's anxious face. 'I'm all right. Really I am. Look.'

She thrust her hand into a pocket of her ski-suit and drew out the little automatic. For a moment the moonlight winked and sparkled on the cold metal, and then she slipped it back again and fastened the pocket with a small steel zipper.

'Do you mean to say you've been carrying that thing around in your pocket all day?' demanded Sarah, illogically shocked.

'Not in my pocket: in its holster, here——' Janet patted her left armpit. 'But I realized at the last minute that no one was going to notice a lump on my ski-suit at this time of night, so I took it out and put it in my pocket instead; easier to get at it there. Not that I shall need it tonight. Or ever, I hope. But I have to carry the whole works with me, because I daren't risk leaving it behind, for fear that some helpful tidy-upper like Meril comes across it and starts asking a whole floorful of agitated questions.'

Sarah said abruptly: 'Janet, what do you get out of this?'

Janet paused, and her face in the moonlight was suddenly sober and thoughtful. After a moment she said slowly: 'None of the things that most people work for. No great material rewards or public success. Excitement perhaps; but most of all, fear. Fear that makes you sick and cold and brainless and spineless.'

'Then why——?'

'My father,' said Janet, 'was a famous soldier. And my grandfather and my great-grandfather. All my family have always been soldiers. But my eldest brother was killed on the Frontier in '36, and John died in Italy, and Jamie in a Japanese prison camp. I am the only one that's left, and this is my way of fighting. One has to do what one can. It isn't enough just to be patriotic.'

Sarah thought suddenly of another Englishwoman, long dead, who had faced a German firing-squad, and whose immortal words Janet Rushton had unconsciously paraphrased: *Patriotism is not enough.*

She held out a hand. 'Good luck, Janet.'

'Thank you. You've been a brick, Sarah, and I'm terribly grateful. I wish I could show you how much I appreciate it.'

Sarah smiled at her; a companionable smile. 'For a sensible girl,' she said, 'you certainly talk an awful lot of rubbish. Take care of yourself.'

'I will,' promised Janet. 'Don't worry.'

She leant forward and swiftly, unexpectedly, kissed Sarah's cold cheek. The next moment, with a strong thrust of her ski-sticks and crisp swish of snow, she was gone — a dim, flying figure in the cold moonlight, dwindling away over the long falling levels of the snowfields to merge into the darkness of the forest. A shadow without substance.

Sarah turned away with a little shiver and made her way back to the hut: suddenly aware of the intense cold which had numbed her hands and feet and turned her cheeks to ice. Janet was right, she thought, shivering. I shall catch pneumonia — and serve me right!

The moonlight slanting over the deep, smooth snow on the ski-hut roof turned it to white satin, below which the log walls showed inky black with shadow. And the night was so quiet that Sarah could hear, like a whisper in an empty room, the far, faint mutter of thunder from behind the distant mountains of the Nanga Parbat range on the opposite side of the valley. But she had not taken more than two steps towards the hut when she heard another sound; one that was to remain with her and haunt her dreams for many a long night to come. The creak of a door hinge . . .

Sarah checked, staring. Frozen into immobility by the sight of the door that she had so recently closed. Someone must have eased it open while she talked with Janet in the snow, and was now closing it again — slowly and with extreme care — and presently she heard the faint click as the latch returned softly to its place. But it was a long time before she dared move, and standing in the icy moonlight she recalled, with a cold prickling of the scalp that had nothing to do with the night air, Janet's carelessly confident words of a few moments ago, when she had spoken of the Blue Run: *'There won't be a murderer waiting down there for me at this time of night.'*

Perhaps not. Perhaps because a murderer had been waiting here all the time. Close beside her under the snow-shrouded roof of the little dark ski-hut on Khilanmarg.

4

It was not until Reggie Craddock's alarm-clock announced with a deafening jangle that it was 5 a.m., and sounds of movements on the other side of the partition betokened the reluctant arising of Messrs Craddock, Kelly and Khan (the remainder of the party being impervious to the joys of pre-dawn skiing), that Sarah at last fell into an uneasy sleep.

She had lain awake for hours, huddled shivering among the blankets in her narrow bunk. Listening to the monotonous rumble of snores that proceeded from the other side of the wall, and the snuffling breathing of Meril Forbes. And seeing again and again the stealthy closing of that door.

Someone had been standing there, watching and listening. And if it had merely been somebody roused from sleep, as she herself had been, surely they would have called out? In that bright moonlight it would have been impossible not to see Janet and herself, or fail to recognize them; and anyone who thought they heard voices and decided to investigate, would have hailed them. Besides ... Sarah shivered again as she remembered that closing door: it had been eased shut so slowly, so very gently ...

There were eleven people in the hut, including herself and Janet. But she could not eliminate any of them, because by the time she had plucked up the courage to move again and re-enter the hut, whoever had closed the door had had ample time to slip quietly back into their own bunk.

Sarah went over in her mind all she knew of the party gathered in the ski-hut.

There was Reggie Craddock, the Secretary of the Club: a stocky little man in the late thirties, who possessed a handful of cotton mills and a consuming passion for winter sports. He had served during the war with an Indian regiment and had only recently been demobbed, and having been born and spent the best part of his life in India, he was well known from one end to the other of that gregarious country. It seemed unlikely, on the face of it, that Mr Craddock of Craddock and Company, lately a member of the Bombay Grenadiers, would be employed in subversive activities or mixed up in murder.

Then there was Ian Kelly. Of Ian she knew a little more since he was a young man who liked to talk about himself, especially to pretty girls — in which connection it may be pointed out that Miss Sarah Parrish was a very pretty girl. But nothing he had told her had led her to believe that he could be in any way mixed up in espionage. In the first place, he had been dancing attendance on her throughout the day of Mrs Matthews' murder, and so could not conceivably have performed that deed himself. He had also, in the last year of the war, won an MC and been three times mentioned in dispatches. That in itself seemed to preclude the possibility of his being employed as a foreign agent.

Johnnie Warrender ... There was very little she knew about Johnnie Warrender, beyond the fact that he possessed an irritating wife and apparently played — or had played — polo. She must ask Fudge about him. He seemed a pleasant enough person; wiry and restless, verging on the forties, and with an open-handed and hail-fellow-well-met disposition. His failing appeared to be drink, for hardly an evening passed without Johnnie getting what he himself described as 'creditably illuminated', while his bar bill at the end of each month must have reached four figures in the local currency.

Mir Khan. Another unknown quantity. She had been introduced to Mir Khan by Ian Kelly during her first day in Gulmarg, but she had never had much speech with him. He was a friend of

Reggie Craddock's, and Reggie appeared to have an enormous admiration for him. Though how much of this was due to the fact that Mir could out-ski Reggie any day of the week, and was reputed to be one of the finest shots in India, she did not know, since she was aware that her countrymen's attitude towards proficiency at games and sports was apt to cloud their judgement, and that provided a man could smite a ball farther, or with more accuracy, than his fellows, and could be counted upon to hit a sufficient amount of birds on the wing, they automatically voted him a 'good chap' and pronounced him to be an 'excellent feller' and 'one of the best'.

Mir possessed these abilities to a marked degree; in addition to much charm of manner and a string of strange prefixes to his name that marked his affiliation to a princely house. He had been shooting snow-leopard beyond Gilgit, and had stopped off at Gulmarg for the Ski Club Meeting on his way south. But there was no reason to suppose, because he was popular and charming and friendly, that he was not also anti-British.

After all, thought Sarah, tossing in the darkness, it *is* his country and we *are* the 'White Raj' — the conquerors, even though we're on the verge of quitting! *Was* it Mir Khan who had stood watching in the darkness from the hut door? Where had he been on the day that Mrs Matthews died? As far as she could remember, with Reggie Craddock and a party on the slopes beyond Khilan. All the same she put a mental query against Mir Khan . . .

That left only the Coply twins. Cheerful, charming, overflowing with good spirits, they had arrived in India at the tender age of eighteen, only a few months before the fall of an atom bomb on Hiroshima had ended the Second World War. To their disgust they had seen no active service, and this was to be their last leave in India before they left to join their regiment in Palestine.

Sarah would have dismissed them as possible suspects if it had not been for two things; both of which, under the present circumstances, she found a little disturbing. There was Russian blood in them, and they had been out skiing alone on the day of Mrs Matthews' death. Their father, now a General in the Indian Army, had married a White Russian, and the twins themselves were bilingual. Sarah had met Nadia Coply in Peshawar, and had written her down, with the cruelty of youth, as being fat and affected.

It was Nadia, a strong-minded woman, who was responsible for christening the twins Boris and Alexis, but time and a British public school had substituted Bonzo and Alec, and Bonzo and Alec they remained. Certainly Nadia, if her own stories could be trusted, had been a member of the old Russian nobility, for she was fond of relating with a wealth of dramatic detail how as a small child — 'and *so* beautiful' — she had sat upon the knee of the Tsar and been fed with bon-bons from a jewelled box. A woman with her antecedents would be hardly likely to have anything but enmity for the Communists. Still — there was Russian blood in the twins and they had been out alone together for most of the fatal Thursday.

Sarah turned restlessly in the darkness. If only it were possible to know exactly when Mrs Matthews had died. But no one would ever be sure of that. The intense cold could play tricks with bodies, and even the doctors would not give an opinion on it. They had said that they thought she must have died roughly four or five hours before her body was brought back to the hotel, which had been at 7 o'clock. But Janet had found her about four, and her body had been stiff already, because Janet had said—— Sarah's thoughts shuddered away from the remembrance of that frozen, contorted corpse.

The Coply twins *could* not be responsible. They were so young. And yet — and yet? Sarah remembered photographs she had seen of German prisoners shortly after the fall of France. Batches of fair-haired boys in their teens and twenties, who only a short time before had been machine-gunning women and children in the streets of small market towns, and dropping high explosives upon roads packed with helpless civilian refugees. No. Youth by itself was no alibi in these days. Youth could be hard and ruthless and intolerant, and without pity for old age and weakness.

What of the women? — for it had been a woman who had made those footsteps, though Sarah was convinced that the faceless creature who had sawn through the latch of Janet's window was a man. Fudge could be written off at once. Meril wouldn't have the guts, and allergic as she was to Helen Warrender, Sarah could not believe that that determinedly elegant and feline woman, with her constant references to the 'Right People', would involve herself with anything so socially damning as murder.

Reggie Craddock, Ian Kelly, Johnnie Warrender, Mir Khan, the Coply twins, Fudge, Meril Forbes and Helen. One of those people. Sarah's aching brain reviewed them all, over and over again in an endless procession, until the muffled whirring of Reggie's alarm-clock broke the evil spell of the night, and she fell asleep at last: to dream of Janet, helpless and panic-stricken, pursued down endless dark verandahs by faceless figures.

She awoke tired and unrefreshed to the smell of burning bacon fat and the welcome sound of a boiling kettle, to find that the rest of the party were already out taking advantage of the early morning snow, with the exception of Meril Forbes, who was preparing breakfast with a vast amount of energy and ineptitude. There was no sign of Janet.

'Mrs Creed said to let you sleep,' said Meril, flapping helplessly at the reeking smoke that filled the living-room from the neglected frying-pan. 'She did try and wake you once, but you seemed so fast asleep that she said we'd better leave you. They're skiing in the Gully; all except Reggie. And Mir, I suppose.'

'Who's they?' asked Sarah, wrinkling her nose at the fumes.

'Oh, all the rest of them,' said Meril vaguely.

In the face of Janet's parting request Sarah did not like to inquire after her, but since Meril had not mentioned her the chances were that she really had got back in time, and without her absence being noticed. She was probably out skiing with the others.

Sarah dressed, shivering in the cold hut, and went outside.

The sun was still hidden behind the rim of Apharwat, but its reflected glow made a glory of the snowfields. The sky was a pale wash of turquoise against which the mountain peaks cut violet patterns, and from somewhere among the pine woods below the *marg* a thin line of smoke from a woodcutter's fire rose unwavering into the still, morning air. But despite the clear radiance of the dawn there was something curiously threatening and oppressive about the breathless chill of the morning; a vibration of unease. And Sarah, looking away across the distant valley, saw that the great rampart of the Nanga Parbat range was hidden by a pall of dark, grey-brown cloud that spanned the horizon from east to west and tinged the sky above it with a foreboding yellow stain. As she watched, lightning flickered in the belly of the cloud and she could hear, faintly, from across the cold mountain ranges, the mutter of a far-distant storm.

Meril Forbes' voice, harried and anxious, exclaiming: 'Oh *bother!* I've burnt the bacon again!' recalled Sarah to a sense of duty, and she offered herself as assistant cook and was gratefully accepted. There was nothing much to be done about the bacon, so she turned instead to the task of preparing large quantities of coffee and toast. But the thought of Janet worried her, and presently, deciding on the indirect approach, she said carelessly: 'Who's looking after Bonzo and Alec? I imagine Reggie didn't take them with him?'

'Not much!' said Meril, clattering cups and saucers at the far end of the room. 'They're as much use on skis as a couple of porpoises. Worse! No, they've gone off to Christmas Gully with the others, to practise breaking their necks. They went off about an hour ago, and if they're not back soon I think we might start breakfast without them, don't you? The others won't be back for hours if they've gone to the Frozen Lakes.'

There was a crisp swish of snow outside and a cheerful voice announced: 'Home is the skier, home from ski, and the hungry home from the hill! Sarah, my beautiful, you are a lazy little grub and a disgrace to your nation. Why didn't you come with us instead of hogging it in your bunk?'

'I am allergic to early rising,' said Sarah firmly. 'What are you doing around here, Ian? We didn't expect you back for hours. Where have you left the others?'

'To their own devices. We decided to go our separate ways. I expect old Reggie's still messing about somewhere at the back of Apharwat, and Mir went off to Mary's Shoulder: said he wanted to practise jump-turns or something. I thought I'd had about enough, after mucking about for a couple of hours admiring the sunrise, so I decided to come back and admire you and the bacon instead.'

'Oh dear! — I'm afraid the bacon's burnt,' said Meril guiltily. 'But you can have a boiled egg.' She went to the door and peered out. 'Here are the others coming now. Where's Janet, Ian? Has she gone to the Lakes with Reggie, or did she go with Mir?'

'Neither,' said Ian. 'She didn't come with us. You forgot we were torn from our snug bunks at the ghastly hour of five ack emma. She'll have gone with the others.'

Meril looked puzzled. 'But she didn't. I mean, she'd gone already when they went, and we thought she must have decided to go with you.'

'Well she didn't,' said Ian firmly, 'and if I may be permitted to bring the conversation back to food, if you think one egg is enough for me, Meril dear, you have committed an error of judgement. I require at least six.'

Meril said anxiously: 'But then if Janet didn't go with you——'

Sarah interrupted hurriedly: 'She must have gone off early on her own, I think. She said something last night about fetching up at the hotel for breakfast; probably wanted to see the beginners' race this morning.'

The arrival of the Coply twins, smothered in the snow of frequent falls, together with Fudge and the Warrenders, put a stop to the conversation; and half an hour later, as they were washing up the breakfast things, Reggie Craddock put in an appearance, having abandoned his proposed trip to the Frozen Lakes owing to doubts as to the weather. There was no sign of Mir Khan, who was apparently still engrossed in the practice of jump-turns on the snow ridge known as Mary's Shoulder.

Reggie ate a hurried breakfast and looked at his watch. 'It's fairly early yet,' he announced, 'so I suggest we slide down and head off the people who are coming up here for the day. I don't like the look of those clouds at all. There's a nasty storm coming up, and I've a feeling it'll be here a lot sooner than we think. I'm not for having a packet of people caught up here by bad weather. What do you say, Johnnie?'

Johnnie Warrender lounged to the door and looked out above Gulmarg to the far side of the valley, where the sky was darkening above the cloud bank that concealed the Nanga Parbat range. The sun still shone serenely, but the curious, dirty yellow stain above the black bar of cloud was spreading rapidly over the cool blue of the sky, and there was an uneasy mutter in the air.

'Perhaps you're right,' conceded Johnnie, who was looking tired and cross in the morning sunlight. There were dark pouches under his eyes and he had cut himself shaving. 'Personally I shouldn't say it'll be here for hours yet — if at all. It may go down the valley and miss us altogether. However, it certainly looks as though something sticky was brewing over there, so I suppose we'd better play safe.'

They had rolled up their bedding and the various items that would be carried down by coolies, packed their rucksacks and strapped on their skis, when Reggie Craddock asked: 'Where's Janet?'

'Gone down ahead,' said Ian Kelly. 'What about Mir?'

'Oh, Mir's quite capable of looking after himself. I couldn't spot him anywhere when I came back, so he's probably gone down too. But in case he hasn't I'll leave a note on the door to tell him we've gone on ahead.' Reggie scribbled a few words on a page of his pocket diary, ripped it out, wrote Mir's name across the front in block capitals, and tucked it under the latch where he could not miss seeing it. 'Come on, we'd better get going if we want to stop the rest of them coming up. We'll go down by Red Run. You two' — he addressed the Coply twins — 'had better stick to the path. I won't have you risking your necks on the top half of the run. We'll give you a quarter of an hour's start. Shove off.'

The twins broke into injured protests, but Reggie was adamant. Fudge volunteered to accompany them to see that they got down without mishap, and after a moment's hesitation Helen Warrender decided to go with them too. She was not a particularly good skier, and disliked fast running except on open snow.

Fifteen minutes after their departure Reggie Craddock gave a hitch to his rucksack and set off down the slope with Sarah, Ian, Johnnie Warrender and Meril behind him. They fanned out on the crest of Slalom Hill and each took their own line, swooping down over the crisp shimmering surface like a flight of swallows; dipping, swaying, turning in a swish of flung crystals, and leaving behind them clear curving tracks on the sparkling snow. The icy air, whipping past them, sang a shrill crooning song in their ears as they swung round the Brooklands Curve and shot over Hill 60, and presently they were among the tall tree trunks; swerving and swinging down the track under the dark snow-laden boughs of pine and deodar.

It is not far short of the first houses that Red Run is crossed by Blue; the junction of the two runs bearing the appellation 'Dirty

Corner' for reasons not unconnected with the frequent and simultaneous arrival at this point of both Blue and Red runners moving at speed and arriving from opposite directions.

Sarah shot down the curving track, jump-turned with expert precision, and emerged into the straight stretch above the junction of the two runs a bare yard ahead of Ian Kelly — only to check violently, in a flurry of snow.

She saw Ian, swerving wildly to avoid her, shoot past and cannon off a tree trunk to fall with a whirl of skis, sticks, snow and startled swear-words into a piled drift, and heard Reggie shout behind her as he came to an indignant standstill a yard or so to her left, the others stemming behind him on the slope. But she did not move. Her eyes, fixed and dilated, were on the two figures immediately ahead of her. The Coply twins, who were standing at the junction of the two runs.

Alec was bending down, dragging frenziedly at the straps of his skis, while Bonzo, his hands cupped about his mouth, alternately shouted something unintelligible up the slope, and pointed down it.

'What the hell — !' said Reggie Craddock violently. He thrust strongly with his ski-sticks and shot away down the track; the others following behind him, except for Sarah, who stayed where she was, held in the grip of a sudden, sickening premonition of disaster. It was only when she heard Ian swearing in the undergrowth and saw Reggie and the others reach the twins that she forced herself to follow them.

Alec had rid himself of his second ski by the time she reached them, and was running down the Blue Run slipping and stumbling on the treacherous surface, while Meril was saying in a high, cracked voice that sounded as if it came from a gramophone: 'But they took Mrs Matthews away — I know they took her away! She can't still be here. They took her away!'

Sarah took one look at the sprawled figure that lay at the foot of the icy slope below them, a dark smudge against the whiteness, and took the slope at a run. She heard Reggie's warning shout and Meril's scream, and then Alec had caught her, and they had fallen together among the snow-covered boulders beside that other figure that lay so still.

It was Janet of course. Sarah had known that it would be. Perhaps she had known it, subconsciously, from the moment when she had awakened in the ski-hut, heavy-eyed and sick with apprehension, to find that Janet had not returned. The Coply twins, gesticulating in the snow, had only supplied the dreadful confirmation of what she already feared to be true.

Sarah reached out and touched her. Janet lay on her side in the snow in a curiously confiding attitude, almost as though she were asleep. Her knees were bent, and her arms lay stretched at her side, her hands still gripping her ski-sticks. There was a little scarlet stain on the snow under her head, and her blue eyes were open. There was no trace of either surprise or horror on her dead face, but rather a faint, definite impression of scorn: as though she had expected death and derided it.

Sarah became aware of Reggie Craddock swearing violently under his breath, of Meril's hysterical sobbing, and of Fudge's arms about her, pulling her away.

'Come away, Sarah. Don't look dear. We can't do anything; she's dead.'

Sarah jerked herself free and stood up. She had seen all she wanted to see in those first few minutes, and verified it when she had reached out to lay her hand on a pocket of Janet's snow-powdered ski-suit.

The narrow metal zip-fastener was closed, but the gun had gone. And it was not until after they had carried the slim, stiff figure up the hill to the hotel, and laid it in an empty room in an unoccupied wing, out of consideration for Miss Parrish's nerves, that Sarah learned — by way of Dr Leonard's wife, Frances, who had assisted her husband to remove the dead girl's clothing, so that he and Major McKay could conduct a thorough examination to eliminate any possibility of foul play — that nothing unusual had been found. Which could only mean that the holster and its sling had also been taken, since its discovery would certainly have aroused a good deal of curiosity and speculation.

5

'Where are you going, Sarah?' Ian's voice sounded as cheerful as ever.

'Out,' said Sarah briefly. She pulled on her skiing-gloves, and picking up her ski-sticks, stepped out of the overheated atmosphere of the hotel lounge into the chill of the darkening afternoon.

'Then I'll come with you and keep an eye on you.'

'No thank you, Ian,' said Sarah, allowing him to adjust and buckle on her skis. 'I'm only going across the *marg*, and I'd rather go by myself if you don't mind.' She drew the loops of her ski-sticks over her wrists as Ian fastened the last strap and stood up, dusting the snow off his knees.

'Don't be silly, Sarah. I know this business has been a bit of a jolt for you, but there's no reason why you shouldn't behave in a rational manner. There's a hell of a storm coming up, and it isn't going to help the situation if you get yourself lost in it. At least let me come with you if you feel you must go mooching about the *marg*.'

Sarah said: 'But I don't want you, Ian. And don't worry, I won't get lost. See you at tea-time — and thanks for your help.'

She slid swiftly away down the snow-covered path, gaining momentum as it dipped sharply downwards, and vanished round a curve of the hill, leaving Ian Kelly to mutter evil words and return moodily to the hotel and the subdued groups of skiers discussing the latest tragedy in the lounge.

At the bottom of the hill Sarah swung to the right, and skirting it, made for the end of the Red Run and turned up into the forest.

The sky was by now completely overcast and, although it was barely two o'clock, the day had darkened to a twilight dimness. Little gusts of wind were blowing across the open *marg*, but under the snow-laden boughs of the forest trees the air was cold and still, as Sarah picked her way carefully between the tree trunks and presently reached the junction of the two runs where the twins had stopped that morning. Brushing the snow from a tree stump she unfastened her skis and sat down facing the slope of Blue Run, and propping her chin on her hand, thought deeply.

Of one thing only she was completely sure. Janet, like Mrs Matthews, had been murdered. Not for one moment did she believe the doctor's diagnosis of accidental death due to a fall at speed and the striking of her head against a rock. She was certain that the blow that had killed Janet had been deliberately inflicted, for to prove it, as in the case of Mrs Matthews, there was the missing gun.

The question was *how?* Sarah went back once more over that conversation with Janet in the moonlight outside the Khilanmarg hut, and once again she seemed to hear Janet's low confident laugh as she said: 'It's all right Sarah. Don't look so horrified. I'll keep to the edge of the run, and I know the route like the back of my hand. Don't worry. There won't be a murderer waiting down there for me at this time of night.'

The edge of the run ...

Sarah stood up, and carrying her skis, walked up the side of the Blue Run, keeping among the trees. Presently she crossed to the other side, and less than a minute later came upon what she was looking for: the track of a single skier on the extreme right-hand side of the run, among the tree trunks.

Turning she followed the track downhill, and at the junction of the runs stopped to fasten on her skis before picking up the trail again. It ran down the hill following the line of Blue Run, passed without pause the small scarlet blotch that marked the spot where Janet's body had lain, and continued for a couple of hundred yards until the trees thinned at the edge of the *marg*; at which point it turned right and was lost among a maze of crossing and re-crossing tracks made by a beginners' class.

Pausing again, Sarah leant against a snow-powdered tree trunk and stared out across the sullen levels of the *marg* with unseeing eyes—— So Janet had not been killed on the way down from Khilan after all. She had kept to one side of that treacherous, frozen run and had gone on across the open levels of the *marg*, to keep her appointment somewhere among the dark pine trees where that red spark of light had shown like a small, evil star on the previous night. That meant that she must have been killed on her way back to Khilan, her mission completed. But there was something wrong there too . . .

Sarah turned and glanced back at the lowering ridge of Apharwat, coldly white against the slate-grey sky, and realized as she did so that although Janet might have come down from the ski-hut by the Blue Run, she would never have returned by that route, since the quickest way down would have proved the hardest way back. She would have come by the forest path. So why had her body been found on the Blue Run?

A theory was forming itself slowly in Sarah's mind, and she leaned her head against the rough bark of the tree, and shutting her eyes, tried to visualize Gulmarg as she had seen it last night from the snowfields of Khilan, following the direction of Janet's hand pointing down at that far small speck of light.

'About level with the Gap,' said Sarah, speaking aloud. 'And not more than a quarter of a mile this side of it.'

She opened her eyes and turned to look in the direction of the hotel, and from there, frowning, to the lowering sky overhead. Then, with a sudden squaring of her small jaw, she set off resolutely towards the Gap.

Fifteen minutes later she was among trees again at the far side of the *marg*, and she had found what she was looking for. Halfway across, a single track had detached itself from the multitudinous tracks of the beginners' slopes and struck off alone towards a point to the right-hand side of the Gap. It was not in a direction ordinarily frequented by members of the Club, and Sarah was fairly certain that she was following the track that Janet's skis had made on the previous night.

The track herringboned up the slope below the road that runs round the edge of the golf-course, and on reaching it, followed the road for several hundred yards, before turning off up a side path between the trees: and following it, Sarah found herself standing before a rickety wooden gateway beyond which, half hidden by tree trunks and snow-laden branches, stood a low, log-built bungalow of the usual Gulmarg pattern.

The log-built 'huts', as all houses here are called, are only occupied during the summer months. When autumn comes and the chestnut trees add their splashes of bright gold to the pine forests, and the snows begin to creep down from the mountain tops, the population retreats to the houseboats and hotels of Srinagar in the valley below, and the huts remain shuttered and empty until the following May. This one was no exception — apart from the fact that there were tracks on the short path leading to the front door and that the top bar of the gate had been swept clean of snow.

At least three people had entered and left the bungalow within the last twenty-four hours. Probably more, for the track Sarah had followed was crossed by others, coming from the direction of the Gap, and there were two more leaving the gate, so close upon each other that they might almost have been a single track. Yet despite this, the house appeared completely deserted.

The roof was hidden under a thick covering of snow, and a fringe of icicles hung from the eaves. The door was closed and there were rough board shutters nailed over all but one of the windows. But the blank, rime-fringed panes of that single unshuttered window looked out, free of the encroaching trees, towards the hotel, and above it to the heights of Apharwat and the long snow slopes of Khilanmarg . . .

It was from this window then, thought Sarah with sudden conviction, that the light that had lured Janet to her death had shone last night. And drawing a deep breath, she pushed open the unlatched gate and walked up the path towards the house.

Her skis slipped and slithered where the tracks of those earlier visitors had hardened the snow to ice, and a sudden thin gust of wind, herald of the coming storm, blew across the *marg* and soughed among the deodars; sloughing off snow from over-weighted branches and whispering about the crude pine walls of the empty house.

Sarah tried the front door cautiously, and finding that it was not locked, took her courage in both hands and pushed it open. The hinges creaked protestingly, and suddenly, daunted by the darkness and the silence inside, she would have turned and run back down the trodden path and out into the open *marg*, but for the thought of Janet setting off alone in the moonlight for that last long ski-run through the lonely woods... 'Sarah!' apostrophized Miss Parrish, in an angry undertone, 'you are a lousy little coward — and anyway, it can't be worse than the V-bombs!'

Unfastening her skis and leaving them beside the path, she set her teeth and stepped over the threshold of the silent house.

The air inside was stale and very cold, and the house smelt damp and musty. But there was a faint scent of cigarette smoke in the small dark hall, and another fainter smell that was barely more than the ghost of an odour: a sickly smell; sweetish, cloying and wholly unfamiliar.

Sarah wrinkled her nose and stooped to pick up a half-smoked cigarette. She touched it gingerly, almost as if she thought it might still be hot, and then dropped it back on the floor with a little grimace of disgust. The door had partially closed and now she saw that a chair stood behind it. It was an ordinary verandah chair with a wooden back and arms and a sagging cane seat, and someone had been sitting in it comparatively recently, for beside it lay a couple of cigarette-stubs and a film of scattered grey ash.

There was something on the arm of the chair that made Sarah's heart leap like a trout on a line: a small, triangular splash of blood that showed wet and vivid against the unvarnished wood. But when she removed a ski-glove and put out a shrinking finger to touch it, it was not blood at all, but only a fragment of thin shiny red rubber, such as might have been torn from a child's balloon, which had caught in a crack of the wood.

The bathos of the discovery, coming on top of that terrified leap of the heart, sent her off into a sudden and uncontrollable gale of giggles that contained more than a touch of hysteria. Oh, for heaven's sake! thought Sarah, mopping her eyes with the glove, I *must* stop seeing horrors at every turn. This isn't getting me anywhere!

She controlled herself with a considerable effort, and looked about her. To the left of the hall in which she stood were three doors which, when tried, proved to be either locked or bolted on the other side, while to the right a narrow passage led to another doorway, presumably a sitting-room. The passage was dark and smelt of rats, pinewood and cheap varnish, and there were marks on the uncarpeted floorboards: smears of damp and traces of discoloured snow. Sarah advanced along it cautiously, and trying the door at the end found that it was unfastened and opened easily.

When the track she had followed across the *marg* had turned up to the gate among the pine trees, she had not doubted that it was to this house that Janet had come last night. But if she had needed proof, it was here—— This, then, was the room with the unshuttered window.

The trees that huddled close about the small house had left this one window clear, so that it commanded an uninterrupted view, in a direct line ahead, of the *marg*, the hotel, the rising wall of forest behind it and, higher still, the distant expanse of Khilanmarg.

There was very little furniture in the room — any upholstered item such as sofas and armchairs having presumably been stored in one of the locked rooms. But there was a small round table drawn up before that single unshuttered window, and on it, among a litter of spent matches, cigarette-ends and grey ash, stood an old but obviously serviceable Petromax lamp. The glass of the lamp was red, and the room was a degree warmer than the rest of the cold house. And once again Sarah was aware of an odd smell that mingled with the scent of stale cigarette smoke. But this time it was a different smell, and vaguely familiar. She stood still, sniffing the close, stuffy air—— *Cordite!* Someone had fired a gun in that little room. Had it been Janet?

A sudden, shuddering horror of the cold, shuttered house and the locked rooms that lay at the far end of the narrow passage overcame Sarah, and turning swiftly, she closed the door behind her, shooting home the bolt with trembling fingers and shutting herself in with the scanty wooden furniture and that betraying lamp.

A low growl of thunder shuddered through the cold air and echoed among the mountains; and once again a sharp gust of wind licked across the *marg* to moan among the pine trees, rattling the window-panes and whining through a knot-hole in the pinewood wall——

No. Not a knot-hole. A bullet hole.

Sarah pulled herself together and walked quickly across the room to verify it. But she had seen too many bullet holes on too many targets to be mistaken, and she turned back to the table. The floor was a pool of shadow in the waning light, but there was a half-empty box of matches beside the lamp, and she stretched out a hand for them and lit one with unsteady fingers. A little flame flared up and sputtered weakly at the end of the match as she held it towards the floor, and a moment later it flickered out. But not before she had seen the ugly, sprawling stain that disfigured the rough planking of the dusty uncarpeted floor.

There was no mistaking what had caused it. Someone had died in this little cold room — and within the last twenty-four hours, for the blood in the cracks between the floorboards was still faintly sticky. It could not have been Janet, because Janet had been killed by a blow on the temple and there had been very little loss of blood, while whoever had made the stain upon the floorboards had lost a very great deal of it — more than a man might lose, and live. Besides, it was out of the question that any murderer would have risked carrying a dead body a mile or so round the *marg* to dump it on the worst stretch of the Blue Run.

Quite suddenly Sarah remembered the ski-tracks she had seen leading away from the gate; the two tracks that had not been parallel, but so close upon each other's heels that they almost seemed a single track. And in a swift flash of intuition she saw the ugly explanation of those tracks, and did not doubt that were she to follow them they would lead round the roadway that skirted the *marg*, and, deviously, through snow-blanketed undergrowth and small side paths to the edge of the Blue Run. Or that they had been made by Janet and her murderer — Janet walking ahead, driven like a sheep to the slaughter-house, with a gun at her back, to stand at last in the bright moonlight at the foot of the icy slope on the Blue Run, awaiting the savage blow that killed her, with that scornful half-smile that death had not been able to wipe from her face.

Sarah straightened up with a little sigh and leant against the table, steadying herself with her hands on the dusty surface. She looked round the room slowly and intently, and down at the ash and the cigarette-stubs on the table, and the single blood-soaked stub that lay on the stained patch of floor. There had been at least two men, then: one who had lit the lamp and waited here for Janet, and rolled and smoked his own cigarettes; and the other who had waited in the hall, sitting on the chair behind the door and smoking a popular and widely advertised brand . . .

Sarah slipped the box of matches into her pocket and forced herself to unbolt the door and return down the dark passage to the hall, and once there she struck another match and held it above her head. But beyond the scattered cigarette ash, the burnt-out stubs and the small triangular fragment of rubber on the chair behind the door, she could see nothing that might give a clue to the identity of the person who had sat there waiting in the dark. Even that strange, elusive suggestion of an odour, that had tainted the close air when she first entered the house, had gone — dissipated by the cold current of air from the open door.

The match spluttered out, scorching her fingers, and she dropped it on the floor and lit another and another, and stood for a long time staring intently about the small shadowy hall as though she could force the silent bolted doors, the dark walls and the blank, shuttered window-panes to tell her what they had seen.

Yet there was, decided Sarah, little they could have told her beyond what they and the ski-tracked snow outside had already shown her; and checking the sum total of that mute evidence she made her own deductions:

The man who had lit the lamp and set it in the window must have waited a long time in the cold sitting-room at the end of the passage, for there were close on a dozen cigarette-ends scattered upon the table top and lying on the dusty floor. Because Janet had been late——

Owing to an unexpected twist of fate that had prevented Hugo Creed joining the party on the previous day, she had, at the eleventh hour, taken his place. With the result that when the signal lamp was lit she was not, as expected, in her room at the hotel, but in the ski-hut on Khilanmarg, and expert skier though she was, that long run down in the moonlight must have taken her over half an hour, so that someone else had got there before her. Someone who carried a gun and must have killed not only Janet, but the agent she was hurrying to meet: the man who had lit the lamp and waited for her in the small cold room at the end of the passage, and who had died on the dusty floor among the scattered cigarette ash.

Yet why hadn't Janet, hurrying silently over the snowy *marg*, heard the reverberation of that shot and been warned in time? The night had been so still. So deadly still that even enclosed within the walls of a room, the sound must have echoed across the *marg*. How was it possible that Janet had not heard it? Or had it been fired after she had entered the dark house? The chair behind the door and the two cigarette-stubs seemed to disprove that theory, for one of the latter had been smoked as far down as possible, while the other had not been lit long before being abandoned, and it had not been pressed out but thrown, barely half-smoked, onto the floor. Both spoke clearly of someone who had waited, sitting at ease in the darkness behind the doorway, and who had not had so very long to wait . . .

It was then that Sarah remembered one of the few sounds that had broken across the silence of the icy night. The sharp cracking of a forest tree as sap froze under the bark or an overburdened bough broke under its weight of snow, and which had sounded like pistol shots. The crack of a distant automatic would have passed for a more familiar sound, and there would have been nothing to warn Janet that she was walking into a trap. Janet, who had said: *'Tomorrow I can go away . . . and be free again!'*

She must have come up the short, snow-covered path confidently, and never known, until she pushed open the door into the dark hall, that freedom of a different sort was waiting for her that night. And perhaps when the spring sunshine had melted the snow from the forest, some wandering woodcutter might stumble across the rotting corpse of the man who had lit that lamp and waited for her, and whose blood had soaked into the floor of the cold, shuttered house among the pine trees. Though even that was unlikely, for there were too many lonely ravines and tangled gullies in the forests, where a body might lie undiscovered until the jackals and the prowling leopards had scattered its bones.

Another warning growl of thunder reverberated among the mountains, and the rising wind slammed the open shutter of the room at the end of the passage, sending Sarah's heart into her mouth. But close upon the heels of that sound there came another and far more frightening one — the soft creak of a floorboard, twice repeated, from one of the three rooms that lay behind those locked doors. It broke Sarah's nerve, and in a frenzy of panic she dropped the matchbox and ran headlong from the house.

Lightning quivered across the *marg* as she snatched up her skis and ski-sticks and fled down the snow-covered path and through the gate that now swung crazily in the wind. But though the instinct of self-preservation urged her to run and keep on running, once out of sight of the house common sense re-asserted itself, forcing her to stop and fasten on her skis — it being obvious that whoever had been lurking on the far side of one of those locked doors could not have been wearing skis, and once she had strapped on her own she could easily outdistance anyone on foot.

Her fingers were so clumsy from cold and panic that it took her the best part of three minutes to fasten the stiff straps. But she managed it at last, and picking up her ski-sticks from where she had dropped them in the untrodden snow, she turned off the road to cross the *marg*.

The first snow had begun to fall as she left the house, but now all at once, with the wind behind them, the whirling white flakes were driving down so thickly that she could not see more than a yard ahead of her. Sarah hesitated briefly, and then changed direction, intending to do a traverse on the slope which would bring her out towards the main road that ran from the Gap to the Club. The road leading up to the hotel branched off this halfway, and though it would take longer, there was less chance of losing herself in the storm. But she had barely gathered speed when a dark form loomed up through the driving snow immediately ahead of her.

She swerved wildly, but too late, and cannoning into something solid, would have fallen but for a hand that gripped her arm and held her upright on the slope. Panic struck her afresh, and she tried to wrench herself away; but the grip on her arm might have been steel, and a man's voice said harshly: 'Who are you? What the devil are you doing here?'

Sarah opened her mouth but found she could make no sound. Her throat seemed contracted with terror, and the wind drove the thick snowflakes into her eyes and blinded her, turning her face to a solid mask of snow.

'What's the matter? Lost your voice?'

Her captor put out a hand in a heavy ski-glove and brushed the snow roughly from her face, peering down at her from the whirling dimness. She had a fleeting impression, blurred by the driving snow, of height, and a pair of eyes, flint-grey and very angry, before her own eyes were once more blinded by snowflakes.

The voice, which she could not recognize, muttered something under its breath, and for a moment the grip on her arm was relaxed. In that instant, with a strength born of fear, Sarah wrenched her arm free, thrust strongly with her ski-sticks and was away.

The slope was in her favour, and since the unknown man was facing the opposite way, it would take him a second or two to turn in his tracks. The storm was in her favour too. She thought she heard a shout behind her, and swinging sharply to her left, vanished into a seemingly solid wall of whiteness.

Twenty minutes later, blinded with snowflakes and buffeted by wind, breathless, shaken, and having lost her way at least half a dozen times, Sarah reached the hotel.

She was only just in time, for the snow that had blotted out the *marg* as she struggled across it was but a fraction of the storm to come. All that night it raged over Gulmarg in a screaming blizzard of whirling snow and shrieking wind. Snow and wind that wiped out for ever the tell-tale tracks across the *marg* and along the deserted forest road. And two months later, when the *marg* was green again and summer visitors came riding up the steep winding track that led up from Tanmarg at the foot of the hill, the *chow-*

kidar, the Indian caretaker of one of the huts among the pine woods, spring-cleaning the hut for the arrival of its tenants, found a dusty, red-glassed Petromax lamp in one of the rooms, and quietly annexed it. There was also a curious stain on the grimy floor, but when the carpet was laid it could not be seen.

The storm had raged for two days and nights: turning from snow to hail, and from hail to driving, blinding rain that washed away the thick snow-caps from the huddled roofs and brought the avalanches thundering down the steep slopes of Apharwat.

On the third day they buried Janet in the sodden little cemetery that the rain had temporarily thawed to a point where the ground was no longer frozen solid. And that done they went down the hill to Tanmarg and the waiting cars, through the slush and the dingy patches of discoloured snow, while a sad wind moaned through the forests behind them.

'Goodbye, Sarah. Pleasant journey. Write to me sometimes. Thal is a boring spot. Not that we shall be there much longer I gather.'

'Goodbye, Ian. Of course I will. Goodbye, Meril. See you again sometime, I hope.'

'Oh, sure to. You'll be up in Srinagar for the summer anyway, won't you?'

'No. I'm going to spend the summer with some friends in Ceylon.'

Reggie Craddock came up blowing on his fingers and looking ill and cold: 'Goodbye, Fudge. You and Hugo are giving Sarah a lift down, aren't you? One of the damned buses hasn't arrived, so I suppose I shall have to hang about for hours just to be sure everyone gets off safely. I'm sorry this show ended the way it did. Ghastly business. I suppose I should have set a guard on that run, or roped it off or something. Pity women hate doing what they're told. Damnable affair. Oh well, hope we shall see you again this summer. I shall be in Srinagar again if I can get any leave. Odd to think it may be the very last time any of us will ever get the chance.

Can't really believe it, somehow. You and Hugo coming up, I suppose?'

'Yes — for a fond farewell and all that. I don't suppose there'll be many people up. See you then; and don't worry too much about — about Janet and Mrs Matthews, Reggie. You couldn't have prevented it.'

Reggie nodded moodily and turned away as Major McKay pushed through the crowd of chattering coolies.

The Major too looked tired and harassed, and it occurred to Sarah that unpleasant as the two tragedies upon the Blue Run had been for the members of the Ski Club, the main weight of unpleasantness must have fallen upon him. He was limping slightly, and his normally ruddy countenance appeared pallid and depressed under the patches of sticking-plaster, souvenirs of his dogged struggles upon the nursery slopes, that adorned it. He shook hands punctiliously with Fudge and Sarah, and having wished them a good run to Peshawar, turned to Meril Forbes: 'You're for Srinagar, aren't you Meril? What are you doing for transport?'

'Oh, I'm all right, thank you,' said Meril. 'Aunt Ena has sent the car for me. It's only your bus for Rawalpindi that hasn't arrived yet.'

'Well it isn't going to be any use to me when it does arrive,' said the Major morosely: 'I've just heard that I have to go to Srinagar again. I thought we had dealt with all the formalities connected with this unfortunate business, but it seems — well, the point is, do you think you could give me a lift in your aunt's car?'

'Of course I can. How horrid for you, though.'

'I'm afraid your skiing holiday hasn't been too pleasant, George,' said Fudge sympathetically.

'I cannot imagine that it has been pleasant for any one of us,' said Major McKay austerely. 'Personally——'

A fanfare of blasts upon an electric horn interrupted him, and Fudge said hurriedly: 'That's Hugo. He wants to get to 'Pindi in time for tea. I must fly. Goodbye, George. Goodbye, Meril dear. Come on, Sarah.'

They left Meril and Major McKay and the remaining skiers standing in the cold wind among the trodden snow-banks and the crowds of jostling coolies. And a few moments later Hugo's big, luggage-laden Chevrolet rolled out of Tanmarg on the start of its two-hundred-and-forty-mile journey down the long, winding, mountainous Kashmir road towards the sun and dust and roses of Peshawar.

one for his Majesty! Goodbye, Georgie. Goodbye, Maddox.
Come on, Teddy!'

They left Ward and Major McKay and the remaining stage [illegible] and stood among the readers – now [illegible] the crowds [illegible]. And a few moments later Hunt [illegible] Chevrolet [illegible] January [illegible] the [illegible] of Two hundred and forty-[illegible] [illegible]

Part II

PESHAWAR

'There needs no ghost, my lord, come from the grave,
To tell us this.'

William Shakespeare, *Hamlet*

6

'That,' said Sarah reflectively, her eyes following the white-clad figure on the racing polo pony, 'is by far the most attractive man in Peshawar.'

Sarah, Hugo and Fudge Creed were seated in deck-chairs at the edge of the polo-ground, watching a knock-up game between two scratch sides.

'I thank you,' said Hugo graciously, tipping his hat a shade further over his nose to keep the sun-glare from his eyes: 'You were referring to me, of course.'

'Oh, I don't count you——'

'In that case, I withdraw my gratitude.'

'Don't interrupt, Hugo! I was going to say, I don't count you because you are a sober married man and therefore technically out of play. If you weren't married to Fudge of course, I dare say I could go for you in a big way.'

'Kindly avoid the use of imported slang, my child,' begged Hugo. 'Besides, the expression you have just made use of never fails to put me in mind of a determined dowager at a free tea making a feline pounce upon the last austerity bun. And to return to the subject of your original remark, which I now take, in lieu of myself, to refer to Charles Mallory, if you are thinking of working up a romantic interest in him you can save yourself a lot of trouble by following Mr Punch's celebrated advice to those about to get married: *"Don't!"*'

Sarah laughed. 'I'm not. But why not?'

Hugo tilted the brim of his hat with one finger and peered sideways at her. 'Can I be sure of that?'

'I'm afraid so. I've tried out my fresh young charms on him for weeks now, without the slightest result. In fact I think he is the only man who has ever snubbed me firmly and with intention, and I don't mind telling you that it's a salutary experience.'

'Hmm,' said Hugo sceptically. 'It also, apparently, has its attractions — judging from the vast sale of novels by women writers, devoted exclusively to square-jawed heroes of the "pick 'em blond and knock 'em down" variety.'

'I,' said Sarah serenely, 'am neither blond nor susceptible to brutality.'

'No. You are red-headed and green-eyed and snub-nosed, and I frequently wonder why the local wallflowers don't gang up on you and scratch your eyes out, instead of eating out of your hand.'

'Charm,' said Sarah complacently. 'Charm and personality, coupled with a sweet disposition. Things you wouldn't know anything about. Stop snuffling at my ankles, Lager!' She bent down and scooped up a small black and tan dachshund puppy who was skirmishing round her chair. 'Tell me more about my Secret Passion, Hugo. Why would I be wasting time and trouble on him?'

'On Bonnie Prince Charlie? Because he's immune, my child. Inoculated, vaccinated and everything. There isn't a woman for miles around who hasn't tried out her technique on him, only to retire with it badly bent and in drastic need of repair. He prefers sport of the outdoor kind to games of the indoor variety.'

'He also, if you want to know,' put in Fudge, who had been idly listening to the conversation from a deck-chair on the other side of Sarah, 'speaks five languages and half a dozen dialects, and is what Reggie Craddock would call "a chap's chap". Finally, alas, he has a revoltingly glamorous girl at home who answers — judging from the outsize photographs that adorn his rooms — to the name of Cynthia, and who wears a gigantic solitaire on the correct finger, presumably donated by the said Charles.'

'Yes,' said Sarah with the ghost of a smile. 'So I noticed.'

'Oh you did, did you? How and when — if it's not too personal a question?'

'Jerry Dugan and I called in on him on our way to the Club the other day. Jerry wanted to borrow a stirrup-leather or something. She is lovely, isn't she?'

'Well up in the Helen of Troy class, I should say. Very depressing.'

'What did I tell you?' said Hugo. 'The chap is a mere waste of anybody's valuable time.'

'Well, maybe you're right. Hello, here's Aunt Alice coming to ask me why I'm not wearing a topee — or whatever those dreadful pith mushrooms are called — and whose side is winning. And I don't know the answer to either.'

A plump, grey-haired lady in a flowered silk dress was bearing down upon them from the direction of the row of cars parked at the edge of the polo ground.

'Sarah dear! No topee! You'll only get sunstroke. Now which side is winning? No thank you Hugo, I'll sit here. Why isn't the Maharajah playing? Rajgore, I mean? — I see Captain Mallory is riding one of his ponies.'

'There's been a bit of a flap in the State. Some enterprising burglar has made off with the Rajgore emeralds,' explained Hugo. Adding with a regretful sigh: 'I wish it had been me! I think I shall set up as a sort of Raffles when I get the sack from the Army. All these Princes and Potentates simply dripping diamonds are an open invitation to crime.'

'So *that's* why Captain Mallory is playing his ponies! Sarah dear, how many times have I told you that it's dangerous for you to be out without a topee before four o'clock?'

'But it's after five, darling,' Sarah pointed out, 'and you know I haven't got a topee, and too much vanity to wear one if I had. And anyway, I don't believe anyone has worn one out here for the last ten years. You haven't got one yourself.'

'Oh, but we're used to it dear. The sun I mean. But coming from Hampshire——'

'Auntie darling, I do wish I could get it out of your head that the whole of Hampshire is a cold and draughty spot full of damp and fogs.'

'Not fogs dear. Blizzards. I remember once when your mother and I spent Christmas with our grandparents at Winchester it never stopped snowing and blowing. I had to wear a woollen vest over my combinations. Which team did you say was winning, dear?'

'I don't know darling. The one Johnnie Warrender is captaining, I suppose. I've been gossiping with Fudge and not really paying very much attention to the game. Anyway, it's only a sort of knock-up, isn't it? Here's Uncle. Uncle Henry, did your lot win?'

'Naturally,' said General Addington, collapsing into a deck-chair and fanning himself with his hat: 'I was umpiring, and saw to it. As a matter of fact,' he added thoughtfully, 'they came very near to losing, in spite of Johnnie's best efforts. That young protégé of the Governor's is hot stuff.'

'So Sarah thinks,' interrupted Fudge maliciously. 'Don't you, Sarah?'

'Does she, indeed? There used to be a song in my young days,' mused the General, 'that said something about

"I've seen the hook being baited,
I've been inoculated;
They can't catch me!"

Don't waste your time, Sarah.'

'Hugo has just been giving me much the same advice. A bit more of this, and I shall get really intrigued.'

'That reminds me,' broke in Mrs Addington brightly, 'I *knew* I'd forgotten something. I've asked that nice Mallory man to dinner tonight. The Charity Dance at the Club, you know. Another man is always so useful. And, as I told him, I had no idea until I wrote out the table plan just after tea, that I'd asked thirteen people, or of course I'd have asked someone else. Some people are so odd about sitting down thirteen.'

Sarah felt a sudden uncomfortable shiver up her spine: where had she heard a conversation like this before? Of course! . . . Hugo had fallen out of the party to Khilanmarg and left it thirteen, which was why Janet had decided to come. She gave a little hunch to her shoulders as though to shrug off the uncomfortable memory and said: 'Aunt Alice, you didn't really tell him that did you?'

'What, dear?'

'Tell him that you were only asking him because you'd discovered at the last minute that you had a party of thirteen?'

'But there aren't thirteen now, dear. He will make the fourteenth, so it's quite all right. Not that I'm in the *least* superstitious myself — except about black cats of course. I once very nearly ran over one on my bicycle and only half an hour later I heard that April the Fifth had won the Derby — just as I said he would.'

'How much did you have on him?' asked Hugo, interested.

'Oh, I didn't have any money on him. I never bet. But it does go to show that there is something after all in those old superstitions, doesn't it?'

Sarah abandoned the unequal struggle and relapsed into a helpless fit of the giggles, while Fudge, returning to the previous topic, said: 'I wonder he didn't refuse, or invent an excuse or something. It's not like Charles to let himself be bounced into going to Club dances.'

'Oh, I don't expect he'll come to the *dance*, dear. I told him that as long as he came to the dinner that was all that was necessary. I'm sure no one will mind *dancing* thirteen. Not that they could, of course. And I can't think what you're giggling about, Sarah dear. He didn't at all mind my being frank with him, whatever you may think. He's a very nice-mannered young man, and I can't imagine why Mrs Crawley and Mrs Gidney, or Kidney, or whatever her name is, and Joan Forsyth and that Roberton woman are so catty about him.'

'Suffering from a sprain in the technique, I expect,' offered Fudge. 'Are they catty about him?'

'Well, dear, you must admit it's a little *odd.* I mean after all the war *was* on still — when he arrived here, that is. And then when his regiment went off to Palestine or the Pyramids, or one of those places where they were always capturing hundreds of Italians — though what on earth they wanted them for I cannot imagine — what did we do with them when we had them? Just *think* how much food they must have eaten! And no spaghetti or anything. Still, I believe they provided one or two quite good dance bands in places like Murree, or was it Mussorie?'

Sarah said: 'Aunt Alice, what *are* you talking about?'

'Captain Mallory of course, dear. You aren't paying attention. A lot of people have been inclined to criticize him severely. For being a sort of ADC I mean — while we were still at war. They feel that he should have been fighting like the rest of them; his regiment I mean — not Mrs Kidney and the Roberton woman, though goodness knows they fight enough. But I must say, we did think it a little *odd* of the Governor to insist on a regular officer when there were so many tobacco people about who were so much cleverer at running things, and danced *quite* as well. But then of course so many people are silly about a man who doesn't do any fighting in a war. So stupid of them, because it's so much more sensible *not* to, don't you think? If we all just *didn't*, I mean, well where would people like Hitler have been?'

'In Buckingham Palace and the White House I imagine,' grunted her husband.

'Don't be silly, dear. How could he have been in two places at once? But as I was saying, Sarah dear, he was always being some sort of an ADC somewhere while the war was on — Captain Mallory I mean, not Hitler — and when it was over he still stayed on here, and now they're sending his regiment off to Palestine, or some place where they still seem to like fighting, and of course everyone thought he'd go, as it couldn't be *too* dangerous now —

I mean not like D-Day, and Burma — but it seems he'd rather stay here instead.'

'I think,' said General Addington, rising from his deck-chair and addressing Sarah, 'that your aunt has said quite enough for one evening. Let us remove her before worse befalls. Come along, Alice, it's past six already and your fourteen guests will be arriving in under two hours.'

'Only eleven guests, dear. The other three are Sarah and you and I. Goodbye, Antonia. Goodbye, Hugo. You two really must come and see us some time. Drop in for drinks some evening won't you? . . . Oh, you're coming to dinner tonight? How nice.'

'Alice!'

'Coming, Henry dear. Come along, Sarah. You mustn't keep your uncle waiting.'

The procession departed down the dusty length of the polo ground to where the General's car waited by the roadside.

7

There was a pile of mail addressed to Miss Parrish on the hall table of the big white bungalow on the Mall: letters that had arrived by the afternoon's post and had been put aside to await her return. Sarah pounced upon them hungrily — aware of a sudden pang of homesickness at the sight of the English stamps on the bulging envelopes — and retired to her room to indulge in an orgy of news and gossip from home.

She was still reading half an hour later when her aunt tapped on the door to announce that she had forgotten to write out the place cards for the dinner table, and would Sarah please try and get down early and do this for her?

Sarah started guiltily, and hastily skimming through the last two sheets of the letter in her hand, bundled them all into her dressing-table drawer. There was still one envelope unopened which she had left to the last because it bore an Indian stamp and looked as though it might be a bill or a circular since the address was typewritten. But there being no time to read it now, she slipped it into her evening-bag before scrambling hurriedly out of her linen frock and into a bath.

It was perhaps half an hour later that she left her room and crossed the hall in a cloud of grey tulle powdered with rhinestones, her red head burnished to a sophisticated smoothness and her green eyes shining like peridots between curling lashes whose natural darkness was a perpetual thorn in the flesh to several of her red-headed but sandy-lashed acquaintances.

There was someone waiting in the unlighted drawing-room. A

too early guest lurking abashed in the shadows, thought Sarah; wondering why the servant who had shown them in had not turned up the lights. The last of the daylight still lingered in the garden, but the drawing-room was almost dark, and she pressed down the switches as she entered and advanced with a smile to apologize for the omission. But her eyes — or was it her senses? — had evidently played tricks with her, for there was no one there.

The big, high-ceilinged room was empty, and Sarah looked around it with a puzzled frown, for the impression of someone waiting there had been so vivid that for a moment or two she found it difficult to believe that she had been mistaken. Probably a shadow thrown by the headlights of a passing car from the road beyond the garden wall, she thought. Drawing up her shoulders in a little shiver, she went out onto the wide verandah where dinner had been laid that night because the approach of the hot weather had made even the big rooms of the old bungalow seem too warm and stuffy.

The sky behind the feathery boughs of the pepper trees at the far end of the garden was turning from lemon yellow to a soft shade of green, and the air was sweet with the scent of roses and jasmine and fragrant with the smell of water on dry, sun-baked ground. But looking out over the fast darkening garden, Sarah was conscious of a disturbing and inexplicable sense of unease; though mentally reviewing the events of the past day she could find nothing to account for this sudden feeling of foreboding that possessed her.

A faint sound behind her made her turn swiftly, expectantly. But it was only a small beady-eyed lizard that had rustled across the matting, and not ... not ... what? What *had* she expected to see? A girl in a blue skiing suit? Yes — that was it! She realized, with a cold shiver of incredulous horror, that she had turned expecting to see Janet!

From the moment that Sarah had arrived back in Peshawar,

over two months ago, everything that had occurred during the closing days of the Ski Club Meeting had seemed to fade into unreality. It was as though it had all been a nightmare from which she had awakened to find herself in a safe and familiar room. And since she had no intention of leaving that room, she had thrown herself with an almost feverish gaiety into what social life there was left in the Station, and thrusting the memory of Janet into the background of her mind had done her best to forget the snowfields of Khilanmarg, the Blue Run, and a line of footprints on a deserted verandah. She had very nearly succeeded in doing so — to the extent, at least, of persuading herself that her imagination, and Janet's, had run away with them, and that the ice of the Blue Run had been the sole cause of those two tragedies.

Of the house among the pine trees she would not let herself think at all, for fear that it might break down her escapist line of reasoning. But now, suddenly, she was remembering Janet again ... Was it because of this party tonight — the party that would have been thirteen? — and because if she herself had not told Reggie Craddock that he ought to get a fourteenth member for the party at the ski-hut, Janet would never have stayed? But that, thought Sarah defensively, would have made no real difference to Janet's fate, since she would still have seen that red spark of light from the hotel and gone out to keep her rendezvous with——

'Sarah!'

Mrs Addington made an abrupt appearance at the far end of the verandah, wearing a gaily coloured kimono over a pair of pink lock-knit bloomers of almost Edwardian aspect, and with her hair tightly screwed into innumerable metal curlers.

'What is it, Auntie? Good heavens! Do you know that it's almost five past eight and you asked your guests for 8.15? Or have you forgotten there's a dinner party?'

'Of course I haven't, dear. I never forget anything. In fact I've just remembered something. The Creeds are coming tonight. Antonia told me so this evening.'

'I know they are,' said Sarah patiently. 'You asked them at least six weeks ago.'

'Yes, yes, dear. Don't interrupt me. I only wanted to say that I'd quite forgotten them when I was writing out the table plan. So of course I hadn't really got thirteen people after all — there were fifteen.'

'Oh darling, you are hopeless! And you black-jacked the unfortunate Charles Mallory into coming to your party entirely under false pretences. I'm ashamed of you!'

'Well that was what I wanted to ask you about, dear. Do you think we can ring him up and tell him we don't need him after all? It's the savoury, dear: Angels-on-Horseback. So *humiliating* if there are not enough to go round. He didn't seem particularly anxious to come, so I'm sure he'd be only too delighted to get out of it.'

'I don't doubt it,' said Sarah dryly. 'But he's not going to get the chance! No, darling: I refuse flatly to let you trump your already ace-high reputation for tact. You and I can either pretend to a loathing for Angels-on-Horseback, or cut the whole course off the menu. Take your choice.'

'Yes, perhaps that will be best. And now I come to think of it, dear, I don't believe it was Angels-on-Horseback after all. I changed it to cheese straws, and the *khansamah** always makes hundreds of those: last time we had them at the tennis tea next day. The ones that were over, I mean. Mrs Kidney said it was *such* an original idea. Good heavens! Is that a quarter past eight? You really shouldn't keep me here talking, dear. I shall *never* be ready in time!'

She disappeared with the speed of a diving duck as the little gilt clock in the drawing-room struck the quarter.

Sarah's wide net skirt whispered along the matting of the verandah as she passed round the long table with its load of silver and cut glass and bowls of Maréchal Niel roses, assisting portly

* Cook.

Mohammed Bux, the *khidmatgar*,* to rearrange the table for the addition of two extra places.

She held her aunt's table plan in one hand and a small pile of name cards in the other, but it might have been noted, had anyone been there to look over her shoulder, that she did not distribute the cards entirely in accordance with the original plan. The revised arrangement, apart from the inclusion of the Creeds, contained one alteration; for when, half an hour later, the guests were seated, Major Gilbert Ripon, who should have sat at Sarah's right hand, had been relegated to the far end of the table, while Captain Mallory occupied that place.

'Not that it was worth the trouble,' confessed Sarah later, leaning over Fudge's shoulder to peer at herself in the looking-glass of the cloakroom at the Peshawar Club, 'because he talked almost exclusively to that hearty Patterson girl, and on the only occasion that we managed to start a conversation, Archie Lovat kept chipping in until in the end they forgot all about me and discussed the last day's hunting across my prostrate form for about ten minutes. After which, of course — *did* you hear her Fudge? — Aunt Alice suddenly noticed the alteration in her dinner plan, and being Aunt Alice, naturally commented upon it at the top of her voice: curse the darling old mothball! And Charles Mallory sort of lifted one eyebrow and looked slightly surprised — damn him — and Gilbert Ripon glared and that revolting Patterson girl giggled. All in all Fudge darling, one of the more frosty of my failures.'

'Not so frosty, really,' commented Fudge consolingly, powdering her nose with care: 'After all, he *has* come on to the dance, hasn't he? — despite all those outspoken comments by your well-meaning but muddle-headed aunt. And that, let me tell you, is no mean concession on his part. He isn't often seen around at dances. Oh well — good luck darling, but don't say I didn't warn you!'

* Butler.

'And if you warn me just once more,' retorted Sarah, 'I shall begin to suspect your motives; so stop fussing about with your face and let's go off and dance.'

Being a popular girl, the queue of would-be partners was a long one, and it was almost halfway through the evening before Charles Mallory was able to dance with his hostess's niece. He proved to be a surprisingly good dancer, which for some reason she had not expected him to be, and Sarah clapped enthusiastically for an encore.

The band, which had been playing a gay and rather noisy quickstep, obliged with a waltz, and when the verse ended its leader crooned the refrain in an adenoidal whisper: ...

'The moonlight and the moon,
And every gay and lovely tune that's played for you,
Were made for you.
The Summer and the Spring,
And that golden wedding ring,
Were only made for you ...'

Sarah's silver-shod feet stumbled and checked and Charles Mallory felt her go rigid in his arms, and glancing down at her saw that her face had suddenly lost every vestige of colour.

'Shall we sit out the rest of this one?' he suggested. 'I'm not very good at waltzes.'

Sarah said: 'Please,' in a small, breathless voice, and Charles led her out of the hot, crowded ballroom into the cool night air of the Club garden, and once there propelled her firmly across the lawn and put her into a wicker chair.

He stood looking down at her for a moment with a slight frown between his eyes: she certainly did look oddly shaken, and he said curtly: 'Wait here and I'll get you a drink.'

He left her sitting in the starlight, and returned a few minutes later carrying a frosted glass in each hand. Sarah thanked him, still in a small voice, and drank in silence while Charles pulled up a second chair, and sitting down, watched her over the rim of his glass without appearing to do so; his own face in shadow.

In the ballroom behind them the band, evidently pleased with their choice of an encore, embarked on a repetition of the song, and Sarah shivered so uncontrollably that her teeth chattered against the edge of her glass.

For the past few weeks life had been so gay that she had thought herself free of the nightmare of Gulmarg. But for some reason it seemed to have returned that evening to haunt her, and though she had tried to push it away it had followed her. Now it was here too — born of a trite, haunting melody — and suddenly she was back once more in the eerie moonlight outside the snow-shrouded hut on Khilanmarg, and Janet was fastening on her skis for her last run and humming that soft, catchy tune . . .

'The Winter and the Fall, and the sweetest words of all, were simply made for you,' crooned the leader of the band.

Sarah said: 'Why *must* they go on and on playing that thing!' There was a sharp edge of hysteria to her voice, and Charles Mallory leaned forward and removed the glass from between her unsteady fingers. 'You'll spill that, and spoil your dress,' he said in a matter-of-fact voice. 'It isn't much of a tune, is it? But they'll stop in a minute.'

He offered Sarah a cigarette, and when she refused it, lit one himself and embarked casually on a surprising story about an impoverished dance-band leader in a Budapest café, who had been born a Prince of an Imperial House: talking to give her time to recover herself and to take her mind off the music that drifted through the opened windows of the ballroom behind them.

Presently the band stopped and as the dancers came streaming out into the cooler air of the lantern-lit garden Sarah said: 'I'm sorry. It was stupid of me to behave like that. I don't know what's got into me tonight. But that tune reminded me of something unpleasant, and . . .'

'What are you two gossiping about?' cut in Helen Warrender

brightly. 'I'm sure it must be something terribly interesting. Can we listen?'

Charles stood up and she plumped herself firmly into his vacated chair, ordered her partner to fetch her a brandy and soda, and turning her back upon Sarah said: 'Isn't it hot, Charles! I'm simply sticking to my frock. That's the worst of taffeta; even though one pays an absolute fortune for a model, it behaves like flypaper in the heat. Thank goodness we shall be leaving for Kashmir the week after next. I really couldn't stand this heat much longer. We're staying with the Douglases at Murree, on the way. I expect you know him, don't you? He's Lord Seeber's son. *Such* a darling. Do fetch another chair, Charles. And one for Tim.'

Charles collected two more chairs and a small green-painted table as Helen's partner returned across the lawn bearing drinks.

'Thank you, Tim. Oh damn! They've put ice in it! Why can't they keep the sodas cold instead of drowning them with ice cubes? Never mind — it's not really your fault. Give me a cigarette will you, Tim?'

The obedient Tim obliged and took the vacant chair, and Helen hitched her chair round to face Captain Mallory: 'Tell me, Charles, what did you think of the polo this afternoon? As a whole, I mean? Do you think we shall ever be able to raise enough people to play at all regularly? Of course if Johnnie had really been playing up to his handicap this afternoon, we'd have beaten you by much more. But then it's not really worth trying against these scratch teams.'

Charles said solemnly: 'Thank you, Helen.'

'What for? Oh! but I didn't mean *you*, Charles. I've seen you play at Delhi and Meerut, and I think it's so sporting of you to play with this rag-tag and bobtail. But I suppose we should be grateful even to them. After all, they do give us some practice games. Oh really, Tim! You know I never smoke gaspers! Thank you, Charles. As I was saying——'

Sarah yawned, and opening her evening-bag pulled out a slim

enamelled vanity-case, and with it something that fell onto the grass at her feet. It was the uninteresting looking envelope that she had not had time to open with the rest of her mail, and had pushed into her bag to read later. Picking it up she glanced at her companions, but as Mrs Warrender's taffeta-draped back obscured Charles Mallory and determinedly excluded her from the conversation, and the unsatisfactory Tim had removed himself and his rejected gaspers into the night, she shrugged her shoulders and opened the envelope; holding it so that it caught the light of the lanterns that hung in the trees behind them.

There was a second envelope inside the first one, together with a covering note from a firm of lawyers in Rawalpindi, dated two days previously, which — when translated out of the complicated jargon so beloved of the legal profession into plain English — informed Miss Parrish that the enclosed letter had been included in a packet placed for safe keeping in the office safe of the Manager of Nedou's Hotel in Srinagar, Kashmir, in January, by the late Miss Janet Elizabeth Rushton. The Manager had handed this packet 'upon her demise' to her bank, to be forwarded to her lawyers who had retained the contents until her will had been proved and probate obtained. Which fully explained the long delay, since lawyers and solicitors, like the mills of God, grind slowly . . .

Sarah turned her attention to the sealed envelope which bore her name and address in her own handwriting, and which Janet must have given, unobserved, to Mr Croal, the Manager of Nedou's Hotel, on the day that she had gone down to Srinagar to attend the funeral of Mrs Matthews. And holding it once again in her hand it was as though a cold breath from the snows and the shadows of black pine forests crept across the crowded lawn.

This, then, was the cause of the queer feeling of uneasiness and foreboding that had awaited her on her return to the big house among the pepper trees: the reason why the wraith of Janet had seemed to stand so close behind her that evening.

Sarah could see her with an uncomfortable vividness, standing in the small firelit room and weighing this same letter in her hand. She had said something about 'taking it down with her' ... To Srinagar of course, where she and Mrs Matthews had taken rooms at Nedou's Hotel for the winter, and where Mrs Matthews had been buried because the snow lay too deep and the ground was ice-hard up in Gulmarg ...

The wax of the seal broke under Sarah's cold fingers and fell upon the soft filmy layers of her skirt like small splashes of blood, and she brushed them away with a shiver of horror and drew out the two sheets of paper that the envelope contained: 'I left a record,' wrote Janet in a firm schoolgirl hand and without preamble or explanation, 'on the houseboat *Waterwitch* owned by Abdul Gaffoor, in Srinagar. Go there as soon as possible and look for it if anything happens to me. I paid in advance for the boat up to the end of June this year, and arranged that if I did not occupy it myself, any friend of mine who held the enclosed receipt could do so in my stead.' Then, in a wavering scribble, as though her nerve and her hand had suddenly failed her: 'I know I ought not to have done this, but I felt I had to. I can't say anything more. I can't. But it's there.'

The letter was unsigned and there was no clue as to the person or persons for whom Janet had originally intended it. In all likelihood it had only been written after Mrs Matthews' death. Probably an hour or two before Sarah herself had run to Janet's door in the moonlight, to warn her of that faceless figure in the snow.

The second piece of paper was a receipt for the rent, paid in advance up to the end of June 1947, for the houseboat, *Waterwitch*; and written on the back of it, signed by the houseboat's agents, were the terms of the lease.

Sarah re-read the short note with its brief, incredible instructions and final agonized cry three times before the words had any meaning for her. It was impossible, fantastic, that she, Sarah Parrish, should be sitting in the Indian starlight, in the ancient city of Peshawar, holding in her hand a clue to international mysteries involving, perhaps, the lives and destinies of countless people. A few lines written by a murdered girl ...

She read it once again, slowly and deliberately, as though she could drag from the paper the hidden thing that lay behind the bald words; the knowledge that had been Janet's when she wrote it, and which, but for this scrap of paper, would have died with her. And yet it told so little. Who had she meant it for when she wrote it? What had she meant to do with it? Why had she written it at all?

To that last question, at least, there appeared to be an obvious answer: because she had been afraid of death. Not so much on her own account, as for the knowledge she possessed. She had been terrified that the knowledge might be lost, and for that reason had been driven to take a desperate risk. Two risks! The chance of written information falling into the wrong hands, and the possibly greater one that her sudden decision to trust Sarah Parrish could prove to be a disastrous mistake.

Mrs Warrender, who had produced a large vanity-case adorned with a regimental crest, and had been powdering her nose as she discussed the old days at Ranelagh and Hurlingham, snapped the case shut and turned to Sarah: 'You'll be going up to Kashmir for the summer I suppose, Sarah? We're going up the week after next. Not that it's any fun now. But I suppose this is the last season we shall ever have, what with the handover set for next year, so ... Oh hello — is that the notice about the races?'

She leant forward and calmly twitched the sheet of paper from between Sarah's fingers.

Sarah did not stop to think. She reached out and struck the letter out of Mrs Warrender's hand, and with the same movement managed to knock her scarcely touched glass off the table, splashing its contents over the scarlet folds of Mrs Warrender's taffeta dress and filling her lap with fragments of half-melted ice. Mrs Warrender screamed and sprang to her feet, and Sarah, standing up, placed a small silver shoe on the forgotten sheet of paper, swished her billowing skirts over both and apologized in a flurry of carefully simulated concern and embarrassment.

Mrs Warrender glared at her like an angry cat and said, in the same breath, that it didn't matter at all and that the frock was ruined; and allowed Charles Mallory to mop off the surplus with his handkerchief.

Sarah said: 'I can't think how it happened. I must have knocked against the table. Perhaps if you went straight home and put the dress into water it won't stain?'

'Nonsense! It's quite impossible to wash taffeta. I shall have to send it to the cleaners. Thank you, Charles. That's enough. It'll dry in a minute or two. No, of course not! I wouldn't dream of taking it off. Look, it's drying already. Tim can — Tim! Where *has* that damn' boy got to? Really, one's junior officers these days are worse than useless! There's the band starting again. Come and dance this one with me, Charles. I was supposed to be dancing it with Johnnie, but you know what husbands are like. Anyway, he's sure to be tight by now and he always cuts my dances.'

Charles said: 'I'm sorry Helen, but I'm afraid I've got this dance with Miss Parrish.' His voice was pleasant but very definite, and he did not look at Sarah. He looked instead at Mrs Warrender, meeting her eyes with a bland gaze.

Helen Warrender, as Fudge had pointed out, was a stupid woman. But there was that in Charles's lazy gaze which even a stupid woman could read, and she flushed a dark and unbecoming red, looked from him to Sarah and back again, and spoke in a voice that was suddenly strident.

'I'm *so* sorry! I didn't realize I'd broken up a tête-à-tête. In that case I'll go and hunt up Johnnie.' She turned to Sarah and said with a metallic laugh: 'Don't take him too seriously, will you? In case you didn't know it, he's *heavily* engaged. Aren't you, Charles darling?'

Charles's expression did not alter, but he drew back a chair as though clearing a path for her, and with a toss of her head she swept away across the lawn, her taffeta skirts hissing angrily over the dry grass.

Sarah stooped down and picked up the sheet of paper, surprised to find that her hands were shaking and her knees trembling with reaction from rage. She sat down abruptly, and reaching for her unfinished drink, drank it thirstily, and putting down the empty glass, looked up at Charles.

'Thank you,' she said with the ghost of a smile. 'That was very good of you. Could you — would you add to your kindness by lending me your lighter for a moment? No, I don't want a cigarette thank you.'

Charles handed over a small silver cigarette lighter and Sarah snapped back the catch and held Janet's letter to the flame. The thin paper, having fortunately escaped being splashed with Helen's brandy and soda, caught alight easily and flared up, burning quickly until at last there were only three words left visible in the bottom corner – *'But it's there!'*. Sarah watched them fade with tears prickling behind her lashes, and thought: Oh! poor Janet! and dropping the blackened fragments onto the lawn she ground them into the parched grass with her heel.

'And now,' said Charles, 'perhaps you'll tell me why you flung that brandy and soda over Helen Warrender? Not, of course, that she hadn't been asking for some such demonstration. Still you must admit it was a little drastic.'

Sarah flushed. 'I didn't — I mean — it was really a sort of accident.'

Charles raised a sceptical eyebrow: 'Yes?'

'You mean "oh yeah?",' corrected Sarah crossly.

Charles's voice held a hint of laughter. 'My mistake; I thought you'd done it on purpose.'

'All right, then. I did do it on purpose and she had asked for it. So what?'

'Nothing. I was merely interested. It seemed a rather forceful way of expressing your displeasure.'

'I'm afraid I did it on the spur of the moment,' admitted Sarah defensively. 'You see, it was rather a private letter and I was afraid she might have had time to see a few words of it. But if she did I'll bet she forgot them the next second, because there is nothing like a really nasty shock for putting things out of your mind.'

'I'll remember that for future use,' said Charles gravely. He lit a cigarette and leant back in his chair watching her through the faint grey curl of smoke, while behind them in the ballroom the band played a slow foxtrot; a dreamy lilting tune that had been popular in the early years of the war.

Somewhere out in the darkness beyond the Club grounds a jackal howled eerily, and as other jackals took up the cry and blended it into a yelling, shrilling chorus as of souls in torment, Sarah shivered, and a sudden horror swept over her. A horror of the enormous, sunbaked land around her and the barren Khyber hills that lay just beyond Peshawar, menacing and mysterious in the starlight. Beyond those hills lay Afghanistan and the fierce and lawless tribes, while away and away to the north-east stretched the long line of the Himalayas, with somewhere among them the snow slopes of Khilanmarg.

A little breeze, rustling across the lawn, brought with it the smell of dust and flowering trees, and scattering the blackened fragments of Janet's letter, blew them away across the deserted terrace ... It's no good, thought Sarah desperately: I know I promised, but I can't go back to Kashmir! I *won't* go. It's nothing whatever to do with me, and I never want to see those mountains again ...

It was as though she were addressing the pale, accusing ghost of Janet. Telling her that as the letter had already been written and the envelope sealed down when she, Sarah, had come to Janet's room that night, it could not possibly have been intended for her, and that but for the chance that had brought her there, Janet would have given it to someone else. To Reggie Craddock, or Meril, or Ian Kelly ... Anyway, it was burnt now so she could forget it. Surely she could forget it ... ?

She saw in her mind's eye the long, winding hill road that climbed and twisted and dipped and turned for close on two hundred miles from the heat and dust of the cantonment town of Rawalpindi to Srinagar, the capital of the cool green valley of Kashmir. But the thought of returning to that valley, with its cold rim of watching mountains and black deodar forests, filled her with shuddering panic. She could not go back — she could not . . .

Charles Mallory's quiet voice broke into the tumult of her thoughts and brought her back to the present: 'What's the matter, Sarah? You're looking like a ghost.'

He had risen and was standing over her, and Sarah rose abruptly: 'I'm sorry. I'm a bit upset this evening. You go on in and dance with Helen. I'm better by myself.'

Her voice, even to her own ears, sounded thin and unsteady, and Charles said: 'Don't talk nonsense. You're shivering like a wet kitten. What's it all about, Sarah? You've been behaving for the last half hour as if you'd just been told where the body was buried. What's the matter? Bad news?'

'No,' said Sarah shakily, fighting a sudden desire to burst into tears. 'It's nothing, really. I – I'm . . .'

'Feeling ill? Would you like me to take you home?'

'No. No. I'm all right. I mean, it's nothing.'

'Well in that case,' said Charles crisply, 'I suggest you take a pull on yourself and come in and dance. You can't sit here looking at ghosts all evening.'

'Oh, go away!' said Sarah, her voice trembling on the edge of hysteria. 'Can't you see I want to be left alone?'

'So that you can work yourself up into an even worse state of nerves, I suppose? But that won't help you, you know. Come on, Sarah. You don't look like the sort of girl who has hysterics. Show some guts.'

'You,' said Sarah furiously, 'would know about that of course.'

'About what?' Charles's voice was softly dangerous.

'Guts,' said Sarah distinctly. 'I understand your regiment's been ordered to Palestine?'

For one frozen second she thought Charles was going to hit her and, instinctively, she took a swift step backwards. But the chair was behind her and she stopped.

Charles looked down at her and laughed; though not pleasantly. And then, she did not quite know how, his arms were about her, sure and hard, and he bent back her head across his arm and kissed her competently.

'You have been asking for that,' said Charles, bored, 'for weeks.' He put her away from him and picked up his unfinished drink.

Sarah stood staring at him for a long moment. Then she snatched up her bag, whirled about and ran across the lawn to the lighted ballroom, leaving him standing alone in the starlight.

Part III

SRINAGAR

'Look for me by moonlight;
Watch for me by moonlight;'
Alfred Noyes, *The Highwayman*

8

It was the last week of May; ten days after the Charity Dance at the Peshawar Club; and the Creeds, accompanied by an unexpected passenger in the form of Miss Sarah Parrish, were on their way up to Kashmir for Hugo's leave.

Only a few hours ago on the long drive from Peshawar to Attock on the Indus, and into the Punjab to the great garrison town of Rawalpindi, from where one of the main routes into Kashmir branches off from the Grand Trunk Road towards the foothills, they had been scorched by the heat and choked by the dust of the plains ... and now they were picnicking by the roadside among pines and firs and deodars, and breathing cool mountain air.

'How did that dear old bolster, your Aunt Alice, take this sudden change of plan?' inquired Hugo through a mouthful of curry puff: 'I shouldn't have thought she would have approved at all.'

'Oddly enough,' said Sarah, 'she took it quite calmly. I think it has at last dawned on her that any girl who served in the forces during the late unpleasantness ought to be able to look after herself. Besides, the minute I said I was going up with you, all was well. Antonia is "a dear girl" and Hugo "such a *nice* man".'

'How right she is,' said Hugo complacently. 'About me, I mean. She has made a noticeable error of judgement in her estimation of my wife, but she can't really be blamed for that. She was probably mixing her up with two other women.'

A car swished past, covering them with dust, and drew up twenty yards ahead with a scream of brakes.

'I wonder what that's for?' said Fudge, waving the dust away from her nose with a chicken sandwich. 'Do you suppose they've run out of petrol, or want to ask the time?'

'As long as they do not wish to borrow beer,' said Hugo, 'all that I have is theirs, including my wife. Oh *blast!* It's Helen. I might have known it. Go and head her off, my sweet. She worries me worse than the hives.'

Fudge said: 'Vulgar brute!' and sliding off the low wall, went to meet the smartly clad figure that was advancing upon them from the car.

'My dear!' — Helen's voice had much in common with a peacock's — 'I thought it was you! I made Johnnie pull up. We've been driving for hours, so I thought we might as well stop and have our lunch with you. I'd forgotten you were coming up today. What luck meeting you. God, how this journey bores me! If only there was somewhere else decent one could go. But of course there isn't. And anyway, none of us will ever go to the place again. At *least* this will be the last time, thank goodness.'

She checked suddenly at the sight of Sarah. 'Good heavens! It's Sarah. What on earth are you doing here, my dear? I thought you were supposed to be going to Ceylon or Singapore or somewhere? Don't tell me you're bound for Kashmir too?'

'Well, it looks that way, doesn't it?' said Sarah sweetly. She had a sudden and quite definite conviction that Mrs Warrender had stopped her car not because she had seen the Creeds, but because she had seen that there was a third person with them, and suspecting who it was, had wished to verify the suspicion. Her surprise was slightly overdone.

'But my dear! How nice. You'll simply adore Srinagar. Personally, I loathe it; but then of course Johnnie says I'm *far* too particular about the people I make friends with. Of course *I* always say one *can't* be too particular in that respect, but I know everyone else isn't quite so—— Well anyway, I'm sure you'll have a lovely time. Not that there'll be anyone up here this year. In fact I hear it'll be *dead* — though I expect you'll find a sort of dying flicker here and there. Why, hello, Hugo!'

'Yes, this is me, Helen. In the flesh. Odd, isn't it? Even Fudge scarcely recognizes me in this pair of socks. What's happened to Johnnie? Is he busy with Mother Nature, or just sulking?'

'He's getting out the lunch-basket. I'm afraid there are rather a pile of things on top of it. Here he is now. Oh, thank goodness you've got some beer, Hugo. I quite forgot to bring any with me, and we're both simply parched with thirst. I could drink six.'

Hugo closed his eyes and moved his lips in what may have been a silent prayer but was probably not, and Fudge said hurriedly: 'I'm so sorry, Helen, but I'm afraid that's the last bottle. However, if you can manage on half each, you're welcome to it.' She dropped her coat neatly over one of the two remaining bottles and turned to smile at Johnnie Warrender who came up carrying a large wicker lunch-basket under one arm and a car rug under the other.

'Hello, Johnnie. Here, don't put that down on top of the sandwiches! What time did you leave 'Pindi?'

'We didn't. I mean we spent the night at Murree,' said Johnnie depositing his burden on the wall. 'Hello, Sarah. I didn't know you were contemplating a Srinagar season.'

'Well, I always meant to do it sometime,' said Sarah vaguely, 'and as this seemed about the last chance I'd get, I decided to cadge a lift off Fudge and Hugo.'

'Good show. Pity you didn't see it in its heyday. It was a good spot once. We used to get some damned amusing polo there too ... Oh well! Good God, Helen! Is this all you've brought in the way of lunch?' He regarded the sloshy mass of tomato sandwiches with unconcealed disgust, and having pitched them down the hillside, helped himself to one of Fudge's curry puffs.

Johnnie Warrender was an ugly little man who looked like a cross between a gentleman jockey and Groucho Marx, but possessed, despite this, a considerable portion of charm. Left to himself he would have been an attractive and cheerful nonentity;

but he was not so left. From the time it had first been realized that Johnnie Warrender of the Lunjore Lancers could hit a bamboo ball farther and straighter, and with greater frequency, from the back of a galloping polo pony than the majority of his fellow-men, the course of his life had been altered, and he became, in a small way, a celebrity.

Gone were the days of happy obscurity and unashamed and cheerful penury, for Johnnie's magic wrist and eye brought him into the circle of the rich, the leisured and the socially prominent. Government Houses and Residencies, together with the homes of every Brass Hat and Little Tin God in India, were open to him, and Maharajahs, Rajas, Nawabs and Princes were quick to follow suit: to lend him polo ponies and invite him to their palaces as an honoured guest.

Unfortunately, there is something about Fame, even in such a comparatively narrow sphere, that is insidious and corroding except to those of steady temperament and balanced judgement. And save in the matter of horseflesh and the polo field, Johnnie Warrender possessed neither steadiness nor judgement. He was still accounted a 'good fellow' and his capacity for gaiety and alcohol remained undiminished. But from being a happy-go-lucky and charming person, he became a spendthrift and a snob; in both of which his wife excelled him.

Helen, who had been a young and unaffected girl, became almost overnight a hard, selfish and scheming woman, and that worst of all Indian pests, an indefatigable social climber. Her goal was not a high one, and by dint of flattery and determination and her husband's prowess on horseback she achieved a fair measure of success — though at a cost. The children she had meant to have were the first casualty, because they 'could not afford the money' — or the time. Not now, anyway: though of course she would start a nursery one day. But somehow that day never came.

The friends of earlier years went next; ruthlessly discarded as she mounted to higher things, while money that Johnnie could ill afford went on the lavish entertaining of their newfound friends. The bills mounted and the Warrender overdraft achieved terrifying proportions. But Helen, if she possessed any fears for the future, refused to face them, while Johnnie's motto was 'sufficient unto the day'. And now their world had crumbled round them, never to be rebuilt.

The first blow had been the mechanization of the cavalry. 'It could never happen,' said Johnnie and his type. But it did; and with the departure of the horses and their replacement by tanks and armoured cars, the standard and opportunities for polo among the less wealthy regiments shrank perceptibly. Then Hitler marched his storm troops into Poland, and the tide of the Second World War, damned for twenty years behind slowly rotting barriers, roared hungrily across the world. And for Johnnie and Helen, as well as for thousands of their class and kind, it was not the beginning, but the end of an epoch. A *Götterdämmerung*; a Twilight of the Gods.

Something of all this was in Sarah's mind as she sat on the low stone wall at the side of the Kashmir Road, listening to Johnnie talking horses and Helen complaining about the impossibility of the British officers who had been sent out to India during the last years ('My dear, half of them simply don't know a racehorse from a tonga pony!'); and seeing, in the merciless midday sunshine, the marks of dissipation and weakness on the one face, and the bitter lines of discontented middle age on the other. Perhaps, with the ending of the war, they and many like them had subconsciously expected the clock to turn back again. But the old days were over for good. India was to be given her freedom and 150 years of British rule would end. There was nothing left for the Johnnies and Helens except memories and debts . . .

Suddenly Sarah felt acutely sorry for them both and for the inevitable tragedy of their kind. There is always something more pitiful in the destruction of petty but prized possessions than in the crash of dynasties, for the latter is at least spectacular and dramatic, while the former is of no more account in the eye of history than the breaking of a child's toy.

Hugo courteously handed the last of the chicken sandwiches to the ever-hopeful Lager and slid off the wall: '*En avant, mes enfants!* "The sun is sinking fast, the daylight dies" — Hymns A. and M. In other words, it's almost five past two and we've been hogging it here for over an hour. If we're thinking of getting to Srinagar this evening we must put on no ordinary turn of speed. I refuse to navigate this tortuous road in the dark. Our headlights are rotten and my nerves are worse. Get off that rug, Helen, it goes in the back of the car.'

Helen rose languidly and, stooping to the lunch-basket at her feet, produced from it a battered-looking watermelon. 'Here, have this Hugo. Johnnie simply loathes watermelon and, after all, we have eaten a good many of your curry puffs. But fair exchange is no robbery, is it?'

'Must I, Helen? Oh well – very thoughtful of you.' Hugo took the green globe with unconcealed reluctance and stowed it gingerly in the boot of the car.

'You can eat it for breakfast tomorrow. Where are you staying in Srinagar, Sarah? At Nedou's?'

'I expect so,' said Sarah. 'I may take a houseboat though. "When in Rome" you know.'

'Oh, then you aren't staying with Fudge and Hugo?'

'Of course she's staying with us,' said Hugo. 'We have hired four houseboats for the season. One for each of us and one for the dog. We are people of large ideas. You must come and look us up some day. Hi! Ayaz!'

Hugo's bearded Mohammedan bearer appeared round the bend of the road where he had been eating his own meal, and Helen said: 'Of course we will. And I must get Gwen to ask you to the Residency one day. We're staying with the Tollivers you know. Well, *au revoir*. Shall I give your love to Charles Mallory when I write, Sarah? But no! — you're sure to be writing to him yourself. All the girls do.'

'Sarah,' said Hugo cheerfully, 'is always too busy reading letters to have time to write any herself. You wouldn't believe the number of people who write to her. In fact, all the boys do. Well, so long. See you at Philippi.'

The car slid away, swung round the corner and was gone.

'Crude,' remarked Hugo, lighting himself a cigarette with one hand, 'but probably more effective than subtle methods. Sarcasm and subtlety are wasted on Helen. Well, it's nice to have you with us, Sarah, and I'm glad you decided to give Ceylon the miss-in-baulk at the eleventh hour.'

'Yes,' said Sarah slowly, 'I think I am too.'

She leant back and closed her eyes against the sunlight and the mountain scenery, and thought again of the events that had led up to her decision to return to Kashmir.

Sarah had returned home after the Charity Dance shaken with fury at Captain Mallory, and determined to leave for Ceylon as soon as possible. But she had been unable to sleep. She had accused Charles Mallory to his face of cowardice, yet she was no better than a coward herself.

It was no good hiding behind the excuse that Janet had never meant that message for her. Of course she had not! Nevertheless it was to Sarah that she had been forced to entrust it. And she, Sarah, who had promised to help — should 'anything happen' to Janet. Well, it had happened. So how could she back out of her promise now? For all she knew, the record that Janet wrote of might be of desperate importance, not only to a few individuals but to hundreds of thousands — perhaps to millions of people.

Yet supposing she did go up to Kashmir herself, and took over Janet's boat, and found it? What could she do with it? No, of course it was impossible! She must forget all about it and let sleeping dogs lie. If only there was someone she could give the letter to. Someone to whom she could hand over the whole responsibility . . . She considered going to the Governor, or the Chief of Police. But she could not forget that Janet had said: 'Of course I can't go to the police! What would I tell them? Give away the results of months of work and planning, and ruin everything at the eleventh hour?'

What could she, Sarah, tell them, when she had burned the only piece of evidence she had — Janet's letter? She wondered now what had possessed her to do it. Cowardice again, she thought wryly. The urge to be rid of this thing that threatened to disturb her peace of mind. Well at least it left the ball firmly in her own court, and sooner or later she would have to make up her mind what she proposed to do about it.

On this decision she fell asleep at last, and dreamt that Charles was kissing her: not scornfully, as he had kissed her upon the Club lawn, but tenderly and with passion. And had been quite unreasonably infuriated when her dream had merged into reality, and she had awakened in the morning sunlight to find Lager enthusiastically licking her face.

Later that day Sarah had gone out into the garden and fought a battle with herself among the flowering jasmine bushes and the beds of yellow and scarlet cannas. In the end it had been Janet's unconscious paraphrase of Edith Cavell's dictum that *Patriotism is not enough*, rather than her own lightly given promise, that had swung the balance. No, it was not enough just to be 'patriotic', to love your own country and your own people, if you were not prepared to take any risks, or make any sacrifices, on their behalf. And if that was 'jingoism', then Shakespeare had been a founder-member, and she was in good company!

She would go to Kashmir and take Janet's boat, and find the record Janet had left there. Though what she would do with it once she had found it, she had no idea. That situation, however, could be dealt with when it arose. In the meantime at least her conscience would cease to trouble her, or torment her with accusations of cowardice. She would send a wire to Ceylon and then ask the

Creeds if they would take her up to Srinagar with them. There would just be time to arrange it . . .

So here she was once again upon the winding Kashmir Road. Being borne swiftly towards the city of Srinagar, and the Dāl Lake where Janet had lived on a houseboat named *Waterwitch.*

9

It was past five o'clock by the time the Creeds' car left the mountains and came out upon the level valley and the long, straight, poplar-lined road that leads from Baramulla to the city of Srinagar — that curious admixture of ancient and modern India that stands astride the Jhelum River, sheltered by a curving arm of the mountains and near a chain of beautiful lakes.

The sun was low in the sky, and its fading rays turned the white snowpeaks that ring the valley to rose-pink and amber; and here the river that had raged through the narrow mountain gorges behind them spread out into a broad and placid stream that flowed serenely between green banks lined with willows and chenar trees.

On either side of the road lay long fields of yellow mustard, the emerald green of crops, patches of late iris, purple and white, and small, huddled villages ringed by willow and walnut. Flocks of slow-moving sheep strayed homeward in charge of brown-robed shepherd boys who played upon small reed flutes, and the twilight was sweet with birdsong and tinged with a sense of nostalgia and lost dreams and the scent of spring.

It was dark by the time they reached Srinagar, so Sarah spent the night on board the Creeds' houseboat; but soon after breakfast on the following morning she set off in a *shikara* — one of the slim, flat-bottomed, gaily canopied boats that are the gondolas and water taxis of this eastern Venice — in search of the *Waterwitch*.

It did not prove difficult to find, and the agency with which the boat was registered for hire accepted Sarah's explanations and the receipt without undue interest, and dispatched her in charge of a polite young Kashmiri to Chota Nagim, some few miles outside Srinagar City where the *Waterwitch* was moored. She had not looked forward to this return visit, but that first trip to Nagim enchanted her.

The *shikara*, once clear of the city, slid away down cool, sun-dappled waterways fringed with willows; past ancient wooden houses perched upon stilts above the stream and crazily reminiscent of Hansel and Gretel. Through villages whose walls rose out of the water, and whose carved and fretted balconies overhung the passing boats. Villages whose main street was the waterway.

As the heart-shaped paddles rose and fell in unison, the boat glided under old, old bridges and by temples whose glittering roofs were discovered on closer inspection to be plated not with silver, but with pieces of kerosene tins. Brilliant blue kingfishers flashed and darted above the quiet reaches of the stream, and innumerable bulbuls twittered among the willows. And at last they came to a quiet backwater near an open stretch of lake where, moored against a green bank and sheltered by the boughs of a gigantic chenar tree, lay a small houseboat.

It was a trim little craft, and according to Sarah's guide contained a living-room, and a small dining-room with an adjoining pantry from which a narrow wooden stair led up to the roof. The forward part of the roof was flat, and supported an orange and white striped awning, and beyond the pantry lay two small bedrooms which led off each other, and were each provided with a minute bathroom.

Unlike the majority of houseboats upon the lake, the sides of the *Waterwitch* had been painted white, while the wooden shingles that covered the peaked roof above the after section of the boat were stained green, so that the whole effect was rather that of a child's Noah's Ark. It formed such a gay and attractive picture, backed by the green of the willows and mirrored in the clear lake water, that Sarah was aware of a sudden and overpowering sense of relief.

She could not have said what she had expected, but subconsciously she had supposed that an air of darkness, decay and mystery would linger about the boat in which Janet had lived and where she had written down and hidden her secret. But there was nothing dark or mysterious about this trim little boat with its freshly laundered curtains fluttering in the breeze.

As the *shikara* drew alongside, a sliding-door in the centre of the boat was drawn back and the red-bearded *mānji*,* the owner, popped out upon the duckboard wreathed in welcoming smiles, and after a brief conversation with the man from the agency, salaamed deeply and hastened to usher Sarah on board.

The *Waterwitch* was furnished in much the same style as any other houseboat upon the lake. The wooden panelling of the walls was unstained and unpainted; as were the low ceilings, which were formed of small sections of wood cut into squares, diamonds and hexagons, pieced together to make a complicated mosaic overhead. There were cheap cotton curtains at the windows and the living-room was crowded with furniture: a sofa, upholstered in faded and much worn plush, whose springs looked to be in urgent need of repair; three armchairs with clean but faded cretonne covers, a large writing-desk, two occasional tables of intricately carved walnut, and several others in brass or papier mâché, in addition to a standard lamp of horrifying design.

A narrow shelf with a fretwork rim ran round the entire room at the level of the top of the windows and was crammed to overflowing with dusty, dog-eared books and out-dated periodicals, and Sarah regarded this tattered array of literature with blank dismay.

There if anywhere, she thought, is where I shall have to look; and her heart sank at the prospect of leafing through all those thousands of musty pages. She had hoped to be able to complete

*A boat-owner.

her search of the little houseboat in a matter of hours, but she had not calculated on several hundred assorted books and magazines as possible hiding-places. It was going to take days, not hours, to conduct a really thorough search through the contents of those close-packed shelves . . .

'Very nice room!' urged the *mānji*, extolling the beauties of his boat. 'Good chairs for sittings. All covers I wash new. Many beautiful books. Many sahibs are leaving books on my boat for long time now. Here is dining-room. Take a look, Miss-sahib, very fine dining-room.'

There was no door across the opening between living-room and dining-room, its place being taken by an old-fashioned bead curtain, and the *mānji* held aside a bunch of the coloured, clashing strings and ushered Sarah through into the next room.

This was better! The dining-room appeared to contain the minimum of furniture and hiding-places, which after the clutter of the living-room was a relief. The table was a work of art in polished walnut wood, oval in shape with a deeply cut and beautifully carved pattern of chenar leaves running round its rim, and Sarah ran her hand appreciatively across its shining surface as she passed on, urged by a lyrical running commentary from the *mānji*, to a small pantry, half of which was taken up by the short wooden staircase that led up through a species of trap-door to the roof.

A bedroom, a small bathroom, a second bedroom beyond it, and another bathroom. The little boat was clean and neat. Swept and garnished and empty of all feeling. An impersonal, placid little boat that gave no hint, no whisper of the secret lurking somewhere within it. Blobs of sunlight reflected off the water outside danced a silent saraband upon the ceilings, the uneven floorboards creaked loudly and cheerfully under Sarah's feet, and the little boat rocked gently to the movement, slapping the water in small gay splashing sounds against its sides.

There seemed to be nothing of Janet here. Janet belonged to the grey skies, the white snowfields and the black winter forests of

Gulmarg; not to the gay green and gold and blue of Maytime on the Dāl Lake.

An hour and a half later Sarah was on her way back to Gagribal Point and lunch with Fudge and Hugo, having completed all the necessary arrangements with the man from the agents, and given orders that the *Waterwitch* was to remain at its present moorings. She had also provisionally booked the next-door *ghat*, or mooring-space, on behalf of the Creeds: 'You won't mind mooring your houseboat there instead of at Nagim, will you Fudge? It's only just round the corner really, and it looked so peaceful and sheltered. Nagim seemed to be full of boats.'

'*Mind?* My dear child, for this I will leave you half of my overdraft in my will,' said Hugo cordially. 'Fudge has a single-track mind in these matters, and merely because some four score years and ten ago, when we first visited this salubrious health resort upon our honeymoon, we parked our barque upon Nagim, she cannot conceive of any other pitch. This regardless of the fact that what was once a blossoming Eden far from the madding crowd, has since had endless monstrosities of wood and stone built all round it, in the form of club-houses, cafés, boarding-houses and what-have-you, and is so thickly jammed with houseboats that one's left-hand neighbour is never ignorant of what one's right-hand neighbour doeth. No. Speaking for myself, I shall be delighted to park elsewhere. For one thing, I do not fancy floating upon sewage; and for another——'

'That will be quite enough!' interrupted Fudge hastily. 'It's a lovely idea, Sarah. We'll have our boat taken out there immediately after lunch.'

The afternoon had been spent sitting up on the roof of the Creeds' big houseboat, as it was poled by a team of husky Kashmiris down the same waterways that Sarah had passed through that morning. And with the evening they came to their mooring.

The *Waterwitch* had been connected, via several hundred feet of wire, to the main electric light cables that ran alongside the Nagim road, and as all her lights were lit, her windows glowed cheerfully in the twilight, and Fudge, who had been trying to persuade Sarah to remain on the *Sunflower*, was relieved at the sight of the gay little boat. 'It doesn't look so bad,' she admitted. 'How did you manage to find it, Sarah?'

'Oh, just looking around,' said Sarah vaguely. 'Don't worry darling. I shall be quite safe. I shall have Lager with me, and your boat is so close that I've only got to raise a yell if I feel nervous.'

The Creeds' houseboat had been moored about thirty yards below the little *Waterwitch* and facing it, so that the cookboat, which housed their *mānji* and his family and would also provide accommodation for Ayaz, lay behind it and out of sight. The *mānji* of each houseboat usually combined the office of cook, head-waiter and *valet de chambre* with that of owner; but tonight Sarah declined the culinary services of her own factotum and dined on board the *Sunflower* with the Creeds.

They were not more than halfway through the meal when a *shikara* bumped alongside in the darkness and a voice hailed the cookboat in Kashmiri. A few minutes later Ayaz, the Creeds' bearer, appeared in the doorway with an envelope on a small brass salver, which proved to contain an invitation to a cocktail party at the Residency on the following evening, addressed to Major and Mrs Creed and Miss Parrish.

'That's quick work,' commented Sarah, as Fudge scribbled an acceptance and handed it to Ayaz: 'How did they know we were here? Helen, I suppose.'

'I don't think so,' said Fudge. 'Hugo and I wrote our names in the book this morning, and put yours in too for good measure. We were having coffee at the Club and met the new P A — an erstwhile acquaintance of yours.'

'Forgive a poor ignorant newcomer,' said Sarah, 'but what exactly is a P A?'

'Personal Assistant,' translated Hugo, helping himself to cream:

'A poor wretch whose job it is to send out the invitations to Residency Tea-Tipples and Bun-Battles. I believe it also includes such onerous duties as translating the *khansamah*'s menus into French, arranging the rhododendrons on the dining-table, fetching and carrying for the Lady Resident, and prompting her in a hissing whisper when she mixes the names of her guests. This sinecure is at present held locally by a bootfaced damsel by the name of Forbes.'

'Forbes? You don't mean *Meril?*'

'The same. No Helen of Troy, as you will be the first to admit. But doubtless oozing with efficiency.'

'I shouldn't have thought she'd be in the least efficient. However, she was a pretty good skier.'

'Was she, indeed? I can't say I ever noticed her performance in particular. It's those spectacles I suppose. I must admit I am sorry for the wench.'

'Why? Because "girls who are spectacled never get their necks tickled"?'

'That, of course,' admitted Hugo. 'But the girl is also gravely handicapped by an aunt who holds the All-India Gold-Plated Cheese Biscuit, open to all comers, for sheer undiluted louse-power.'

'Hugo!' expostulated Fudge indignantly.

'I apologize, m'dear. An ill-chosen simile, but doubtless Sarah gets the idea.'

'I have heard rumours,' admitted Sarah, recalling certain forcible remarks of Janet's on the subject of Meril's aunt. 'What's the matter with her?'

Hugo said: 'You will undoubtedly meet the lady at this binge tomorrow, and be able to judge for yourself. Speaking for myself, she fascinates me, and I cannot help regretting that upon her demise it will not be practicable to have her stuffed and placed in some public museum.'

'And they say that women are cats,' commented Fudge, selecting a banana from the fruit dish. 'For sheer concentrated cattiness, you can't beat the male!'

'Nonsense!' said Hugo. 'I speak but the limpid truth. Lady Candera is the Original Boll Weevil. She has an eye that can bore holes through six feet of armour-plating, and a tongue that could skin an elephant. Take it from me — a tough baby! Strong men blench before her and women take cover.'

'Is she quite as formidable as Hugo makes out?' inquired Sarah of Fudge.

'Well, almost,' admitted Fudge, dipping her banana thoughtfully in the coffee sugar and ignoring Hugo's outspoken criticism of the action. 'I'm scared of her myself; but then I take jolly good care to avoid her.'

'Worm!' observed Hugo, removing the coffee sugar.

'Worm yourself! You're terrified of her. She prides herself on always saying exactly what she likes as rudely as possible. And that's always pretty unnerving to the general public.'

'Tell me about her,' said Sarah, interested. 'She sounds full of entertainment value.'

'She is, in a way,' admitted Fudge with a laugh. 'I've often thought that life would be a lot duller if it were not for these highly coloured characters. If everyone were all a nice pink, like the Hoply girl or Mrs Ritchie, how bored we should all be! I appreciate the addition of a few nice splashy reds and purples myself. They add a dash of paprika to the mixture, if nothing else.'

'Lady Candera,' pronounced Hugo, 'is a type that is, or was, fairly common all over the world. But we grew a special brand of them in the Indian Empire. Next year there will be no Indian Empire, and so that brand will become extinct — along with the Johnnies and Helens and their ilk. They won't go to ground in England, because it will not be able to give them what they want; so the Lady Canderas will retire to infest places like Cyprus and Madeira, while the Johnnies and Helens will probably get themselves dug into Kenya. *Ehu fugaces!* And if you shove that slimy chunk of fruit into the coffee sugar once more Fudge, I shall arise and assault you.'

'You still haven't told me much about this Lady Whatsiz,' complained Sarah. 'What's she like?'

'Nothing on earth,' said Hugo promptly.

Fudge threw him a withering look. 'She is tall and thin and, as Hugo says, she's got an eye like a gimlet. I believe she's half French or Afghan, or something of that sort. They say she used to be a raving beauty when she was a girl. She must be about ninety by now — well anyway pushing eighty — and she looks like something that has been dug up from the ruins of Byzantium.'

'Miaow!' said Hugo, handing over the cream jug. Fudge ignored him.

'Her husband was something or other in the ICS — the Indian Civil Service. Or am I thinking of the F and P?'

'Foreign and Political Department,' translated Hugo kindly, 'the chaps who only had to keep breathing in order to end up with a four-figure pension and a handle to their names.'

'Well anyhow, he was something big in some Indian State,' said Fudge. 'But he's dead now, and she lives in a houseboat near Gagribal with Meril and a sort of dim companion-woman called Pond.'

'And a very suitable name too, if I may say so,' interpolated Hugo: 'I have seldom encountered anyone so damp as that female. If there is a breeze about, she ripples.'

Fudge ostentatiously returned the cream jug: 'Where was I? Oh yes. They live somewhere near Gagribal in a huge houseboat.'

'Chiefly noticeable,' said Hugo rapidly, 'for the outsize telescope erected on the roof, by which means they are enabled to keep an indefatigable eye upon the misdeeds of the unwary.'

Fudge giggled. 'They used to spend a lot of time peering through it, and years ago Lady Candera tried to start a "Purity League" in Srinagar. She said that the goings-on she observed in other houseboats and passing *shikaras* were flagrantly immoral and should be stopped. She even tackled the Resident about it, and he apparently replied that he would consider taking action provided he could have a good look at the "goings-on" through the telescope first. She never spoke to him again.'

'Poor Meril!' said Sarah. 'No wonder she looks so harried.'

'Let's go and sit up on the roof,' suggested Fudge, rising. 'There's a moon tonight.'

'Not me,' said Hugo firmly. 'I have no desire to waste my last leave in Kashmir scratching mosquito bites.'

'Is it really that? Our last leave in Kashmir?' sighed Fudge. 'Oh dear! Somehow I can't believe it. We've spent so many leaves up here. Do you suppose we shall ever come here again?'

'No,' said Hugo. 'Unless, of course, the Amalgamated Brotherhood of Mangle Manufacturers, of whom you will by then be an unwilling member, come here for their Communal Workers-of-the-World Jamboree and Butlin Binge one day. Then, standing by the rows of cosy, communal, Comrades Dormitories, and gazing out at the Concrete Lido that will have blossomed by the lake, you will drop a tear into its medicated waters and murmur, "Ah me! How lovely it used to be when it was merely sewage!"'

'Disgusting brute!' said Fudge. 'There was a time when you used to spend hours holding my hand in the moonlight.'

'Undoubtedly. But that was in the days when I was merely betrothed to you, or endeavouring to become so, and that was all I could do about it. However, having successfully pressed my suit, should I now be overcome by the romantic yearnings that once drove me to moon-gaze, there are other things I can do about it.'

'Hugo!'

'Not before the child!' said Hugo. 'Shove off and shiver on the roof and leave me and the port in peace.'

'I think I shall go to bed, if you don't mind Fudge,' said Sarah. 'It's been a long day, and I feel sleepy.'

'Very sensible of you,' said Hugo, yawning. 'We will see you onto your yacht.'

They escorted Sarah down the gangplank and along the few yards of turf that separated the two boats, Lager frolicking and barking in the moonlight and chasing imaginary cats in the shadows.

'Are you sure you'll be all right?' asked Fudge anxiously. 'Shout if there's anything you want.'

'Quite sure. I will. Good-night Fudge. Good-night Hugo. Come in Lager, you little pest.'

Sarah turned and walked up her own gangway, and the little *Waterwitch* rocked and creaked to her footsteps. At least, she thought, it would be impossible for anyone to come on board without instantly advertising their presence, since even the lightest step on a houseboat could be both heard and felt. The floorboards creaked and the boat vibrated slightly to every movement of those on board.

She closed and latched the sliding-doors behind her and snapped off the lights in the living-room, dining-room and the small pantry as she passed through them on her way to her bedroom. After which she undressed and got into bed, suppressing, with an effort, a strong desire to look over her shoulder and jump at every slight sound aboard.

Lager leapt onto the foot of her bed and curled himself up into a small velvet ball, and Sarah turned out the light and lay for a while staring into the darkness, until, moved by a sudden impulse, she reached out a hand and pulled back the curtain from the window beside her bed.

The glassed frames had been pushed back into the thickness of the wall leaving a wide square, screened by wire gauze against flies, mosquitoes and night-flying insects, that looked out across the moonlit lake to the shadowy mountains beyond.

Gulmarg lay somewhere over there — an unseen hollow below the white levels of Khilanmarg and the long ridge of Apharwat.

The moonlight would be shining on the little ski-hut, as it had shone that night when she had talked to Janet in the snow. It would be lying cold and clear along the verandah of the silent hotel, as it had lain on the night that she had stood and stared down at a line of betraying footprints on a thin film of snowflakes; and it would peer into the garden of a deserted house near the Gap, where the wind swung a gate idly to and fro on a broken hinge . . .

Sarah shivered, and closing the curtains against the white night, fell into an uneasy sleep.

10

The late evening sunlight shone warmly upon the smooth lawns and towering chenar trees of the Residency garden where peonies, roses and canterbury bells bloomed in gorgeous profusion in the long flowerbeds, and wafts of scent from the direction of the kitchen gardens spoke of sweetpeas already in bloom.

In an ordinary year the British Residency in Srinagar gave many parties during the course of the season; but this year was not as others. It marked the end of an epoch — of an era — and something of this feeling seemed to pervade the present party. A tinge of restlessness; of farewell to familiar things. Next year there would be no time for parties. Only for packing and goodbyes. So let us eat, drink and be merry, for tomorrow we shall be scattered as chaff before the wind and the familiar places will know us not . . .

Their hostess greeted Sarah and the Creeds in the dim hall of the Residency, and directed them into a spacious green and white drawing-room full of guests and flowers.

'Hello, Meril!' said Sarah, turning to accost a hurrying figure.

'Oh, it's you Sarah! I heard you were up here with the Creeds I thought you said you weren't coming to Kashmir again.'

'I wasn't,' admitted Sarah, 'but it seemed a pity to miss what may be my last chance of seeing this place. It was rather a spur-of-the-moment idea.'

'Well, I hope you'll like it. It isn't going to be very gay this year, what with everyone trying to get home. Still, you'll like being out at Nagim. The bathing's quite decent.'

'What's quite decent?' inquired an all-too-familiar voice behind them. 'Personally, I've yet to find anything decent about this place.'

'Oh hello, Mrs Warrender. May I introduce Miss Parrish? Mrs — oh of course, how stupid of me! You've met before. You were both at the Ski Club Meeting, weren't you.'

'Yes. Sarah and I know each other well. *Do* tell me, how is Charles? And what do you think of Srinagar? *Quite* deadly of course. No life in it. Gulmarg is the only place worth going to in Kashmir, but even that is simply finished this year. Anyway, it was becoming too shatteringly provincial. Isn't that George McKay? What on earth's he wearing that frightful blazer for? It looks exactly like a striped awning! Some ghastly Cricket Club or other I suppose ... Hello, George. I thought you were busy doctoring people in Sialkot?'

'I was until yesterday. At present I am on embarkation leave.' Major McKay shook hands with Meril and bowed to Sarah. He was a solidly built man of medium height and in his late thirties, with a pleasant but rather humourless face and a certain primness of manner that made him seem older than his years.

'Yes, I'm really off,' he said in answer to inquiries. 'I thought I'd give Kashmir a last look before I left. There are more people up here than I thought there'd be. All doing the same thing I suppose. Saying goodbye.'

'Well I hope for your sake that Srinagar will leave a better taste in your mouth than Gulmarg,' said Helen with a laugh. 'All those post-mortems must have made it rather a busman's holiday, and I hear our hardworking Secretary, Reggie, didn't see eye to eye with you about one of them. Was that true?'

'I'm sure I don't know,' said Major McKay stiffly. 'It's a subject I cannot really discuss.'

'Oh dear! Have I said something I shouldn't? How awful of me! Where are you staying?'

'At the Nagim Bagh Club, for the moment; but I hope to get some fishing later on. Is your husband up here?'

'Yes, Johnnie's somewhere around. Heavens! Here's that Candera woman. Why on earth Gwen asks her I don't know. Oh sorry, Meril. I forgot she was your aunt.'

Meril smiled wanly and glanced over her shoulder with a somewhat hunted expression at the latest arrival: a tall, elderly woman clad in impeccable tweeds, who stood in the doorway surveying the assembled company through a pair of jewelled lorgnettes. No; not elderly, corrected Sarah mentally – old. But despite her age she was holding herself with that erect carriage so admired by the Victorians.

'If she's coming over here, I'm off,' said Helen Warrender, and removed herself swiftly.

Meril looked as if she were about to follow her example, but a harshly imperious voice arrested her.

'Ah, Meril,' said Lady Candera bearing down on the shrinking Miss Forbes: 'Gossiping, I see? I understood you had certain official responsibilities connected with these functions. Obviously, I was mistaken.'

Meril flushed an unbecoming shade of red and shuffled her feet like a small child: 'I'm sorry, Aunt Ena. Can I get you anything?'

'Yes. A brandy and soda please. You know I detest cocktails.'

'Yes, Aunt Ena. Of course, Aunt Ena.' Meril left at what was almost a run, and Lady Candera turned her lorgnettes upon Sarah, observing her from head to foot with the peculiar rudeness of the undisputed autocrat. Sarah remained unruffled and returned the old lady's scrutiny with equal interest.

Lady Candera showed little signs of the beauty that legend credited her with. Though perhaps a hint of it lingered in the modelling of jaw and temple and the line of the thin, beaked nose. Her face sagged in innumerable yellow wrinkles and was curiously blotched, as is the skin of some elderly Indian women, and her eyes were an odd, pale grey that appeared lighter than the tone of her somewhat swarthy complexion – and were certainly a paler shade than the iron-grey of her hair. She wore a magnificent rope of misshapen pearls, and her bony fingers were loaded with diamonds and emeralds in heavy, old-fashioned and not over-clean settings.

Sarah's appearance, or possibly her calm gaze, appeared to interest her, and raising her lorgnettes she addressed Major McKay in commanding tones: 'Major McKay, who is this gel? She's new. Not like the usual run of cheap stuff we get up here this time of year. Or is she?'

Major McKay, his ruddy countenance betraying a mixture of embarrassment and frigid disapproval, said stiffly: 'Lady Candera, may I introduce Miss Parrish. Miss Parrish——'

'— of London and Hampshire,' interpolated a gentle voice as Hugo drifted up, glass in hand. 'How are you Lady Candera? Hello Doc, nice to see you up here again.'

'One of these tourists, is she?' said Lady Candera, with a sound that in anyone less majestic would have been termed a sniff.

'Please! Please!' deprecated Hugo, waving his glass in a pained manner. 'Let us say "A bird of passage" — and what a bird! In my opinion, a golden oriel.'

'Ah,' said Lady Candera, bringing the lorgnettes to bear again. 'Very interesting.' She nodded briefly at Sarah, turned abruptly and walked away.

'Hugo, that was outrageous of you!' said Sarah, attempting severity and relapsing into a giggle.

'Why? I am a keen soldier and believe in keeping in practice.'

'What were you practising then?' inquired Major McKay.

'Counter-attack,' said Hugo solemnly. 'Have a sausage?' He collected a plate of small hot sausages speared on cocktail sticks, and a glass of sherry for Sarah. 'The sherry is a far, far better thing than that weird mixture they are dishing out,' said Hugo.

'I recommend it. Here's cheers! By the way McKay, perhaps you can——' He stopped. The Major was no longer with them. 'Odd,' commented Hugo. 'He was around a moment ago.'

'Why, hello Sarah!' a tweed-clad figure was pushing its way between the guests towards them: Reggie Craddock, whom Sarah had last seen in Tanmarg, superintending the departure of the Ski Club members: 'Oh ... hello Hugo; I didn't see you ...' Reggie sounded less than pleased. 'Up here again?'

'What do you mean "again"? I am practically a fixture. In fact they are considering according me the status of a Protected Monument. What brings you here, Reggie?'

'Last spot of leave in Kashmir,' said Reggie. 'I'm due home soon. We're selling up, you know. Nearly seventy-five years and three generations in this country, and now — oh well. You know the Nawabzada, don't you?'

He caught the arm of a slim, flannel-clad figure and dragged him out of the crowd.

'Yes, of course,' smiled Sarah. 'We met skiing.' She held out her hand to Mir Khan who bowed over it gracefully.

'It is nice to see you again, Miss Parrish. I do not ski now. The snow has gone. So I play tennis and golf instead. Do you play these games also?'

'A little,' said Sarah.

'Don't you believe her, old man! She plays both with distressing competence,' said Hugo.

Sarah laughed, and catching a glimpse of Johnnie Warrender through the crowd, asked Mir Khan if he included polo in his list of sports?

Mir Khan shrugged. 'When I can find it,' he said. 'But polo is dying in India; even among the Princes.'

Reggie said: 'Don't you ever do any work, you idle plutocrat?'

'Not if I can help it,' admitted Mir with a disarming grin. 'One of these days work may catch up with me, but just now I run very fast and so I keep just out of reach. For the moment I am what the Americans would call a playboy.'

'And very nice too,' sighed Hugo, accepting a fresh and brimming glass from a passing *khidmatgar*. 'I only wish I was in a position to follow your admirable example. But what with an expensive wife to keep in socks and headgear, not to mention keeping myself in pants and footwear, I am reluctantly compelled to apply my classic nose to the grindstone. It's all very sad. "Skin off your nose,"' said Hugo.

'And what do you think of Srinagar?' asked Mir Khan turning back to Sarah.

'Well, we only arrived the day before yesterday,' said Sarah, 'but I like what I've seen of it so far.' The talk turned for a time to the valley and the various beauty spots Sarah must visit before she left, until Hugo said: 'By the way, Reggie, there's another member of your skiing flock here this evening. McKay.'

'Oh,' said Reggie Craddock briefly; his pleasant face all at once blank and uncommunicative. The oddly uncomfortable silence that followed was broken by their hostess, who bore down upon Mir Khan and whisked him away to meet a Frenchman who wrote travel books and knew his father, while Hugo was removed to entertain a Mrs Willoughby.

Sarah was left with Reggie Craddock, who began to talk skiing; but she was not really listening to him, being more interested in gazing around the crowded room to see how many faces were known to her. Surely that was one of the Coply twins talking to a pretty blond girl by the piano? The boy half turned his head; yes, it was Alec. Or was it Bonzo? She never could tell which was which unless they were standing together, when it was possible to pick out the small differences that distinguished them from each other. Apart, few people were aware which one they were addressing.

Reggie Craddock talked on and on. But now he was speaking of Janet Rushton, and the name served to jerk Sarah out of her inattention . . .

'Damned shame about Janet,' said Reggie. 'She was a really good sort: and one of the best women skiers I ever saw. Kandahar class. Why the hell women jib at obeying perfectly clear and rational orders, I'm hanged if I know. It wasn't as if I hadn't expressly ordered everyone to keep off Blue Run, and explained why. Good Lord, you'd have thought one fatal accident was enough to scare 'em off the run, apart from a direct order. Never been so upset in my life. Gives the Club a bad name too. Puzzles me though; she was no fool, Janet. Not the sort to do a damn' silly thing like that. To tell you the truth, Sarah' — Reggie dropped his voice to a confidential undertone — 'I've never been quite satisfied about that business of Janet.'

He stopped and looked at Sarah intently, as though he had perhaps expected to surprise some flicker of agreement on her face. His eyes were very bright and as curious as a bird's in his brown, nutcracker face.

Sarah felt herself flushing under his gaze and was furious with herself; it was a trick she had never outgrown and which she mentally designated as Victorian and 'missish'. She spoke quickly to hide it, and with perhaps a shade too much emphasis: 'What rubbish, Reggie! I didn't suspect you of being imaginative.'

'Imaginative in what way?' asked Reggie Craddock. He lowered his gaze and examined the contents of his glass with exaggerated interest, but Sarah did not reply, and after a moment he said, apparently at a tangent: 'You knew Janet quite well, didn't you.'

It was not a question but a statement of fact, and the suspicion darted across Sarah's mind that he said it casually — too casually — in order to ... what? Was she herself getting over-imaginative? Why should she suddenly imagine that Reggie Craddock, of all people, should be laying a trap for her? Fishing slyly for an unguarded statement?

Reggie's eyes were upon her again, bright and bird-like. No, not bird-like, thought Sarah. A bird's eyes were bright and soft and inquisitive. Reggie's eyes were bright and inquisitive, but they were hard too. As hard as flakes of steel; and somewhere deep down in them there glimmered something that was wary and alert.

His question seemed to float in the air between them and she realized that she must answer it as casually as it had been asked. 'No,' said Sarah, aware of an odd constriction of her throat. 'I can't say I knew her at all well. I'd spoken to her, of course. But then I spoke to most people at the Meeting.'

'She had the room next to you in Gulmarg, didn't she?' Reggie was once more intent upon his glass, twirling it slowly so that the lights moved on the olive at the bottom.

'Yes. But I didn't see much of her. She was in a different class from me as a skier.'

'I see,' said Reggie Craddock slowly. He poked at the olive in his drink with a small cocktail stick. 'I thought you must have known her well, since you've taken on her boat.'

His glance flicked upward to Sarah's face, and something jumped and fluttered in her throat, and her mouth was suddenly dry. She lifted her glass with a hand she was surprised to find steady, and sipped at her sherry before replying.

'Yes?' said Sarah with a composure she was far from feeling. Her tone was gently interrogative and her slightly lifted eyebrows managed to convey a faint suggestion of polite surprise at this inquiry into her personal affairs.

Reggie Craddock flushed an unbecoming red and looked away. He said hurriedly: 'I knew Janet pretty well. She was here last summer when I was up on leave. We were on one or two parties together; and of course we were both interested in skiing.'

He paused to eat the olive and tuck the discarded stick absently into a bowl of pansies that stood on the grand piano at his elbow: 'She had a rather jolly little houseboat,' continued Reggie more slowly. 'I remember her telling me last year that she'd taken it on a long lease for this year as well, because one of the best moorings on the lakes went with it, and decent moorings were often hard to get. When I came up here this year I thought I'd take it on, but the man from the agents was out when I called in about it, and the next time I went along, which was this afternoon, they told me you'd taken it.'

Sarah said nothing and continued to sip her sherry.

Reggie cleared his throat and fidgeted with the stem of his glass. 'I suppose you wouldn't consider sub-letting it to me? I wouldn't ask except that — well I know it sounds damn silly, but I've rather a hankering to take on that little boat. Reasons of sentiment, and all that rot, and this looks like being my last chance. Of course I'd get you another one just as good, and you could keep the same *ghat*. I don't suppose it makes any difference to you what boat you're on, as long as it's a decent one and you're next to the Creeds. Tell you the truth, I was a bit cheesed off when I heard you'd got in ahead of me with Janet's boat. Well — er — how about it?'

Sarah regarded Reggie Craddock thoughtfully over the rim of her glass. An assortment of quite incredible theories were running through her mind, whirling and flaming like catherine wheels on Guy Fawkes night.

Reggie had known Janet well. Reggie had taken the trouble to find out, or remember, that Janet had occupied the room next to hers at the hotel in Gulmarg. Reggie had tried to rent the *Waterwitch*, and having failed to do so was trying to persuade her to give it up to him. He had, it was true, issued a strongly worded edict against the use of the Blue Run; but supposing that had been a blind?

Added to all that there were two other facts worthy of note: Reggie Craddock had been in the ski-hut at Khilanmarg, and was the only skier up that year who was entitled to wear on his lapel the little gold K on a blue enamel ground that was the badge of the Kandahar Ski-Club.

All these things and many others raced and jostled each other through Sarah's brain, intermingled with a feeling of blank incredulity. It was, of course, utterly fantastic, and she was letting her suspicions run away with her. It was ridiculous, absurd, impossible, to imagine for one moment that a man like Reggie Craddock ... And yet Janet Rushton was just as absurdly and impossibly dead, and all at once words that Janet had spoken repeated themselves in Sarah's brain: 'If anyone had told you a few hours ago that I was a Secret Service agent, would you have believed them? ... Of course you wouldn't! Because I don't look like your idea of a Secret Service agent.'

'Well?' said Reggie Craddock.

Sarah collected herself with an effort. 'I'm terribly sorry to disappoint you Reggie, but I'd rather not. I've taken a fancy to that boat, and once I've got settled into a place I hate having to move.' Her tone was light and friendly, but perfectly definite.

A rather ugly look crept over Reggie's face, but he answered easily enough: 'Oh, that's all right. I merely thought it was worth asking. But of course, as you were a friend of Janet's ...'

'I've already told you,' snapped Sarah with some asperity, 'that I barely knew the girl.'

Reggie finished his drink and put the glass down upon the piano with a brisk clink. 'I think I forgot to mention,' he said, 'that when the agents told me that you had taken on the *Waterwitch*, they also told me that you held Janet Rushton's receipt for the boat, without which you could not have moved in.'

There was a brief moment of silence. Then: 'What month were you up here on leave last year, Reggie?' asked Sarah.

'August. Why? What's that got to do with it?'

'Only that it interested me to hear that Janet had told you last August that she had paid for the *Waterwitch* in advance for this year.'

Reggie's brows drew together in a scowl. 'I don't see ...' he began.

'That receipt,' said Sarah softly, 'was dated December 3rd.'

Somebody in the press of guests stepped back and inadvertently jostled Sarah's elbow, jerking the remains of her sherry in an amber stream down her grey linen dress, and a breathless voice began to gasp incoherent apologies: 'Oh dear! Oh, dear me, I am *so* sorry! How *exceedingly* clumsy of me!'

Sarah turned with overwhelming relief to find a small, anxious woman struggling to extract a handkerchief from a large and overcrowded handbag, with which, when she had succeeded, she made futile little dabs at the stained dress. At any other time such an accident would have been annoying, to say the least of it. As it was, Sarah could have kissed the offender, since but for this timely interruption she would have become involved in some impossible explaining. For her retort to Reggie Craddock had been a double-edged weapon.

If, as she had insisted, she had barely spoken to Janet Rushton, how was it that Janet's receipt for a lease of the *Waterwitch* was in her possession?

Turning away to reassure her rescuer, Sarah was aware that a large, hearty woman wearing puce-coloured crêpe de Chine had borne down upon Reggie Craddock and swept him away on a spate of voluble chatter, and she breathed a deep sigh of relief. She really *must* learn to keep her temper and guard her tongue. It had been stupid and foolhardy to make damaging admissions merely to score off Reggie Craddock, and she was not at all sure that by doing so she had not allowed Reggie Craddock to score off her!

'I *cannot* apologize sufficiently,' the small woman was saying unhappily. '*Most* careless of me. Your pretty frock! But these parties — so crowded.' She groped agitatedly for a pair of rimless pince-nez that had fallen off her diminutive nose and were now swinging aimlessly from the end of a thin gold chain.

'Please don't bother,' urged Sarah with her most charming smile. 'As a matter of fact, I'm really terribly grateful to you.'

'To *me*?' said the small woman blankly. 'Now you are making fun of me!'

'No, really,' Sarah assured her earnestly, 'I mean it. I was involved in a most awkward conversation, and your bumping into me like that simply saved me. Sherry won't stain. I'll rub it down with a sponge when I get home, and it won't show a mark, I promise you.'

'It is so kind of you to say so,' fluttered the small woman. 'I am sure you cannot mean it, but it has made me feel a little better about my clumsiness. May I introduce myself? My name is Pond. Miss Pond.'

'Oh!' said Sarah with interest. 'I'm Sarah Parrish.'

'How do you do,' said Miss Pond primly.

'Fine, thank you,' said Sarah. 'Here, let's sit down, shall we? That sofa looks quite comfortable.' She steered her companion towards a chintz-covered sofa from which they could look out over the garden, and having seated herself, turned with frank interest to look at the companion of the formidable Lady Candera.

Pond, thought Sarah. Hugo was right. It really was a most suitable name. A small patch of somewhat weedy water; the haunt of homely, foolish things like ducks and tadpoles.

The little woman seated beside her might have been any age from thirty to sixty, and her features seemed to consist of a series of buttons: a small flat button of a nose, a primped button of a mouth and a pair of brown boot-button eyes. She wore, in addition to an anxious expression, a haphazard collection of garments that gave an impression of having been flung together in a hurry, and Sarah's fascinated eye observed that she was wearing short buttoned boots in addition to such miscellaneous items as a Batik silk scarf, mustard-yellow fabric gloves, and several strings of assorted beads.

Her voice was soft and breathless and she appeared to speak in a series of gasps. Was this Sarah's first visit to Kashmir, and what did she think of the dear valley? Where was she staying? And did she not think that the Lake was *too* beautiful?

Sarah, grateful for her escape from Reggie Craddock, replied suitably, while outside the windows the daylight faded and the garden filled with shadows and the scent of mignonette and night-scented stock.

They were still talking when, well over a quarter of an hour later, a stentorian voice cut through the cocktail party hubbub as a knife cuts through cheese: 'Elinor!' trumpeted Lady Candera.

Miss Pond sprang up as though she had been stung in a sensitive spot by a hornet. 'Oh dear! I'm afraid that is for me ... Yes Ena, I am coming. So nice to have met you, Miss Parrish. I am so sorry. About the sherry, I mean. Yes, Ena, yes ... I'm coming.' And gathering up a scattered collection of gloves, handbag, handkerchief and scarf, she scuttled out of the room.

'What are you giggling about?' demanded Hugo, plumping himself down on the window-seat near Sarah. 'Has the human doormat been amusing you? Incredible creature, our Pondy. How do you suppose she does it?'

'Does what?'

'Puts her clothes on. I have a theory that she first covers herself with glue and then crawls under the bed, gathering up fluff as she goes.'

Sarah burst out laughing. 'You *are* an idiot, Hugo. But possibly you're right, at that.'

Fudge came across the room and leant on the back of the sofa: 'What are you two laughing about? Do finish that drink, Hugo. It's quite time we left. They'll be sweeping us out with the crumbs soon. Sarah! What on earth have you spilt on your dress?'

'Sherry,' said Sarah. 'And believe me, I was never more grateful for anything in my life. Is Reggie still around?'

'Reggie Craddock? No, I think he left about twenty minutes ago with Mir.'

'Thank God for that,' said Sarah devoutly. 'Come on. Hugo.'

They said goodbye to their host and hostess and moved out

into the hall to wait while a red-robed *chaprassi** went off to summon the car.

Twilight was merging into dusk, and the lights of the Srinagar Club twinkled through the trees beyond the Residency gates as Sarah went out onto the front steps — Fudge and Hugo having stopped to talk with some friend — and stood looking up to where the bright blob of light glittered from the summit of the Takht-i-Suliman temple, high above the chenar trees of the garden.

A lone figure, obviously one of the departing guests, appeared suddenly at the far end of the drive near the gateway, from the shelter of a clump of bushes. There was a strong light above the gateway, and as the figure passed through, Sarah noted that it was wearing a striped blazer and wondered idly what Major McKay had been doing in the garden? A moment later someone came swiftly out of the shadows across the gravel drive from the direction of the tennis-courts, and ran lightly up the steps.

'Hello Meril,' said Sarah. 'You're just in time to see us off.'

Meril stopped, and putting up an uncertain hand to push back a lock of hair that was straggling untidily across her brow, said anxiously: 'Is it late? I felt I couldn't bear that stuffy room a minute longer, so I went out to walk round the garden. The flowers all seem to smell so much sweeter at night. I didn't realize it was so late. Are people leaving?'

'They've mostly left I think,' said Sarah, turning to look over her shoulder into the lighted hall: 'Your aunt is still there — telling Hugo where he gets off, judging from her expression! And at a guess there are still quite a few people left, so you don't have to worry: you're in time to speed at least a dozen departing guests.'

Meril looked alarmed. 'Oh dear, I suppose I shouldn't have gone out.' She pushed ineffectually at the errant lock of hair, and inquired abruptly: 'Why did you come up here again?'

*An office-servant.

Sarah raised her eyebrows, more at the tone than the question itself, and said with a laugh: 'It's a free country!' and Meril blushed suddenly and hotly in a wave of scarlet colour that temporarily eliminated her freckles. 'I – I didn't meant it like that,' she said. 'I only wondered——' Her voice trailed away as she turned to peer anxiously over Sarah's shoulder to where her aunt stood among a small group of departing guests in the hall, and Sarah suffered a pang of conscience: poor Meril! It was a shame to snub her. She must lead a dreary and frustrating life with that aged autocrat of an aunt. No wonder she was such a milk-and-water nonentity!

'As a matter of fact,' she explained, 'the Creeds were coming up, and everyone told me that I really ought to see Kashmir without its snow before I left India. So here I am. We're parked in a sort of backwater just outside Nagim. You must come out and bathe and have lunch with me some day.'

'I'd like to do that,' said Meril absently, her eyes still intent on the group in the hall: 'We don't get much bathing here.'

'Then it's a date. We're just the other side of the Nagim Bridge. Chota Nagim, I think they call our backwater. My boat's the green and white one. It's called the *Waterwitch*.'

'The *what*?' Meril turned quickly.

'The *Waterwitch*.'

'But – but that is — that was Janet's boat!'

'Yes,' said Sarah pleasantly. 'Was she a friend of yours?'

'Janet? Well no — not really. I knew her of course. She was up here all last year. She lived in that boat out at Nagim, but she went about a lot. Tennis and parties and things. Everyone knew her. Aunt Ena doesn't like me going to parties. Not that I get asked to so many,' added Meril with an uncertain smile.

Sarah said: 'Would you say Reggie Craddock had been a special friend of hers?'

'Of Janet Rushton's? I don't know. Why do you ask?'

'Oh nothing. Idle curiosity, I suppose. Something he said this evening gave me the idea.'

'Reggie Craddock and Janet,' said Meril thoughtfully. 'Perhaps he did like her. I never thought about it before. He was up here on leave last year, of course, and Major McKay said——'

But what Major McKay had said was lost, for at that moment Fudge and Hugo came out of the hall and swept Sarah down the steps and along the wide gravelled drive towards the car park and home.

11

Sarah devoted the next few days to an exhaustive search of the *Waterwitch.* But the task proved far from easy, since Fudge and Hugo were apt to appear on the boat at all hours of the day, demanding her presence at bathing parties, picnics or expeditions, and she found it hard to produce an adequate supply of plausible excuses for not accompanying them.

On more than one occasion she had been sorely tempted to tell them the whole story and ask for their assistance in her search, and the only thing that restrained her from doing so (apart from a conviction that this was a matter best kept to herself), was the fact that she possessed no shred of proof with which to support her incredible story, and did not relish the prospect of its being received with polite or derisive incredulity.

Examined in the cold light of day it frequently appeared, even to her, as both fantastic and impossible, and she still sometimes wondered if she had not dreamt or imagined the whole thing. But the evident anxiety of some person unknown — Sarah suspected Reggie Craddock — to obtain possession of the *Waterwitch* did little to support that theory, for it was on the morning after the Residency party that a Kashmiri who said he came from the agents had endeavoured to persuade her to exchange the *Waterwitch* for another boat.

Sarah had refused to consider it, and suspecting bribery, had sent the man away with a flea in his ear. But though she remained on the boat and continued with her solitary search, she found it wearisome and disheartening work.

She had begun by looking in all the obvious places — enthusiastically assisted by Lager, who barked and scratched and evidently laboured under the impression that he was being encouraged to hunt rats. But her main difficulty lay in the fact that life on a houseboat could only be compared to living in a goldfish bowl, since apart from the sudden and frequent appearance of one or other of the staff, who were liable to walk in on her at any moment, the attention of water-borne hucksters requesting her to examine their wares, or attempting to sell her fruit or flowers, was as maddeningly recurrent as the clouds of mosquitoes and midges: and less easy to repel.

On one occasion she had been surprised by the *mānji*, while engaged in unpicking a section of her mattress in order to make sure that no folded paper had been concealed among its lumpy, raw cotton stuffing. (Lager had been particularly noisy, and she had been cross and preoccupied, and had not noticed the *mānji*'s approach.) Her explanation, that she was in search of some sharp object that had pricked her from the mattress, was not well received. The *mānji* informed her that never before had it been suggested that evil insects inhabited his boat, and not so much as the smallest flea would the Miss-sahib find — unless perchance one had entered the boat upon the person of the Miss-sahib's dog, and for this he accepted no responsibility. Sarah's attempts to clear up the misunderstanding merely made matters worse, and the *mānji* had retired, offended dignity in every whisker.

But since it was impossible to move noiselessly on a houseboat — and nothing larger than a mouse could have stirred without advertising its presence — thereafter Sarah saw to it that Lager did not run excited races with himself while she was searching.

Unfortunately, there was nothing she could do about the numerous vendors of shawls, carpets, papier mâché and underwear, whose *shikaras* — drifting silently over the water — would appear suddenly outside the windows with the request that the Miss-sahib should 'Only look — do not buy!' The sudden and unheralded appearance of these gentlemen never failed to startle her, and she began to wonder how Janet had ever been able to make a record of anything without the entire population of Srinagar being aware of it! She must have written it and hidden it by night; when the lamps were lit and the curtains close-drawn, and every door and window bolted and barred . . .

Only when all the obvious hiding-places had been exhausted did Sarah turn resignedly to the bookshelf in the living-room, and taking down the volumes one after another, go methodically through them. It proved to be a weary, dusty and thankless task, for the books were for the most part old and tattered, and they smelt of dust, mildew and mice. The dust made Sarah sneeze and her head ache, but she plodded doggedly on: occasionally coming across one that had been Janet's and which bore her name on the flyleaf — written in that sprawling schoolgirl hand that Sarah remembered so well from her one sight of it in the letter she had burnt at the flame of Charles Mallory's cigarette lighter.

These particular books she had examined page by page, and in one of them she found several sheets of paper covered with Janet's handwriting and stuffed between the cover and the dust jacket — and for a marvellous five minutes was convinced that she had found what she was looking for, since it appeared to be a code. But its appearance was deceptive, for it proved to be a laundry list.

On the following day she had barely settled down to work when an unexpected caller arrived in the person of Helen Warrender.

Helen had evidently driven out to the Club at Nagim, which lay only about a quarter of a mile from where the *Waterwitch* was moored, on the far side of the narrow strip of land that separates the Nagim Bagh lake from the backwater of Chota Nagim. Leaving her car there, she had walked across the fields to call on Sarah.

A flurry of barks from Lager announced her approach and gave Sarah just time to push the day's quota of unsorted books under the frill of the sofa and hurriedly brush the dust from her hands, before going out to greet her. Helen, it appeared, had come to make her an offer for the boat.

Friends of hers, explained Mrs Warrender airily, had specially wanted this particular boat, and been most disappointed at hearing that it was already occupied. But on hearing that Helen knew the present occupant they had asked her to approach Sarah with a view to an exchange of boats: 'And of course dear,' concluded Helen, casting a disparaging eye about the cluttered living-room of the *Waterwitch*, 'I knew you couldn't possibly have any objection, so I told them they could consider it fixed. That's right, isn't it?'

'No,' said Sarah coldly. 'I'm afraid it isn't. I have absolutely no intention of giving up this boat, and when you next see Reggie you can tell him that from me!'

'Reggie?' exclaimed Helen Warrender blankly.

'You can add,' continued Sarah, with a dangerous sparkle in her green eyes, 'that I am a moderately easy-going person, but I don't like being pushed around.'

'I don't know what you're talking about,' said Helen Warrender. Her customary drawling voice had suddenly lost its veneer of affectation and was quick and harsh: 'Reggie? What Reggie? You mean Reggie Craddock? The man who — but *he* can't be ...' Helen stopped abruptly and bit her lip. 'I'm sorry,' she said more slowly. 'There seems to have been some muddle. It wasn't Reggie Craddock who wanted the boat. It was — oh well. Someone you wouldn't know. A friend of mine.'

She turned and stood for a while staring out of the houseboat window in frowning concentration and tapping her teeth with the edge of her sunglasses. She seemed to have forgotten about Sarah.

Presently she swung round and said: 'Why did you think I was trying to get the boat for Reggie Craddock? Has he been after it too?'

'It looks that way, doesn't it?' said Sarah. 'I'm sorry I was rude, Mrs Warrender, but——'

'Oh, call me Helen,' said Mrs Warrender impatiently. 'There's no need for you to apologize. I didn't realize your boat was so much in demand. Why did Reggie Craddock want it?'

'Sentimental reasons,' said Sarah. 'Or so he said. I didn't really go into it. Srinagar is full of houseboats and most of them appear to be empty this year. But as I happen to have taken this one, I prefer to stay on it.'

'And that goes for me too, I suppose?' said Helen.

'Well, yes; I'm afraid so. I'm sure your friends will be able to find a dozen boats as good as this one, and probably at half the price. After all, prices should have fallen considerably this year.' She realized suddenly that she had made a tactical error and stopped.

'Oh,' said Helen Warrender in an interested voice. 'So you booked this boat last year? But you can't have done that. You weren't here. How did you come to take it? And why are you paying higher than you need for it?'

Sarah considered for a moment. She was strongly tempted to tell Mrs Warrender to mind her own business, but realized that this would only create an impression of secrecy; in addition to being rude. It was not that she had any particular objection to being rude to Helen Warrender (who in Sarah's opinion had asked for it), but she particularly wished to avoid a suggestion of any mystery being attached to her occupancy of the boat. She therefore decided that an edited version of the truth would serve her best: 'I took over this boat from a friend of mine,' she said carefully. 'Janet Rushton.'

'You mean the girl who killed herself skiing in Gulmarg? But I knew her!'

'Yes, that's the one. She had this boat last year, and she'd taken it on for six months of this year as well. Then she changed her mind about it, and happened to tell me one day that if I ever wanted to come up here later in the year before the lease ran out, I could take it on. I thought it might be a good idea, so I took over her lease, hoping that I could sub-let if I didn't come up after all. But I did, and I like the boat; and I like this *ghat*. But I don't expect I shall stay up here long, and as soon as I've gone your friends and Reggie Craddock and the agent's uncle's brother-in-law, and anyone else who wants it, can fight it out between them. Until then I intend to stay on it myself.'

Mrs Warrender said 'Oh' in an uncertain tone of voice, and sat down on the arm of the sofa. 'Well that's that, isn't it? It's damned hot all of a sudden; I shouldn't be surprised if we were in for a thunderstorm. I could do with a drink if you've got one around.'

'I'm so sorry. I should have offered you one before,' apologized Sarah. 'What'll you have? Lemon squash?'

'As long as you put plenty of gin and a spot of bitters in it, yes.'

'Sorry, no gin on board. But if you'll wait a minute I'll run across to the Creeds' boat and hijack some of Hugo's.'

'That would be darling of you,' drawled Helen, dragging off her sun-hat and fanning herself with it. 'I confess I loathe soft drinks, and I could do with a stiff John Collins.'

Sarah ran down the gangplank and across the short strip of turf that separated the two boats, but it took her a minute or two to locate the gin which Hugo had left behind a flower vase on the writing-table, and when she returned it was to find Helen Warrender sitting on the floor with a pile of books strewn around her. She had one in her hand and looked up, unabashed, as Sarah entered: 'Funny place to keep your books,' she observed. 'Your sausage puppy started rooting them out from under the sofa, so I thought I'd better rescue them. Your *mānji* must be an untidy devil. There are lots more under there.'

'Are there?' said Sarah, in what she hoped was a disinterested voice; and mentally consigning Lager to perdition, she mixed a John Collins and handed it to her unwelcome guest. 'I'm afraid there's no ice. Do you mind?'

'Not at all, darling. Thanks. Well, here's cheers.'

Helen downed half the glass while continuing to gaze at the book in her hand, and Sarah saw that she was looking at a flyleaf across which Janet had written her name.

'This Rushton girl,' said Mrs Warrender. 'Wasn't she supposed to be rather a spot skier?'

'Yes,' said Sarah briefly.

'Damn silly thing for her to do. She ought to have known better. I rather wonder at your wanting to take over her boat after that.'

'Why?' inquired Sarah coldly.

'Oh, I don't know. Rather gruesome, don't you think? Still, if you don't mind. It's been an unlucky year for Kashmir in the way of accidents, hasn't it? First the Matthews woman and then the Rushton girl. I keep on saying there's bound to be a third one. These things always go in threes, don't they? Well, I suppose I'd better be going.'

Sarah did not attempt to dissuade her and Helen stood up and brushed her skirts, and tossing Janet's book onto a chair, walked over to a looking-glass in an atrocious Victorian frame of plush and shells hung on one wall, and replacing her sun-hat, peered at herself and exclaimed: 'Heavens, what a mess I look! It's this heat. Let's hope we get a good storm to clear the air.'

She dabbed at her nose with a rather grubby powder puff, and having touched up her mouth with lipstick, said: 'Well, my visit seems to have been rather abortive, doesn't it? Sorry you don't feel like giving up the boat. Still — there it is. If you feel like changing your mind, let me know.'

Sarah continued to say nothing, and Mrs Warrender snapped shut her handbag, adjusted her dark glasses and trailed out of the boat into the sunlight. At the bottom of the gangplank she turned and said: 'Thanks for the drink. I do hope you won't regret it. The boat business I mean.' Upon which cryptic remark she waved a languid hand and walked off between the willows.

'Now what was that intended for?' mused Sarah, addressing herself to Lager: 'A threat or a promise? Either way, I'm not sure I like it. No. I do not like this set-up one little bit and I've half a mind to—— No, I haven't! I won't be pushed around!'

There were two gangplanks on the *Waterwitch*. One that led from the bank to the pantry, and was used almost exclusively by the *mānji* and the other houseboat servants, and a second that led to a small open space on the square prow of the boat from which one entered into the living-room. Sarah stood on the prow in the hot sunshine and watched Helen Warrender take the field path that led between young corn and a blaze of yellow mustard towards the Nagim Bagh road, and presently she said again, and with more emphasis: 'No, Lager. I will *not* be pushed around!'

12

Having replaced the books so tactlessly exposed by Lager, Sarah postponed any further search through the houseboat's tattered library, and spent the remainder of the day with the Creeds.

I'm beginning to imagine things and to be suspicious of everything and everybody, she decided ruefully; and that's fatal. After all, why *shouldn't* Reggie Craddock's story be true? How do I know it isn't? He did know Janet, and for all I know he may have been fond of her. Suppose Mrs Warrender's friends really do want this boat, and for quite unsinister reasons? It *is* rather an attractive little boat, and quite a reasonable size compared with most of these outsize floating palaces I've seen. I must try and cultivate a sense of proportion ...

With this laudable object in view she lunched with the Creeds, accompanied them in the afternoon on a picnic to the Shalimar Gardens, and returned to dine with them on the roof of their houseboat, though their original plan had been to dine and dance at Nedou's Hotel, and they had booked a table there. But since Major McKay, who was to have made the fourth member of the party, had sent an eleventh-hour message to say that he had pulled a muscle while playing tennis, they abandoned the dance with some relief and ate a scratch meal, hurriedly concocted by the houseboat staff, instead.

The day had been hot and breathless, but with nightfall a light wind began to blow from the mountains, ruffling the surface of the lake and driving little waves in crisp slaps against the side of the houseboat.

Normally, on moonlit nights the lakeside was noisy with frogs; but tonight for some reason the croaking chorus was silent, and though the sky overhead was still cloudless, away to the south-west summer lightning licked along the distant ranges of the Pir Panjal, and there was a mutter of faint, far-off thunder in the air.

Beyond the willow trees a line of tall lombardy poplars bent their heads before the freshening breeze, the *mānjis* came out upon the bank and began to tighten mooring-ropes and chains, and Hugo, who was dispensing coffee, got up from the table and went to the roof's edge to observe the operation.

'Ohé, Mahdoo!' called Hugo in the vernacular: 'What dost thou do?'

'Perchance there will come a storm in the night, Sahib. We make the boats secure so that should the wind be great, it cannot pull them away to drift and sink in the lake.'

'That's a jolly thought!' said Hugo, returning to his seat. 'Nice thing for yer uncle to wake up in the small hours and find himself drifting rapidly away from the home bank and about to turn turtle at any moment.'

Sarah yawned and got to her feet. 'Well I'm off to bed, I think. Good-night, and thanks for a lovely day.'

'Good-night Sarah. Sweet dreams.'

Sarah strolled along the bank in the moonlight and waited at the foot of her gangplank while Lager scampered off into the shadows to chase imaginary cats. He was away for an unconscionably long time and Sarah, growing impatient, whistled and called. She could hear him scuffling about somewhere in the shadows beyond the willow trees, but he would not come to her, and when at last he reappeared he was licking his whiskers and prancing in a self-satisfied manner.

'Lager, you little horror,' reproved Sarah sternly, 'you've been scavenging! What have you been eating? You know you aren't allowed to eat rubbish!'

Lager's ears, nose and tail drooped guiltily and he pattered docilely up the gangplank at Sarah's heels.

The *mānji* had left the lights burning and Sarah made a tour of her little boat, checking that the windows and doors were fastened before returning for a last look round the living-room. She had already commented caustically to Fudge upon the feeble lighting in Srinagar, for the Power Station being unable to supply the load demanded of it, even a 60-watt bulb produced only a feeble yellow glow. But tonight, for some reason, it seemed to her that the lights were suddenly over-bright and garish and that in their glare the small houseboat appeared larger and less overcrowded and strangely empty.

Outside, the night was full of noises. The slap of wind-driven water against the sides of the houseboat, and the jar and whine of the ropes and chains that moored it to the bank; the sough of the wind through leaves and branches, and the chorus of creaks and groans from the boat itself as it rocked and jerked and fidgeted at its moorings. But inside the small living-room it was comparatively quiet.

The harsh yellow light poured down on the faded covers of the chairs and sofas, the tortured carving of the over ornate tables, the shabby Axminster carpet and the long row of dusty books and tattered magazines. And looking about her, Sarah was seized with the uncomfortable fancy that everything in the boat — each piece of furniture — was endowed with a peculiar life of its own, and was watching her with a curious, sly hostility. So must they have watched Janet. Janet scribbling her record with fear-stiffened fingers and repeated glances over her shoulder. Janet hiding it away somewhere on this small boat.

The room knew. The room was aware. The blank eyes of the window-panes blinked and brooded, reflecting a dozen Sarahs in lilac linen dresses. The cheap cotton curtains billowed faintly in the draught, and the bead curtain in the dining-room doorway swayed and clinked softly as though some unseen presence had just passed through it . . .

Outside the wind was rising, and as the boat began to rock to the gusts, Lager pattered restlessly about the room sniffing at the skirting-boards and the shadows of the chairs, and whining. Sarah spoke to him sharply, and having pulled the curtains to, snapped off the lights and marched determinedly to bed.

She turned off the dining-room lights as she passed through, but left the pantry light burning so that when she was settled in bed with Lager curled up at her feet, and switched off her bedroom light, she would still see its glow through her half-opened door. It gave her a vague feeling of reassurance, like a nightlight in a nursery, and she fell asleep lulled by the rocking of the boat and the wail of the wind through the branches of the big chenar tree. But some two hours later she awoke suddenly and sat bolt upright in bed. She had no idea what had awakened her: only that one moment she had been fathoms deep in dreamless slumber, and the next moment wide awake and with every sense tense and alert.

The threatened storm had skirted the lake and passed on down the valley towards the mountains of the Banihal Pass, but the boat still rocked and creaked at its moorings, and the water still slapped noisily against its sides. The wind was blowing in savage gusts, and in a brief lull between them Sarah could hear the scuffle of rats in the roof and the steady snoring of Lager, who had burrowed under the blankets. It was several minutes before she realized, with a sharp pang of alarm, that the pantry light was no longer burning and the entire boat was in darkness.

Stretching out a hand she groped for the curtains of the window near her bed and pulled them aside, but no moonlight crept in to lighten the little room, for the sky was covered with clouds and a light rain was falling on the uneven surface of the lake. Sarah felt for the switch of the bedside lamp and heard it click as it turned under her fingers, but the light did not come on and the room remained shrouded in darkness.

It's the storm, she thought. The wind must have torn down the wires or blown a branch of a tree across the line somewhere. There's nothing to be frightened of...

Then why was she frightened, and what had awakened her? Why was she sitting so rigidly upright in the darkness, listening intently for the repetition of a sound?

And then she heard it: and knew that this was the sound that had jerked her from sleep into tense wakefulness.

It came from the front part of the boat. From the dining-room, thought Sarah, trying to place it. She heard it quite clearly in a pause between the gusts of wind, despite the multitudinous noises of the night: a muffled scraping sound that was quite unmistakable. The sound made by one of the sliding houseboat windows being drawn stealthily back in its groove.

Sarah knew those windows. They were guarded by outer screens of wire flyproof mesh that also slid back into the thickness of the houseboat walls when opened. They had no bolts, but were fastened together on the inside by inadequate latches of the hook-and-eye persuasion. And as the frames, owing to warping and slapdash workmanship, hardly ever fitted quite accurately, it was a simple matter to slip a knife blade between them from the outside and lift the latch.

Somebody had just done that. Someone who was even now easing the stubborn ill-fitting frames apart, inch by inch.

Sarah sat rigid, her heart hammering; waiting for what she knew would be the next sound. Presently it came: a barely audible thud, followed by a slight extra vibration of the uneasy craft as someone stepped down through an opened window into the boat.

A scurry of wind drove the rain against the window-panes by her bed, and in the resulting rocking and creaks from the *Water-witch* she could not pick out any further sound of footsteps.

If I just sit here, thought Sarah frantically, and don't move or make a sound, perhaps they won't come in here. Perhaps it's just someone after the spoons. If I keep still ... But she could not do it. There was Janet — and Mrs Matthews. Why had she been so stupid and so stubborn as to sleep alone on this ill-omened boat? It was all very well to tell herself not to panic or do anything silly because nothing really bad could happen to her. Look what had happened to them? No: she dared not sit still and wait. She must get away quickly. But she had forgotten Lager. If she got out of bed he would wake up and bark ...

Of course! That was it — Lager. Lager would save her! He would race off into the darkness barking defiance, and create a diversion, for darkness would be no problem to him, and he could, when the occasion demanded it, make as much noise as a hurdy-gurdy. It might well be sufficient to frighten away the intruder — though on this wild night it would not wake the Creeds — and under cover of the noise Sarah herself would escape by the back of the boat and rouse the cookboat.

She leaned forward in the darkness and dug Lager out of his nest of blankets. He was warm and velvety and relaxed, and he continued to snore gently. But he did not wake. Sarah shook him and spoke urgently into his floppy ear in a tense whisper: *'Lager! Lager! Wake up. Rats, Lager!'*

But the dachshund puppy did not move. Sarah shook him violently. He's doped! she thought incredulously. He's eaten something. Where? When? And then she remembered how he had scuttled off into the shadows when she returned from the Creeds, and had reappeared licking his chops. He had eaten doped food. Food that had in all probability been put there for this special purpose ...

A sudden fury of rage shook Sarah, temporarily submerging her panic, and clutching the unresisting Lager under one arm she slid to the floor and groped her way across the room.

For one wild moment she had considered opening the window and shouting. But she knew that the wind would tear the sound to tatters and it would only be a waste of breath. She would have to go through the empty second bedroom behind her and through the bathroom and out at the back of the boat, from where she could rouse the *mānji*. Or better still, feel her way along the narrow duckboards that ran along both sides of the boat, until she reached the gangplank by the pantry door, and go down it and along the bank to the Creeds.

The *Waterwitch* rocked to another sudden buffet of wind, and Sarah banged her head violently against the open door of her cupboard and dropped Lager. For a moment she clung to the edge of the cupboard door while a variety of coloured sparks shot through the darkness: she must have forgotten to latch it and the draught and the uneasy motion of the boat had combined to swing it open.

After a moment or two she stooped dizzily and groped about in the darkness. Lager still snored gently, and guided by the soft sound she gathered him up and made unsteadily for the spare bedroom door, moving this time with more caution.

It seemed a long way in the dark. The door was ajar — presumably the wind again — and Sarah passed through it. There was no gleam of light from the black night beyond the curtained window-panes, and the wind shrilled through the cracks in the houseboat and sent cold draughts along the floors. Once something touched her cheek and she started back, her heart in her mouth. But it was only a curtain billowing out on the draught.

She tried to remember how the room was furnished. A bed against the wall, and the door into the bathroom to the left of the bedstead; the dressing-table under one window. Was there a chest of drawers under the other? She could not remember, but once she touched the bed she would get her bearings.

Sarah moved forward an inch at a time, one hand held out before her. Where *had* the bed got to? And then suddenly her hand touched polished wood. But it was not the end of a bed. It must be the dressing-table. No, it was too high for that and too smooth, and it had a carved edge. Surely there was no table in the spare bedroom that had a carved border to it?

She stood still, confused and uncertain, her head still aching and dizzy from its violent contact with the cupboard door. And as she stood there, she became aware of something else: a curious clicking sound somewhere near her. She could hear it between the blustering gusts of wind. *Click ... clack ... click ...* Very softly, like someone telling beads. *Beads!* The garish bead curtain that hung in the open doorway between the dining-room and the living-room ... That was it! ... it was here, close beside her; swaying and clicking in the dark. And with a sudden, sickening shock of panic she realized what she was touching. It was the oval dining-table with the deep, carved, chenar-leaf border.

She wasn't in the spare bedroom at all. She was in the dining-room! She must have lost her bearings when, confused by the blow on her head, she had stooped down to grope in the dark for Lager. And the curtain that had touched her cheek was blowing out from an open window; that was why this room was so much colder. There was a window standing open in it; which could only mean that the sound she had heard — the sound of a window being opened — had come from here.

She was in the wrong room. And in the same instant she realized that someone else was in the room with her.

Sarah stood frozen, not daring to move. Even her heart seemed to have stopped beating. She could hear no sound other than the noises of wind and water and the creaking of the boat as it rocked and strained at its moorings, but she did not need any sound to tell her that someone was there, close to her; almost within reach of her hand. Sheer animal instinct, that sixth sense which warns us of the near presence of one of our own kind, was sufficient ...

I mustn't move, she thought frantically. I mustn't breathe ... She felt the floorboards under her feet vibrate, and the air about her stirred as though something solid had passed her in the black dark.

There was a sudden lull between gusts of wind and in the brief silence Lager gave a loud snuffling snore.

She heard someone draw a hard breath in the darkness, and something — a hand — brushed against her bare arm.

Sarah dropped Lager, backed wildly away, and screamed at the top of her voice. And as she did so a light flashed on; the white glare of an electric torch, full in her face, and an incredulous voice said: 'For God's sake! Sarah!'

The next moment arms were about her holding her closely, and she was struggling frantically, still in the grip of terror. Her captor held her with one arm and with his free hand turned the torch onto his own face.

'Charles!'

13

Sarah burst into overwrought tears, and Charles, holding her, said: 'I'm sorry, Sarah. I didn't know there was anyone on board. Don't cry, dear. It's all right now. There's nothing to be frightened of now.'

No, there was nothing to be frightened of now. All at once Sarah knew that. The terrors and confusions and doubts that had haunted her since that white night in Gulmarg when she had awakened in the moonlight were over: Charles was here and she was safe. For a long moment she let herself relax against his shoulder, and then jerked away; aware of a sudden and entirely unfamiliar feeling of shyness.

'Here,' said Charles. 'Handkerchief.'

Sarah accepted it thankfully, blew her nose and sniffed childishly.

'Could we turn on the lights do you think?' said Charles. 'I'm not sure how much more life there is left in this battery.'

'There aren't any,' said Sarah unsteadily. 'I think the line must be down somewhere. But there are candles in the next room, if you've got any matches.'

'I've got a lighter. That'll do instead. Good Lord! What on earth's that?'

Charles retreated a swift step and flashed the beam of his torch onto the floor.

'It's Lager,' said Sarah, dropping onto her knees beside the limp velvet bundle: 'I'd forgotten him, poor lamb. I dropped him when you touched me. I was so scared.'

'What's the matter with him? Is he ill?'

'No. He's doped.' Sarah lifted wide startled eyes to Charles's face above her. 'Did you do it?' she asked sharply.

Charles went down on one knee and turned the puppy over. 'Do what? Dope him?'

'Yes,' said Sarah in a whisper.

'No. Why the hell should I want to?' said Charles impatiently. He turned back one of Lager's eyelids and studied the eye for a moment. 'Opium, I should say. He'll be all right.'

Sarah said in a shaky whisper: 'Someone did. If it wasn't you, then there's someone else who meant to get on this boat tonight.'

'What's that?' said Charles sharply. 'Look — it sounds to me as though something pretty tricky has been going on around here. This is no place to talk. Let's find these candles.'

Sarah got up holding Lager in her arms and they went into the living-room and lit two dusty, yellowed candle-ends that still remained in a pair of tarnished candlesticks of Benares brass. The flames flickered wanly for a moment or two in the draught and then steadied and burnt brighter, and the small room was once again just a room: overcrowded with furniture of a vanished era, shabby, over-ornate, uninteresting and uninterested. And remembering the vivid impression of tense and watchful awareness that it had given her earlier that night, Sarah wondered at herself.

She looked up to find Charles watching her with an unreadable expression in his eyes and the shadow of a smile about his mouth, and became abruptly conscious of the fact that she was wearing nothing but an exceedingly flimsy chiffon and lace nightdress: and in the next instant, with fury, that she was blushing.

'You look very nice,' said Charles pensively. 'All the same, I think you'd better put on something else or you'll catch cold. Besides,' he added, there happen to be a lot of things I want to talk about, and I'd like to be able to keep my mind on the job.'

'Oh!' said Sarah breathlessly. 'Oh! You ... you ... Give me that torch!'

She thrust Lager into his arms, snatched the torch from his hand and fled. To return a few minutes later wearing a severely tailored dressing-gown of dark green silk that clothed her from throat to ankles, and with her bare feet thrust into small green morocco slippers. An observant spectator might have noticed that she had also found time to apply a discreet amount of lipstick and powder and to run a comb through her red-gold curls.

She found Captain Mallory lying on the sofa nursing Lager in his arms and blowing smoke rings at the ceiling. 'Please don't get up,' said Sarah frigidly, seating herself in the armchair opposite him. 'And now, if it's not too much to ask, will you please tell me what you were doing on my boat?'

'I didn't know it was yours,' said Charles, 'and I didn't know anyone was on board. So few of the houseboats have been taken this year that it seemed a safe bet that it was unoccupied.'

'Look,' said Sarah leaning forward, 'do you see any green in my eye?'

'Yes,' said Charles with disconcerting promptness: 'emeralds and peridots and jade, sprinkled with gold dust and steeped in dew. Perfectly lovely.'

Sarah flushed rosily and drew back with a jerk. 'Thank you. But what I wanted to point out was that though I may have green eyes, I'm not all *that* green. If you thought the boat was empty you'd never have come creeping into it in the small hours of the morning.'

Charles blew another smoke ring and regarded her meditatively over the tip of his cigarette before replying. He appeared to be turning something over in his mind. After a moment or two he apparently came to some decision, for he swung his heels off the sofa and sitting up spoke in a voice that was wholly free from flippancy: 'All right. I didn't think it was empty. I had been told that it was occupied by a "maiden lady". The description is my informant's, not mine. Her name was given as Harris. It rang no bell. I was further informed that she would be attending the dance at Nedou's Hotel tonight and would not be back until well after midnight. By the way, do you mind my smoking? I should have asked.'

'No,' said Sarah. 'Go on. Why were you on this boat?'

'I wanted to have a look at it, and at the same time I did not want to appear in any way interested in it. I decided that the task of scraping an acquaintance with a maiden lady called Miss Harris in order to take a look at her boat, might take more time than I had at my disposal. So I came along to give it the once-over unofficially. I was therefore surprised, to put it mildly, to find Miss Parrish not only in residence but remarkably vocal.'

Sarah said: 'That's not true either. Is it?'

'What makes you think so?'

'Because I don't believe that you're the kind of person who makes mistakes. Not when it really matters.'

'I appear to have made one this time,' said Charles dryly.

'No you didn't. You thought I'd be at the dance. So I should have been if Major McKay hadn't strained a muscle. And as the dance goes on until one o'clock tonight, and it takes nearly an hour to get back here by *shikara*, you knew you had plenty of time. You didn't expect to find anyone on this boat, but you knew I had taken it, didn't you?'

'Maybe,' said Charles noncommittally, watching Sarah with half-closed eyes. 'Why do you think this is an occasion that really matters?'

'Because——' Sarah checked suddenly. 'No. Tell me first why you came here.'

Charles hesitated a moment, staring down at the glowing tip of his cigarette and frowning, and then he said slowly: 'I knew the girl who had this boat last year. Her name was Janet Rushton.'

Sarah drew a sharp breath and Charles looked up swiftly: 'You knew her too, didn't you. That letter you burnt on the lawn of the Peshawar Club was in Janet's writing. I was fairly sure of it. We checked back on you. You were in Gulmarg for the Spring Meeting. You had the room next to Janet's. You came up here and took over her boat, using the receipt signed by her. How about it, Sarah?'

Sarah did not answer. She sat quite still, her eyes meeting Charles's level, penetrating gaze while a minute ticked slowly by.

The wind blew another flurry of rain against the window-panes and the candle flames swayed and flickered to the draughts, throwing leaping shadows onto the panelled walls and the intricately inlaid woodwork of the ceiling, as the houseboat jerked and rocked, creaking and groaning at its moorings.

Sarah spoke at last, and uncertainly: 'I don't understand. If you are — one of them — if you were keeping tabs on me ... What *is* it all about, Charles?'

Charles transferred Lager to a sofa cushion, and coming to his feet took a restless turn about the small room, and came back to stand over Sarah, frowning down on her and fidgeting with his cigarette.

After a moment he said abruptly: 'I've no idea how much you know, but it's obviously a good deal more than is healthy for you. I think you'd better tell me. Everything please, right from the beginning and without leaving anything out.'

Sarah told him: sitting in the shabby armchair that Janet must have sat in, in the boat that had been Janet's boat, with the guttering light of the candles that Janet must have used throwing leaping shadows across her white face. And as she talked, it was as though she was reliving the incidents that she described: as though she saw again the lamplight glint along the barrel of Janet's automatic, and stared unbelievingly at a line of footprints in the blown snow on a moonlit verandah. Once again she seemed to hear Janet's voice in the shadow of the ski-hut on Khilanmarg, and to watch the flying shadow swoop across the snowfields and vanish into the darkness of the forest: once again to stare down across the shadowy bowl of Gulmarg at a far-off pinpoint of red light ...

She told, her voice a dry whisper with the returning terror of that moment, of the thing that had followed upon Janet's departure — the sound of a door stealthily closing among the shadows under the snow-hung eaves of the ski-hut. Of the finding of Janet's body in the Blue Run, and her own visit to the house by the Gap. Every incident seemed etched so clearly in her mind that she could tell it all as though it had only happened yesterday. The tracks on that snow-covered pathway. The darkness and silence of the empty house. The faint odours that lingered in the cold rooms — cigarette smoke, damp, cordite, and that other cloying, elusive scent that she could not place. She told him of the bullet hole and the stain upon the floor. Of the man in the snowstorm, and, finally, of the arrival of Janet's letter months later in Peshawar.

She told it all in meticulous detail up to the burning of Janet's letter, while Charles sat on the arm of the sofa and listened; his face expressionless and his eyes intent. And when she had finished she shivered convulsively, and gripping her hands tightly together in her lap to hide the fact that they were trembling, said: 'What's it all about, Charles? I don't understand, and I'm scared. Yes I am! I'm scared stiff. I wouldn't mind if I thought it was just some of the usual anti-British stuff ... Indian terrorists. But it isn't. There was someone listening in the ski-hut. And then Reggie Craddock trying to get me off the boat, and someone who said he was from the agents, too. And this morning Mrs Warrender turned up with a story about a friend who wants to swop boats with me. What's it all about — ? or am I going crazy?'

'Say that again?' said Charles sharply.

Sarah laughed on a high note. 'I said, "Am I going crazy?"'

'No, I mean about Reggie Craddock and Helen Warrender. Let's hear about that: word for word, please.'

So once again Sarah took up the tale and repeated all she could remember ...

The cigarette burnt out between Charles's fingers and he swore and flicked the smouldering fragment into the ashtray. 'Hell!' said Charles. 'This needs a lot of thinking out. Go to bed, Sarah. You've had enough alarms for one day. We'll defer any further explanation until the morning.'

Sarah's mouth set itself in a stubborn line and her green eyes sparkled in the wavering light of the candles.

'I am not budging,' said Sarah firmly, 'until you tell me what it's all about. I shouldn't sleep a wink, and you know it. It's no good trying to be discreet and hush-hush and Top Secret, because like it or not, I'm in this too. Up to my neck, as far as I can see! What's it all about, Charles?'

'If you mean Reggie Craddock and Co., I don't know. As for the rest, I can't tell you much more than Janet told you ...' Charles stood up and began to pace the small expanse of faded Axminster carpet once more; his hands in his pockets and his frowning gaze upon the floor.

'A year ago,' began Charles slowly, 'one of our agents sent word that he was onto a big thing. He didn't even give a hint as to what it was, but he sent a – a signal. One that we only use very rarely, and which means that we are onto something white-hot and must be contacted with all possible speed.'

Sarah said: 'Janet told me that Mrs Matthews had sent for help last November. Before they even moved into Nedou's Hotel.'

'She had. And a Major Brett was sent off as soon as it was received. But——'

'Wasn't he the man who fell out of the train?' asked Sarah on a gasp.

Charles nodded, and turning away, resumed his pacing: 'But the first warning arrived last May. It came from Srinagar and had been sent by my best friend. We sent someone to contact him at Murree, but Pendrell never got there. The car he was travelling down in was involved in an accident on the way, and he was killed. It was a very well-staged accident.'

'Like – like that Indian who came up in December to meet Mrs Matthews,' whispered Sarah.

Charles glanced at her and nodded again. 'Ajit; yes. Mrs Matthews was sent up to take over after Pendrell died. There were a few lines to go on, but nothing very much; for though there were several of our people up here, they weren't in the same class as Mrs Matthews. Janet came up as a sort of Number Two to her, and we heard nothing more from either of them until we got that signal from Mrs Matthews towards the end of November. It meant that she had got the goods and to send someone at once.'

'I still don't see why she didn't go herself,' said Sarah frowning: 'Janet said they weren't allowed to, but——'

'They weren't. If Pendrell had sat tight he might be alive today; who knows? But he decided to leave Kashmir, and the move was fatal. He must have been suspect already, and when they heard he was leaving for 'Pindi they obviously decided to take no chances. They played safe and rubbed him out.'

'But Janet——? And you said there were others ...'

'It's far easier to send a new agent who has nothing against him or her, to contact one "on the ground". Any move on the part of Mrs Matthews or Janet Rushton to leave Kashmir would perhaps have been construed as suspicious; supposing the other side were in any doubt about them. It was safer, in theory, to stay where they were — though unfortunately it didn't prove to be so in practice. And after Ajit and his car and his driver were swept over the edge of the road by a convenient avalanche, we realized that the chances were that Mrs Matthews and Janet had been spotted, and that there was a far more efficient team operating against us up here, and in northern India, than we had hoped.

'With Ajit dead, it was decided to use the Ski Club Meeting as protective colouring and send up a skier, ostensibly just another winter-sports addict, to contact one or other of those two women.

The agent was to arrive after dark and the meeting would take place in great secrecy. After which he would stage a second, and public arrival, on the following day, and for the rest of the time avoid being seen speaking to either of the women except in the middle of a crowd.

'The meeting-place and the signal — that red light you saw — was worked out and sent to Mrs Matthews by catalogue. It was a risk of course, but after what had happened to Pendrell and Major Brett and Ajit, less of a risk than trying to send any plan by word of mouth. One or other of them, Janet or Mrs Matthews, were to have watched for that light every night after they arrived in Gulmarg: if it had been noticed by anyone else it would only have been taken to mean that the *chowkidar* — a watchman — was cooking a meal or sleeping the night in an empty hut. Having seen it, either Mrs Matthews or Janet would have visited the hut. They were both excellent skiers and it would have been a great deal easier than it sounds for one of them to have slipped out of the hotel in the small hours and skied over, and back again half an hour later, without being observed.'

'But suppose there was a storm or something, and they couldn't see it?' asked Sarah.

'If they didn't come the first night, the messenger was to remain two more nights. No longer.' Charles stopped in front of one of the candles and said irrelevantly: 'These things will burn out soon.' He stood staring down at the unsteady flame for so long that Sarah moved restlessly in her chair and said: 'Go on.'

Charles lifted his head with a jerk as though he had temporarily forgotten about her.

'That's about all,' he said curtly. 'You know the rest.'

'No I don't,' said Sarah, her voice barely above a whisper. 'What happened to the man? The messenger. They killed him too, didn't they?'

'There wasn't a messenger,' said Charles slowly. 'He was held up on the road and arrived too late.'

'But how ... ?' Sarah found she could not complete the question.

'We don't know how they found out,' said Charles bleakly. 'About the hut and the signal I mean. But there's obviously been a bad leak somewhere, because the light was a trap, and Janet walked into it.'

'But somebody else *was* there. I've told you! I saw the bullet hole and — and there was blood on the floor.'

'I know,' said Charles. 'I saw it.'

'You!' Sarah's voice was a whisper.

'Yes,' Charles's eyes, watching her over the guttering candle flame, reflected small dancing glints of yellow light. 'You see I was the messenger. I was the man you bumped into in the snow-storm on the *marg*.'

'Oh!' said Sarah on an indrawn breath. 'I didn't know. I only knew that —' she stopped abruptly.

'Only knew what?' asked Charles curiously.

Sarah flushed and bit her lip. 'Nothing,' she said curtly. She did not intend to explain to Charles that the intense interest she had taken in him in Peshawar had sprung partly from a strange and persistent conviction that she had met him before.

Charles regarded her curiously for a moment but did not press the question. He sat down again on the sofa and pulling a thin gold cigarette-case from his pocket offered it to Sarah, and when she shook her head took another cigarette himself and lit it at one of the candles.

Sarah, studying his face as it bent above the wavering flame, was astonished at herself that she should not have instantly recognized him as the man of the snowstorm. How could she have forgotten the line of cheek and chin, even blurred as it had been by darkness and falling snow? The grey eyes, or the voice with its faint suggestion of a drawl and its unintentional but instinctive note of command, which could only belong to Charles?

Charles looked up suddenly and caught her intent gaze. His

mouth curved in a shadow of a grin and he said: 'It was easier for me. You had red hair.'

Sarah blushed rosily and for no apparent reason, and to distract attention from the fact, said hastily: 'Tell me what happened. What did you do?'

'There wasn't much I could do,' said Charles soberly. 'It had been arranged that I should be among the later arrivals at the Meeting — there were several people who could only manage the last few days — so that I could leave with the rest of the crowd not too long after collecting the information. Just long enough to be seen to have no contact with Mrs Matthews and her supposed niece! But though the reasoning behind that decision was sound it turned out to be a mistake, because the weather was obviously batting for the opposition——

'A flash flood on the Kabul River meant that I took a full day to reach Rawalpindi, then just beyond Uri I found that the road was blocked by an avalanche that had brought any amount of rock and trees with it, and no motor traffic was likely to get through for three or four days. So I came on foot and skis, which was slow going and delayed me badly. I was met near Babamarishi by one of our men, a Kashmiri, who acted as a guide as far as the outskirts of Gulmarg and happened to mention, casually, that an elderly memsahib had been killed in a skiing accident. His version of her name was near enough for me to realize who it was. So I had that much warning, at least. But there was still Janet.

'I went on, keeping to a woodcutter's track through the forest that Kadera had shown me, in order to keep out of sight as much as possible. I had a key to the hut, and I meant to lie up there until it was dark enough to light the signal lamp that was in my pack. I wasn't far short of the hut when I met a coolie who was employed by the hotel to collect and carry wood — he had a great load of it on his back and had stopped to rest, and he asked me for a cigarette. He too told me about the old memsahib who had died, and he said that the young Miss-sahib who had come up with her had been killed that very morning in a similar accident; which he attributed to evil spirits. That was how I learned about Janet . . .'

Charles was silent for a time, twisting the cigarette between his fingers and looking tired and grim. And at length he said: 'Since it seemed that they had both died on one of the ski runs there was no reason to suppose that anyone knew about the hut near the Gap, so I went there anyway. Because I badly needed somewhere to rest before tackling the long slog back to Babamarishi, and there was obviously no point in staying on in Gulmarg any longer, or in turning up officially as a latecomer to the Meeting. I meant to turn back and say I hadn't been able to make it because of the hold-up on the road, and that it hadn't been worth waiting for the way to be cleared. Which is what several other people did——

'It wasn't until I got to the hut and saw those tracks on the path and found that I didn't need my key because the door was open, that I realized that a fuse had blown somewhere — and at a very high level. *You* know what I found inside. It didn't take long to work out what had happened, or realize that who-ever stage-managed those two "skiing accidents" also knew all about the hut and the signal. In fact there was only one thing I couldn't understand.'

He paused for a moment, frowning, and Sarah said: 'Why they didn't lay for you too?'

Charles nodded. 'Yes. If they knew so much, why didn't they wait for me? They obviously knew that another contact was com-ing and what he was going to do; though it's doubtful if they knew his identity, because any one of a dozen people might have been detailed for the job. Well, why not wait until I arrived and gave the signal, knock me off, and then wait until Janet arrived and do the same by her?'

'Perhaps they had meant to do that,' said Sarah, 'and then something happened to hurry them up?'

'The storm,' said Charles. 'I came to the conclusion it must have been that. They probably waited in the hut for me for a night or two, and then realized that there was a storm brewing.'

'Bulaki said so,' interrupted Sarah in a half whisper.

'What's that?'

'My bearer. He told me on the morning we left for the Khilanmarg ski-hut that there was bad weather coming.'

'That would be it,' said Charles. 'If they waited any longer for the contact to show up they might hit bad weather and be unable to use the signal: so they decided to get Janet. After all, she was the main objective. Once she was dead it didn't really matter how many messengers came up to the hut. It's some consolation to realize that she must have got one of them. She carried a gun, and I'm prepared to bet a good deal that the bullet that made that hole came from it.'

Sarah said: 'Were you in that house when I came into it?'

'I don't think so. I must have missed you by a pretty narrow margin. I don't mind telling you that I didn't stay long! I saw everything I needed to see, and then I went up through the trees at the back and did a recce to see if I could find the body of the man who was shot in the sitting-room. There were tracks running slantways up the hill, and I followed them for a while; but I didn't like the look of the weather, so I came back, and I only noticed then that there was a broken latch on a side door. I went in by it to see if I'd missed anything, but there was nothing there but a pile of dusty furniture, and as I saw that it had started to snow I chucked my hand in and came away. I cut across the back garden and came down parallel to the path and onto the *marg*, and I hadn't gone far when I hit into you. Gave me a considerable jar, I assure you.'

Sarah laughed a little shakily. 'Not half as bad a shock as it gave me! So it was you I heard in the hut.' She sat silent for a moment and then said, 'Then — there is nobody who knows.'

'Knows what?'

'The – the "Big Thing" you talked about. The thing your friend found out — and Janet and Mrs Matthews too. Now that they are dead, does no one else know?'

'No one human,' said Charles slowly.

'What do you mean,' asked Sarah sharply.

'There is still something that knows. This boat knows.'

In the little silence that followed upon his words a candle flame flared and went out, sending up a thread of evil-smelling smoke into the deepening shadows of the room.

The draught whined along the floor and lifted the worn carpet in uneasy ripples as the boat lurched to a wilder gust of wind, and once again, as earlier on that same night, Sarah became aware of the inanimate objects that furnished the small room. Once again they seemed to her imagination to become endowed with a sentient personality, a mysterious entity of their own, so that even with her eyes held by Charles's steady gaze, she could still see them. The carved tables, the shabby chintz-covered chairs, the cheap brass trays and the rows of dusty books upon the shelf. All those things that had watched Mrs Matthews: that had watched Janet, and were now watching her, Sarah Parrish . . .

'Yes,' said Sarah in a dry whisper. 'Yes, the boat knows.'

A savage gust of wind raged across the lake, accompanied by driving rain, and shook the little houseboat as a terrier shakes a rat. The tables and chairs jerked and shifted and the candlestick that bore the last remaining candle toppled onto the floor, plunging the room into darkness.

Then, as suddenly as it had come, the wind died away. One moment the night was riotous with sound, and the next it was quiet save for the slap and splash of water against the sides of the boat, the whisper of light rain falling on leaves and lake water, and a faint mutter of far-off thunder.

Silence seemed to flow into the valley, smoothing out the

turmoil of the storm as oil smooths out rough water. And in that silence, though there was no sound of footsteps, the boat jerked suddenly to a different rhythm as someone trod quietly up the gangplank and scratched very softly on the pantry door . . .

14

Sarah's terrified gasp was loud in the silence, and Charles switched on his torch, and throwing an arm about her shoulders felt the tension of her accumulated fear as vividly as though he had touched something charged with static electricity.

He said quickly: 'Don't, dear! It's only Habib. I'm sorry — I ought to have warned you. But what with one thing and another, I forgot. I put him off on the bank and told him to keep an eye on the approaches, and to come aboard if anything worried him. I left the boat outside the dining-room window.'

'Who — who's Habib?' quavered Sarah, struggling to collect herself.

Charles released her, and stooping to pick up the fallen candle-stick, replaced it on the desk before replying.

'Officially, my bearer-cum-driver,' said Charles, relighting the candle with the flame of his cigarette-lighter: 'Actually, an invaluable assistant. I'd better go and see what's up.' He walked to the doorway, and then turned and came back again.

'Can you use a gun, Sarah?'

'I . . . I think so. But——'

Charles drew out a small black Colt automatic barely larger than a cigarette-case and tossed it into her lap. 'Be careful of it. It's loaded. I'm going out to talk to Habib and do a bit of reconnoitring, and if anyone you don't know comes onto this boat before I get back, don't wait to ask questions. Shoot first and argue afterwards! I won't be long——'

Without giving Sarah a chance to protest, he turned and

vanished into the darkness of the dining-room, and a moment later she heard the sound of the pantry door being eased open in its groove, and then the boat vibrated again to noiseless footsteps descending the gangplank.

Sarah sat tense and still, straining her ears to listen in the stillness, and fighting a frantic desire to follow him and run screaming down the bank to take refuge with the Creeds. But between the prow of her own boat and theirs lay almost thirty yards of wet darkness, bounded by reeds and scrub willow: and Charles had taken the torch. Her fingers tightened round the tiny gun, and the feel of the cold metal steadied her; but she was still sitting tensely on the extreme edge of the sofa, listening, when Charles returned some fifteen minutes later. The candle had guttered out, and the entire houseboat was in darkness.

This time Charles came from the shore and up the gangplank, and Sarah collapsed onto the sofa cushions with a sob of relief at the sound of his voice. He spent some time moving about in the pantry, from where she could see the reflected gleam of his torch, and presently he came into the room carrying a lighted hurricane lamp that he had found in one of the cupboards. It flared abominably and the oil smelt, but Sarah was grateful for any form of illumination.

'Well?' she inquired, trying to make her voice sound cool and casual: 'What was worrying him?'

'Habib? Nothing much,' said Charles shaking the wet out of his hair. His clothes were patched with damp and leaf mould and his shoes were caked with wet earth. 'Your electric line is down: he tripped over the end of it on the bank, and was afraid that it might have been cut on purpose. Which would have proved that someone other than myself had designs on this boat tonight. However, we managed to trace the other end without drawing attention to ourselves by showing a light, and it was probably brought down by the wind.'

He broke off to fiddle with the wick of the hurricane lamp

that was flaring lopsidedly and darkening the glass with smoke, and poking at the wick with a matchstick, observed in an abstracted voice that judging from the ease with which he had been able to break into her boat earlier in the evening, he suggested that she fit the door and windows with some strong bolts tomorrow. If, of course, she intended to stay on it.

There was the faintest suggestion of a query in those last words, and Sarah replied shortly that she had every intention of doing so. But though the words were brave enough, the effect was somewhat marred by the fact that she had been unable to bring them out without her teeth chattering. Because even as she spoke she wondered what would have happened to her, and if she would still have been alive, if it had been someone other than Charles who had forced the latch of the dining-room window that night?

Staring at him with dilated eyes, she said in a harsh whisper, and as though the words were forced out of her: 'I'm afraid. Charles, I'm afraid.'

Charles knelt swiftly, and catching her cold hands held them tightly against him. His own were warm and steady and very reassuring, and he smiled at Sarah; a smile that did not quite reach his eyes.

'No, you're not. Brace up, Sarah darling!'

'It's easy for you —' began Sarah on a sob.

'That's where you're wrong,' interrupted Charles roughly: 'It's damnably difficult for me!'

He dropped her hands, and standing up abruptly returned to the dining-room where Sarah, following him, found him hunting in the cupboard under the sideboard with the aid of the torch. 'Don't you keep anything to drink on this boat except orange squash and soda water?' demanded Charles irritably.

'There's brandy in the corner cupboard.'

'Thank God for that! We could both do with some.' He splashed a generous amount into a glass and held it out. 'Drink that up and you'll feel better.'

'No thanks,' said Sarah distantly.

'Don't be so missish,' advised Charles with a suggestion of a snap.

'I'm not. I just don't like brandy!'

'Who asked you if you liked it? Just drink it up, there's a good girl. We still have a lot of the night before us!'

He pushed the glass across the table and grinned unexpectedly. 'You needn't worry,' he assured her, 'I fully realize that I am alone on this boat with you, and that it is long past midnight. In fact not one of the charms of yourself or the situation has escaped me. But I'm not trying to make you drunk.'

Sarah glared at him furiously and instantly drained the glass, and Charles reached out and patting her shoulder approvingly said: 'Good girl.'

'I believe you said that on purpose,' accused Sarah, thinking it over, 'just to make me mad enough to drink the stuff. Did you?'

'Well, it worked anyway,' said Charles equably. He poured a strong peg for himself and taking Sarah by the elbow returned to the living-room.

'And now let's get back to business,' said Charles, ensconcing her on the sofa with Lager on her lap. 'First of all, what was in that letter of Janet's that you burnt? The sooner we get that clear the better. Try and remember it word for word.'

Sarah told him, knitting her brows in an endeavour to remember the exact wording, and Charles said, '*Hmm*; now I wonder why on earth she didn't—— Oh well, she didn't, and that's that. At least we know that she hid something on this boat. The trouble is that several other people appear to know it too. Or so it would seem. But how? — and why? Did you tell anyone else about that letter?'

'No.'

'Could anyone else have seen it at any time? Did the envelope look as if it had been tampered with when you opened it?'

'N – o,' said Sarah doubtfully. 'I don't think so. You see, I didn't think of looking for anything like that. I came back to the house that day — it was the evening of Aunt Alice's party for the Blue Cross Ball — and I was late back and there was a big mail in. I read all the home letters first, and I hadn't time to read this one. It looked dull, so I put it into my bag to read later.'

'How long had it been on the hall table?' asked Charles.

'I don't know. Two or three hours, maybe? I had been out since about three o'clock and I didn't get back until past seven.'

'Then anyone could have seen it there and steamed it open and read it and put it back again?'

'Of course not!' said Sarah indignantly. 'Only someone in the house; and as we were all out watching polo that afternoon, there would only have been the servants, and none of them would read or write English. Anyway, what would have been the point? If anyone had wanted to see it, it would surely have been simpler just to steal it and be done with it? Then I should never have known about it.'

'Oh well,' said Charles. 'Let it go. What then? Did you leave your bag about anywhere?'

'No. You see it was one of those bags that are meant to go with a certain dress. It had grey roses on it and hung on a band round my wrist. The only time it was out of my hands was during dinner, and then it was hung on the back of my chair. You were there. You could have touched it. No one else.'

'Yes,' said Charles slowly. 'That's true. To think I had the damned thing not six inches from my hand for nearly an hour on end! If I'd only known—— Well, go on.'

'I didn't open the letter until halfway through the dance, and as I didn't know what was in it I didn't think of looking to see if the envelope had been tampered with. Anyway, there wasn't very much light. Only those paper lanterns. And then Helen Warrender interrupted and — well you know what happened after that. You were there. You——'

Sarah was struck by a sudden thought, and sitting upright with a jerk that almost dislodged the comatose Lager from her lap, she stared accusingly at Charles: 'Was that why?' she demanded.

'Was what why?'

'You know! Did you come to the party because of me? Was that why you seemed to be around so much and yet never——' She stopped and bit her lip.

Charles's lips twitched, but his voice was perfectly grave: 'But of course,' he said. 'How could I keep away?'

Sarah flushed pinkly. 'I didn't mean that,' she said with some heat. 'You know quite well what I meant! I mean was it because I had known Janet? Were you only keeping tabs on me?'

'Yes,' admitted Charles frankly. 'I was — interested.'

Sarah laughed. It was, despite herself, a somewhat bitter little laugh. 'And I thought —' she said, and stopped again.

'Did you?' asked Charles softly. He watched the smoke from his cigarette spiral slowly upwards for a moment or two; then: 'But you see Sarah, you might have been the one.'

'What one? What do you mean?'

'The one who killed Janet.'

Sarah's gasp of rage made a soft explosive sound in the quiet room and she struggled for words: 'You – you – you think that I — you thought that I——'

'All right,' said Charles calmly. 'I'll take it as read.'

'Do you really think —' began Sarah.

'No,' said Charles, as one giving the matter his consideration: 'I don't. Not now. But it was perfectly possible. It has also been said — and proved with regrettable frequency — that most female criminals are also good actresses. You knew Janet and Mrs Matthews. Your fingerprints were on the brass poker in Janet's room, and I met you in that snowstorm not a hundred yards from the hut by the Gap. You had to be watched.'

'And you watched me,' said Sarah tartly.

'Among others, yes,' admitted Charles with a grin. 'And as

luck would have it, I happened to be present when you opened Janet's letter. I even had to watch you burn it — and with my own lighter! — when every instinct was urging me to reach out and grab it.'

'Then why didn't you?' demanded Sarah. 'Oh! ... Oh, I think I see. If I *had* been the one, then ... yes, I see. Very difficult for you.'

'Damnably,' admitted Charles cheerfully. 'Still, even if I didn't know what was in that note, I knew where it had come from, and could check up on it to a certain extent.'

'How did you know that?' asked Sarah sharply. 'Did you know her so very well?'

'Who? Janet? No. Hardly at all.'

'Then you are asking me to believe that you could recognize her handwriting from just that glimpse? The letter wasn't signed and I held it so that it couldn't be read.'

For answer Charles drew out a leather pocket-book from his breast-pocket, and after hunting through it, extracted a small sheet of folded paper that he tossed onto Sarah's lap.

Sarah jerked it open and stared at it incredulously. It was the covering note from the firm of lawyers in Rawalpindi that had accompanied Janet's sealed envelope.

She looked up at Charles and discovered that he was watching her with the same curious intentness that she had observed before, and she said a little unsteadily: 'I – I don't understand. How – how did you——?'

'How did I get that letter? I picked it up off the lawn. You'd forgotten it.'

'But I couldn't ... I would have noticed ...'

'No you wouldn't. You see you gave me an excellent piece of advice — have you forgotten? When you knocked that brandy and soda all over poor Helen Warrender you said that there was nothing like a good shock for putting things out of people's minds. You then very obligingly presented me with an opening, and I provided the shock. Remember?'

A slow wave of colour, starting at the base of her throat, mounted to the roots of Sarah's hair, and she stood up, dropping Lager in a velvet heap onto the floor: *'Oh!'* breathed Sarah stormily. 'You – you——'

'Go on,' urged Charles. 'Let's have it. What about "You cad, sir!"?'

Sarah sat down again abruptly, and Charles laughed.

'It's no use, Sarah darling. All's fair in love and war, you know. And it worked. It worked like a charm! You swept off like an insulted Archduchess, entirely forgetting that letter, which had fallen onto the grass and which I had carefully edged under your chair. What's more, the shock was apparently sufficient to keep you from realizing you'd lost it right up to this very minute. And — if it's any consolation to you — I enjoyed it very much, thank you.'

'I think,' said Sarah with dignity, 'you are the most insufferable man I ever met.'

'And you,' said Charles, 'are without any doubt at all, the most attractive and infuriating woman I have yet encountered in the course of a long and varied experience of crime.'

A dimple appeared unexpectedly in Sarah's cheek and she collapsed into a sudden fit of slightly hysterical mirth.

'Oh dear! I am sorry. But I suddenly thought of "Olga-Poloffski-the-Beautiful-Spy" and all those. Is it really true, do you suppose? I mean, do you meet dozens of ravishing female spies?'

'You'd be surprised,' said Charles. 'And now let us abandon these fascinating personalities and get back to business. How long have you been on this boat?'

'Five days,' said Sarah promptly.

'Found anything yet?'

'No. I've made a start though. I looked in all the obvious places first of course, and then I thought it was probably in one of those wretched books up there. I've been through about half of them, but it's a tough assignment; specially when you don't know what you're looking for.'

'Well now you'll have me to help you. A "record" she said?'

'That's it. There were some old gramophone records in the bottom drawer of that desk. I thought at first she'd used the word literally, so I had them out and played them over on the Club radiogram. But they were just tunes; and cracked at that.'

'A *record*,' said Charles thoughtfully. 'Might be anything. Scratched on a window-pane, written on the underside of a floor-board. Hidden behind one of those fiddling little bits of wood on the ceiling. Hell! It isn't going to be easy. But we've got to get it even if it means taking this boat apart plank by plank. And the sooner we find it the better, for it seems to me that too many people are interested in this boat.'

'That reminds me,' said Sarah slowly. 'You never answered a question of mine. If you were keeping tabs on me, how was it that you didn't know I was on this boat?'

'I did,' said Charles. 'But as you surmised, I was assured that you would be at the Nedou's dance. A nasty accident of the usual sort overtook one of our local agents, and the understudy wasn't as efficient as he might have been.'

'Accident? You mean — *murder*?' Her voice cracked oddly on the word.

'It isn't so unusual, you know,' said Charles gently.

'Yes, I know,' said Sarah with a little catch of her breath. 'I saw it happen to Janet. I didn't believe it, but I saw it happen.' Her fingers twisted together in her lap and she said jerkily: 'Charles, why is it only now that I've taken the boat that so many people want it? After all it's been empty for months. Why do they want it now?'

'Ah, that's the question,' said Charles. 'I'd like to know the answer to that one myself. The way I see it is that our lot aren't the only people who linked you up with Janet Rushton. The chances are that someone else, or possibly several people, have been keeping a watchful eye on you as well — just in case. You can also bet your bottom dollar that this boat was searched pretty thoroughly after Janet died, if not before.'

'Then if you think that, what's the use of our searching it? The record was probably found weeks ago!'

'Use your head, Sarah,' urged Charles. 'If it had been found, no one would have taken any further interest in the boat. Whereas quite a surprising amount of people are taking an active interest in it. So it stands to reason it wasn't found.'

'But I don't see——'

'Listen,' said Charles patiently: 'Janet lived in this boat, and paid a cash deposit on it, reserving it up to the end of June this year with the proviso that should she be unable to make use of the boat herself, whoever held the receipt for the money could do so instead. That clear?'

'Quite, but——'

'*Ssh!* Janet dies, and you can be sure that this boat was searched from top to bottom. Not because they had any idea that she had hidden anything in it, but just to be on the safe side. Nothing is found and the boat ceases to be of any interest. Then, suddenly, a Miss Parrish, who had been present at the January Meeting of the Ski Club, occupied the room next to Janet Rushton's and been seen talking to her in the moonlight outside the ski-hut (you say there was someone watching), and is therefore, in all probability, an object of suspicion, receives a mysterious letter.'

'But no one could *possibly* have known about that!' objected Sarah.

'Don't interrupt. On receipt of this letter she suddenly changes her plans, and instead of going to Ceylon, decides to return to Kashmir. Now I don't suppose that anyone else got onto that letter of Janet's. We did — through you! But I admit I think it's unlikely that anyone else did. *But* — Miss Parrish, still almost certainly under surveillance, arrives in Kashmir *and produces the receipt for Janet Rushton's boat*. Now do you see?'

'I suppose so,' said Sarah slowly.

'There's no "suppose" about it. Why has Miss Parrish decided to come to Kashmir? And where did she get the receipt for the *Waterwitch*? Obviously, from Janet Rushton. The *Waterwitch* immediately becomes worth watching again — and so does Miss Parrish!'

'But if, as you think, they have already searched the boat —' began Sarah.

'Of course they've searched it. But that doesn't mean they feel any easier about letting someone whom they have every reason to be suspicious of do a bit of independent searching. Because you *have* been searching; and I bet you any money you like, your *mānji* has reported to that effect. In fact the whole set-up is probably causing a lot of uneasy speculation. Why are you here? How did you get hold of Janet's receipt for the *Waterwitch*, and what are you looking for? The sooner they get you off the boat the better.'

'Of course,' said Sarah slowly, 'there's another thing. I might even find it for them.'

Charles gave her a curious slanting look and said softly: 'That, I should imagine, is pretty well at the top of their list. For all they know you may have been told where to look. If so, and supposing they can't shift you off the boat, the next best thing is to keep tabs on you and let you do the finding. Should you turn up anything——' Charles broke off and frowned.

'Go on,' said Sarah. 'And should I turn up anything?'

'Oh well,' said Charles lightly. 'I imagine they'd find it fairly simple to steal it off you. They'd have saved themselves a hell of a lot of brainwork, and pinching the solution off you would be child's play.'

'That isn't what you were going to say,' pointed out Sarah.

Charles stood up suddenly and walked restlessly across the small room, his hands in his pockets. Then he turned and came back to Sarah and stood in front of her, frowning down at her.

'I've changed my mind,' said Charles shortly. 'The sooner you get off this boat and out of this country the better. You can pack up and move into Nedou's Hotel tomorrow morning, and we can get a car to take you down the hill the next day.'

Sarah smiled disarmingly at him. 'Suppose I don't want to go?'

'You'll do as you're told,' said Charles curtly. 'As long as you are here you are a nuisance and a liability.'

'Oh no, I'm not,' corrected Sarah firmly. 'That's where you're wrong. As long as I'm here there is just a chance that I may be merely a simple-minded tourist after all, who has got mixed up in this entirely by mistake and doesn't know a thing. And who quite possibly *bought* the receipt off this Miss Rushton, at that! For all they know, Janet may have decided she didn't want the boat, and seen a chance of getting her money back by selling it to someone who wasn't likely to know that houseboat rents would fall considerably this season. Don't you see? They can't be sure.'

'That's not the point,' said Charles roughly.

'Yes it is. And there's another thing. If I go, this boat goes to the next applicant on what seems to be a nice long list.'

'No it wouldn't. I should take it on.'

'And become a marked man at once? You've said yourself that once anyone in your job becomes suspect his usefulness is reduced to a minimum. That's right, isn't it?'

'Yes, but——'

'No, it's my turn to hold the floor. I'm not going! It isn't because I don't know exactly what you were going to say just now when you pulled yourself up. You were going to say that if and when I find anything, I should go the same way as Janet.'

'Exactly!' agreed Charles grimly. 'In fact the chances of your being allowed to survive any discovery on this boat are nil. That's why I'm packing you off to Ceylon tomorrow.'

'Charles — wait a minute. All this that you're working on, it's very important, isn't it?'

'Very.'

'How important? Is it only going to affect one or two people or hundreds of people — or what?'

'I don't know,' said Charles slowly. 'That's the hell of it. We simply do not know yet. But it could be millions.'

'Well then, do you think you've got any right to take chances with something like that? Suppose they *are* suspicious of me? It doesn't really matter, because they can't be quite sure. As long as I'm on the boat you stand a better chance of keeping other people off it, and unless it can be proved that I'm up to my neck in this, I doubt their doing anything very drastic just now. Can't you see that?'

'Maybe you're right,' said Charles thoughtfully. He stood still, his hands deep in his pockets, staring down at the faded carpet, and presently he jerked his shoulders uncomfortably and said: 'All right, you win. But with conditions.'

Sarah said: 'It depends on the conditions.'

Charles ignored the remark. 'First of all,' he said, 'you will carry a gun with you always, and use it without hesitation in a crisis. If you shoot some innocent citizen by mistake, I'll get you out of it. But as I've said once already this evening, the golden rule in the present situation is shoot first and argue afterwards. I'll give you a heavier gun. That one hasn't much stopping power. Next, you will get a set of bolts and fix them to every available door and window. You can do that, can't you?'

Sarah nodded.

'Finally,' said Charles, 'you will go nowhere by yourself. Always keep in company when you leave the boat. Is that clear?'

'As pea soup,' said Sarah flippantly. 'All right. I'll do it. But where do we go from there?'

'We take this boat to bits if necessary,' said Charles. 'And as we haven't any time to lose, we may as well get on with it now. Sleepy?'

'At the moment,' confessed Sarah, 'I don't feel as if I shall ever be able to sleep again.'

'Good,' approved Charles callously. 'In that case let's get on with it. How far did you get with the books and what were you looking for?'

'A loose sheet of paper or else pages marked so that you could read off a code. That was all I could think of!'

'And not a bad idea either. Oh well, let's get to work.'

They settled themselves on the floor, surrounded by stacks of novels, and proceeded to go through each one methodically; looking down the spine of each book and investigating the thickness of each cover with a penknife. The night was at last both quiet and still, and although they could occasionally hear a far-off growl of thunder no breath of wind returned to disturb the lake, and the houseboat lay motionless at her moorings in a silence broken only by an occasional soft arpeggio of plops as a frog skittered across the water from one lily-pad to the next, the splash of a leaping fish or the cheep of a sleepy bird from the branch of the big chenar tree.

They worked methodically, stacking each book to one side as they finished with it, and reaching for the next. Hour after hour seemed to slip by, and Sarah's back began to ache and one of her feet had gone to sleep. She began to listen for sounds on the bank outside and to start nervously at each tiny night noise.

Charles, who had apparently never once glanced in her direction, appeared to be aware of the state of her nerves, for now he looked up from his work and smiled at her.

'It's all right,' he said, 'I told you no one would come back tonight. I think we've done enough for the moment. Let's put this lot back. Sorted on the right-hand shelves, unsorted on the left. OK?'

He stood up, and reaching down a hand pulled Sarah to her feet.

'Ouch!' said Sarah, collapsing on the sofa and massaging her left foot to restore the circulation while Charles replaced and stacked the long line of books. 'As a matter of fact,' she said defensively to Charles's back, 'I wasn't thinking of anyone trying to come on board — not with that man of yours on the bank. But suppose someone was watching from much further off? After all, they'd be able to see that a light was burning in this room, even though the curtains are drawn.'

'You forget,' said Charles with a grin, 'that you are a nervous spinster living alone. You would be more than likely to have a lamp lit in reserve on a night like this. In fact I bet you left one on when you went to bed, didn't you?'

'Well, yes. The pantry one,' confessed Sarah a little shamefacedly.

'I thought as much. You'd have to be an exceptionally strong-minded woman not to. No, I don't think you need worry about a light in this room being suspicious. And if your boat should happen to attract any more visitors tonight, Habib will deal with that.'

'How much does he know?' asked Sarah curiously. 'About all this, I mean?'

'Enough to be going on with,' said Charles noncommittally. 'No one knows much more than that — except for one, or possibly two men at the top.'

'Janet said something like that,' mused Sarah. 'She said that she and Mrs Matthews were only links in a chain . . .'

'Mrs Matthews was a little more than a link,' said Charles. 'But Janet was right. Too much knowledge too widely spread can be very dangerous. That's been proved over and over again: this particular business being a case in point! Somewhere along the line someone has either been bribed, blackmailed or tortured into telling what they know. We've got a reasonable number of people, like the man who met me in Babamarishi, up here in Kashmir: all of them working on their own particular line, and by no means all of them knowing each other. They are the real nuts and bolts of the whole system; but not the spark or the petrol. And, unfortunately, not at a level to be handed the kind of information that Mrs Matthews and Janet Rushton seem to have stumbled upon — which was their bad luck.'

He was silent for a time, staring unseeingly at the flame of the oil lamp that etched harsh lines and hollows in his face, and presently Sarah said: 'Charles——'

'Yes?'

'Who are *"they"* — the ones you call the "opposition"? The people who killed Janet and Mrs Matthews and – and all the others? I asked Janet that, but she wouldn't tell. So I supposed that they were the usual Freedom Fighters — the "Quit India!" lot. But now that we're quitting anyway, and they know they've won, I can't see that there would be any point in that.'

'There isn't.'

'Then who?'

'Work it out for yourself,' said Charles unhelpfully.

'That's no answer and you know it. You can't fob me off like that now — not after scaring me nearly out of my mind tonight; let alone in Gulmarg! Is it politics, revolution, mutiny, drug-smuggling, or what? You say "nobody knows". But you must have *some* idea.'

Charles sat down on the arm of the sofa, and said slowly: 'Yes. We have an idea. You see Sarah, every country in the world has an Intelligence Service — a Secret Service, if you prefer to call it that. Here in India it's often kept busy with what Kipling called "The Great Game". That game runs from beyond the Khyber to the frontier of Assam, and further. We have to keep an ear to the ground all over India, because a whisper heard in a bazaar in Sikkim may touch off a riot in Bengal. We have to keep eyes and ears in every town and village——

'Well, something very queer has been happening in India during the last year or so. Something beyond the usual underground stuff. There have been, for instance, a phenomenal number of burglaries. Not just the usual line in theft, but really big money. Carefully planned robberies of State Jewels worth millions. Things like the Charkrale rubies and the Rajgore emeralds, that are almost beyond price. Some of these jewels have turned up in surprising places, but we have discovered that for some reason most if not all of them have passed into or through Kashmir. This State has been a sort of collecting house — a pool.'

Sarah said: 'I remember about the emeralds. I mean, that was why you were playing polo the day that —' she stopped suddenly, and Charles looked at her curiously. 'Those emeralds,' he said after a pause, 'are here in Kashmir.'

'How do you know?' asked Sarah, startled. 'Have you got them?'

'No. But we know they are here. We thought we had taken every possible precaution against them getting over this border, but someone's been too clever for us. They are here.'

'But what for?' asked Sarah.

'Well, in the first place, for re-cutting. A great many of the stones have been re-cut here, in grubby little jewellers' shops poked away among the back streets of the city. But the best of the stuff has gone out across the passes by Gilgit and over the Pamirs.'

'Where to?'

Charles looked at her slantingly under his lashes. 'Your guess is as good as mine,' he said dryly: 'I told you to work it out for yourself.'

'But – but they're our *allies*!' protested Sarah, horrified.

'They are no one's allies. They never have been ... Except just for as long as it happens to suit their own book, and not one second longer! They will even ally themselves — and will continue to ally themselves — with the most blatantly fascist, reactionary and brutal regimes, solely to serve their own interests — and no one else's! There are a lot of things that the people of other nations will stick at doing because of that outmoded idea, "moral principles"; but they will stick at nothing, and their goal is always the same. Themselves on top; and everyone else either kneeling, or if they won't kneel, flat on their backs or their faces and very dead!'

'But the money — those jewels ... I don't understand why ... Do you mean it could be needed for starting something against us — another mutiny?'

Charles laughed; and then sobered suddenly. 'No. It's not that. As you've just told me yourself, there wouldn't be any point in starting one now that the British are quitting India.'

'Then why should you worry about it? Surely it's no longer your affair when you're clearing out?'

'Because the world has shrunk, Sarah. It's shrinking every day. It is no longer a matter of indifference to people in South America when a Balkan State blows up. Whatever is going on here is something that may affect us all, and we've got to find out what it is. We've *got* to!'

Sarah said: 'Is that why Mrs Matthews came up here? Because of the money, and the jewels and all that?'

'Yes. Because every single lead we followed seemed to end up in Kashmir. We thought at first it was merely theft on a big scale and nothing more; but it had to be stopped. We put a lot of people onto it, but they were mostly small fry. Pendrell was a fairly big fish, and he got onto it. And he died. So we sent along another of the same — equally good — Mrs Matthews; and they got her as well. Two people have sent us the Top Secret signal, the one we only use for something white hot. Something's brewing all right, Sarah. Something black and damnable. And we've got to get onto it and scotch it before we quit this country, because after that——'

'The deluge,' finished Sarah.

'Perhaps. In the meantime, as I've already said, your guess is as good as mine. How many more of these beastly books have we got left to go through?'

'About forty,' said Sarah with a sigh. 'I'll do them tomorrow. *Ouch!*'

'What's the matter?'

'Pins and needles again. I've rubbed them out of one foot, but I've been sitting on the other and now that's died on me too.'

Charles went down on his knees, and pulling off the small green slippers, rubbed the circulation back into Sarah's numbed feet.

'Isn't it lucky that I have such nice ones?' mused Sarah complacently.

Charles looked up and laughed. 'Frankly, no,' he said. 'At the moment I should prefer it if they were the usual twentieth-century bunch of radishes that one sees so often on the bathing boats.'

'Why?' inquired Sarah curiously.

'Because they are distracting my attention. And also because I should feel distinctly better if I could find something about you that I didn't like.'

'Oh,' said Sarah in a small voice. Charles replaced her slippers and stood up, brushing his knees.

'Would it be any help,' suggested Sarah meekly, 'if I told you that I snored?'

'Do you?'

'I don't know.'

'I'll think about it,' said Charles gravely, '— and take the first opportunity of finding out. Thanks for the suggestion.'

'Don't mention it,' said Sarah primly. 'I am always happy to oblige any gentleman with whom I pass the night.'

'Good Lord!' said Charles, 'it's morning!'

'I was wondering when you were going to notice it.'

Sarah went to the window and drew back the curtain. Outside, the lake and the mountains were no longer black but grey, and to the east the sky was faintly tinged with silver and saffron. Birds were beginning to cheep and rustle in the trees, and faint but clear, from the direction of Nasim, came the melodious cry of the muezzin of the mosque of Hazratbal, calling the Faithful to prayer ...

'Damn!' said Charles softly. 'I shall have to move quickly! Good-night, Sarah — I mean, Good-morning. Go and get some sleep. You'll be all right now. I'll be seeing you——'

There was a soft whistle from the bank.

'That's Habib,' said Charles; and was gone.

Sarah heard the muffled rasp of the pantry door being shut and then the boat trembled to swift footsteps upon the gangplank. There was a rustle among the willows and then silence.

Lager yawned and stretched and thumped his tail sleepily. 'Well thank goodness *you're* all right!' said Sarah.

15

It was past ten o'clock when Sarah awoke to find Fudge Creed standing by her bedside, shaking her.

'Wake up, you idle creature!' said Fudge. 'Do you usually oversleep to this extent? Anyone would think you'd been on the tiles all night!'

'You'd be surprised,' said Sarah yawning. She sat up, ruffling her hands through her red curls. 'Morning Fudge. Is it a nice day?'

'Heavenly!' pronounced Fudge pulling back the window curtains and letting in a ballet of sunblobs that danced across the ceiling. 'Your *mānji* reports that your breakfast has been ready for the last hour and a half, so I imagine it's uneatable by now.'

'Tell him I'll be ready for it in fifteen minutes,' said Sarah, sliding out of bed and stretching to get the sleepiness out of herself.

'Will do. And when you've finished, you're coming out shopping with us. We want to get some papier mâché bowls to send off as a wedding present; and as Hugo thinks you'd like to see the city and the river, we thought we'd go to the Fourth Bridge shops. They make lovely stuff there. What about it?'

'It sounds just what the doctor ordered,' replied Sarah buoyantly, relieved at the prospect of getting away from the boat for an hour or two. Charles had said, 'Don't go anywhere alone,' but he had not told her to stay on the boat, and she felt she had had quite enough of the *Waterwitch* for the time being. Having dressed she asked the *mānji* to buy a dozen bolts complete with screws and sockets in the bazaar, before sitting down to a belated breakfast which, as Fudge had predicted, was considerably the worse for wear and bore signs of having been kept hot over a charcoal brazier.

Sarah presented the kidneys to a grateful Lager and distributed most of the scrambled egg to a pair of friendly little bulbuls who hopped and twittered and flirted their pert black crests on the duckboard outside the open dining-room window, and drinking the lukewarm coffee she wondered why, after the alarms of the past night and her recent order concerning bolts for repelling intruders, she should feel so exceptionally gay and lighthearted?

'Oh what a beautiful morning!' sang Sarah. *'Oh what a beautiful day!'*

'Hell and damnation!' yelled a voice outside the window. There was a crash and a thump, and Hugo erupted through the window clutching a dripping paddle: 'Why is it,' he demanded heatedly, 'that although I was presented with a Rowing Blue by my misguided University, I remain incapable of paddling these flat-bottomed, over-canopied punts for five yards without turning at least three complete circles and soaking myself from the waist up? 'Morning, Sarah. You're looking almost as good as you sound. Do you feel as good as you look?'

'I feel terrific!' said Sarah. 'It must be the air or something. I feel like rushing out and doing pastoral dances in a cornfield.'

'Well how about rushing out to the Fourth Bridge and holding my hand while Fudge reduces me to bankruptcy among the papier mâché merchants?'

'Are you thinking of rowing us there?' inquired Sarah cautiously.

'Have no fear! I am, alas, too corpulent for prolonged exercise and too incompetent a performer with one of these beastly fancy paddles to attempt it. I propose to drive. We might have lunch at Nedou's on the return journey: how does that strike you?'

'Wizard!' said Sarah. 'Just wait while I get a hat. *"I've got a*

beautiful feeling, everything's going my way ...''' She vanished, singing, in the direction of her bedroom, while Hugo abstractedly finished off the toast and marmalade.

It was midday by the time they reached Ghulam Kadir's papier mâché shop at the Fourth Bridge, for Hugo had insisted on stopping at the Club for a beer *en route*, where they had found Reggie Craddock and Mir Khan, who had decided to accompany them.

Ghulam Kadir's showrooms overlooked the river and were stacked and piled with articles in papier mâché. Bowls and boxes in every conceivable size and shape, vases, candlesticks, dressing-table sets, lamps, platters, tables and dishes. On all of which birds and butterflies, leaves, flowers or intricate oriental designs had been painted in miniature and embellished with gold leaf.

Several brown-robed assistants wearing spotless white turbans of impressive size hurried forward to display the wares, uttering polite murmurs of greeting, and to the evident satisfaction of the aged proprietor — and the unconcealed amusement of Mir Khan — the pile of Sarah's purchases soon grew to alarming proportions.

Hugo, losing interest, eventually wandered off through a curtain-hung doorway, and they heard his voice raised in greeting in the next room.

'*Blast!* It's that old Candera pest,' grumbled Reggie Craddock, who was holding an assortment of finger-bowls while Fudge debated the respective merits of chenar leaves, kingfishers, lotuses and paisley patterns. 'Can't stand the woman. How Meril can stick it, beats me. Gossiping old bully!'

Lady Candera's astringent tones could be heard uplifted in comment and criticism from the next room: 'Well Hugo? Wasting your time and money as usual I see? Where's your wife? Why people buy this rubbishy trash I cannot imagine. No taste. No discrimination. I've just been telling Ghulam Kadir he's lucky that there are still so many tasteless tourists left in Srinagar. What are you doing here?'

'Imitation being the sincerest form of flattery,' said Hugo, 'I am following your example and acquiring — reluctantly and by proxy, so to speak — a collection of this rubbishy trash.'

Lady Candera gave vent to a high, cackling laugh. 'I like you, Hugo Creed. You are about the only person who has the gumption to stand up to me. But you malign me if you think I am buying this stuff. Heaven forbid! I am merely seeing that Meril's deplorable taste does not lose her her job. The Resident wants about two dozen pieces of papier mâché work and similar local rubbish to send to some charity bazaar, and has asked my niece to get it. The man must be entering his second childhood to entrust the selection to Meril who, if left to herself, is certain to be grossly cheated over the price and return laden with all the unsaleable hideosities in Srinagar. Major McKay has very kindly come to support me.'

'Oh, God!' muttered Reggie Craddock.

Meril Forbes' voice was heard to say in trembling protest: 'But Aunt Ena, you know it was your ...'

'Hold your tongue, child!' snapped Lady Candera sharply. 'I will not stand being argued with. Now run along and look out some nice powderbowls. I don't like the last two that you have shown me. Major McKay can advise you.'

The dusty, heavily embroidered curtain swung back and Lady Candera entered, her lorgnettes at the ready: 'Ah Antonia,' she observed to Fudge, 'increasing your husband's overdraft, I presume?' She turned the lorgnettes upon Reggie Craddock, inspected him silently and added: 'I see you have brought your faithful cavalier. Ah me, what it is to be young——! Though to be sure, in my youth, we missed a great many opportunities by observing a stricter regard for the conventions. You are about to drop one of those bowls, Major Craddock.'

Reggie Craddock scowled, and in an effort to retrieve the sliding bowl, dropped three more.

'Why don't you put them on the divan?' asked Lady Candera.

'So much more sensible. There you see, you have cracked that one and will have to buy it. However, I have no doubt you can use it as an ashtray. You are looking a little flushed, Antonia — or else you should use less rouge. If you modern women must use make-up, I do wish you would learn to apply it with a more sparing hand.'

Fudge said placidly: 'Dear Lady Candera, how you do love to torment us. But this morning I am determined to disappoint you. I refuse to rise.'

'You and Meril are two of a kind,' observed Lady Candera, seating herself regally upon the divan: 'No guts.'

Fudge smiled and said: 'But we are all scared of Lady Candera. She knows everyone's secrets and nothing is hid from her. Isn't that so?'

'I know yours, if that's what you mean,' snapped Lady Candera.

'Aha!' said Hugo. 'I see that you belong to the "All is discovered!" school.'

'And what is that, pray?'

'Kipling put it very neatly once: "Write to any man that all is betrayed, and even the Pope himself would sleep uneasily." In other words, if you whisper *"All is discovered!"* in a chap's ear, nine citizens out of ten will immediately take the next boat for South America, on the off-chance of its being true.'

'You mean, because there is no one who has nothing to hide?' asked Mir Khan.

'That's about it,' agreed Hugo. 'In fact if someone hissed *"All is discovered!"* in my ear, you would be unable to see me for dust.'

'That I can *well* believe!' said Lady Candera tartly. She turned her back on Hugo, and raising her lorgnettes surveyed Sarah at some length. 'Ah, the rich Miss Parrish,' she observed.

'I'm afraid not,' said Sarah.

'What? Oh — But I thought all trippers who could afford to come out to India were rich.'

'Not this one, I'm afraid,' confessed Sarah with a laugh.

'Well, it's a good story, girl. Spread it,' advised Lady Candera. 'To be thought rich is the next best thing to being it. You will find it a great aid to popularity. You too are buying this rubbishy trash, I see.'

'Yes,' said Sarah. 'I think it's charming.'

'Before the war it had certain merits,' admitted Lady Candera. 'But like everything else, its price has quadrupled and its quality deteriorated — thanks to our various allies, who paid fantastic prices without any discrimination whatsoever so that it soon ceased to be worthwhile to maintain a decent standard of workmanship. Any trash would sell.'

It was perhaps fortunate that at this point they should have been interrupted by the arrival of Helen Warrender, accompanied by Captain Mallory.

Charles, who had included Sarah casually in a general greeting, did not look in the least as if he had spent a sleepless and strenuous night. Or that the proprietary hand that Helen kept on his arm was in any way unwelcome. And Sarah, noting these things, felt unaccountably depressed and irritated. Mir Khan had left her side to discuss the rival merits of candlesticks and table-lamps with Meril Forbes and Major McKay in the next room, and as the others had fallen into a group about the divan where Lady Candera held court, she found herself temporarily alone.

There was a small archway on her left, half covered by a heavy fringed and embroidered curtain, and driven by that feeling of irritation she pushed the curtain aside and slipped through, to find herself in yet another showroom; dim, dusty and crowded with tables.

The walls here were hung with folds of brick-red cloth embroidered in geometrical designs in reds and browns and lavishly strewn with small pieces of looking-glass no bigger than a man's thumbnail, while underfoot the floor was thick with Persian rugs. In the centre of the room and against the walls stood innumerable tables of carved and inlaid wood, piled high with articles in papier mâché, and yet more bowls and vases and boxes were stacked upon the floor in dusty pyramids upon the rugs. There appeared to be no exit from the room, other than through the archway Sarah had entered by, but on one side of it intricately carved shutters of painted wood guarded a window and a balcony that overlooked the river.

The shutters were closed, so that the only light in the small, dim room filtered through the interstices of the carving, and the atmosphere was both cold and stuffy. It smelt of dust and sandalwood and slow centuries ... And of something else. Something that Sarah could not for the moment place.

She wandered about the room restlessly, picking up and examining various pieces of papier mâché and putting them down again without really seeing them, and listening with half an ear to the voices in the next room: Charles's voice, Hugo's, Helen's and Lady Candera's, which presently blurred together and grew fainter and faded to a mere murmur of sound. They have all gone somewhere else, thought Sarah.

The small, dusty, cluttered room was very quiet: quiet and cold and – and what? Sarah could give no reason for it, but all at once she found herself gripped by a feeling of panic that made her want to turn and run out of the room and after her companions. It was as if on entering this place she had somehow stepped out of the ordinary everyday world, for there was something here that frightened her. Something ...

Quite suddenly she realized what it was. The smell that had been in the dark deserted hall of the hut by the Gap. It was here too! Faint but distinct, in Ghulam Kadir's showroom by the Fourth Bridge.

Sarah stood motionless: holding her breath and unable to move. There was no sound now from beyond the curtain, and even the noises from the river and the city beyond the carved wooden shutters seemed to sink into silence. Something rustled behind the drapery upon the walls, and the little mirrors winked and twinkled to the faint movement — a hundred sly, glinting eyes that watched Sarah and reflected her endlessly upon the dark, dusty hangings.

She did not hear footsteps upon the thick rugs, but the curtain that hung over the archway was jerked back and Charles stood on the threshold.

'I've been sent to round you up —' he began, and then the fear in her white face checked him, and he dropped the curtain quickly. Sarah's voice was a croaking whisper: *'The smell! The smell in the hut. It's in this room . . .!'*

'Hush!' said Charles. He took a swift stride forward and gripped her wrist in a clasp that hurt. 'Pull yourself together, Sarah!' he ordered in an urgent whisper. 'Quickly . . . That's the girl.'

'That smell . . .' repeated Sarah.

'Yes, I know. What the hell were you doing in here?'

'I just came in to see——'

'No. I mean here in this house?'

'Fudge wanted to do some shopping.'

'Are you——' There was a very faint sound from beyond the curtained doorway and in almost the same moment, as swiftly and surprisingly as he had done once before, Charles caught her into his arms and kissed her, holding her hard and close so that she could neither move nor speak.

The curtain behind them swung aside and Major McKay stood in the archway, looking pink and startled. His already ruddy face gradually assumed the hue of a beetroot, and he gave a small dry cough of embarrassment and stood back as Sarah, released, brushed past him with flaming cheeks.

She ran across the big showroom and through a doorway into another room beyond. A twisting wooden staircase led up from it, and from somewhere overhead she could hear Reggie Craddock arguing with Fudge, and Helen Warrender's high, affected laugh. Sarah stopped abruptly; daunted by the thought of Helen's mocking eyes, Mir Khan's clear, perceptive gaze, and Lady Candera's deadly lorgnette all levelled at her flushed face and ruffled hair.

She wished she could remember what she had done with her bag. There was a small square of looking-glass in it, in addition to a powder-puff and a comb. Had she given it to Mir Khan to hold or was it on some table in the room behind her? As she hesitated, Charles walked quickly through the door. His face was perfectly blank and he looked at Sarah with a faint frown as though he had for the moment forgotten who she was.

'I suppose,' said Sarah in a low, furious voice, 'that that was some more shock treatment? What am I supposed to forget this time?'

Charles's frown deepened. He caught her elbow, and jerking her round began to propel her up the narrow stairway.

'Don't be a fool, Sarah,' he advised brusquely. He paused for a moment at the turn of the stair to look swiftly upwards and behind him, and spoke in an undertone: 'Someone was coming in, and as I had no way of telling who it was I had to establish an alibi damned quickly. I've probably put years on McKay's life in the process; the poor chap was incoherent with apology. But that's his look-out; and for all I knew it might have been—— Well the fact of the matter is that I can't afford to be discovered deep in private conversation with you just now, Sarah. Not unless I can provide a very obvious and innocent reason for it. So there was nothing for it but to provide the reason.'

'I see,' said Sarah.

'I doubt it,' said Charles with an edge to his voice. 'This is an unhealthy house to visit just now, Sarah, and the sooner you're out of it the better.' He smiled down suddenly at her sober face. 'All right, I apologize. It was abominable of me, and that's the second time I've offended. If there is a third you'll know I really mean it! And now if you think you could try and look less like a girl who has discovered a body in the basement and more like one who has recently been kissed in the conservatory, we'll join the others. Think you can manage it?'

'I'll try,' said Sarah meekly.

'That's the spirit,' approved Charles, and followed her up the stairs to a large upper room where the remainder of Ghulam Kadir's customers were admiring furniture and carved ornaments of polished walnut wood.

'Oh, there you are,' said Fudge from the window recess. 'Where did you get to, Sarah? I told Charles to collect you in case you got lost among all these rooms and staircases. What do you think of these little walnut-wood tables? Aren't they sweet? I really think I must get a set of them.'

Hugo groaned audibly as one of the assistants, a fat little brown-robed man with a face deeply pitted by the marks of smallpox, hurried to stack the nest of small, polished tables one within the other, and surround them by vast sheets of paper and copious loops of string. Another assistant, a stately gentleman whose grey beard had been dyed an impressive shade of scarlet, was engaged in performing a similar office for Meril Forbes' purchases under the critical eye of Lady Candera, while a third assistant made out the bills.

Ghulam Kadir appeared in the doorway and gave a low-voiced order and the red-bearded assistant vanished through a curtained archway and reappeared with a large brass tray loaded with tiny cups of black coffee which Ghulam Kadir handed round with flowery compliments.

Charles proffered his cigarette-case to Helen Warrender who looked at it and laughed. 'Thank you, but I won't deprive you of your last one.'

'Sorry,' apologized Charles: 'I didn't realize I had only one left, but for you, Helen, I will even sacrifice my last cigarette!'

'Dear Charles, I wish I could take you seriously! You know I never smoke anything but Sobranies, but after that I shall honour you by accepting your last gasper.' She bent her head over Charles's proffered lighter as the pockmarked assistant hurried up with a box of cigarettes, and Charles accepted one with a word of thanks and glanced at his watch: 'I hate to hurry you, Helen, but it's past one o'clock, and since we are supposed to be joining Johnnie and the Coply twins for lunch at Nedou's Hotel at 1.15, we shall be a good half hour late even if we start now.'

Helen gave an affected little shriek of dismay and began to hunt through her bag. 'What is it I owe you for, Ghulam Kadir? Oh yes — the powder-bowl and the tray and the eight table-mats. That's seven rupees eight annas, and twelve rupees, and let me see — the mats were four each, weren't they? I'm sure not to have brought enough money. Charles darling, your arithmetic's better than mine, how much do I owe?'

'Fifty-one rupees eight annas,' said Charles promptly. 'Here, I've got it, you can pay me back at lunch.' He handed over a collection of crumpled notes while Helen said: 'You *are* an angel, Charles! Don't forget to remind me, will you?' and Lady Candera remarked, 'A nice morning's work, Helen,' in acidulated tones.

'Shift ho, for all of us,' said Hugo. 'My stomach has been commenting on the lateness of the hour for some time past. What is the ghastly total, Fudge? ... Heaven save me! Here you are, Ghulam Kadir, you old robber. Pity we didn't arrive in a pantechnicon. Good God, Sarah! You don't mean to say you've acquired all that? On second thoughts, I regret that we did not come in two pantechnicons.'

They went down the twisting staircase in single file, and when they reached the main papier mâché showroom, Ghulam Kadir, who had preceded them, produced a handful of small objects — little papier mâché containers made to hold a box of matches — and formally presented one to each of his customers.

'Oh, thank you! they're charming,' exclaimed Sarah, examining her gift which bore a design of gold chenar leaves and brown, furry chenar buds on a cream ground.

'And now we really *must* go,' said Fudge. 'What are you looking for Sarah?'

'My bag,' said Sarah. 'I left it somewhere down here and I haven't paid my bill yet.'

'Ah, Captain Mallory; your cue again, I think,' observed Lady Candera with malice.

Sarah flushed angrily. 'I must have put it down somewhere here.'

'Anyone seen Sarah's bag?' demanded Hugo. 'Anyone ever seen any woman who did not end up a shopping expedition by mislaying something? Is there a doctor — I mean a detective — in the house?'

Parcels were abandoned while the party hunted through the rooms. 'Oh dear — I am sorry,' apologized Sarah contritely. 'It's a white one. Not very big. I can't think where——'

'Is this it?' inquired Hugo patiently, fishing up a white suede bag from between a carved sandalwood table and the end of the divan.

'Bless you, Hugo!' Sarah reached gratefully for her property and paid her bill, and the party once more collected its respective parcels and pieces and went down into the street where they were joined by Major McKay, who had been soothing his ruffled feelings with a quiet cigarette on the river steps.

Lady Candera, Meril and the Major, who were also apparently lunching at Nedou's Hotel, were going as far as the First Bridge by *shikara*, and Charles, who had left his car on the other side of the river, accepted a lift for himself and Helen as far as the opposite bank. Sarah, Reggie Craddock and Mir Khan piled into the Creeds' car, and were driven away through the maze of narrow and tortuous streets that twist and turn through Srinagar City.

16

It was almost two o'clock by the time Hugo's car drew up outside Nedou's Hotel and decanted its passengers.

'You and Reggie will lunch with us, won't you, Mir?' asked Hugo, disentangling himself from a pile of paper parcels.

'I should be delighted.'

'What about you, Reggie?'

'Well,' said Reggie doubtfully, 'I didn't warn out for lunch at my pub, so——'

'Oh give 'em a ring, if that's all that's worrying you. They'll have given you up by now, anyhow.'

'You're probably right,' admitted Reggie. 'In that case, thanks very much: I'd like to.'

Nedou's Hotel, in contrast to its recent crowded years, seemed very quiet and sleepy, and there were only a few people in the entrance hall as Fudge and Sarah passed through. From the bar came a subdued murmur of voices and the clink of glasses, and Sarah, glancing in through the open door as she passed by, caught a glimpse of Johnnie Warrender and the Coply twins throwing dice.

Hugo led the way to a table by the window and presently Helen, followed by Johnnie, Charles and the Coply twins, took their seats at one nearby. But there was something curiously depressing about the vast, echoing room with its sea of empty tables, and even Hugo seemed oppressed by it and to have temporarily mislaid his customary good humour.

Lunch was for the most part a silent meal, and when it was

over they took their coffee out into the entrance hall where they sat facing the empty spaces of a big dance floor. There was a stage at the far end of it — the scene of many amateur performances and cabarets in past years — and the heavy, dark curtains of crimson plush that hid it from view seemed to add to the gloom of the deserted ballroom.

Hugo, Reggie and Mir drifted away to the bar in search of liqueurs, while Fudge and Sarah sat on, sipping their coffee and making desultory conversation to Major McKay, who appeared to have lost his party, and presently Charles came across the hall and sat down on the arm of Fudge's chair.

'Cigarette, Fudge? You don't, do you Sarah? Well St George, what have you done with the dragon?'

Major McKay was betrayed into a smile. 'If you are referring to Lady Candera, she went to sleep over the coffee. We had luncheon in the private dining-room upstairs to avoid having to mix with the *hoi polloi* — that's you, Charles.'

'Touché,' said Charles with a laugh. 'Well good luck to you. I hope you pull it off. If you do, you'll deserve the Albert Medal with bars.'

Major McKay turned a rich shade of beetroot and Sarah said: 'Pull what off?'

'George knows,' said Charles with a grin.

'On the contrary, I have not the least idea what you are referring to,' said Major McKay frigidly. He consulted his watch, and rose. 'Well — er — time's getting on. I suppose I'd better go and see if Lady Candera's car is back. I shall be seeing you all at the Nagim Club this evening, I expect.'

He made his escape, and Fudge turned reproachfully to Charles: 'You really shouldn't pull his leg like that, Charles! It's too bad of you. It upsets him. Besides, it may only put him off.'

'I find it irresistible,' said Charles. 'George is a good old stick, if only he'd stop taking himself so seriously. And if that sort of thing is going to put him off, he's not worth any woman's time.'

'What *are* you two talking about?' demanded Sarah, bewildered. 'Put him off what?'

'Meril, of course,' said Fudge impatiently. 'You don't suppose George McKay is dancing attendance on that old dragon for fun, do you? We're all madly hoping that he'll run off with Meril.'

Sarah laughed. 'What an old matchmaker you are, Fudge! But why run off with her? I'm quite sure that Major McKay would never do anything so unconventional.'

'Well he'll never get her if he doesn't,' predicted Fudge. 'The minute Lady Candera realizes that it is not her witty and stimulating conversation that the gallant Major is interested in, but her despised niece, she will show him the door in no uncertain manner. And Meril, poor child, will never have the courage to do anything about it.'

'I don't believe it!' said Sarah flatly. 'Not in this day and age. That sort of thing went out with Victorian novels and the vapours. Meril isn't a minor. She doesn't need anyone's consent. Besides, you're wrong when you say she hasn't any courage. I've seen her take a slope, skiing, that *I* wouldn't dare face.'

'Ah, but that's quite a different sort of courage,' said Fudge wisely. 'Lots of people with plenty of physical courage haven't an ounce of moral courage to go with it. Meril's one of that kind, and where her aunt is concerned she behaves like a hypnotized rabbit.'

'Sounds as if she'll make the Major a perfect wife!' commented Sarah caustically. 'But what makes you think he's interested in her, anyway? Lady Candera seems to hypnotize a lot of people. Maybe he's one of them too?'

'Well, he was up here last year and he went around quite a bit with them. But it certainly wasn't Lady Candera who drew him up to Gulmarg. Meril used to give him skiing lessons every day. Now here he is again, in spite of the fact that he could have taken his leave in England instead. Of *course* it's Meril! Besides, didn't you see the beautiful shade of puce he went when Charles pulled his leg about it?'

'Personally,' said Charles, 'I can imagine nothing duller than having to go through life tied to such a model of rectitude and propriety as George McKay. No woman of spirit could bear up under the strain.'

'Nonsense,' said Fudge firmly. 'He's a good man. He's kind and he's reliable. Besides Meril isn't a woman of spirit. She'll make him a perfect wife, and they will stodge along together and be as happy as ... as ... well, I can't quite visualize George as a lark, I must admit. Anyway, it's too late in the afternoon to think up suitable similes. Where on earth has Hugo got to? It's time we were making tracks for home.'

Fudge got up, and accompanied by Charles, crossed the hall and disappeared in the direction of the bar, and Sarah, left alone, turned to look across the gloomy spaces of the deserted ballroom.

The sun was shining brightly outside the line of tall windows that ran down one side of the room, but between the windows and the dance floor stood a row of pillars that supported a long gallery overhead, and formed an open corridor between the windows and the ballroom below: a corridor that was furnished with sofas, chairs, tables and writing-desks, but which owing to that line of pillars, kept much of the daylight from the ballroom floor.

It was a gaunt and not very attractive room, and in the afternoon light, gloomy and bare and unfriendly. But Sarah was peopling it with the gay dancers of other years and picturing it ablaze with lights and full of noise and music and laughter; and presently she moved out onto the polished floor, humming softly to herself and took a few dancing steps across the shining surface.

Except for her own tuneful humming, it was very quiet in the big ballroom. And indeed the whole hotel seemed to be taking a siesta, for she could hear no sound from the hall or the passages beyond the ballroom. Even the subdued murmur of voices from the bar had ceased, and beyond the tall windows the garden drowsed in the afternoon sunlight, empty and silent.

The sprung floor vibrated under Sarah's feet as she swayed and turned to the strains of an imaginary band: *'The moonlight, and the moon, and every lovely lilting tune ...'* hummed Sarah, and stopped. That song again! Janet's song. Perhaps this ballroom *was* haunted. Perhaps Janet had danced to that tune here last year — and other years ...

Sarah stood still in the middle of the dim, deserted floor, trying to visualize Janet in a ball dress, and thinking of all the young men up on leave who had danced there during the war years, and gone away to die in Burma and Malaya, North Africa and Italy; in Japanese prisoner-of-war camps and on the infamous Death Railway ...

As she stood there, her eye was caught by a faint movement. The curtains that hung in front of the stage rippled very slightly as though someone had drawn them an inch or two apart in order to peer out between them, and then dropped them softly back into place.

Sarah stayed very still, listening. Yes. There was someone on the stage behind the curtains, for in the stillness she could hear, very faintly, the pad of quiet feet moving across bare boards. A dog or a cat? But the curtains had moved at the height of a man's head. A hotel servant, then? — snatching a brief siesta in the shelter of the curtains.

A hundred to one it's only a servant! Sarah told herself firmly. It was silly to start imagining things even in innocent places like this, and she would go and see for herself.

She ran lightly across the floor and up the short flight of steps that led to the stage, and taking a deep breath, pulled aside the folds of the curtains and went through onto the stage behind them.

It was much larger than she had expected, but nothing moved upon it save the lazily drifting dust motes in a shaft of sunlight.

The wide stretch of uncarpeted boards sloped slightly upwards towards the back wall in which there was a single tall window, and after the gloom of the ballroom the stage, on this side of the curtains, seemed full of light.

The sunbeams streaming in through the high window made symmetrical patterns on the bare boards and slanted across the piles of chairs and tables that stood against the walls of the stage, one upon the other. On one side a small flight of concrete steps led down to what were probably dressing-rooms, while on the opposite side, where the sunbeams did not penetrate, a steep, enclosed staircase wound up into the shadows of a gallery above. A gallery that was the continuation of the one that ran overhead along one side of the ballroom.

There was someone or something on that staircase; though Sarah did not know why she should be sure of this. Perhaps a board had creaked, or something had flickered among the dusty shadows... The empty stage stretched silent and still in the drowsy afternoon light and the heavy folds of the curtains hung dark and unmoving; and no sound came from the ballroom behind her. The furniture against the walls, the neatly stacked tables, the wicker chairs turned one upon the other, the smug outlines of cretonne-covered sofas and armchairs and the red plush curtains seemed to hem Sarah in, and she straightened her shoulders and walked steadily across the stage to the foot of the spiral staircase and looked up into the dusty dimness overhead.

Something moved sharply above her on the stairway and for the flash of a second she glimpsed a face that peered down at her from the shadows overhead. Then its owner turned and she heard a scurry of bare feet on the staircase, followed by the swift pad of retreating footsteps in the gallery overhead.

Sarah whirled about and running across the stage, slipped back between the curtains. From the front of the stage she could see up into the ballroom gallery and she was just in time to see a figure whisk out through its far door: a figure wearing the brown voluminous robes and white turban of a Kashmiri, and that she might have taken to be a member of the hotel staff if it had not been for the brief glimpse of its owner's face that she had received from the dark stairway.

She had a good memory for faces, but even if she had not, there would have been little excuse for forgetting this one, since she had seen it only an hour or so ago. It was the pockmarked face of the fat little assistant in Ghulam Kadir's papier mâché shop at the Fourth Bridge in Srinagar City.

As she stood there, staring up across the ballroom to the half-seen door of the gallery, the curtains at her back moved again and Sarah whirled round, her heart in her mouth.

'Charles!'

'Hello, Sarah.'

'Gosh!' said Sarah in a gasp. 'You gave me one hell of a fright. What were you doing back there?'

'Watching you,' said Charles. He lit a cigarette and his eyes regarded her thoughtfully over the small yellow flame of his lighter. 'You know Sarah,' said Charles softly, blowing out the flame, 'you are too curious by half. Too curious and too courageous. And in the present circumstances, that is an unfortunate combination. I would feel a lot happier about you if you'd allow discretion to be the better part of valour for a change.'

'Do you know who was behind that curtain?' demanded Sarah. 'Well I'll tell you——'

But she was unable to, because Charles had taken a swift stride forward and the palm of his left hand was over her mouth.

'Ssh!' said Charles softly. 'There are too many eyes in this place, Sarah, and too many ears.' He raised his voice, and said as though continuing a conversation, '— it was a pretty good band too. Run by a man in the Police called Chapman, who played a darned good game of golf and——'

But it was only Meril Forbes who came hurriedly through the

doorway below the stage that led out of the ballroom into the long, whitewashed cloakroom passage.

She was wearing her usual air of distressed uncertainty and she checked at the sight of Charles and Sarah: 'Oh! ... Have – have either of you seen Aunt Ena? She sent me to get some cigarettes, and I've got them. But goodness knows where she's gone to: I've looked everywhere. She does so hate to be kept waiting. Oh dear, anyone would almost think she did this sort of thing on purpose!'

'Of course she does,' observed Hugo, strolling in through the doorway, hat in hand: 'Didn't you know? *"She only does it to annoy because she knows it teases."* You should refuse to rise, Meril dear. As a matter of fact your elderly relative is outside in her car, sizzling slightly.'

'Oh dear!' repeated Meril helplessly, and hurried away across the ballroom.

'Poor kid,' observed Hugo kindly, watching the retreating figure. 'Pity someone can't make her a present of some backbone. Ah, there you are, Sarah. I've been sent to hunt you up. My spouse has been demanding your immediate apprehension. She is thinking of making a beeline for home. Coming?'

'Yes,' said Sarah gratefully. She turned and ran down the steps from the stage and joined Hugo on the ballroom floor.

'Charles been taking you on a Cook's Tour?'

'Yes,' said Charles, coming down from the stage: 'I've been telling Sarah all about the Gay Days.'

'Believe it or not,' mused Hugo, 'there was even a historic occasion when I myself performed upon that bally stage. If memory serves, I sang a duet with a girl called Mollie someone. A tasteful ditty about a bench in a park — or was it something about tiptoeing through tulips? I can't remember. I do recall, however, that my braces lifted the occasion to the heights of immortality. They gave under the strain of a high C and my trousers descended. It went well with the audience. In fact, I think

I may say without vanity that I was a riot. The customers rolled in the aisles, and had anyone been able to supply a piece of string, or a safety-pin of suitable dimensions, I could have taken a dozen encores. As it was, our prudent stage-manager blacked us out and hurried on with the show. Ah me! Those were the days!'

From somewhere in front of the hotel came the sound of a car horn blown in a series of impatient toots.

'That is undoubtedly my better half beginning to simmer at the edges,' said Hugo. 'Come on, Sarah. Let us leg it with all speed.'

17

Sarah had tea that day on the flat roof of the Creeds' houseboat, looking out across the lake to the mountains behind Shalimar. Willow boughs made a swaying curtain of green lace above the tea table, and a trio of perky little bulbuls flirted their crests among the leaves and twittered for crumbs.

The lake seemed to drowse in the late afternoon sunlight, the reflections mirrored in its placid surface broken only intermittently by the passing of an occasional country boat or *shikara*, or the splash of a brilliant-hued kingfisher. And Sarah, toying abstractedly with a cucumber sandwich as she tried to make up her mind whether or not to return to the *Waterwitch* and continue her search, decided against it. The thought of leaving the sunlit peace of the comfortable deck-chair at Fudge's side to rummage through the dark, dusty corners of the *Waterwitch* was repellent, and though conscience fought with inclination, inclination won, and Miss Parrish stayed on: watching the shadows lengthen across the water and the mountains turn saffron and pink and rose in the rays of the setting sun, while Subhana, the Creeds' *mānji*, cleared away the tea things.

Lager, entirely recovered from his last night's adventure, snuffled and skirmished among the reeds and willows on the bank, and Fudge and Sarah sat idle, their hands in their laps, looking out across the lake through the soft blue shadows while below them homeward-bound *shikaras* and country boats from Nasim passed down the water lane towards the Nagim Bagh Bridge, their paddles splashing in musical rhythm.

A scent of woodsmoke drifted across the quiet air, and presently, like the first star in a pale sky, the light on the top of the little stone temple that crowns the hill of the Takht-i-Suliman shone out, wan in the warm evening light, and from somewhere in the Creeds' cookboat a voice began to sing a plaintive Kashmiri song full of odd trills and quavers.

'Where's Hugo?' asked Sarah suddenly.

'What?' Fudge woke from her reverie with a start. 'Hugo? He went along to the Nagim Club to meet some chap who's putting up there, and who's advertising a trout rod for sale on the Club's noticeboard. Hugo wanted to have a look at it. I think this must be him now——'

There was a sound of voices from beyond the willows that screened the field path leading from the houseboat to the Nagim road, and Fudge sighed and said: 'Damn! he's brought somebody back with him; and I did so want a peaceful evening doing nothing. Now we shall have to sit about drinking short drinks and making polite conversation for hours on end. I suppose it's this rod man.'

'No, it isn't,' said Sarah, who had risen and was peering down through the willow boughs. 'It's Charles.'

'Oh,' said Fudge on an odd note. She looked sideways at Sarah and laughed. 'Still interested in him, Sarah?'

'No of course not,' said Sarah hastily.

'Which means you are. Well — now's your chance.' She stood up and waved to Hugo who had arrived on the bank below.

'I've brought a guest,' called up Hugo. 'Rustle us up a drink, darling. We're coming up.'

Fudge crossed the deck and called down to Subhana, as Hugo and Charles, enthusiastically greeted by Lager, came up onto the roof of the houseboat.

'I found him at the Club,' said Hugo, waving an explanatory hand at Charles. 'I hadn't realized he was staying there. He wishes to take you poodlefaking in the moonlight, Sarah.'

'Hugo!' said Fudge. 'I do wish you wouldn't use that disgusting expression.'

Charles laughed. 'As a matter of fact,' he said mildly, 'I wondered if you would all dine with me tonight? There is apparently a gramophone dance on at the Club, and though I don't imagine the attendance will be large, it might be quite fun. The Secretary has put out a plaintive appeal for support.'

Fudge smiled and shook her head. 'That's sweet of you, Charles. But I don't think I could face a gramophone dance tonight. I've got a bit of a headache and I feel like a peaceful home evening and early bed. You take Sarah. I'm sure her Kashmir education will not be complete without a dance at Nagim on a moonlight night.' Fudge turned her head and looked out across the lake to where the setting sun was transforming the Gulmarg range into a flat lilac silhouette against a saffron sky: 'It's going to be a lovely night,' she said.

Charles turned to Sarah. 'What about it, Sarah? Would you like to come? I'm afraid I can't promise you a very amusing evening: we shall be lucky if half a dozen couples show up at the Club.'

Sarah hesitated a moment, looking from Fudge to Charles and back again, and Charles, turning a little so that his back was to the Creeds, lowered one eyelid for a fraction of a second. 'Yes, I'd love to,' said Sarah promptly. 'Are you sure you and Hugo won't come, Fudge?'

'*Quite* sure!' said Fudge firmly. 'Thanks all the same, Charles.' She smiled across at him, and Hugo said sadly: 'I, you notice, get no say in the matter.'

'Oh, darling!' said Fudge remorsefully, 'do you really want to go? All right then, I'll go if you'd like. I can easily take an aspirin.'

'Nonsense,' said Hugo. 'I was only pulling your leg. I could do with early bed myself after the ghastly schemozzle of that storm last night. I hardly got a wink of sleep. Besides, I am reaching the sere and yellow leaf. My dancing days are done. It is now up to young and sprightly creatures like Charles and Sarah here to carry on the good work of making the nights hideous with revelry. All that I shall now contribute to the racket will be a snore.'

Subhana and Ayaz Mohammed appeared upon the roof with an assortment of drinks and glasses, and Hugo having dispensed sherry and whisky with a liberal hand, the four of them sat on into the green twilight, talking and laughing, while a huge, apricot-coloured moon lifted above the mountains beyond Shalimar and laid a shimmering silver pathway across the lake.

Eventually, glancing at her watch, Fudge inquired of Charles what time he was thinking of dining?

'Round about eight, I suppose. The dance won't begin until after nine.'

'Well it's nearly eight now,' said Fudge. 'I don't want to hurry you, Sarah, but if you intend to change you'd better think about moving.'

Sarah jumped up, and Charles said: 'I'll wait for you. Then we can go along to the Club together. That is, if you won't mind looking at the papers while I change? Or would you rather I came back and fetched you in about half an hour's time?'

'No. Wait for me here. I won't be more than ten minutes,' said Sarah; and vanished down the hatchway staircase, calling to Lager to follow.

Abdul Gaffoor, her *mānji*, was switching on the lights in the *Waterwitch* when she reached the boat, and pausing only to tell him that she would not be in for dinner, she made for her bedroom — conscious of a little shiver of distaste as she passed through the silent rooms, and grateful for the scuttering patter of Lager's feet and the sound of his small excited snufflings and whimperings as he sniffed at the floorboards, beneath which lurked an entrancing smell of rats.

Strewn all over her bed was the untidy heap of paper-wrapped parcels that she had bought that morning and which

Abdul Gaffoor and the Creeds' bearer had carried in from the car; and Sarah was annoyed to see that every parcel had been opened, the string round each one cut and the paper roughly replaced. Abdul had evidently been curious as to her purchases and had peered at them all with the inquisitiveness of a squirrel. 'He might at least have had the decency to do them up again tidily!' said Sarah aloud and crossly.

She bundled the entire collection hastily into an empty suitcase, and had removed her shoes and dress when a sudden and unpleasant thought slid into her mind and she stood still, staring down at the bed where the parcels had lain. A moment later she whirled round to open the cupboard and have her suspicion instantly confirmed; for it needed no second look to see that someone had been going through her belongings.

Neat piles of underclothing were not quite as neat as she had left them. A nest of carefully rolled stockings had been disarranged, and the order of the line of shoes on the bottom of the hanging cupboard had been changed — Sarah invariably put walking shoes at one end of the line, followed by house shoes and then evening slippers; but now a pair of gold evening sandals stood between blue suede house shoes and brown brogues...

There were other indications too; small in themselves, but enough to show that someone had been taking an exceedingly thorough look at all her possessions. Was it only curiosity on the part of Abdul Gaffoor, or was there some other less pleasant explanation? Sarah was suddenly intensely thankful that she had taken the precaution of carrying Charles's gun with her in her bag which had not been out of her sight, except——

She snatched up her bag in a panic and opened it, but the gun was still there, wrapped about with a chiffon scarf, and she drew a deep breath of relief and regarded it thoughtfully. She really could not carry a gun to a dance! Besides, she would be with Charles, and since her room had already been searched it was highly unlikely that anyone would search it again for some time. On that decision, she took out the gun and stuffed it under her pillow, and straightening up, saw with dismay that according to the little travelling clock that stood on her bedside table she had already overstepped the ten minutes she had promised to be away.

Heavens! thought Sarah, I'm going to be appallingly late, and Charles will think I'm one of those deadly women who say ten minutes and mean thirty! She turned hurriedly back to the cupboard, selected a deceptively simple evening dress of white linen boldly patterned in black leaves, and slipped her feet into a pair of white satin sandals. That should do for a gramophone dance, thought Sarah — and for Charles.

A few minutes later she was dressed and ready. She gave a final glance at herself in the inadequate mirror and looked in the cupboard for an evening-bag. But the assortment that presented itself to her proved unsatisfactory, and with another look at the clock and an exclamation of annoyance, she snatched up the white suede one from which she had removed the little automatic, and having reached for a brief fur cape, switched off the lights, and with Lager frisking at her heels, returned to the Creeds' boat.

Charles must have been watching for her, for he came down the gangplank as she arrived opposite the boat. 'Are you intending to bring that pup?' he inquired, 'because he won't be allowed inside the Club rooms you know.'

'Don't worry, I'm going to ask Hugo to keep an eye on him: Lager dotes on him, and he'll stay quiet as long as Hugo is around. It's only when I leave him alone that he behaves abominably and yelps non-stop like a lost soul. We left him behind this morning in the charge of the *mānji*, but I'm afraid he's a snob. He doesn't consider that *mānjis* are "company", and I gather he hardly paused for breath. He started yelping when we left and we could hear him still at it from the Nagim road when we got back at half past three. But he behaves like an angel with Hugo, don't you ager, you little horror?'

'Who is taking my name in vain?' inquired Hugo appearing in the open doorway at the top of the gangplank.

'Me,' said Sarah ungrammatically. 'Hugo, be a darling and look after Lager for me. He's had his supper, and if I leave him alone on my boat he'll only howl until I come back.'

'OK,' sighed Hugo. 'Sling him along. Here, Lager boy — no, there is no need to chew holes in me to show your appreciation of my person. Good-night, Charles. Have a good time, Sarah.'

'I intend to,' promised Sarah. 'Good-night, Hugo.' She raised her voice and called up through the willow boughs: 'Good-night Fudge,' but there was no reply from the roof of the boat and Hugo said: 'She's gone to bed — it's that headache, I'm afraid. I'll say good-night for you.' He waved a cheerful hand, and they turned away along the bank to pass round the shadowy trunk of the big chenar tree and come out onto the moonlit path that ran across the fields towards the Nagim road.

'Nice work,' said Charles, taking Sarah's arm and hurrying her down the path between the young corn. 'I need an alibi tonight Sarah, and you're it. Damn that thing!' ... he had trodden on a piece of rusty tin, laid down by one of the *mānjis* to cover a depression in the path that the last night's rain had filled with muddy water, and it had creaked loudly and protestingly under his feet as though a nightjar had screamed in the fields.

'I had to ask the Creeds to come along for the look of the thing,' said Charles, 'but that providential headache of Fudge's has saved me a lot of trouble.'

'What do you mean "want me for an alibi"?' asked Sarah.

Charles glanced over his shoulder before replying, but the moonlit expanse of field offered little or no cover, and they were out of earshot of the boats and the trees. Nevertheless he dropped his voice to an undertone: 'I have an assignation for tonight,' said Charles, 'on an island in the lake. Not the sort of place I should have chosen for it myself, but I suppose it has its points. However, under the circumstances I do not want to go floating about the lake by myself. It's not the sort of thing I'd be likely to go in for, and might well give rise to comment and curiosity. On the other hand, if there is one thing that chaps go in for more than another in Kashmir, it is floating round the lake in a *shikara* with a girl. So no one is likely to consider it in the least odd if I take the beautiful Miss Parrish for a moonlight ride. Even if Fudge and Hugo had decided to join the party, it would still have raised no more than a tolerant eyebrow and an indulgent laugh if I had gone off with you in a boat for an hour or two.'

'What is this assignation?' asked Sarah, her eyes sparkling with excitement. 'Who is it with?'

'One of our men. You saw him today — twice, if I am not mistaken. In fact you scared him considerably the second time!'

Sarah checked to stare up at him, her brows wrinkling: 'I don't understand,' she said. 'I haven't seen anyone I don't know today except——' She drew her breath in on a sudden gasp and stood still. 'Not – not the man from that shop?'

'That's it,' said Charles. 'The assistant with the pockmarked face. You saw him again at the hotel I think.'

'But – but I don't understand,' said Sarah again. 'What was he doing at the hotel?'

'Trying to see me,' said Charles, hurrying her onwards. 'He's one of our best men. We planted him there two years back. A pretty neat bit of work it was too. He had hoped to get an opportunity to speak to me this morning during the time that we were all at the shop, but due to the mob of customers who turned up he was kept too busy and didn't dare risk it. The most he could manage was to make me a sign to that effect, which he did when he handed me the cigarettes.'

'What was it?' asked Sarah in a whisper.

'Nothing in the least exciting, I'm afraid,' said Charles with a grin. 'He merely scratched his chin with the little finger of his left hand, in a gesture that is shorthand for NBG, or "sorry, no can do — over to you". So I immediately mentioned Nedou's Hotel and that I was lunching there, and talked of the stage.'

'Yes,' said Sarah slowly. 'I remember.'

'Ahamdoo is pretty quick, and that was quite enough for him. But the meeting at Nedou's was a frost — largely due to you, I may say! You walked in on us before he had time to say a word. We heard you coming, and he whisked round and was halfway up those stairs to the gallery when you appeared on the scene positively radiating suspicion. By the time I was able to catch up with him he'd got the wind up good and proper — either he thought he'd been followed or he'd spotted someone he was scared to death of, because he was in a blind panic and couldn't wait to get away. He merely hissed at me that he'd be on the Char-Chenar island at eleven tonight, and was off like a scalded cat: I wasn't given time to draw breath, let alone argue the toss; and I have to admit that when you bust up that initial meeting I could cheerfully have strangled you!'

'You ought to have warned me,' retorted Sarah, employing the popular tactic of attack being the best form of defence. 'And anyway, where were you?'

'Sitting in one of the armchairs that had its back to you. The back was a high one, but I don't mind telling you, Sarah, that you gave me a few very nasty moments. You couldn't see me unless you started peering round among the furniture; but I couldn't see you either, and I didn't know who the hell it was. I didn't dare move until I heard you walk away towards the staircase, and believe me it was a weight off my mind when I realized it was you.'

'Why didn't you tell me at once?' demanded Sarah indignantly. 'I was scared stiff. You might have explained!'

'With the place simply teeming with people? Not much!' said Charles firmly.

'What people in particular?' asked Sarah curiously.

Charles looked down at her and shook his head, for by now

they were near a small village, and a few yards further on the path left the field, to wind between a handful of tall, ramshackle Kashmiri houses before joining the main road that stretched away on either hand, white and deserted in the moonlight.

The acacia trees that bordered it patched the dusty road with shadows and filled the air with fragrance, and the few shops — rickety buildings hurriedly constructed of unseasoned deodar-planks during the brief boom years of Nagim Bagh — were for the most part shuttered and silent. Once safely past these and walking in the direction of the Club, Sarah repeated her question.

'Well,' said Charles meditatively, 'there's Reggie Craddock for one.'

'But he couldn't be mixed up in a thing like this?' gasped Sarah, horrified. 'Yes I know he tried to get me off the boat, but—— Oh no! He couldn't. Not really. Besides, he's an Englishman!'

Charles said dryly: 'My dear Sarah, money talks in all languages. And there has been big money spent here.'

'Then you think that Reggie ... ?' began Sarah.

'I don't know,' said Charles curtly. 'He might be in debt. When chaps get into the hands of Indian money-lenders they can end up in some ghastly tangles. I don't say he is; but I'm curious about Reginald Craddock. He knew Janet Rushton, and for all I know he may have been genuinely fond of her; though somehow that doesn't strike me as sufficient reason for wanting to get you off Janet's boat. Craddock was a member of the party at the ski-hut, and he was at Ghulam Kadir's shop this morning at a time when a very important message was due to be passed to someone there.'

'What's that?' Sarah stopped for a moment on the moonlit road. 'Oh, you mean the one that pockmarked man meant to give you?'

'No, I don't. That shop is used as a cover for a lot of things. Not active things: strictly passive ones. I think you would find that its aged and respectable proprietor is careful to know nothing f plots or plans. He merely allows his premises to be used, in return for a nice fat sum, as a sort of post office and receiving centre that collects and passes on information for the opposition. Something was due to be passed today: Ahamdoo was onto that much. I have my own ideas as to how it was done, but I can't be sure. We've had a check on everyone who entered or left that shop today, and Reggie, of course, was one of them.'

'So was I, for that matter. And so were lots of other people — including you,' retorted Sarah.

'I know. But all the same I am distinctly interested in Major Reggie Craddock ... Left turn here — this is the Club.'

They turned in through an open gate, to walk down a long, tree-shaded drive that wound through an orchard and ended in lawns, neat flowerbeds, and a low Club building on the extreme edge of the Nagim Bagh lake. As they neared it Sarah, who had been silent for a few minutes, said thoughtfully: 'I wonder if you could work up a case against everyone who was in that shop this morning?'

'Of course,' said Charles cheerfully. 'I can produce a different theory to fit each one of you; and yours is still the best of the bunch.'

'In that case, I'm surprised that you trust me with all this information,' said Sarah with a laugh.

'How do you know I do?' asked Charles softly. Sarah stared at him blankly, but before she had time to frame an indignant reply Charles had steered her inside the Club and seated her in a chair on the edge of the ballroom floor, and having ordered tomato juice and promised not to keep her waiting long, vanished in the direction of the Club's residential block, leaving her alone with a pile of illustrated papers and two bored Club *khidmatgars* who were whispering together by the bar at the end of the room.

On the far side of the ballroom floor a row of french windows faced the lake and gave onto a long, roofless verandah, supported on wooden piles and set with chairs and tables. Sarah left her chair and went out onto it, to find herself looking across a sheet of moonlit water bounded on the far bank by a row of dimly seen houseboats, from which an occasional square of light threw a thin quivering line of yellow across the lake. The majority of them, unlike the many boats that were moored to the near bank, appeared to be unoccupied, and behind them, above the dark, distant tree-tops, rose the crouching bulk of fort-crowned Hari Parbat; silhouetted blackly against the moonwashed plain and the long line of glittering snow peaks that fringed the far wall of the valley.

Sarah leaned her arms on the verandah rail and gazed out across the water to where, shimmering in the moonlight, the snowy slopes of Apharwat lifted above the dark tree-line that marked Khilanmarg. Somewhere over there, a dot in the waste of whiteness, was the little ski-hut, and somewhere below it, among the miles of trees, lay the rambling hotel buildings and the small hotel room where, for her, this fantastic adventure had begun. And once again, as she looked at those far mountain ranges she wondered why she stayed on in Kashmir, where so many frightening things had happened to her since the night that she had been awakened by the moonlight on her face.

She had quitted the place with such deep relief, feeling thankful that she need never see it again. But a mixture of curiosity, bravado, and a promise given to the dead girl had brought her back, and ever since her return she had been living in a constant state of fear and tension. So why did she stay, when it would be so easy to send a cable to the Pierces in Ceylon, to hire a car and be in Rawalpindi in less than a dozen hours, and on the Frontier Mail speeding south the same day? If she were in her right mind she would be thinking of packing and leaving immediately, for none of this was any concern of hers. Yet she knew that she had no intention of going, and was, on the contrary, conscious of a feeling of intense exhilaration, even though last night on the *Waterwitch* she had experienced pure, undiluted terror, and again that morning, both in Ghulam Kadir's shop and as she stared up the dark staircase at the side of the stage in Nedou's Hotel. But it did not seem to matter. All that mattered was that she was young and alive, and life was glorious and exciting — because she was going to dine with Charles.

Sarah smiled to herself a little ruefully in the moonlight, and thought: You may as well admit it, you're not staying on here and allowing yourself to be scared out of your wits just for the fun of it or from any altruistic motives. You are staying because you've fallen in love with a man who is engaged to a beautiful blond called Cynthia! You've had a lovely time playing at being in love and enjoying having men fall for you, but now you've burnt your fingers. And Cynthia or no Cynthia, you don't really give a damn *how* many people get themselves bumped off, or if the whole British Empire and the sub-continent of India goes up with a bang, as long as you can stay around near Charles.

Women, decided Sarah cynically, are wonderful! At which point her musings were interrupted by Captain Mallory, correctly dinner-jacketed, who joined her at the verandah rail carrying two glasses of sherry.

'Here's to you, Sarah.'

'Thanks.' Sarah sipped her sherry and looked at Charles over the rim of her glass. 'Who is Cynthia?' she demanded abruptly.

'Cynthia? Sounds like a song: *"Who is Cynthia, what is she, that all her swains commend her?"* What Cynthia — or should I say which Cynthia? Or do you mean my sister?'

'Your sister! Have you got a sister called Cynthia?'

'I have indeed. You'll like her.'

'Oh,' Sarah smiled widely and dizzily. Yes, she was young and alive, and life was glorious and exciting because she was going to dine with Charles . . .

Except for a depressed gentleman wearing tweeds and a pince-nez, and a youthful couple who were holding hands under the table-cloth and conducting an intense conversation in whispers, the dining-room in the residential block of the Club was empty, and Charles and Sarah dined in the comparative privacy of a table set by a bow window, from where they could look out over the lawns and the lake to the mountains. The depressed gentleman finally departed, to be followed shortly afterwards by the intense couple. But Charles and Sarah sat on deep in conversation . . .

Sarah was enjoying herself. Her green eyes sparkled and her copper curls glinted in the wan light of the drably shaded ceiling bulbs, and the conversation, by mutual consent, did not touch on the business that had brought Charles to the valley. It was not until almost the end of the meal that she remembered to tell him of the search that had been made of her room and the opening of her parcels. 'You hadn't anything there, had you?' asked Charles frowning. 'Anything incriminating, I mean?'

'No, thank goodness. The only incriminating thing I've had was that little automatic, and I'd carried that about with me in my bag. Lucky I did!'

'Very,' agreed Charles soberly. 'But I can't understand why anyone would have been interested in the stuff you bought this morning. That makes it look as if it could be only a bit of curiosity on the part of your *mānji*. Let's hope so, anyway.'

A white-coated *khidmatgar* appeared with coffee and inquired if they would prefer it served over in the ballroom or out on the lawns, but Sarah did not want to move: 'It would be cold by the time it got over there anyway, and the kind of coffee they make in this country is bad enough when it's hot.'

She poured out the pale, unappetizing brew and handed a cup to Charles, inadvertently spilling some on her dress in the process. '*Bother!*' exclaimed Sarah cheerfully: and reaching for her bag, opened it to pull out a handkerchief. Something else came out with it and fell onto the table-cloth — the little papier mâché matchbox container that Ghulam Kadir had presented to her that morning.

'Complete with box of matches, I see,' said Charles, idly turning it over with one finger. 'You've been favoured. Mine was only the case without the box of matches.'

'So is this one,' said Sarah. She put away her handkerchief and picked up the little box. 'No it isn't! But I'm almost sure ... Why, it's not mine at all. Look! Mine had almost the same design, gold chenar leaves on cream. But it had those little furry chenar seeds in the pattern where this has got bulbuls. I know what must have happened! We all put our things down when we were hunting for my bag just after we'd been given these boxes, and I suppose I must have picked up someone else's by mistake. They're very alike.'

'You did *what*?' said Charles sharply. 'Here! Give me that box! It's a thousand to one chance, but——' He drew out the box of matches that the little case contained, but there were no matches inside it. Only a small slip of folded paper.

'A thousand to one chance,' repeated Charles in an awed whisper, 'and, by God, we've pulled it off! This is what they were searching for of course, when they went through your room with a small-tooth comb.'

He smoothed out the scrap of paper on the palm of his hand. It bore a single line of graceful curving eastern writing, and Charles studied it, frowning.

'What is it?' asked Sarah urgently. 'Can you read it?'

'I can read it all right, but I haven't an idea what it means. It's a line from a poem in Persian.'

'What does it say?'

'Well, rather freely translated, it says "the author" — literally, the teller of tales — "threads his bright words as beads upon a string".'

'"The teller of tales threads his bright words as beads upon a string",' repeated Sarah slowly. 'What on earth does it mean? Is it a code?'

'God knows,' said Charles. 'It may mean anything. Perhaps it's a password. Anyway, we've got something at last. And what is better, the very fact that it hasn't reached the person it was intended for will almost certainly have thrown a largish-sized spanner into the works. I should imagine that no ordinary hair-tearing is in progress somewhere.'

Charles rolled up the small scrap of paper and tucked it into his breast-pocket. 'Now for heaven's sake Sarah, try to remember where that match case was when you picked it up. Can you get any picture in your mind of where it was lying or whose things it was with? If we could only get a line on who had it originally, the battle would be practically in the bag. Think, Sarah!'

Sarah put her head between her hands and frowned down at the table-cloth for a long minute.

'It's no good,' she said. 'I'm terribly sorry, but I just haven't got an idea whose it could have been. Someone found my bag for me — Hugo — and I saw this box and thought it was mine. It was so like, and I hadn't had time to look at any of the other people's boxes. I suppose I just picked it up and stuffed it into my bag. I think I picked it up off the big carved table. Or it could have been on the divan? I can't be sure. But – oh *no*——!'

'What is it?'

'Don't you see, if this really is the message that was due to be passed to someone, then that someone must be one of *us*! One of the party in the shop. A European. English . . . !'

'Not necessarily,' said Charles slowly, turning the little box between his fingers. 'We've got to think of everything. Every possibility. There were several other people who visited that shop this morning besides the ones we met there, and it is just within the bounds of possibility that someone who had left before we arrived made the same mistake that you made. Put a box down and picked up the wrong one. There were quite a few of these matchbox cases scattered around the showroom tables.'

'But you don't think it's likely?' said Sarah shrewdly.

'No,' said Charles slowly. 'I don't think it's likely.'

'Then you think it could——'

'I think that the sooner we dispose of this ornamental trifle the better,' said Charles grimly. 'Under the circumstances, I imagine you'd be safer walking about with a time-bomb in your pocket than with this box.'

'I don't believe it!'

'No? Then the sooner you do the better.'

'I don't mean what you've just said, I mean I don't believe that's the message. Why would anyone bother to wrap it up like that? — be so devious? It sounds silly and complicated and – and far-fetched to me!'

'What you don't realize is that the East *is* devious. It will always prefer to walk bye-ends to an objective rather than march up to it from the front; and it's the failure of the West to understand this that trips us up so often. Besides, as I've already told you, that shop was no more than a post office — for collecting and being collected from only. Whoever sent that message would not have delivered it there personally, or gone anywhere near the place. It probably passed through several hands *en route*, just to muddy the trail and make sure that it could not be traced back to its source.'

' "Bye-ends", in fact,' said Sarah.

'That's right. Everyone who touched it would certainly have taken a good look at it, and made nothing of it. But you can bet your bottom dollar that it would have made sense to the one it was intended for — and to no one else! Come on, Sarah, let's go and dance ...'

He stood up, and taking her arm led her swiftly out of the house and along the moonlit path to where strains of music from a large radio-gramophone in the ballroom showed that the dance had officially begun.

By this time, the Club was looking considerably gayer. Several of the high bar-stools were occupied by partnerless males, while between eight to ten couples were dancing to music provided by the Club's radio-gramophone: among them, several people whom Sarah knew ...

Meril Forbes, wearing pale blue taffeta, was dancing with Major McKay, and one of the Coply twins was partnering an unknown blond. Reggie Craddock was there, and so was Helen Warrender: the latter wearing a décolleté creation, glittering with green sequins and more suited to a Viceregal Ball than a Club gramophone hop, was dancing with a tall bowlegged man with a vast straw-coloured moustache whom Charles said was a Colonel Grainger; adding that he was a four.

'What on earth does that mean?' inquired Sarah blankly.

'Polo handicap. He was considered to be worth four goals to any side he played for. Johnnie was a seven.'

'What is he now?'

'A has-been,' said Charles briefly.

'Isn't that Johnnie at the bar?' asked Sarah.

'I expect so, that's his usual pitch and that is what it did for him, poor devil.'

The record ran to a close and the dancers stood about the floor and applauded in a desultory manner while the Club Secretary put on another one. 'Hello Meril,' said Charles, pausing beside Major McKay and his partner. 'Your Aunt Ena here to-night?'

Meril started nervously and turned. 'Oh! ... Oh hello Charles. Er ... No. Aunt Ena wasn't feeling very well. She was coming. I mean ...' Meril fumbled nervously with a small evening-bag embroidered with multi-coloured beads and sequins, dropped it and made a clumsy dive to retrieve it.

She was forestalled by Charles who handed it back and said with mock severity: 'Do you mean to tell me that your aunt thinks you two are sitting soberly at the Institute?'

'Well — well, yes,' said Meril on a half gasp.

Charles looked at Major McKay's blushing countenance and whistled expressively. 'George, I'm surprised at you! I had no idea you concealed so much duplicity and rash courage behind innocent façade. Have you considered what Aunt Ena is going to say when she discovers that far from escorting her niece to a lecture on "Three Years in Borneo" — with hand-coloured slides — you have taken her out on a round of mad revelry?'

'Well — er — as a matter of fact,' began Major McKay uncertainly, 'I — er — that is——'

'I asked him to bring me!' interrupted Meril defiantly. Two bright patches of colour burned in her usually pale cheeks and Sarah noted with surprise that she looked positively pretty. 'I hate lantern lectures and I hate the Institute, and I didn't see why I shouldn't dance instead. After all, it can't really matter a bit to Aunt Ena. She went to bed.'

'And I wouldn't put it past George to have slipped something in her coffee,' said Charles cheerfully. 'You want to watch these doctors, Meril. Darned dangerous chaps.'

'My dear Charles,' said Major McKay huffily, 'a joke's a joke, but you really should not——' he caught Charles's eye, grinned, and said unexpectedly: 'Thanks for the suggestion, all the same. I will bear it in mind.'

Charles laughed and pulled Sarah back onto the dance floor.

'I have misjudged George,' he said. 'I believe he may even be capable of rousing Meril to stand up for herself, when Lady Candera finds out what he's up to and orders him never to darken her doorstep again.'

'If you ask me,' said Sarah with some asperity, 'Meril won't need any rousing. If she is to be believed, it was her idea that they duck this lantern-slide lecture and take in the nightspots instead. So it's my bet that you and Fudge, and anyone else who is interested, can go ahead and buy the fish-slices and plated toast-racks in perfect safety.'

'You sound a little crisp, Sarah darling. But then to you, Meril is only a sort of Boneless Wonder. You haven't seen as much of her aunt as we have. If you had, you would realize why we get such a kick out of seeing old George advancing cautiously to the rescue. It gives us the same feeling we'd get watching some solid London Bobby, backed by the full resources of the local fire brigade, crawling up a forty-foot ladder to rescue a kitten that has got itself stranded on a factory roof.'

Sarah laughed. 'I know. And I'm not really being crisp. It's only that it goes against the grain to see one of my own sex — specially one who can ski like Meril and has a nice figure and could even be pretty if she made the least effort — behaving with such – such *hysterical* flabbiness!'

'That's what comes of serving in the WRAF and wearing uniform,' said Charles with a grin. 'The sight of a really womanly woman, complete with fluttering nerves, timidity and the vapours, not to mention migraine and a horror of mice, inspires you with acute irritation.'

'It does indeed! This is the Atom Age — more's the pity — and anyone as spineless as Meril Forbes should be dumped straight back into a Brontë novel where she belongs. However, if she can sneak off dancing the minute her aunt's eye is off her, I feel there's hope for her yet. If she has any sense she'll get roaring drunk and go home and recite——'

Sarah checked, frowning, and missed a step.

'What's the matter?' asked Charles.

'Nothing — it's just that I suddenly had a funny feeling that I was quoting something that someone else had once said ...' And even as she spoke, she remembered.

Of course. It had been Janet, speaking impatiently in the Khilanmarg ski-hut: 'What you need, Meril, is to get roaring drunk and recite the Declaration of Independence to your aged aunt ...' But she refused to think of Janet tonight, and she thrust the memory resolutely away from her and was grateful that the ending of a record at that moment gave her an excuse to ch[illegible]e the subject. The Secretary dutifully played a few more [illegible] and then closed the gramophone for a break, and the [illegible]attered to various tables on the edge of the ballroom [illegible]r or the verandah.

Charles led Sarah to a chair on the lawn outside and hailed a loitering *khidmatgar* to order drinks. Twice a car purred past them, bringing late arrivals; dances came and went, and they had been there for some little time when they heard the crunch of gravel on the path beyond the lawn as someone walked down it in the direction of the car park.

'Who was that?' asked Charles, turning in his chair.

'Reggie, I think,' said Sarah, peering through the mixture of moonlight and shadow. 'But I couldn't really see. Why?'

Charles did not answer, and presently they heard a car start up. It drove off and, by the sound, turned to the left in the direction of Nasim, and when they could hear it no longer, Charles stood up and said: 'Let's go back and dance. We've got about another quarter of an hour to fill in before we need start.' They walked back together across the lawn, and as they re-entered the ballroom, he glanced down at her and said: 'Do you think you could look as if you were romantically interested in me? In about a quarter of an hour's time we are due to leave this Club, ostensibly to go moon-gazing together. Try and look the part, will you?'

'*"Merely corroborative detail intended to give verisimilitude to an otherwise bald and unconvincing narrative"?*' murmured Sarah wickedly.

Charles laughed and pulled her into his arms. 'Perhaps. Anyway they've put on a suitably inspiring tune for us to dance to.'

They moved out onto the floor as a rich and fruity tenor voice from the gramophone announced that *'People will say we're in love!'*

'Let us hope so,' said Charles. He was an excellent dancer and Sarah dropped her long lashes and relaxed to the sweet swing and sway of the music:

> *'Don't sigh and gaze at me —*
> *Your sighs are so like mine,*
> *Your eyes mustn't glow like mine,*
> *People will say we're in love . . .'*

'You're doing it beautifully,' approved Charles, his mouth at her ear. The music stopped and Sarah opened her eyes and applauded automatically.

Although the dance had still over an hour and a half to run, several people had apparently already left, and looking about the room, Sarah could see neither Reggie Craddock nor Helen Warrender. A Coply twin was sitting out in the verandah talking to some girl whom Sarah couldn't see, but whom she imagined, judging by the fold of blue material just visible beyond the open doorway, to be Meril Forbes. However, there were several new arrivals: among them Mir Khan in a party of six, all of whom were strangers to Sarah. He bowed and smiled, but did not speak.

Johnnie Warrender was still at the bar and appeared to be rapidly approaching a state of extreme truculence. His voice was clearly audible through the babble of voices and the latest record whirling on the gramophone.

'Helen?' said Johnnie thickly, 'how sh'd I know? P – probably off p – poodlefakin' shomewhere. She dish – dis – pises me. Thash what. Like that Sh – Shakespeare woman. *"Infirm of purposh, g – gi' me the dagger!"* Thash Helen!'

'Hmm,' said Charles, swinging Sarah past the bar. 'Very illuminating. I wonder——' He did not finish the sentence, for at that point Johnnie Warrender slid off his stool with a crash of breaking glass, picked himself up with the assistance of his neighbour and left the building, walking unsteadily.

The music changed again, and a moment later Sarah shivered.

'What is it?' asked Charles quietly. 'Cold?'

'No. It's that tune. It seems to haunt me.'

'The moonlight and the moon,
And every gay and lovely tune
That's played for you . . .'

harles gently.

tside the ski-hut on Khilanmarg; while she

was strapping on her skis. And – and it seems to have kept cropping up ever since. They played it that night in Peshawar. The night I read her letter——'

'Yes,' said Charles, 'I remember.'

'And now here it is again!'

'Perhaps it's an omen. A good one this time, let's hope.'

The big clock on the wall struck the quarter hour. 'Come on,' said Charles. 'This is where we make a move.' He glanced down at his watch and gave a sudden exclamation of dismay. *'Damn and blast!'* said Charles furiously, under his breath. He seized Sarah by the arm and hurried her off the floor.

'Why? What's the matter?'

'It's my own bloody fault,' said Charles savagely. 'I shouldn't have taken my time by that clock. It's almost fifteen minutes slow. Come on, Sarah. Step on it!'

'I'm sorry,' said Sarah firmly, 'but as I gather this is going to be a longish trip, I'm going to dive into the Ladies Room first.'

'Must you? Oh all right, only make it snappy! I'll go and get my *shikara*. Meet you at the top of the water steps. Turn right at the end of this building. *Hurry!*'

He disappeared into the night and Sarah whisked into the Ladies Cloakroom.

The Ladies Room at the Nagim Club was entered through a small vestibule leading off the entrance hall, and Sarah closed the door behind her, and putting her bag down upon a dressing-table took a swift look at her face in the mirror. Light, running footsteps sounded on the path outside the window, followed a moment later by a slight sound from the end of the passage that led out of the dressing-room to the left, where the lavatories were, as though someone had either quietly opened or closed a door.

Sarah flicked her nose with a powder-puff and ran across to the passage. She tried the door of the first lavatory and found it locked, but the next in the line was open, and as she closed the door behind her there was a faint scuffling sound from the passage outside followed by a smothered laugh. Sarah paid no attention, but when she turned the handle again to leave, the door would not open. Oh bother the thing! thought Sarah frantically. It *would* take this opportunity to stick! She tugged at the handle, but the door remained obdurate.

A system of oriental sanitation prevailed at the Club, as in most of Kashmir, and therefore each lavatory had two doors: the back one opening into a narrow passage reserved for the use of lavatory attendants. Sarah hastily unbolted it, only to find that this door too was fastened from outside. Fastened . . . That was it of course! The doors had not jammed. Someone had locked her in. Some silly fool of a practical joker, thought Sarah, remembering that smothered laugh. But Charles had said 'Hurry!' and he was waiting for her at the foot of the water stairs: she *must* get out.

She hammered at the door with her fists and shouted at the top of her voice until the noise echoing loudly round the little whitewashed cell almost deafened her. But when she stopped to listen she could hear no sound from outside except, very faintly, the strains of the radio-gramophone in the ballroom, and she realized with a stab of dismay that until some other woman entered the Ladies Room, she could shout herself hoarse without a chance of anyone hearing her above the noise of voices and music in the ballroom. There was nothing for it but to wait until someone else entered the cloakroom.

Locked in a lavatory, of all places! thought Sarah furiously. Of all undignified, silly, stupid situations!

The words of a ribald song of her earlier schooldays rose unbidden to her mind:

'Oh dear, what can the matter be?
Three old ladies locked in the lavatory!
They were there from Monday to Saturday.
Nobody knew they were there . . .'

Sarah giggled hysterically and immediately afterwards was seized by another stab of panic. *'Nobody knew they were there.'* That was the trouble. Charles knew where she was, but he could hardly come charging into the sanctity of the Ladies Cloakroom in search of her. However urgent his desire for speed, she was sure that a proper Anglo-Saxon respect for decorum would forbid such an impossible breach of etiquette.

But it appeared that she had over-estimated Charles's respect for the conventions.

She heard the door into the dressing-room open violently, and shouted again, and Charles's voice called: 'Where the hell are you?'

'In here!' called Sarah. 'I've been locked in!'

There was a sound of quick footsteps and of a bolt being jerked back, and the door swung open suddenly and precipitated her into Charles's arms.

'Are you all right?' demanded Charles sharply. 'What happened?'

But Sarah was unable to answer, for she was suddenly overcome by a gale of unseemly mirth.

'For God's sake stop giggling!' snapped Charles.

'I c – c – can't help it,' choked Sarah. 'It's so s – s – silly! Three old ladies l – locked in a lavatory. Oh gosh——!'

Charles gripped her shoulders and shook her until her hair resembled a red-gold Japanese chrysanthemum. 'Pull yourself together, Sarah!' he said urgently. 'How did it happen?'

'I don't know,' said Sarah, dabbing her eyes. 'When I went in there I heard a slight sound and someone laughed, and when I wanted to come out again I found that some idiotic humorist had locked me in, so I banged and yelled for a bit and then you came. That's all.'

'Who was it?'

'I tell you, I don't know! I only heard someone laugh. I suppose they thought it was frightfully funny. It must have been a practical joke.'

'Let's hope so,' said Charles grimly. 'Come on, we've got to get out of here. Where's the back door?'

He caught her by the elbow and hurried her down the passage past the bathing cubicles and out at the far door, but once in the open he was forced to slow his steps, and they walked decorously down the path.

Something glinted and sparkled with a flash of green fire on the moonlit gravel near the dressing-room window, and almost without thinking, Sarah stooped and picked it up. It was a small green sequin.

18

Charles led the way along the path and round the end of the Club building to a flight of wide stone steps that descended to the water's edge where a number of *shikaras*, their crews sleeping soundly and small oil riding-lights blinking smokily in each prow, lay moored in the shadow of a big chenar tree.

A single *shikara* was drawn up at the bottom step, and a shadowy figure in Kashmiri robes stood with one foot on the prow and one on the stairs, steadying the boat. Charles handed Sarah in, murmured a few words to the man and followed, and the man pushed the boat off from the shore, and leaping aboard, passed them and swung himself into the stern where the rowers sat.

They drew away from the shadows of the bank and out into the brilliant moonlight on the lake, and Sarah, leaning out to peer around the high padded partition that served as a backrest for the passengers and screened them from the crew, saw that there were four men paddling the boat. She turned to Charles who was sitting beside her, his shoulder touching hers, and said in an undertone: 'Is it safe?'

'Is what safe?'

'Going off on this sort of trip in a public *shikara*.'

'It isn't a public *shikara*. It's a private one — and they're all picked men.'

'You mean they're British? In disguise?'

Charles gave a short laugh. 'Don't be such a little owl! Of course not. There are all creeds and classes in our job. Hindus, Mussulmans, Sikhs, Dogras, Pathans, Parsees, Punjabis, Bengalis — any amount of 'em. One of our best men is a quiet little *bunnia** who keeps a shop in a Delhi bazaar. Another drives a *tonga*† in Peshawar City.'

'Um,' said Sarah, and was silent for a space.

'What's worrying you?' inquired Charles in an undervoice; aware that she was troubled.

'All these people,' whispered Sarah, 'and the man who was watching out for you last night — Habib. And there was the one you met at some place near Gulmarg, and the pockmarked man in the shop, who we're going to meet . . .'

'What about them?'

'Well, weren't they here when Janet and Mrs Matthews were alive?'

'They certainly were — except for Habib, of course.'

'Then – then why weren't they able to help them? Why didn't one of *them* leave Kashmir and carry a message to someone in British India?'

'I thought I'd already told you why,' said Charles with a trace of asperity. 'The fact that we have a certain number of people, such as these men tonight, whom we can call upon to help us, doesn't mean that they know more than a fraction of what is going on. Any more than a junior employee in some big Multi-National Corporation knows what is going on in the mind of the Chairman of the Board of Directors! Unfortunately, whatever those two women stumbled upon was too hot to be handled by any of the resident helpers in this State. And even more unfortunately, neither of them realized — according to what you told me about your conversation with Janet — that they themselves had been spotted, until it was too late to call up a squad of watchers to keep an eye on them. Or perhaps Mrs Matthews

*A shopkeeper.
†A two-wheeled horse-drawn vehicle.

considered it wiser at that juncture to refrain from hedging her bets? That's something else we shall never know.'

'I suppose so,' said Sarah, and relapsed into silence.

The paddles fell softly, rhythmically, with a soothing monotony of sound as the boat slipped smoothly through the water. There was no wind on the lake that night, and the breeze of their passage was barely enough to do more than stir the faded cotton curtains that hung from the decorated canopy overhead.

Charles shifted restlessly and though he was lying back against the cushions in apparent relaxation, Sarah was aware that his body was tense and strained.

'What's the matter? Why don't you tell them to hurry?'

'I daren't,' said Charles briefly, shifting his shoulders again in a small jerky gesture of anxiety. 'There may be people watching and we mustn't look as if we're in a hurry until we're well out of range of the Club. We're supposed to be out for a sentimental moonlight row, not a boat-race. The trouble is that we're badly behind time.'

'But surely he'd wait?' asked Sarah anxiously.

'Ahamdoo? Of course. But it could be dangerous for him to hang around for too long. I suppose he chose the island because it would be a comparatively easy place for me to reach. And a much safer spot to get to because I'd have to come by water, instead of by land through all those bazaars and mean streets. But it still seems a pretty dicey choice to me.'

'Then why did you agree?' whispered Sarah.

'I told you. I hadn't any choice!'

'I'm sorry. I – I forgot.' Sarah fell silent again, and Charles turned and looked back to where the lights of the Club were mirrored in the lake behind them. A minute or so later he said: 'OK, I think we can safely step on it now.'

He gave a low-spoken order to the rowers, and immediately the tempo of the paddles quickened. Sarah would not have believed that the shallow wooden boat could move at such speed.

The four heart-shaped paddles dipped and rose as one, driving the pointed prow through the water with a sound of tearing silk, while the curtains fluttered and flapped in the draught of their passage.

As they neared the end of Lake Nagim, where the wide expanse of water breaks up into the narrower channels that lead towards Srinagar or to the main stretch of the Dāl Lake at Nasim, Charles gave another order. And once more the pace slowed, and swinging left, they passed under the shadowy arch of the Nagim Bridge in a leisurely manner.

There was a figure upon Nagim Bridge. Some night idler who leant against the wooden rail at that end of the bridge where a tree threw a patch of shadow, and whose cigarette-end made a spark of orange light against the darkness.

Beyond the bridge and away to the left stretched the backwater of Chota Nagim, and Sarah could see the outlines of the Creeds' boat and, behind it, the solitary riding-light that marked the *Waterwitch*. Then they were paddling past reedbeds and dark patches of lotus leaves, and presently the *shikara* entered a willow-bordered channel between banks that were not more than a dozen yards apart, so that the thin boughs arched over the water, interlacing above it and breaking the moonlight into a thousand silver fragments that powdered the black water below. But even here the paddles still did not change their rhythm.

Charles jerked back his cuff and peered at his watch, and the greenish, luminous circle of the watch face, glowing faintly in the shadows, reminded Sarah that she was still clutching the small green sequin she had picked up on the gravel path outside the window of the Ladies Room at the Nagim Club.

As the *shikara* left the gloom of the short willow-shadowed channel and came out again into open water, she examined her find. The small green sequin lay on the palm of her hand winking and glittering in the clear moonlight, and she was just about to drop it overboard when something seemed to click like a shutter in her brain.

A green sequin. Helen Warrender had worn a dress embroidered with green sequins. Then sometime that evening Helen Warrender must have passed along the path that led to the back door of the Ladies Cloakroom at the Club. Why? Only someone wearing a bathing costume would be likely to make use of the back door. Anyone else would naturally enter it by the main entrance in the hall.

Sarah's mouth tightened and her green eyes sparkled dangerously. Practical joke nothing! thought Sarah angrily, she wanted to make me look silly to Charles, and anything sillier than getting oneself locked in a lavatory I can't imagine. She'd like Charles for herself. Well, she can't have him, that's all——!

'Cat!' said Sarah, unaware that she had spoken the word aloud.

'What's that?' asked Charles, startled.

'Nothing,' said Sarah, flushing guiltily. 'I was just thinking of something.'

She flicked the little sequin overboard, where it flashed briefly in the moonlight like a wicked little green eye, and was whirled away in the wake of the paddles — for now they were moving swiftly once more.

The *shikara* passed through a narrow neck of water where a grassy island bearing a row of tall poplars reached out an arm towards the shores of Nasim, and entered the wide, glimmering expanse of the Dāl Lake. On their left, among the dark masses of trees along the curving shore, lay the village of Nasim and the mosque of Hazratbal; and away in the distance, at the far side of the lake, lay the Shalimar Gardens and the mountains, misty with moonlight.

The lake stretched before them like a vast mirror, smooth and shining, and the night was so still that the dip and thrust of the paddles seemed intolerably loud in that silver silence. Yet theirs was not the only boat on the Dāl that night. There were a few little low-lying native boats, barely more than dark streaks on the gleaming water: fishermen out spearing fish, or houseboat *mānjis* returning from visits to friends in the villages. And further out on the lake, their white canopies ghost-like in the moonlight and the oillamps on their prows pricking warm pinpoints through the silver, were two more *shikaras*.

By now their own *shikara* was heading away from the Nasim shore towards the centre of the lake, and Charles had ceased to lounge back against the cushions. He was sitting upright, leaning a little forward with his hands clenched on his knees, staring intently ahead; and Sarah, following the direction of his gaze, saw a ghostly shape afloat on the water ahead of them, and realized that it was an island. A tiny island with tall trees upon it, lonely and lovely in the middle of the moonlit Dāl.

At first it was only a shadow, a silhouette in silver point; but as they drew nearer to it the outlines sharpened and darkened, and she could see that there was a small building on the high ground in the centre of it, while at each corner a huge chenar tree leaned its boughs out over the water.

As she looked, Sarah's eye was caught by a movement away to the right of the island. There was yet another *shikara* out there on the lake, a white moth in the moonlight. But since this one carried no light at its prow, it was impossible to tell if it was moving towards the island or away from it.

Charles had seen it too, for he gave a curt order to the rowers and they checked their paddles. For a moment or two their boat moved ahead on its own momentum, the water whispering along its sides; then it slowed and drifted quietly to a stop.

Sarah moved, her dress rustling on the cushions, and Charles made a brief imperative gesture of the hand, demanding silence. He was staring out into the moonlight, his head a little on one side, and Sarah too sat still, listening. In the silence she could hear the quick breathing of the rowers behind her and the *drip*, *drip* of water from a paddle. A fish jumped and a frog croaked from a patch of floating weed. Then, very faintly, she heard the sound of paddles and realized what it was that Charles was listening for.

The sound of those other paddles was not growing louder, but softer; which meant that the boat beyond the island was moving away: and there was yet another sound from somewhere far away out on the lake. So faint that it was little more than a vibration in the stillness. The *pht – pht – pht* of a motorboat . . .

Charles turned his head and gave a brief order, and the *shikara* moved forward again; softly now, as though the need for haste were gone; and almost before the prow grated against the bank he had gone forward and leapt ashore. Sarah followed more gingerly, her boldly patterned frock nearly invisible against the chequered black and silver of moonlight and chenar shadows.

The little island could not have been more than thirty yards square. The four great chenar trees were rooted on the level turf, while in the centre the ground rose in a series of artificial terraces banked with Persian lilac, to a small summer-house. It did not take more than a couple of minutes to walk round the entire island. But there was no one there.

Charles looked at his watch again and stared out across the water to where a faint white dot showed against the reflections of the mountains. It was the *shikara* that they had seen beyond the island and it was moving in the direction of Srinagar.

A bird rustled among the lilac bushes, but no other sound broke the stillness, for the faint beat of paddles and the throb of the motorboat had both died away: and watching Charles's tense profile, white against the inky shadows of the chenar trees, Sarah was seized with a sudden shiver of fear and unease that made her glance quickly over her shoulder, as though she half expected to see someone standing behind her among the shadows.

'Why isn't he here?' she asked, forming the words with an effort. She had meant to speak them aloud, but somehow they had been spoken in a whisper. And it was in a whisper that Charles answered: 'I don't know. Either he never came, or else . . .'

He did not finish the sentence and after a moment Sarah said uneasily: 'Or else what?'

Charles turned slowly, and his face in the clear moonlight showed drawn and rigid, the face of a stranger. It was as though he had aged ten years in as many minutes. He said under his breath and as though he had forgotten Sarah and was thinking aloud: '... or else — he's still here.'

Sarah took a swift step backwards, her hands at her throat. 'Still here? You mean — on the island?' Her voice cracked oddly: 'Don't be ridiculous, Charles! There's no one here but ourselves and the boatmen.'

'Perhaps,' said Charles curtly. 'Anyway, we can make sure.'

He turned away abruptly and began to search among the lilac bushes, and it was a moment or two before the full significance of that dawned upon Sarah. Her brain felt cold and numb and stupid and she did not seem able to move. She stood as though frozen, staring unseeingly ahead of her into the dense shadows, while the bushes about the little summer-house rustled as Charles searched among them.

Directly in front of her, outlined blackly against the expanse of moonlit lake, stood one of the four huge chenar trees that gave the island its name. Its massive trunk was hollow with age, and as Sarah's eyes became accustomed to its darkness, detail after detail emerged from the shadows as though it were a photograph in a developing tray.

Charles had made the circuit of the lilac bushes. 'He's not there,' he said.

'No,' said Sarah. Her voice sounded husky and strange and as if it did not belong to her — as though it belonged to some other girl who stood there in a black and white patterned frock among the black and white patterns of shadow and moonlight. She lifted one arm and pointed stiffly, like a jointed doll: 'He's over there. In the tree ...'

And suddenly, as though her legs would no longer bear her, she sat down abruptly on the dew-damp grass and began to laugh.

Charles leant down and quite deliberately struck her across the cheek with the back of his hand.

Sarah gasped, choked, and caught her lower lip between her teeth, and for a long moment she stared up into Charles's quiet, unwavering eyes, and seemed to draw strength from them.

'I'm sorry,' she said in a subdued voice. 'I'm – I'm behaving very badly.'

Charles said: 'I shouldn't have let you come. Go and sit in the boat, darling.'

'No,' said Sarah. 'I'm all right now. Let me stay, please.'

'It won't be pleasant.'

'I know,' said Sarah: 'Janet wasn't pleasant ... or – or Mrs Matthews, either.' Charles did not argue further, but turned and walked over to the tree.

Sarah had been right. The sprawled fingers of a plump, clutching hand that showed so still among the dead leaves and grasses at the foot of the old chenar tree were Ahamdoo's. The rest of him lay huddled inside the hollow tree-trunk with the haft of a Khyber knife protruding from his breast.

Charles and the tall rower who had stood at the bottom of the water steps by the Club lifted him out and laid him on the grass in the bright moonlight. The round, pockmarked face that had been ugly in life was uglier in death: the dark eyes wide and staring, ringed with white, the lips drawn back from uneven teeth in a grimace of agony or fear.

Charles knelt and searched through the voluminous brown robe, and pulling off the curled-toed leather slippers, felt inside them and examined the soles. But if Ahamdoo had carried any tangible message, it was not there. Only ... only ... about the folds of those robes there lingered, faint in the fresh night air but quite distinct, that same curious odour that both Sarah and Charles had met with twice already: first in the deserted hut by the Gap, and then again, that very morning, in the dusty showroom of Ghulam Kadir's shop at the Fourth Bridge.

Now it was here too; on a little island in the middle of the moonlit Dāl, clinging about the robes of a murdered man.

Charles lifted a fold of the robe and sniffed at it, frowning. Letting it drop again, he rose to his feet and spoke to the tall rower, who fetched a torch from the boat, and together the two men searched the island inch by inch: the grass verge, the terraces and the steps up to the little summer-house, the bushes of Persian lilac and the hollow trunks and twisted roots of the old chenar trees. But they found nothing there but dead leaves and the debris of old picnics. And though there were footmarks in plenty, it was impossible to tell who had made them or when, because too many country boats stopped at the island on their way across the lake.

Charles returned to the *shikara*, and lying prone along the shallow prow, peered into the water around the shore with the aid of the torch while one of the rowers paddled the boat in a slow circuit of the island. He had obviously forgotten Sarah, who stood backed against the lilac bushes in a patch of bright moonlight, her hands gripped tightly together. Now and again she shivered, but she did not move.

The *shikara* completed its circuit of the island and Charles returned to the body of Ahamdoo. There was no other boat, and nothing to show how Ahamdoo had come to the island. Charles stood for a while in silence, staring down at the huddled figure with an intense, frowning concentration, as though he could wrench the secrets from that dead brain by an effort of will. Then abruptly he went down on his knees again.

Ahamdoo's right hand, which Sarah had seen protruding from the hollow trunk of the chenar tree, was lying with clawing, outspread fingers on the grass. But the other one was clenched, and Charles knelt again and lifting the closed fist, forced it open. Rigor had not yet set in and the body was still warm, but the fingers had been so tightly clenched that it was only with difficulty that he opened them.

There was something in the palm of Ahamdoo's hand on which, at the moment of death, he had clenched those podgy, brown fingers; something that gleamed dully in the moonlight. A single blue china bead.

Charles picked it up and turned it over between his fingers, smelt it, shook it, looked through it and touched it gingerly with his tongue. Finally, with a faint shrug of the shoulders, he produced a handkerchief in which he wrapped the bead carefully, and having replaced it in his pocket, rose to his feet, dusted his knees and spoke to the tall rower in the vernacular.

Together they lifted the small, plump body of Ahamdoo and placed it in the shadow of the chenar tree, and a second man came over from the boat carrying a coarse blanket with which he covered the body. Charles spoke to them in a low voice and they nodded without speaking. The tall man thrust his hand into the bosom of his robe and for a moment Sarah thought she saw the glint of a revolver. Then Charles touched him on the shoulder, and turned towards her: 'I'll take you home,' he said curtly. 'There's nothing more we can do here.'

He took Sarah's cold arm and led her back to the boat, while the tall man and the man who had brought the blanket squatted down, India-fashion, in the shadows near the shapeless dark heap that had been Ahamdoo. And presently the *shikara*, now with only two rowers, drew away from the island.

Sarah found that her teeth were chattering, though whether from cold or shock she could not be sure, and Charles picked up her fur cape from where it lay on the floor of the boat and fastened it round her unresisting shoulders. There was a folded travelling rug on the forward cushion, and he shook it out and drew it up over her knees.

Sarah said, trying to keep her voice steady: 'What are those two going to do?'

'Wait here until I send the boat back for them.'

'Aren't you going to send for the police?'

'No,' said Charles curtly. 'The less the local police, or anyone else for that matter, knows about this, the better.'

'But — the body. You can't just leave it there. What are they going to do with it?'

'Dispose of it,' said Charles bluntly.

'How?'

Charles shrugged his shoulders. 'Oh there are ways. It's better for everyone concerned that Ahamdoo should just disappear. I assure you it isn't an unusual occurrence in this country.'

He relapsed into silence; frowning down at the tasselled shadow of the canopy fringe that jerked in time to every thrust of the paddles; his hands clasped about his knees.

Sarah drew the fur cape closer about her throat and shivered again, and Charles evidently felt the slight movement, for he glanced round at her.

'Cold?'

'No,' said Sarah. 'I – I was thinking. Did they — was it because we were late? If we hadn't been late——'

Charles shook his head. 'We were bound to be late. If one thing hadn't delayed us, another would. I've been too sure that they weren't onto me.'

Sarah drew a sharp breath and jerked round to face him: 'You mean, you think they know about you?'

Charles laughed; but without amusement. 'Of course. But I'd like to know how they spotted me. I've walked on eggshells for years, waiting for this to happen.'

'What difference will it make?'

'Don't be silly, Sarah,' said Charles impatiently. 'It's the chap who isn't suspect who is useful. The others are about as much use as a sick headache.' He struck his knees with his clenched fists: 'I should have been on the island before moonrise if necessary, and stuck there until Ahamdoo arrived. Instead of which I go putting up a lot of unnecessary smokescreens and providing myself with completely redundant alibis at the Club, and allow myself to be neatly delayed there while someone else keeps my appointment and rubs out Ahamdoo under my nose.'

'But you couldn't know —' began Sarah.

'Couldn't know what?' demanded Charles bitterly. 'I knew Ahamdoo would arrive at the island at the exact time he said he would. Our people don't arrive late or early on a job I assure you: it isn't considered healthy. I had taken the trouble to find out exactly how long it would take me to get to the island from the Nagim Club, and I should have taken my time by my own watch. But I didn't. Instinct made me keep an eye on the Club clock because I happen to know that it is checked daily by the wireless, and it was easier to keep an eye on it rather than be continually looking at my own watch. And because I was too sure of myself I fell into a trap that shouldn't have caught a baby!'

'What do you mean?' asked Sarah. 'What trap?'

'The clock, of course. Tonight, for some unaccountable reason, that clock which was right by mine and the wireless at five this afternoon, was nearly twelve minutes slow. To have made it any slower would have been to run too great a risk of having it spotted — but a lot can happen in twelve minutes. It probably didn't take more than twelve seconds to kill Ahamdoo! All the same, twelve minutes is cutting it a bit fine, so they take another chance ... Nearer a dead certainty than a chance, when you come to think of it!'

'How do you mean?'

'I mean that as soon as you and I arrive together at the Club, obviously intending to dine and dance, they realize what I mean to do. And they bet on your paying a fleeting visit to the Ladies Room before setting off for an hour or so on the lake! All things considered, it was a dead cert that you would, and someone was probably alerted hours ago to keep an eye on you and the moment we looked like making a move to leave, to delay you — using that particular ploy for starters! There would have been other ones in reserve, in case that one failed. But it didn't. It worked like a charm, and as a result another eight or ten minutes are wasted, so that even by making up what time we could by paddling flat out whenever possible, we arrive at the island a good twenty minutes beyond time.'

Sarah said desperately, remembering the green sequin: 'But how can you be sure that it wasn't a coincidence? The clock I mean? And locking me in *might* have been only a joke? You *can't* be sure!'

'I'm not much of a believer in coincidences of that type,' said Charles. 'Especially when I arrive at a rendezvous to find that someone has beaten me to it. It's all too convenient.'

'But – but surely it was far too risky? You could have looked at your watch and not at the clock — there could have been other women in the cloakroom who would have heard me and let me out, and stopped them from trying anything else.'

'In that case,' said Charles grimly, 'you can be quite certain that something equally innocent to the eye would have delayed us. And even if all the innocent-seeming devices had failed, I still do not believe that we should have been allowed to reach the island in time. Some nasty accident would have occurred.'

'What sort of accident?' asked Sarah in a small voice.

'God knows. But... Well just think how easy it would have been for instance, for someone who had seen us leave on time, to get into a car or onto a bicycle — or even to leave pretty briskly on foot! — and reach the Nagim Bridge, or better still that neck of land just beyond it, ahead of our *shikara*? We'd have been a sitting haystack in the moonlight at that range. They couldn't miss!'

'You mean you think — you can't really think that someone would have tried to *shoot* us?'

'Not us; one of us. It wouldn't really have mattered which one, if the object was either our late arrival or non-arrival at the island.'

'I don't believe it!' said Sarah breathlessly. 'I won't believe that anyone would——'

'Oh, possibly not,' interrupted Charles impatiently. 'I'm merely telling you that some way would have been found to stop us getting to the island in time, and that if the simpler ways of preventing it had failed, something damned unpleasant would have been substituted!'

He paused to stare out across the moonlit lake, and after a moment spoke as though he were thinking aloud:

'Whoever did it must have been waiting on the island. The motorboat of course. That would cover the time problem. A motorboat could drop a man on the island and be away again in a matter of minutes, and Ahamdoo would never have landed if there had been another boat there already. He would have made certain there wasn't one before he went on shore. And the murderer, of course, would have used Ahamdoo's boat to get away in. The only thing that doesn't make sense is why didn't they remove the body?'

'Why should they?'

'Oh, just to confuse the issue a bit. If there had been no sign of him I couldn't have been a hundred-per-cent certain that he hadn't developed cold feet at the eleventh hour. And they can't really have supposed that they'd scare me off by demonstrating what they were capable of. Sarah, somehow I've got a hunch that leaving him there was a mistake on the part of the murderer, and I trust it's going to prove a pretty costly one.'

'What doesn't make sense to me,' said Sarah, 'is why they didn't wait a bit longer.'

'You mean until I turned up, and then dispose of me too? Well for one thing, they would have known that I wouldn't have arrived there alone, and that I and anyone with me would certainly be armed. And for another, that a gun battle at this hour, on a night as quiet as this one, would create a hell of a racket — not to mention the resulting blaze of publicity! You notice that to date nothing noisy has been used. A blow on the head for Mrs Matthews and Miss Rushton, and a knife for Ahamdoo——'

'But you've just said that someone on the bridge or that neck of land, could have shot us!'

'If they had, they'd have used something like an air-gun — it would have been enough, at that range! Or a silencer. But they couldn't bank on us doing the same. They had to stop Ahamdoo's mouth, and the moment they'd done so they knew they had to leave pretty smartly — and did!'

Charles relapsed into silence, occupied by his own thoughts, while Sarah stared ahead of her seeing not the beauty of the moonlit lake, but a small glittering green sequin, winking up at her like a little evil eye from the gravel of the path outside the Club.

If Charles was right and locking her in had all been part of a plan, then Helen ... No! it wasn't possible! It couldn't have been Helen. It must have been someone else. Then what had Helen Warrender been doing on that path this evening? How long had the sequin lain there? Or was there anyone else who had worn a dress with green sequins on it? People one knew did not do these things — plot and spy and lend themselves to murder. It could not possibly have been Mrs Warrender. And yet ...

Sarah's mind went back to the story that Johnnie Warrender was badly in debt. It was no secret, for Helen was eternally referring to the extent of his overdraft, and she also made no attempt to disguise her preference for the society of those who were socially and financially better off than herself. All the same would any amount of money tempt her to involve herself in murder? It did not seem credible ...

Sarah's thoughts ran round and round in a helpless circle of suspicion and denial, like a squirrel in a cage, as the *shikara* turned out of the Dāl and crossed a small open stretch of water, heading for the dark, willow-bordered channel that led into Chota Nagim where the *Waterwitch* and the Creeds' houseboat were anchored.

The moon was sinking towards the mountains beyond the bulk of Hari Parbat Fort, and the *shikara*'s canopy no longer threw a shadow down upon its passengers. The cold clear moonlight illuminated every corner of the boat, and Sarah turned her head and looked at Charles. He was frowning thoughtfully down on something that he turned over and over between his fingers, and she saw that it was the cheap, blue china bead that he had taken from Ahamdoo's clenched hand.

For some reason the sight of it filled Sarah with shuddering repulsion: a renewal of the horror she had experienced as she made out the outlines of those plump, rigid fingers among the dead leaves at the bottom of the hollow chenar trunk. She said suddenly and violently: 'Throw it away Charles! How can you touch it?'

Charles tossed it lightly into the air and caught it again. 'Throw it away? Not much! This means a great deal Sarah, if only we can work it out.'

'Why should it mean anything? It's only a china bead.'

'You're forgetting something,' said Charles, rolling the bead in the palm of his hand.

'What?'

'The writing on that bit of paper in the matchbox.'

Sarah caught her breath. 'Of course! I'd forgotten. It was something about beads——'

'*"The teller of tales threads his bright words as beads upon a string,"*' quoted Charles. 'Quite a coincidence, isn't it?' He tossed the bead in the palm of his hand, throwing it and catching it again.

'I thought you didn't believe in coincidences,' said Sarah.

'I don't. That's why I'm interested in this bead. Very interested. That line out of a poem would obviously have meant quite a lot to the person for whom it was intended. And I don't believe Ahamdoo was carrying this for fun. There's a link between the two, and I mean to find it. This may not be much to go on, but it's something.'

Sarah looked at the small blue oblong as it glinted in the moonlight. It was about half an inch in length, made of coarsely glazed china, and the hole through it was large enough to take a fairly thick piece of twine. One saw strings of these beads in shops in the native bazaars and round the necks of *tonga* ponies: they were said to bring good luck and avert the evil eye, and even the wiry little pack-ponies who had ploughed through the snow on the Gulmarg road had worn ropes of them slung round their necks.

'Could there be anything inside it?' she asked.

'No,' said Charles, squinting through it at the moon. 'Not a thing. However I will crack it up when I get back, just to be on the safe side. Hello, here we are in the home stretch. I hope Fudge and Hugo haven't been waiting up for you. I promised Fudge I wouldn't keep you out too late. Do they take their chaperoning duties at all seriously?'

'Lager's the only one who is likely to be awake,' said Sarah. 'I only hope he doesn't bark and wake everyone up.'

The *shikara* had turned out of the main stream and was now being paddled softly up the backwater of Chota Nagim, and Sarah peered ahead to where the *Waterwitch* lay moored in the shadows of the willow trees beyond the Creeds' boat. She had turned out all the lights in the boat before she left, with the exception of one over the front door that lit the prow and the top of the forward gangplank. But the *mānji* had evidently considered this insufficient, for now a welcoming orange glow lit up the drawing-room windows, adding a warm note of colour to the waning moonlight and the black shadows as the *shikara* nosed its way gently through a patch of lily-pads and bumped alongside.

There was no one on board except Lager, warm from sleep and whimpering an enthusiastic welcome, and Charles looked about the narrow crowded drawing-room, and having tried the lock on the door, said: 'Did you get those bolts I told you to put on your doors and windows?'

'Not yet,' confessed Sarah. 'But the *mānji* said he'd have them fixed by tomorrow. I'll be all right. Lager will protect me, and this time I'm going to lock myself into my bedroom as well, and anyone who likes can come on board and burgle the boat — I shall put my head under the bedclothes and refuse to move.'

Charles frowned and jerked his shoulders uneasily. 'Can I count on that?' he asked, unsmiling.

'I promise,' said Sarah. 'I've had enough of rushing in where angels fear to tread. And quite enough "alarums and excursions" for one night. Don't worry. Look at Lager. He's simply bursting with beans and bounce, and if anyone puts a foot in the boat tonight he'll bark his head off and wake up everyone for miles. There's no storm tonight, and you could hear a mouse move in this quiet. Listen.'

She held up a finger and the silence seemed like a wall about them.

'You see? It was different last night. The storm was making such a racket that a troop of elephants could have boarded the boat without my hearing them; and Lager had been drugged. But you could hear a pin drop tonight, and if I yelled, Hugo and Fudge and the *mānjis* and Hugo's bearer would all be buzzing round like bees. Besides, I shall turn all the lights on and no snooper is likely to come sneaking up on a brilliantly illuminated boat in the small hours of a night like this.'

'No, there is that,' said Charles slowly. He went over to the nearest window and stared out into the moonlight: 'It will be dawn in less than four hours.' He swung round on Sarah. 'Have you got that gun?'

'Yes,' said Sarah. 'It's under my pillow, if you want to know.'

'Good. Well you do just as you said. Lock yourself into your bedroom, and if you hear anyone move on the boat before morning, yell the roof off and don't hesitate to shoot.'

'I know,' said Sarah: 'I hear someone trying the bedroom door, and *"Bang!"* — I've shot the *mānji*, who was trying to bring me my morning tea. I hope you'll bail me out?'

Charles laughed. 'I'll do that. We'll move you off this boat tomorrow, anyway. It's not worth the risk. I wouldn't leave you on it tonight if I hadn't got it under pretty close observation.'

'You've *what*?' said Sarah. 'You mean——?'

'Oh, I've had some of our people watching this boat in shifts since this morning — I mean yesterday morning,' corrected Charles, glancing at his watch.

'Where are they now?' asked Sarah, interested. 'I didn't see anyone.'

'You weren't meant to. One of them is keeping an eye on the approach from upstream and another from the bridge end, to keep a check on anyone who comes past here by water; and a couple of chaps are posted on the landward side. Anyone who looks as if they are coming towards this boat will be followed. I want to know the names of any intending visitors.'

'Where are you going now?' asked Sarah. 'Back to — back to the island?'

'No. I've sent the boat back there. That's a job they can do better without me. I'll walk back to the Club from here.' He turned away, and Sarah accompanied him out onto the prow.

The night air was cool and fragrant after the stuffy atmosphere of the little houseboat drawing-room, and Charles walked down to the foot of the gangplank and stood there, peering into the shadows beyond the big chenar tree. He drew the torch out of his pocket and flashed the light briefly, twice, and a figure detached itself from the shadows fifty yards or so from the boat, where the willows grew thickest, and moved into the moonlight.

Sarah heard a faint rustle of footsteps on grass and presently a tall Indian stood at the foot of the gangplank. He wore a dark blanket wound about his shoulders and drawn over his head so that it threw a deep shadow over his features, and Sarah could only catch a gleam of eyes and teeth.

Charles spoke in a low voice in the vernacular and the other answered as softly.

'Has anyone been near the boat?'

'No one Sahib; save the *mānji* who has returned to the cook-boat and is now asleep, and the big sahib who brought back the Miss-sahib's dog. There have been no others as yet, either from the water or the land.'

'Remain then and watch. Now that the Miss-sahib has returned, allow no one to enter the boat before morning.'

The man saluted and withdrew noiselessly into the shadows, and Charles turned and came back up the gangplank, and said: 'Wait here, Sarah. I'm just going to take a look round the boat to see that the *mānji* hasn't left anything unlocked.'

He went away down the narrow duckboard that ran all round the outside of the boat on the level with the window-sills, trying each window and door as he passed, and disappeared round the far end. Presently he reappeared again from the opposite side having completed the circuit of the boat.

'OK. Everything appears to be locked up safely. You'd better bolt this door too, just to be on the safe side.'

'All right,' said Sarah slowly. She felt a sudden aversion to entering the stuffy atmosphere of the cramped and shuttered little boat in which Janet had lived and worked, and hidden her secret.

A bittern called from a reedbed on the far side of the backwater: a lonely, mournful cry. Sarah shivered, and seeing it Charles said: 'You're quite sure you're all right? You don't think you'd better go over and ask Fudge and Hugo for a bed?'

'No I don't,' said Sarah with asperity. 'Good-night, Charles. I won't say "thank you for a lovely evening" because it's been the most gruesome evening I've ever spent, and I hope I never have another one like it. But thanks all the same.'

Charles smiled down at her, his face drawn and tired in the moonlight. He laid the back of his hand lightly against her cheek in a brief caressing gesture and said: 'Go on in and let me hear you bolt the door,' and she turned away obediently and went in.

19

The bolt shot home and Sarah leant tiredly against the closed doors and listened to the sound of Charles's footsteps descending the gangplank.

The little boat rocked and creaked for a moment, and then steadied again and the silence flowed back once more.

Lager came pattering back into the room from some expedition into the darkened rooms at the other end of the boat and frisked about Sarah's feet, and she gathered him up into her arms and sat down in one corner of the shabby sofa, feeling very tired. Too tired for the effort of getting to bed, and yet not in the least sleepy.

Sitting huddled and relaxed, her chin resting on Lager's silky head, she remembered that she had told Charles that the night was so still that you could hear a pin drop. It had been true while he was beside her, but now that he had gone and she was alone the night seemed full of little sounds: the soft lap of water against the side of the boat, the scutter of a rat somewhere beneath the floorboards, the creak of a board contracting in the night air and the croak of frogs from among the lily-pads; Lager's gentle breathing, and the soft *click, clack* as the bead curtain in the doorway between the drawing-room and the dining-room swayed in a draught.

Slowly, very slowly, a queer sense of uneasiness stole into the cramped little room: a feeling of urgency and disquiet that was almost a tangible thing. It seemed to tiptoe nearer to Sarah and to stand at her elbow, whispering — prompting — prodding her tired brain into wakefulness and attention. As though, perhaps, Janet herself had entered the room and was trying to speak ...

For a moment the feeling that someone — was it Janet? — was watching her was so vivid that Sarah jerked round and looked behind her. But the room was empty and there was no gap between the motionless folds of the cheap cotton curtains that shielded the dark squares of the window-panes and shut out the moonlit night.

But there was still something there that clamoured with a wordless persistence for attention, and Sarah's tired brain shrugged off its lethargy and was all at once alert and clear. She sat quite still; tense now, and very wide awake, staring about her.

The room was just the same, and nothing appeared to have been moved since she had left it. There were the chairs with their shabby cretonne covers and the sofa on which she sat. The over-ornamented tables with the dust of long years lingering in the endless crevices of their intricate carving, and the lines of tattered books and aged periodicals that leant limply against each other on the long wooden shelf that ran round the narrow room. A yellowing calendar dating from the restless, long-ago twenties still hung from a nail on the wall beside the carved walnut-wood desk, and the time-worn Axminster carpet that had been made in some murky factory of Edwardian England, and travelled ten thousand miles from the loom of its birth to end its days on the floor of a houseboat on the Dāl Lake among the mountains of Kashmir, still spread its faded reds and blues under her feet ... That carpet could tell a tale, thought Sarah, gazing down at its worn surface. *'The teller of tales threads his bright words as beads upon a string ...'*

A frog skittered across the water outside and a soft breath of wind from off the mountains ruffled the leaves of the chenar trees. The draught lifted the threadbare Axminster in a soundless ripple and stirred the quiet cotton folds at the windows, and the curtain in the doorway that led into the dining-room swayed and clicked. Beads — red and green and white and yellow: glass beads, winking and glinting; china beads, opaque and smooth. Blue china beads ...

Click ... clack ... click. A small voice in the silence saying over and over again, *'Look! ... look! ... look!'*

Something clicked, too, in Sarah's brain, like the shutter of a camera, and she was unaware that she spoke aloud: 'Of course!' said Sarah. '"As beads upon a string!" Of course. Why didn't I think of it before? — it's there — in the curtain. Janet's record!'

She dropped Lager onto the floor and stood up.

Why hadn't she noticed before that there was no design about the curtain? That the beads fell into no pattern? Small beads interspersed at brief irregular intervals by large blue china beads. That was it — irregular intervals. Dots and dashes, short beads and long beads, with blue china beads to mark the divisions. So simple. As simple as a page of Morse code ... and so very quick and easy to make——

Sarah found herself trembling with excitement as she ran to the desk and snatched up her writing-block and a pencil, and pulling forward a carved chair, sat down facing the curtain and began to write down the order of the beads from the top to the bottom of each string in turn.

The letters made no sense but they read off smoothly in dots and dashes. Long beads and short beads and blue china beads. It'll be in code of course, thought Sarah, but Charles will know it. She scribbled on in the silence.

A night bird called again from among the reeds, and another breath of wind from across the lake ruffled the lily-pads and sent the water lapping softly once more against the side of the boat. Lager snored peacefully on the sofa, but all at once Sarah's pencil slowed and stopped, and her eyes became fixed and still ...

Someone was watching her. She was quite sure of it. A queer, unmistakable, prickling shiver of awareness crept up her spine and tightened the skin of her scalp, and she had to force herself to look over her shoulder. There was nobody there, and with the curtains closely drawn no one from the shore or the lake could possibly see into the room, while if anyone had come up onto the duckboards or paddled close in a *shikara* she would have heard them in this stillness. Her nerves must be playing tricks on her.

Yet the feeling of being watched, and the awareness of another presence close at hand, persisted and grew stronger and stronger until it was not a feeling any more, but a deadly certainty, and Sarah sat rigid, straining her ears to listen.

Somewhere in the darkness on the other side of the bead curtain a board creaked sharply, and a faint tremor of movement shook the floor beneath her feet. So she had been right! There *was* someone on the boat. A creaking board by itself was nothing — they creaked all night and for a dozen trivial reasons — but that quiver of movement that had run through the *Waterwitch* was unmistakable. Someone, somewhere on the boat, had taken a step in the darkness.

Sarah listened, tense and trembling: thinking that no one could come on board, either from the lake or from the land, without making far more noise and a great deal more vibration than that which had been produced by a single stealthy footstep ...

It was only then that she remembered, with a wild rush of relief, that Charles had left a watcher on the bank. Several watchers! The one out there now must have put a foot on the gangplank and caused that slight tremor, for no stranger would have been able to come onto the boat without being seen by one of Charles's men. It was stupid of her to panic. She was perfectly safe.

She picked up her pencil again. And once more a board creaked in the darkness and the little boat vibrated to soft footsteps. Once — and again — and again ...

Lager stopped snoring and lifted his head, his eyes bright and alert and his head cocked a little on one side.

Someone was moving on the boat. No. Not *on* the boat. *In* the boat——

The doors and the windows were locked and barred and there were watchers on the bank; but none of that was any use. No one was trying to board the boat, for someone was there already. Someone who had been there all the time, waiting in the darkness beyond the sly, winking lines of the bead curtain.

Sarah sat quite still, not daring to move, her body rigid with fear and her mind darting about like a terrified animal in a trap.

Charles had said she was safe — she had a gun and there was a watcher on the bank not twenty yards away. She had only to cry out. But the gun was under her pillow in the bedroom, away in the blackness beyond the bead curtain, and she seemed to have lost the power to move or breathe. She opened her mouth to call out, but her throat seemed to have dried up. It was as if she were trapped in a waking nightmare.

She heard Lager jump off the sofa behind her and land with a little *flump* on the floor, and he pattered over and stood beside her, peering into the darkness beyond the glinting beads. The boat vibrated gently to soft footsteps as someone moved across the dining-room, and now it seemed to her that she could hear breathing — or was it only the wild thudding of her own heart that sounded so loud in the silence?

Something flickered and moved in the darkness beyond the bead curtain: eyes were looking at her and a hand came forward to draw aside the curtain — a horrible hand . . .

Sarah tried to scream, but no sound came from her fear-constricted throat, and Lager, beside her, thumped the floor with his tail as the curtain swung aside. And it was only Hugo who stood there in the doorway looking down at her.

'*Hugo!* Oh Hugo — oh God! you gave me such a fright! Hugo you *beast* — I nearly died of heart failure I suppose you've just been snoring away on my bed ever since you brought Lager back — and I thought—— *Oh Hugo!*'

Sarah collapsed in a limp heap, gasping, choking, sobbing in hysterical relief, and after a moment or two she dashed the tears from her eyes with the back of her hand and laughed up at Hugo.

But there was something wrong. Something out of true. Why wasn't Hugo laughing? Why didn't he say something? Why did he look so – so——

The cold hand that had for a moment released its clutch upon Sarah's heart, began to close again — very slowly — and she struggled to her feet and stood staring at Hugo, her hands clutching the back of the spiky, carved chair. There was an odd smell in the room — so faint that had the windows been open she would not have noticed it. A smell that conjured up terrifying memories . . .

Hugo said: 'What were you doing, Sarah?'

His voice was the voice of a stranger; soft and without any expression — almost a whisper.

Sarah said: 'Hugo! Don't look at me like that! What's the matter?' Her voice cracked oddly.

Hugo did not take his eyes off her face. He said again: 'What were you doing, Sarah? You were taking it down, weren't you?'

Sarah did not answer. She could only stare numbly, her eyes held by that curious fixed look on Hugo's face.

Hugo said: 'I saw you. I was watching from the pantry doorway. You were writing it down, weren't you? I never thought of it being here. How did you find out?'

Sarah's brain seemed to be full of wavering, ludicrous thoughts that swooped and darted like swallows. Incredible, impossible, fantastic ideas that chased themselves across her brain, whirling and absurd; gone before she could see them clearly or put them into words.

Hugo leant down and picked up the writing-block and Sarah's eyes, released, flickered and closed and opened again.

Hugo — Hugo's hands holding the writing-block. Bright red hands: shiny, slippery, horrible . . . Why, he was wearing gloves!

Rubber gloves ... *Red rubber gloves*, drawn up over his wrists, smooth and taut except where a jagged tear at the edge of the left-hand glove showed a small triangular patch of sun-tanned flesh ...

He was holding the writing-block in his left hand, and in the right a curious object that looked like, and yet unlike, a gun. And he was speaking again, though his words did not seem to make sense to Sarah. She could only stare at those smooth, slippery, red hands and try to remember something——

Red ... like blood ... and shiny; and that smell ... the smell in the dark, musty hall of the house by the Gap. That was it! — the tiny triangular patch of wet blood at the edge of the chair, that hadn't been blood at all but a fragment of red rubber——

Hugh was saying: 'I'm sorry, Sarah, but there it is. You know too much. You shouldn't have meddled. Why the hell couldn't you leave well alone?' His voice was all at once absurdly querulous and aggrieved, like that of a spoilt child.

Sarah forced her gaze away from those scarlet hands and up to Hugo's face. She said, her voice a frozen whisper: 'Then it was you in the hut, waiting for Janet. Oh no! No, I don't believe it. It's crazy — you couldn't, Hugo!'

'I had to,' said Hugo, still in the same queer, querulous voice. 'You don't suppose I liked doing it did you? The damned girl was too clever for her own good. Besides, the end justifies the means — you believe that, don't you? The individual doesn't matter — can't matter. Janet was just grit in the machine. She had to be removed.'

He's mad, thought Sarah wildly, he's quite mad! He *must* be. She said: 'Hugo — don't! You don't know what you're saying.'

Hugo laughed suddenly and when he spoke again his voice was quite normal. He came forward into the little cramped drawing-room, and as the bead curtain clashed behind him he glanced at it, frowning, and said: 'I shall have to cut that damned thing down, or our dear friend Charles might drive up to it in the same way you have. Odd to think I've been through this bloody boat with a small-tooth comb and missed what was right under my nose. Damned smart of you to spot it, Sarah: I always knew you were a smart girl. How did you do it?'

Sarah said wildly: '*Hugo* — Hugo I don't understand. Why did you . . . ? Oh, I think I must be going mad!'

Hugo sat down astride a chair facing her, his arms along the back of it and his chin on his sleeve, but he kept the odd-looking object in his right hand pointed at Sarah. His hand was quite steady, and suddenly Sarah was afraid as she had never been before, even when she had first heard the footsteps in the dark behind the bead curtain. And curiously enough, her fear steadied her.

She looked at Hugo, and it was as if she were seeing him for the first time.

The Hugo she had known, the gay, babbling, easy-going Hugo, was no more a real person than a piece of painted canvas scenery is real. That Hugo was merely a façade; a smokescreen; and behind it lived the real Hugo. Looking at him now, Sarah could not understand why she had ever thought those hard, implacable eyes were gay, or had failed to notice the cruelty of the small tight mouth. I suppose, she thought dazedly, it was because he was always laughing — or talking. His mouth was always open and his eyes crinkled up. One listened to him and laughed at what he said, and didn't really look at him at all . . .

She said desperately: 'But why? — What did you do it for?'

'The Party,' said Hugo; as one who says 'for God'.

'What party? I don't understand — you're English! — you can't mean——'

'As a matter of fact,' said Hugo, 'I'm half Irish, but——'

'Oh God!' interrupted Sarah. '*Cromwell*, I suppose!'

Hugo threw back his head and laughed; but the unaffected gaiety of that sound did not deceive Sarah any longer. It was a habit and no more. Part of his stock in trade. It went no deeper than the surface.

'I'll spare you that,' said Hugo, 'but if you think that any waving of the Union Jack is going to affect me, you waste your breath. No, it was always the Cause. One life, Sarah, that's all we get, and we're a long time dead. Have you ever thought of that? No, I don't suppose you have. You're young yet. But there are millions of people who spend it in misery and sickness and grinding poverty, slaving their guts out to earn power and money and leisure for a pampered handful of profiteers or effete layabouts who still think of themselves as "the Aristocracy" and regard all those who work with their hands, or are less well born or well connected than themselves, as "the Common Herd" ...

'Now that this war is over the scum will be coming up to the top once more and imagining that they can carry on in exactly the same way as they did before. Well they are due for a series of nasty shocks! Much nastier ones than the election results that put a cat among the pigeons last year! The People are moving, and nothing can stop them now.'

'You mean — you're one of *them*?' gasped Sarah. 'A *red*?'

'If you like to call it that. Though it's not a word we use much.'

'But you're a serving officer ... you can't ... Doesn't your country mean anything to—— No, I can see it doesn't. But Janet — and Mrs Matthews — and, and — Ahamdoo—— Oh God! was that you? How many were there? How *could* you——'

'Don't be a fool, Sarah!' said Hugo roughly. 'They were on the other side, and they knew the risks of the game. They took a gamble and lost. That's all there is to it. Do you suppose that any of them would have hesitated to shoot me if they'd been able to get off the mark quicker? Of course not! Your precious Charles wouldn't hesitate to shoot me in the back if he had half a chance. And quite rightly. I'd do the same to him if I thought I could get away with it. I'd only just tumbled to Charles. Clever chap. Makes me boil to think I never dreamt ... Oh well——!'

Sarah said uncertainly: 'Does – does Fudge know?'

Hugo's face changed. His brows twitched together in a black

frown, and his voice was suddenly harsh and rasping: 'No she doesn't! Fudge has nothing whatever to do with this. She knows where my sympathies lie of course, which was why she insis ... persuaded me to give up my job in Intelligence — because she was afraid I might be "too biased". She hadn't the remotest idea that it was much too late in the day for that, or that the damage, from her point of view, was already done. She still doesn't know. Not yet, anyway.'

Sarah said: 'Then how did you manage about Janet? You were at Khilanmarg with her when ... No you weren't! That was why Janet stayed: you said you'd strained a tendon. You hadn't, I suppose.'

'No. I merely didn't want to go to Khilan because I was still hoping to catch whoever came to that hut near the Gap: Charles, I imagine? Oh yes, we'd cottoned onto the hut all right. It wasn't too difficult, because one of the great advantages of having worked for Intelligence is that you get to know a reasonable number of your fellow-workers, and to learn how some of them tick. For example, that a select few of the more erudite, who are not all that certain that their Indian servants don't understand English and may not be averse to accepting bribes and listening at doors, elect to conduct their top-secret discussions in Latin, in the belief that not a word of it will be understood by any inquisitive ear. And how right they would have been if I hadn't got wind of it and contrived to plant a few exceedingly innocent-looking Indian ears here and there, whose owners, convincingly disguised as humble servitors, were all in possession of Classical degrees acquired at English universities——.

'That hut scheme was only one of several interesting bits of news we managed to collect in this way: and very useful it proved—— Though I admit it never occurred to me that Janet would take my place up at Khilan just when it had become a case of "Now or Never", with the possibility of the weather turning nasty and still no sign of any ruddy lamplighter. Fortunately it made no odds, since she came anyway. I nipped across from the hotel and lit my own signal lamp, on the off-chance that it might fetch her down, and it did. All I had to do was wait. The only casualty on our side was that idiot Mohan Lal, who apparently hadn't realized that she'd be bound to have a gun. She plugged him very neatly.'

'Who – who was Mohan Lal?' asked Sarah shakily.

'Oh, just one of the boys. Rather a nasty bit of work and no loss. But it annoyed the third member of the party, who we'd managed to plant as a waiter in the hotel, quite considerably. I had the greatest difficulty in preventing him from shooting the girl out of hand, which would have caused no ordinary mess. Nothing like a purely accidental death for closing a tiresome episode without trouble. Missing bodies, or corpses with bullet holes in 'em, are a hell of a nuisance and stir up streams of awkward questions.'

Sarah said: 'How did you do it? Why didn't they——' Her voice failed her and she could not go on.

'Why didn't they make a fight for it? Ah! See this little gadget?' He gestured with the curious weapon he held. 'Gas. A very clever invention of an exceedingly clever man. It can either stupefy, anaesthetize, or kill instantly. Depends on your trigger finger and how much you wish to use. It leaves no trace and it makes no noise. A whiff of this, and then it's a simple job to knock someone on the head in the sort of place that they might be likely to hit themselves if they'd had a bad fall. Or stick a knife into them with no fuss at all: not a cheep . . . !

'I've got an excellent staff, but the brains are here,' Hugo tapped his forehead, and suddenly flung back his head and laughed loudly and uproariously: 'God, how I've laughed up my sleeve sometimes at all our pompous brass-hats and gilded Foreign and Political snobs — the lordly "heaven-born"! If only they'd known that all the time I held 'em here – here, in the palm of my hand!' The hard blue eyes held for a moment a fanatical glow and his voice dropped to a whisper: 'But nobody knows. I've been too clever for them. Nobody knows. Good old Hugo — the station silly ass.'

Sarah said, trying to keep her voice steady, trying to keep the wild panic from showing in her face: 'Why are you telling me all this?'

Hugo looked at her for a moment as if he had forgotten she was in the room. He said petulantly: 'Now don't be silly, Sarah. You know quite well why. You know too much. Far too much. I'm sorry, but there it is.'

'But – but——' the words seemed to dry in her mouth, 'you can't kill me, Hugo! You can't. If – if I promised ...'

'You wouldn't keep it, and I'm too near the end of the job to take any chances. The stakes are too big. No, my dear. A little whiff of this and the question will be settled. I'm not sure what they will decide that you died from. However the local MO is not likely to amount to much, and the chances are that he'll put it down to some heart trouble and leave it at that. In your fall, suffering from this inexplicable attack, I think you will have stumbled against the bead curtain and pulled it down with you. Yes, that will be the best idea. Two birds eliminated with one stone. And if you are considering screaming, I shouldn't. This stuff can work like chain lightning.'

Sarah fought with blind panic and managed to steady her voice. She said: 'It's no use, Hugo. You can't get away with it this time. There are men watching this boat and they must have seen you come on board.'

'You mean the bird in the bushes along there?' said Hugo with a laugh. 'That's all right. He's the only one within sight of the boat. The others are merely watching the various approaches.'

'You mean, you *knew*?' Sarah's grip tightened on the back of the chair.

'Of course I knew. I'm no fool. The chap over there saw me come on board. In fact he couldn't have missed me: I made as much noise as possible. And why should he worry? He sees you hand over Lager to me when you leave, in the presence and with the approval of his boss — Charles was a party to that transaction, remember? Then not long before you return I come along the bank complete with dog, and go onto your boat turning on the drawing-room light in the process — always a disarming act. No criminal turns on a light. As you could see, he's not posted near enough to overhear much, and he undoubtedly supposed that you and Charles were greeted affectionately by me when you came on board.

'I hope you've noticed that I haven't kept my voice down? Your amateur watchdog will have heard loud voices and laughter proceeding from this boat for the last ten minutes or so. The Miss-sahib having a jolly chat with the stout sahib who is her friend. No sounds of alarm. Not a bark from the dog. When I've dealt with you and set the scene here, I shall go out, chatting merrily, call back a gay "good-night" to you, and leave with the same amount of ostentation as I arrived. The watcher will think nothing of it. I shall then — which is a bore but necessary — have to deal with him. A very simple business.'

'You couldn't!' breathed Sarah. 'You couldn't! He'll have a gun ...'

'Oh, almost certain to. But what more natural than that you or Charles have told me — the old familiar friend — that he is there, lurking in the bushes? I shall hail the bird in a conspiratorial whisper and say you have a message for him. Naturally he will bite. Here is a sahib who is obviously in on the whole thing. And at close range he can get a whiff of this, and since we don't want to overdo the heart-failure idea, he can be found in the morning — drowned, I think. All very murderous and harrowing, but absolutely nothing to do with that nice Major Creed, who will be simply prostrated with manly grief and emotion. See?'

'Yes,' said Sarah slowly. 'I see.'

Her brain seemed suddenly to have cleared. Hugo was not mad: it was worse than that. He was a dedicated, dyed-in-the-wool fanatic in his loyalty to his own ruthless dogma and his equally ruthless masters, and he meant just exactly what he said. He would kill her without a qualm; as he had killed Janet and Mrs Matthews and Ahamdoo — and how many others? He would deem himself justified, because to those of his kidney the end would always justify the means — any means! However brutal and degrading. And what he had said was true — no one would ever suspect him. Even Charles would never suspect. Those who were employing Hugo had chosen a good tool, for like Caesar's wife, he was above suspicion.

There must be some way out. This could not be happening to her — Sarah Parrish.

The light. Could she make a jump for it and smash it? In the dark she would have a chance, for the weapon Hugo held had one disadvantage. Except at point-blank range he could not use it without grave risk to himself. And if he tried to use it in the dark he might himself fall a victim to it.

The switch was near the far door and out of Sarah's reach; but the single bulb that lit the room was nearer, and though it was still too far away, the wire that led from the switch sagged across the ceiling, held in place by a few rusty nails, and if she could jump for it and wrench it down the lights would go out. But would it break or hold? And even if it did break, would the shock from the current knock her out? If so, she would be in as bad a position as before ...

Hugo followed her gaze with complete understanding, and grinned.

'You can't do it, Sarah. Well, I must be getting along. Any last messages or anything?'

And then Sarah heard it. Coming from that distance it was a very faint sound, and if all her perceptions had not been screwed to their peak by panic her ears would never have caught it.

Someone was coming down the field path, and whoever it was had trodden on the sheet of tin that lay over the wet patch.

Lager had heard it too. He lifted his nose from his paws and his eyes turned to the window behind Hugo's head.

'Lager —!' pleaded Sarah desperately.

Lager dropped his head back on his paws obediently, and Hugo said: 'I'll look after him. Don't worry.'

I must talk, thought Sarah, I must keep him talking. There's a chance . . .

Hugo sat up and lifted his right hand. His eyes had widened curiously so that the whites showed all round the irises. Odd, pale eyeballs, hard and glittering like wet pebbles. That small, cruel mouth. Henry VIII — who had said that? It had seemed funny once, but it wasn't funny now. How could they all have been so blind? 'Bluff King Hal', who in spite of his bluffness and his bulk and his joviality had been a killer. This was a killer too.

Sarah said frantically: 'Listen Hugo — if I tell you — all that I know — what they know . . .' her voice was coming in gasps, and Hugo's eyes narrowed a little, but his right hand did not move and Sarah realized that he too was listening. She began to talk loudly, wildly: 'Look, Hugo — I can tell you things. I can tell you everything you want to know — anything you like, I——'

Lager lifted his nose again and said *'Wuff!'* and Hugo turned his head.

Sarah could never remember very clearly what had happened then. It had all been a churned-up horror of panic and noise.

She only knew that Hugo's eyes had moved aside from hers at last, and terror lending her strength, she jerked up the chair she had been clutching. It caught Hugo under the chin and he fell over backwards.

She had a confused recollection of Lager barking, Charles's voice calling her name and someone else shouting: a crash of breaking glass, and then blackness.

*

Sarah recovered consciousness to find herself lying in the open on the prow of the *Waterwitch*, with Charles bathing her head with cold water. The drawing-room seemed to be full of people and there was a queer sickly sweet smell in the air — a smell that she knew.

She stared up at Charles and said: *'Hugo!'*

'I know,' said Charles. 'He's dead.'

'Dead?' Sarah sat up with a jerk, clutching at the wooden edge of the prow with frantic hands. 'Did you — did you——'

'No,' said Charles quietly. 'He killed himself. He knew the game was up, and so he turned that devilish weapon on himself.'

Sarah stared wildly into the small brightly lit room where every window and door had been thrown open, the curtains drawn back and the night air was swiftly dissipating the sickly odour. There were three Indians in the room and Reggie Craddock: two of the former wore Kashmiri dress and the third was Mir Khan. Reggie Craddock was kneeling on the floor beside Hugo's body, stripping off the rubber gloves from the limp hands.

Charles stood up and went back into the room, and Sarah dragged herself to her feet, and following him, subsided onto the sofa and began mechanically to brush the water from her face with the backs of her hands, while staring down incredulously at Hugo . . .

Hugo lay on his back. His eyes were closed, and the small, cruel mouth had fallen into the lines he had trained it to take in life. He was smiling, an amiable and vacuous smile, as Mir Khan went through his pockets, removing papers and replacing cash, a cigarette-case, a box of matches and other objects of no interest.

Reggie got up from his knees and handed the gloves to Charles, who wrapped them gingerly round the weapon that Hugo had held, and picking up a carved wooden box from a table beside him, emptied out the oddments it contained and placed the whole bundle inside it. Mir spoke to the two Kashmiris in their own tongue, and they went out, one of them carrying the box, and Sarah heard the sounds of their footsteps on the gangplank, and then silence.

Mir rose and offered her a cigarette, and when she shook her head, lit one himself, and Charles left the room — to return almost immediately with a small glass of brandy which he handed to Sarah without speaking.

She swallowed it down with a grimace, and Charles said gently: 'Do you think you could tell us what happened?'

Sarah nodded dumbly, and as the brandy began to take effect she pulled herself together with an effort, and told him all that had happened since he left her, in a voice that she did not recognize as her own as it repeated, tonelessly, everything Hugo had said and what she herself had done.

At the mention of the curtain, Mir Khan turned sharply away from the window and going over to it stood fingering the beads while she spoke. But no one interrupted her.

There was silence for a while when she had finished, and Reggie Craddock said, looking down at Hugo: 'Can you square the doctor?'

'Yes,' said Charles curtly.

'You'll ha˙ e to explain things to him a bit.'

'Of course.'

Mir swung the beaded strings, and listening to them click and clash together, said: 'It is better this way. We cannot afford a public scandal. But can you be sure he spoke the truth when he said she did not know?'

'I think so,' said Charles.

Sarah looked helplessly from one to the other. 'I don't understand,' she said wearily.

Charles turned and walked over to the open door, and stood looking out into the night towards the Creeds' boat, his hands in his pockets. 'We were talking about Mrs Creed,' he said.

Sarah caught her breath in a little gasp: she had forgotten about

Fudge, and suddenly she found her eyes full of tears. 'But I told you that Hugo said she didn't know anything about this!'

'I can believe it,' said Charles quietly, 'and I see no reason why she should be told.'

'But you'll have to, now.'

'No we won't,' Charles turned back from the doorway. 'I think this is what had better be the official version. Mir, Reggie and I escorted you home after the dance, and found Hugo here on the boat having brought Lager back. We were all sitting round having a drink, when Hugo had a heart attack and died before any of us could do anything. We're all witnesses to it, and as that foul stuff appears to be everything that Creed claimed, I think you'll find that we won't even have to square the MO. The medical verdict will be heart failure. I'd better go and collect the MO now.'

'Take my car,' said Mir. 'It's standing in the road.'

'Thanks, I will.'

Reggie said: 'What about Fudge? Hadn't you – hadn't one of us better go over and tell her?'

'No,' said Charles curtly. 'We'll have to get the doctor first.'

'But surely she'll miss him and come over?'

'I doubt it. It's my guess that you'll find Hugo slipped his wife a sleeping-draught on every occasion that he wanted to do any night work. He was too clever a chap to take chances. Come on, Sarah. Time for you to go to bed.'

'I can't,' said Sarah. 'I couldn't sleep. And – and — I'd better be here when the doctor comes and when Fudge comes. It would look all wrong if I'd gone to bed.'

'She's right,' said Reggie briefly. 'Cut along and get your medico. The sooner we get this beastly business settled the better.'

'And I,' said Mir, 'shall take down the rest of this bead code.' He stooped and picked up the fallen writing-block.

Sarah heard the sound of Charles's footsteps die away and the night was quiet again.

Mir's pen made a small, monotonous, scratching sound in the silence as it marked down line after line of dots and dashes, and Reggie leant against an open window, staring out into the night while the sky paled to the first, far-off, whisper of morning. And on the floor, Hugo lay and smiled.

Sarah found that tears were pouring down her cheeks, but she was too tired to lift her hand and brush them away.

20

It was three days before Sarah saw Charles Mallory again: by which time Hugo had been buried and the stir caused by his sudden death was already subsiding, for his had not been the only death in Srinagar that week.

Within a few hours of the news of Major Creed's death from heart failure, there had been another tragedy; equally sudden and unforeseen. Johnnie Warrender had broken his neck while exercising some of His Highness's polo ponies.

There had been other happenings too; arrests and disappearances. But since these had been among the crowded mazes of the city, they had not come to the ears of the European visitors, and it is doubtful whether they had aroused much attention even in the city itself, owing to the surge of rumour, counter-rumour, speculation and uncertainty aroused by the imminent passing of the British Raj.

Sarah was sitting on the grass under the willows, looking out across the lake and the open strip of water where the *Waterwitch* — now paid off and retired to some mooring on the Jhelum River — had recently lain. It was almost six o'clock, and the sun was moving down the western sky towards the mountains of the Pir Panjal. Lager was snuffling and digging among the roots of the great chenar tree, and overhead a pair of bulbuls were conducting a vociferous domestic argument.

Someone was walking down the field path, for the battered sheet of tin was still in place, and though the hot suns of the last few days had baked the ground beneath it to a bricklike hardness, it still creaked protestingly when trodden on. Sarah heard that familiar sound and turned swiftly; and all at once there was a tinge of colour in her cheeks and something strained and stiff in her attitude relaxed. A few moments later, Charles came towards her across the grass.

He looked very tired, and there were lines in his face that she did not remember having seen before. But his eyes were quiet, and the watchfulness that had been in them had gone.

'Don't get up,' said Charles and subsided cross-legged on the turf beside her. 'Where's Mrs Creed?'

'She's gone for a walk.'

'Alone?'

'Yes. I wanted to go with her, but she preferred to go alone. She's all right; I mean——'

'I know,' said Charles. 'She has a lot of courage, and I'm very sorry for her. But not nearly so sorry as I would have been had her husband lived, and she had found him out.'

'Do you think she would have done?'

'Of course. In the end it would have been unavoidable. For one thing there were the children, who are both in England at the moment. Like a lot of British kids, they were here in Srinagar at the Sheik Bagh School during the war, and their parents took them home as soon as it ended and put them into boarding-schools in England. But Hugo had planned a family holiday in the Lebanon at the end of the summer term, and it's beginning to look as though from there they would all have vanished — to end up in some comfortable dacha outside Moscow, where the kids could have been educated and brainwashed and transformed into rabid little Stalin-worshippers.'

'Oh no!' said Sarah unhappily. 'He couldn't have been so cruel! Fudge would have *hated* it so!'

'Maybe. But she couldn't have done anything about it, because once you walk into that particular spider's parlour, your chances of getting out are nil. And even if she did get the chance, she'd never have been allowed to take the children with her, and she wouldn't have abandoned them — not in a million years. At least she's been saved that.'

'Didn't she ... do you think she ever suspected anything?'

'Not the real truth. That's something she can't have conceived of. But she's told us that she was afraid her husband was involved in something that he didn't want her to know about, and that was why he was under stress. I think she suspects some kind of black-market deals. No more than that. They had been poor, and suddenly they seemed to be rich. Money was coming from somewhere and she didn't know from where. There were other things too that she couldn't account for. Mir says she has been lucky, and that there is a verse in "one of your Christian books" (it's in the Psalms, as a matter of fact) that says: "Keep innocency and take heed unto the thing that is right: for that shall bring a man peace at the last," and that Mrs Creed has kept innocency and so will gain, perhaps, peace at the last. I hope so.'

Sarah said: 'She loved him ...'

'Yes, she loved him. Very much, I think. But there are worse things than losing someone you love. There is finding out that they are not *what* you love. Mrs Creed is a truly "good" woman, and she admired his political views because they seemed to her compassionate and kind and caring. He never let her know more than that, and she could not have borne to discover the truth, and find that her beloved husband was not only a traitor but a murderer. And a thoroughly bad hat into the bargain!'

Sarah said restlessly: 'Nobody can be *all* bad.'

'That's true, and there was one good thing in him: though he himself would probably have considered it a weak spot. His love for his wife and children. All the rest was bad. Not even grandly bad: only mean and vain and cruel and egotistical.'

'Why? *Why* Charles?'

'I'm not sure. But from what we've learned, and from what his wife has unconsciously given away, he was a man who was eaten up with envy of those who had more than he had. More money, more brains, more personality, a better education, a better social background. It is an only too common failing in these days,' said Charles bitterly.

'But he *was* clever. And popular — people liked him. Everyone liked him.'

'Oh yes. He was clever. But not clever in the right way. He was cunning. His childhood had bred in him an envy of those who had more than he, while his vanity made him wish to lead in everything. He went to a university where he fell in with a very radical and distinctly precious set, most of whom had enough pull to get them into cushy jobs when they left. Hugo hadn't, so he plumped for the Army where he found, as so many find in so many walks of life, that an average man with money and a good social background could get ahead of a better man with neither.'

'But a brilliant man —' began Sarah.

'A brilliant man will rise to the top anywhere. You can't stop him. But Major Creed was not brilliant. Only cunning: and in his own view, "penniless", because he had very little in the way of a private income. He was passed over once or twice in favour of men he considered were inferior to him except in pocket and background, and he could not rise above it. He allowed it instead to sour him and destroy him. He had already acquired strong Communist sympathies at his university, but now he went over to the Party heart and soul, and for the meanest of motives: "Envy, hatred, malice and all uncharitableness!" He transferred into the Indian Army in 1933, and shortly before the war broke out managed to get himself attached to the Intelligence Corps of all things.'

'Yes, he said something about that. About knowing people in it and being able to find out about that hut in Gulmarg because they ... But I didn't believe he could ever really have been in it. I thought he was – was just inventing. Lying again, I suppose ...'

'He wasn't, worse luck. No; Hugo of all people was involved

in intelligence work, and what's more he was carefully vetted for the job; which proves that he must either have covered his tracks very well, or else the "vetting" was pretty slack in those days! That's one reason, of course, why he was above suspicion. And why the opposition always knew so much about what was going on. It seems that he organized and ran a very effective under-the-counter Intelligence Service of his own, at one and the same time as the official one; and without anyone ever suspecting it! Oh, he was clever all right. I suppose all traitors have to be — those who get away with it! And all the time he remained, on the surface, "Hugo the Good Fellow", "Hugo the Joker", the "Life and Soul of the Party"—— 'Pity no one ever dreamed *which* Party . . . !'

Charles paused and began to tear up the grass stems, shredding them between his thin, tanned fingers, and presently Sarah said: 'Tell me about it, Charles. What was in Janet's curtain?'

'Everything,' said Charles. 'Everything except a name: Hugo's! That was something they hadn't yet discovered. You know, of course, that there is to be a transfer of power from Britain to India.'

'Of course,' said Sarah with the ghost of a laugh. 'Nobody around here talks of anything else these days.'

'Quite,' agreed Charles dryly. 'But what you don't know is that the transfer will not take place next year, as was originally announced, but in August of this year.'

'What!' Sarah sat bolt upright. 'But – but——'

'Unfortunately, it's true: you'll hear the announcement very soon. As far as that part of it is concerned, we have found Janet's curtain too late.'

'Why? What difference could that have made? And why do you say it's "unfortunate"? Don't you want them to run their own country? How would *we* like it if——' She saw that Charles was laughing at her, and stopped and bit her lip. 'I'm sorry. I should have known. What were you going to say?'

'I was going to say that it's a great pity that so many people fail to realize that the war that has just ended is only a taste of what is to come. That this "Peace" we are enjoying is only the lemon, the very sour lemon, that both teams suck at half-time. The big struggle is to come, and it is going to be far more bitter: because it will be between ideologies and not nations.'

'But what has this got to do with the transfer of power?' demanded Sarah. 'Everyone knew it must come one day.'

'Of course. But there are those who profit enormously from chaos and disaster, and who will therefore ensure that both occur when that day comes. To this end, money has been spent. It has been poured out!'

Sarah said: 'But, Hugo? What was he doing in all this?'

'Hugo handled the money. And from here. What better place was there? This is not "British India". It's a protectorate: an Independent Native State ruled over by a Maharajah, who is "advised" by a British Resident and can only be deposed — and that only as a last resort — if he behaves *really* badly. Even then, he must be replaced by his heir. Kashmir is, in a way, national — almost international — ground; and moreover, it has a largely Mohammedan population and a Hindu ruling class. That was an asset to begin with! But it had a better one. It was a famous holiday resort for both Indians and British. People from all over India came here, and needed to give no explanation for doing so beyond that they were on holiday.

'Huge sums of money came in here: American dollars, brought by American Communists wearing American Army uniforms. Oh yes, some of them were in it too! English pounds and Indian jewels, bar gold, and silver rupees. All kinds of money was collected here: much of it the proceeds of large-scale robberies. Here it was changed into whatever currency was needed, and here the leading plotters and agitators came for orders and pay, and for funds. There were a great many helpers — among them British men and women.'

'I know,' said Sarah soberly. 'Johnnie Warrender was one, wasn't he?'

'No, not Johnnie. Helen.'

'*Helen!* Then it was—— But why — I mean Johnnie is dead. I thought . . .' said Sarah incoherently.

'Oh yes, Johnnie killed himself. It was no accident, but he faked it very well. You see he had learned about his wife. And besides, I think he was a dead man already.'

'What do you mean?'

'He was finished. What Americans would call "washed up". There was nothing any more for him. He had been living on an overdraft for years, and now there was no hope of paying it off, or of paying his other debts. Or playing polo again. With the transfer of power the world of people like Johnnie Warrender will come to an end. It was Helen who worked for Hugo. I don't think she really knew what she was doing: she probably didn't want to! She is a stupid woman of limited outlook, who thought only of the money and nothing else at all. A perfect tool for Hugo. Do you remember the theft of the Rajgore emeralds?'

'Yes,' said Sarah. 'There was a lot about it in the papers; and you mentioned them too — you said they were here.'

'So they are. We suspected that those emeralds would come to Kashmir, as a good many other stolen jewels had done, and we set a watch for them. But they slipped through. Mrs Warrender brought them and passed them to Hugo on the road.'

'But she couldn't have done that!' protested Sarah. 'I was there: and Fudge too. She didn't give him anything!'

'She's told us herself. She gave him the emeralds. They were inside some fruit — a grapefruit or a papaya or something.'

'No,' said Sarah slowly. 'It was a watermelon. I remember now . . .'

'Helen Warrender would have done almost anything for money. There are too many people like that.' Charles pulled up a long grass stem and sat chewing the end of it thoughtfully, looking out over the lake, and after an appreciable interval, Sarah said: 'You can't stop there. Tell me about the rest of it. There are so many things I want to know. That message in the matchbox — how did they find out? About the curtain, I mean? And how did that pockmarked man, Ahamdoo, know?'

Charles said thoughtfully: 'Now that he's dead, I don't suppose we'll ever know the answer to that. We can only guess.'

'Then how did *they* know?'

'That question,' said Charles with a faint smile, 'should be "Why didn't they find out sooner?" — considering how little privacy there is on a houseboat!'

'You're telling me!' sighed Sarah with deep feeling: 'That's why I can't imagine how Janet managed to make that curtain without every Kashmiri within a radius of ten miles knowing all about it.'

'But they *did* know. That's the whole point. It is also a beautiful illustration of why the thought-processes of the East so often succeed in baffling the West. There is an old saying, which originated in this part of the world, that "It is always darkest under the lamp". Janet Rushton knew that to be true, and being a smart girl, she put it to good use. She knew very well that if she attempted to make that record in secret — say, after dark when the curtains were drawn — she would undoubtedly have been found out, and however carefully she had hidden it, it would have been discovered. So she did it openly and in full view, and when it was finished, she hung it up where everyone could see it. Therefore, because it was common knowledge, no one even thought to mention it...

'From what the *mānji* now tells us, she must have planned it all very carefully. And since she had the advantage of being born in India and spending a good slice of her childhood here, she knew a lot about the mind of India. She knew, for instance, that because it was inclined to be devious, it could be deceived by openness: and she traded on that knowledge.'

'But the bead curtain?' prompted Sarah.

'The *mānji* says that there had always been one on the *Water-*

witch; apparently many boats had them in the old days. But one day in late November, Rushton Miss-sahib destroyed it. She seems to have tripped and fallen, and grasping at the curtain as she fell, brought it down with her. It was old, so the strings broke easily, and he says that the Miss-sahib was very upset and insisted on replacing it. When she found that such things were no longer made locally, she sent him to the bazaar to buy string, and also extra beads, since many of the original beads had fallen between the floorboards and been lost.

'This, of course, ensured that the maximum number of people would hear the tale. She even went to the bazaar herself and bought more beads, and as there was a last sunny spell towards the end of the month, she sat out on the roof of her boat and threaded them in full view of every passing *shikara*, while Mrs Matthews sketched on the bank. She worked on it for the best part of ten days, and by the end of that time it had become such a familiar sight that it was taken for granted, and ceased to be of the slightest interest. In other words, she deliberately sat under the light and flaunted the thing that must be hid.'

'Yes ... yes, I see,' said Sarah. 'It was a sort of double bluff.'

'Exactly. And it succeeded in fooling everyone. It might have continued to do so if a certain dealer in carpets (now behind bars and telling us a lot of interesting things in the hope of escaping death!) had not been a lover of Persian poetry. He was one of the many who had actually seen Janet Rushton working on her curtain when he came alongside in his *shikara*, hoping to sell her a carpet, and he had also been one of the people who searched the *Waterwitch* after her death, just in case she had left behind anything either useful or incriminating; and found nothing. But only recently, happening to read that poem, the connection between words and beads suddenly struck him, and he began to wonder ...

'Since he does not live in Srinagar — his main shop is in Baramulla — he sent this line of verse by a sure hand (whose owner is also now in jail!) to Ghulam Kadir's shop, concealed in a matchbox inside a papier mâché cover, with instructions that it must be passed to Creed-sahib whom he knew would be visiting the shop on a certain day. The man who took delivery of it had the bright idea of presenting similar boxes to any customer who happened to be in the shop at the time, to cover this simple transaction. And as a result of trying to be too clever fell a victim to chance, because your box happened to be too like Hugo's.'

'And I suppose Ahamdoo saw the message?' said Sarah slowly.

'That is the assumption. It wouldn't have been too difficult, since he was one of the assistants in the shop, which — as you saw — has plenty of hiding-places. And he had sharp ears and excellent eyesight! He'd already overheard enough to let us know that a message was to be passed to a *feringhi*, a foreigner, who would come to the shop on that particular day, ostensibly to buy papier mâché, and he suspected either Lady Candera, or her niece Meril, whom he thought might be working for her as a spy. Presumably he managed to take a look at the message — a glance would have been enough! — and when you interrupted us at the hotel, and he saw both Lady Candera and Meril Forbes there, he fell into a pond of panic, and decided to meet me on that island instead, because he thought it would be safer.

'He'd worked with Mrs Matthews, and he too had seen the bead curtain that Janet was making. He had also, on our behalf, searched both their boats after they were dead. So when he read that line of *Farsi* (Persian) — which it seems he must have done — he too would have begun to puzzle over it. And when he set out for the island he took a blue bead with him, presumably to illustrate a theory that the blue china beads could have been stops at the end of words. Though that, of course, is something else we shall never know . . .'

'Is that all?' asked Sarah. 'I mean all that was in Janet's curtain? Just – just about the money and jewels ... to pay the agitators and saboteurs?'

'No,' said Charles slowly. 'No, there was something else.'

'I thought there must be. You needn't tell me if you don't want to, you know.'

'If I didn't, it would be because I still can't quite make myself believe it. You see it was a plan, a very well worked-out plan, to take over Kashmir as soon as the British moved out, and turn it into a Communist State.'

'But what ever for? What would be the point of that?'

'The point would be that with a Communist Government in power the President, or the Dictator, or whatever he liked to call himself, would, in the name of the new Government, call upon Russia for help if either India or the Muslim tribes of the Border country tried to move against them.'

'But what *for*?' repeated Sarah.

'Come on, Sarah, use your head! For a bridgehead, of course! For a base from which, in due time, Russian troops could move against Afghanistan or the North-West Frontier, or India herself, eventually. Just take a look at the map. Any of the nearby territories could be knocked off one by one by anyone who was strongly entrenched in Kashmir, if Kashmir itself was a fully paid-up member of the USSR.'

'I don't believe it. It couldn't be done!'

'No? Think again. On the day of the transfer of power — and probably for some weeks before — the communal hatreds that have been so carefully fostered by the paid agitators will be given their head. And if the country is *really* partitioned, there will be riots and killing and terrible disturbances. Under cover of that, and while everyone's eyes are elsewhere, Kashmir was to have been cut off from the world. Believe me, it would have been quite easy! Far easier than anyone thinks possible. There are not many ways into this country, and those ways are through high mountains and easy to block: and there is only one aerodrome — not a very good one, either! With riot and bloodshed breaking out all over India, it would not be considered so very extraordinary if no news came out of Kashmir for several days. And by the time anything was done about it, it would have been too late ...'

Sarah said: 'Do you really believe it would have been possible?'

'Yes. I think so. The ownership of the State is already in dispute, so there would be a well-built façade for agitators to shelter behind. The battle cry would be: "We are neither Indians nor Pakistanis! We are Kashmiris! — *Kashmir for the Kashmiris!*" And with the troubles that the new Government will have upon its hands, a *fait accompli* in Kashmir might have proved very difficult to deal with.

'Oh believe me, it may sound wild and improbable, but it was perfectly possible! A handful of men could close the airfield and cut every road into this country — and defend it against an Army. Besides, possession is still nine points of the law! Then later on, when India was ready to turn her serious attention to re-taking Kashmir, the new junta and its boss would yell for help to the Kremlin, who would hurry to assist a defector from the tyranny of capitalist countries, and rush in troops and bombers and fighters and Uncle Tom Cobley and all. Yes, I think they could do it all right.'

Sarah moved restlessly, her fingers pulling off the heads of the daisies that starred the grass. 'But you were in time?'

'Yes, we were in time. We've rounded up a good many people, and some of them have talked, so that we have been able to fill in the gaps in the knowledge Janet Rushton recorded. We've been able to make raids and we have found scores of documents and blueprints. It has been like a net pulled in from the sea. At first you do not even know where the net is, for the marking corks are small and the sea rough. Then you find the first mark and begin to pull the net in, foot by foot. To begin with you pull in only net and water and bits of weeds. But when the last bit of the net comes up it is heavy with fish who can't escape. That's how it's been with us.'

Sarah shivered suddenly, as though the evening air had become cold. 'Were they going to use that – that gas?'

'What gas? Oh, you mean that gun of Hugo's? No, that was just one of the many nasty little inventions that scientists of every nation like to come up with. Hugo thought this one would be useful, and got his friends to make that little gun for him. He used it to stupefy his victims, thereby making it easier for him to polish them off in a way that could be made to look like an accident, and probably the only person to be actually killed by it was himself! It had one bad drawback: that smell. That's why he couldn't store refills on his own boat, and kept a few stashed away in that shop at the Fourth Bridge.

'I'm inclined to think that Ahamdoo must have found one and brought it along to show me, because the amount that was used on him to prevent him yelling and running ought to have been dispersed by the night air, as it was used in the open. But his clothes smelt strongly of it; as if he'd carried some hidden under the folds of that smock. They'd have found it when they took his gun, of course. That was missing; and so was his own knife. He wouldn't have come out unarmed.'

Charles flipped the stub of his cigarette into the lake where it broke the reflections with a little hiss and sent a tiny ripple out across the quiet water.

'What about Mir Khan?' asked Sarah. 'Did he know, all the time?'

'Know what?'

'That Janet was an agent; and Mrs Matthews. And you.'

'That I was, yes. The others, no. We don't all know each other: as I told you once, it isn't considered necessary, and often it only adds to the risks. Mir had been on a job in Gilgit and was in Gulmarg only by chance, and because he likes to ski.'

'And Reggie Craddock?'

'He's not one of us. But it seems that he was more than half-way in love with Janet Rushton, and he didn't believe her death was an accident. Also, because he was interested in her, he noticed what no one else did and what you yourself only discovered by accident. That she was very much afraid of something. People in love often do not need words to tell them things ... You ought to know that!'

Sarah flushed faintly and turned her attention to the daisies once more, and Charles said slowly: 'Reggie watched Janet Rushton, and he knew. It was he who stood in the shadows of the ski-hut and watched her go away across the snow. It was he whom you heard close the door.'

'Was it Reggie who made those footsteps on the verandah?' interrupted Sarah. 'I suppose he—— No, of course it wasn't ... They were too small.'

'Helen,' said Charles. 'She told us about that. The Warrenders had the end room on that block, and the reason for that surreptitious bit of snooping was nothing more than curiosity. She happened to be suffering from an attack of insomnia, and remembering that George McKay was a doctor, decided, Helen-like, to wake him up and demand a sleeping-draught. By chance she opened her door at the exact moment that you started scratching at Janet's; and retreating hastily, she watched you through a crack and saw you let in and the light go on. It stayed on for a long time, and then suddenly went off again — that was when Janet looked out! — and when it came on once more she couldn't resist sneaking along to see if she could find out what on earth was going on. However, by the time she got there Janet had put the radio on, so she couldn't hear a thing and retreated, baffled. Thereby letting George enjoy uninterrupted slumbers, as I gather she'd forgotten all about the insomnia by then!'

Sarah laughed, and felt the better for it: she had been wondering if she would ever laugh again after the shock of that appalling night. Remembering that she had interrupted Charles when he had been telling her about Reggie, she said hastily: 'Go on with what you were saying about Major Craddock. How much did he hear when he was listening to Janet and I talking outside the ski-hut?'

'Very little; he says you were both whispering. But that wasn't what worried him. You see, he is a skier: possibly one of the best who have ever come to Kashmir. So he did not accept the explanation of Janet Rushton's death, because she too was a good skier; and a good skier would not have fallen in that particular way. He suggested as much to Major McKay, but George was no skier and paid little attention. They had a difference of opinion about it, and McKay was angry.

'Reggie is not very clever, but he's stubborn. And it is surprising how much information a stubborn and dogged man can ferret out if he really sets his mind to it. Reggie set his mind to it and decided to carry out some investigations of his own. At one time he suspected you.'

'*Me!* Good heavens!' Sarah sat bolt upright.

'Only because he had seen you talking to Janet outside the ski-hut that night, and you had never mentioned it. Later he became convinced that there was something on the boat — Janet's boat — that you were after. When he found he couldn't get you off it, he watched it.'

'Oh he did, did he!' said Sarah, stormily.

Charles noted the fact, and smiled. 'You owe your life to him, all the same! To him, and to your dog.'

'To *Reggie*? How? It was you——'

'Not entirely me, I'm afraid. I didn't suspect Hugo. But Reggie had been secretly watching the boat, and he had seen Hugo searching it. He had also seen Hugo put down, very carefully, a piece of meat among the roots of the chenar tree on the night that Lager was drugged.'

'*Hugo* did that?'

'Of course. Who else?'

'The beast!' said Sarah wrathfully. 'The *beast!* And he always pretended to be so fond of Lager! I have had moments of feeling I could almost be sorry for Hugo, but I shan't have them again!'

Charles leant back and laughed delightedly. 'Oh the inconsistency of the British! How is it that we will always be able to feel "almost sorry" for a murderer, but have no mercy for anyone who ill-treats an animal? I'm sorry, Sarah. It was rude of me to laugh.'

Sarah was compelled to laugh with him. 'You're quite right of course. Oh dear, it's disconcerting to find out how childish and unreliable one's reactions can be! I suppose Hugo meant to come on board that night, and didn't because of the storm. Or else he saw that there was a light on and thought it meant that I was awake. Poor Lager! Go on about Reggie, please.'

'Reggie didn't fully understand what he'd seen. But then he had never liked Hugo—— You knew that?' for Sarah had nodded, and now she said: 'Well Hugo was always very friendly to him, but I did sometimes think that Reggie seemed to find him irritating. That's all.'

'Reggie began to wonder if it were not possible that Hugo had had an affair with Janet Rushton. If perhaps she had become too demanding, and a threat to his marriage and reputation. Even that he might have killed her to rid himself of that threat. It's curious that his romantic imaginings should have led him so near to the truth! He thought that there could be letters hidden on the boat — love letters from Hugo to Janet — and he went away and brooded on this. Do you remember that when I left you that night I spoke first to one of the watchers?'

'Yes. Why?'

'I asked him if anyone had been near the boat, and the man replied that no one had, except the *mānji*, who had returned to the cookboat and was now asleep, and the big sahib who had brought back your dog. He didn't add *"and who is still on the boat"*, because it didn't occur to him to do so; any more than it occurred to me to notice that although the man had mentioned that the *mānji* had gone back to his cookboat, he had not said that Hugo had returned to his boat. You see Hugo was above suspicion. The watcher, seeing Hugo go on board, supposed later that you and I had been talking to him. But what more natural, if there was danger to the Miss-sahib, that Creed-sahib should remain when Mallory-sahib left?'

'That's what Hugo said. So he was right.'

'Yes, he was right. All the same, I was worried. It seemed to me that there was something not quite right; something that didn't fit. A false note. But I couldn't pin it down. It nagged at me in the way that a name or a face that one can't quite remember does, and then just as I reached the gate of the Club, I suddenly realized what it was — Lager! You had told me that when you left him alone he would whine and bark without ceasing.'

'Yes,' said Sarah. 'It was true. He's a little beast that way. He'll yelp and howl for hours on end.'

'But he was not yelping or whining when you came back to the boat that night.'

'No, but that was because —' Sarah stopped suddenly.

'— because Hugo was on the boat,' finished Charles. 'Exactly. That's what suddenly occurred to me. The pup had been making no noise. Why? Because someone was with him. Someone he knew. It was then that I remembered what the watcher had said — or rather, what he had *not* said. He hadn't said that Hugo had left the boat: only that he had gone on board. Then Hugo was still on the boat. Where? Why hadn't he shown himself? Had he taken a nap on one of the beds and fallen fast asleep?'

'Yes, that's what I thought when I first saw him,' confessed Sarah, and shivered suddenly and uncontrollably. 'So what made you come back?'

'Because I met Reggie, and because Reggie had been talking

to Mir Khan. The dance was over and Reggie and Mir had stayed on talking in the Club garden. Reggie had probably had too much to drink, and he was worried and lonely and off his guard. And when Hugo's name happened to come up in the course of conversation, Reggie confided to Mir that he didn't trust him — he was "up to no good", was the way he phrased it — and he went on to say that he himself had been watching your boat, and what he had seen ...'

Charles drew out another cigarette and lit it, and said through the smoke: 'Fortunately, Mir is an Indian. Had he been British the chances are that he would automatically have been on the side of a fellow-countryman, and so Reggie's information would have meant very little. As it was, he had no reason to be biased for or against Hugo; but since he knew we were suspicious of anyone who was interested in the *Waterwitch* — and clearly, Hugo was interested — he told Reggie to come with him at once and they'd wake me up. Mir seems to have thought I'd be in bed and asleep by then but that the matter was too urgent to be left. They were actually crossing the drive on their way to my room when they met me coming up it, and Mir told me what Reggie had seen.

'A few minutes earlier and it might not have meant very much. But now, when I'd just realized that Hugo must already be on your boat, it meant the end of the world — or that's what it felt like!' Charles laughed suddenly, and said: 'It's a long time since I won the quarter mile at my school. But I must have lowered my own record that night! There wasn't time for explanations. I just said, "He's on her boat now!" and turned and ran, with Mir and Reggie pelting behind me——

'We had to slow down a bit when we reached the field path, because it was vital to move quietly and there was that damned piece of tin somewhere on the path. Even then, Mir put a foot on it, but otherwise we made no noise. We could hear voices; and then the dog barked, so I called out——

'Hugo couldn't expect to explain away a dead body, or those gloves and that smell. Had it been anyone else who called, I think he would probably have killed you at once, and then gone out with some story that you were asleep, and tried to bluff it through. But he knew I would come on board.'

Sarah said: 'He had that awful stuff. He could have killed us all. Why didn't he?'

'Because he couldn't have got away with it. He must have realized within seconds that I wasn't alone, and he can't have known how many people I had out there with me: though he would have known that some if not all of us would be armed. And then he'd be coming out from the light into the dark — the moon was down by then — so we'd see him before he could see us. Worst of all, from his point of view, that filthy weapon of his was only useful at short range and against a single target. It would have been useless against an unknown number of men whose positions he couldn't pinpoint. The odds against him were too great, and he must have realized it and turned that foul gun on himself.'

A silence fell between them. The smoke of Charles's cigarette spiralled up slowly in the quiet air, and behind it the lake lay like a sheet of topaz in the twilight. The sun had dipped behind the Gulmarg range, and the mountains behind Shalimar were no longer rose and cyclamen, but slate-grey and cold blue against a pale jade sky flecked with tiny apricot clouds as soft as a fall of feathers from the breast of a wounded bird. A veil of wood smoke from the evening fires drifted across the darkness of the trees at the far side of the lake and a lone frog began to croak among the reeds.

Charles said: 'That's Mir coming across the fields. I suppose someone told him I'd be here.' He came to his feet and stood waiting.

'I have only come to say goodbye,' said Mir walking towards

them. 'No, do not get up, Miss Parrish. I cannot wait.' He shook hands with Charles and smiled down at Sarah: 'I shall see you again, I hope. But tomorrow I leave Kashmir.'

'More ... work?' asked Sarah, standing up to shake hands and brushing daisy heads off her lap.

'I am afraid so.'

'Why do you do this kind of work?' she asked curiously. 'You don't have to.'

Mir laughed. 'There you are wrong, Miss Parrish. We all have to do the work we were sent into this world to do. This is my work: I do not know why it should be so, but I know that it is. And I help my country, also. There is some satisfaction in that. Goodbye — and ... I wish you much happiness. *Khuda hafiz!*'

He sketched the graceful Oriental gesture of farewell and turning away among the willows, walked quickly back along the field path.

There were so many more things that Sarah had wanted to know. So many questions that she had meant to ask. But suddenly they ceased to matter. It was only Charles who mattered, standing before her in the dusk under the willow trees.

The moon had risen while they waited, and now it floated silver and serene in a sky that still held the last faint glow of sunset. It laid a shining pathway across the quiet water and lost itself among the lily-pads at the lake's edge.

Charles's tall figure seemed etched against it in black on silver, while Sarah's white face and pale frock gleamed from the shadowy background of the willow boughs, silver on black.

Charles reached out and took her hands in his, and Sarah said softly: 'You said that if there was a third time, you'd really mean it.'

'This is the third time and I really mean it,' said Charles gravely.

'Good,' said Sarah contentedly.

The two figures, the black and the silver, drew together and became part of the moonlight and the shadows: so still that a heron, alighting in the shallow water at the lake's edge, remained within a yard of them, pricking between the lily leaves, until Lager, returning from a foraging expedition beyond the chenar tree, sent it flapping out across the moonlit Dāl.

Postscript

For those who are interested in facts, the first ski-hut on Khilanmarg was destroyed, together with its occupants, by an avalanche that roared down from the ridge of Apharwat, leaving a track that is still there — a long, wide, silver-grey smear on the mountainside. The ski-hut in this story, which was built to replace it, has by now, I am told, been demolished and replaced in turn by a hotel with a ski-lift that connects it with Gulmarg.

The original H.B. *Sunflower* (there could be a new one of that name by now), which I have allotted to the Creeds in this book, was our houseboat — rented by my father for several years, together with its mooring in Chota Nagim ('small' Nagim), the *ghat* with the huge chenar tree, massed willows and the field path that one followed to reach the Nagim Bagh Road and the bridge of that name, or the Club. I should not be surprised to learn that the piece of rusty tin on that path, laid down by our *mānji* to cover a depression where rain would collect in wet weather, was still there.

The Club certainly is. And so too is the bridge and the little island known as the Char-Chenar — four chenars — though the central pavilion and the tiers of rising ground on which it stood have been bulldozed to the level of the surrounding turf, and the thickets of Persian lilac have gone. Sadly, so has the ancient wooden mosque of Hazratbal, the sacred hair; so named because it enshrines a precious relic in the form of a hair from the Prophet's beard. It has been demolished in favour of a showy white marble mosque from which the once melodious and haunting voice of the muezzin, calling the Faithful to prayer, has given place to a metallic and vociferous one that emerges, at full blast, from a cluster of outsize loudspeakers, wired for maximum sound at the top of the new minaret.

Importunate salesmen in *shikaras* loaded with every kind of local produce from Kashmir carpets to cabbages and cut flowers, still tout their wares alongside every occupied houseboat; and the old, picturesque, wooden houses where the makers of papier mâché, carved wood and embroidered *pashmina** live, still crowd together on either side of the Jhelum River where it flows through Srinagar City. The one-time British Residency, standing among its green lawns and gardens in the shadow of the Takht-i-Suliman, looks much the same as it did in the old days, though nowadays it houses a series of showrooms for the display and sale of the many arts and crafts for which Kashmir is famous.

I suspect that by now both of the Nedou's Hotels — the stone-built one in Srinagar and the rambling, ramshackle, much-loved wooden one in Gulmarg — have been modernized and 'improved' out of all recognition. But as far as I am concerned, they will always be there unchanged and unchanging. Enshrined, like flies in amber, in my memory; complete with the stage upon which I appeared more than once in charity cabarets. For I was the girl to whom my fictional Hugo Creed refers briefly near the end of Chapter 15; the 'girl called Mollie someone' with whom he once sang a duet: 'A tasteful ditty about a bench in a park — or was it something about tiptoeing through tulips?' Hugo could not remember. But in fact it was both, though on two separate occasions; and my partner on that bench was not in the least like Henry VIII, being a lissom young officer in an Indian Cavalry regiment, one 'Bingle' Ingall of the 6th Lancers.

Oddly enough, there is a postscript to that particular duet. Years later — over forty of them I fear, during which I had completely lost track of him — we suddenly met again in, of all places, the

*Handwoven cloth of goat's wool.

Book section of a famous department store in San Francisco where I was signing copies of *The Far Pavilions* and *Shadow of the Moon.* He had, it seemed, become a professional actor, married an American girl and settled in a suburb of that city; and having seen in some local paper that I was in town signing books, had dropped in to say, 'Fancy meeting you here!' It is a far cry from Kashmir to San Francisco, but as Hugo would probably have said: 'If I may coin a phrase, "It's a small world."'

It is indeed! And getting smaller every day.

READ MORE IN PENGUIN

In every corner of the world, on every subject under the sun, Penguin represents quality and variety – the very best in publishing today.

For complete information about books available from Penguin – including Puffins, Penguin Classics and Arkana – and how to order them, write to us at the appropriate address below. Please note that for copyright reasons the selection of books varies from country to country.

In the United Kingdom: Please write to *Dept. JC, Penguin Books Ltd, FREEPOST, West Drayton, Middlesex UB7 OBR*

If you have any difficulty in obtaining a title, please send your order with the correct money, plus ten per cent for postage and packaging, to *PO Box No. 11, West Drayton, Middlesex UB7 OBR*

In the United States: Please write to *Penguin USA Inc., 375 Hudson Street, New York, NY 10014*

In Canada: Please write to *Penguin Books Canada Ltd, 10 Alcorn Avenue, Suite 300, Toronto, Ontario M4V 3B2*

In Australia: Please write to *Penguin Books Australia Ltd, 487 Maroondah Highway, Ringwood, Victoria 3134*

In New Zealand: Please write to *Penguin Books (NZ) Ltd,182–190 Wairau Road, Private Bag, Takapuna, Auckland 9*

In India: Please write to *Penguin Books India Pvt Ltd, 706 Eros Apartments, 56 Nehru Place, New Delhi 110 019*

In the Netherlands: Please write to *Penguin Books Netherlands B.V., Keizersgracht 231 NL–1016 DV Amsterdam*

In Germany: Please write to *Penguin Books Deutschland GmbH, Friedrichstrasse 10–12, W–6000 Frankfurt/Main 1*

In Spain: Please write to *Penguin Books S. A., C. San Bernardo 117–6° E–28015 Madrid*

In Italy: Please write to *Penguin Italia s.r.l., Via Felice Casati 20, I–20124 Milano*

In France: Please write to *Penguin France S. A., 17 rue Lejeune, F–31000 Toulouse*

In Japan: Please write to *Penguin Books Japan, Ishikiribashi Building, 2–5–4, Suido, Tokyo 112*

In Greece: Please write to *Penguin Hellas Ltd, Dimocritou 3, GR–106 71 Athens*

In South Africa: Please write to *Longman Penguin Southern Africa (Pty) Ltd, Private Bag X08, Bertsham 2013*

BY THE SAME AUTHOR

The Far Pavilions

'A *Gone with the Wind* of the North-West Frontier' – *The Times*

The Far Pavilions is a story about an Englishman – Ashton Pelham-Martyn – brought up as a Hindu. It is the story of his passionate, but dangerous, love for Juli, an Indian princess. It is the story of divided loyalties, of friendship that endures till death, of high adventure and of the clash between East and West.

Shadow of the Moon

When India bursts into flaming hatred and bitter bloodshed during the dark days of the Mutiny, Captain Alex Randall and his superior's wife, the lovely raven-haired Winter de Ballesteros, are thrown unwillingly together in the struggle for survival.

Trade Wind

The year is 1859 and Hero Hollis, beautiful and headstrong niece of the American consul, arrives in Zanzibar. It is an earthly paradise fragrant with spices and frangipani, it is also the last and greatest outpost of the Slave Trade. A passionate opponent of slavery, Hero is swept into a turmoil of royal intrigue, abduction, piracy, smuggling and a virulent cholera epidemic. There in Zanzibar, the most cruelly beautiful island of the Southern Seas, she must choose her love and unravel her destiny.

and

Death in Berlin
Death in Cyprus
Death in Kenya
The Sun in the Morning
(Autobiography)